DR. JOHN
On Assignment

by John M. Keshishian

INKWATER PRESS
PORTLAND • OREGON
INKWATERPRESS.COM

AUTHOR'S DISCLAIMER

This book is a composite of events, real or imagined, but not completely a work of fiction. Some but not all names and incidents may be the product of the author's imagination. In those imagined events, any resemblance to actual events, places and persons, living or dead is wholly coincidental. Additionally, liberties have been taken when recounting certain events to conform to time frames and to continuity as needed to preserve confidence. The protagonist, John M. Sundukian, is a thinly veiled version of the author, as befits this slightly fictionalized version of Dr. John's activities.

Copyright © 2013 by John M. Keshishian

Cover Design by Philip Chalk
Cover layout and interior design by Masha Shubin

This story, while fictional, is based on actual events. In certain cases incidents, characters, names, and timelines have been changed for dramatic purposes. Certain characters may be composites, or entirely fictitious. This story is created for entertainment purposes. Opinions, acts, and statements attributed to any entity, individual or individuals may have been fabricated or exaggerated for effect. The opinions and fictionalized depictions of individuals, groups and entities, and any statements contained herein, are not to be relied upon in any way.

All rights reserved. No part of this book may be reproduced or transmitted in any form or by any means whatsoever, including photocopying, recording or by any information storage and retrieval system, without written permission from the publisher and/or author. Contact Inkwater Press at 6750 SW Franklin Street, Suite A, Portland, OR 97223-2542. 503.968.6777

Publisher: Inkwater Press | www.inkwaterpress.com

Paperback
ISBN-13 978-1-59299-840-1 | ISBN-10 1-59299-840-2
Hardback
ISBN-13 978-1-59299-841-8 | ISBN-10 1-59299-841-0
Kindle
ISBN-13 978-1-59299-842-5 | ISBN-10 1-59299-842-9

Printed in the U.S.A.
All paper is acid free and meets all ANSI standards for archival quality paper.

1 3 5 7 9 10 8 6 4 2

Scan this QR Code to learn more about this title

"... a nerve-jangling, heart-pounding account of espionage and danger featuring just about every heroic and every evil character and event possible. These are the recollections of a distinguished Washington surgeon who found himself playing the role of a reluctant spy. Enjoy this rollicking tale and try to imagine what you would do if you were in Dr. John Keshishian's globe-trotting shoes."

– Mary G. Smith, Senior Assistant Editor, ret., *National Geographic*

"John Keshishian's *Dr. John...On Assignment* is proof that real life beats fiction every time. Keshishian is an authoritative, engaging guide to the shadowy world of Cold War espionage, filled with adventure, betrayals, danger, and surprising twists that keep readers on the edge of their chairs. With this book, this distinguished surgeon and gifted photographer proves that he is a masterful story-teller as well."

– Robert M. Poole, Author of *On Hallowed Ground: The Story of Arlington National Cemetery*

"Imagine enjoying the pleasures of an exotic location when suddenly you find yourself wrapped in intrigue and surrounded by guns, spies and assorted deranged bad guys. Dr. John has been there, done that, got the T-shirt. Somehow he does what any surgeon-photographer-adventurer-writer does and comes back from the edge of the precipice time and again with amazing tales. Much of it may even be true. After all, he does have the photos and very convincing stories. A good time was had by all.

Well, at least by Dr. Keshishian."

– Bill Allen, Former Editor, *National Geographic*

"It is difficult to categorize the writing of Dr. John M. Keshishian, ranging as it does from a Tolstoyan breadth of vision to the anecdotal deftness of a Guy de Maupassant. His photos of Central Asia, his archaeological analyses from Egypt and Israel to Guatemala, and his scientific studies over a fifty-year span are remarkable. The ultimate sadness of the tribute to his only son, deceased prematurely, reflects his ability to touch everyone."

— Allen M. Johnson, PhD

"Dr. Keshishian is great at medicine, great at photographs, and great at writing. In this fascinating book he does all three. At the *National Geographic* magazine, he also did all three."

— Bill Garrett, Former Editor, *National Geographic*

"Renaissance man John Keshishian, surgeon to stars and spies, has been just about everywhere and done just about everything, including some secret, dark-of-night operations for U.S. intelligence. Now he has written a rollicking memoir that may not quite tell all, but tells quite enough to keep the reader awake until the wee hours of the morning."

— Charles McCarry

DEDICATED TO THE MEMORY OF MY SON

William Wrather Keshishian

November 24, 1954 – December 4, 2010

Books by Author

Autopsy for a Cosmonaut, with Jacob Hay

The Mayan Shard Caper

Table of Contents

Books by Author vii
Acknowledgments xi
Prologue xiii
Chapter 1: How I Got Myself Sizzling in the Fire 1
Chapter 2: To Vietnam 4
Chapter 3: Saigon, Pearl of the Orient 9
Chapter 4: François Sully 15
Chapter 5: Antoine Nicolai 24
Chapter 6: Nha Trang 57
Chapter 7: Saigon—Again 86
Chapter 8: Bangkok 98
Chapter 9: Vientiane 110
Chapter 10: Muong Sing, Laos 131
Chapter 11: Goodbye, Muong Sing 135
Chapter 12: And the Fun Begins 144
Chapter 13: Inside Red China 154
Chapter 14: By Hoof and Mouth Through Yunnan 168
Chapter 15: A Lift from Birddawg 184
Chapter 16: Thailand, Once Again 197
Chapter 17: The Security Officer 205
Chapter 18: Back in Bangkok 215

Chapter 19: New Delhi 217
Chapter 20: Sheremetyevo International Airport 223
Chapter 21: Sklifasovsky Institute 237
Chapter 22: Amsterdam 284
Chapter 23: Washington DC 310
Chapter 24: London, Brown's Hotel, Mayfair 327
Chapter 25: Beirut, Lebanon 329
Chapter 26: Doctor, We Have a Problem 333
Chapter 27: Washington, and The Beat Goes On 339
Chapter 28: Clearmont Mews, McLean 345
Chapter 29: Cairo, Egypt 354
Chapter 30: Cairo on the Nile 368
Chapter 31: The Gezira Sporting Club 389
Chapter 32: Return to DC 407
Chapter 33: Andrews Air Force Base 414
Chapter 34: A Shark Is Hatched 424
Chapter 35: Dr. John Strikes Back! 426
Chapter 36: The Bahamas 431
Chapter 37: General Archie S. Koffman 448
Chapter 38: London Calling—It's Mandy 454
Chapter 39: The Chinese Photo 465
Chapter 40: Return to the Abnormal 473
Chapter 41: The Cosmos Club, Washington 476
Chapter 42: Abu Simbel on the Nile 481
Chapter 43: Aswan Port 488
Chapter 44: The Plan 497
Chapter 45: The Tunnels 509
Chapter 46: The Panel 518
Chapter 47: Dr. Grosvenor and a Future Path 531
Chapter 48: The Past and the Future 538
Author's Note 541
Photos 543
About John M. Keshishian, MD 553

Acknowledgments

WITHOUT THE ASSISTANCE, CRITICISM AND ADVICE BY MY WIFE, NANCY Lee, I'd have had difficulty putting these sentences together. Her previous editorial experience came into play as she commented on each and every page.

And so too, constant input from Dr. Allen McTavish Johnson, Soviet Studies expert, scholar, friend, journalist and severe critic.

But there were many others:

Cameron Akbari, surgeon and colleague, who provided comfort and support during difficult days.

Lew Biben, cardiologist, advisor and source of medical information.

Riess K. "Brownie" Brown, flight instructor, Woodbridge Airport, Virginia. Brownie could do and did things with aircraft that are not found in flight instructors' manuals.

Robert Core, advisor, former Marine officer, legal expert, and friend who is very knowledgeable in matters outside normal everyday events of life, including extensive knowledge of weaponry and things that go bang.

Bill Garrett, former editor of *National Geographic* magazine, a genius with words and pictures, for his constant advice and occasional criticisms.

The late Jeffrey C. Kitchen, former State Department officer, who provided advice and insight into certain arcane government activities.

Antoine Nicolai, chief pilot for Michelin, Vietnam. And sometime flight instructor.

Dr. Francis Robicsek, surgeon, archaeologist and colleague, who helped and guided my research on tombs, both Egyptian and Mayan.

François Sully, journalist and friend, who met an untimely death from a helicopter event.

Dr. Lucy Van Voorhees, lady cardiologist and horse farmer who watches over me.

Dr. George Watson, former head of the Division of Ornithology at the Smithsonian Institution, whose knowledge of birds is more than just encyclopedic. It's downright amazing.

The late Dr. Alec Wetmore, former head of the above division in the Smithsonian and dean of all bird men—possibly in the whole world—who recognized instantly the Nile Ibis from a handful of bones. A friend and colleague.

Philip Chalk, wordsmith extraordinaire, and Becky Krueger for their careful examination of the contents, and grammaticians of the first order.

Brad and Martha Taishoff for their support and encouragement.

All the good folks at Inkwater Press...and a few others who have requested anonymity.

Prologue

It is good for a man that he should bear the yoke in his youth.
—Lamentations 3:27

IT'S REALLY HARD TO KNOW WHERE TO BEGIN ALL THIS. I REALLY HADN'T planned any literary work about my past. In fact, I rarely thought about my times back in Southeast Asia and other interesting spots until Grey Palmer interviewed me about a famous but now long-dead Texas oil tycoon. I had performed a tricky operation on that Texan—a portacaval shunt, rerouting blood from his scarred liver back to his heart. Against all odds, he'd survived, and we remained friends for the duration of his life. So too his son.

Shortly after this interview session ended, I found myself sipping cocktails and chomping pistachios with Duane "Dewey" Clarridge, an ex-CIA officer. Dewey had just written a book about his life in the Agency. We were in the Ritz Carlton Bar at Tyson's Corner, exchanging lies and recounting some of our strange activities in Southeast Asia. After a few drinks, memories flooded back. (I can't handle too many drinks.) Dewey listened, and then shook his head unbelievingly.

"Man, he said, "you really gotta stick some of this shit down on paper. Write a few chapters and get some friendly editor to go over it. This is great stuff, man, you should get it published."

I thought about it. How the hell does one go about getting books published these days? Not since my *Autopsy for a Cosmonaut* had I written anything that interested any publisher.

Bill Garrett's name. He, the highly respected former editor of *National Geographic* Magazine, came immediately to mind. But Bill said he was busy doing his own book. After shopping around like an out-of-work actor, I couldn't get anyone to read my chapters. Publishers were kind, but not interested. In fact some chortled when they skimmed through some of the events I reported. "Great imagination" was the usual comment.

Dewey was convinced it would make interesting reading and urged me get on with it. "Keep in touch," said Dewey, "lemme me know if I can be of help when you get it all done." I promised him I would. So, here goes.

CHAPTER 1

How I Got Myself Sizzling in the Fire

I STOOD THERE SHIVERING IN THE DARK WAITING FOR THE GO SIGNAL. WE were snugged in a copse of bushes in the street just outside the home of this precious padré.

We'd trundled here as quietly as possible in those golf cart–like buggies after the quiet Porter had landed us in Red China. Red China? It had finally hit me. Was I nuts? What the hell was I doing here in the first place? How had I let myself be talked into doing this ridiculous little stunt? Why hadn't I refused? Well, too late now, my friend. The fat was in the fire; in for a penny in for a goddam ton.

Here we were, a group of madmen, and a woman or two, skulking in the weeds, waiting for the Go signal. The high arcing cigarette flipped out by one of our advance people, tossed high, followed by a small shower of sparks when it hit ground. That would be the signal for us. I was aware my shivering was not entirely from the cool evening. The truth was I was scared shitless.

Once the cigarette showed itself, we'd enter. Each of us had our assigned task. Simultaneously, we'd enter what appeared to be a dilapidated old shack, in reality, more a hovel, and extract the highly diseased, very sick padré, load him into the Porter, then fly him back to some hospital in Thailand. And his lady too. But first, I had to jam a million units of Uncle Sam's finest penicillin into his miserable, scabrous butt in hopes it might save him. Then lug him out to the plane and we'd all fly out together, right?

Wrong! Well, let's say not quite right, as things would turn out. But that was the plan as I had understood it; possibly I hadn't read the fine print

At the moment, the padré's future was my responsibility. The rest would come later. I got ready to do my chore.

As I'd stood there shivering, I'd laughed inwardly. I'd finally been told why I, me, the idiot Dr. Sundukian, had to go in with the team and do the grab-and-go exercise. At what point, I wondered, had I lost my senses and agreed to go on this not so very jolly lark into Red China? Knowing damn well if we got caught I might at best get shot. How stupid of me to have even considered this ridiculous caper. It was because his woman, Mei Ling, had said, "no tickee, no laundry"...or something along those lines. I was the tickee. And if I didn't show up, there would be no tickee and then of course, no laundry. And that just wouldn't do. So I, the gullible Doc, had been snookered in and here I was. OK, let's see what's next. Oh *merde*.

I mused some more. Of course, I damn well knew the answer. I'd just neglected to admit it to myself. Because like most vain males, I had willingly, it seems, allowed myself to be set up by that lovely siren...Gigi. More *merde*!

I had to admit, though, she'd given me fair warning about what might happen if one got caught. And what happens to big shot local natives not in line with the folks up north. But nothing about what happens to do-gooders like me if I get caught. But then never mind, that would never happen since I was with the pros, right? Men who did this for our military. Goody.

So yes, I'd made a deal; a *quid pro quo*. I'd go traipsing in with them if they guaranteed me a flight to Saigon after the rescue. Little did I know the possible ramifications? So it was a deal. Because the unpalatable alternative was that I was stuck in Laos with no foreseeable way of getting out of Dodge. I wasn't in any way considering floating down a wild river in a dilapidated boat all alone with no earthly idea where I'd go ashore, possibly running aground on a midstream sandbar. And there would endeth me. So I'd taken the only logical alternative, hadn't I?

I stood there still shivering and thought back to the hospital where I would never, ever forget that lunatic Dooley with his maniacal laughter, cackling on about Radio Hanoi knowing I was in the valley...and that I was a marked man. It didn't require a degree in astrophysics to realize that my ass was in serious danger. I had to get the hell out and this was my only chance.

Once again, that same lame question popped out: What the hell was I doing here in the first place? How could I have been so stupid? I knew the answer, but again, too proud to admit it to myself. Suckered once again by a hank of hair, blonde, and a whiff of fancy perfume.

Suddenly a lighted cigarette tip flew through the air. It arced then fell, hitting the ground with a shower of tiny sparks. Show time. Off we go.

But, whoa, John...I precede myself. How did I allow this mad episode in my life to ever get this far? This needs some serious explaining.

CHAPTER 2

To Vietnam

I N 1959, THE FRENCH WERE WELL ON THEIR WAY OUT OF VIETNAM. THEY'D gotten their asses shot up at Dien Bien Phu five years earlier and then agreed shortly afterward in Geneva to bid adieu to Indochina. By the end of the decade, French citizens in Saigon were no longer welcome, and they knew it. Yet many had lingered, some haughtily announcing they would leave only when they were quite ready. Bankers, businessmen, doctors—for these unhappy Gaulists, empire had meant a life of favor and comfort. Moreover, it was the only real home many of them had ever known. Instead, France was itself a kind of colony for them, half a world away and uncomfortably different.

Edgy and embittered, some of these hangers-on descended into petty vandalism as they departed, exacting street-level revenge by ripping fixtures, wiring, and equipment from government and commercial buildings. The vandalism resulted in widespread chaos, with some medical facilities, including hospitals, left in shambles.

Quick to respond, the United States rushed in to help through "Operating Missions." These "USOMs" were a new branch of the State Department and forerunners of what would become the Agency for International Development. Through them, America would try to help the foundering country of South Vietnam get on its feet,

TO VIETNAM

in part by restocking medical institutions with supplies, equipment, support—and personnel.

So it was that in 1959, I, a young surgeon in Washington DC, was asked to go to Vietnam. In one sense, heading to Southeast Asia would be a homecoming of sorts for me as I'd spent the better part of World War II as a naval officer in the South Pacific. In fact, that was even how I'd ended up a surgeon in the first place.

During my senior year at Washington DC's Woodrow Wilson High School, I was offered a football scholarship to Bucknell University. I figured I'd go to Bucknell, get my degree, and then—who knew?—maybe medical school. When I arrived on campus in the fall of 1941 and reported to the coach, he smiled and said, "Fine, get over there and start snapping to the kicker."

Several months later after the bombing of Pearl Harbor, Coach announced that our country was now at war and that we were all going down to the local federal building to sign up for the military: And so we did. I chose the Navy, having a bit of small-boat experience. The Navy recruiting officer assured me that eventually I'd be sent to medical school depending on where the openings were and that I had nothing to worry about. I signed up.

I finished one year at Bucknell, and then began my military service on a work detail in Plattsburgh, New York. It was a hot, summery day, and I was sweating in an old, abandoned building that was being renovated. I was part of the renovation crew, when suddenly a Jeep pulled up and the driver yelled something, which sounded like Sunkjan. That had to be me. He zipped me to the commandant's office where a bored yeoman told me I'd passed my exams, to get my duffel bag together and head for the bus station. I was being sent to Cornell University for officer candidate school.

After graduating as an Ensign in May of 1943 and getting my thirty days' home leave, I reported to the 12th Naval District in San Francisco for further transfer to the South Pacific. I was being sent to the 7th Fleet Amphibious Forces. I couldn't wait to get on with my life, to get to where the action was. Many long weeks later, I finally shipped out on a naval transport called the Sea Cat *PA225* and eventually reached Hollandia, New Guinea, where, of course, no one was expecting me. My flotilla was nowhere in sight, and no one knew where it was.

That evening at the Officers Club, I sat alone, morose and nursing a ten-cent gin-and-tonic, unhappy that I'd have to find a spot in Bachelor Officer Quarters to bunk. Just then, a rowdy bunch of Aussies invited me to join them for dinner and later invited me to their airstrip station thirty miles up in the mountains at a place called Sentani. I spent the next six weeks trying to locate my flotilla from there, using a Jeep shuttle to keep in touch with the harbormaster. As it happened, those were the best six weeks anyone could imagine: great weather, great food and drink flown in daily from Australia, fresh game, and movies at night. It was an idyllic existence even when we captured Japanese soldiers skulking around in the bush watching the movie. Eventually, though, word came from the harbormaster that my ships had steamed in; I said my goodbyes to the Aussies and rode down to the port. My farewell dinner hangover would take days to clear.

I reported aboard the flotilla flagship, the LST *466*, and was promptly berated by the operations officer for hiding with the Aussies, avoiding duty, keeping an officer from returning home, etc., etc. I finally got it through to them that there was no space for me at the BOQ in Hollandia and I'd had no place to stay. The Aussies had been heaven sent. Realizing my plight, they invited this poor Yank to join them at their mountainside ranch quarters at Sentani. I explained how I'd kept in touch with the harbormaster but for security reasons could never be told when and where my ship was located. But only, I think, after my explanations, which they reluctantly accepted, and with a touch of envy I suspected, things quieted down and I was assigned to communications and deck duty.

Our ships, each formally dubbed a "Landing Ship, Tank," were known as LSTs for short, which many took to mean "large, stationary targets." We often were exactly that.

After fifteen months of sea duty, I was transferred to Washington and began shore duty at Main Navy in August of 1946, in my spare time garnering needed undergraduate credits at night school. It was while I was at Main Navy and taking night school courses that I applied directly to medical school and—*mirabile dictu*—was admitted after my Navy discharge without an undergraduate degree. Acceleration of this sort was not unheard of as the country demobilized in the mid-1940s, but still, it did mean that I became an MD with just one year of college. I didn't do too badly, though, and by the late 1950s, I'd become a specialist and had even been anointed with the rank of Clinical Professor of Surgery.

So when the offer came to head back across the Pacific, it felt like being asked to dig out my uniform from fourteen years earlier. But I wasn't in the military any more. My years of dodging Japanese bombs in the South Pacific were now well behind me. As a civilian, I could have left Vietnam alone. I could have said, "No."

Somehow, I didn't.

I was, admittedly, a prime candidate for the job in question. Not only was I serving on the board of the international relief agency CARE, but I also was part of its Medico in-field service branch, and it was clear enough that I would fit right in with a team of physicians, nurses, technicians, and anesthetists being organized hastily at the request of the USOM in Saigon. The head of Medico, a Dr. Peter Comanduras, leaned on me heavily to go, as did the dean of George Washington University Hospital, John Parks. They both had twisty, circuitous connections to the State Department, and were determined that I be part of this team headed to Saigon for a few months—an All-American Surgical Team. It would consist of nurses, technicians, and doctors from top U.S. teaching institutions. Famed Dr. Richard Overholt from Boston, one of America's top lung surgeons and a pioneer in surgical treatment of tuberculosis (TB), would be one of the team surgeons. Another was Dr. Carl Almond, a highly trained disciple of the famed heart surgeon Michael DeBakey.

Comanduras assured me it was the right thing to do; my surgical and teaching skills were needed for just a few months, I was told, to help in Vietnamese hospitals and medical schools. America would be grateful, I was assured; our struggling Vietnamese friends needed our help. A specific selling point was that tuberculosis was prevalent in Vietnam. If medicines couldn't melt the TB-bug from diseased lungs, this team would remove it with scalpels. Dean Parks concurred with somber nods of his shiny, bald head. Parks gave me a sweeping leave of absence from my teaching rounds, clinics, and classes and arranged for my patients to be covered. It was all set—a done deal.

Honestly, I thought the whole grandiose sales pitch was bullshit even then. And why I agreed to go remains a mystery to me still. I was just coming into my own professionally and otherwise in Washington, and running off to Southeast Asia on a do-good venture could not possibly help my career. And soon after I accepted the invitation—indulging whatever suppressed appetite for adventure it seemed likely to satisfy—a familiar, inner voice of guilt started kicking in at night, often waking me from sleep. At times, it was deeply disturbing: Doctor, are you nuts? Are you scared? Why are you running halfway around the world, away from all your responsibilities?

To this day, I don't know the answers. I just kept reassuring myself that I would only be forsaking my personal and professional life back home for just a few months. That made it thinkable, at least.

Off to Saigon we went.

CHAPTER 3

Saigon, Pearl of the Orient

SAIGON WAS A DIRTY, NOISY, AND TENSE CITY IN 1959. THE BUSY STREETS were filled with rickshaws, bicycles, mopeds, motorbikes, hordes of little taxis, and still more hordes of people. Sidewalks were crammed as people crowded each other to buy their daily *chao dai*, or egg rolls, and noodles from street vendors. At the edges, chattering little women in traditional *ao dai* tunics minced gracefully along, carrying little string bags loaded with the day's shopping.

The atmosphere was murky, with fumes from all the vehicles and some assistance from animal droppings. Like all cities in Southeast Asia, Saigon had a distinctive scent, a mixture of jasmine, sandalwood, smoke, and night soil. One became aware of this miasma the moment a plane's doors opened and one stepped out into it. The malodorous fog also gave a bluish tint to the air. The climate was saved only by an occasional draft of air from the nearby Saigon River.

From the moment our team stepped foot in the city, our Vietnamese counterparts greeted us with open arms. We were heroes, feted nightly by physicians, embassy personnel, and ministry officialdom. These social obligations soon became exhausting, and for westerners not used to the oppressive humidity, it was a wearying pace. To make things worse, almost everyone spoke a strange tongue, and English was odd man out. I didn't fit. Within the first week I was homesick, wanting only to salve my feelings of guilt, serve my sentence in no-man's land, and get back to my home base in Washington.

USOM had quartered me in the venerable Majestic Hotel, a lovely turn-of-the-century building at the intersection of Quai Belgique and Rue Catinat overlooking the busy Saigon River, itself teeming with junks, passenger ships, and sailboats of all sizes and shapes. At any hour of day or night, huge freighters were loading and unloading cargo at riverside wharves. Lights, noise, and occasionally cruise liners with dance bands blaring livened up the waterfront. Why there were no collisions on the river was a mystery. At times, racing shells manned by the few remaining French knifed through the water, missing other boats by inches. Curses at them in many languages flew across the river intermingled with other noises.

Across the river from the Majestic, in the Chinese sector of old Saigon, was the Cho Rai Hospital. There, I was assigned a small office without air conditioning. It was typical of French colonial buildings and hospitals: open verandas, wide pavilions, louvers, and shuttered windows. The French knew their colonies well. The arrangement was functional but not comfortable, assuring that one didn't spend too much time sitting. The desk chair didn't even tilt backward.

There was an X-ray viewbox on the wall, of German make. A telephone, which occasionally worked, was a Swiss make, and the desk lamp of uncertain origin. Here I conducted my medical business, wrote reports and completed charts. The hospital gardener always had a vase of fresh flowers on my desk to break up the drabness. Oddly colored flowers were everywhere, and almost all smelled like gardenias or frangipani. Their combined aromas were so overpowering, however, that I often placed them out in the hallway.

Cho Rai was no cutting-edge hospital, especially its operating rooms, which were open to the elements—no windows, just shuttered blinds to keep out the burning sun's rays and to allow the rare stirrings of air to pass through. In some rooms, ancient overhead fans reminiscent of an old Humphrey Bogart movie actually swished round and round. Floor fans circulated hot air, dust, and an occasional sparrow that had gotten too close to the blades. But with no air-conditioning and Saigon a very hot place, any air movement was a blessing.

Above us, geckos—Asian, fly-eating lizards— suspended upside down by sticky finger-pads scooted across ceilings. I wondered if they ever fell, but the Vietnamese nurses assured me that not only did this never happen but that, in fact, their presence was a sign of good luck, especially when they croaked. OK, I thought, thrice blessed am I, because there were always several scooting around when I operated.

My team and I held clinics, reviewed X-rays, gave advice, consulted with our counterparts, and made suggestions for Western-style treatment. On operating days, I spent hours resecting sections of lung ravaged by tuberculosis—lungs resistant to all medicines. Some patients had been subjected first to pneumothorax, a technique during which air was leaked deliberately into the chest to cause the lung to collapse. In theory, this also delivered a blow to the TB by depriving the bugs of space to grow. It sometimes worked, but it was more often a failure and just slowed the healing process.

Operating on those patients was a ball-buster. Lungs were hideously scarred and stuck fast to everything inside the chest. Shaving a diseased lung off the heart and carefully peeling it off the pulmonary artery and veins can be scary. But my former chief of surgery back in Washington DC, Brian Blades, had schooled me well. I could do the toughest of these cases without much sweat, thanks to his training.

Underneath their clean, white garb, operating-room personnel sweated buckets. Performing an operation usually does that to all team members, and the tougher the case, the more one sweats. It's stress—pure, unadulterated, raw stress. When someone's life hangs on a surgeon's ability to dissect cleanly, it can be unnerving. But the ability to put aside stressful aspects of the case is what separates a master surgeon from an ordinary hacker. Some surgeons never bridge that gap.

Two hospital events brought me face-to-face with reality in dramatic fashion. I had just removed part of a tuberculous lung from a senior Buddhist monk. It was a tough resection, and he'd lost some blood. Postoperatively, the patient had been hooked to a ventilator, and when we tried to wean him off, he couldn't tolerate it. Things didn't look good, so back to the ventilator.

During early rounds on his fourth postoperative day, I entered his ward, but the monk's bed was empty. There were fresh sheets, the bed neatly made up. There was no sign of its former occupant. Two of his priests were waiting for me; they were smiling. They went through the ritual of prayerful clasped hands and head bowing.

"*Bac Si* [Doctor]," they said, "our brother asked us to thank you for all you did for him. But he knew that he would never breathe on his own, and so it was time for him to move on to another life, and we obeyed his wishes. We removed the breathing machine." They had turned off the ventilator, and the old monk had quietly died.

No sorrow, no rancor, no sign of anger—the monks stood smiling their innocent smiles, grateful for what we had done, and especially for my efforts. As they left, they presented me with a small arrangement of flowers: frangipani.

I was speechless. The loss of my patient stunned me. This Buddhist monk had deliberately opted to die, and I was totally unprepared for this. In hindsight, it was part of my maturing as a surgeon, but at the time, I blamed myself for the monk's death. This went on for days. My moods shifted from anger over having done such a poor job to guilt because I'd not had sense enough to realize the old guy couldn't tolerate losing that much lung. Looking in the mirror, I saw only a grim creature with hollow eyes, dark patches underneath, and a haunted look. Could this be me, Johnny Sundukian? I cringed. Then I went through the agonies of self-reproach that surgeons often face.

I was a mess on the inside, but no one would know it merely by watching me work. Years earlier, I'd discovered an ability to switch off all emotion by seizing on a mantra: Go cold. All feeling would be erased from my affect and my face. On those rare occasions when an operation was going to worms, with panic setting in among my team, I'd go cold. To my crew, I'd say calmly and firmly, "Just do what I tell you, and stay cool." The team would sense this confidence, take heart, and move ahead. It was an example of basic leadership in action, and it almost always worked.

If going cold protected me emotionally as I tried to make sense of the monk's suicide, I also began to develop an appreciation of the beliefs and habits of this strange country I was in. The Vietnamese sincerely believed in their afterworld; they had no fear of death. They grieved for the loss of the temporal presence of their departed, for he was no longer there. But he was with his ancestors, and that's what really mattered—what was, in fact, more important. Prayers were directed to him, as they were to other ancestors as well.

I wasn't sure I could embrace such a concept, but then I wasn't really all that religious a person. For that matter, the monk had left temporal earth happily and willingly, so who the hell was I to question his choice, just because my ego had been bruised?

There was other drama as well. Earlier that week, I'd been spat upon by a patient who, it turned out, hated white people, especially Americans. The hospital administrator was aghast when he learned of this and insisted that the patient in question was a communist. This was part of the communists' effort to try to drive the Americans off, he said. "A thousand pardons, *Bac Si*."

(Hell, I thought, I'd had worse things happen to me right in Washington. Try talking to a demented patient who barges into your office cursing obscenities and waving a large pistol at you. I'd resected his malignant lung tumor several months earlier, but his wife, thinking he was dying, told him she was leaving him. "You should have killed me on the operating table!" he screamed.)

And so it went, day in and day out, week after week. Operate, lunch, nap, and head back to the hospital. My hotel room was air-conditioned, and at slack times, I just hung out there. It was my space for answering correspondence, making notes, and hiding. My life assumed a monastic, monotonous character, and I was already decidedly tired of it.

Then, however, a normal social life began to creep in. I befriended a fellow named François, who would drop by to chat with the gloomy, lonely American doctor. One day, I asked him about a car I noticed, an ancient Citroen waiting in front of the hotel and full of what had to be Americans. A window decal, surely placed there as a gag, read MSU, and underneath, in small print Michigan State University. That certainly was surprising. What the hell were these people doing here?

"Hah," François said, "those chaps are American police on contract with some crooked government, yours or this one here, I don't know wheech. Maybe secret police, maybe even your CIA. The official story is they are here to train the Vietnamese police in Western crowd-control. What lies—they are probably commandos waiting for something to happen."

So that's how come they all had fuzz cuts. Obviously, they were military or law enforcement of some kind—MPs, probably.

But why?

CHAPTER 4

François Sully

*We are here on Earth to do good to others. What
the others are here for, I don't know.*
—W.H. Auden

I'D FIRST MET FRANÇOIS ONE DAY AT CHO RAI. I WAS DIGGING MY WAY through X-rays and patient lists; there were some nasty resections coming up. All were bad cases of TB, one a possible carcinoma, and one a chest-wall tumor. I was betting that a certain round tumor which showed up on X-ray was a tuberculous abscess, well "encapsulated." In medical parlance meant encased in a cocoon of scar. We'd see.

A steward knocked on the door, clasped his hands, and did a little head bob. "*Bac Si*," he said. "Visitor," pointing to the front of the hospital. It was an easy amble out there, and sure enough, there stood a pipe-smoking man in a safari jacket with huge rings of sweat under the arms. A soiled ascot was strung around his damp neck. He wore rumpled chinos and ankle-high, rough-out boots—clearly military. He had a friendly smile and extended a huge, gnarled paw. His name was François Sully, he said.

"They sent me over from the CARE office," he said, adding that he was a reporter, a stringer for Agence France Presse. When AFP had learned our team was coming to Saigon, François was assigned to do a story, and he'd picked me to write about. He was hoping to shadow me for the next few weeks, hanging around with notebook and camera, snapping photos of me in operating rooms, clinics, wards, restaurants, and even on trips—a complete portrait of the bleeding-heart American doctor.

I thought that an article would be all right, but I didn't want a lot of fawning publicity, and I had no idea where he was going with his information and photos. But gradually, I loosened up and became more comfortable with him. François began to fill me in on how life was lived out here. In time, he became my introduction to the dying French empire in Southeast Asia, where life, he said, would be impossible without anisette, Pernod, whiskey, and oversexed women.

François took me in tow, insisting that I get out and see both the city and the countryside—that I get the flavor of the country. Being a people-watcher, he opined, would be a great way for me to become more worldly, as he couldn't believe how naive I was about almost every political topic he brought up. He spent hours explaining the political world in Southeast Asia—matters about which I was, frankly, totally clueless. As François began "smartening" me, I began to get a glimpse of the problems America faced, never mind the French and others before them. It was all about power and the communists' determination to take over this part of the world. And at some point, I realized that my guide was far more well rounded, informed, and savvy than just a bummed-out China hand. He was somebody's spook; he had to be. But whose?

François always wore a safari jacket in various stages of clean. Its many pockets were crammed with bulgy items that included a notebook and writing tools. Occasionally he also wore a straw hat, and sometimes shorts worn Australian-style with a belt buckle off-center. Most of the time, he wore those same U.S. Marine rough-out boots and wouldn't give a straight answer where he got them. His sunglasses were strictly Hollywood, and I assumed they were there to cover his often-bloodshot eyes, which went along with strong curry and garlic fumes. His nose was not Gallic but rather squat and puffy, yet it had only a few of the veins seen in heavy boozers. But François was still young. His features all blended into the look of a beefy local who sweated furiously, stained his hat, and at all times appeared unhappy and in need of a drink.

One day he asked in his delightful colonial-French twang, "Doctor, we shall 'ave lunch at the Cercle Sportif Saigonnaise today? Ees ok wif you?"

"Sure François, whatever you say."

The Cercle Sportif was a city club for the French and certain genteel, Francophile Vietnamese. Inside a vine-covered fence was a huge pool, tennis courts, and dining facilities. At cocktail time, an ancient piano's keys were caressed by a downtrodden French pianist. He played on the veranda and plinked out nostalgic tunes à la Hoagy Carmichael, occasionally crooning cocktail melodies with a throaty, whiskey-altered voice and the occasional cough. On most Fridays, there was a dance band and cocktail-style dancing. *Quelle* civilized? I thought.

My lunch with François at the club was to be my first foray into the local social scene, below the formal circuit of embassy receptions. As we made our way to the dining rooms, François introduced me to certain of the local citizenry. Some were denizens of the fourth estate—reporters from France and Australia, a couple said to be Polish—as well as women workers from various charities. Of the latter, some of the more unattractive ones wore unusually large, silver crosses suspended on their chests, though for what reason I would never know. All were in there for the same purpose, supposedly: to help the poor downtrodden of Vietnam. But after a few minutes of listening to their inane conversations, I realized that these people didn't give a rat's ass for the locals or their welfare or that of anyone in all of Vietnam. As we moved on, François confirmed my suspicions.

"John, you see that little bastard with the goatee?"

"Yeah."

"What you think of him?"

"Well, he told me he was a reporter for an Australian news syndicate."

François stopped me with an upraised palm. "Don't believe a word of it. All these bastards are spies or fuckin' commie sympathizers who pretend to be reporters, or workers in God's name. Actually, all they do is snoop and spy, so watch what you say. They may say they like you, but they hate you. Especially that chubby woman over there—the one wif the big tits and the huge silver cross. What you think of her?"

"Hard to say—she has this big cross on her chest. Is she a nun?"

"Ah-hah, *M'sieu*. She *was* a nun. They caught her fuckin' wif the Monsignor and kicked her out. So now she is out here doing her penance, while also fuckin' that commie Australian reporter and still wearing her big cross on her fat tits. Ugh. Avoid her, *mon ami*, she may have the big eyes for you next. Anyway, you wouldn't like her. She wants to make the world commie, and she stinks—always she needs a shave and bath."

I made a mental note: Avoid the cross.

Frankly, I'd never been in the presence of such people. Real persons involved in mind-numbing goings-on: spies, hanky panky, and undercover do-gooders. Clearly I had some more growing up to do. The thought of what François had told me and what I'd seen made me shrink up inside a little.

"Come, John, we eat."

We ate. The food was fabulous, a delicate combination of the French and Asiatic: cold, cracked crab; langoustines; marinated squid; fresh salads; and fruits. And exquisite pastries. Almost everyone drank drank tea or *Bamibam*, the French beer with the numerals 33—Bamibam is 33 in Vietnamese—on the label.

I was on my second helping of cold shrimp when I sensed something glide by, trailing an exotic lemony perfume. I looked up, but by then the source had passed us.

François noticed my craning and chuckled. "*Docteur*, avoid that one."

"Huh? Why? Whatever for and just who in the hell is she? She sure smells nice."

"*Attendez*. She works for the Michigan people. She says she is a secretary there or sumsing like zat. But she is more, I theenk. She has a United Nations passport and an Irish one, too. Her husband is a pilot, flies the big white plane for the U.N., always flying big shots back and forth. And sometimes visits Saigon to say "*'allo*" to wifey dear. And she 'as a good fran—maybe a companion, some say her lover, but I don' theenk so—who also is a pilot here in Saigon, for the Michelin tire people." He squinted, touched the side of his nose, and nodded his head knowingly.

He went on: "Some call her the Ice Maiden. She is like Ingrid Bergman—nice figure, magnificent chest, and built maybe a little like your Grace Kelly. *Mon dieu*, when you see her in the bikini, you will understand. Me, I theenk it's all a mask, this cool façade. Some women are like that, you know—dull-looking until they get you between the sheets, then *ma foi*, look out! I theenk a light secretly burns under her skirt. But then I have no knowledge of zis. Finish your drink, *mon ami*."

I made note of all this, wondering when the hell I would ever see her in a bikini.

Reading my mind, François said discouragingly, "She only eats here—never swims. She never looks at you, either, and if you look at her, she gives you the *tout rien*, the nothing smile, like the Mona Lisa's. *Rien de tout*! Nothing more. You wonder what she's thinking. But she knows what you're thinking: You want to fuck her. Zat makes some men nervous. Other men are attracted to her like a moth to the candle. I theenk she gives them that cool smile to make them uncomfortable. But in small groups, she can be very charming, very cordial, very *classée*. She is educated, cultured, and very *au courant* on important events. And she is very clever. But I have warned you, *mon ami*: Don't get your dick caught in the zipper, or your wings burned in the candle flame, you hear me?"

A short while later, I noticed a figure leaving, making her way on the opposite side of the pool, and there was no doubt: this was the woman that François had described. Spectacular body, a regal bearing, and long, tawny legs. She was chesty, make no mistake, but she didn't flaunt it. Still, when she firmly put down each short-heeled sandal, her boobs jiggled a bit. And I had the feeling she knew it. In fact, there was a practiced rhythm to her gait, like a U.S. Marine. Step, click, step clack, jiggle, jiggle. Jiggle jaggle.

I made her to be in her late twenties or early thirties. Hair the color of pale honey, with a few lighter streaks. And definitely not from a bottle. She allowed a quick glimpse of slim ankles on long, tanned legs inside a revealing, wrap-around skirt. And did I see, as she moved her arms, a flash of tapered fingers with red nails and matching toenails? Indeed, I did. Quite a package she displayed, and she wanted to display it. And did I imagine that she swayed her backside as she flounced out, that she knew we were watching?

She looked straight ahead, as though she were on parade, on display—as though she knew I was looking and was giving me a private show. Of course this was all fantasy on my part—wasn't it? Looking neither left nor right, still very much the regal one, she strode out of my sight towards the exit onto the Quai Bourgogne. It had only been a few seconds, but looking at her had given me an odd stirring in my groin, which, at the moment, was a tad embarrassing.

My interest in Saigon had just risen, too.

— - • - —

FRANÇOIS'S TALK OF PILOTS AND small planes was a kind of omen for me, as it turned out. Several days later, the local CARE people contacted me, asking if I might fly to Cambodia and examine the son of a prominent French family. Local doctors had said the boy had a hole in his heart, and my going to check him out was pitched to me as a chance for our ambassador in Phnom Penh to do an important favor. The trip would take just that day. I would be ferried to and from Cambodia in an embassy plane. It sounded to me more like a subtle command rather than a request; how could I refuse?

"*D'accord*," said I, and I packed my stethoscope and blood pressure cuff (which was all I really needed), plus camera, lenses, and extra film. A safari jacket seemed right—lots of pockets. Khaki slacks and broken-in combat shoes.

At Tan Son Nhut Airport, a shiny DC-3 waited. Civil Air Transport, it said on its sides; two pilots loafed alongside. The captain spotted me, and waved me over.

"Hi, I'm Gerald Smith with CAT, and this here is Serge Evans, my number one. We have this little beauty gassed up and ready to go to Phnom Penh. You ready to fly, Doc?"

I looked them over. I'd wager these two men were red-blooded Americans from the Midwest. For all the world, I could have been at National Airport in Washington. They were in white shirts, ties, dark slacks, and snappy airline pilot's caps. So very proper even this far from home. But there was something else. It's hard to describe, but something about their stance and mannerisms screamed military pilots, either present or past. But no matter, they looked competent—and damn well had to be competent, if they were flying in this part of the world.

I gave each a firm handshake and my best big smile and climbed on board. Within minutes, we were airborne.

We flew across miles of rice paddies, ponds, foreboding jungle, forests, and huge plantation spreads. After about an hour in the air, I caught the glint of gold-capped spires off in the distance. Gradually, we descended into the city area; we slowed some more, and suddenly we were zipping by amazing sights on both sides of the plane: brick, red-tiled temple roofs and tall spires of bright, shiny gold that reflected the sun in a dazzling—almost blinding—blast of light. I knew from reading that this was gold-leaf appliqué, lovingly applied by Buddhist adherents over hundreds of years. It had to be inches thick and was surely worth a fortune.

Upon landing, we were met by a driver, and I was shuttled off to the embassy. The pilots had things to do with the plane and were quite happy to stay behind. They mentioned that after the plane check, they'd head for the Green Latrine, a notorious bar and restaurant that could accommodate lonely men. Be back after lunch. OK with me?

Certainly.

After obligatory social niceties at the embassy, I was led with my frightened but brave young patient to a room set aside for the exam, his anxious parents trailing. Notably, the boy was slightly underdeveloped for his age, which is often seen in such cases: not enough oxygenated blood makes it to the body's tissues, reducing nourishment to the growth centers. With a disarming smile, I slipped on my stethoscope and listened over his chest wall. Sure enough, I heard a familiar, continuous murmur just to the left of his scrawny sternum, up high—the signature of a "patent ductus lesion" that connected the aorta to the pulmonary artery, an errant holdover from birth. At the same time, it could have been a "septal defect," a flaw from one heart chamber to another. I needed special equipment to make a more definite diagnosis. There was no such equipment here, and just as well. Phnom Penh wouldn't be the place to do any tests. Far better he go home and see the doctors there. If it were a ductus, it needed to be fixed, and soon, since he was old enough now and should have a good result from an operation. I turned to speak to the parents.

"I think you should take your son back to Paris to have an operation to repair this little problem with his heart. It is a fairly simple operation to tie off the still-open connection. Paris is your home, isn't it?"

The boy's mother answered. "Yes, of course, Doctor, but can you not operate on him here? We wish to stay here for now, and we have many reasons not to return to France at this time."

"Well, your son probably has a small artery from the artery above his heart which didn't close off after birth. He needs to have certain X-ray studies to show the location and size of this little artery so that the surgeon knows where to go and what to do. It would be best for your son to go to Paris or some other city in Europe or even America for proper diagnosis and treatment. I speak from experience; I've done many such operations. I strongly urge you to have it done by your own surgeons near your home. Have I made myself clear? Do you have any other questions?"

They said they understood and thanked me repeatedly. As I made ready to leave, they presented me with a small package of French Cabernet—in cans! Cans? I remembered that Air France served me wines poured from cans. These wines I was being offered were identical to the Air France bottled brands, which had been excellent Cabernets. The boy's parents recognized my surprise and assured me that the cans kept the wines from oxidizing or aging. A cork, they said, doesn't last in the tropics; there, cork's only use was in safari helmets.

"*Bon,*" said I heartily, "*Merci beaucoup.*"

Not thirty minutes later, Gerald, Serge and I were winging our way back to Saigon.

"Wanna ride in the cockpit?" Captain Smith pointed to the jump seat.

"Absolutely!" I said. "Can I get some photos from up here?"

"Sure. In fact, why not hop in the co-pilot seat and fire away?"

I couldn't believe my luck. I quickly switched seats with the grinning co-pilot, and there I was, in the right seat, the co-pilot's seat in a fixed wing aircraft!

"Wanna steer ?"

"Sure," I answered, still in heaven. The captain showed me how to do it: push the rudder pedals and turn the steering wheel, which work the ailerons in coordinated turns. Anyone on the ground might have wondered at the aircraft doing some funny S-turns over Cambodia. Let 'em. At that moment I knew that someday I would learn to fly.

CHAPTER 5

Antoine Nicolai
Chief Pilot for Michelin, S.A.

So it came to pass that I met the chief pilot for Michelin, the French megabusiness and granddaddy of rubber plantations the world over. As a result of this meeting, I learned, among other things, to fly.

It happened this way: I had just arrived at one of the small soirées that François held at his little home in a suburb of Saigon. As I first stepped inside, I glanced at a group of people nearby, among them a red-faced, beefy Brit squiring a tiny Vietnamese woman who spoke passable English with some French mixed in. I noticed that almost all were smoking and chattering away like so many small birds. Many were clutching long drinks, too. But all conversation had stopped when they saw me coming up the walkway with François. They knew who I was, it seemed, and I didn't take comfort from the looks I saw on their faces—a mix of curiosity and hostility.

"Allo...attention," yelled François. "I have the pleasure to introduce to you peasants," he chuckled, "the American surgeon, Dr. Johnny Sundukian."

I felt myself reddening as I felt their eyes on me. I knew I was getting the once-over.

"The doctor," François continued, "is here to save our Vietnamese hosts from the ravages of tuberculosis, to teach them medicine, and make them members of the new world in the mold of America." Why he said all that I'll never know. I think it was a ploy to put conversation on a new tack, and possibly, in a perverse way, to irritate his guests. He succeeded. There wasn't a single welcoming expression or even the faintest smile on any face—nothing but a palpable dislike of me.

Slowly, the assembled turned back to their conversations. Many couples were chatting in French, there was a bit of English, and I recognized some Vietnamese. I looked them all over; this was a motley crew of people. One fellow spoke with an Australian accent, touting the virtues of Asti Spumante. It was the only champagne readily available in this area, he proclaimed, and quite good. Cases were supplied him by the Italian attaché. His companion was one of the ugly women, a social worker affectedly smoking a tiny cheroot. From time to time she poofed little spurts of smelly smoke from pursed lips, the upper of which sported a thin mustache. Ugh, thought I. Would anyone sober ever kiss her?

Near them stood a small, mousy couple who kept awfully still, eyes furtively glancing around as though being hunted. I had the feeling they were almost quivering, but whether from excitement or fear wasn't clear. The mousy man seemed unsure as to whether he was to be friendly with me. During François's introductions, he had handed me his card accompanied by a stiff nod. It said he was Polish. The card read:

> Tadeus W. Piwinski
> Wicekonsul,
> Ambasada Polskiej
> Rzseczypospolitej Ludowe w Saigon

I smiled and shook hands, nodded, and accepted a glass of bubbly—Asti, they said—and nibbled on some hors d'oeuvres. I fell into a discussion with some news correspondents about America's intentions in Vietnam. No, I had no idea what our intentions were, but I kept the banter up.

I was stunned when told it was widely known that our president was planning to assassinate Ngo Dinh Diem, the new Republic of Vietnam's first president. The idea was that the U.S. would install its own puppet and then make peace with the North. "After all, why do you think he has so many commandos hiding here in plain clothes?" I was asked. "There is a commando training camp up at Nha Trang."

I was taken aback by this allegation and about to say something unpleasant when François spotted my clenched jaw muscles, a dead giveaway. He grabbed my arm, stopping me in mid-flight. Just then, the Aussie piped up.

"Tell us, Doctor, do you think smoking causes lung cancer?" Whether he was changing the subject or setting me up made no difference, because, whoops, here was my chance: it was my favorite alarmist topic. My old teacher and chief, Professor Brian Blades, had forbidden me from telling medical students outright that smoking did cause lung cancer, but I always finessed him by quoting what others said about smoking—that yes, it did.

I smiled, looked around, hesitated for a moment, then said in somber professorial tones, that "Yes, unfortunately, studies are now beginning to show that lung cancer did indeed appear to be on the rise, and especially in smokers. And that now, slowly, we are beginning to see the identical disease in women—that is, male-pattern lung cancers. But," I hastened to add, "please do not let this stop you from smoking, because if everyone were to stop, it would be very bad for my business. And I make a great deal of money for my hospital operating on fools—I mean," as I corrected myself with mock regret, "people who smoke."

Silence. I scanned the crowd. My little *pronunciamento* had put a slight damper on the evening's fun. In no time, however, I was back in the hot seat, required to defend America against this or that preposterous claim. As I parried one petty jab after another, I allowed my eyes to wander. And they landed on a most welcome sight: There across the room, lifting a glass from a tray, was the tall, leggy woman I'd seen at the Cercle Sportif! She was a knockout, no question, and right at that moment even more so. Her hair was swept up to showcase a long, graceful neck, and she was clad in a loose dress of light green silk that looked at once fashionable, comfortable, and somehow inviting. I had trouble looking away.

Amid my sudden distraction, dinner was announced, and I stumbled my way to the dining room while doing my best to disguise repeated glances cast her way. I managed to find my place, only to arrive just as she herself slid into the seat to the left of mine! With studied aplomb, I took my chair, and she turned to me with a cool smile. "Giselle Prudhomme," she said. "My friends call me 'Gigi.'"

The ice broken, we chatted amiably. She wasn't so stiff after all; I relaxed and allowed myself to show more interest. She said she was half Scottish from her father and half French-Canadian from her mother. Now, though, she was an Argentinean citizen.

"Don't ask me how my father got to Argentina, but I think he retired from British government service and got as far away as he could," she said dismissively. "He never said much about his past. My mother's family has been there for at least a hundred years. I was born there, and I have dual citizenship—U.K. and Argentine—and my husband, an Irishman, holds a United Nations passport. It's complicated, don't you think?"

As the evening wore on, a certain camaraderie grew between us. She had an electricity about her that was exciting, but there also was something I couldn't quite identify, some element of concealment. Whatever it was, I decided then and there to find out. So I told her bits and pieces of my background, and I chatted at times haltingly—maybe shyly, even, which isn't my style at all. When I mentioned that I was still single, I noticed her eyes widen almost imperceptibly. But conversation was difficult, given continuous interruptions from her other dinner partner and a couple seated across the table. The meal finally ended, and after cognacs on a patio in back, I glanced at my watch. By most diplomatic protocols, it was time to leave.

I rose to say my goodbyes and then made a point of passing Gigi one more time. As I did, she reached out, grabbed my wrist, and gently pulled me down to ear level. Speaking softly—it was still noisy as hell, but maybe she didn't want anyone else to hear—she said, "Stop by for a nightcap. You should get to know Antoine and me better. He is so very much like you. I think you two would get along famously."

"Antoine," I had ascertained, was Antoine Nicolai, her friend and frequent companion with whom she had come to François's party. We had been introduced at the end of dinner, and I was relieved, if a little surprised, to detect no displeasure whatsoever in his greeting, given that I'd spent the last hour or so transfixed by Gigi. He was in fact genuinely kind (and so stood out in that crowd), and I was only too willing to take advantage of that kindness if it meant spending another hour or two with her.

Of course I would, I mumbled, adding that I'd make my own way to her home. She gave me directions, and as I made to leave once more, I found myself trapped yet again by the newspapermen arguing about Diem—about how he would have to go along with the North's demands, and how the French had to endure insolence from these little people. I pleaded total innocence of world affairs and asked them with faux eagerness to educate me. After all, what should I know?

I was a willing target, and I quickly got their drift. South Vietnam was a pigeon, and the hawk was waiting. I shrugged. I didn't know who the hawk was—probably the Russians, as they seemed to be behind much of the unrest in this world. Well, no, I thought, not exactly…maybe the Chinese, or the North Vietnamese, and behind them all, playing the innocent, would be the Russians.

Their dismissiveness was unmistakable—eye-rolls and shared glances that said: "Oh you Americans, you really don't know anything."

Right, I thought—I'm an American doctor, and doctors know very little about anything except maybe medicine, golf, and the stock market. Of course, I knew that didn't apply to me, but these chumps didn't.

-- • --

A WILLING FRANÇOIS OFFERED TO drop me off at Gigi's house. He was puffing on a on a huge Cuban cigar.

"Ahem, Doctor, please be careful you don't get tangle up in a spider's web…eh? Better I should find you a nice young Vietnamese girl to rub your back. It would be best for you, believe me." He said rub with a definite French intonation—ghhhhrub, almost like an Arab.

He was worried that I might get myself involved with Gigi and suggesting it could mean trouble—just in case my thoughts were running that way. And just maybe in case her thoughts were running that way, too.

Well, hell, I was a big boy. But François had been chuckling all the while between puffs on his cigar and delivering his veiled comments, so it was hard to tell how serious he was. Maybe he knew more than I did about women. Probably—he was French, wasn't he? And maybe he had his own little back-rubber.

"Thanks, but I'm OK—don't have problems there," said I. "But I thank you all the same. I'll let you know if I need a back-rubber, OK?"

Selling me on the idea of some other woman was a tall order just now. This Gigi had a captivating air about her. Still, I knew I needed to stay in control. For the moment, I'd just observe and infer.

-- • --

GIGI'S BUNGALOW WAS IN A small, secluded residential enclave a few miles from my hotel. Not to my surprise, Antoine was already there, sipping something green and evil-smelling—probably Chartreuse, a liqueur whose flavor I'd always detested. He poured a small one for me, with a single cube of ice. To be polite, I sipped; it tasted horrible. I bravely chin-chinned with him before sneakily pouring the whole dreadful mess into a jardinière.

"I say, old chap," I asked in a mock thespian voice, "Is it possible to get a plain gin tonic?"

"For you, Doctor, we have anything you wish. Bombay Gin is O.K. wif you?" I nodded almost eagerly.

I took the drink and looked around to see what the room revealed of its occupant. Soft, indirect lighting bathed the ceiling and walls. Little clusters of votive candles set in colored demiglasses were artfully scattered around the room, casting warm glows. Vietnamese sculptures, placed where they would make the greatest visual impact, stared out from eye-level wall shelves. A few primitive paintings were scattered here and there, as were several shelves of books. On a small cocktail table lay a world atlas, newspapers, and a fashion magazine—on its cover a smiling, bare woman. And over in one corner was a small table, crowded with silver-framed photos. I scanned them. They appeared to be her mother and father as well as a military man—her husband, I figured. He was very tall and handsome in his dress uniform. Navy, I thought.

I try not to pry, but a quick look tells a doctor a great deal about a patient; using those same senses, the same thinking process, it takes only a few glances at someone's living room get the "feel" of the owner—books, photos, arrangements of furniture, color combinations, and the general ambience.

My quick take was that this Gigi woman was all class—good breeding and a hint of old money. Clearly well traveled and well read, and probably well educated. The whole bungalow gave the impression that she was a genteel person. But it occurred to me that it all could all be a facade, to hide something.

I hadn't noticed, but Gigi had joined us quietly. She was perched in a corner settee, her legs tucked up under her. She'd made a quick change into very tight Levis, a pale, yellow shirt open down to the third button. (I'd counted.) It was a simple but very effective look. I may have been staring at her like a high school freshman.

Around her neck shone a thin gold chain with a tiny gold Buddha pendant—a grinning, fat, little Buddha with tiny, green eyes. Somewhere in the house, a phonograph softly played French jazz. Geckoes were still sounding off, competing with the low din of an army of crickets. Out in the courtyard torches cast flickering shadows across patio flagstones. The night air was heavy, humid, and still, but from time to time I caught whiffs of exotic jasmine floating on unseen currents.

"Please come in, Doctor," she said without moving. "Make yourself comfy. I see Antoine has fixed you something nice, and we do use ice—not like the French or the Brits." I smiled my thanks.

I could smell ginger and cilantro from somewhere. I looked over at the kitchen area where a slim Vietnamese girl with a chignon like a shiny cat's tail slid silently around, preparing food.

"Gigi, you're not still hungry," I said with contrived alarm.

"It's nothing much, doctor—just a few munchies before Minh goes home. What we don't finish tonight is my breakfast." I nibbled something salty and tasty—crabmeat, I hoped—and washed it down with green tea.

Antoine looked at his watch. "No more drinking for me tonight. I fly in the morning, so now I have one Evian for the road, and I go home."

Fly? That got my immediate attention. "Fly?" I asked.

"Yes, fly," he answered. "Tomorrow I fly the payroll to three of our rubber plantations. Boring, really, but the only way to pay workers out in the back country."

"Could I come along?" I blurted out.

"Why you want to go? I tell you now, is boring, maybe dangerous, and will take most of the morning. But you want to come along—is fine, I can use the company. So, seven o'clock at the civilian side of the aerodrome," he said, using the French term. "You will see my Beaver getting ready."

"Can I bring my camera?"

"Of course. Bring also a bottle of water, and strong sunglasses, too."

I was genuinely excited at the prospect, and I guess it showed. Gigi chuckled softly. "Doctor, this man flies a little crazy because he is former military, and they are all a little crazy. But he is the best pilot in Vietnam. In fact, if you ask him nicely, maybe he will teach you to fly."

How could she have known?

Now I was anxious to get to the hotel and sleep. But I had no transportation, and no taxis were out at this time of night.

The hotel wasn't too far a walk.

Antoine: "Wait, Doctor, I drop you."

-- • --

At seven sharp the next morning, I was at the airport. I'd seen photos of deHavilland Beavers in flying magazines, and I already knew of its reputation as one tough workhorse. It's a single high-wing with a powerful 450-HP, radial engine—a real mule and a bitch to fly until you get the hang of it. It's used in the bush, the desert, and the outback. It can land and takeoff from anywhere; with floats it even lands on water. Now, right in front of me, one of these stubby machines sat near the terminal, gleaming in the early morning sun. On the pilot-side door was painted: MICHELIN.

Antoine was there, fussing at a mechanic in Vietnamese. Both were looking under the cowling. Antoine was speaking and gesturing, too, just like a true Frenchman.

A vehicle pulled up close to the plane. Quickly, two men transferred heavy, white canvas bags into the cargo section; they carried sidearms. One climbed in the rear section and plopped down.

Antoine checked a clipboard, counted bags, and signed for them. "OK, we go."

I climbed into the right seat, my camera suspended around my neck. My safari jacket held a bottle of Evian, a notebook and pencil, my passport, and some money. I was ready and fairly bursting with excitement. Imagine: I was headed out over the jungle in a small plane to land at plantations? Amazing.

While we waited for clearance, Antoine grumbled at the slow tower operators. He pulled out a chart. "We fly first here and then here, we buzz the strip, and if the recognition flags are OK, we dump the money on the runway and fly off; if not, we keep the money and keep flying. The VC and other bad peoples know about the money run but don't know when until I take off. Word then gets to the backcountry fast. Sometimes they want to rob us, but we have guards on the ground, and we shoot the bastards. Is dangerous at times, but you are with me, so not to worry."

He went through his checklist, mumbling to himself. It was funny in a way: He would yell a question at himself then answer it: "Altimeter? Set; two niner niner two, Fuel Pump? On!" And so it went, until the checklist was completed.

"Tower. Michelin, you are cleared runway three eight, immediate takeoff...contact one two zero decimal six on departure, altimeter two niner niner two: Climb and maintain three thousand your departure altitude until further advised, *adieu*."

"Roger, tower, we move now," Antoine answered. "OK, Doctor, hang on. Don't touch nothing, don't put your foot on the pedals. Touch only your camera, take all the damn pictures you want—you strapped, yes?"

"Yes."

He had the control yoke on his side, but I noticed it could flip over to my side too—cute. When Antoine started the engine, it caught with a deafening roar. He wore earphones and spoke to the tower with his face mike, but he'd left the overhead speaker on for me to listen. Just now it was playing music from some Armed Forces station….jazz. It made for a crazy cacophony of sounds, a bit disconcerting for the uninitiated.

"Michelin, Tower. We are rolling. *Adieu*."

He advanced the throttle, and suddenly we were roaring down the runway. After a short distance, he gave a gentle pull on the yoke. The Beaver leapt up like a scared squirrel—and just like that, we were zooming out and away over the city.

Wow, was my first response; it was my first pop in a small plane. An exhilarating feeling, a "freeness," spread over me. Just below, rows of houses with red-tiled roofs, sampans, and small sailboats on the Saigon River, then oceangoing ships and little skiffs, and then we were zipping over rice paddies, all the while climbing slowly. Ahead of us in the distance was an unbroken blanket of bright-green jungle.

Antoine was busy adjusting throttles, pitch, and mixtures. He called tower to advise he was nearing 3,000 feet, the air-speed indicator reading 120 mph. Below us now was a solid, green carpet as far as the eye could see. About twenty minutes later, I was still open-mouthed at all the strange sights below us. We were now flying level and this high up, the air, mercifully, was a trifle cooler.

Antoine signaled me to put on my earphones. I heard lots of clicks and static…then, "Doctor, out there is the first plantation. All what you see is rubber trees. In five minutes we make our first run. OK?

"Fine."

I looked at my watch; it had only been about thirty minutes since takeoff. We must have gone nearly seventy miles, and now were heading south. Antoine pointed; off in the distance I saw a reddish gash in the green carpet. It looked like a dirt road, laid out next to a huge complex of buildings. We dropped closer and buzzed across ranch houses, a pool, tennis courts, a wide patio with a smoking grill, cars, trucks, and suddenly Antoine banked hard to the left and powered down, then dropped his flaps. We began our approach to the long, dirt airstrip gouged out of raw jungle.

Off to the left sat a large hangar, atop which spired a huge flagpole with a large green pennant hanging, sad and limp. Antoine smiled, gave me a thumbs-up, and waggled his wings as he zipped past the hangar. Then gunned the engine, zoomed back up, banked hard left, left again, and abruptly nosed down toward the strip.

I had been clicking away furiously, changing film once—a neat trick under the circumstances. Antoine turned and yelled something at the guard, and a moment later I heard rushing air from the back. The guard had kicked open the cargo door and held it out with his foot, simultaneously tossing out three of the canvas money bags. The door then slammed shut, and we zoomed upwards, circling the strip.

As we banked, I saw a small Jeep race out to the bags which had landed dead center in the middle of the runway. Two rifle-toting men retrieved them; they waved, and we waggled our wings in response.

We quickly climbed back up to 3,000 feet and headed off again. Antoine opened the chart, put a finger where we'd been and pointed ahead to where we were going. Frankly, I was a touch airsick with all the acrobatics, but no way was I going to let him know. I sucked it in, smiled weakly, and took a sip from my Evian bottle. I had a sneaking feeling that Antoine knew and was snickering up his sleeve, but after a few minutes of straight and level flight, things settled down for me.

The next drop site was done much the same way, but it was getting on to lunchtime now. Antoine looked at his watch. "Doctor," he yelled into the mike, "maybe we stop here and visit with our friends." He pointed to the next spread coming up about five miles ahead. As before, he buzzed the field, which looked perfectly calm: another green flag hung limply from a flagpole atop a hangar. Antoine turned to a guard, gave him a flat hand-sweep, and then began a flaps-down "crabbing" descent, landing with only a few bumps and a huge cloud of red dust behind him.

At the end of the runway, he made a power turn, and we trundled practically up to the front steps of a charming ranch house beneath a huge copse of shade trees. At the last minute, Antoine wheeled the plane smartly, gunning the engine as he cut the ignition. A sputter, and then all was quiet. He set the brakes.

"How you like zat, *docteur*?"—this time using the French pronunciation. I smiled. What else would one do? Although I was still a touch lightheaded, I wouldn't own up to it. Shoulder on, I said to myself.

Several men and an attractive woman ran down to greet us "alloing" and us waving. There was lots of laughter, rapid French, and then my introduction: the *Americain docteur*. Our greeters were the managers of the plantation, and we were just in time for lunch, they announced. Come in and wash up, then please join us.

We left the guard with the plane and were ushered to the veranda. Extra plates, iced tea, Citron soda, and huge platters of food: cheeses, fruit salads, and bread. Everywhere were pots of shrubs and jungle flowers—even orchids. A nice lunchtime setting, with an overhead fan to keep us cool.

I asked about the guard. Antoine said, "Don't worry for him. The kitchen staff will take him food. He can't have any beer, but I can—just one," he chuckled, and our idle chatter continued.

About fifteen minutes into the luncheon, one of the kitchen helpers came over and whispered urgently to the manager in Vietnamese, who quickly relayed the information to Antoine.

"*Faché merde!*" he yelled. "I should not have landed. I didn't listen to myself. *Alors*," he spoke rapidly in French to his hosts: A stakeout truck loaded with armed bandits had appeared at the end of the runway. They probably were planning to stop our takeoff, having learned of the payroll aboard, but for the present they were too afraid to come near the house. Instead, they were watching and waiting.

The plan was first to retire inside the house—leisurely, slowly, acting as though nothing was out of the ordinary. We did, and as soon as we were inside, Antoine grabbed a pair of field glasses and slid over to a window.

"Hah, a motley group of ragtag bandits...not any military bearing...not communists, just bandits. OK, I call the Army."

Antoine picked up the phone. Dead. The lines had been cut.

"Bastards," he said through clenched teeth. "Yes, well, you bastards, so you think you are clever, eh? Hah! OK, then, I have another plan."

He asked for the keys for the company car and checked his sidearm, a mean-looking .45 automatic. Then looked at me. "Doctor, can you shoot?"

"Yeah," I said. And it was true: I'd had a sidearm in the Navy, a 1911-model .45-caliber pistol. Antoine tossed me a holster holding a similar Colt .45 and a spare clip.

"Strap it on, and let's go out through the side door."

"Mind telling me where we're going?"

"Yes, *mon ami*, we are going to sneak down the back lane to the local army garrison, and if any of the half-assed soldiers are there, maybe they will come and chase those bastards away. These bandits are afraid of their shadow—otherwise they would have attacked the plane and the house by now. They will run faster if they see more than five people."

Antoine was angry: nostrils flaring, eyelids narrowed, and little beads of sweat—more than the usual tropical sort—rolling down the side of his face. He adjusted his hat. Speaking rapidly, he told the ranch foreman and his wife to lock the doors and shoot the first bandit that approached the house.

As it turned out, this would not be a problem: the ranch was equipped with a cabinet full of shotguns, rifles, handguns, and one huge, serious-looking weapon that was almost a blunderbuss. Antoine pulled out the mammoth rifle and patted it, almost fondly.

"This, Doctor, is an M 209, one of your military guns. Blow the shit out of anything. You load a 40-mm. grenade in the lower chamber, then when you get mad at someone, you shoot bullets from the rifle to make sure he understands before you fire the grenade. I love this monster." There were two of these weird-looking weapons. (I learned later that they were used mainly for taking care of unruly elephants!)

We slipped quickly into the huge barn adjacent to the house. There were trucks, spray machines, motorcycles, and equipment of all sorts. Bird droppings were prominently splattered over the trucks, as many had nested overhead. Over against one wall sat an ancient Citroen sedan; we hopped in. It had been maintained in good running shape, low mileage; the battery was kept charged. On the first key twist, the engine caught and purred quietly. One of the servants raised the latch on the barn doors as Antoine nudged the car up against them and slowly pushed. The doors opened silently, and he eased the Citroen out just as quietly. One could barely hear the engine, and better yet, we were shielded from the runway and the baddies by the house.

A mile down the road was the army garrison, and we were there in minutes. It had a flea-bitten, terracotta-colored exterior, like a sheriff's office in an old Western movie. Antoine pulled up in front and ran inside.

I don't know what he said, but a moment later, a dozen soldiers carrying old Enfields, bolt-action rifles, and shotguns boiled out and piled into a large lorry. Driving furiously, we roared back towards the ranch house with the lead truck creating billows of suffocating dust. But Antoine kept pace.

At the ranch house we circled off the driveway and onto the runway at full throttle, and then directly towards the bandits' truck. Suddenly, from both sides of the army truck, soldiers leaned out and began firing, mostly in the direction of the bandits. Antoine pulled alongside but out of their line of fire, his right hand on the wheel. Leaning out, he cocked his .45 and began blasting away at the baddies. He looked over at me and yelled: "Goddamit, Doctor, start shooting!"

I did.

It was momentary bedlam. Anyone would think he was witnessing a western horse opera...an American one. But at the moment

I had this one slight problem; my goddam Colt .45 wouldn't fire; no response to my trigger finger. I kept pulling, then I, the village idiot, remembered...the safety. I loosed it and fired off a clipful; it bucked madly. I reloaded and blasted some more.

Seeing firepower coming their way, the baddies and their smoke-belching truck bolted for the jungle fringe. I could see a narrow road, and they were heading for it. But as they drove off, they fired a final salvo in our general direction. Hornets were zipping by, and as bad luck would have it, one slammed into our left front wheel, shredding the tire, and another into our windshield which exploded in a dangerous shower of glass shards.

Antoine screeched "Shit!" as he held the Citroen, momentarily out of control, in check. Still, it slewed back and forth from side to side as he slowed and finally stopped. Hands slippery from sweat, he had grimly gripped the steering wheel. Even so, we had nearly turned over once when his hands briefly slipped. In the end, he rode that ancient truck to a halt.

We both glistened with small chunks and slivers of glass. Anyone who says windshields don't shatter is an idiot, and French windshields are no exception.

Antoine began blasting his horn, finally getting the army truck's attention. He waved them over. They circled back, then pulled up alongside. If any bullets had hit the truck, there was no sign of it.

We were covered with those sparkly glass shards, mixed with little rivulets of blood that trickled down our faces and arms. Not a single slug had hit them or their truck. Looking at us, they were in total disbelief.

In rapid French, which I was beginning to understand, Antoine suggested they not chase the bandits any further. He explained tactfully, but forcefully, that as they well knew, these guys would try to lure us into the jungle, with some of their men having been dropped off to ambush us. "Ambush, boom-boom, and we are dead."

They understood. On the other hand, maybe the bandits would circle back and attack the military garrison, the barracks. Highly unlikely, it seemed, but they saw the wisdom of Antoine's remarks.

Antoine got out, saluted the lieutenant, not a military salute, just a kind of recognition salute, followed by a grim handshake and weak smiles.

I watched Antoine deftly slip a wad of bank notes to the officer, and it was understood. Some soldiers would go back; others would stay as guards. It was a pact sealed with that wad of money.

Antoine looked at me and I at him. He threw up his hands, leaned back, and roared with laughter.

"Look at you, Doctor, you look like a goddam Christmas tree decoration."

"How very damn Gallic of you, Antoine," I said, now beginning to shake as the excitement and delayed fear set in. "You trying to get me killed out here?"

"No, no, Doctor…you know, I actually like you. For a bloody American, you're OK. Here, have a smoke."

"I don't smoke, and you know it…and if I did, it wouldn't be those smelly French things." Gauloises really stunk.

"OK, *mon ami*, but I need one of these things so we can fly home. Come, we get cleaned up and change clothes."

I don't think I'd ever been shot at point blank. I'd been shot at in New Guinea and Halmahera Island during WWII, but mostly I'd been safe aboard ship, even while watching and counting any number of torpedoes that missed our hull. But this was different.

Fortunately our hats had protected our hair and sunglasses our eyes. The little rivulets of blood quickly congealed, as did some spatterings here and there on our torsos and clothes. We were both still a touch shaky, but nothing serious. A Jeep came out from the house to retrieve us.

At the ranch house, Antoine and I gingerly peeled off our shard-spangled clothes. Clad only in our soiled shorts, we stepped under an outdoor shower. Rubber plantation work is grimy, dirty, and sticky, so there were soap, detergents, rubber solvent, and other nasty-smelling things on the shower ledge for cleanup. But shampoo was what we used, and after many rinses, we were finally clean.

Spare clothing was plentiful, so we chose from a collection of khaki shirts, jackets, and trousers. I ended up looking like a raffish French Foreign Legionnaire....not bad.

Then there was the question of our unfinished luncheons. We'd lost appetites, so, forsaking food, Antoine knocked back half a tumbler of brandy to steady his nerves. So much for his abstinence talk the other night.

"OK, Doctor, now we get the hell out of here."

The plane's doors were wide open. It appeared the money guard had been watching from his shady vantage point under the nearside wing. He had his shotgun in hand, but clearly he'd hopped to the side, away from trouble. As the plane aired out, we checked for any possible damage. Flaps, rudder, controls. Everything seemed OK. No leaks from the fuel tanks. Good to go.

"So, the hell with our unfinished lunch, the hell with coffee. We go."

The ranch manager and his wife and almost all the workers walked out to the plane to wave us off. They were relieved to see the plane intact but remained apprehensive about bandits being nearby. The bandits were still out there in the jungle somewhere, but tracking them down would be a waste of time. We might find the truck, but the bandits gone...and there was that danger of the bushwhack. I think Antoine and Michelin made a deal with the army because half of the soldiers had off-loaded, and my interpretation of the chat with the lieutenant was that these men would bivouac at the plantation for the next week. Smart. They would be Michelin's rented guards.

We did another careful ground check of the plane, very carefully. The guard assured us he had protected the craft, had unsheathed his weapon just in case and that all was well. He had secured the big over-and-under grenade weapon in a rack behind Antoine's seat—again, just in case.

Antoine said nothing. Neither of us believed the guard. In all likelihood he'd probably cowered under the plane. But in truth, the plane was unscathed. I stole a glance at my watch and was shocked to see that all the drama had chewed up more than six hours. We needed to get going.

The big 450-HP engine started with a roar, the cowling shaking and rattling as Antoine did the checks—props, carburetor, fuel pump, cowl flaps. I was getting the hang of the routine by now. He set the directional gyrocompass, slowly trundled over to the end of the runway, swung the craft around, gave it 40° of flap, and aimed for the center of the runway.

The ruined truck had been moved off and the runway swept clean of all large debris. No matter, that big prop would blow off loose stuff, but it might also suck stuff into the engine, which could ground the plane and us with it.

"Now Doctor, this will be different takeoff, not like Saigon. Here we are in the jungle—we have about 3500 feet runway, we have tall trees at the end of the runway, so we must to climb fast. We make a short field takeoff. I only need about 1400 feet of runway to get up off the ground, then we climb very steep. You follow?"

"Yes, I follow." I also gulped.

"OK, we go like hell down the runway, when I go fast enough, I pull back on the stick, pull up the nose just a bit, then we fly. Make sure your seat is set fast in its position. I don't want you suddenly sliding back when I pull back on the control yoke. Understand?"

I said I did. He went on. "Friend of mine, a pilot, he forget. When he pull back on the yoke, the nose went up, but the loose seat slid back with him holding the yoke…it went back too far, and just like that, it was too late: the nose shot up, he stalled, the plane rolled over on its back and slammed back to the runway. He limps very badly now, and he don't fly no more. So straps tight, seat fastened, OK?"

I did a double check. Antoine slowly eased down towards the thick white strip crossing the runway. Then standing on the brakes, he revved to full power. The Beaver shook and rattled, the cowling vibrating so hard I thought it would come loose; then he throttled down. "Is running OK!" he yelled, and then he rechecked his flap setting: two notches of flap, then full props and full power. Off we roared down the runway.

We'd only gone about 500 feet when Antoine yelled. "Shit *alors*! Those assholes sneaked around to the other side." Sure enough, there were the bandits off to the side ahead of us—and the accursed truck parked crossways about three quarters of the way down the runway we were on.

"Is OK!" Antoine shouted. "We go up now. Hold on."

At this point, we'd only gone a third of the way down the strip. Still, Antoine gently pulled back on the yoke, causing a small shudder to course through the plane. We eased off the runway a few feet, and that was all Antoine needed. He leveled off quickly to gain airspeed, and we flew another few seconds straight towards the truck. Behind it, trees—very tall trees—loomed. We had to get up now or crash.

The bandits had climbed out and were aiming rifles at us. I'll never know if they fired a shot, because suddenly Antoine yanked back on the yoke and horsed us into a quick climbing turn, spiraling up and away from the truck and the bandits. We were airborne, speeding off in the opposite direction. My clean clothes were drenched with sweat, and more sweat fogged my glasses. I glanced over at Antoine: he wore the face of a savage. Feral lips pulled back in a snarl, nostrils flaring. He was quite pissed.

I sensed he was going to do something half-crazy, but what, I had no inkling. My only thoughts ran along the lines of dear sweet Jesus, what next? By now we had plenty of airspeed, and he'd retracted flaps to one notch, which meant something was in the works: one notch of flap will keep you aloft at slower-than-cruising speeds. Plus, it helps when maneuvering, which is what I assumed was coming next.

"Hah—how you like zat, Doctor, eh?" Antoine asked, not looking for an answer. "We fool those bastards, eh? Now I gonna fix them good." He turned to the back and yelled something unintelligible to the guard.

I turned to find the guard easing two huge metal gasoline cans toward the cargo door. Antoine banked the craft sharply left and left again, lining us up with the runway. Then, like a fighter pilot, he zoomed straight down towards the still-parked truck. As we dived, the guard opened the cargo door and at Antoine's command kicked out the fuel canisters. I couldn't see them fall, but they had to hit the ground in front of us. We were doing about 100 mph.

Once again, Antoine pulled up sharply to the left, went into another short climbing turn, and then turned back down into a long, sloping approach. He then opened his side window and yelled for the grenade launcher, which the guard had primed with a grenade at Antoine's command. Antoine muscled it out the window and aimed it straight ahead. On the opposite side of the plane behind me, the guard was aiming his Very pistol, his signal gun, directly at the truck. Antoine yelled, "FIRE."

The grenade launcher fired and bucked, and at the same time, I saw red smoke from the signal flare streaking towards the truck. Both flare and grenade hit just next to the truck a split second apart as Antoine banked away. Whoosh....Kaboom! A huge ball of orange and sooty black flame blossomed upwards, followed by another explosion and more black clouds. We felt the blast and heat even at 100 feet. The truck's diesel fuel had exploded, and the cans of fuel which we had splattered all over the runway had splashed the truck, too—a double whammy.

Not content, Antoine flew over again for another look. The truck was now engulfed in flames. On the far side of the runway, a few bandits waved their fists, and some fired at us, which made me a touch nervous.

Enough, I thought. Finally satisfied, Antoine pulled up, flew low over the ranch house, gave a final waggle of the wings, then leveled off for the flight back to Saigon.

Once up and cruising, he checked his instruments, then turned to me, "Doctor," he said, flipping the yoke over, "I am ver' tired. You will steer the plane to Saigon on this heading and course, OK? And you stay on this heading, OK? I have trim the plane, because in half an hour we start to climb just a little. If you feel the plane climbing too soon, wake me, OK? Don' worry, I only sleep with one eye close. And now you will remember: hundred-octane gasoline makes more boom than a dynamite bomb. Gasoline vapor, it spread fast and cover more space, then when it go boom it makes lots of trouble, unner-stan?" He'd demonstrated his point. I felt like I'd done the roller coaster ride at Glen Echo Park just outside Washington. Having imparted that obvious information, he leaned back and pulled his floppy combat hat over his eyes. The plane was mine.

Sure enough, in about twenty minutes, the plane began climbing just a bit; the vertical indicator dial said so. We were just a tad above horizontal, and sure enough, Antoine opened one eye, reached over, adjusted the trim wheel, and winked at me. He gave me a half-smile, and returned to his hat-down, catatonic position.

I realized then that he had incredibly blue eyes set in a rugged, deeply tanned face—a French Clint Eastwood with a touch of Errol Flynn, all with sandy hair and moustache. This guy Antoine was either harder or tougher than he appeared or both....but he put on a helluva good show. Either way, I was impressed by his bombing skills. Not many civilian pilots were this combat-wise. No question he was or had been French military. So once again, I wondered: what the hell was this person doing out in this godforsaken place—other than flying the mail for Michelin? On the other hand, the French did keep their eyes and ears open in all their possessions. Regardless, I already liked the guy, and I knew I'd keep him as a friend. He had a certain *savoir faire* that I identified with in moments of self-flattery.

When Antoine went to "sleep," we'd only been about an hour out of Saigon, and in radio contact with the tower there. We'd called to give our departure and arrival times, only to find the airwaves jammed with babbling in French and Vietnamese. Later, when we had a clear space, Antoine called Saigon tower in English. (Alas, the French tongue was no longer the *lingua franca* of the aviation airwaves; and now—*merde*—it was English.) We got our instructions and landed at Tan Son Nhut.

Taxiing over to the Michelin tie-down area, Antoine looked over at me and chuckled: "Eh, Doctor, we have fun, no?"

"Oh, Yeah—yes indeedy!" I replied. Now it's true that "fun" was hardly the word to describe what had just happened, but I wouldn't have missed it for the world. It was an adventure that money couldn't buy: how many times in a few hours had I cheated death? It was all a question of timing—picking the right time and place.

"Antoine, you do this sort of thing often?" I asked sincerely.

He just smiled and winked, which made me wonder all the more. In rapid French, he gave orders to his ground personnel to have the plane cleaned, washed, and refueled. Replace the jerry cans we'd used in the bombing run. Return money sacks to the bank. We'd do another run in two or three days.

"First I go in and sign the damn flight closure papers—is required. They don't give a damn, no way, but is for the government rules. Then, Doctor, I take you to your hotel. I advise you, take nice shower, take a little walk, and go out to a nice restaurant instead of that lousy hotel food, OK? After dinner you go to bed. You gonna be tired after your first fighter mission," he chuckled. "I catch up with you soon."

I took a shower and put on some clean clothes. Suddenly it occurred to me: How many frames had I snapped during that harrowing ride? And how would they come out when processed? Quickly I brought my daily log entries up to date and got all the exposed film labeled. That was important: label the film while the information was still clear in the mind. I had to recall where each shot was taken, what film was used, what exposures I used, even the time of day. It might not seem important at the time, but consider that Admiral Peary's location on the ice pack was determined years later from photos by noting the position of the sun's shadow on the ice: he didn't quite get where he thought he had. I still had plenty of film, but I'd be very chary of what subjects to shoot. And I would be careful to document each frame.

It was nearing dinnertime. I strolled down Rue Catinat, walked into the Continental Hotel, and asked for an outside table in the courtyard. There was no way I could drink a whole bottle of wine, so I ordered a Bamibam, then soupe Chinoise, rolls, and a small salad.

As my eyes adjusted to the darkness, I looked around. Little candles flickered everywhere. Strings of tiny lights had been draped artistically along the walls. The ever-present jasmine perfumed the air, and somewhere a gecko croaked its approval. From hidden speakers came tinny, whiny Vietnamese music, which to me was maddening. It was the only music the Vietnamese seemed to like, save the occasional French crooner.

I looked up at an impossibly dark sky, like a velvet blanket studded with tiny diamonds. The southern stars were much larger and brighter out here. And that nagging question popped up again: What the hell am I doing here? When would I come to my senses and get out?

I lowered my eyes to the courtyard around me. Good God—what do I see some thirty feet away? None other than the willowy Gigi. And her escort? Our gallant fighter pilot, Monsieur Antoine Nicolai, the bon vivant of Air Michelin—and, it seemed, a real ladies' man.

What a guy! I felt a rush of jealousy but suppressed it quickly with feelings of guilt. Shame on you, Sundukian! Ignore them...mind your own damn business!

I stuck my nose into the soup and slurped away. But wait just a damn minute. Hadn't he told me to avoid hotel food and go to a good restaurant? So what the hell was he doing here in a hotel veranda munching hotel food? I chuckled at their appearance here. Did I still believe in coincidence? Well, I had to accept that my being here was a coincidence. And they looked so cozy. I wondered again, were they lovers? None of my damn business, but one can't help but wonder at times.

Between spoonfuls of this fine soup, I flicked my eyes up. Antoine's back was to me, but Gigi was looking in my general direction, and there was no question she had seen me. In fact, she may have even seen me enter. As she stared in my direction, I'd swear she was striving to make eye contact. And then—God's truth, guvner— she winked at me! True, it was dark. I could have been wrong. Maybe it was wishful thinking. But I saw her wink looking right at me, and give a momentary smile! What kind of a woman would do that while sitting with another man? A slippery one, that's what. It made me wonder: Was this wink an invitation of sorts, or just a sort of "Hello, sorry, but having dinner?" Or was she merely teasing in some obtuse way?

The veranda was dimly lit, but still I could see she was wearing a wispy, yellow, chiffon-looking material. Around her long, graceful neck she wore a strand of large luminous pearls that glowed in the table's candlelight. And I could also see one sandaled foot swaying slowly, but no further sign of recognition. After the wink, she never looked my way again.

"Uh-uh, ain't she something?" said one of my many inner voices. "She sure do like yellow, and she sure do like lemony perfume. And she may even like you a tiny little bit." Ah, lemon—a favorite aroma of mine.

I finished my salad, paid, and quietly left. I needed sleep.

— - • - —

ONE OF MY CALENDAR NOTATIONS, at the request of the Medico-CARE office, was to visit an orphanage run by a certain Madame Vu Thi Ngai. Mme. Ngai was quick to tell you that she was Tonkinese—an elite people, a class above all the rest hereabouts, she explained proudly. She had moved this orphanage from Haiphong down to Saigon because, as she loudly proclaimed, she did not wish to have these children raised by barbarian communists.

Dutifully, I visited. François accompanied me, snapping photos at every opportunity. There were others from my office as well, including one or two of my nurses, dragging along behind us. When she appeared to welcome us, Mme. Ngai was clad in a strange combination of what seemed to be silken knickers and a fashionable silk blouse, tightly buttoned over a very generous bosom that I was told enhanced her ability to euchre funds for her orphanage from government officials.

All around us, little children dashed, laughing and tittering like tiny birds. They seemed happy, were mostly clothed, and apparently adored Mme. Ngai. Knowing my role, I said all the proper things about her orphanage, promised to speak to the CARE brass about increasing her support, and joined her for high tea.

"Have you heard of Dr. Dooley?" she asked me once we were seated.

I remembered hearing about him, how he and Dr. Comanduras had put Medico together, but confessed I didn't know him personally.

"Well, we keep in touch. He is up in Muong Sing—that's Laos, you know. He has this hospital there and treats those savages in that area. They come from all over—Burma, China, northern Vietnam, even China. But mind you, the North Vietnamese"—she pronounced it "Vitnamees"—"think he is running a spy center. He told me you had been invited to see his hospital. So, tell me, when are you going? I would like you to take a small package for him."

"I'm not sure what you mean, Mme. Ngai," I answered honestly. "I don't know anything about any visit. And I have a very full schedule for the next few weeks."

Frankly, I found it unnerving to learn from a virtual stranger about an invitation I hadn't even received yet. Fortunately, the nurses interrupted with a flurry of questions about the orphanage. I hung around for a bit and then said my goodbyes, promising to return and to see what I could arrange for the orphanage in the way of additional supplies. At heart, though, I just wanted to get away before I found myself sucked into something.

Of course, a few days later came the inevitable: A message from our embassy in Saigon to Medico, plus a message left at my hotel desk. Dooley had sent word through the American embassy in Laos, saying, in effect, that it would be nice if I, Dr. Sundukian, would visit his hospital and make rounds with him—on his patients. A second message of the same date from Chuck Miller, head of USIS in the Laotian capital of Vientiane, said the same thing, adding that it would be a show of U.S. support for Dooley's project. Clearly, this was an orchestrated invitation.

I mulled this over. I was rapidly becoming disenchanted with my role as a do-gooder. It was wearing thin. If this were a genuine invitation and not a Mae West one, I could use it as an excuse to get out of Saigon while continuing to roam the world. I just wouldn't admit to myself that it would amount to running away.

And isn't that really what you want to do, old chap? Why all this posturing about being a savior of the downtrodden, the sick and miserable people of the world? All you wanna do is to keep running away—but from what?

I was no Albert Schweitzer. Actually, I felt like some overgrown kid who had run away from home. Instead of touring Europe like the rich kids did, I was doing Southeast Asia. Worse yet, I had run away from my responsibilities, my practice, my career, and my social life—all on the home front. What a no-good bum! Another burst of self-loathing, to which I added a dollop of despair. Things needed to change.

I went to the Embassy to speak with the Political Officer and the Cultural Attaché about this possible visit to Dooley. They were occupied with other more important things, they said, and suggested I speak with a travel agency. I took the hint: If I wanted to visit Dooley, it would have to be on my own, because my government had no interest. It could not even be an official visit, said a low-level Embassy person. I would have to take leave.

Suppressing the impulse to seek out our ambassador himself, I walked down the street to the Alcan Travel Agency, just around the corner from the Majestic Hotel. A sweet young Vietnamese lady greeted me and asked how she could help. She assumed I was at least a high-ranking officer, as many of her clients were off-duty members of the military needing arrangements for weekend jaunts. Upon hearing my plans, she wondered aloud why any civilized person would even consider going to Muong Sing in Laos. It was in dangerous country—did I not know? Still, she outlined a ten-day itinerary that included a side-trip to the temples of Angkor Wat. She would take care of visas, tickets, hotels, everything. The price seemed quite reasonable.

Smiling again, she told me, "Please let me know when you wish to go."

Now I had some thinking to do. The Angkor Wat suggestion was intriguing; I'd read about this remote religious complex that had been built deep in the jungles of Cambodia and then, for no apparent reason, abandoned. It had been the home of a vanished empire, the Khmer, and according to the article, its soaring temples rivaled some Western cathedrals.

I gave the Alcan Travel lady some possible dates. Could she work out a schedule? Meanwhile, I told the CARE-Medico folks my plans: It was now mid-July; sometime in early August I would be leaving on my hegira to visit Dooley. I left out the part about a side-trip to Angkor Wat.

I found François and told him my plans; we talked it over. He listened, nodding his head like the village priest. He was smoking his foul-smelling pipe and when not sucking on it, puffed a Gauloise.

"Good idea, Doctor," he said, not using the French pronunciation this time. "You are not happy here, and deep in your heart, you wish not to be here, no?"

I didn't answer. He was probably right, but I hadn't gotten to that part of the confessional yet.

"So you wish to go off on another lark. OK, why not? You only live once, neh?"

I told François he was basically correct. I'd seen all I wanted to see of Saigon. And I despaired of helping the sick here. What we were doing was Band-Aid work, taking care of immediate problems but with no strategic planning for the longer term. OK, perhaps that planning was going on at higher levels. Still, it was mostly hair-shirt work by bleeding hearts who also had strong and dangerous political views. A bad combination for do-gooders. Mainly, I was fed up with the futility. And the more I thought about it, the less I wanted to do with it. I was burnt out and ready to leave.

-- • --

WHILE I WAS GETTING THINGS in order with Alcan Travel, two other interesting matters popped up. The first was an invitation from yet another embassy-connected outfit. Our medical team was invited to be guests of MAAG, which, I learned, was the Military Advisory and Assistance Group helping the Vietnamese military. The Military Attaché at the embassy said they would like to host us at their coming weekend retreat in Nha Trang, a resort area north of Saigon and smack dab on the shores of the South China Sea.

Fabulous! Our visit would coincide with a major festival during which most Vietnamese would be on holiday. So why not?

I replied that I would be delighted to accept along with any of our nurses and doctors who were not on duty. This was Tuesday; we would be leaving on Thursday afternoon. All guests would fly up to

Nha Trang on Air Vietnam. Tickets and lodging would be arranged by the Embassy.

Goody! Nha Trang, I learned further, was a beachfront getaway for the wealthy of Saigon. Accessible from the city and not too far by air, it was the perfect resort spot. The area was described as exquisitely beautiful: rock formations cropping up through a cerulean blue sea; sparkling white beaches and exquisite little coves ideal for sunbathing, picnics, or whatever. In the city of Nha Trang were wonderful restaurants featuring fresh seafood; grilled langouste was a regional specialty. And Nha Trang was also the home of an Oceanographic Institute.

This being Vietnam, there was more to the story, of course. Missing entirely from the slick brochures was this little tidbit: a short distance from those sparkling sands was a training site for a U.S. Special Forces contingent made up of men from the Army, Navy and maybe even some Marines.

I learned this from a laconic François, who had to be chuckling secretly at my astonishment.

"How do you know all this stuff, François?" I asked.

With a deep puff on his foul-smelling pipe—puff…puff—and then carefully choosing his words, François said, "What the hell do you think I do out here, just eat drink and fuck Vietnamese girls? This is true, of course, but I also listen, I watch, I look, and I read. Just like it says at the *Chemin de Fer* crossing: I listen for fast-moving trains. I read faces, I read newspapers, and I talk to other reporters. I take military people to lunch—they love to brag, especially the American ones. I take embassy secretaries out, mostly the ugly ones—they love to have a Frenchman take them for the petite drinkypoos and dinner, and then confide to me what goes on inside their embassy. Makes them feel so important, and of course, I sit there with my mouth open. I act so stupid. But I don't take them to bed—well, maybe some of the nicer new ones—because sometimes they become complicated and demand more. You follow, no?"

I was getting the drift.

"And so, what do you do with all this information?"

"Why, I send in little news notes to my agency, Agence France Presse, and they write little stories with my name on it and it makes me famous, that's what I do. I even send them stories of the nice American doctor I know named John Sundukian, and his pictures, too. They know you in France, you know? Tell me, Doctor, has anyone done a story about you in America?"

The answer was no, but I didn't care. "I don't need a story."

OK, so François was a Vietnam watcher for his government. I might be naive, but I wasn't stupid. But if he was a French watcher, then I wondered who our watchers were?

François continued his merry pranks by telling me he was thinking of flying up for the weekend in Nha Trang, too. It would be more fun than staid old Saigon, he said, and anyway, Antoine told him there was space on his plane. Tired of tracking all the machinations, I shrugged off this additional coincidence.

"Just what are American Special Forces people doing up there, François?"

"Hah," he shook his head sadly. "Silly boy," he said. "Why you don't ask them when you get there? And then you tell me what they tell you, OK? *D'accord?*"

I agreed. What the hell could I possibly learn that he didn't already know?

--•--

THE NEXT HAPPENING: A LETTER from my father in Washington. He'd spoken to friends at State and asked them to send a letter to his son in Vietnam. The letter was duly placed in the embassy pouch, and, just like that, it was hand-delivered by embassy driver to the CARE office.

My dad had connections that defied description. Born in a town called Hadjin in 1894, a town no longer in existence, having been destroyed by the Turks in WWI, he attended local schools and eventually ended up in the Syrian Protestant University in Beirut, which was later named American University in Beirut. While a medical student at the AUB in 1915, he was arrested, then drafted into the Turkish (Ottoman) Army serving with the 4th Army in Syria.

From this unpleasant happening, he defected from the Army, vowing revenge for what they'd done to him and his family in Hadjin, where many of them were slaughtered and others herded into the death march through Syria.

Now a fugitive, Dad and some outlaw cohorts pursued the lucrative wartime career path of contraband: carpets, dried apricots, fancy gold-tipped cigarettes, whatever. Dad must have made and lost several fortunes along the way. Mainly, however, he stayed one step ahead of the law and the Turks. It certainly helped that he spoke some ten different languages.

In one especially memorable case, Dad entered into an agreement with German forces stationed in Ottoman territory. With the European war in its late stages, the Germans, who had no idea that Dad was AWOL, probably wouldn't have cared if they'd known. What they needed was a local supply contractor—a dry-land chandler—and for these Krauts, Dad delivered: cigarettes, potatoes, flour, meat, and other necessaries, much of it obtained in Damascus. Payment was always in gold, half in advance; the Krauts were flush with gold, much of it from the Turks. (This was Dad's private revenge. The Turks owed him for taking his family's lands.)

On one occasion, he delivered to these German clients a large flock of sheep—stolen, as it happens. Not a week later, he and his rustler pals sneaked back, re-stole the remaining flock, drove them a few miles to a hidden valley, and put them out to graze. The Germans, again desperate for meat, contacted Dad for help. Straight-faced, he sympathized. Returning to the valley, he sheared some sheep to avert their recognition. Others he smeared with mud, and laced their wool coats with bits of bramble. When he turned this disguised flock over to the Germans yet again, the ruse worked: The Krauts paid as usual in gold.

Somewhere in his travels, Dad met Margaret Devletian, a lovely, slim, dark-haired woman of breeding and education. She was a student at Roberts College in Istanbul and the daughter of Artin Bey Devletian, Surgeon General of the Turkish Army and head honcho at Istanbul's Haydarpaşa Hospital. Artin Bey was a talented and well-trained surgeon—and, notably, an Armenian Christian, a rarity in

Turkish military circles. He and his family occupied a mansion in Kadiköy, an exclusive suburb of Istanbul, where they were protected (as well as watched) by a retinue of soldiers, servants, drivers, and gardeners, as befitted a General and a favorite of the Sultan.

My father spotted the General's daughter, and it was love at first sight, he later claimed. He wooed this damsel and married her after careful screening by her family. One point heavily in his favor: his net worth at that time exceeded the General's.

Then flush with Kraut gold, and fearful of capture by the Turkish Army, Dad took mother and slipped out of Turkey forever. They finally landed in the Ionian Greek island of Corfu where Dad founded an orphanage, became a member of the Lord Mayor's Fund of London, and opened a carpet factory in which skilled orphans' fingers wove carpets. And, for that matter, where I was born one summery August day.

Eventually, Dad made his way to Washington DC, where he became the owner of a premier Oriental rug salon bearing his name. Speaking many languages fluently, and several passably, Dad became the darling of the upper crust and diplomatic set, which flocked to his salon to buy, haggle, sip coffee, and make idle chatter. He also became a friend and later an advisor to Eleanor Roosevelt, who referred him to later occupants of the White House for whom Dad served as a consultant. He did likewise for the State Department and many embassies. (His other sons, my brothers James and Harold, nobly carried on his tradition. But Momma made me become a doctor, just like her father.)

His commercial success aside, Dad remained in some ways a mystery; my brothers and I grew up aware that he had contacts—if that's the word for it—in unusual circles. This was confirmed for us at his funeral, of all places. As we sat waiting for the service to begin, four large, stone-faced men strode into the chapel and without a word went directly to Dad's casket, where they swiftly draped the flag of Armenia over his casket. They were Dashnak strongmen, members of the Armenian Revolutionary Federation, a nationalist independence movement which included certain extrajudicial projects. Then, looking neither left nor right, they departed. It was rumored they had flown in from Beirut. Amen.

Getting back to the matter at hand: What the letter from Dad said was that Soviet Premier Anastas Mikoyan had recently come to Washington on a diplomatic visit. At the Russian Embassy reception, he and Dad had met, conversed, and got into a helluva shouting match that made all the local papers. It was a real verbal brawl, and it sounded to me like Dad got the best of it, with Mikoyan having to tread softly and handle the fallout in his own sneaky way.

Dad had accused him of being a traitor to Armenia. Mikoyan had turned against his own people by subjecting them to intolerable living conditions, Dad said, and even worse, he'd lured Armenians back to the motherland from America, then confiscated their property and reduced them to penury. When these hapless returnees realized it was all a sham and asked to leave, their pleas were denied. They were trapped in a Soviet nightmare.

Mikoyan put on a brave show of face, arguing that Dad was all wrong and challenging him to come to the USSR as his guest and see for himself. But Dad had spoken in Armenian, and when Mikoyan had some slight difficulty understanding Dad's dialect, Dad accused Mikoyan of forgetting his native tongue. He announced that Mikoyan, a former Seminarian in Georgia, had fallen completely from grace.

This was getting a bit much for the crafty old Armenian. "Margos," he shouted at him, pointing his finger, "You are wrong, you will come and visit, you will be my guest, and then you will see for yourself how mistaken you are—and you will apologize."

Shortly thereafter, Dad had received an invitation on official stationery, delivered by the Soviet embassy. It was a nice conciliatory message with assurances of friendship and ending with "Come at your convenience, signed Anastas." Dad included a copy in his letter to me, and explained what he wanted. "Sonny,"—one of his names for me—"read this letter and newspaper clipping of my fight with Mikoyan. Stop by Moscow on your return and visit the old son of a bitch and see what he has to say. You might learn something about

Russians. You know I am a Dashnak, and if I went, it could be my death sentence. I might accidentally die there."

I had never talked to Dad at any length about his ties to the Dashnaks, a shadowy revolutionary movement dating from the late 19th century that demanded the reformation of Armenia into a republic. But I knew enough to know that if he indeed was a Dashnak, Dad was a marked man.

In an instant I made up my mind: I'd stop by Moscow on my way home. It would be a rare opportunity, and I'd get some photos, too. But I had a feeling getting there was going to be tricky.

CHAPTER 6

Nha Trang

An embassy car drove us to the airport. In our party were two of Dr. Overholt's nurses, a technician from the Lab and one of the gas-passers—anesthesiologists. If I had to bet, I'd say that I wasn't one of their favorite doctors, but I was the fastest surgeon they'd ever worked with, and that was a plus. The nurses liked fast, neat, and no shouting. I was that.

At the airport we checked in to Air Vietnam, showed passports, got stamped, went to the boarding area, and waited. Glancing over to the hangars where the smaller planes were parked, I noticed activity around Antoine's Beaver. It was being readied for flight. Hmmm. I had an idea, a wild one. How could I get away from this bunch and fly with Antoine, in that Beaver?

The flight to Nha Trang was announced, and we boarded the old tail-dragger DC-3. My first hint that things were bad was the smell of vomit—recent vomit. I searched the aisles and seats, and there was the source: Tiny Vietnamese women barfing into tiny barf bags. The engines hadn't even started. The smell was awful, enough to turn anyone's stomach. That settled it.

I turned to Kay O'Donnell, our senior nurse and chaperone of the other little nursies: "Kay, be a good soul and bring my small bag to the villa...I'll meet you there. Something just came up." Not waiting for an answer, I hurried back to the hatch and hopped out. Dodging a cart and several scooters, I hustled over to the Beaver. Antoine was smoking a Gauloise, awfully close—dangerously close—to the fuel truck, chatting it up with the ground personnel.

"*Allo* John, Doctor John. You go to Nha Trang for the holidays, no? And maybe you want to ride wif me? Hah, is OK. We will have the glamorous Ma'mselle Gigi, then, Peter Jenkins, the pharmaceutical chap, and our friend François. Doctor, you will be my co-pilot. OK?"

"Sure." I found myself grinning like a monkey. This was my lucky day. I'd fly right seat again and I was getting to like it.

Within minutes, all the passengers had arrived. There were the perfunctory smiles and handshakes all around. Then at Antoine's command, we boarded, and I took the right seat...the co-pilot's spot! Antoine did the preflight checklist himself—I didn't blame him, as this time we'd be in commercial space—and then clicked the mike and hurled greetings to the tower.

I took a moment to check out our glamour girl. A cool one, this. I was coming to realize that every move she made was planned—every facial expression, every body position, all calculated for effect. She had an agenda, that was clear, and she seemed to be on stage, performing for some audience. But whom? I'd wait and watch to find out. I could be cool, too.

Today she wore a safari jacket, open several buttons down, with a filmy, mauve scarf tucked into the open neckline, discouraging cleavage-peekers. Below the jacket, fashion chinos and delicate sandals, pink toenails protruding. Slung over a shoulder, a tan, designer tote bag. She glanced toward me in a mechanical, impersonal way, raised an eyebrow, and offered, as always, that mysterious, knowing smile.

Antoine pushed the throttle, and the powerful engine revved up. He'd gotten clearance, then told the tower he was leaving. After a long runway roll, we were off and climbing out towards the northeast.

There was a guarded, but festive air aboard. Antoine's voice came out loud and clearly over the engine's roar. "*Allo, 'allo*, zis is your Capeetan. Please sit back and relax, keep your belts tight, and someone please pass me a cold beer." The last with a nasal, Gallic chuckle.

We flew steadily and smoothly for about an hour toward the northeast. We crossed fields, paddies, patches of jungle, and then burst out over the South China Sea almost at Nha Trang. A few miles out beyond the city, Antoine contacted their tower and was cleared to land. We descended, passing over some magnificent craggy islands off-shore which appeared to be floating in the loveliest blue water imaginable. The approach came quickly, though, and suddenly we were dropping into the runway center stripe and then taxiing to the terminal, where I saw the Air Vietnam DC-3 already parked.

A small Michelin Renault bus was there with a grinning driver looking expectantly at Antoine. We piled in. I thanked Antoine profusely for the ride and said I'd hope to see him later. The driver knew exactly where to drop me: Villa Neptuna, number 32 just off the main drag. "Soldier's home," he announced.

During the noisy flight, there'd been no chance for conversation with the other passengers, but the glamorous Gigi had given me a quick, raised eyebrow—which could mean anything. But I chose to take it to mean, "Now whatcha gonna do, big boy?" I hardly knew the woman, but she seemed to want to know me. I decided I could afford to be patient.

I found my hospital crew sitting on the veranda of the lovely, French-ranch-style building, smiling with cool drinks in hand. Two very attentive military types sat alongside the younger nurses, who had changed into shorts and blouses, their pale skins a sharp contrast with the deeply tanned, fit-looking men. One chap was tall, lean, rangy, and rugged-looking with a certain hardness to him that somehow said "Don't mess with me." He was laughing and chatting amiably with two nurses, who seemed spellbound. The other chap was also rugged, though a tad more compact and just a hair shorter, and wearing what passed for tropical military dress: shorts, shirt and sandals. Both had crew cuts. I saw my bag on the ground next to the entryway.

"Welcome Doctor, I'm Jim Rothbard, Navy, and that there's Buck Webber, Army." Steel grip handshakes, but not crushers.

"Hi gentlemen, thanks for the invitation," I said. "Neat-looking place you've got and I'm delighted to be here. I feel like we just won a contest prize, right, ladies?" Smiles and head-nodding.

"Well, sir, Buck there is an ordnance expert, and I'm what you call a Frog man, a squid. You'll meet Commander Bill Hiers, chief of this MAAG unit, at dinner; we'll make sure you have a pleasant stay. We have a suggested itinerary for your time up here. We want you all to enjoy yourselves—orders from the ambassador, and probably Washington."

I was puzzled by that remark, but not enough to distract me. I wasn't too interested in itineraries, which really translated to guided tours. I just wanted to hit the beach, grab some sun, and think.

We were shown our rooms on the second floor by a Vietnamese maid. Each had a private bath and huge windows, with double doors that opened onto a spacious porch and a view of the sea. This villa was situated on the main drag, facing the beach. A wide strip of palms, separating us from the ocean, lightened the constant breeze, served as shade, and provided coconuts for our cooks.

These were first-class digs, and I sensed this was going to be fun. Lying on my bureau was a neatly typed sheaf of papers. "Greetings from the MAAG commanding officer," it said. Warnings about sun, weather and food, and several choices of things to do: a boat trip to see offshore islands; visits to pagodas, visits to the Oceanographic Institute, shopping, and a list of restaurants. There was food and drink available at any time, and a car and driver as well. Just contact the concierge. The only item that really interested me was the offshore islands boat trip scheduled for two days later. I signed up, foreseeing an opportunity for some great photos for Mel Grosvenor at *National Geographic*.

--•--

AT COCKTAIL TIME, CANAPÉS AND a bar appeared as if by magic. Several of the military types showed up to shmooze, dressed with medals and aiguillettes flashing, the arms of their uniforms encircled by gold stripes and, to further dazzle the onlooker, bright neck ribbons from which dangled decorations. They were here under orders, I was sure.

Commander Rothbard, Major Webber, and a fellow I assumed was Commander Hiers were ordering drinks. But it wasn't Hiers at all—it was a chap named Hank Peters, who smiled shyly and said "Howdy" when introduced. I took an instant liking to him. He was tall, rangy, and had the widest shoulders I'd seen since my football days at Bucknell. Sandy hair, with sky-blue eyes set in deep sockets in a grizzled, tanned face. He seemed completely relaxed, almost sleepy. Every movement was easy and languid.

"Right pleased to meet you, Doc," he said. "We heard you was coming but never saw you get off that DC-3."

I explained.

"Oh yeah, that there French fella, Antoine—he's quite a guy. You know him?"

I explained some more. He nodded. I kept on. "Are you part of the MAAG group here?"

"Well, yes and no. You see, I'm assigned to the training unit here."

The next question was obvious: "What do you do with them? He gave me a sidelong look, which gave me the feeling I was getting a quick evaluation.

"Well, I'm what you call an ordnance expert, I'm an explosives man. I teach the men up here what they need to know about explosives—all kinds. How to use them, what kind to use in a given situation. Things like that." He stopped there.

As our conversation went along, I learned that he was an Army Warrant Officer, and a senior one at that. He said he'd been in the Army for about twenty years, having grown up in Tennessee, where his uncle worked at the Holston Army Ammunition Base and from whom he inherited an interest in explosives.

"Some people have a knack for dealing with explosives," he said. "And some don't. If you don't, then you find out right early in the training period. The smart ones get out, the dumb ones get dead."

I wanted to explore this train of conversation, but a maid passed through the room gently tapping the dinner gong. For the moment, the end of the conversation.

My place card put me next to Jenny Adkins, one of the less attractive nurses— terribly sweet but difficult to converse with. Dental extractions were not my forte, and I finally tired of getting her to talk. I'd wanted to sit next to Hank, but he was seated next to old Kay.

Commander Hiers made a brief welcoming address, after which a magnificent meal was served: Lobster bisque, grilled fish, garlic bread, and a huge salad to the side. There were iced drinks and a Napoleon for dessert. After demitasse coffees, the evening's events were coming to a close.

I saw Hank leaving, but he spotted me and came over: "Doc, if you'd like to have a look-see, I'd be happy to show you around our base. Just call me and let me know if you want to come up."

Was I interested? "Absolutely. Hell, yes."

"OK, fine. Just let me know, and we'll give you a tour of the base."

"How about bringing a camera?"

"No reason why not, Doc. Far as I'm concerned, it's OK."

— - • - —

AT BREAKFAST THE NEXT MORNING, a sheet of stationery was on my plate. Someone had written "Please call M. Antoine, 35612." I first wolfed down fresh chunks of mango, melon, and pineapple, and accepted a small cheese omelette from the smiling Asian cook. Satisfied, I went to the phone.

"*Eh bien*, Doctor, you are having a good time?"

"Yes, thank you."

"Well, *mon ami*, maybe you would like to fly wif me this morning, eh? I am to fly up along the coast for some sightseeing, then later maybe we see the bird-nest gatherers. OK? Then we land, and I get our little rubber boat, and we go sit in the sun. *Tutto bene*, OK?" Antoine spoke Italian and Vietnamese in addition to French and English, and I once heard him say something in Chinese. Nothing about this guy surprised me.

"Great."

"So, then meet me at the airport in maybe the next hour. Bring some water, your swimsuit, shirt, take a towel from your room, and don't forget a hat. I bring food and drink. Oh yes, I also bring the lovely Giselle with me, is OK?"

"Fine," I said, and fine, I thought. I was beginning to wonder about those two. And I always had just a teeny, tiny touch of jealousy about her. I'd never admit she interested me. After all, she was married, but she didn't act married. That bothered me slightly, but Antoine not at all. Europeans are different, no question.

— - • - —

A DRIVER TOOK ME TO the airport. I walked over to the tie-down area. The sun was high in a cloudless sky, and it was already hot, despite a slight breeze coming off the ocean. Sea gulls and Frigate birds were wheeling around garbage piled behind the hangars, and an Air Vietnam DC-3 was getting ready to leave, doors still open.

Within minutes, Antoine pulled up in an open mini-Renault. In the passenger seat, Gigi herself. Wow. This one knew how to dress for any occasion, and today was no exception: hat, long and dangly earrings, a pale yellow sun shift that touched her ankles, sandals, and a large tote bag.

Antoine: "Hello, Doctor, waiting long?"

"No, no. Just got here."

Wonder if they had separate rooms? Careful—None of your damn business, Sundukian.

"What we gonna do, Doctor, we gonna fly up the beach and find one of those tiny little coves, then later we take the boat there for the picnic. We have food, and I cook for you, me, Gigi, and her friend Vera. What you say, is still OK?"

Sounded fine. I'd brought camera, film, water, two oranges, and my small bag with the necessaries. I was prepared.

Antoine opened the plane doors and did the preflight walk around. Gigi climbed into a back seat and plunked herself down. A few minutes later, we were ready to roll.

This time Antoine handed me the checklist. I called out the items; Antoine checked and confirmed, with a tiny smile at my obvious delight. He set the altimeter, adjusted the mix, and started that big horse of an engine. We finished the preflight check while lumbering down the taxiway, leaving the doors open as long as possible to keep cool. I noticed that Gigi knew the drill perfectly well; obviously, she had flown many times with Antoine.

Doors were now closed and latched. Antoine set flaps, adjusted trim, flipped on the fuel pump, and then looked over at me.

"Doctor," he said, flipping the yoke over to my side. "You gonna take off—OK?"

"HUH?"

"Just listen. You hold the control wheel. You don't gotta do nothin.' I gonna increase the throttle slowly, we roll down the runway and this plane, she take off by herself. She fly herself. *Capisce?*"

"Yeh." But suddenly I was just a tad scared.

"Keep your feet flat on the floor, I handle the rudder pedals. When we get up one thousand feet, then we gonna level it off, OK? You don' worry, I have my hand around the column."

He advanced the throttle, we started rolling; shortly—and amazingly—the plane lifted off ever so gently...all by itself. I was both terrified and ecstatic at the same time. All I could do was look straight ahead; I whimpered that the plane was going a little steeper than my comfort zone allowed, but Antoine chimed in with "Fine, fine, fine—is going fine."

He kept talking me up: "Fine, now we gonna push the yoke forward just a little...not too much...that's right. Now with your left hand, pull the throttle back just a bit, enough, OK, fine." Antoine was adjusting switches, but I was glued to the yoke—not frozen and not really scared now...just anxious. And, at the same time, as excited as a kid at the circus.

"OK doctor...is fine. You did good, now I take it." He flipped the yoke over to his side, immediately goosed the throttle, retracted flaps, and banked hard towards the ocean. We were zipping. And I was still aglow. My first takeoff!

"Well whadda you know—you just had your first flight lesson," said I to myself, inwardly screaming whoopee! Just to think, I'd had my first flight lesson. This sort of activity could become catching.

I felt a hand patting my shoulder, gently but firmly. Gigi was smiling at me and gave me a thumbs-up. She was wearing the same perfume—light, with just a touch of the lemon that always gives me the sense of coolness. Hiding her eyes were fashionable sunglasses. She sat sideways, legs facing left, her shoulders just behind me. This was apparently to call attention to her legs, and it worked. I smiled back and mouthed "Thanks." She gave an approving wink.

We flew up along the coastline. Sandy coves whizzed by beneath. Stands of palm trees, tall clumps of sea grass, and scattered shrubbery clung to high, craggy cliffs on the landside. Nature had carved each tiny cove from the most inaccessible part of the cliffs; most appeared approachable only by water.

The South China Sea was a clear, greenish blue; small waves lapped against dazzling white beaches. One storybook cove had a heart-shaped shoreline with its own tiny island just offshore, and extending from either side, a coral barrier reef put there by nature to protect swimmers from sharks. Antoine pointed to this particular one and gave me a thumbs-up, meaning, I guessed, that this would be our picnic site.

Antoine circled and banked out to sea again, and then began descending almost to wave tops. By now, I'd grown accustomed to his flying style, but at times he still made me nervous. We zoomed by a sunken coastal freighter, its deck and superstructure jutting above the waves. We could see clear down to the clean, white bottom where the hull lay trapped forever in sand. "Bad storm," yelled Antoine, pointing down.

A minute later, we were speeding towards tiny offshore islands, volcanic eruptions of lava which had bubbled up from the ocean bottom, hardened and now thrust out like so many huge spear points. A black junk with two weathered, red sails was anchored in the lee of one of those islands. We circled at low level, and I spotted three small, round dories being poled to the base of the cliff, on which, to my amazement, youngsters scampered from one crag to the next. Each carried a string bag stuffed full of bird nests, Antoine said—some with tiny, just-hatched birds still inside. Swarms of angry parent birds zoomed at the intruders.

As Antoine circled for a better look, I aimed my Nikon and shot frame after frame. Dangling from one crag down to the beach was a long line that the boys used to slide filled bags down to the dories. Antoine shouted over the motor, "For Bird's Nest Soup—you wait, you like." I wasn't so sure.

One or two more circles, and then it was on to the airstrip.

--•--

AT THE MICHELIN TIE-DOWN AREA, a slim woman sat astride a Vespa, clad in a large, floppy hat, dark eye shades, shorts, and a long-sleeved shirt. Was this Vera? Apparently. Hugs, kisses, plenty of chatter in French, and I was introduced. Vera gave me a quick once-over, and I guess I passed: I got a big smile and a melodious "How do you do, Doctor? I've read about your visit to Vietnam." It came out that she was a French civil service employee, reluctant to leave and delaying departure as long as she could. She had a small apartment on the beach here, and this was possibly her last visit. *"C'est la vie,"* she sighed.

We headed over to the marina to pick up the boat, as our cooler and other supplies would be sent ahead by military Jeep.

Zipping over the waves at breakneck speed, our orange-colored Zodiac was really quite gentle. Barely touching the water, it still managed to shower us with spray. I noticed a 40-HP Evinrude stuck on the back, sucking fuel from a flat tank in the stern. Antoine said the entire package was old military. He didn't say whose, but I guessed French.

We slid over the barrier reef with plenty of clearance and beached the boat. As a safety measure, Antoine jammed a little anchor into the sand, then deployed the inventory of supplies that already had been delivered for us: small folding chairs, an umbrella, a small collapsible table, and a cooler. How they got there puzzled me, but then again, we were dealing with commandos. These guys have their ways, I figured. The umbrella was jammed deep into the sand and provided much-needed shade. While Antoine and I slipped into shorts, Vera and Gigi retreated behind a small clump of palms, beach bags slung over their shoulders. Antoine tossed a container of French suntan lotion at me, which I spread liberally. Antoine smeared some on my back; he snickered all the while.

"I suggest you still keep a shirt on, Doctor—you with the lily-white skin will burn like toast, eh?"

A few minutes later, the ladies came mincing out from their palm-screened changing area...and I guess my jaw may have dropped. I'd never seen women in bikinis except in magazines, and certainly not as skimpy as these. Here before me were two very well endowed, shapely women wearing very damn little. And they were totally unconcerned; I imagined that they could have been naked with equal aplomb. It was slightly flustering, and I found myself gawking. I decided to act totally nonchalant, and, after a while, succeeded.

We chomped on little sandwiches, cold chicken, shrimp, wine, and beer. Gigi and Vera decided it was time to get wet and ran for the water, splashed each other, then swam out to their little island.

I found shade under the umbrella. But I was restless. This was not real, it was not what I had come out to Vietnam for, and a small sliver of guilt began digging into my brain. On the other hand, I assured myself that this was only a short break, a small segment of loaf-time. I'd already been working my camera, and after all, Mel needed pictures for his magazine. *Et voilà*—I had begun thinking in French—have at it.

So, camera in hand, I shot several rolls of the cove from all angles. I climbed a short way up the volcanic cliff, recoiling when a lizard zipped past. With palms framing the women in their bikinis, I got excellent shots of the beach, cliffs, and trees. But what suddenly froze my eye to the viewfinder was completely unexpected: I was on a crag some twenty feet up and framing scenes with palm trees when I realized the ladies had doffed their halters and were merrily splashing in the surf. Fortunately, I already was employing long-lens photography, so I shot another roll, from various angles—these to titillate Mel and his editors back in Washington.

Shortly, Gigi and Vera splashed back to shore still topless and began perching on folding chairs in floppy hats and eye shades, toweling off, and preparing to laze and read magazines. Mel might never use these shots, but they might come in handy for a lecture, I thought—a Luis Marden lecture on the tropics. I fired, deftly bracketing my exposures. Since sand reflects light upwards, I recalled calmly, it eliminates shadows and gives a more even skin-tone.

The ladies were totally unconcerned with my shutter clacking. Finally, I came down and headed over to my camera bag. As I shuffled by, Gigi looked up with a mischievous smile and winked. I think I blushed.

Antoine was fussing with a long bag in the Zodiac. He extracted a pair of water skis and towline, and for the next hour, Antoine and the ladies—now wearing shirts for protection during their frequent tumbles—took turns on the skis. I handled the boat; I'd been in the Navy and small boats were my element. After one more long run, Antoine announced it was time to leave. It was getting late, and we'd had enough sun and wind for the day.

Back at the marina, we disembarked and headed for the cars. Giselle slid in next to me and said quietly, "Doctor, if you have some time this weekend, could we have a chat? Just let me know at the Villa. You have the number. OK?"

"Well, yeah, sure. Just let me see what's been laid on at our place. I'll call as soon as I know, OK?"

What the hell did that mean...chat?

"Fine." She smiled slyly, a cutesy little Mona Lisa smile...almost a smirk. What did she want to chat about? A dozen possibilities zipped through my mind. Patience, Sundukian.

Antoine dropped me off at the Villa Neptuna. I thanked him profusely, said my goodbyes to the ladies, and headed for the showers.

That evening, dinner proved to be a boring affair, but possibly I had too much on my mind. The food was delicious: Fish Kiev—like Chicken Kiev, except a local fish stuffed with crab, shrimp, and octopus. The chef was a Vietnamese Cordon Bleu–type and not just your ordinary military hash-slinger. But I was preoccupied with my

NHA TRANG

upcoming visits with Dooley in Laos and to Russia and Mikoyan. This was pretty heady stuff for me, not to mention that I had this ongoing guilt about having left my practice and teaching to do good out here. Instead, I was just a world-traveler, a bum with portfolio, a boondoggler. These were sobering thoughts.

I skipped dessert and coffee and excused myself. The commander announced that some stateside movies had arrived for those who were interested and the nurses promptly seized the opportunity for film entertainment. And, I think they were hoping to make a night of it; if I were in their place, I would too. There were some lonesome men out here.

-- • --

"*Allo*. Michelin," the phone answered on the second ring.

"Madame Prudhomme, please."

Pause. "*Mom-ent*, please."

"Hello."

"Hi, Sundukian here. Busy?"

"No, no, not at all. I was just making some notes. The others went into town for dinner. There's a popular seafood restaurant in the city, and they wanted langouste. But I begged off."

"Well, look, I have some time tonight, and you wanted to chat with me. Would this be a good time?"

"It would be just perfect. Would you like to come over here, or possibly buzz out to a small restaurant for some munchies and coffee? Yes? We could chat there?"

"I think maybe the restaurant would better. I'm still a bit hungry."

I must have sounded hesitant. Actually, I was reluctant to be seen alone visiting this woman in her villa. Public places are always safer. And I wasn't sure what she had in mind.

"Fine then, just wait for me in front. I'll be along in a few minutes. Ciao." The connection ended.

OK, she'd be along in a few minutes? How? Walk, fly? Whatever. I got a little pad and pencil and a small penlight and then slipped my passport into the room safe.

Downstairs, the after-dinner conversation was getting a touch louder, between the delighted giggles from the nurses and deep laughs from the men.

I slipped out front, and heard it before I saw it—a tiny headlight bouncing down the boulevard. It was attached to a motor scooter, which slid to a halt right in front of me, with Gigi sitting athwart the front seat in slacks, safari jacket, and open-toed sandals. A scarf was wrapped snugly around her head, and a pocketbook slung over a shoulder. My face, no doubt, reflected my surprise.

"Where the hell did you get this rig?"

"Like it? We have several at the Michelin villa," she said, waving her hand airily. "But don't just stand there, Doctor—hop on my little Vespa."

"Hop on?"

"Yes, silly, there's a seat behind me—hop on. You can hold my waist or the hold bars next to your seat, whichever is better for you." She had an inviting grin, eyebrow raised on one side.

I couldn't find the holds, and by now she'd pulled away. I waved my arms to maintain my balance, she turned and yelled, "Hold on to me, silly, and don't be afraid. I don't bite."

I slipped both arms around her waist and hung on. She smelled nice, and felt soft and firm at the same time. The more the scooter jiggled and bounced, the more I found myself getting aroused.

I wondered: was she doing a number on me, or was I too quick to imagine? I'd have to be clinically observant. In any event, she had to know that her body was getting my full attention. But what about her? The word icy came to mind. That's what François had said about her.

We zipped north along the main boulevard, and then suddenly she cut left. One hard bump pushed my hands and arms up an inch or two, jostling her generous breasts. "Oops" was all I could say as I slid my arms back to waist level.

I felt her chuckle. "It's OK," she hollered.

We were now speeding across a long bridge. After a few more minutes of level zipping, she slowed and made a left turn across a small rickety bridge onto what looked like a little island in the middle of a river. We sped on down a dirt road towards the water, and I just could make out a small, lighted pier with a thatched hut at the far end. It was lighted inside by candles and small lamps and appeared to be an old fisherman's shed converted into a bistro. Nets hung from the rafters, and strains of music were coming from the direction of the shack's kitchen, as were strong aromas with traces of jasmine, sesame, ginger, and fishy things being cooked.

Gigi pulled up beside the pier, parked, and locked the scooter. Then using her own little penlight to light the way, she took my hand and led me up some steps onto the rickety pier. The shack was something out of a Hope-and-Crosby road movie: candles stuck in wine bottles; several couples busy with bowls of noodles; some old trawl nets hanging from nails; hooks, gaffs and some old oars nailed to the walls. A large opening in the middle of the floor was surrounded by a two-foot wooden railing. At its bottom, waves softly lapped against pilings, and occasional thrashing sounds could be heard, too.

"That's where they keep live seafood," Gigi said. "It's a huge holding tank with bamboo slats and netting. They keep everything—turtles, fish, lobster, crabs. You order what's available, they pull it out, and hand it to the cook."

"You been here before?"

"Yes, my husband and I often ate here. But that's been awhile." A wan smile. She offered nothing more.

We selected a table facing the water. It was a calm sea. On both sides of the pier were other piers. Large boats tied alongside mostly looked like shrimpers and trawlers. Lights bobbed on their decks. Across the water, a quarter moon was peeping just above the horizon. Our candle was shrouded by a paper shade, preventing the breeze from dousing the flame.

I was still unsure what this was all about and a touch uncomfortable. But whatever the situation, I could handle it, I assured myself.

A tiny woman came over and bowed gently. "I just realized I am hungry," said Gigi, "Must be the ocean air. I'm ordering a small bowl of soup, some *chai giao* and white wine. Will you join me?"

"Sure fine, I'd love some. How come you're suddenly hungry?"

"It must be the salt air. And maybe you make me a little hungry."

Oh boy. I may be dumb, but not stupid. Don't touch that line, say nothing, let it play out.

I smiled and said, "Oh."

The wine was bottled, corked, and cold. We didn't go through the tasting foolishness. Instead we both took large swigs. Gigi sipped a little more, nodded and declared it good French white Burgundy. It was good, but then I knew damn all about wines. The soup was delicious, a kind of fish stew.

We sipped, slurped, smiled some more and had more wine.

"Wondering what's going on, Doctor? May I call you 'John'?"

"Of course. All my friends call me 'John.'"

"Good. First I want to ask you something personal. No offense, OK? Would you mind telling me your age?"

"Me? I'm thirty-five. Why?"

"I already knew, but some men lie."

"How old are you," I asked.

"Oh, ho, good. Touché. I'm thirty-eight."

"Christ, you don't look it. You look much younger."

"How kind of you, John." I could tell she was pleased, "You see, I'm trying to make a point. Things aren't always what they seem, especially out here. Try to remember that, always keep that in mind when you see something that doesn't make sense. Now, you must be wondering what kind of a person I am, one minute the demure lady, the next minute a bit forward. I know you're not married, and you know I'm married. Still, to me, you're a very attractive man, and I am attracted to you. Are you shocked? Don't be. At times I am shameless and play games. But tonight, I'm going to be serious with you. Because I'm worried for you, and maybe I care just a little…about you."

She had averted her eyes for a moment, looking down at the table, but now she leveled them and locked eyes solidly with me. She'd done some clever things with her eyeliner and the faintest application of sparkly eye shadow, which set off purplish irises. In this light the effect was dramatic and hypnotic.

"John, what's so damn maddening about you is that you seem so naive about world affairs, about what goes on in this world. I get the feeling that you don't really care. It's more than maddening. And that's what I want to talk to you about."

She leaned forward just a bit more. "Oh, one more thing, John. If things were slightly different, you'd have difficulty getting away from me."

I was taken aback. Was she serious? Me? Is that so? Wonder how she feels about Antoine, I thought. She spends enough time with him. I scolded myself for being catty.

With a studied lack of emotion, I looked into her eyes. She would be an interesting woman to know better, no question. But that might not be the right thing, given, as she'd reminded me, that she was married. She sure didn't act married. Then again, that could work two ways—as a deterrent to unwanted attentions, and as a lure. "If things were different" was like baiting a hook. I wasn't biting just yet.

I called for more wine, needing time to think, to plan and respond. I'd had women flirt with me, proposition me, and even berate me for not following up their overtures. But I was a bit off-balance now.

"By the way, what do you think of me?" she asked abruptly.

"Well," I started with a wave of my hand, "I..."

"Don't," she said. "Leave it. I shouldn't have asked. I already know. Sometime soon, I want you to tell me about yourself. I need to know more about you."

Like hell she did.

No question, I was damn sure attracted to her, but I wasn't going to do or say anything stupid. I'd give her my biography if she wanted—but later, not now. I decided I had better stop drinking wine for the evening.

"OK, John, let's talk about what you're slated to do soon. I've got to make sure you know what you're getting into. You're going to visit Tom Dooley in Muong Sing, in Laos, then go to Russia. Right? So, you want to tell me why? What's this got to do with medicine? What is John really doing out here? Who do you work for?"

"Gigi,...I can call you 'Gigi,' right?"

She smiled, "But of course."

"I'm not sure why you ask. But to answer your question…" I then told her the highlights of my life, from my childhood in London up to the present. I explained about Medico, CARE, and my being volunteered to serve as a surgical specialist. Finished, I pressed her back. "And I'm not quite sure what brings you out here. You say you work for Michigan State University. Your husband is a pilot for some International Control Commission—a man who you rarely see, right? So what the hell are you; and what's Michigan State doing out here? What is Gigi really doing in Vietnam?"

She nodded. It was a fair question, she said. Then slowly, she moved her chair closer. I suspected she wanted to keep her voice down, but as she moved her chair, her pocketbook strap slipped off the chair back and fell on the wooden planking floor; making a heavy clunking sound when it hit. The flap popped open. Clearly visible was her penlight, as well as the dull metallic sheen of a handgun. It looked like a flat, automatic SW .32 cal, if memory served. In her pocketbook? Why not in her waistband, in her jeans?

From the expression on my face, she knew I'd seen it. Deliberately, she closed the flap and rehung the strap on the chair-back.

"A woman needs protection," she said, with no change of expression. That was pure bullshit, and we both knew it. I let it go for the moment, but it had me thinking. What kind of a woman would carry a gun in her pocketbook?

"OK. Let's start," she said, with a slight toss of her head. "You're going to Laos, which right now is a very hot spot in Southeast Asia. Do you know anything about that place?"

I confessed that I didn't.

"Oh dear, I knew you were an innocent." She shook her head, her dangling earrings flopping at each movement. Oddly, I found that sexy. Still, I knew the head-shaking was out of frustration and dismay.

"John, you are innocence personified. You need to have some idea of what you're getting into, both from this Dooley jink and then going to Russia. Tell me—assure me—you're not having flights of fancy, or that you're not doing, what should I say, something else.

Can you tell me? Will you tell me?" And in the same breath, "Did anyone from the embassy brief you about anything?"

"Nope."

"Shit!" It didn't slip out; she said it conversationally as though it were in her everyday lexicon. Which suggested she was a lot tougher than she looked, especially since she was packing. At that moment, I knew she was a lot more than just Michigan State.

"You ought to have a small briefing before you go up there; I can do a quick sketch now; we've got time and it's still early. So listen while I give you a brief history lesson, you poor lad." The last comment she followed with a smirk.

She pulled a pair of eyeglasses from her pocketbook, narrow with thin black frames. Her scarf had settled down around her neck and her hair was gathered in the back like a pullet tail, secured by a silk twist. For all the world, she looked like an attractive librarian or schoolteacher, but I knew better—she was anything but. Again I caught a whiff of her faint lemony smell.

From that tote bag, she pulled out some notepaper on which were scribbles. Clearly she'd planned for this. "For starters," she said, "intelligence reports suggest Dooley is a homosexual." Whoops, that got my attention. I'd been only half listening.

"Say that again…"

"You weren't listening, were you?"

"Yes and no."

"You mean no."

"I don't know what I mean." She did sound like a goddam schoolteacher now, which was annoying. I had disliked schoolmarms since early in my school days.

"Let me start again. You should first know that Dooley's hospital is part of the American military, and it's part of an intelligence setup. It's a listening post for activities in parts of Yunnan. Did you have any idea? And by the way, does it bother you that he's allegedly a homo?"

"No."

"OK. The CIA is using him, maybe others, too. I'm not sure whether he's tumbled to that; if he has, he doesn't care; if he hasn't, well, he must be dense. Frankly, I think he knows, is pleased and doesn't care. It gives him some credibility. Do you see that?"

She continued: "The hospital takes care of indigenous natives in the valley there. It's right on the border between China, Burma, and Laos. The natives know no boundaries. They wander freely in and out of the neighboring countries, and often in and out of North Vietnam. All the natives in the valley of Muong Sing will know about you, just as they already know about the famous *Thanh Mo*—Dr. Dooley, the white doctor. That's what you'll be called too, John, the moment you set foot in the valley. The word will get out, and you'll be the other *Thanh Mo*."

I listened, knowing I had no choice.

"Dooley's hospital has a large following, which will amaze you. You'll see all this for yourself. But the place also takes care of wounded KMT fighters and other mercenaries used by Americans. You know anything about that—who the KMT are?"

"Uh, no."

"I thought so." She frowned slightly and continued. "Ten years ago, in 1949, the communists finally defeated Chiang Kai Shek and his Kuomintang Nationalists. This is the KMT—Chiang's leadership corps, who fled to Taiwan and set up the Republic of China there. Now, some of the KMT generals and troops had been co-opted by the CIA and taken to the Muong Sing valley area in Laos. They set up their own villages there—families, crops, horses, cattle, everything. And they are still supplied by unmarked CIA couriers out of Hong Kong. The CIA looks the other way on another lucrative pastime: the refugees grow poppies, and the raw product is flown to Bangkok for processing.

"The CIA coordinates missions up there, usually into Yunnan, inside China. The old KMT generals are contacted and told when to strike. When the time comes, they'll mount their ponies and ride into Yunnan, just like their Mongol ancestors. They shoot up communes, targets of opportunity—whatever will cause the commies the most discomfort. Occasionally they seek out a particular person—usually a party official—and kill him. This does two things: it keeps terror afloat in China, and it lets Mao know that the KMT lives. You may see some of this for yourself, John dear, so keep your eyes open.

"The North Vietnamese are always sending teams of killers and assassins into Laos to return the favor. I'll tell you this: they'll know you're coming, and they may want to hurt or kill you. Every Asian in the valley knows they're at risk from the commies, too. So, tell me, are you prepared for this? Did you have any idea of what you might be getting into?"

I shifted in my chair. "Well how the hell would I?" I asked. "All this is certainly sobering and scary. But how come you know so much, Gigi? Quit the mysterious stuff and level with me. You know too much for just a worker for Michigan State, OK? I'm not completely stupid."

She rolled her eyes slightly and sighed. "Wait till I finish my wine and my lesson for the night, Johnny boy."

By now it was getting late. She downed her wine and waved for more. I stopped her.

"You have any more wine, and I don't ride back with you. Clear?"

"OK, fine. Citron-soda," she said to the old lady who'd taken our order.

Gigi went on. "Let me tell you more of what the communists do in that part of the world—Dooley's world, and in Cambodia, too. In all their radio broadcasts, they accuse the Americans of espionage, imperialism, colonialism, and planning to take over their countries. All Asians who work with Americans are called traitors and warned they're marked for revenge. When the communists decide to go on a terror campaign, they select a village, trap all the villagers inside, and pick out a few to make examples of—usually the elders and the most intelligent-looking men. Then they hack off their heads and impale them on stakes, right in front of the assembled villagers."

I grimaced. She noticed. "There's more. They pick out a few others at random, slash their knee tendons—just like they do with cattle—and let them fall helpless on the ground for later. Once they're ready to leave, they walk over and hack them to death. It's not a pretty sight. They sometimes rape one or two of the youngest women in plain sight and take a few along for trophies when they go. These bastards are mostly North Vietnamese, plus a few Chinese trained specifically for this kind of terror. So the villagers and tribes up in Dooley land know all about this terrorist activity. I think Dooley knows he's in danger, but he's crazy and doesn't care. We've urged him to leave, but he refuses. I'll stop here. It sickens me to talk about it."

We, she'd said. Who the hell was "we"?

It was getting late…I waved for the check. I wanted to drive the scooter back, which was fine with Gigi. This time, she held on to me, and quite firmly I thought. But I didn't care. Actually, I liked it. I could feel her body and those oversized breasts jammed up against my back. And yes, they certainly did arouse me. But I tried to keep my mind on the road.

It was an easy ride back to the Michelin villa. There were still a few lights on and some candles flickering, and someone smoking nearby. I smelled that strong Gauloise tobacco, but no one in sight. Gigi was still leaning firmly against my back, her head laid sideways across my right shoulder. She apparently had no notion of getting off.

"Hey, we're here," I said. I still had to get back to my villa.

I made to climb off. That roused her.

"Listen," she said, straightening, "you take the scooter. I'll get it back tomorrow."

"OK, yeah. Sure." I knew that we were being watched, and she did, too. Something in her body language had changed slightly, as if she were going onstage. Otherwise there might have been more than just a moist peck on the cheek.

"Goodnight," she said with a big, tired smile. "Thanks for the after-dinner drinks. Ciao." She started for the front door.

The scooter, now much lighter, handled fine on the short ride back to the Neptune. I pulled around to the back of the villa and put it into a shed. I was sore, I noticed as I walked away. It could have been the scooter seat, but I think it was something else. My groin was still aching. It felt like my first date with that cute blonde cheerleader from Wilson High—what the hell was her name? It was a boy's name…something like Lloyd or Gil. But she'd been just a tease, damn her. Said I was her football hero and she'd wanted to reward me. I ended up with sore balls for two days.

I climbed into my bed but tossed and turned, thinking about this woman and the gun in her pocketbook. Finally, sleep caught up with me.

The next morning, Hank Peters picked me up in a dusty Jeep. We drove down from Nha Trang towards Cam Ranh, the low, beachside road twisting and turning, empty of traffic. Hank glanced over and read my mind. "This is our road, Doc."

We passed through scapes of tall trees and shrubs, then a swampy area, and finally out onto a dazzling vista of rocks, beach, and water. Off to my left in the azure sea was yet another cluster of small barrier islands, and then I noticed something unusual. A cable hung from the cliff top just before me, sloped down and out just about head high above the water to one of those islands, where it angled upward and disappeared into some rocks.

"Know what that is, Doc?"

"Cable," I said. "Cable car?"

"Nope, not quite. It's a slide cable. I'll show you how she works later."

We turned inland, drove up a long, curving road, and pulled onto a level area at the top of a massive cliff. Surrounding us on this vast promontory were sheds, shacks, basketball courts, buildings that looked like barracks, a helicopter pad with an orange windsock, and paths leading down towards the trees and vegetation through which we had just driven. There were no signs anywhere, and no writing of any sort on any of the building exteriors. It looked for all the world like an abandoned installation except for one thing: The place teemed with soldiers in military fatigues, some in MP armbands and most with rifles posted along the road and arrayed around the camp perimeter.

"These boys also keep an eye on us, Doc," said Hank. "They watched us enter and drive up the road. There's no other way in, and if you ain't a friend—boom." He chuckled.

We pulled up to one of the long, low buildings. "There's chapel this morning and orders are everybody goes and prays, and they do, else they draw down some bad duty," Hank said. "At noon on

Sundays, after prayer services, we have some mighty fine chow, so it's a well-attended service. But let's start by getting you in some fatigues."

I changed into camouflage gear, slapped on a floppy campaign hat and large combat boots. I kept my camera and hung my clothes in Hank's quarters. Hank was a Warrant Officer, the highest of the low, he explained. He'd been an enlisted man and risen up as high as an enlisted man can, after which he was commissioned a Warrant Officer. He could have been made 2nd looey, but he preferred the respect and kinship a Warrant Officer receives from the troops. Enlisted men see Warrant Officers as one of them—one of their boys who made good. Hank's choice had been all about pay, respect, and a safe harbor between two levels of military life. Warrant Officers drew more pay than 2nd looeys, after all.

During the next few hours, we toured rifle ranges and jump towers built for parachuting proficiency. I saw bayonet dummy targets, obstacle courses—the whole place was a training and fitness arena. He showed me classrooms decked with chalkboards covered with colored directional arrows and attack formations. Another was a classroom for learning the Vietnamese language.

"Now, Doc, let me show you my workshop," Hank eventually said. We walked off towards a dun-colored group of buildings set off by themselves. Outside one of them, a small generator purred; alongside it, an air conditioning unit. He unlocked doors and flipped on lights in what was a large and well-used workshop. There were guns and parts of guns, plus hand grenades and wooden boxes with various markings—but on all, clearly visible, a hand grenade painted in black. I knew what that meant: explosives.

Hank opened a large refrigerator and extracted a brick-shaped gray object that looked like artist's molding clay. "Here, catch," he said, tossing it. "That's 'plastique,' Doc."

I didn't know what "plastique" was, I said, but just the same, I was very glad I'd caught it.

He grinned and then explained it was something called C4, a very powerful explosive that's easy to handle, cut, carve, and mold but that can only be detonated with a blasting cap, like Primacord. He cut off a hunk with a knife, rolled it into a ball, and threw it forcefully against the near wall. It made a splat sound, flattened out, and stuck. Hank walked over and peeled it off with a mischievous smile. Next, he opened a drawer, pulled out a length of heavy line, and cut off a length. Then he plucked out some small, fuse-like objects and a box with a rotary timer switch, stuck them all in his pocket, and led the way outside to a deep pit about 100 yards away.

There, Hank showed me how to mold C4 into any shape needed for a particular job—how to insert detonators into C4 just so, how to blow huge holes in the ground, how to girdle and blast a huge mahogany tree trunk clean through. Fifteen minutes in, my ears were ringing, and I reeked of dirt and something like burnt grass. At an hour, I was tiring, but Hank was indefatigable, insisting on showing me how to use Primacord as a fuse, detonator, and explosive in its own right.

"OK, Doc, we'll finish up our little bang session," he finally said. "For my last trick, I'm gonna show you how to blast a hole in solid concrete. It's gonna be a huge hole. Then we go fishing."

"Fishing?"

"Yep, we'll take a rubber boat out and catch some dinner."

"I got a problem, Hank." I explained that I already had a dinner laid on.

"No problem, I'll get you back in plenty of time. Let's go."

Back at the shed, he pulled out a small bicycle inner tube and some more C4; he also grabbed a small, bulging satchel that looked heavy. We trudged over towards some massive, roofless walls that once had been part of some French military barracks, now in ruins. The nearest wall was quite thick and after all these years, still looked redoubtable.

Hank extracted the inner tube, filled it from a cylinder from the satchel. "That's water in there," he said. Then he pulled a thick rope of C4 from the satchel and handed it to me. "Hold this, Doc—don't worry, it won't do a thing right now."

Reaching in again, he withdrew a small pointed-tip hammer and a mean-looking spike. With a mighty smack, he drove the spike into a crack in the wall. Then he suspended the inner tube over the spike, took the rope of C4, and quickly taped it to the inner tube using wide strips of duct tape. Finally, he stuck a detonator into the heart of the C4 rope, its wires leading to a clump of trees. We got behind them, and Hank mashed a button on the little black box in his hand. BLAM! Another ground-shaking blast, with rocks, dirt, chips, and dust flying in every direction, along with the smell of something like gunpowder. Hank was enjoying himself; I was getting deaf. When the dust began settling, sure enough, before us in this enormous wall gaped a hole. I found it hard to believe, but there it was. The wall had to be at least three feet thick, and it had been cut through like soft butter.

"A hole big enough to climb through, dontcha think, Doc?"

We walked over for a closer look. It damn sure was. In fact, it was big enough for one or two persons at a time to get through. I was impressed.

"Neat trick," I declared. "How'd you figure out how to blast a hole that large?"

"Well, it has to do with physics, I can't completely explain it, but some people at Quantico, the Marine demolition men, first explained it to me. The exploding C4 slams against the water-filled tube, and the water, which doesn't like to be compressed that hard or that violently, slams through whatever is in its way, like that wall back there. The water-filled inner tube acts like a powerful hydraulic press, a piston driven by the exploding force of the C4. It happens really quickly—in fractions of a second they tell me. It's almost like a guillotine in speed and action—zingo! One or two rigs like that, with maybe a central kicker—a small wad of C4 in the center of the circle—can level the side of a building. But it has to be set up just right. No room for mistakes." He paused for a minute, glanced at his watch. "Tell you what—let's head for the beach."

"I left my trunks at the villa."

"No problem, we got plenty of GI bathing trunks."

NHA TRANG

-- • --

DOWN AT THE BEACH, a large orange zodiac bobbed alongside a well-protected pier. Clean, white sand covered the bottom beneath it, and brightly colored fish darted among the pilings. A number of other zodiacs, plus some rubber boats and john boats—all well used—had been pulled up on the beach.

Hank started the small motor on the first pull; it didn't purr but just burbled quietly. "Muffled," he said.

We zipped out onto the open sea and up the coast, scooting around huge cones of stone and lava that stabbed up through the azure water, pointing sharp fingers to the sky. Some were joined at the waist, others separated by small channels. The water, while clear, also seemed more aquamarine, and in spots it looked very deep. I could see coral heads and small reefs where still more colorful fish floated, motionless.

After maneuvering us over a notably larger reef, Hank cut the engine and dropped a small mushroom anchor. I heard whoops and shouts nearby and quickly spotted the source: some of the men were sliding down the cable I'd seen earlier, dropping from the cliff above us toward a small island. At the low point, they'd let go of the strap they'd been holding and plummet into the ocean with a huge splash. It seemed great fun—for them.

Hank chuckled as I watched. "Those are the UDT men—Underwater Demolition Team," he explained. "We call them Frogmen or squids. They're happier in the water than on the beach. And they're all crazy. Now I'm going over the side and catch us some fish, maybe a lobster or two. But I have to let them know to wait for me to come up—you'll see why in a sec."

By now Hank had slapped on a mask, fins, weights, and a small tank. He shouted out to the daredevils, saying he'd only be a few minutes. Then, grabbing a harpoon gun and spears, he rolled effortlessly over the side of the boat. Over the next few minutes, he speared five huge lobsters, several groupers, and one or two other fish, stashing them in his net-bag. Back on board, he tossed them into a wet burlap sack and sat on the gunwale to rest before moving away from the reef.

83

The sun was still hot, but it now was angling down towards the horizon. Hank hailed the other crews, telling them he was done and all clear, which brought a raucous response of laughter and waving. "Watch," he said. "Those guys figger on getting a couple of dozen lobsters for their Sunday barbecue. Don't rightly approve their methods, but they work."

Shortly, a huge spout of water rose some ten feet in the air, followed by a dull shock and a muffled boom. Hank explained: "Those guys laid a very small charge of C4 alongside one of those reefs, and now they're gonna have a passel of fish, lobsters, octopus, and maybe some shucked clams. What stays whole goes onto the grill, and the chopped-up, mangled stuff goes into chowder. Sure wish you could stay, Doc—these crazy Texans make great barbecue."

I thanked him and wanted to stay, but begged off.

"Hank, I've got a question for you. I'm asking because you obviously know explosives, so you must know guns, right?"

"Well, yep, I do know a thing or two. What's on your mind?"

I told him about when Gigi had dropped her pocketbook, and about the weapon I saw inside. I also told him a little about her, including the Michigan State story she'd told me—which I'd had trouble believing—and about her so-called husband and Antoine.

"You keen on this gal?"

That shook me. Was I? I wasn't sure, but not necessarily keen, just interested, I said.

Hank did a lip tug, looked at me for a full five seconds.

"Tell you what. They's two kinds of women who carry. Little yap-yapping women who want to feel safe often stash a little trouble-maker, like a .25 caliber auto. They may know how to use it, they may not. Chances are, when they need to use it, they'll freeze up, wet their pants, and miss their target. A woman like you've described, though, doing what she does and carrying what sounds like something larger—a Beretta or maybe a 9mm.—she's probably a professional of some sort and is authorized to carry. If I had to guess, she's with some intelligence-gathering outfit, and nowadays they's so damn many of them she could be anything. Michigan State sounds like a great cover for intelligence gathering. She's probably got a network of informers, puts all the gathered stuff together and interprets it, and forwards it all onwards somewhere else. It sounds like she's had weapons training; I wouldn't be surprised at all if she gets in harm's way at times. Just a guess, though."

I'd been thinking along those lines, and Hank's conclusions made perfect sense. So Gigi had to be a spook of sorts. Humph. I wasn't too surprised. Better watch myself. But why? I was of damn little use as a source of information for her.

I thanked Hank and climbed aboard the Jeep. He drove me back to the villa.

"B'fore you leave for up north, Doc, give me a whistle. I may have some names for you."

Again, I thanked him for everything. He smiled, "En-joyed it. You take good care, and watch yer topknot, hear?"

CHAPTER 7

Saigon—Again

THINGS AT THE HOSPITAL WERE HUMMING AGAIN. THE OPERATING ROOMS had been repainted, fans repaired. Several resections were awaiting my return, as was a full day of diagnostic bronchoscopies—which I hated, given that most patients needing bronchoscopic examination of their airways would spit up blood mixed with green stuff. It was usually infected, smelled putrid, and made most nurses run to the hall trying not to barf. If that wasn't bad enough, most of these patients had bad breath for starters.

I buried myself in work, letting the weeks slide by. At times, I was working harder here in Saigon than I had at home. And there was that word again—home. It always triggered a guilty feeling for having virtually abandoned my teaching and practice responsibilities. Still, the fat was in the fire now. I had to follow through with what I'd set out to do; my time in Saigon was winding down.

Between operations and hospital work, I managed to get my Dooley visit lined up. I'd first fly to Bangkok, then on to Laos's capital, Vientiane, and then board an Air Laos feeder to Muong Sing. On the return flight to Bangkok, I'd get my visa for Moscow.

— • —

SAIGON—AGAIN

DAYS BEFORE I WAS TO leave, the embassy sent over a fat envelope, which had arrived via diplomatic pouch from Washington. It was from Dad; as usual, he'd prodded low friends in high places at State to do him a favor. Dad had a magic way in such matters. I often wondered if he was on someone's secret payroll.

The envelope contained pertinent clippings about Anastas Mikoyan's visit to Washington, including the now-famous one-on-one encounter with Dad. Here also was Mikoyan's subsequent invitation, in writing, approving my visit to Moscow.

As for my departure, things were falling into place. I had some lunch meetings with François and Antoine and told them I might not return to Saigon from Russia. They seemed saddened by that remark. I realized then that we'd struck up something along the lines of a good friendship and my leaving had caught them off guard. I promised to keep in touch, but we all knew that's not always the case when people leave. Antoine seemed saddened to hear that I'd be leaving. He tossed back a drink and we did a Salud thing. Again, I'd keep in touch, I promised.

Next, a meeting with Ernie Kline, the political officer at the embassy, covering my reasons for visiting Moscow. It was highly unusual, he told me, for someone of my status to receive an invitation from Mikoyan; was there something else he should know? He seemed to be talking down to me, and I guessed that he wasn't thrilled with my upcoming adventure.

Indeed he wasn't, and he made that clear: There were some misgivings about my trip at the embassy's highest levels, and Washington would, of course, be notified. All this meant that someone was envious, I figured, jealous that an unconnected, no-name physician could get to do something that Foreign Service officers hungered for. I feigned innocence, smiled, and said something like "Yeah, it's real strange, isn't it?" And let it drop. Kline was not at all certain I'd actually get my visa from the Russkies, but in case I did, I should please check in at our Moscow Embassy on arrival straight away, he said. I assured him I would.

My whereabouts, anyway, would be monitored closely for my own safety, Kline added. And I should keep in mind I would be an object of great curiosity to the Soviets. They'd surely keep me in sight at all times and ply me with questions. Maybe I'd keep notes on those sessions—yes? Sure.

I'd cleaned up all loose ends at the hospital and my bags were finally packed. I'd be traveling light. So I tossed all unnecessary clothing and articles into a bag for the maid. I was ready and anxious to leave now; in fact I was getting restless.

One last thing I had to do, along with cleaning out my office and clearing things with the Medico team, was to get Gigi to tell me the rest of her story—what she was doing out here. I'd try to catch up with her once more. I called her office, only to learn that she was in Bangkok but expected back on that evening's flight. She called next morning, and why sure, we could have dinner at the Cercle Sportif that night—my last in Saigon.

--•--

LATE THAT AFTERNOON, THE HOTEL porter brought me a message instructing me to contact a Sergeant Mishawy at a certain phone number.

I did. My phone call was answered by a male voice that said only "State your name and business." I did, adding that I was returning a call from a gentleman named Mishawy. My call was disconnected immediately, right then. Odd, but then nothing surprised me in this place anymore.

Within ten minutes, there was a knock on my door, and the sergeant introduced himself, producing documents that ID'd him as a communications specialist at the embassy. (I learned later that he was billeted at the nonexistent military residence just down Tu-Do Street from the Majestic Hotel.) He held up a small gym bag that looked too heavy to be toting tennis shoes or gym gear. "This here's a present from Hank Peters."

He then opened the zipper, extracting an automatic pistol.

SAIGON—AGAIN

"Hank wanted you to carry this with you," he said. "Don't worry, sir—nobody will spot it. It's got hardly any metal in it—it's made of ceramic and bonded plastic components. And it comes apart easy and can be scattered in your dopp kit and baggage." The gun was designed by Hank and some other ordnance people and had no official name, he added. It was just a weapon—one Hank thought I needed.

Watching me heft the lightweight piece, Mishawy went on, noting that Hank and a guy named Stoner actually had developed several weapons. "Stoner invented guns for the Army," he said. "The two of them were working on a better version of the M1, and they ended up creating an automatic they designated the '63.' The gun you're holding uses the same small round that the 63 did."

I must have seemed unconvinced somehow, as Mishawy went into a sales pitch. "This little baby works, sir—I've tested it. It's automatic, real light, and doesn't have the kick of the forty-fives. And it comes with a special slug that tears the shit out of whatever it hits."

Reaching into the little gym bag, he pulled out three clips wrapped in oil paper within a soft cloth bag, followed by four boxes of ammunition and a small holster. One clip was elongated forward and bent like a small banana. The others were stick clips, one short, the other long. Mishawy jacked a single cartridge from the long clip. He pointed out that the casings were ceramic, but the slugs were metal...lead. Some slug's business ends were cross-hatched, which, Mishawy advised, you didn't use unless you absolutely wanted to blow someone away. He showed me the settings for auto and rapid fire, and finally produced a thin frame which looked like a clothes hanger, but was actually a plastic portable stock that converted the piece to an automatic rifle. "You might call this gun a mini-Uzi, sir, because when you slip this stock on, it's a rifle, too. Something they might-a borrowed from the Israelis; not sure on that."

He spent the next half-hour showing me how to load, strip and dry-fire the piece. When he was satisfied that I wouldn't blow my foot off, he shook hands gravely, wished me luck and left. "If you wanna reach me, sir, just call that there number and leave a message. I'll find you."

Inside the gym bag I found a folded note with "Doctor John" on it. Within was Hank's spidery handwriting: "Doc, keep this with you. Separate the parts and stow them in your baggage when you're traveling. Mishawy will check you out. You may need this where you're going. Hope you have a good dinner. Hank"

Good dinner? How did he know? What did he know? A number of people seemed to know my every move. Why?

Weary of feeling watched, I dressed for dinner and made my way to the Cercle Sportif, where I was directed to a corner booth. Gigi showed up shortly; flashing a big smile, she slid into the seat beside me, at the same time ordering a Citron-soda with Bombay Gin from the hovering bar-boy.

Still smiling, "Johnny boy," she announced, "I'm taking you to dinner tonight." There had been no hello, no greeting, just the announcement. Huh? And for the first time I realized she'd slid over just close enough that I felt the warmth of her upper thigh against my thigh. It could have been an accidental thing, or a well-planned move. I pretended I'd not noticed it. I'd just go along with this woman's games and let things play out. At times like this she frightened me.

Gigi had gone to Bangkok to visit friends and take care of a few business matters, she said. And she mentioned casually that her husband had flown a group of UN diplomats into Bangkok to meet with North Vietnamese representatives, giving her a few precious, rare hours with him. Somehow, it was unconvincing.

When I mentioned our previously unfinished dinner conversation, she said—also unconvincingly—that she couldn't remember much of that dinner discussion. So I reminded her, as the waiter prepared our salad, the gist of that chat.

"Oh, yes." Now she remembered.

She pondered for just a moment. Then, looking me in the eye with that disconcerting stare and her left eyebrow raised, she told me that she was an economics consultant with Michigan State on loan to our State Department. She did economic analyses, studied local trade and bank activities, changes in currency values—that sort of thing. She and her assistants put this data into formulas and graphs, generating projections as to how well a given country was doing. It was all very technical and very boring, she said. And why in the world was I interested?

As she talked, she paused from time to time to take dainty forkfuls of salad and tiny sips of white wine. I took in what she said, but it sounded to me like so much bullshit.

"What branch of our State Department looks at this sort of stuff?" I asked.

She was in no rush to answer.

"Well, Johnny boy, I think the State Department intelligence people," she said. "Their Intelligence Agency does. And I'm sure they share it with other interested agencies, so I guess that's what I do for them, and for Michigan State."

So you see I'm really an employee of the State Department Intelligence Agency, silly boy!

So that was it: Gigi was a spy for our State Department—and she wasn't even an American.

"And of course, Johnny dear, you won't talk about me to your friends, will you." It was not a question, but rather a declarative statement. "No one would believe you anyway, and you do care for my safety and well-being, don't you?"

No answer was necessary. I nodded. Finally she'd explained the gun in her pocketbook.

"This is for you," she said in a new tone of voice, as she produced a folded sheet of paper and held it out for me. When I reached Bangkok, she announced, I was to look up a Jim Thompson whose fabric shop was on Surawong Road, just down from my hotel. How did she know where I was staying? Also, she said, there was a Chuck Miller from Vientiane who'd leave a message at my hotel if I wasn't in. Their names, along with a short list of suggested things to do in Bangkok, were typed on the sheet. I slipped the list into a pocket; with everything I had on my mind, it would have to wait.

Our food was delicious: soupe Chinoise, crab rolls, salad, grilled things on tiny skewers, and a good French Chardonnay. We made aimless chatter, her eyebrows doing their up-and-down dips as she rambled. I noticed she was drinking more wine than I as we chatted about my future plans on return to the States. At some point after the skewered things, we switched to beer, the wine long finished.

This was probably a serious mistake. By now it was late, and we'd consumed several beers in addition to the wine. We'd also chatted ourselves out; we'd reached a state of total relaxation. The alcohol, I mused, had released many inhibitions on both sides of the table. For food, anyway, I was sated.

By her previous arrangement, there was no dinner check. So would I please escort her home, just down the street? I'd been there before, knew the way.

Only a cad would refuse.

Gigi took my arm. As we sauntered along the Quai Belgique, she holding my arm—tightly, I thought—and still chattering away, she pointed out the boats and small sampan-like craft lining the river banks on either side. Many had families clustered on the stern decks, cooking the evening meal. On some, sleepers in their hammocks swayed as these little boats rocked from passing waves.

Shortly, we reached her home and entered through the veranda entrance. A host of lighted candles gave a soft luminance to the room.

Gigi's lemony scent was in the air now, mixed with a rich coffee aroma from the tiny kitchen. A maid had arranged small trays with cups, goblets, serviettes, and nibblings, placing them on the coffee table and silently disappearing. Clearly something was afoot, and suddenly, I wasn't hungry. In fact I was apprehensive and maybe scared.

"Wait just a moment before you leave," she said quietly. "I have a little something for you."

She disappeared around a corner, reappearing shortly in a robe—something flowing, flimsy, and diaphanous. *Gulp.* With a mischievous smile, she poured a large brandy and a coffee for herself, a smaller one for me. I sipped the coffee; the brandy could evaporate, for all I cared. I'd had enough alcohol for the evening.

She walked over, bowed gravely, and handed me a jewel box covered with soft black velvet. It was open, and inside, a thin gold chain from which dangled a fat, golden Buddha. It was exquisite—the Buddha even had tiny green jade eyes!

"Johnny, boy, this is your good luck talisman," she said. "This tiny Lord God Buddha will watch over you, protect you, and where you're going. Anyone who sees it will know you're under his protection. Promise me you'll always wear it."

"OK," I said gravely, "I will."

She reached for her brandy snifter—really a giant goblet—and I saw that it was nearly empty! She was now like a debutante after too much champagne, quite high. It was after midnight, and as I screwed up my courage to leave, she spotted my move, pirouetted gracefully, and plunked down beside me on the couch. It seemed I was not to leave yet.

Damn, I'm trapped!

By now I was truly nervous, with a sense of impending disaster. There was more here than just sex. It was an ominous feeling of something about to happen out of my control. Stupidly, I was immobilized with indecision.

Maybe she sensed this, I'll never know. She was already barefoot, and now she artfully propped her slim ankles and bare feet on the coffee table in front of us. She leaned hard against me, and if I'd been even half a man, I'd have jumped up and run out right then.

But I didn't. Instead, I was frozen...partly by fear and partly by curiosity, suspecting what was developing yet too timid, too weak. I was completely spineless.

All the while this was going on, my mind was racing and that inner voice chortling at my predicament: this must be how a mouse feels when a cobra has raised its monstrous head and zeroes in on it. I'd had these same feelings when a lusty student nurse dragged me into a hospital linen closet years ago in Pittsburgh. "Finally gotcha," she'd said. Sure, it was wrong, wicked, and likely to be trouble, but I sometimes feel powerless to correct matters. I needed help. I needed to bug out. Damn.

Without interrupting her chatter, Gigi swung herself upward suddenly, threw both arms around my neck, and kissed me full on the lips. Exhaling, she began wiggling her tongue in my mouth while muzzling my ears, and then she dug her long nails into my back through my jacket. Sitting upright, she gave a gymnastic wiggle to her shoulders, shrugging off her robe. And just like that she was gorgeously naked from the waist up.

The adroit moves and gorgeous breasts captivated me. My mind was racing, and a warning and a sudden impulse to leave tugged at me one last time, but it was no use and no matter; things had gone too far.

In the dim light, her bulbous breasts gleamed as though oiled; she had huge nipples and areolas, and I was shocked to see that she had painted her breasts—red rouge on her nipples, and dark circles around areolas, which were now outlined in black, like targets. Atop all this was a cloud of sparkling glitter, sprinkled across her chest. I was mesmerized.

Ever so slowly, she moved her hands behind her head and thrust out her chest, her eyes half-shut and glazed over. The tip of her tongue jutted out to the side, and she began swaying from side to side, hips in one direction, shoulders in another. She appeared to be doing some sort of sexual dance, and suddenly the thought occurred to me: Is she on drugs? Wouldn't be cocaine. Is it hashish? This is clearly not just a drunken woman—I've seen them dance on bar tops in Washington. No, this has to be some sort of drug-induced behavior—but what? And when had she had time to take it?

I let myself stare at this apparition straddling me: immense breasts thrust out, hands moving over her chest and then behind her body, all while slowly swaying from side to side. Grinning and looking down at me with a vacant stare, she gently wiggled her shoulders to set her breasts a-sway. It was seductive—and oddly terrifying. Was this a conscious thing, or was she actually in a trance?

OK, so now what do I do?

After a few more shoulder-wiggles, she stood up, reached down, and undid a waist-tie, sending what little she still was wearing cascading to her feet. There before me, in the flickering light of the candles, stood a naked, swaying woman with glittering, painted breasts—and, to my shock, no pubic hair.

Dear God, what next?

Still wearing my dinner clothes, I sat there like a ninny—a very aroused ninny. My legs began trembling, my kneecaps shuddering. Gigi leaned forward and put her hands on my shoulders, pulling me forward so as to remove my jacket by the lapels back and down. Then she swiftly straddled me like a tame mount and began loosening my buttons, all the while eyeing me with a fixed smile and unfocused stare.

Her fingers did their work. I did nothing. I couldn't. I was a person transfixed, detached, loathing myself for weakness but lost all the same in the prospect of what was about to happen.

Astride me, she pressed against the monster rising in my trousers. I groaned in dismay; I was undone and heard myself panting like a pig in heat. Gigi took this as an admission of lust and lifted herself enough to slide off my trousers. She tossed her head back and laughed. "So, Johnny boy—finally noticed, huh?"

And that settled it: She wasn't drugged. She was perfectly aware of every move she was making. *What a slick actress* was all that zipped through my brain.

She did another shoulder-shake, which made her sparkling breasts jiggle again, and then, unerringly, she mounted me! A form of reverse skewering, so to speak. I was now well and truly, firmly and helplessly, skewered!

Abandon all hope, ye who have been skewered.

She began to have her way with me, and I realized she had skills of a sort that I'd never encountered—and I'd had a few wild ones here and there. But this one put them to shame.

When she'd had her fill of me—and I guess I of her—she let out a loud, shuddering sigh, and slid off of me onto the carpet at my feet. Her breathing gradually slowed, and as I sat there, catching my own breath and admiring her shadowed form in the candlelight, I was surprised to hear her snoring softly. She had fallen asleep.

Compared to her screaming just moments before—oh, yes, she was a screamer—the snoring was a relief, its own kind of farewell. Staggering to my feet, I made my way to the lavatory, dressed, and stepped out onto the verandah. As I did, I thought I heard her giggle.

That was odd—one minute snoring, the next minute giggling? I tiptoed back and stood over her. She smelled strongly of brandy, sweat, and sex. Her eyes were shut and completely relaxed; the giggle had come from a deep dream state.

I spread her robe across her and left.

--•--

SAIGON WAS NOT AN INVITING city at this time of night. The streets were mostly deserted, and my footsteps echoed loudly as I made my way back to the Majestic. Fluorescent lights cast shadows on sleeping figures in doorways. I was anxious to get back to the brightly lit Quai Belgique and walked faster.

As I did, my mind jumped wildly. When the hell did Gigi have time to apply all that nipple makeup? One minute, she'd been normal, and the next, a wild woman. I'd only been in her home for minutes before the fireworks erupted.

More to the point, why me? What could she have accomplished by doing that number on someone who was leaving and whom she'd most likely never see again?

As I thought about how easily I'd been seduced—how completely I'd been subjugated and how incapable I had been of resisting—a certain self-disgust welled up in me. Gigi had oversexed me, for want of a better term, and done it as neatly and slickly as a carnival hustler on a country bumpkin. But why? Possibilities raced through my mind as I plodded along. Power? Had she been affirming that she had power over men, power to be in command of any situation? Well, hell, I was no one to impress. I was like a punching bag, a practice target. And

perhaps that was it: perhaps she was just fine-tuning her skills, the way an athlete does to stay in shape.

No, something else seemed at work here. Rounding a corner, I realized what scared me now: that Gigi had set me up, that she had made me beholden to her. But at that moment, on the couch...that hadn't crossed my mind. After all, I had no reason to think I would ever see her again. Whatever. At least that episode was over.

SAIGON—AGAIN

Unfortunately, the main doors were locked at The Majestic Hotel, and I'd left my keys with their bulky door tag at the desk. Of course the doors are locked, you idiot! It's after midnight. I rattled and banged on the door, yelling curses and my room number at the sleepy night watchman. Finally, he shuffled over and let me in. I took the cage elevator to my floor, unlocked my door, washed again, and fell in bed.

— - • - —

THE NEXT MORNING I LEFT for Bangkok; the embassy had kindly sent a car for my trip to the airport. I'd left goodbye notes for François, Antoine, and the CARE team.

CHAPTER 8

Bangkok

MY FLIGHT WAS UNEVENTFUL—A LUMBERING, OLD AIR VIETNAM DC-3 from Saigon direct to Bangkok. Once airborne, I pulled out my Nikon and got aerial shots through the window of paddy after paddy, plus the occasional gleaming spire of a temple, soaring through carpets of verdant jungle. The filthy windows lent the images a certain softness, a kind of ghostly halo. (No one at *National Geographic* ever figured out the dirty-window angle, and several of the shots ended up accompanying Laos and Cambodia stories.)

I'd been booked into the Erawan Princess Hotel. From my taxi, I noticed a nearby street sign for Surawong Road—where Jim Thompson's shop was located. I marked it on a map I was carrying.

As soon as I was in my room, I made a list of things to do—and my mind flashed back to that sheet of paper from which Gigi had been prattling off items for me. I shuddered momentarily before putting her out of my mind for the time being.

Let's see: Check with the Soviet consulate offices in Bangkok. Buy some trinkets and baubles for friends, have them shipped home. Visit Jim Thompson at his boutique, then wait for a call from Chuck Miller. And make damn sure to catch my flight to Vientiane and Dooley.

The Soviets were simple: Yes, they knew of my visa request. No, I would pick up the final papers in Delhi, from which I would fly to

Moscow. Yes, they knew when I was arriving and had already put me in a hotel for the night before my departure. So that's how it is, I thought: if my travel agency in Saigon knew, so, too, would Aeroflot.

Jim Thompson had been advised of my stopover in Bangkok and contacted me at the Erawan Princess. Could I join him for lunch the next day? We had much in common, he said. He was from a small town in Delaware, and I was from Maryland, right? Well, yes, close—it was Virginia, but I let it go. But how did he know? Who'd told him?

-- • --

SURAWONG ROAD WAS A NOISY, clattering boulevard crammed with large and small trucks, three-wheeled bicycle-rickshaws, jitneys, motorized tricycles, and occasionally an ox cart—all vying for space. They carried unbelievable loads of everything from trays of food and live animals to birds, people, and building materials—often in combination. It was a bedlam that reminded me of Seventh Avenue in New York City, almost.

After we exchanged pleasantries at his boutique, Jim Thompson suggested we make our way toward the Bangkok Royal Sporting Club, which turned out to be a lovely place with pagoda-like buildings, each roof covered with red tiles. All around were spacious verandas, well-tended gardens, and bursts of hibiscus, dainty little jasmines, and bougainvillea. Waiters in starched shirts, pantaloons, and miniature turbans scurried around. On one side, a swimming pool; to the other, fountains and more plantings.

Jim had a very relaxed air and a charming smile; he easily could have been a well-dressed man-about-town, gracing a magazine cover. After working as an architect in Delaware, he told me, he joined the military, then moved over to the Office of Strategic Services, which decided to send him to Bangkok to start a business. After carefully considering the possibilities, he decided that it would be almost impossible to launch a business in the city, and anyway, since his real work was to gather information, he figured somewhere up-country might be a better starting place. The OSS concurred.

After poking around a bit, Jim eventually entered into a joint venture with villagers up and down the Mekong River, with the aim of producing fabrics with native motifs. He supplied the raw materials and such essentials as dyestuffs and improved looms, while the villagers wove the fabric, usually producing a beautiful, raw silk, in plain or local tribal patterns. At an agreed-upon time, Jim would show up on a boat, going village to village along the river and paying cash for finished fabric.

Once in Bangkok, the new inventory would be indexed and made into bolts ready for the showroom marketplace; selected fabrics were given to skilled seamstresses who produced items for sale in the boutique. Especially lustrous silks were appliquéd with heavy borders of spun-gold thread. Not incidentally, this business was a wonderful medium for backcountry newsgathering. In a short time, Jim developed a network supplying him with information about local activities, particularly what the bloody Commies—Chinese and North Vietnamese—were up to. This information was regularly communicated via our embassy to Washington. Not many in Bangkok knew what Jim's real activities were, but Thai society readily accepted this lavish entertainer who threw large dinner parties for upper-crust officials and gave gifts of exquisite fabrics to their wives.

(Jim later presented me with several yards of material to take home as presents. I tried to refuse his generosity, but he insisted, whereupon I explained I had no way to carry them back with me. Ah, but he had already arranged to send them on to me in McLean—he'd thought I would be a while getting back, he said. How would he know? What made him think that? Did he know something I didn't? Or was I getting overly suspicious, paranoid? I thought about it, and then it made sense. I would be going up to Dooley's, so no sense lugging that stuff up there with me. How silly of me, he was just being thoughtful. Surely my concerns were pointless.)

After a casual lunch, Jim insisted that I take a sightseeing trip in his car with his driver. I wasn't too keen on the idea. The heat, humidity, and masses of humanity were oppressive and made me grumpy: for as far as I could see during my taxi rides, the whole town teemed with jostling bodies that clogged streets, canals, everywhere. And I began to get the restlessness common to travelers with lengthy itineraries; I wanted to get the hell out of here and be on my way. But Jim's car had air-conditioning, and the English-speaking driver knew his way around, which put me at ease, at least for the time being

Driving through downtown Bangkok, I became aware, again, of a strong odor—actually a horrible stink. It was a now-familiar mix of diesel fumes, dung—both animal and human—rotting garbage, and roasting meat from outdoor grills. The stench just hung there; it penetrated the car, the mind, and, there being no breeze, stayed there. As we drove along through the canal districts, we passed hovels and shacks, many perched precariously on stilts, their entire structures hanging over canals. A rainbow of drying clothes was strung from each shack to the other. Inhabitants could be seen releasing their urine and feces directly into waterways that were used simultaneously by women a few yards away to rinse vegetables. Next to them were happy, screaming children, jumping into the filthy waters. From to time, high-speed motorboats roared by, throwing off fumes and sheets of spray, adding to the general chaos. My medical mind could not assess the impact of this on the locals. These smiling, laughing, uncomplaining people had no idea how this unhealthy situation was affecting their lives.

Soon it all seemed the same. Everything I saw was a repetition of what I'd just seen, and now fatigue was setting in. I'd had enough. I told the driver to return me to my hotel, which he did, reluctantly.

As I left the car, he bowed and handed me an envelope. It was from Master Jim. The driver would call for me at 7 p.m., it said in elegant lettering, for dinner at the Bangkok Royal Sporting Club with Mr. James Thompson and guests. I smiled at the driver, "Please thank Mr. Jim. I should be delighted to join him, and I will be ready at seven." More bows and he was off.

But dammit, I didn't have a fresh shirt or pressed slacks or anything suitable for dinner; I had barely passed muster for lunch in my traveler's uniform of rumpled khaki. The hotel concierge advised that a jacket and tie indeed would be required, and furthermore, that this "is most certainly not a problem, sir." He would quickly obtain a summer-weight jacket, white shirt, and suitable tie from a local tailor on call for such situations. In fact, he already knew that I going to dinner with "Tuan Thompson."

Just after six-thirty, the concierge rang my room: My car and driver were at the entrance. As I walked out, I saw it was the same driver, who stood smiling proudly in front of a gleaming, tan Bentley. I was impressed. And I'd cleaned up nicely, I thought, having donned a white cotton shirt, a Jim Thompson silk tie, raw silk fawn slacks, a blue silk blazer, and Italian loafers. A square of bright, yellow silk hung from my breast pocket. The mirror reflecting a well-dressed man-about-town, thanks to the tailor and my concierge.

At the club, another smiling attendant greeted me. "This way, sir, to Mr. Thompson's group." He ushered me inside, where still more staff members smiled and bowed as we passed by. It certainly did give a visitor a friendly feeling. At the same time, standing impassively beside the reception desk was a huge, bearded Sikh in full Punjabi regalia. He might well have been a statue, except that his pale blue eyes missed nothing. (Blue eyes didn't really fit, but history has recorded that a band of lost Crusaders did once somehow get to his part of the world.) If I had to guess, I'd say he was something between a bouncer and a guard. Formidable would be an apt description.

I was shown into the bar, where Jim Thompson was seated at a low table, chatting with a tall, lanky fellow—an American, by his looks and dress. In contrast to natty me and Thompson, this fellow wore a rumpled shirt, a crooked tie, unpressed chinos, and a worn safari jacket. On his feet were dirty field boots. A long slender cheroot, Burmese by its looks and smell, was clenched in his teeth. Glistening on the table were drinks in tall, frosted glasses.

I took a glance around. The setting was impressive. It had a quiet, dignified, and low-key ambience. A delicate aroma of sandalwood, mixed with light incense, wafted through the room, caressing my smell center. Despite subdued lighting, the polished teak and mahogany furniture gleamed impressively. Scattered everywhere were rattan chairs, bamboo side tables, and plump couches with beige silk upholstery. In some areas, lacquerware plaques showing dancing girls and strange script were suspended from silk-covered walls. Massive jardinières were displayed on hand-carved stands, some holding tropical plants that brimmed with huge, green leaves. Miniature statues of Buddha, lit by oil lamps, sat in niches and alcoves along hallways. Ceramic dragons glared from side tables, and rubbings from temple walls were artfully displayed to impress the viewer. This was one sophisticated setting.

Jim saw me and beckoned.

"Doctor, you look smashing in that outfit. Looks like they took good care of you at the hotel. I hope you take time to get some rest before you head north—and I mean some real rest. This climate doesn't agree with everyone." Then, nodding to his rumpled guest, "I'd like you to meet Chuck Miller—he's our information man in Vientiane." We shook hands, more smiles all around. I didn't miss the "our information" man sobriquet.

Jim ordered a Rum Punch for me. "Best you'll ever taste, Doctor," and he was right. He said it was fine, aged rum with fresh lime juice. It tasted so good, like some exotic fresh fruit punch, that my thirst nearly undid me. I started to quaff it down but stopped when I considered the possible consequences. I needed to stay awake and alert this evening, and this deceptively strong drink could be my doom. I had one more day in Bangkok before leaving for Vientiane, so there was no sense waking with a hangover on my last morning. I sipped more slowly, grabbing handfuls of giant cashews from a huge teak bowl before us.

We chatted, I sipped. Chuck Miller was a decidedly low-key guy who probed politely for my reasons for being out here. It was the usual what-I-was-doing-out-here routine. Why was I going to see Dooley? And did he understand correctly that I was on my way to Moscow, too? I filled him in with as much as I thought he needed to know, as he clearly would be passing this information along. But that wasn't my concern. I understood, and Jim was just doing his job, I assumed. Jim must have known, too, that I had been briefed about Dooley and the area up there by someone, but again, that was just an assumption. So here was this silly doctor on his way up there. And as always, the burning question: Why?

I answered Miller's questions, told him about my medical experiences in Saigon, and sipped my Rum Punch. At one point, as I was reaching for what was now my nearly half-finished drink, I caught a whiff of a something exotic, and it wasn't coming from my glass.

Surely not—that's impossible. Isn't it?

She was here! It was that all-too-familiar lemony scent. Looking up, I saw no one, but the fragrance wasn't coming from the bar. Deciding I was way off, I dismissed the possibility, guardedly accepted one more Rum Punch, and turned back to Jim and Chuck Miller. But not a moment later, there entered into our area a man about my size and, to my surprise, balanced delicately on his arm was none other than Gigi, the houri of Saigon!

Once more: Now what?

I checked her out from my vantage point beside Jim Thompson. I had to admit, she looked so very elegant, as regal as a queen entering her palace. Her hair was swept up in back, perfect for showcasing a three-strand necklace of gray-blue matched pearls, fronted with a pale jade cameo. The jewelry was chosen, no doubt, to draw one's eye first to the pearls and then to the tight, straight neckline and striking cleavage below. Her knee-length silk dress was a sleek, smooth, black sheath that fitted every contour, every hollow, every protuberance with not so much as a ripple to mar its surface. I marveled at how she managed to look that chic and relaxed all at once.

Jim introduced her escort, a certain Cecil Montague, as a dear, old friend of his—and, from generations back, a relative.

"Really?" I asked, happy to shift the attention away from Gigi.

Yes, in fact: Montague was related to a great-great-uncle on Jim's grandmother's side, one Sir Alphonse Montague. The line, it seemed, went all the way back to the Montagues of the Surrey area south of London. "You know, the Montagues are really Italians," Jim elaborated. "Montchessi or something like that."

Then, slipping smoothly along, he did the honors for Gigi. "And of course you know Mrs..." he turned to introduce his lady guest and used her married name: "Prudhomme." But, curiously, I think he mispronounced it.

"Yes, of course," I replied quickly, "we met in Saigon. How nice to see you," I said to her. "I had no idea you were coming to Bangkok."

Gigi responded with a devastating smile. "Oh, Doctor, it's my work. I never know when I have to travel around this part of the world. There's work here with Cecil," she said, waving a hand airily in his direction, "and then sometimes I have to visit Hong Kong. I just never know where duty takes me. Cecil's from our Hong Kong office and we needed to meet with Chuck Miller here. So dear, kind Jim Thompson thought it would be ever so nice for us all to have dinner tonight, didn't you, Jim? And here we all are. Isn't this just wonderful?" She ended with a quick lowering of the lids and a sly smile, which I felt certain was aimed at me.

An elegantly dressed maître d' was now whispering in Jim's ear, whereupon Jim announced that dinner was ready. With Gigi on his arm this time, Jim led us to our private dining room. It was lavish, but not ostentatious. We sat at place-carded seats at an elegantly set table.

The first course was a gigantic shrimp cocktail, followed by several more courses, most of which were sumptuous, tropical; I recognized chicken, meat, and fish. For some, however, I had no idea what was on my plate, so I played safe and just took a few bites. I drank only bottled water and iced tea. I had no intention of getting a stomach bug.

The enchantress was seated directly opposite me, looking absolutely stunning and seemingly avoiding eye contact with me. The conversation around us ran to what New York designers desired from Jim in the way of designs and fabrics. Chuck and Cecil talked about the communist menace in northern Laos, the poppy shipments from Burma, and the powerful warlords in the hills extracting levy from all—especially the many caravans loaded with raw opium. Payoffs, they said, had to be in gold.

This reminded Cecil of some pigeon-blood rubies from the Mogok valley region, recently seized by Thai authorities from the satchel of an American smuggler. The exquisite gems were now in government

DR. JOHN...ON ASSIGNMENT

vaults in Bangkok and the smuggler in prison. Jim allowed that he was negotiating the purchase of those rubies but had little hope, mainly because local officials could be expected to snag them for themselves. But he expected that he'd be able to buy at least a few for the boutique.

There were diplomatic problems galore in this case, Chuck pointed out. The smuggler could face a firing squad unless the U.S. could act quickly through back channels. And then there would be payoffs needed, as was so often the case in these situations. Interestingly, funds were available from embassy accounts.

While all this was going on, something happened to me that I can't say I'd ever experienced before. Imagine, if you will, a midget elephant under our dinner table. And, during the dinner, this midget elephant runs its trunk up my leg and begins tickling my knee and my inner thigh. That would be disconcerting, no doubt.

Well, this barefoot Contessa seated opposite me had extended her long, slender leg across several feet of distance and slid her bare foot up inside my pant leg. She wiggled her big toe against my knee cap and then moved her little toes right up my thigh! I looked across at her in surprise. How the hell could she do that gymnastic trick without moving her body? But then, I should have remembered: she was a first-class acrobat, as I'd just recently learned.

Uh-oh. She couldn't reach that high...could she? Gigi gave no outward sign that she'd noticed my stunned look. It was time to bring this to a halt this before she further proved her adroitness.

Reaching down as though for my napkin, I grabbed her big toe and twisted it firmly, but not quite so hard as to evoke a squeal. Immediately, the foot disappeared from my pants leg. No one at the table had any inkling of the drama underneath.

She sat nibbling at her dinner daintily, her head cocked charmingly to one side as she chatted animatedly with this Montague chap. Only later did I get a sidelong glance...with a squint and tiny tip of tongue stuck out. This woman loved to play games. I fleetingly thought of kicking her over backwards—two could play this game! But sanity prevailed.

I had dessert, a sort of lichee compote layered with delicate slices of mango and vanilla ice cream. Then, coffee *avec* before after-dinner liqueurs in the adjoining lounge. My knowledge of after-dinner drinks was limited, but I'd once heard someone order a B&B in such a moment, so I asked for one on ice. The others had ordered brandies of their own and took up serious political discussion. My Seiko indicated it was getting on to my bedtime, so I decided on an early exit and made my goodbyes.

Cecil said he'd catch up with me in Vientiane; Chuck was staying in town, and we'd made plans to lunch the next day. Jim said he would send his car to drive me around and help with last-minute items. But silly me was getting suspicious: why the sudden concern and interest in me, a nobody in their world? My paranoia was kicking in again. Was I being watched, "helped"?

I thanked everyone again for their kind wishes, said my goodbyes, and in return got a sweet smirk and lifted eyebrow from the Contessa. (This would be the last time I would see Jim Thompson, though he and I did keep in touch. Some time later, he disappeared—murdered, it was thought, in Malaysia, according to official reports. But that's another story.)

Jim's driver let me off at my hotel. A message awaited me from the consular service of the embassy of the USSR, advising that my visa had been confirmed and that my passport would be stamped at the New Delhi office at such time as I wished to travel to the Soviet Union. Great!

And now to bed.

-- • --

I'D HAD A LONG DAY and grown more than a little weary, despite enjoying the dinner and Jim Thompson's affable hospitality. So I was well into a deep sleep when I suddenly became aware that my door had opened and closed and that someone had entered the room. Long years of responding to hospital calls had trained me to waken instantly when roused, and now I jerked upright. With a sinking realization, I saw her standing beside my bed in the dim light, twirling a door key on a chain and grinning hugely. She smelled of lemon and strong brandy.

"How the hell did you get in?" I croaked, falling back onto my pillow in a show of displeasure.

"Oh, shush, silly boy. I told them I was your wife, and they gave me the extra key. Any more questions?"

I said nothing. I should have gotten up, tossed her out, and slammed the door. But I just lay there, tired and unwilling to create a scene in my shorts. Any such commotion would be hard to explain, and heaven knew what she'd do to make it worse. She had tossed the key on the dresser with a loud clank and kicked off her spiky pumps.

She flipped on the bathroom light and stood silhouetted against it, pirouetting slowly before closing the door. I heard water splashing.

Now I had a dreadful, sinking feeling, the kind of feeling one gets, I guess, before the onset of a disaster. *Oh, shit! This can't be happening again. Just like the Saigon thing. Please let this be a dream, a short, bad dream.*

A dream, however, it was not. She was very much there. Emerging, like a high-class stripper, she began undressing. I started to protest, but she shushed me with a finger to her lips. Now she was completely naked...and, I saw once more, had a fabulous body. Her breasts seemed to be glowing, catching reflected light from invisible sources.

"Don't say a word, silly. I'm your Suzy Wong tonight."

What the hell did that mean?

"Dammit, I don't want any Suzy Wong tonight, and I don't want you here, either! What the hell gets into you, why the fixation on me?" And half-heartedly, "Please get the hell out of here now!"

Gigi was having none of it. Her slight stagger reminded me that she was still carrying on board a load of the finest drinks money could buy. She gave me a withering stare, and then grinned as she stood at the bedside cupping her breasts in her hands.

"You are so goddamned silly. Just quiet down, and you'll see why I'm attracted to you. Nobody has ever ignored me like you do. No man has ever not made a pass at me. And you? You totally ignore me. You cannot be such a boob. Well, I'll show you," she said with a wicked smile. "I'll let you know what you've missed, and I promise you, you'll never forget me." Another giggle.

The small part of my brain that was still working wondered: What does her husband think of these goings-on? Had he a clue? Was he going to hunt me down and kill me? These thoughts whirled through my brain as I waited to see what she had in mind. Dammit. She was beginning to excite me.

--•--

WHEN I AWOKE THE NEXT morning, she was gone, her side still damp and just barely warm. But the lemony scent was still there; it had been ever since she'd entered the room.

No note, no nothing. She'd sneaked out earlier while I'd been zonked out. The dinner, wine and after-dinner workout had done me in. I'd slept well.

CHAPTER 9

Vientiane

T HAT EVENING, I FOUND MYSELF IN LAOS'S UNASSUMING LITTLE CAPITAL, sitting with Chuck Miller and Cecil Montague on a porch outside a hotel bar and looking at military maps. Both of them had marked sites in Thailand and Northern Laos, trying to familiarize me with the area before I ventured northward. Patiently, they tried to explain the complicated political maneuvering among the various factions and America's posture in the face of all this. It was confusing and not very interesting, but I listened politely. How much I'd remember was problematical.

Dr. Tom Dooley's headquarters were in the far north of the country, near a village called Muong Sing. He had selected this area because of its proximity to several borders, and also because the indigenous clans had at best a shaman for their ills. Dooley likened himself to Dr. Albert Schweitzer, the famed Swiss physician who plunged into central Africa to bring medical services to the natives—so much that, like Schweitzer, he even brought an organ along. (In Dooley's case, however, a generator was employed to power the instrument.)

Muong Sing lay in a wide valley between towering mountain ridges, just south of a point at which the borders of Laos, Burma, and China touched. Chuck indicated that this was an area of constant concern to the U.S., not least because of the KMT guys— mercenaries,

VIENTIANE

that is—who were doing at least part of the job that Laos's own soldiers seemed unable to do. (I was aware of some of this, thanks to my briefing and Gigi's little lecture.) This valley was guarded, if that's the right word, by a reputedly lackluster Lao military force housed in an old French military outpost. The site was now dilapidated, in no way resembling its once-formidable appearance when garrisoned by French Moroccan troops. If challenged by armed intruders from the north, the current Lao military troops would respond pathetically, and the locals knew there was no true military force here that they could count on to protect them.

Chuck Miller was perfectly frank about wanting intelligence from me. "While you are up at Dooley's, be sure to take notes and photos whenever you can," he said. "It would be a kindness to a grateful government if someone from our branch, Information Services, could meet with you when you return to the States." I told Chuck and Cecil that I kept a diary of sorts, as well as a log of my photographs, and I mentioned my commitment to *National Geographic*. This was fine; it didn't present a problem to them.

"Just give us a chance to peek at your pictures. We can make instant copies and return the whole batch back to *Geographic*. You might even consider keeping doubles for yourself. But we'll be in touch with the *Geographic* people ourselves, so it's not going to be a problem."

That sounded reasonable to me, but they were forgetting that *National Geographic* would be developing the film and so would have first peeks and first choice. After all, Mel Grosvenor, the executive director, had first rights to everything from my camera, and it was his film in the first place. I kept this to myself; I wanted no chance of a delay for any picayune reason. So I smiled and mumbled an accord.

Chuck Miller helped me get my stuff together for the flight to Dooley's hospital. I took only a light kit; Chuck would store the rest of my baggage at his home. This meant, I knew, that on my return I'd find all my soiled laundry cleaned and pressed by his coterie of household servants—standard hospitality in these parts. Chuck's wife, Anne, popped in to bid me adieu. She worked in Chuck's office in town, doing something related to the distribution of reading material about America in several languages—and more, I suspected.

--•--

AT THE LOCAL AIRPORT, I was directed to a huge, single-engine deHavilland Otter. The French pilot, Miguerre Devlet, introduced himself as an old China hand, and in some ways, at least, he looked the part: He was wearing a khaki shirt, shorts, and hiking boots, but just before takeoff, he switched a well-worn Stetson for an Air Laos captain's cap. By now, he'd already checked weights, baggage, and passengers—and turned away two passengers carrying pigs, though he did allow several boxes of trussed ducks to be jammed in the back with all the bags and a couple of bicycles. The Otter was a true bush plane, developed in Canada to serve towns and villages scattered across that great northern expanse. Its single engine was a huge radial with plenty of power—so much, in fact, that this little, snub-nosed plane could carry almost as much cargo as a small transport.

During his preflight walk-around, Miguerre prodded tires and rechecked the plane's fuel and oil and flight surfaces. As he finished, I stepped over and showed him my *Geographic* ID and press pass, asking if I might ride in the co-pilot seat so as to get a few aerial photos. "No problem, Doctor—an honor to have you." We finally climbed aboard, and a few minutes later, three robust-looking American men climbed aboard. They nodded at me silently and took places in the rear.

WE TOOK OFF FROM VIENTIANE easily; we were fairly light. Miguerre had shown me the French military aerial chart with our course and heading marked and our estimated flying time noted on the right side. It might be a problem, he said, if the cloud cover was too heavy: we had to cross an 8,000-foot mountain ridge before descending into Muong Sing valley. He planned to play it safe and cross at 10,000 feet—he used feet, not meters, in his calculations since the Canadian altimeter was in feet with sub-markings in meters. But if he couldn't find a cloud-hole to drop through, we would divert to a village called Nam Tha as an alternate landing site. He showed me the spot on the

VIENTIANE

chart, and I noticed the red course line heading from Muong Sing to Nam Tha, as well as a direction arrow and compass heading written in pencil. He'd had this problem before.

—-•--

ONCE ALOFT, WE CLIMBED OVER paddies and low hills. I loaded my camera and settled on a lens while casually scanning the horizon, only to spy in the distance the most spectacular cathedral spires one could imagine. It was as though someone had dropped Washington DC's National Cathedral right in the middle of a vast, green jungle—with parts of the spires and rooftops gleaming with gold!

"The faithful," Miguerre yelled over the sound of the motor. "Those stupid idiots, they cover it with gold leaf—imagine that. *Alors*, one day I steal that gold." He chuckled. Actually, he might have been serious, for all I knew. One never knew with the French.

"What is it called?" I yelled.

"Sonamabitch," he hollered back.

He circled slowly as I shot several rolls of film, capturing the cathedral's every angle. This meant sharp banking at times, much to the discomfort of our fellow passengers. It was worth it, though, for it was surely a once-in-a-lifetime opportunity, and indeed, my aerial photos, it turned out, were the only ones in existence at the time. And may be still, in fact. (Disappointingly, the *Geographic*'s research staff told me that they couldn't be certain of the identity of that site, and so these temple photos were never published. But they did publish some aerial views of mine taken near Angkor Wat in an article on Cambodia.)

I gushed my thanks to Miguerre for allowing me to get those aerials. He waved me off with a smile. "Save your thanks," he shouted over the roar of that huge engine. "We still 'ave some ways to fly yet, and there is much more to see."

We roared on, climbing slowly, heading northwest. Miguerre checked his compass, then his watch, and the indicated air speed. He held up five fingers and gave it the open and close three times, then pointed to his watch, which I took to mean "fifteen minutes."

The minutes passed quickly, and after checking his compass again, he went into a slow left bank and began circling. He pointed below us and then put his finger on the chart; it was Muong Sing. Still looking at me, he began slowly shaking his head: we weren't going to land. There was solid cloud cover below us, and no sensible pilot would drop through it and risk splattering his craft into a mountainside. Actually, Miguerre had done it, he said—but only on rare occasions, when he'd had at least a peek at the terrain below before losing visibility. But today, there wasn't a prayer of dropping through.

Miguerre made two more turns, then pointed to the fuel-tank needles, which gave me a start. One read a quarter full, the other a little less. My heart did a little extra lump-thump; I tensed up. Flying was not always fun, and this was altogether different from my carefree seaside flights with Antoine. I gave Miguerre the raised eyebrows. He pointed and shouted, "Petrol Nam Tha"; we'd have to refuel there. Now I realized that this was indeed true bush piloting; it had its serious moments, and right now, this was one.

He circled once more, and then increased power and turned right to another heading, I assumed for Nam Tha. Just for the hell of it, I checked the gyrocompass heading against the chart. They were the same. Drawing on my newfound skills of bush-flying navigation, I estimated another fifteen to twenty minutes' flying time.

--•--

IT WAS BRIGHT AND SUNNY with good visibility at Nam Tha, which seemed little more than another smelly village dotting the countryside in the northern tip of Laos. As we approached, I could make out a great, long, glistening runway, and I thought nothing of it at first...a wet runway, right?

Wrong. It was mud. We half-landed, half-splashed down into the thick muck and then taxied to a quick stop near a shed. The three local passengers were told to offload with their baggage and crates of ducks, at which they began to complain loudly. They'd been told they were going to Muong Sing, so why were we pushing them off here? Miguerre spoke to them quietly but forcefully in their own language, which quickly quieted them. (Hearing a foreigner speak in their language always surprises the locals and makes dealing with them much easier. I had picked up on this watching Antoine and the Michelin people during our gunnery practice from the air.)

So the native passengers piled their possessions on heads and backs and silently trudged off. They could not have been happy, but their faces showed no emotion. In all likelihood, said Miguerre, they would walk to Muong Sing, several days away. For them, time was not that important.

The other Americans stayed aboard the plane. Miguerre yelled orders and instructions to the scruffy local airline agents in their dialect and then climbed back aboard. The agents shooed everyone away from the propeller in preparation for our takeoff.

"*Attention,*" Miguerre told us, "We may not be able to take off if the mud on the runway is too deep. But we try, this horse can do it sometimes. We see."

Miguerre had done such a superb job of landing on the mushy, sticky runway that I hadn't thought much of it at first. But glue-y mud grabs plane wheels with octopus-like tenacity, restricting ground speed and preventing lift-off. Sure enough, after two hairy aborted takeoffs, Miguerre yelled, "*faché merde*" and called it quits. "So," he announced, "we spend tonight here, my friends," and that was that. Finis.

Stepping out, we all slogged back dejectedly to the runway shed, which doubled as the airline office. A wheezy Mercedes truck went out with Miguerre and towed the mud-stuck plane back to the shed. He locked all doors and secured the flaps and rudder, and then ordered a guard for the plane. Next stop: the local hotel.

Hotel? Surely there was not a hotel here? But there it was, just off the end of the runway and tucked back into the shadow of the jungle.

I retrieved my kit from the plane and fell in behind Miguerre as he led us over to the ancient building. It looked awful; I heard chickens squawking and the unmistakable sound of grunting pigs. Watching us silently from the windows were hotel employees. We must have been a sight: wide-eyed children giggled as we straggled in.

Miguerre secured places for us. He and I would share a small, musty room. Our bureau held a large tin basin and a cracked pitcher of water. I was grimy, sticky, and in general, bushed. So was my pilot. Silently, we washed up.

Downstairs, Miguerre ordered cold beer. It was a good European beer, in bottles. How it was cooled was a mystery; how it got up here, even more so. I learned that the bottles were kept covered with wet burlap, so that water evaporation removed heat and thus cooled the beer—a simple law of physics, and clever of the locals to use it. Once refreshed, we planned the next day's activities.

It was now late afternoon. I wanted to walk around the village and shoot photo scenes for the *Geographic*. Miguerre grabbed my arm: "No, no, *docteur*. Not on your life. You might not come back! Understand? You must trust me, eh? Some very bad peoples around here. Some are eyes for the North, and maybe they think of a reward if they capture you. So you stay with me. You want to take pictures, go up on the balcony, put on your telescope lens and shoot from there. Anyway, you see much better and farther. You must trust me, doctor. These people won't bother me, but you? *Alors*, you are another matter."

"OK, I get your message, Miguerre."

Looking down, I saw he'd strapped a huge revolver to his thigh. I thought of the handgun I'd left behind. It might have been handy and reassuring, so it was just as well not to be burdened with something unfamiliar and risky.

So grabbing my camera and extra film, I climbed some rickety stairs to an equally rickety second-story balcony and propped my long lens on the railing. A bamboo stool made a perfect seat; I could see and aim my lens without much movement. No one would notice me from this marvelous vantage point. I waited, and not for long.

Within minutes, all manner of subjects came by: Boys, yellow-garbed monks with shaved heads who were begging for rice, teams of snorting oxen, bicycles, two men carrying a slaughtered hog slung on a long pole, its fly-covered hide lain atop the carcass.

I got marvelous shots of all this. Then, just at dusk, a single line of a soldiers—about a dozen, weapons slung loosely across their shoulders and dressed in olive khaki and slouch hats—suddenly came trooping silently along the jungle edge. They had appeared as though from nowhere, and within minutes, they disappeared just as silently back into the jungle. I watched fascinated. None of them had said a word or glanced to the left or right; they just glided, almost slinked, straight ahead. Then, gradually blending in with the jungle, they disappeared. It was eerie. Miguerre said later that they were probably irregulars from the North. They'd never bother anyone in this village, since the local villagers probably supported them. No one gave them a second look. This was everyday life here.

Still crouched on my vantage point on the balcony, I had an ideal view, and true to my calling as amateur photographer extraordinary, I fired off two more rolls of precious high-speed film before dinner.

Miguerre had ordered the manager to switch on the hotel generator to provide light for his guests, but the manager protested, complaining about the price of diesel fuel. Very high, he bleated along with other unintelligible squeals. Miguerre silenced him with a look. Soon a sputtering engine from somewhere outside caught, and three feeble lights came on. Miguerre had made it clear: if the manager wanted his diesel fuel delivered on the regular air-freight run, he damn well better get lights glowing tonight.

After tea, Miguerre went out to check on the plane—a precautionary routine pilots perform. I went along, happy to get out of that dismal hotel. Unlocking the Otter's door, he climbed aboard, flipped the radio switches to on, and tuned in to his home frequency. Then in rapid French told home base his plight. I could make out a few of his curses and a portion of his status report. Then satisfied for the moment, he switched off; we locked up and made our way back. There was no sign of any guard.

-- • --

UP UNTIL NOW, I HADN'T paid much attention to the three Americans who had drifted off after checking in. They'd gone towards the village and just disappeared. Miguerre was unconcerned; they knew their way around and were safe. They spoke the native lingo and knew the locals from past visits. As we returned to the ramshackle hotel just after dark, the trio sauntered back into the hotel, as if on cue.

Miguerre made the introductions, and we shook hands all around. Two features the men had in common were hard-calloused palms and powerful handshakes; desk workers these guys were not. The biggest of them was a burly chap with shaggy eyebrows above a rugged face and a prominent, even portly, tummy. He wore an amused smile. The other two were thinner and wore identical safari jackets, Levis, and hiking boots. They looked very much like men I'd seen at Chuck Miller's place.

I introduced myself again: "Hi, men, I'm Sundukian."

The burly one stuck out his hand and with a Boston Irish accent, said, "I'm Rich Davis, pleased to meetcha." Then one of the others, named Ted Brawner, did likewise; I would remember him because of a small strawberry mark at the corner of his mouth hidden partly by a sandy mustache. The third was Art Swirsky, who wore a small tattoo on his left forearm—a fire-breathing dragon with the words Semper Fi beneath.

OK, these rugged guys were obviously military. And tomorrow we all would be passengers again on that huge Otter. We nodded and exchanged smiles. At that moment, Miguerre piped up: *"Allo,* time for another beer." He held up four fingers, and promptly the manager of this flea-bitten hostel produced four bottles of an excellent Czech pilsner. Its name apparently started with a U, but the label was wet and crumpled; no matter, it was cold and delicious.

Between pulls on the beer, I explained that I was a surgeon on my way to Dooley's place for a medical consulting visit. From their blank looks, I wondered if they heard me. It appeared I'd made no impression. Maybe they knew.

"You guys know Dooley?" I asked.

"Oh yeah, we know Dr. Dooley," said Rich. I didn't like the way he said that.

I raised my eyebrows inquiringly at him.

Rich put his beer down, swallowed, and looked at me for a second before explaining. "You gotta understand, Doc, this guy Dooley's nuts. He thinks he's gonna save the world and bring happiness to those miserable people up in that part of Laos and maybe north of there, and that just ain't gonna happen. They won't give a shit about him in the long run. It's probably true that while he's there he might do some good, but in the long run—nah! Nobody out here gives a shit for anyone or anything. You'll see. By the way, you got a sidearm?"

"Not with me; I left mine with Chuck Miller."

"Yeah, well, we better get you one. Some guy might want to take your fancy camera and stuff."

A tiny quiver of worry pierced my chest.

It was curious, I thought, that they didn't ask any more probing questions. By their mannerisms, it was clear that these men looked and listened, but spoke little. This told me a great deal: that they were disciplined and the product of training, just like my surgical residents. It was very reassuring and gave me a welcome sense of security. We sat there at first, quietly sipping our beers. What kind of men were these?

"What do you fellows do up at Muong Sing?"

"Well, sir, we go up there from time to time to see how Dr. Dooley is getting along. We check on any problems he may be having, what he needs in the way of supplies. And we also make sure his mechanical equipment is functioning and that there's enough fuel at that little airstrip. Then we talk to the locals and find out what's going on, what kind of chatter's in the air, the marketplace—that sort of thing."

That seemed to cover it all, I thought, and it was the most information on any matter I'd had this whole trip. And so these guys were information gatherers, too, just like almost everyone I'd met out here.

"Any of you speak or understand the local languages?"

They chuckled in unison. "Doc, between us we speak everything up here including Russian, but not Hungarian. And we monitor some of that on our radios. They got Russkies up north, believe me, and they get the Chinese and them other slopes all riled up against us. The fact that there are Americans up here has 'em real ticked off. It's just a question of time before they start some trouble. When the Chinese decide what they want to do, they're gonna do it, and it don't make no difference what we want—it's gonna happen. They plan to take over this whole fuckin' area, build a two-lane highway right up into Yunnan. Then they can roll their trucks and equipment up and down that whole valley. But that ain't gonna happen—not yet, anyway. There's still the KMT and us, and maybe we and them got some things to say about it. So we just gotta wait and see."

Chugalug. We drank our pilsner in silence.

— - • - —

THE DINNER WAS GOOD. UNBELIEVABLY, that tiny kitchen and the owner, who was also the part-time cook, put together a meal of chicken soup, dumplings, grilled duck, and vegetables. Platters of pork, chicken, beef, and huge grilled shrimp came steaming out from the kitchen. Shrimp this far from the sea? Miguerre explained that jungle streams nearby provided freshwater shrimp and crayfish, which locals considered a delicacy. That was reassuring, so I ate some—and I had to admit, they were tasty. Pots of black tea were served along with the dinner. Eyeing the food, the three men who had snacked earlier in town decided to join us.

After dinner, Rich checked his watch, then reaching into one of his black bags, pulled out a small battery-powered shortwave radio and dialed in a few frequencies. He brought in BBC World Service, listened to the news, then switched to the Armed Forces Network news for comparison. Then Rich pulled out another small radio, into which he plugged a small microphone, then from its back panel uncoiled a small length of thin wire antenna which Brawner fastened outside to a tree. He powered up and started transmitting.

"Mustard, mustard, this is hot dog, over."

Silence.

Once again, "Mustard, mustard, this is hot dog, you read?"

Static, more silence, more static, and then suddenly:

"Hot dog, wait one." A short silence, then "Come in, hot dog, we read you three by, I say again three by."

This was the parole (password) used by mustard; then hot dog was to give his parole, the codes prearranged for each mission.

"Mustard, hot dog, you coming in about two by, turn it up a notch, over."

"OK, hot dog, go ahead." The paroles had cleared.

"We have ketchup and rolls, we need relish."

Then Rich read off a series of numbers, perhaps coded messages and probably coordinates from the chart he held. The transmission went quickly and ended with "Hot dog copies. Relish in jar. Out." We have ketchup and rolls. Need some relish?

"Rich, what was all that?"

"Well, Doc. We just gotta let our folks know where we are. Now they know we're OK, and that we have stuff waiting for us at Dooley's. We don't stay on the air long, somebody might be tuning in on us. So we say goofy stuff which don't make no sense to the baddies who may be snoopin'; won't mean nuthin' to them, but our people understand. And maybe you will too, soon. 'Cause you see, *you are ketchup*!

Huh? Me, ketchup?

"Care to explain that, Rich?"

"Don't get upset, Doc. We just have to let them know you're safe, and we're safe, and where we are. I gave them map coordinates. Everything is fine. If we need help, it can be here pronto; we have some support and planes. So for now, all is just fine. You got nuthin' to worry about."

"How did they know it was you on the air and not somebody forced to sound like you?"

"Good question, Doc. Here's how it works. We use the 'rule of seven' this week—the number changes from week to week, and we never know what the number is until we leave home base—but the numbers have to add up to seven this week. Let's say I call in to base, and they answer and say I'm coming in, oh, 'four by.' Ordinarily radio transmissions are five by five when we're fully powered and right on frequency. So I answer that I hear them 'three by.' Their four and my three make seven. It's that simple."

The hotel generator was cut off at about ten. Then to provide light, a few smelly, smoky kerosene lamps were lighted. It was feeble yellow light at best, giving the place an eerie cast—strange shadows where none had existed before. I'd become frustrated with the delay and was anxious to get going. Why I wanted to get going was not clear to me, but it was something internal...a sort of urge, an inner force that was telling me to get moving. But for now, I didn't have any choice. I decided to cool my racing engine and turn in.

Grimy and sweaty, I just couldn't bring myself to sack out in this condition, so I rinsed off with a washcloth, put my kit bag beside me on the floor and wearily stretched out. Our beds were Asian pallets—a lumpy mattress and sheet. No pillow, just a smelly headrest. I stripped down to my shorts and didn't need the sheet at all. Miguerre had done the same. Our pallets were next to each other.

But as he got ready to turn in, he slid that big revolver under his pillow. From his flight bag, he extracted another weapon—a small, dull-finish automatic, which he shoved under his mattress on my side.

"Doctor, these men with us. They know who you are, but they don't ask too many questions. They have their orders, and I am sure they have been told to keep one eye out for you. You are an important traveler, so they just keep you under observation at all times. That's in addition to other things they do—just in case you're wondering. And also they have to keep an eye on this madman Dooley; he is crazy, you know."

He switched his attention to the weapon. "Now this small thing under the mattress, I keep it facing your side, understand? You know how to work it, so, risky, but I have taken off the safety, OK? If you need to use it, just start pulling the trigger and it fires seven rounds. I'm sure you won't need it, but if you do, use it, but for Chrissakes, you don't shoot me, eh?"

He went on. "Now about this Dooley, he sometimes does things to get the Lao Kings and their Chinese neighbors upset, so sometimes we have to keep him a little quiet. Let him put bandages on sores and lumps, let him fix broken legs. Let him smear medicine on the lepers. But not much more."

Lepers? Oh shit! But it's not that contagious. I'll just stay away; stay clear of any of them.

"But when he starts preaching good-good for mankind, then, we have to speak to him. We tell him very gently to shut his fucking mouth, to stop preaching; leave that to the Abbés and others. Otherwise, he's gonna get lots of people killed, including maybe himself. The Chinese have told the Lao to keep this man from arousing the natives. So they—and maybe your people—are always sending memos and short, tiny-brained officials up to Muong Sing to talk to Dooley. Me, I think he should be kicked out, sent home. That's what many think."

He went on." Trouble is, Dooley, he don't give a damn. I think he wants to die. He's a crazy Catholic do-gooder. Which is good, don't misunderstand, but just right now things are in a very delicate state in this region. *Vous connais*, eh, you know? So we tell him, yes, he is doing many good things, but we say, please, for the love of God, don't get the local people too upset, because they may rise up against us, and we have lost all our political work. And that then he definitely will get chased out. He doesn't want this, so he quiets down for a while. But it needs to be repeated from time to time. You understand Latin?"

"Well, just what I learned filling out prescriptions."

"Yes, well, sometimes Dooley says a Latin Mass on Sundays since there is no real priest around. He calls himself a lay priest and says it is permitted, and so on. I'm afraid he is a touch *fou*, a little crazy. Nice, kind, and good-hearted, but a bit tooty-frooty."

I thought about all that.

"Miguerre, I thought you were only a pilot. But for just an ordinary pilot, you know a lot. Don't get me wrong, what I mean is that you seem to know more about political things than most pilots."

"Eh, well, you see, Doctor, the DSD has pilots too."

The DSD, I guessed, was the Sûreté, and I remembered that François Sully told me that the French would never really give up in this part of the world. Wherever France has an interest, the Sûreté are there in one form or another. Somewhere you wouldn't normally expect them. France hoped to reclaim Indochina, and they wanted to make sure nobody else did, and of course, they were suspicious of Americans as well as the Chinese! So France had its watchers.

My mind slowly stopped racing. I could hear Miguerre purring as he slept. I must have fallen asleep too, and then my wild dreams started again. This time, a bad one.

I saw a face in the mirror pointing at me. It called me some dreadful names—shameless womanizer! And said some nasty things about what I had been doing. I awoke with a start, covered with sweat; my luminous dial indicated three in the morning.

That face in my dreams was me...I was pointing to myself and making accusations. Sweaty and with my heart pounding, I plopped back on my pallet, but sleep came hard now. When it finally did, I had another tiring episode of mirror-and-face, and this time it was the houri of Saigon. She was in the mirror, looking out and crooking her finger at me. She had a huge smile, long, blonde hair, and was completely naked! Whoops. Even in the safety of my dream I was still terrified. I had to get away from her, so I started running. And once again, I awakened, panting and sweaty.

Enough. At that moment, I wished for a Phenobarbital capsule.

As a physician, I recognized the dreams for what they were—a form of anxiety, a panic attack, instigated, no doubt, by a clash between my conscience and what I, now a consummate idiot, had lately been up to.

Hell's fire. Well, since it was nearly six in the morning, I might as well stay up.

Proud roosters announced their presence nearby, but Miguerre was gone, his pallet empty. I wondered if he had a mission or I'd chased him off.

I smelled coffee and bacon; someone was preparing breakfast. I shaved and sponged off, slipped on a dry shirt, and collected my thoughts. I looked under the mattresses. Both weapons were gone.

— - • - —

IN THE TINY DINING AREA, a smiling servant poured a mug of delicious coffee for me.

"Mister Miguerre, the pilot, where is he?" I asked.

"Oh, *M'sieu* is at the *avion*." The waiter pointed in the direction of the landing strip.

Without another word, he placed a huge bowl of fruit in front of me—not at all what I expected. Large chunks of fresh pineapple, papaya, orange, banana, lichee fruit, and one or two other creamy white chunks of something. All very delicious. Next came a platter with bacon, omelet, toast and some form of jelly, and more coffee. Things were improving.

While I was munching buttered toast, I heard the unmistakable drone of an aircraft engine. The sound got louder by the second, and through the doorway I saw the huge Otter flying towards us. I dashed out, and there it was, roaring by at treetop level like some airborne monster, its engine barking down at us as it zoomed past. I noticed that Miguerre had his flaps down for slow flight, and waggling its wings to get our attention. It went by so quickly, Miguerre must have worried that no one had noticed the wing waggle, so he circled, and came over once again, lower and slower. By now the clatter had everyone up and dashing around. I looked up and could see Miguerre, waving his left arm out through his little side window, with a big, gold Rolex reflecting the early sun's rays. The plane swept by and headed towards the rice-paddy landing strip. Moments later, I heard the engine's roar stop. He had landed. I was sipping my second cup of tea when a decrepit lorry with a smiling Miguerre at the wheel pulled up in front.

"Allo, docteur. Ça va?"

"Yeah, just fine, Miguerre. How the hell did you manage to take off from that gummy field?"

"Hah, these mud fields which grow mosquitoes and very sad rice, they also drain fast. This morning, instead of going down the runway, I went across it. The long rows make it bumpy, but now the mud can't hold me down; the faster I go, the higher I bounce. Once I have enough air speed, I am up. Is an old bush-pilot trick. For me, it's no problem. I've done this before. But I have to make sure. So now, I have my second coffee, and we go."

"Hold it a minute," I said.

I wasn't quite prepared to go up in that roaring creature that had just been flung around from muddy field to roof top and back down.

On the other hand, my logy brain knew that Miguerre also valued his own life. Still, I had to ask. "Doesn't that bouncy-bouncy across the paddy rows do bad things to the plane, the wheels, the struts, the...?" He waved his hand to stop me.

"Hah, you don't know that Otter. It can take all the punishment you can give, and more. It's like the elephant: it may be slow, it may look ugly, but, *ma foi*, it's one tough and powerful son of a bitch! We go to Muong Sing, no problem. *Allons nous!*"

That was good enough for me. I was ready. My kit bag and cameras were ready. I planned to fire off a few frames for Mel; it would be my last opportunity in Nam Tha.

"Oh, one thing, Doctor," Miguerre said, as he motioned me over. "You ride up front wiz me again, is OK? Just to let you know, things might be a little, how you say, tight on our flight to Muong Sing. At some point red lights will show on the console but I don' want you should worry."

We hadn't gotten any fuel here? Oh my.

Miguerre knew I had some familiarity with airplanes, and he may have heard that I'd handled Antoine's Beaver, but I wasn't prepared for this. Should I wait for another flight? There weren't any—I'd be stuck here with smelly natives, strange troops oozing out of the woods, and nothing to look forward to. It was crystal-clear: I was leaving.

Miguerre went on: "You see, these cretins here used up my cache of fuel, my spare barrels of gasoline, to drive their goddam Mercedes truck and their other lorries. They said they had no fuel, and it was a desperate situation for them. I was so fucking mad, but what's the use? That goddam Mercedes will burn anything, cooking oil, kerosene—even eau de cologne, which, of course, these people never heard of. Anyway, all together there was less than half a barrel of petrol left for me. I ran it thru the chamois first. So, anyway, we may be running a bit close. *Vous comprenez?*"

Goddam right, I *comprenezed*. Low fuel and a flight over mountains, with the possibility of a heavy cloud cover: a formula for disaster. Shit!

"Miguerre, how do you figure we do it?"

"We do the time-distance formula. I know the distance and the air speed, and I figure the wind at one or two knots. So I know the actual ground speed, and when my trusty Rolex watch tells me we are there, I start down."

"What if you're wrong? What if...?" Again, he waved me off, slightly irritated

OK, Doctor, I said to myself, shuddup!

"Doctor, if I fly you, then you leave the worrying to me. You are the doctor, I am the pilot. This is not my first tight flight, OK?"

I nodded dumbly and felt slightly ashamed. I'm not ordinarily a nervous Nellie.

At the plane, we clambered aboard. No one spoke much. Miguerre had walked around, checking ailerons, the rudder, and other parts—a little more carefully than usual, I thought. But the knot in my gut confirmed that I was nervous. Fact was, we were low on fuel, and there was no room for mistakes. All I could do was suck it up and tough it out.

Once seated and strapped in, I looked behind me in the cabin. I couldn't believe my eyes. The burly one had gone to sleep, and the other two were cleaning their nails with wicked commando daggers. The guys in the back had no idea what the situation was, and then it occurred to me that they probably would have shrugged it off, anyway.

The start-up was smooth. Miguerre did his run-up, ran through the checklist. All was fine. He turned the Otter at right angles to the furrows in the rice field and started the takeoff roll. He did a two-notch, short-field takeoff—a trifle bumpy, but it seemed quite easy. Once up, he gained air speed and began climbing ever so slowly. He circled to his heading, and we were off.

In a loud voice over the laboring engine, he said, "We go at slowest most economical rate of climb to ten thousand feet. We have to clear all these mountains—most of them not on any charts—and then it should be no problem. OK?"

I nodded vigorously and flashed a smile—"*d'accord*." But I was still worried. We had damn little fuel. What if we ran out over the mountains? We drop like a rock on some mountaintop. And who would be there to help us? No one. I decided that at least I could take photos—maybe someone would develop the film and figure out what happened. My frightened mind was behaving stupidly.

Suck it up, I told myself. I took a swig of Evian from Miguerre's bottle. Someone once had said something to me about French water having a calming force. It also made me want to pee...badly.

I wasn't scared—not really.

Miguerre looked at his watch every few minutes; flying time should be around thirty minutes from Nam Tha to Muong Sing. We were climbing up through fluffy stuff, with an occasional break admitting a glimpse of bright blue sky. I kept hunching forward in my seat, subconsciously urging the Otter and its huge, reliable Pratt & Whitney radial engine onward. But this great laboring beast obeyed only the pilot. It just climbed steadily, without a sputter.

Miguerre's best rate of climb was a fuel saver—a bit slow, but a wise choice. As we droned along, mountaintops popped up occasionally through the cloud cover like so many snaggly teeth. These peaks were something like three or five thousand feet above sea level, but whatever—we still had to fly over them, and then find the valley of Muong Sing and land!

— - • - —

WE DRONED ALONG, WITH A carpet of clouds below us, stretching as far as we could see. Then, without warning, things went red on the dash. Miguerre looked over at me and winked! Then he calmly reached for a handle, turned it to switch fuel tanks, and the red light went off! We flew on for a few more minutes, but soon we had an orange indicator for one tank and red for the other.

Oh boy, here we go, I thought, terrified. We are out of fuel in one tank, and on warning light for the other. Marvelous! We have about seven or eight more minutes' flight time to Muong Sing, and are almost out of fuel. When that orange light goes red, we will have bought a mountaintop! *Merde!*

But Miguerre had a few tricks left; he'd started descending and then reduced engine power. He was saving fuel, and whatever fuel was left would be slanting down from the wing tanks. And maybe we would arrive flying the last few miles on fumes alone. I repeated the obvious question to myself: Why hasn't the engine quit?

Miguerre had throttled back more, and began turning the fuel tank handle back and forth from tank to tank. I shot several frames of this whole scenario—the console lights, the fuel gauges, and Miguerre switching tanks—just in case someone should develop the film after finding our wreckage high atop some uncharted mountain in this goddam backwater. My anger at my helplessness had gotten my adrenaline going, which was no help to my now-loosening bowels, and never mind that I also had to pee badly. I was just plain shit-scared.

Then, in quick succession, several things happened that soothed my mind and my innards and made Miguerre my hero for life.

"OK, Doctor," he said loudly, a huge smile creasing his face from ear to ear. "Look down below—we are here."

"Where?" I yelled back, too panicked to accept the obvious.

He pointed below. "Muong Sing. Now we glide down, because any minute our engine goes poof."

Sure enough as we started down, our engine began sputtering, just as they do in movies. Miguerre hit the flap controls, giving us a notch of flap for more lift.

"We have to use the best angle of descent at this speed"—the air speed indicator read 80 mph—"because our engine is no help now. We have to glide, so we reduce our angle and stretch out the glide distance. I do it many times."

Easing down almost silently now through the clouds, we all at once burst into the open. There below us was a bright-green valley with little touches of red here and there on the slopes (the significance of which would come to me later). Immediately ahead of us: a beautiful, long, grassy runway, with markers on each side and about 5,000 feet long.

My eyes were glued to that runway and the small shacks and other buildings on each side; we kept floating down, down. Miguerre had feathered the huge, three-bladed props so that they would offer less resistance as he stretched out his glide. Soon we were floating just a few feet above the runway.

Miguerre's last move was to flare out, tipping the nose up at the last second to lose all speed just before touching down. It was as perfect a dead-stick landing as I'd ever seen—because it was the only one I'd ever seen.

Miguerre had done it! He was amazing, really: the only signs of stress I could see were big, wet patches under each arm. He glanced at me and winked. It was only then I saw tiny rivulets of sweat on his forehead, dripping over his sunglasses. This was one very cool guy.

Our momentum carried us quietly off the runway towards some parked Jeeps, and finally we stopped. Miguerre set the brakes, sunk back into his seat, and smiled at me.

"Here we are, Doctor—a little off schedule, but I hope you enjoyed the ride."

I couldn't think of what to say, so I said something stupid. "That was great navigating, Miguerre, but your gyrocompass was not set to conform to your magnetic compass."

"You noticed, eh?"

"Yeah, I noticed."

"Well, the goddam gyrocompass was not working on this trip. Why, I have no idea, but anyway, I always prefer the old-fashioned, trusty, magnetic one. Even the caveman used it, you know—the chunk of magnetic iron rock tied to a sinew. They knew how to get around, and so does my old-fashioned compass. I get the new one fixed when I get back. So, now I get some fuel and some food, and maybe tomorrow I start back. You were a good co-pilot."

He chuckled again, clapped me on the back, and we got unstrapped. The men in the back had been silent since Nam Tha. Whether frightened or totally relaxed, I never knew. Maybe somewhere in between.

Miguerre opened his side door and dropped out, leaving me to wonder what I'd gotten into, yet again.

CHAPTER 10

Muong Sing, Laos

Two Jeeps came racing toward us with some fellow standing in the front of one, wildly waving a skivvy shirt and mouthing something. Through clouds of dust, I saw that it was Dooley, with some nurses in white and one or two other people hanging on.

By now, we had piled out into bright sunshine. There was a refreshing breeze coming off the runway, carrying the familiar smell of manure; I saw oxen grazing nearby.

Dooley extended a hand and began babbling, laughing, and gesturing emphatically all at once.

"Thanks for coming up, Dr. Sundukian. Wonderful to have you here! You must be tired. Let me take you to our hospital and show you your quarters. Then we'll get you and this gang of merry men taken care of right away." What about Miguerre, I wondered. He should come to the hospital with us and get something cool to drink.

Pulling away momentarily, I went back to this anointed pilot, now busy with the huge beast's refueling. Several workmen were towing the plane towards a cache of 44-gallon fuel drums that were stacked on their sides in the only patch of shade near the runway.

"Miguerre, you OK?"

"Not to worry, Doctor—I watch these addicts take care of my Otter, then I come in and have tea with you." Tea? Hah. I had to

131

laugh; his little triumph over death called for something besides tea, and I was certain that Miguerre had more than a little brandy hidden away in his kit.

Dooley drove us across the field towards his hospital, down yet another rutted dirt road. The large French Colonial–style building had once been a private home and, given that it had been surrounded by a war for years, it was in remarkably good condition. A huge veranda wrapped around it, and a large sign that hung over the front proclaimed it to be "Dooley's Hospital" in English and Lao.

At the front, a motley collection of locals sidled around as though awaiting some event. I could see great activity inside, with people scurrying from room to room—some in white, some in native dress, some in shorts and sandals. The scene was one of subdued bedlam. There was high-pitched twittering of the tribespeople, along with children crying and frantic parents trying to quiet them. On a couple of patients I noticed huge goiters—cheek swellings that were probably parotid tumors—and then gasped involuntarily at the sight of large, open sores on several noses and cheeks: Leprosy! Still others showed gruesome scars on their lips and cheeks, as though from an animal bite. I recognized the deformity; it was "Noma," a bacterial ravaging of the mouth and labia.

All the indigenous people were bare-footed and dressed in tribal regalia, and all carried something, from babies and oxbows to fishnets and baskets suspended from yokes. Some even had baskets on their heads, effortlessly balanced. These were mostly Akha Kho tribesfolk, I learned—members of a nomadic group that wandered with impunity between China, Burma, and Laos. They were Dooley's source of information, too, and were why, I guessed, he had come here in the first place.

My tour continued, as Dooley led me around the porch and pointed farther down the rutted road. A few hundred yards away was an ancient French military fort now flying a tattered Laos pennant. It was like something from an old Foreign Legion movie, except that the troops in front, rather than parading or drilling, were instead dawdling around, giggling, and chattering. Many wore only sarongs, and several of these sarong-clad troops were doing their laundry in an irrigation canal right in front of their fort—a canal that was filled, I was certain, with filthy water. I shuddered to think what organisms were present in that water; no wonder I'd seen all those deformed mouths and lips. But, of course, this was Southeast Asia, after all.

All this time, Dooley had been rattling away in a high-pitched, rapid-fire ramble, and though I tried to take in as much as I could of what he said, my tired mind was numbed and not registering everything. I did catch, however, that dinner was to be at seven sharp, and figured that gave me time to clean up and get rested. Before leaving the veranda, I took a look around. The outside horde had begun to melt away, and it was pleasantly quiet. Out back I heard the lowing of some huge, horned animals from a nearby field, and I assumed these were the iconic, local water buffalos. Their smell was strong, in fact they downright stunk!

As we prepared to go in, Dooley indicated where the outdoor toilets were a short distance away, and then he showed me the showers and wash-up areas on the porch, just off to the side of the living quarters. Mirrors were suspended from overhead beams above three large washbasins—not your country guesthouse, but under the circumstances, functional and acceptable.

Inside, I followed him down a corridor to my quarters, a bright, airy little room set off in the front of the building and away from the clinic and patients. It was fairly large, with whitewashed walls and a small cot against the wall opposite the door. He explained that this space had been built to accommodate visiting officials, and since I was a ranking dignitary, it was mine for this visit. I smiled gratefully, shook his hand, and within seconds was on the cot in a moment of welcome solitude. An extra day in Nam Tha and a hairy flight into Muong Sing, I thought. Well, anyway, we made it.

— - • - —

AFTER A SHORT REST, I removed my sweaty clothes, slipped on a pair of swim trunks, and headed for the showers. I ignored signs asking that water be conserved, blissfully enjoying a good head of pressure.

(Another sign announced that water was "purified" for showering and boiled for drinking. Dooley, it seemed, was a bit of a clown, too. The sign to conserve water was printed in several languages; I congratulated myself for understanding three.) I returned to my room to dress.

Cleaned and refreshed, I headed to the dining room, where I was surprised to find a piano, along with several tables and a long desk that was Dooley's personal work area. The latter was covered with scattered papers, open books, and piles of unopened mail. A member of the staff motioned me toward a chair by a window, where another poured me a tall glass of iced tea.

I raised it, sipped, and sat back to wait. Now I finally would find out just why Dr. Dooley was so anxious to have me visit.

CHAPTER 11

Goodbye, Muong Sing
or
How I Came to Hate China

*Not everything which has taken place among persons
of the lowest class is worth narrating.*
—Ammianus Marcellinus, Roman historian, A.D.
Fourth century, Rerum Gestarum, *28-1-15*

THE NEXT FEW DAYS WERE SPENT WITH DOOLEY IN HIS CLINIC, SEEING patients with horrible conditions: diseases of the skin, gut disorders, birth defects, and a host of other problems I had neither seen nor read about in medical books. He showed me advanced cases of leprosy, tracing the spread of ugly lesions on the cheeks, noses, and foreheads of several men and women. He pointed out tubercular patients whom he'd diagnosed by history and physical alone, as he had no X-ray capacity. (Amazingly, he could percuss out tuberculous lung cavities by tapping a patient's chest with his fingers.) Next, terrible examples of damage from bacterial infections in the mouth and gums, and even lips: young men and women with lips missing—sometimes both their upper and lower lips. The resulting scar was permanently disfiguring. Dooley mumbled something about performing plastic surgery on these unfortunates. I pretended not to hear; this was no place to perform such operations. (Somewhere in the back of my mind, I remembered that Indian surgeons performed nose flap operations to cover syphilitic lesions—successfully, in open-air market places. I pushed that to the back of my mind, too.)

Trying to stay out of the way, I spent several hours watching groups of natives straggling up the road to the hospital. Each group would send one man to speak to Dooley, and to Dooley's credit, he spoke with them in their tongue, with an occasional assist from a Lao hospital worker. Between them, they spoke most of the languages and dialects in that area (this to the likely annoyance of China, for these groups bore information from deep inside nearby Yunnan province). From Dooley's descriptions, I recognized members of the Thai Lus, Ka Khos, Thai Dams, Meos and others, many of whom I could not identify and whose names I would never remember.

Amid the commotion, I managed to get quite a few pictures of leprosy, parotid tumors, and goiters the size of tennis balls—larger than any I'd seen. And just beneath the skin on each side of these goiters, I saw the hugely enlarged thyroid arteries pulsating like coiled snakes. I couldn't stop thinking about how difficult it would be to operate on these patients. The huge arteries were so intimidating—but how did they get so large? And how could anyone treat these patients?

Dooley had the answers. Given their heavy diet of freshwater fish from mountain rivers and streams, locals in the valleys around the hospital were often iodine-deficient. (Ocean fish, it turns out, are much richer in iodine.) If dietary iodine isn't enough, Mother Nature makes more cells in the thyroid gland to compensate—even to the point of creating a huge gland. Actually, Dooley wanted to feed them iodine and see whether these glands could then be removed without growing back. "But I don't have any Iodine," he said, "So that's that!"

Dooley's face took on a clever, coy look as we were speaking, one that made me wary. "So, would you consider removing some goiters, Doctor Sundukian?" he asked, not once looking me in the eye.

I thought of a million possible complications: unwanted operative events, a collapsed trachea, a fatal thyroid crisis. "Not a chance," I said.

I had absolutely no intention of operating on those patients. As far as I was concerned, no surgeon in his right mind would operate on such patients out in that setting—if anywhere else, for that matter.

After all, just one bad outcome in Muong Sing would be a medical and political disaster. How long would it take Radio Hanoi, Radio Peiping, and Radio Anything to get that kind of incendiary information out on their airwaves? Certainly not long. They surely had eyes and ears everywhere, even among workers at the hospital.

I smiled but politely, and firmly, declined.

— - • - —

His bravado notwithstanding, Dooley's medical impact was impressive, beginning with his overflowing waiting room. In the four years or so since he'd opened up shop in the mid-Fifties, word of Dooley's training and dedication had spread widely throughout the local clans, and now every morning the hospital's waiting room was packed with wailing children and ailing adults. As he passed through the throng, Dooley would go from one group to another smiling, laughing and speaking in Lao, chucking an infant's chin, rubbing a baby's scalp—in general imparting goodwill and bonhomie. And each week, dozens of patients would be treated each week for afflictions that otherwise were sure to be fatal, with a much larger number receiving treatment for conditions that, while not life-threatening, were still debilitating, painful, or personally devastating. (Suffering was less acute, it should be noted, among those whose constant grins made clear that poppy was in use.)

After my first few days, then, it wasn't hard to decide what I'd be telling the rest of the board and the brass back at CARE in Washington regarding Dooley: the many thousands of dollars we'd sent to this isolated, ramshackle compound were paying off well enough. But all that money was landing in unreliable hands.

This was not because I doubted Dooley's clinical skills. As a doctor, Dooley was not only very capable, but he could be remarkably compassionate, in contrast with his occasional brash outbursts and brusque behavior with clinic personnel and even visitors. Instead, my doubts drew more from what I saw as a streak of intense, almost manic frustration in him—something close to madness. He had a certain look, an intensity of purpose rarely seen save in the overachiever.

His unblinking, straight-ahead gaze fixed his eye contact with the person with whom he spoke—he was talking only to that person, only to them. And, he never stopped talking, or laughing or babbling as he moved about. Speaking English, a phrase in Lao, and at times in French, sometimes in all three, with an assist whenever needed from an ever-present Lao aide.

Similarly, he took a kind of manic pleasure in his celebrity. There was no mistaking the satisfaction he took in the dependency of his impoverished, uncomprehending patients on his medical judgment, and it left me seeing him as something of a charlatan, a false savior. Years earlier, he had been a talented orthopedic surgeon in St. Louis, only to serve as a shipboard Naval surgeon off the coast of Vietnam. The tour of duty had shown him firsthand all the diseases, malnutrition, and high infant mortality of Indochina, along with the common lack of any medical or other sort of help. It must have seemed an ideal place to launch a cause, a stage on which to play a grand, paternalistic role, even if it was in the middle of nowhere.

In short, he had run away. He learned quickly to use his flair for self-promotion and for describing the plight of poor natives to play on the emotions of sensitive folks in far-off lands, and thus obtained funds to support his grand project. He was part doctor, caring for those who otherwise would not have medical care, and part religious zealot. In his own way, I decided, he imagined himself to be a clone of the famed Dr. Albert Schweitzer—complete with the piano, like Schweitzer's organ, as well as the deliberate isolation in some God-forgotten, long-suffering corner of the world.

All the drama of being the Savior of Muong Sing, however, was wearing visibly on Dooley. He seemed a bit pale, a bit wan. Could he be anemic? Other signs struck me, too: His freckles were too prominent, he had bloodshot eyes, and he was thin rather than lean. I had the feeling that he was overly tense, possibly from lack of sleep. In short, the guy was not well physically, and, in addition to all this, he seemed wound up like a tightly coiled spring. He seemed likely to come to an explosive end—but how, and when?

For the moment, I just shrugged, mentally. So many of these hair-shirted ones eventually came to strange endings. I had no desire to be around at such an ending for Dr. Dooley.

— - • - —

AS IT WAS, DOOLEY'S ENDING seemed to be closing in. Manic and vainglorious as he may have been, the ill of Muong Sing sought him out just the same. He was giving this isolated region its first real look at medical science, and the locals clearly liked what they saw.

The Viet Cong and Communist-Chinese sympathizers lurking in the mountain ridges nearby, on the other hand, were less enthusiastic. Dooley was trouble for them, and it wasn't hard to appreciate their displeasure. He was a living contradiction of their propaganda denouncing the society he represented. Surely there were ways to deal with this man and his hospital—and soon, before he became an even greater cult figure.

For some time, Radio Hanoi had been lambasting Dooley and his hospital as a center for espionage agents, a place where Yankee malefactors co-opted refugees by "poisoning their minds." Radio Hanoi was required listening for the native population, as part of the ongoing Chinese master plan to overrun the entire area, especially Muong Sing. At this point, it was a slow, cat-and-mouse game. Still, Dooley's renown clearly had made him a top target. Radio Hanoi now was loudly condemning the little hospital complex, and dark denunciations of Dooley personally were issued repeatedly.

I promptly learned that even my own arrival had not been overlooked.

At dinner one night, Dooley casually mentioned the Radio Hanoi attacks and then looked over at me, adding, "They say you, Doctor, are a spy—a poisoner, here to kill little children, seduce women, and steal their gold and silver. And it's all my fault. So they want you captured and killed. How do you like that?" With that, he grinned and let out an ugly cackle, making sure that all at the table had heard him and shared his humor. I felt like strangling the son of a bitch; how could he think Radio Hanoi's calls for murder amusing?

I didn't sleep at all that night, lying in bed wondering about how many Viet Cong and Chinese partisans were up in the mountains—and how reliable the unimpressive Lao troops stationed in a former French outpost nearby really were. In the darkness, I scolded myself for having agreed to visit this off-the-map dump and unwittingly making a target out of myself. When morning came, though, I decided to damn the torpedos: I would head right for the village center and get some shots for *National Geographic*'s Mel Grosvenor, who had loaded me up with film. It would be a relief to escape the noise and disorganization of the hospital compound, and anyway, my camera was like an old friend, like a pacifier for a toddler. The distraction would be welcome, and since Mel had told me the magazine had never had anyone—even an amateur like me—visit here, I figured the marketplace of Muong Sing would be a good bet to get some exotic shots to submit.

I cadged a bumpy ride on a Jeep heading for the village and got off in what looked like a main square crowded with locals and reeking with animal waste. Teams of oxen and water buffalo snorted and lurched along, straining against impossible loads as their flanks were slapped with bamboo rods. In a small shop facing an open-air market, I found walls covered with cigarettes and hands of local tobacco, along with packages and cans of food from China. The smell of fresh animal hides destined to be made into pigskin articles rose from a pile by the door.

As I made my way along the perimeter of the market, many of those I passed smiled, bowing with hands clasped before them. Some had blackened teeth. ("White teeth belong only to dogs," it was later explained to me.) As they smiled and bowed, they said something that sounded like "*sambadee than mo.*" I smiled back, advancing my film and pressing the shutter release; I got some marvelous shots and promptly used up most of the film I had at hand. Heading back to the Jeep, I found it loaded and its driver preparing to head back to the hospital.

On the way into town, the driver, a Lao hospital technician, hadn't shown much interest in me or my camera, instead shouting in the local dialect to passersby and muttering under his breath at wayward oncoming carts. Now, though, he pointed to me as I approached him and grinned wickedly, saying, *"Than Mo...Radio Hanoi."* He then made a sweeping gesture with his finger across his throat. I couldn't tell whether he was pleased at the idea or mocking the broadcasts as empty threats, but I knew what he meant. My mouth went dry, and a chill ran across my sweaty shirt-back. Something seized hard inside my chest and gut all at once.

The whole ride back, my mind raced as I wondered how close this threat really was. Dooley's own example was hardly reassuring, given his blithe disregard for his own safety. And then it dawned on me: Dooley knew he was in a dicey situation, and, in his would-be-martyr fashion, he even relished it. I now remembered the pilots and Rich's group telling me that he was a nut who possibly wanted to get killed. They had already distanced themselves from him and his hospital, figuring that disaster loomed.

Suddenly I felt my interest in the fate of this quirky, frenetic American evaporate. I already had my personal impressions to pass on to CARE and some photos for my friends back at *National Geographic*. Now I just wanted to get the hell out of Dodge.

-- • --

GETTING OUT, HOWEVER, WAS LOOKING increasingly more difficult. After offloading us, Miguerre and his Air Laos Otter had departed for Vientiane. While my departure had been scheduled—rather loosely, it seemed—for a week or so from the day of my arrival, just exactly when he'd return to extract me had been dismissed as anyone's guess. Miguerre himself had been given no idea. His next flight to Muong Sing would be according to a schedule given him by his station manager, or perhaps when there was nothing else to do. A full week had now passed, and I was stuck. There was a good chance that I'd get killed if I hung around long enough.

Frustrated and anxious, I resolved to ask Dooley to radio out a request to have me extracted. I hadn't seen much of the Americans who'd flown in with me; they'd had chores to carry out in the village,

I was told, shoring up the village chieftain and providing material and other support. Now and then, these men would show up at the hospital for meals, chat amiably with whoever was there and then, after coffee, just fade away. Where they went was never clear, and no one seemed concerned.

Neither was I. Until now.

After dinner one night I buttonholed one of them, the burly Bostonian named Rich. He looked more hard than tough, though I had no doubt he was both when the occasion demanded. What he was and what he really did, I didn't care. That he had military or paramilitary experience was pretty obvious.

"Say, Rich, could we talk?" I asked, trying to sound calmer than I felt.

"Sure, Doc, what's on your mind?"

"Well, Dooley said something about Radio Hanoi."

Rich snorted. "Don't let that stuff bother you. Nobody pays any attention to that crap; they don't believe half of it themselves. It's just bullshit for the masses. You're not scared, are you?"

"Damn straight I am," I answered, "wonder if I could borrow a handgun from you."

He could tell I was serious and gave me a sidelong glance. Then his face broke into a lopsided smile. "Sure, Doc. In fact, I've been holding a piece for you from Hank Peters. Here, come with me."

His mentioning Hank, who had already surprised me by slipping the pistol to me back in Saigon, once again gave me the eerie feeling that I was being watched—or watched over. Luckily for me, Hank Peters had been thinking ahead again.

"Wait here," Rich said, as we reached a staircase at the end of a corridor. When he reappeared, he was carrying a towel, which he unfolded to reveal a well-used Colt 911 .45-caliber pistol.

As I hefted the gun, I asked him, "By the way, where do you get these old, unlisted weapons?"

"Did I say it was unlisted? Never said that, Doc. Guess you got that from Mishawy in Saigon, right?"

I searched my memory. Maybe I just inferred that from the way Mishawy had acted.

"Yeah, guess so," I said.

"Well, you're pretty close to right. We have some Chinese friends who came here when the Nationalists beat it to Formosa. You'd be surprised at the number of different hand weapons these guys brought with them—automatic pistols, parabellum pistols, Lugers, Shmeissers, Mausers, and some old Russian pieces. They even had old, bolt-action Enfield rifles from World War I. And crates of ammo, too. Where and how they got them is anyone's guess. But you can bet they didn't buy 'em. Collected 'em along the way would be my explanation."

He pointed to the weapon he'd just given me. "This works great for big-assed guys like me," he said, pointing to the small of his back with a chuckle. "You want to make sure you keep the safety on back there, 'cause even skinny guys like you can get your asses shot off."

And in fact the .45 did fit nicely there in my butt crease, its handle supported by my belt. For the moment, I felt safe. At least I could defend myself, and having a gun at the ready put my mind at slightly greater ease. I double-checked the safety and then slipped it back under my belt so that the handle pointed to the right. I practiced snaking it out and releasing the safety at the same time. I was fast becoming a regular John Wayne.

"Not bad, Doc, and you might want to keep that handy," Rich said. "I don't trust that guy Dooley, if you follow what I mean."

I just looked at him, trying to appear innocent.

"Let's get some tea," he said. "I need to talk with you, anyway. Private-like."

CHAPTER 12

And the Fun Begins

THE LOCAL LAO RAISED TEA PLANTS ON THE THEIR MOUNTAIN SLOPES, MY favorite a Chinese tea called Lapsang Souchong that smelled like smoky, tarred railroad ties and that Dooley's larder had in abundance. It was dark, strong, and left a pleasant taste. I took it black, with a dollop of honey or a cube of sugar.

Rich and I sat in the evening silence with our cups, sipping the tea and nibbling on homemade macaroons. I watched him expectantly, wondering what he could possibly have to say. I waited and then waited some more; still he coolly sipped and nibbled, as though this were high tea in Cricklewood.

Impatient, I started some idle chatter about tea. Rich was waiting for an opening, as it turned out. "Did you know it's OK to slurp tea here, Doc? Makes it cooler and lets your host know you're enjoying it."

"Yeah," I said," a lady back in Saigon told me that."

"Bet it was that lady from Michigan State—right, Doc?"

How the hell did he know about Gigi?

"What makes you say that, Rich?" I asked in a slightly reproving voice. Once again, I had the feeling that everyone in Southeast Asia knew what I was doing—all the time. Was nothing safe from prying eyes and ears? I answered myself once again. No, it isn't. Nothing I did was a secret to anyone. OK, so my trysts with a bombshell acquaintance in Saigon were common knowledge. But why did anyone care? Could it be that all these people were keeping tabs on me merely because I was set to visit Russia?

"No offense, Doc," Rich said. "We've been told to keep our eyes on you and make sure nothing happens. We're a form of protection—Consider us bodyguards."

He paused as though fishing for words. "But there's more, too." Putting his teacup down, he leaned forward slightly. "You're a lung specialist, right?"

I nodded. "Guilty as charged," I said, warily.

"Well, here's the thing. I have to bring you up to speed about a problem that's come up. We, uh"— he broke eye contact momentarily, searching for how to proceed—"we have a man, a couple actually, over across the border in Yunnan," he said, pointing toward China. "They're in a little village; he's an American missionary-type, born and raised in old China, and she is outwardly his wife, as far as anyone is concerned. She's Chinese, born in China, wealthy parents sent her to the United States for college, which is where she met this guy.

"Anyway, this woman, who we call 'Mei Ling,' has been in place with this man for several years now. I'm not really told what information she gathers, but I'm betting it has to do with a nuclear research site the Chinese operate about 60 clicks away at Xuanching. Now we've just learned that he's down with bad pneumonia—fever, chills, a heavy, gurgling cough—and has been sick as hell for months. And sometimes he gets delirious and starts hallucinating and babbling—in English and Chinese. As far as we're concerned, this is really bad. If he says anything at all that he's not supposed to say, he could expose not just himself and Mei Ling, but others, too. Local medics have brought him herbal medicines that only made him sicker. What he needs is a big dose of penicillin and someone to stick it in him."

For the last minute or two, Rich had been glancing around as he spoke. Now he fixed his gaze on me. "And so we're wondering if you could help us with that."

Help? I'm supposed to make an illegal house call in Communist China to stick penicillin in some guy's ass? I was already on Hanoi's shit list. The last thing I wanted was to get caught sneaking into a communist country. And was his mentioning my nights with Gigi supposed to be some kind of threat if I refused to go along?

Before I had a chance to say anything, he held up his hand, palm out.

"There's a whole lot more here. You're probably wondering why this guy is so important to us and why we need a doctor instead of just a medic to go in with us." He looked down for a moment.

"What I can tell you right now is that first off, you wouldn't be going alone. A team is going into China, and we're actually going to bring out that poor sonovabitch. We'll go over there to his little hidey-hole, give him some medicine, and then get him and his lady outta there. This is what we do—we're extractors. When something goes to shit or somebody needs to be moved, we get the call. We could use you here because this missionary guy's so sick, he may be dying. He's coughing up green and brown junk that reeks, and our medical folks are thinking that he has a bad lung abscess, full-blown pneumonia, empyema, or even all of those together."

He took a longer sip of tea than before and then looked over at me. "And yeah, Hank Peters put the finger on you. He said you'd do it."

This last line hit me pretty hard—and not just because I'd come to feel indebted to Hank. At least I'd been singled out and surveilled because I was considered trustworthy, rather than out of fear that I wasn't. But did it even make sense to try to sneak into China if this fellow was that sick? Good Lord—any one of the conditions Rich had mentioned could be a killer if not treated quickly and still could be fatal even then. Could this guy be that important?

As my mind raced at the prospect that I might end up undercover in China, Rich delivered the roundhouse. "What I think we'll be doing—as soon as I hear from our control folks—goes like this: In a day or so, a plane will come in, pick us up and drop us near our target point. There we get picked up and taken to where our man is. We grab him and her, get back to our plane, and come back here. Simple, right?" Standing up, he raised a finger. "Just a sec—I'll be right back."

A day or so? As in, tomorrow or the next day? As Rich disappeared around the corner, I tried to square my own plans with Rich's request. Hours ago, I'd resolved to beat it back to Saigon no matter what, and now I was being asked to join a bunch of fake-named spooks on a midnight flight to the Chinese outback.

When he reappeared holding a case, Rich surely could sense the shock I felt but acted as though he didn't. "What I need you to do is this," he said. "Check out this medical kit and make sure it has what you'd need for keeping a very sick man alive for the trip back here. Tell me whatever else you'd need, and we'll try to get it here at Dooley's place. You'll want to pack a small overnight kit, just in case, and I have some special gear for you to wear on the trip."

"Whoa," I said, "hold it right there." Reeling a little and unsure how to phrase my misgivings, I reflexively picked up the blocky, zippered case Rich had put on the table between us. Someone with some medical training had assembled its contents. The kit contained just about everything that would likely be needed: two bags of IV fluid and tubing, morphine ampoules, Demerol, Compazine, epinephrine, a canister of dried plasma, surgical instruments, catheters, bandage material, and packages of iodoform gauze. The instruments were feather-light, and I guessed that they were titanium. The whole kit weighed only about five pounds.

Meanwhile, Rich pressed on, pulling out a paper bag holding clothes made of sturdy, thin cotton that was printed with a green-black camouflage design. There was also a floppy cotton hat and matching bandana. "It keeps sweat and hair out of your eyes. Trust me. It works."

Overwhelmed, I stammered, "Listen Rich, I gotta know more—I'm not going over there just to satisfy some higher-up that a real doctor was along for the trip."

Again, he held up his hand. "John, I've told you all I know up to now. Nobody tells me more than I'm supposed to know, either. We're going to go in—my team, you, and maybe one or two others—to extract this sorry bastard and bring him back here; end of story. We'll have to work out the kinks as we go. Like I told you, this is what we do—only this time, you'll be going with us. Swirsky, Brawner, and I, we work together, we've done this kind of thing countless times, and we have the drill down almost to—"

"What kind of a plane?" I asked, interrupting. "Where's it come from? How do you know where to land?" A million questions flooded my brain.

Rich answered with a weary patience. "The plane comes from near Chiang Mai. It's a Porter—they land anywhere and take off almost straight up."

Porters? I'd heard of them—Swiss-built, originally used in the Alps to rescue skiers. They could land on mountain slopes, meadows, wherever. But what were Porters doing in this part of the world? Then it dawned on me: If Air America had them; it was for work behind the lines.

Realizing that an entire chunk of the U.S. government was in one or another way behind these plans reassured me now, and I accepted that if I were to agree to go, I would never know very much—that I would be along to play a medical role and otherwise needed to stay out of the way. Standing up restlessly, I exhaled long and slowly and then told Rich I'd sleep on it.

— - • - —

IN FACT, THOUGH, I'D ALREADY decided—or rather it all seemed decided for me. Quite simply, I'd be safer casting my lot with these commando-types than I would be alone in northern Laos by myself after they left. I could fly out with the team and then fly back in the Porter to wherever it went next. I'd be out—back in Saigon within a couple of days, even. But for some reason I didn't want to just sign up with a smile. I had at least a little leverage as long as they needed my consent, so what I'd do was negotiate a straightforward deal with Rich. I'd go in with them and help get their precious cargo out, provided that they fly me out to Saigon directly afterward.

When I presented my terms to Rich the next morning, he quickly said, "That certainly sounds reasonable to me. I can't see a problem with it."

"One last condition," I blurted, "since you guys agree to fly me out, then cancel my outbound flight from here with Air Laos. I'd hate to have Miguerre fly in for nothing."

He looked at me blankly for a moment. "OK, John, I'll pass that along, too."

Satisfied, I retreated to my room to kill time as though packing, when in fact my tidy little duffel was ready to go. Thinking of the empty day ahead, I began wondering what photos I might still get and was sorting lenses and film when I heard an airplane make a telltale pass over the airstrip next door. Heading outside and past a copse of low trees, I scanned the foothills nearby and spotted a single-engine aircraft making a wide turn to set up its approach. As it lined up with the runway, the stubby craft tilted oddly downward and, more alarmingly, kept coming at full speed. I watched spellbound as huge flaps extended from the back of the wing, making the plane appear to halt in mid-air like a sea gull and then drop effortlessly on the runway. The engine's high-pitched whine lessened as its huge propeller slowed to a stop. This was no piston-prop engine—the whine gave it away; it was a powerful turbine. This was the Porter.

From my perch on the hospital's veranda, I gave this strange-looking aircraft a quick once-over. Its engine jutted way out in front with the prop stuck on like a huge pinwheel. Being a tail-dragger, the Porter rolled along the ground with a kind of pugnacity, as though at all times looking up. Under each wing was hung a bullet-shaped auxiliary fuel tank, added for extended range. Goody, I thought, those will get me back to Saigon. But why those huge wing flaps, so much larger than I'd seen on similarly sized craft? Then it came to me. Those flaps could generate tremendous lift and provide tremendous slowing power too—ideal for backcountry work. Right about then I realized something else: Unlike any other aircraft I'd ever seen, this one was painted a dull gray and bore no markings at all.

The plane now had taxied off the grass strip and came to a stop in the same spot where Miguerre had parked his Otter when he'd flown me in. These are the mysterious folks who will get us in and out of China, I thought, and I shielded my eyes to get a better look as the cabin doors swung open. A pilot and co-pilot in flight suits emerged, and as they stepped out of the wing's shadow toward a Jeep waiting nearby, I felt a rush of confused pleasure. The pilot of the Porter was Miguerre!

After a pause, I set out for the driveway at the front of the hospital where Miguerre would be brought and promptly reproached myself. Why should I be surprised? He had told me that he had flown on French military missions, so the two governments must be working together on this. Regardless, he was a crack pilot, so his presence in the cockpit was reassuring, to say the least. And furthermore, he was my friend, which was no small matter, given how isolated I'd been feeling. The happy thought made me laugh a little as I made my way along the walk and again glanced over my shoulder at the plane.

What I saw then brought me to an abrupt standstill, and I felt my knees go weak. From the open cabin doors had stepped a third figure—none other than Mrs. Gigi Prudhomme, the wicked witch of Saigon. Like Miguerre and the co-pilot, she was wearing a flight suit, but there was no mistaking her distinctive backside. Her gait, despite the outfit, still had that familiar, devastating sway. What the hell was she doing here?

Frozen with surprise, I watched as several small valises were loaded into the Jeep and the passengers climbed on for the short drive over to the main hospital entrance. My mind was swimming: What had seemed to be just a pleasant, even giddy, moment had instead turned into Alice in Wonderland, with strange people showing up suddenly in strange places. Gigi was the last person I'd expected to see. Rich, Hank, even Miguerre—I had the vague feeling that their roles could be explained, but what the hell did Gigi have to do with any of this?

I retreated to my quarters and grabbed my notebook and camera bag. For some reason, it suddenly seemed important that I not let on how desperate I had been to leave. Camera and film in hand, I slipped quickly out a side door of the hospital on a trumped-up errand, wanting time to work things out in my mind. I followed a footpath leading down to the Mekong River, which I could hear burbling in the near distance. Overhead, I thought I saw sea gulls. What the hell would sea gulls be doing this far from the ocean? And how far back in all this subterfuge did Gigi go?

I trudged about half a mile and distractedly shot some scenery using a conventional 50mm lens, switching to a macro-zoom for close-ups of some perched dragonflies. It was one of those moments in which my camera functioned as though it were a living thing, able to know on its own what speed and shutter settings I wanted. I worked without relying on my light meter; there was no calculating f-stops or shutter speeds. I busily framed and shot, finding consolation in the complete control over my camera that I so patently lacked over everything else at the moment.

The heat and whiny bugs began to get oppressive; sweat ran into my eyes, making focusing difficult. They'd be looking for me at the hospital; I'd need to say just the right things, to keep my composure and not look like a naïf. My little photo session was over, I knew, and during its swift half-hour, I'd come to accept what was obvious: I really had been set up. It had been a set-up the whole bloody time, from the moment they learned that I, the cocky young chest surgeon, was coming to Saigon. The parties, the seating assignments, the chance encounters at the Club—yes, even the sweaty hours in the darkness of Gigi's flat. The flying invitations, the gun delivery, the timing of my visit to Dooley's. All of it choreographed, set in motion to strand me here at a jumping-off point, with little choice but to go along.

The full extent of my deception became clearer and clearer, and I felt a surge of anger toward Gigi. She'd played me well, and I'd been easy. Females, cynics say, are born with the ability to corrupt while appearing pure at heart; one could harken back to Adam's Eve. Gigi had done so with me. I was her assignment, and if it involved duping me while roping me in, well, so be it. The mortifying sense that I had been manipulated so easily and so visibly left me feeling exposed and sheepish.

As for the bare facts, there they were, laid out before me like a map: Gigi & Co. were this Mei-Ling's remote handlers, her control. Without a medical doctor to treat her failing, hallucinating husband and fly him out, Mei-Ling wouldn't agree to leave, either. So what to do? Fill the hole, find the part. Locate some naive lung doctor, get him on the hook, and put the plan into motion. I was that doctor, and now my job was to fly in, keep quiet, shove a massive dose of penicillin into this padré's buttock, high-tail it to the airstrip, and sit tight on the flight out. Realistically, what choice did I have?

Returning to the hospital, I headed quickly to my room, wanting time to prepare for an encounter with Gigi. With a loud, nervous sigh, I tossed my camera and film bag on the bed and turned to close the door—and jumped a mile in my skin. There she was, perched nonchalantly in a chair in the corner, legs crossed and staring at me. Her hair was pulled back in a businesslike manner, and she had changed into a sober cotton blouse and long shorts with espadrilles.

"I don't want you to hate me," she said evenly.

"Too late," I mustered, trying for a measure of cool resignation.

She continued looking at me, and just as I began to wonder what I might do next, she stood up and took two measured steps in my direction, positioning herself immediately in front of me with her hands on her hips. Her haunting, lemony scent filled my head, and I could do little more than wait for her to say something.

"Anyway," she finally said, pausing again. "Thank you for going."

"Yeah," I replied, wishing I had something more to do than stand there sweating and trying not to look away.

She stepped back toward the door and opened it, and then turned to look at me again. Our eyes met for a moment. Then she pulled the door shut behind her, and I listened as her footsteps retreated softly down the corridor.

— - • - —

Knowing that I needed to say my farewells to Dr. Dooley, I set out in time for the clinic, only to run into Miguerre and the co-pilot poring over notes and charts with Rich, Swirsky, and Brawner. Smiling, Miguerre stepped toward me and put a welcoming arm around my shoulders, at which I resolved to overlook whatever role he had played in this whole little plot regarding me. I couldn't bring myself to think that his affection for me wasn't genuine, and he seemed to want me to know that it was. Beyond that, I found it enormously comforting that this adventure was just another day at the office for him. Maybe it really could be just a quick grab-and-go after all.

Rich motioned me over to stand beside him. "You might wanna listen in on this—we're going over the drill, what we're gonna do with this snatch."

So I did. Lines, dots, and more lines. All led into China and out, but in different directions. The implication of that escaped me at the time.

CHAPTER 13

Inside Red China

*Ils n'ont rien appris, ni rien oblies. (They have
learnt nothing and forgotten nothing.)*
—Charles de Talleyrand (1754–1838).

AS THE SUN DROPPED BEHIND THE MOUNTAINS THAT EVENING, I JOINED Miguerre for his preflight look at the plane. He had brought along a flask of very fine medicinal-grade brandy and had a few more small flasks stored aboard the aircraft. He insisted these were for medical necessities only. *Oh, yeah—sure they were.*

As we chatted, I told him I had concerns about this whole idiotic project. He smiled patiently and told me not to worry. "These little operations go on all the time out here. Would you like a brandy to calm yourself?" he asked with a grin.

"No, thanks. You mean pulling people out?" I asked.

"*Absolutement, mon ami,* we do this frequently, and for many American dollars each time."

I knew from the planning session our pilots would be doing time-and-distance flying. Take off, get on course, set your RPMs and watch the chronometer and the Rolexes. Given the distance and guessing on wind to calculate ground speed, a pilot would know that a certain RPM setting would put him over the landing spot at a certain time. The trick was to do it.

Once darkness had fallen completely on the airstrip, our whole little group was herded into the odd-looking plane with the dull paint job and no markings. Our light travel kits and weapons were stowed, and we were strapped in. Miguerre double-checked the doors and made certain that no internal cabin lights were on. Gigi sat stone-faced in the second row next to Rich, Brawner, Swirsky, and me. We were jammed together. I may have been trembling.

After Miguerre checked that we were strapped in and the doors locked, he and his right-seat pilot began clicking switches on the consoles. I heard a slow blowing sound and then felt the engine start up. It was a gentle throbbing sound at first with a whine to it. The sound rose steadily, and then the plane began moving slowly to the runway. Miguerre would have to climb to 8,000 feet before clearing the mountaintops, but I was sure this plane could do it.

I felt the plane turn and line up on the runway. It was hard to see anything outside, but these guys knew what they were doing; they'd done it so many times before. All at once, the engine whine mounted; I felt the plane shuddering against its brakes. Suddenly we were moving, faster and faster, and then we tilted up. And then, just as suddenly, it was quiet…no more rumbling below us. We were up and climbing, in the space of just a few seconds.

We'd be flying into the night both invisible and blind—showing no lights of any kind, and with no visible points of reference outside. But these were skilled pilots who had the latest autopilot setups; furthermore, they had calculated the distance and time factors carefully. It would be a dead-reckoning flight, to be sure, but an educated one.

In the cockpit, it was quiet, with only the dim, red glow of instrument lights. Outside, the whispery drone of the powerful turbo engine and air rushing over the fuselage had settled into a steady, low tune; it was hypnotic. But the occasional bump and my high adrenaline titer—along with the knowledge that I hadn't the foggiest notion where we were going, other than some hamlet in Yunnan—kept me fully awake.

As of this moment, I had become a board-certified coward just thinking about the upcoming grab-and-scoot operation. A hard knot in my stomach hinted that I was ready to vomit, but I gulped, sucked in some air, and grunted. I was under control—barely.

The step-by-step details of the next few hours had been thought out as best they could be. As instructed, we wore our camouflage gear for the flight—just in case we had to "land early"—and the plan was to change into local dress once we were on the ground. Touchdown would be near a small village on a remote field known to the pilot, and friendly contacts would be waiting for us. A hooded light-recognition signal in response to a series of blinks from the plane would give us the all clear. We would land, off-load, and be given a route to the padré's home. Once we reached his door, Gigi would knock and announce herself. Mei-Ling would be expecting our arrival; she had been advised to be ready to move—and fast. We were to be back at the strip, ready to take off with our new passengers, within so many minutes. If the plane could not wait for us and took off early for some reason, we would make radio contact with it at set times, advising Miguerre and his co-pilot of our status and whether to come get us or wait for another message.

As we droned along, I sneaked glances at my companions. No expressions, just blank stares. They were looking straight ahead, and the red glow of instrument lights created eerie shadows on their faces—almost like Halloween masks. We were flying straight and level, just above the mountaintops I'd seen on the navigational charts, I hoped. There was only an occasional bump as the plane hit a small pocket of turbulence over hills and under small clouds. But the engine never changed its steady drone as we bore on through the night.

Our estimated flight time was one hour and ten minutes. We carried more than enough fuel, I knew, especially given those little auxiliary wing-tanks, each with fuel for about two hours of flight time. When these were empty, they were dumped like empty rocket boosters, leaving the engine to draw on its internal tanks. Our plan had been to climb to 10,000 feet and clear the mountains, then proceed on course until we'd neared touchdown point. The minutes dragged on, and my feeling was that we damn well should be there by now. Still, we flew on and on. I glanced at my watch again. We'd been airborne about sixty minutes, so we should be approaching the designated landing spot. We hadn't started down yet, but it had to be soon.

There are several ways to land a Porter. In our case, Miguerre planned to fly directly to the designated target site, go nose down, "dirty up" with speed brakes, flaps, and leading edge flaps. Then at about 250 feet, we'd make a "Beta mode" landing. We'd reverse props while still heading nose-down, then flare out just above ground, and finally land silently like a sea gull alighting on a beach. Descending quickly from that height also meant a quieter intrusion, which lessened the chance of detection.

Miguerre checked his Rolex, tapped the co-pilot, and pointed to the time. The co-pilot nodded, eased back ever so slightly on the throttle. I felt us tip and begin sliding down. At some point several minutes later, we were hanging in mid-air, seemingly stopped in mid-air. After another minute or so like this, the engine had powered down to a mere whisper and suddenly we leveled off and touched the ground. We'd landed, but were still moving ahead, taxiing silently. Bouncing a little, we trundled along the dirt runway for a few more minutes and then came to a stop. That the Porter could be so quiet at idle and so noisy at full power certainly had its advantages. It was an amazing plane.

If there had been a light signal from the ground, I hadn't seen it—my only view was from a side window. Miguerre popped his door, then someone on the outside opened the passenger-side door. We were now somewhere inside hostile Red China! Holy cow. My first thought was that the outside air in China smelled like every other place in Asia these days: night soil or whiffs from a nearby piggery or swamp. It all smelled the same.

With a stiff shove, Rich brought my focus back to the task at hand, pushing me to climb out. In the gloom, I saw a pair of three-wheeled lorries parked alongside the dirt runway. "This way, Doctor," said an unfamiliar, hushed voice as a strong hand led me by my elbow to one of the lorries. "Here, change into these." The voice was definitely American, but maybe Chinese-American, and despite the darkness, I could make out glasses and some crooked teeth. "Here you go—put these on now!"

I shed my camouflage gear and donned baggy, black trousers tied around my waist, a Mao shirt, and a goofy-looking cap, keeping the shoes I'd flown in with. I transferred my penlight to my shirt pocket and my automatic into the small of my back; my tightened sash-belt would hold it there. I stashed my Bowie knife and mini compass into leg pockets and a tiny canteen of water into a hip pocket. My baggy pants with my floppy jacket covered a lot of body and hid my stuffed pockets—and, I hoped, me. I was a round-eye in Asia, and I knew only too well that there were damn few of those anywhere near where I was standing.

"Call me Charlie," the voice said. "Be sure to stick close to me, I'm going to be with you while you're here."

"OK," I answered—my voice audibly trembling, but only slightly.

I was led to the back of the first lorry, which was about the size of a large golf cart, its engine purring like a lawnmower. Apparently this one would lead the way, with the other to follow in a minute or two for appearance's sake, in case anyone was watching. From the way Rich, Brawner, and Swirsky darted into the other one, it was obvious that this was serious business. They didn't just shuffle over—they sprinted to their vehicle in a crouch and jumped aboard.

Out of the darkness, Gigi slid in and squatted on the low platform behind the driver's seat, next to me. This was a woman I now didn't recognize. Her eyes were squinty, her lids unnaturally slitted, and she wore a grim look. I could sense her body next to me, now hard and taut. Part of that tautness had to do with a loaded shoulder holster she'd strapped on outside her jacket. And for once, there was no lemony fragrance—just sweat.

Suddenly I realized that while we'd been changing clothes, the Porter had gone, and my innards immediately tightened up. What? Where was our way out? Then I spotted the faint outline of the plane's tail tucked in bushes under some huge trees. Miguerre had silently sneaked off, taxiing over to a secluded spot off the strip. The propeller was still turning slowly; ready to move at a moment's notice—even to take off almost straight up, if needed.

Charlie stretched a dirty, foul-smelling canvas cover over us, turning the lorry into a mini-motorized covered wagon. We pulled away softly and quickly found ourselves on badly rutted back roads. As we lurched and bumped along, Gigi and I tried to keep our heads down and to avoid breathing any more of the noxious diesel fumes than necessary. I noted gratefully that the engine drowned out the sound of my heartbeat, which moments earlier had been so loud that I was sure anyone nearby could hear it.

We putt-putted along for what must have been about twenty minutes and then felt the lorry pull to a soft stop, the engine still running.

In the darkness, Gigi startled me with a brusque whisper over the hum of the lorry. "You have the kit?"

"Yep."

"Get the antibiotic ready. You're going to give him the shot as soon as we get in there. Then we grab him and get back to the plane."

In other circumstances, her officious manner would have rankled me. I was far too nervous for that now, though, as I rested on my elbow under a rotting canvas, trying to fill a syringe by the paltry light of a penlight held in my teeth.

I shut the little case, the syringe inside, and then tried to ask coolly, "So that's all I do, right? Just stick him in the ass with the penicillin?"

I was trying to muster a little bravado, but Gigi slapped me right down. "Yes, that's all you do. Just stick him," she said, adding, "and then stay clear of any other activity. OK?"

We moved out on what felt like cobblestones but soon came to a halt again. The engine cut, and several seconds passed before Charlie pulled back the canvas enough for us to see where we were, parked some 200 yards away from an unlit crossing with one or two houses and a few shacks tucked into a copse of trees and undergrowth. Charlie pointed to a run-down, scruffy house set back off the street. I could make out tall shrubs, a thatched roof with a flowering vine draped over one side, and a dim light in the window.

"That's it. That's the house," Charlie said. "Get ready."

I marveled at the smoothness of the operation so far. My adrenaline rush now had reached its peak. I was trembling, and my kneecaps were jerking. As we waited for Rich and the others, I watched Charlie toying with something that looked like a small Cupid's bow. Noticing me, he said matter of factly, "Mini-cross-bow. They fire very small darts, very accurately. Not a heavy, pull, metal-tipped darts. Darts are quieter and cheaper than bullets. For close-in work, it's real quiet. If you get them in the neck or the throat, they only make a tiny squeal." He chuckled quietly.

Within a few minutes, the other lorry pulled up behind ours, and all the passengers piled out quickly. Sore from the ride and fighting off a leg cramp, I allowed myself a quick stretch and then crouched down in the darkness with Rick and the rest.

--•--

WHAT HAPPENED NEXT WOULD REMAIN firmly etched in my mind forever—just like the bombing run with Antoine. It all probably lasted only a few minutes, but it seemed so much longer. I first heard Rick ask Charlie, "What about the guards?"

"No signal yet," said Charlie.

"What guards?" I whispered to Gigi, panicked to hear that we might have been expected.

"Didn't you notice those guys standing around in the shadows, smoking?" she whispered back sharply. I hadn't seen anything.

"Those are guards, they're local cops," Rick muttered to me. "Our first group will take them out before we go up to the house. One of our men will flip a lighted cigarette butt towards us with a high arc. That's our signal to move up to the house."

Take them out. Just like that. I'd served in the wartime Navy and then spent years as a surgeon, so I had seen more than my share of death. But I'd never sat waiting for anyone to be killed in the darkness just a stone's throw away, and I now was sweating bullets under my jacket. Busying myself, I made sure I had my syringe ready, its needle "safed" into a little glass container through a rubber dam on top.

Looking up, I saw the red light of a cigarette arc through the darkness and land in front of the house. Someone's little cross-bows must have done their job. Charlie stood up and said, "No more cops—let's go." Running quietly, we sped along a narrow gravel path through uncut grass, approaching the house from the side. The door opened as we crossed the tiny porch, and the whole group slipped quickly inside.

Two kerosene lanterns provided a surprising amount of light in the gloomy hovel. There was much movement—lots of quick shuffling and muted whispering. Each one of us had a specific task, and apparently, each was doing it. Gigi was helping a tiny woman jam clothes, folders, and pamphlets into a carryall.

As I readied to do my part of the drill, a dreadful stench assailed me, and I realized that in fact, the whole house stank. It was the smell surgeons encounter when draining a lung abscess, the fetid odor of rotting meat. The likely source was the padré himself—his coughed-up pus and just plain dirty surrounds. I couldn't imagine anyone living in such a hovel; to be ill and confined in such a place taxed the imagination. It was little more that a death chamber, and we needed to get out fast—all of us.

Charlie motioned toward the back room. "He's in there—get ready." I stepped under a pinned-back piece of fabric and was able to make out a lanky figure sprawled on a large pallet next to a kerosene lamp and a host of bottles and jars. This was our patient, the padré, and obviously, he was a very sick critter. He couldn't have weighed more than a hundred pounds and only moved when his chest heaved. I could hear him gurgling and coughing with each breath, at times almost suffocating. Actually, that coughing could save his life if he could keep it up. It was his body's feeble effort to clear out the copious fluid in his throat. Unfortunately, though, the poor bastard was almost too weak, which meant that he'd soon drown in his own pus. What he needed was a bronchoscopy, for certain, and maybe even a tracheotomy to keep his airway clear, plus an antibiotics-and-drainage regimen. All that meant getting him to a real hospital—Without it, he'd soon be dead. Looking at him, I had serious doubts that this guy would make it anyway. So what were we waiting for?

Cautiously, Charlie and I approached the figure, unable to tell in the dim light if he was awake. I called out to him. No answer. I took out the syringe and signaled to Charlie to roll the padré over on his side—I needed a buttock. Charlie rolled him over; I pulled the sheet back, tugged down a sagging waistband, and promptly sank the 18-gauge needle into what was left of his scrawny, almost emaciated rear end. The needle slid in without resistance—in fact, I felt it bounce off some bone, but the ailing padré didn't even flinch. Pushing the plunger quickly, I drove a million units of Uncle Sam's finest penicillin right into this fellow's godly ass, and just as the syringe emptied, the old boy reacted. He sat up suddenly and let out a raspy howl, at the same time coughing up a mouthful of dark, rotten-smelling goo that dribbled out of his mouth onto the thin sheet that had covered him. I could hear more bubbling in the back of his throat, and the stench was as putrid as anything I'd ever smelled—living or dead. The poor son of a bitch smelled like a bloated, rotting carcass—the sum total of pus, effluent, and body odor. The injection had hurt, to be sure, but for once, those CIA medical folks in Washington had guessed right. The penicillin probably would buy the padré at least a little more time, and now that he had it, my part was done. I just wanted out.

Charlie took a cloth and wiped the slobber off the padré's chin. Then he grabbed Rich's arm and began talking quietly into his ear. Both did some head shaking. Then I heard "OK."

At a hand-signal from Rich, the two lorry-drivers grasped the four corners of the padré's bottom sheet and hefted him up, out, and down the walkway to the nearest of the two lorries. Now Rich was speaking quietly into his hand-held transceiver. It was almost check-in time, so it must have been Miguerre or the co-pilot on the other end. Looking at his wristwatch, Rich gave a final affirmative nod and then snapped his fingers softly. Swirsky, Brawner, Gigi, Mei-Ling, Charlie and I filed out behind him, exiting the fetid little house. The front door was closed quietly, with nary a squeak from hinges that Rich had oiled when we entered. Glancing sideways as I stepped off the porch, I saw no trace of any Chinese cops and guessed that their bodies had been dragged off and hidden. No one had said it, but I knew exactly what we all wanted right now: for these cops not to be missed before we got in the air.

Moving quickly, we all piled into the purring lorries and started back to the landing spot. So far all had gone well, without incident. No one, no police, had been expecting us at all. On our entry route, we'd seen only a few lights—mostly kerosene lamps and an occasional harsh sodium vapor lamp set high above an intersection. As for people, all we'd seen was an occasional bicycler. Not one single pedestrian.

From a home we passed as we rumbled along, I caught a savory whiff of cooking. I hadn't eaten all day, and the scent of garlic and ginger made me realize that I was hungry—which meant my adrenaline was wearing off and that soon fatigue would set in. I was tiring sooner than the others, it seemed, but I knew that would improve when I clambered back aboard the Porter. I couldn't wait to get back on that plane and fly out.

The lorries slowed to a halt alongside the open field, I looked around, again my heart began drumming in my chest Damn! There was no Porter in sight—not even the sound of an idling motor! When we'd left, it was hidden in the nearby brush, but by now it should have taxied back to us. I strained my senses, hoping to hear the high-pitched whine of Porter's engine. Still nothing. No cricket chirps, not even a night-bird call. All I could hear was the padré's gurgling—sadly the only sign that he was alive. There was nothing anyone could do for him here or now, and it was obvious that he didn't have long. The rest of us stood waiting, staring at the darkened field.

Momentarily, Mei-Ling sat on the ground with her knees pulled up to her chin and the padré stretched out beside her. Standing next to her was Gigi, who was now all business. In the last few hours, she had barely acknowledged my presence at all, making mostly fleeting eye contact with no change of expression. Instead of the hauntingly beautiful face, there now was only a cold, bleak look, like that of an unhappy mother-in-law. This was one cool, controlled woman. Could this be the same hot-blooded siren I knew in Saigon? Yes, it was, and I understood. This was business, it was show time. A mission had to be completed, extracting a terrified Mei-Ling, sitting there at her feet, along with the extra baggage—the padré. No time for niceties.

Where the hell was the plane?

I was close to panicking, but no one else seemed especially concerned that the Porter hadn't appeared out of the dark mist. We waited and waited some more. Five minutes passed; then five more. It was altogether too calm, at least for me. But the group's tension level had dropped appreciably by now, and I decided I knew why. The job was almost over, and we were almost out. At least we haven't been discovered, I told myself. Right?

And just then, as though out of nowhere, a large, dark blob materialized quietly out of the gloom to our left and rolled to a stop in front of us. One minute nothing, the next a whispery whine announcing the Porter's return. Hallelujah!

Charlie and his men quickly unlatched the cargo door and shoved the padré aboard atop a pile of blankets. Mei-Ling and Gigi hurried into seats along the bulkhead, and I prepared to climb aboard and join my patient.

Then disaster struck.

Above the subdued whine of the turbo engine came the sound of a coughing motor approaching. A small car with its engine racing came hurtling out on the field. It turned and headed straight for us—horn honking, headlights flashing, high-pitched voices shrieking. Suddenly there were blinking flashes and popping sounds.

Gunfire! Shit! The jig was up! The dead cops had been found—or maybe one had survived and reported the padré's removal. Maybe relief guards had showed up, maybe an officer just checking. Whatever had happened, we'd been found out, and there was nothing to do but fight it out as best we could.

I fell to the grass as Rich and his gang spun into action, returning fire with automatic weapons fitted with sound suppressors—no roaring gunfire, just muffled pops. After being hit by a few rounds from our weapons, the oncoming car veered sharply to one side, than tumbled over and skidded to a stop. The driver had been hit; I could see holes in the shot-up windscreen.

That took care of that, I thought as I got to my feet. Two of our men had been grazed by handgun fire, but nothing serious. The plane had taken several rounds, but of no real consequence, either. Rich barked an order for everyone leaving to get aboard, and I stepped over to the plane.

Looking within, I noticed the plane's insides had been converted. The few remaining seats now were along the sides to accommodate our stretchered patient on the cabin floor. And in the dim cabin lights, I could see a huge splotch of blood standing out starkly on the patient's shirt. Startled, I looked closer and had my fears confirmed: The padré had taken a round. He'd been shot in the chest!

As I leaned over him, I saw pulses of thick, putrid pus bubble out of the fresh chest wound. With each labored breath, the rancid fluid was oozing and spurting all over his shirt and running down onto the blankets. Raising a hand to quiet Gigi and Mei-Ling, I listened closely to the padré's breathing, and sure enough, there were still bubbling sounds, and while the breathing continued, the sounds were growing weaker. I laughed involuntarily and then realized that I better explain myself. This gunshot wound, of all things, was helping. It meant pus and gases were escaping from the lung abscess. Imagine: a man is shot in the chest, and instead of killing him, it might actually be saving him. Pus was draining out of the wound and not burbling up into his trachea to threaten his airflow. Sure, the padré still had to be taken to a hospital where trained surgeons could attend him, where they could insert a drainage tube into his chest and even clean out his windpipe. He'd need antibiotics and heavy-duty care. If he were lucky, he might even live.

I looked for a seat and suddenly got a sinking feeling. We had added two passengers, and the plane only carried six the way it was configured. I could do the math but was stunned at what seemed like the answer. I wheeled and looked at Rich behind me and noticed he had taken a small bag out of the plane.

"We gotta send these folks on, Doc," Rich said offhandedly. "They've got fuel in the tanks, and they should make Chiang Mai easy—that's where the military has a medical setup."

Raising the bag's strap to his shoulder, he squared up and looked me in the eye. "You, me, and Charlie are going to hike out."

Huh?

Hike out? Me? But we all knew I was supposed to be on the plane! That was the deal!

Dumbfounded and infuriated, I looked quickly at stone-faced Gigi sitting across from the open hatch where I stood. She had known, too; it explained her strained expression. I leaned toward her in an accusatory manner to add to her discomfort. She pursed her lips, but there was no change in her taut features, which were grave with concern. Still looking at the padré at her feet, she gave a riffled finger wave, a sort of goodbye. No smile, no eye contact—nothing.

And that was it. There was nothing I could do about it. There would be no plane trip, no disembarking with my patient in Chiang Mai. Instead, I was to be left behind in the early-morning darkness of rural Communist China with two commandos who had just killed a couple of policemen and surely would be blamed for the deaths of the others at the house. I didn't need any old hand at the spying game to tell me that there was a good chance I'd get caught and executed. And once I had, no one would ever know what happened to that silly American surgeon who left Saigon for Laos and never came back. Pity. *Merde*.

Hope and luck had deserted me. But still, I was a doctor—I had a responsibility. I leaned back into the cabin and said brusquely, "Well, whoever's taking charge of this guy, make sure you keep him lying on his bad side. The pus will drain faster that way. Keep his head up, his mouth clear, and his face clean. If you can call ahead by radio, alert the base hospital. They'll have to do an emergency bronchoscopy, maybe a tracheotomy, and definitely insert a chest tube. He may need blood and IVs. Try not to fly above ten thousand feet. If you do, slap an oxygen mask on him."

Glaring furiously at Gigi, I stepped back from the plane. Charlie and Rich slammed the cargo hatch shut and slapped the fuselage like a horse's backside. The turbo engine revved up, and in a few seconds, they were all on their way. The plane did a very short roll before disappearing into the gloom.

Just like that it was quiet. The Porter was gone. And here I was, quite possibly a goner, too—duped into getting myself dropped in

Communist China and now left here in the darkness at the end of a trail of dead bodies.

Now what?

CHAPTER 14

By Hoof and Mouth Through Yunnan

Out where the handclasp's a little firmer, out where the smile dwells a little longer, that's where the West begins.
—Arthur Chapman, Eastward Ho! *(1603)*

If I had known I was to be left to forage my way back to freedom, I might have brought a map. Instead, this is the complete list of what I was left with to make my way out of China: a change of clothes, a knife, a pistol, a flashlight, a handful of medical supplies, a camera, some film, and a fountain pen.

At least I am in the company of seasoned commandos, I told myself. After all, Rich and Charlie—in whose hands my safety now rested—were still alive and had got me this far. That counted for something. Didn't it?

"Come on, Doc, give us a hand," I heard. Together, we pushed one of the lorries towards the overturned sedan and tipped it over, too. Charlie tore a long strip from a towel and yanked open the fuel cap, sliding the towel into the tank. Then he pulled it out and tore it once lengthways, turning it into a long, shaggy fuse. Calmly, he pulled out his cigarette lighter, struck up a flame, and held it under the wet fringe of the towel's end. Blue flame began licking along the wick: it was time to move. Rich, Charlie, the other driver, and I quickly scrambled into the remaining lorry and putt-putted toward the far end of the field—a maddeningly slow ride, I thought. I wanted to get away, and much faster.

We turned onto another rutted road and began chugging down it when the fuel tank in the first of the two vehicles ignited, lighting up the darkness behind us and finally setting the other tank aflame. I heard a low whooshing sound and then a muffled whoomph. Amazingly, the tanks didn't explode. "Why not?" I asked.

Rich explained that properly set, a gasoline fire would burn rather than explode, reducing both vehicles to charred, unrecognizable masses that would include the local cops who had chased and fired on us. It wouldn't do to have those bodies found. Charlie offered that he had considered burning down the padré's manse, too, but decided against it. No sense making a commotion while we were attempting to put distance between us and the authorities, who would soon be on the lookout for us. One comforting thought was that someone who heard the Porter depart might convince our pursuers that we'd been aboard. But knowing the Chinese, they would still put out an alarm. It was imperative for us to move out.

Shifting into a higher gear as a straight stretch of road appeared, Charlie muttered that we had some fast traveling to do. Glancing at my luminous dial, the time was just after one in the morning. Amazingly, what seemed like just a few minutes had taken four hours. I saw my medical kit and camouflage clothes in the lorry with us. For now I'd hang on to them; no telling when they might come in handy.

--•--

CHARLIE HAD OFTEN PASSED HIMSELF off for a local; he even spoke the Yunnan patois. But Rich and I were going to be a problem. At some point, Rich had changed into a nondescript, rumpled jacket and some wrinkled pajama pants, and from a safe distance he might just pass for a coolie. Still, he and I were both taller than the average Chinese and were likely to attract attention. Pale faced and round-eyed, we surely would have trouble being taken for anything but what we were: two white men in the wrong place.

Disguise and all, Rich was a study in serious: a commando knife tucked in his boot, a flat-bladed throwing dagger sheathed under his skivvy shirt behind his neck, and a small machine pistol slung across his back. He was one formidable, tough-looking chap.

After a couple of hours or so at the wheel, Charlie stopped to let the other driver off at a dark crossroads. Not long afterwards, he pulled up at a small house in the countryside, where there were two occupants waiting up, expecting us. Charlie spoke with them briefly, and Rich and I drew furtive glances. Charlie passed over some money and said *sheh-sheh*, which I guessed meant thanks. We slipped inside.

The tiny cottage was sparsely furnished. It was little more than a primitive hut with pallet beds and sad-looking headrolls, plus a charcoal fireplace for cooking and an outdoor toilet. Chickens and ducks left the back yard nothing but mud and fowl droppings, and from the smell, there may even have been a pigsty nearby. I saw a few other shed-like structures immediately behind the cottage in various stages of disrepair. One had a sagging roof. No observer would be interested in this place, would they? Who in his right mind would want to hide here?

The answer: We would. The plan, Rich said, was for us to hole up here for the next day or so while the initial swarm of police activity died down. Then we'd make our way out of China by a southwestern route. Following my companions' lead, I lay down on a pallet to get some sleep.

-- • --

IT WAS MIDDAY WHEN I woke up to the sound of Rich's steady breathing across the room and animals in the yard. Aching, I realized that I'd been so exhausted by the adventure with the padré that I'd slept for a solid seven hours on little more than a hard wooden platform.

The rest of the day passed slowly, as we listened for any sign of trucks or car and discussed what we'd be doing next. Pointing to his thin, oilskin map, Rich located us near the town of Yumchao, about 400 miles north and slightly west of Muong Sing in Laos. I was relieved to hear that there indeed was an extraction plan for us, taking us directly southwest to a little town at the foot of the Ail Shan Mountains called Oolong, not far from Kunming. Locals there didn't much respect orders from Party headquarters and did what they damn well needed to get by, Rich added. The older ones would remember the dashing American pilots during World War II who flew the China-India-Burma route, bringing planeloads of material in by the back door of a Japanese-occupied country.

We would drive the lorry in that general direction, maybe changing vehicles once or twice. At Kunming, Rich would use his transceiver and try contacting our military in the Udorn and the Chiang Mai regions of Thailand on a preset frequency to arrange a land-and-grab operation. Patrolling the Yunnan-Burma border with swift twin-engine craft, these U.S. crews would be monitoring the Signal Corps Radio frequency assigned to Rich. If one of those planes was airborne when Rich was transmitting, contact would be likely—but only then. We'd have to be lucky. If we ran into trouble, our first contingency plan was to hike over to the Mekong River and float down, offloading in Thailand. If worse came to worse, we had yet another option, the Salween River that would carry us down into Burma. These were longer, arduous, and more dangerous routes, to be used only if the pick-up near Kunming fell through.

As the sun came up the next morning, we climbed back into the lorry to test our luck.

--•--

KUNMING WAS ABOUT 200 MILES away. Allowing for crowded roads, stops to rest, and vehicle changes, Charlie had estimated that we'd be lucky to make 75 miles a day—and we absolutely had to avoid the military, the police, and the just plain nosy. For cover, we had loaded our small lorry with several baskets of local produce and set out, going from one town to the next trying not to attract attention—just like legitimate farmers or peddlers. Remarkably, it seemed to work: no one paid any attention to us. Rich and I kept our heads down, stayed in the lorry, and never looked or made eye contact with anyone. Rich and I pulled dirty coolie hats down over our faces, with wisps of scraggly hair hanging below the hat-brims and lightly-shaved chins to make us resemble local peasants—which we did, as long as our round eyes weren't visible.

That first morning and afternoon passed uneventfully. As the evening approached, Charlie stopped at a roadside stand, gladhanding vendors and buying cooked rice and dumplings. We then found a place to overnight in a copse of trees by some fields, unloading the baskets and stretching out—the three of us, head-to-toe—in the back of the lorry.

The second day was similarly quiet, and as it wore on, I began to wonder if there really was anyone looking for us at all. That night, we stopped outside the town of Hangping, far enough away from the main drag to avoid the curious and the police. Through his network, Charlie had made arrangements for us to stay in a shed behind a farmer's cottage, set back from the main road.

Once we were safe inside the shed, our farmer host and Charlie began speaking in the local dialect. There was a great deal of loud chatter back and forth, and it seemed like shouting, but apparently it was just an ordinary conversation. From their polite facial expressions, I surmised that everything was going according to plan. Soon we all supped on huge bowls of noodles with onions, pieces of meat, and huge kernels of horse corn all mixed together. There was also a large bowl of steamed greens on which we sprinkled soy, and for dessert, several locally grown oranges—small, thin-skinned, and delicious.

Between seed-spitting—these oranges were extremely seedy—I struck up a conversation with Charlie. "How did you ever get in this line of work?"

Charlie smiled, said, "Beats working for your father," and turned away.

When we were done, the farmer and Charlie carried bowls and other dishes back to the cottage, and when Charlie returned, the three of us bunkered down, hoping for sleep. Crickets chirped outside in the darkness; somewhere an owl hooted. Unlike earlier nights, Rich never quite seemed to sleep; he just appeared to be in a continuous, semi-dozing state. After some time, we were all stirred by a soft, shuffling sound outside the shed, and Rich sat up, instantly alert. His pig-sticker knife had been kept at the ready, point-down in the soft earth beside his headrest. Near his butt, within easy reach, was his handgun, and he could flip off its safety and aim in seconds. His other weapon, the machine pistol, had been horizontally stashed under the wide flap of his backpack. Obviously, Rich had done this sort of drill before.

Charlie had hand-weapons and a knife, too. But I'd noticed earlier that his palms—especially the outer edges—were calloused, a sign of a martial-arts man; those palms could be killers. Just in case, he carried a small automatic tucked in his boot as backup. I had my weapon and my knife—and was terrified at the thought that I might have to use them.

A moment later, things were quiet again, but the excitement meant that no one was going back to sleep anytime soon. Since we were awake, I goaded Charlie into finishing his story about how he'd gotten into the undercover-spook business.

— - • - —

FROM CHILDHOOD, CHARLIE HAD WORKED in the family restaurant in San Francisco's Chinatown, he said, his family having made their way originally to Vancouver and then southward down the coast. As he grew into his teens, Charlie found work at the family restaurant a drudgery; being studious and intelligent, he badly wanted to break out of the narrow, crowded confines of Chinatown. Out of the blue, he converted to Catholicism, won an academic scholarship to a Catholic college, and was on his way—or so he thought. When graduation came, he found himself back in Chinatown, of all things, working yet again at the family's now-sprawling tourist-attraction restaurant. The turn of events dismayed him; he had a college degree and was still shoveling out dumplings.

One afternoon, two men came into the restaurant. Charlie noticed their glances and began to wonder if they were scrutinizing him. They ordered, sipped tea, and finally one of them called him over.

"Good evening, gentlemen—everything OK?"

"Sure. We just wanted to talk with you. Are you Chai Cheng Huang?"

"Yes, I am," Charlie answered, surprised.

"Father Wintermeyer told us you'd just finished college. He's a good friend of ours, and when we told him we were looking for someone that fit your background, someone like you, for...a particular position, he mentioned you. He thinks very highly of you. Is there some place we can talk?"

"Sure."

Charlie led the visitors to a side dining room where the men introduced themselves as recruiters for the U.S. government and asked him if he might be interested in a new career. He jumped at the offer.

In time, Charlie had become a valued and busy operative, sent time and again into the country from which his family had come—while always remaining a loyal American, he was quick to add. ("I am Chinese-American, true, but the communists in China are brutal to their own people and their neighbors," he said, "while America took my family in.")

As he spoke, Charlie never referred to "Central Intelligence" or any "agency." And it occurred to me that Rich didn't, either. I was finally learning not to ask too many questions—developing a feel for what I could and couldn't bring up. Anyway, the important part was what was obvious: Charlie was a San Francisco man of Chinese extraction, out here in the land of his ancestors with two round-eyed American compadres—potentially in very deep shit. If we were caught, things would go bad for all of us, but probably worst of all for him.

The prospect was too terrifying to think much about, lying here in the dark in a filthy shed a couple of hundred yards from the road to town. For the moment, the only escape was sleep.

— - • - —

RICH AND I ROSE AT the din of rooster calls to find Charlie squatting by the shed door, looking preoccupied—knitted brows, squinting eyes. Something wasn't right.

We cleaned up as best we could and then downed sticky rice cakes, chunks of cold duck meat, and tea that Charlie had set aside the night before. Carrying our little bundles of weaponry, flashlights, and clothing, we slipped out and made our way behind the main hut to the lorry's parking place. Coolly, Charlie muttered that by his calculations, we ought to make it to Kunming within the next twelve hours. At that, Rich checked his SCR batteries; he'd be making his first call around noon to see what was flying.

Then Charlie let out a breath and delivered a shocker: the farmer's dead body was under the baskets in the lorry!

What the hell was going on?

No wonder Charlie had seemed tense when we awoke. He explained quickly: Our farmer host had procured a group of local ladies, who had been waiting inside the cottage for us, to keep us men warm at night—for an extra fee. When told this upon our arrival, Charlie had politely declined: We were tired, he said; maybe we'd stop again on the return leg of our trip, but not this time. The farmer was insistent, saying that he was already out some money for the women and that we were not showing proper respect for him and his hospitality. To quiet him for the moment, Charlie had given him a small amount of money but concluded that this man would likely squeeze him for cash again in the morning and then blow the whistle on us as soon as we'd left.

When Charlie had helped carry the dishes back to the house, he was relieved to find the women gone and the house empty; once the farmer turned away from him, Charlie had swiftly delivered quick chops to each side of his neck, mashing his carotid arteries, killing him on the spot. Knowing that we had nowhere else to sleep but that someone could come by and find the dead farmer, Charlie had stashed the body in the lorry and covered it. I was totally dumbfounded. This man had been alive and chatting with us last night, and now here before us he lay dead in the cart. Charlie had calmly killed him. I felt saddened and remorseful, but at the same time I was aware that the other way around, leaving him alive, would have meant we might end up dead. That brought some solace to my concerns. But there was no time for recriminations. We had to move, and quickly.

The plan now, he said, was dump the lorry with the body in a ravine, load and all. It would appear that the farmer had driven off the road with his truckload of goods and gone into the ravine, breaking his neck. It would be a while before anyone figured out what really had happened, if ever.

We started out and before long came to a drop-off a few stories high with a rocky creek at the bottom. With no one in sight, we pushed the throttle lever to high, depressed the clutch, and held it down with a short length of bamboo tied to a piece of string. Then we gave the truck a shove, and Rich yanked the string: the clutch engaged, and off she went. Adios to one greedy farmer.

We were now on our own, on foot and in China. Oh, bully!

Taking off down the road, we agreed that we needed some other form of transportation, and soon, if only to get the hell away from the crash scene.

We pushed on. I was thirsty and hot—and, worse, I'd developed loose stools and needed to run behind a bush every ten or fifteen minutes. Blessedly, I found that my medical kit had antidiarrhea pills; I popped two, and all gut activity ceased almost instantly. I also lost my appetite. No matter.

After a half hour of trudging, with no one giving us a second look, Charlie pointed out a warehouse surrounded by fences a short distance from the road. Inside the compound were a number of small vehicles parked in orderly rows. This looked promising to Charlie and Rich, and from a nearby clump of bushes, we watched silently as cars and trucks came and went through a guard gate. We noticed that some vehicles appeared to exit behind the buildings then suddenly appear on the main road. Rich and Charlie would reconnoiter: there must be a back exit. I settled down behind some high grasses and, drowsy from pills, drifted off.

Without warning, a hand soon shook me. I tried to jump up, but the hand held me down. Rich chuckled, "It's OK, Doc, it's us."

Sitting down, he explained: "Looks good. We found some pickups parked behind the main building. I think I can hotwire one, get it running. Tonight, we'll go to the back exit. Charlie will give the guard some bullshit about taking the truck for repairs to deliver it to the next town by dawn, and we'll just wing it from there. There should be only one guard, and if we have to, we'll take him out."

Groggy and worried, I asked, "How do you guys start an engine without a key?"

Rich and Charlie looked at each other and grinned. I think Rich snorted.

"I been boosting engines since I was thirteen." said Rich. "You don't need a key—you just find the right wires at the ignition, scrape off the insulation and touch them together. The starter kicks over when contact is made. Some of these factory vehicles don't even have a key, just an on-off switch. The important thing is to have a vehicle with a hot battery, so you pick a vehicle which shows recent use, like fresh mud on its tires."

This plan did nothing to allay my already seriously jangled nerves. But these guys were pros, and I was under their protection. For them, I sensed, killing was something they did when the occasion demanded. It wasn't an emotional act, but rather a simple matter of business—totally impersonal.

We sat in the bushes and waited. Charlie had some food and water from the farmhouse in his knapsack. I still wasn't hungry, but I sipped fluid—replacement water, I figured—and chewed a rice cake. We'd nap until midnight and then make our move. As I dozed, my mind drifted to thoughts of pilots and others who had crashed in the jungle, waiting for rescue. They were alone, frightened and maybe hunted. I wondered how many had survived. With me here, though, were two seasoned men who seemed quite at home in this sort of caper. Were I more religious, this would have been the time for prayer.

Finally it was time. Rich planned to use his Swiss Army knife for the hotwiring, and I gave him a roll of surgical tape and a hemostat, thinking that the clamp might come in handy as a substitute pliers and the tape could hold the crossed wires together. I, being the least skilled in these events, was directed to wait in the high grass at the roadside while Charlie and Rich slipped in, found a vehicle, and drove to the main road where I'd be waiting.

Stealthily, they moved out. When my watch showed that twenty minutes had passed, I grabbed my stuff and made my way to the main road. It was dark, but there was enough starlight for me to make my way; I would have five minutes to spare. Except for a night bird calling from the woods, all was silent.

From the direction of the tiny guardhouse at the main gate, I heard high-pitched, whiny music, probably a radio. Otherwise, all was still; this early in the morning the road was empty. Moments later, I heard an automobile engine laboring toward me on the main road, coming from the direction of the rear exit. A blue, four-door sedan covered in dust pulled up, and the rear door popped open. Rich's voice croaked urgently: "Get in, Doc—we gotta haul ass."

I did, and that was that. Did the guard die? I never knew. Fixated on getting out of sight and on to our pick-up site, I forgot to ask what happened in the parking lot and never found out. That's how trusting I had become of Charlie and Rich's training and preparation. When I thought about it, I could only marvel at what we'd done so far: We had now gone undetected in Red China for three days, which had to be some kind of record. Unbelievable! How much longer could this charade last?

We came upon a wide shoulder on the road, where Rich pulled over and switched seats with Charlie so that he could keep his face lowered in the hours to come. We pushed on to Kunming.

--•--

THE FUEL TANK WAS REGISTERING half-full, but this was a four-cylinder, fuel-sipping job that we'd swiped, and Charlie figured we had enough for the time being. He drove steadily and cautiously, avoiding larger towns and doing nothing to draw attention.

Under his lowered brim, Rich stared straight ahead, scanning the countryside; I stayed hunched over in the rear, quivering at times. As the miles rolled off, the countryside began to rise, and gradually the terrain became hillier and much prettier. The rushing streams and tall trees even reminded me of West Virginia. A few minutes later, in the far distance and through a bluish haze, I could see faint outlines of a mountain range. This had to be the Ail Shan range, and my heart leapt. Calculating by mileage, we were nearing the point at which radio contact with the airborne patrol might be possible—this was it, wasn't it? I fervently hoped so.

When we came upon an unmanned road-repair site, Charlie pulled off to the side and tucked our car behind the largest pile of gravel. "Pit stop," he declared. We got out, stretched and peed. Behind us, road traffic was picking up now—bicycles, small motorbikes, and any number of noisy trucks belching the usual black diesel exhaust. As we watched from our place of partial concealment, a big, two-wheel cart drawn by a team of two oxen came crawling along, going in our direction. We'd have to pass the snorting beasts and creaking wood once we got back on the road, and the sooner the better. We hurried back inside the car, grateful to find the road ahead clear around the cart. Charlie zipped past with no problem, and for the moment, our fortunes seemed to brighten. Still, I felt the occasional shudder of apprehension.

Rich began measuring distances on the chart with his thumb, and nodded, muttering, "Maybe." Powering up his SCR, he extended the antenna, put the receiver to his ear, and held up a pair of crossed fingers for my benefit.

"BirdDawg, BirdDawg, this is Skunk, over."

Nothing.

"BirdDawg, BirdDawg, this is Skunk, over."

Still nothing.

"Any Dawg, any Dawg, if you read, come in, over."

After a minute of fiddling with the squelch control and volume knobs, Rich snapped off power. All he'd heard was static.

"We're still too far away, or maybe the batteries are too weak, or nobody's up there right now. We'll just keep going and try again later."

I couldn't help but glance at the sky. Somewhere up there should be a swift, twin-engine, spotter-and-reconnaissance aircraft on patrol. New ones from North American Rockwell had made it to Asian bases now, Rich had said, using a two-man crew seated in tandem: one piloting the aircraft, the other observing, navigating, managing instruments, and handling radio and ground-surveillance radar. They even had automatic radio-frequency scanners that monitored preset radio frequencies—designed for just this kind of situation. Where were they?

We were coming up on noon now. The roads were filled with all manner of transport—wheels, feet, and hooves—and Charlie was noticeably more tense. Rich was expressionless. I remained slouched down in my seat, imagining the worst. The dead policemen at the padré's and the torched vehicles at the airstrip would have been reported to furious authorities two days earlier. By now our dead farmer and his lorry would be found and combed over, too. Someone could easily put two and two together, deducing our direction and alerting police all around us. Moving quickly was more important now than ever, but we could do little but crawl through one crowded hamlet after another on our route to the mountains.

Remarkably, no one paid any attention to us. No one even noticed us at all.

--•--

THE TIME FINALLY CAME TO turn toward the foothills to our north, and as we did, our path began curving and rising as we approached the mountain range. Also about this time, the now-laboring engine began missing and showing signs of strain. Surprisingly, the fuel gauge still showed just under a quarter tank. On the dashboard, I made out the word "Wartburg," written in Cyrillic—the car had been made in East Germany! God only knew how many miles it had on it, but it still chugged along, carrying us up to our point of departure. At this particular moment, I thanked East German engineers.

Rich suddenly piped up, "Bingo!"

"What is it, Rich?"

"Doc, look out there—see that soybean field? See that windsock on that pole at the end? That means only one thing. Cropduster planes. They fly over that field, so somewhere around here is an airstrip. We just gotta find it."

We searched along the foot of the range, skirting the hills until we came upon an area that was long, and flat, with no roads or water crossing it. This was the logical place for an airstrip.

Rich pointed and once again, a low "Hey, lookee yonder." About a half-mile ahead, we could just make out a cleared space of dirt running at a slight angle to the road. Rich took a quick chance and tried calling on his SCR; again lots of static, but no response. He shut it down again.

"These things work on line-of-sight at times," said Rich. "If our guys are up, they'll still be cut off from us by mountains. But if we can just find an airplane, like a parked one on a field, maybe we can rig something."

Charlie found a road that wound down through some trees, pulling over for a passing bicyclist at a nudge from Rich. The cyclist gave us a wave and said something like "Ho, hah," and Charlie gave back a "Ho, hah," adding something else. The bicycle man smiled and bobbed his head, pointed ahead, then pumped away towards the strip. When he was out of sight, Charlie pulled the car over beside a copse of trees and turned the engine off.

Rich pulled out his little telescope and surveyed the field in the distance. "Here's what we've got," he said. "I see two crop dusters that look Russian; an old DC-3 with no engine in one nacelle; an old Curtis C-46 on blocks; and a small German plane, like a messed-up old Fieseler Storch. And I see wires leading from the shacks to a pole, so they must have power. We ought to just watch a while."

We sat quietly, the minutes ticking by. Nothing. With no role to play, I was quickly losing patience; my mind would race with scenarios in which police, shrieking in Chinese and pointing guns at us, suddenly surrounded us.

I saw Charlie stiffen and point to the road. The cyclist was coming back our way.

"Guys, stay in the car, and don't move. I got an idea."

Charlie jumped out and waved at the cyclist. They chattered back and forth, the cyclist nodding agreeably as Charlie pointed to us and to the plane and to him. Then Charlie smiled and pointed to his wristwatch. More head bobbing, then the cyclist hopped on his bike and turned around, heading to the strip. Charlie came back.

"OK, listen up, my brave friends," he said, climbing in. "This guy is the manager of this crapped-up field. I showed him a Ministry of Information card with my picture on it and told him that you're a couple of visiting Russian newspapermen working on a story about the glorious farm communes and new pesticides and other baloney. We were just on the road, spotted his place, and thought it would make an interesting story—we'd walk around, take his picture, that kind of thing. So he's invited us over. I slipped him some Hong Kong dollars as a tip."

--•--

I COULDN'T SHAKE THE THOUGHT: when something seems too good to be true, it almost certainly is.

The first effect of survival genes, which mother had passed on to me, was to be wary. The three of us had just spent three days laying low and staying out of sight, and now we were going to try a little role-play, too. It seemed reckless: What if the strip manager spoke Russian? Would he be able to tell we were frauds? Tiny hairs on the nape of my neck were standing straight up—less out of fear than a feeling that something just wasn't right. I couldn't believe this fellow had bought such a cock-and-bull story, and I wondered if Rich had similar doubts. Still, I kept my mouth shut. To comfort myself, I fondled the handle of my pistol, pretending I was scratching my ass.

We drove up to the shack, got out, and walked up to the door of the larger shack. Charlie and Rich leaned in and took a good look around. Rich looked back at me and said, "There's big batteries charging up in there, and our man is boiling water, making us some tea. I think we go in and accept his hospitality here. We two are supposed to be Russians. I'll talk Russian to you, Doc, while Charlie does Chinese. When I look at you, just say '*da*.' If I rub my nose, nod and say '*spasiba*.'"

Inside the shack, we were greeted with bows and smiles and offered cups of steaming black tea and hard, almond-flavored biscuits. Following Charlie's lead, we stuck cubes of coarse sugar between our teeth and sipped at the tea—conveniently, I thought, because it kept us from having to talk for the moment. Charlie did his bit, chatting in Mandarin, then turning slowly to us and saying something in Russian. We nodded, "*da*" and "*spasiba*."

When we finished, Charlie pointed outside and led us back to the car. Facing our host, he gave a short bow and said something that had to be "thank you," and then he pointed to a parked crop-duster. Bicycle Man nodded rapidly and smiled widely, showing dingy yellowed teeth. He gestured as if to encourage us and then returned to the shack where we'd had tea.

The three of us walked idly around to the backside of the plane, preferring to be hidden from our host and from the road. The old, bi-wing duster was a huge Russian model, a monster of a plane with a big radial engine, lots of struts, a cargo door gaping wide open, and one tire half flat. Inside, we saw large tanks strapped to the cabin walls and patches of white crop-dusting powder lying in the bottom along with crushed paper cups, cigarette butts, and yellowed newspapers. All signs indicated "Nobody home." This thing wasn't getting airborne anytime soon.

"An Antonov," said Rich. "An AN-2, maybe. Anyway, a hell of a plane. Let's see if it has a radio." He climbed in, and a minute later his head appeared in the cockpit window. He gave us a thumbs-down and came out.

"It's got the frequency spread I need, but no batteries—what we really need right now is one of those batteries back there in the shack," he said in a low voice. "You know, I could probably fly this plane out too, if I had to, but we probably wouldn't get far. I bet they only leave enough fuel to keep the tanks wet between flights because they don't want defectors."

We were tantalizingly close. All we needed was to hook up a battery and power up the radio.

It was time to make that happen.

CHAPTER 15

A Lift from Birddawg

O Lord, thou hast searched me out and known me: thou knowest my down-sitting, and mine up-rising.
—Psalm 139:1, 2a (KJV)

Rich and Charlie had barely begun to plan something when the shack door swung open, startling us. Bicycle Man came out and walked slowly out to us. More smiles, head bobbing, and chatter, during which Charlie's face suddenly fell and then took on a look of rapture. Charlie promptly spread his arms as if praising the Savior. Still smiling, he reached into his pocket for what I now knew were paper Hong Kong dollars, but Bicycle Man waved him off. Charlie held up a hand, reached in his knapsack, and instead offered the real prize—a stack of solid-silver Hong Kong coins. Bicycle Man smiled broadly and took them.

"OK," said Charlie, pointedly not minding if he was overheard speaking English. "The fucking jig may be up around here, because this guy knows who we are. Government radio is all over the place, saying the police are looking for two 'foreigners'—three, if you include a 'China boy,' which means me. But we may be OK, 'cause this guy says he likes Americans. He says he worked at the airstrip at Kunming as a kid, unloading the planes that had flown the Hump. He says he even remembers General Chennault and the Flying Tigers. So he's going to help us power up the radio, I guess. And he let me know that the planes don't have enough fuel to take us very far, in case we

A LIFT FROM BIRDDAWG

had any other ideas. I gave him some silver *kumshaw*, but we better jump on this before he gets cold feet."

Moving quickly, we backed the car up to the shack door, lugged one of the bulky batteries out, and loaded it in the trunk. Once at the plane, we horsed the battery into its compartment onboard, which oddly was located in the rear of the fuselage. The now-helpful Bicycle Man hooked up one of the terminals.

As we worked, Charlie went on. "He also told me where to go to get us pulled out. About fifteen miles from here there's a hidden meadow up the mountainside, and smack-dab in the middle of it is a long lake that runs east-west. He told me the road to take. There's woods there, so we can hole up and wait."

Rich scurried into the cockpit and began flipping switches. I heard the whine of small motors and controls and instruments powering up. A few seconds later, we heard the radio speakers come to life with humming and scratchy static. Rich dialed in our SCR frequencies; grabbing the hand mike, he pushed the transmit button.

"BirdDawg, BirdDawg, this is Skunk, over."

Silence.

Once again. "BirdDawg, BirdDawg, this is Skunk—" and a voice came rattling back through the tinny overhead speaker.

"I read you four by four, Skunk, This here is BirdDawg. ID me one time."

"BirdDawg, we're Skunk from ComFive. Have no current ID. We're in deep. We need BirdDawg and his birdy right now, *muy pronto,* you catch? Over."

"Wait one."

"Roger that," Rich said. Several seconds passed.

"Skunk, this is BirdDawg. We need some better info. Stand by."

"Roger that, Dawg. Skunk standing by." This time, Rich shut his eyes and sighed.

"OK, Skunk. Who plays catcher for the Yankees?"

"Mostly Yogi Berra," said Rich without moving.

"What's Yogi say sometimes?"

Rich shot upright and yelled into the hand mike: "Yogi says I'm gonna kick the livin' shit outta you guys if you keep jerking me around, Goddamn it! We're in a bad situation here, and we gotta get the hell out! You copy? Right now is when you do the hero thing and come get us. Drinks on me at the nearest VFW. You copy?"

"OK, Skunk, we copy," the little speakers announced, with laughing audible in the background. "Read me some numbers."

"Dawg, stand by one." Grabbing his chart, Rich gave the grid coordinates without any coding. Then he gave his military serial numbers to be checked out via radio verification to somewhere. The minutes dragged on, but once Rich was identified, BirdDawg most likely would be told who was with him—or so I told myself.

Rich limited his remarks to bare essentials in case others were listening on the same frequency. I had already heard that the Chinese rarely monitored the alternate international distress frequencies— China was too big a country, and international distress calls were rarely made inside their territory. But a little caution couldn't hurt.

Skunk and BirdDawg had matching sector charts on which they confirmed grid numbers. Then Rich's aircraft transmitted what he and Charlie guessed were the coordinates of the mountain meadow from his chart. They'd have to re-transmit once we actually found the place.

"BirdDawg, we're heading over there, and we're gonna wait on you. We'll be hanging there in maybe two hours, max. We got an SCR, monitoring this frequency but can switch to 121.5 MHz if necessary. Give me a radio check one time for my SCR."

Rich clicked on the SCR, and reception was verified, which meant the transmitter was working, too: "Birdy, Birdy, radio check, you read?"

BirdDawg answered on the SCR: "Skunk boys, we read you five by five." That was the best news yet. Our aerial angels had heard our weaker SCR.

"That there's a Roger," said Rich. "We'll squawk you on this channel every twenty minutes. You guys gonna stick around?"

"Roger, Skunk, you men keep in touch. We gonna pick you up chop-chop from last coordinates. Us angels will guard this frequency and monitor the pick-up. Stay loose. Adios for now."

"Roger that. Be advised we have red flares. If we see you, and you don't hear us, we'll pop a flare, over."

"Hold off on that, Skunk—don't be shootin' no flares. Don't fuck up the lift. We're gonna get you, so stay loose, and wait for instructions. Dawgs is out."

--•--

WE HAD TO SUPPRESS OUR excitement at the prospect of getting yanked out. At last we'd made contact, and help would be waiting for us just a few miles away.

We returned the battery to the shed, and after more fast chatting, Bicycle Man handed us a package wrapped in a green leaf: his afternoon meal of rice, sliced duck, and squash. After Charlie expressed our gratitude, we waved and left. The staggering good fortune of running into Bicycle Man left me feeling protected by Providence. America's alliance with pre-Communist Chinese had ended with World War II fifteen years earlier; the odds of running into someone in China now who remembered U.S. airmen fondly had to be preposterously long. Surely this had to end well now, didn't it?

Out on the road, we once again chugged off in our heaven-sent escape chariot. These last few miles would clearly be difficult: there were no signs out here, so Charlie needed to be navigating—studying landmarks, checking the chart, and calling the shots. This put Rich behind the wheel, which clearly was risky. So he slumped a little and pulled his hat down again, just enough to see, but not be seen. We drove along for a maybe twenty minutes and then turned right at one intersection onto a muddy, one-lane road now winding directly into the mountains and, we hoped, to our place of deliverance.

Now we were climbing slowly through ruts and gullies. At times we spun our wheels, slithering dangerously close to the road's edge, green vegetation above and below us. After rounding one curve, we confronted a waterfall that had cut a deep trough across the road— too wide and deep for us. Rich turned the engine off, and we jumped out to fill the gap with downed branches, stones, and gravel. Finally, filthy and exhausted, Charlie and I got behind to push as Rich gunned across the loose, slippery pile. Looking at each other, we were a study in slate-gray mud, but our spirits were still rising, propelled by the anticipation of getting out.

After another hairpin switchback, we came suddenly upon a group of hikers filling their canteens from the same waterfall, but farther up the hillside.

"OK," Rich said, braking quickly, "We gotta stop." He pulled up, set the handbrake, and lowered his chin to hide his face. Then, in a whisper, he told Charlie to go over to the hikers and learn what he could about the road ahead while filling fill his canteen. Was there a meadow up here, or were we in the wrong place?

Charlie stepped over to the waterfall and laughed, pointing to his muddy appearance and back at us and waving his arms toward the mountaintop, chattering non-stop. One of the young lady hikers smiled at him shyly and said something. She opened her knapsack and handed him a bulging paper bag. Charlie offered exaggerated thanks, filled his canteen, and then walked slowly back to the car, waving farewell.

"OK, we just missed some solidarity picnic for workers at the meadow, which is up ahead here," he pointed towards the top of the road. "She thought I looked hungry and gave us their extra food. I told her we'd gotten lost but that we'd head up to the meadow now to eat." Charlie put the bag on the floor by my feet and took his place again up front. Rich revved up the engine, and we were off again, two of our hats tilted to hide our faces. More smiles and waves from the trekkers as we drove by. Beyond the next bend, we broke out onto a clear stretch of road. There in the distance was the meadow, and directly in front of us, the lake. In what was now a late afternoon sun, the setting was tranquil and heart-warming.

Now to call BirdDawg and meet the plane.

-- • --

AS WE APPROACHED ON THE hard-dirt road, we could see a picnic site with a wooden platform near a cluster of trees by the lakeshore. Two log structures nearby looked deserted, but smoke still rose from a stone fireplace, and we could smell the doused embers and what we guessed was the remains of pork grease cooking.

We were still some fifty yards from the cabins when the engine of our redoubtable stolen car spluttered and coughed, and its German heart stopped. As it died, Rich maneuvered it off the road, rolling a few feet downhill toward the water. We hadn't thought to refuel at the airport, and now we were on foot again; the car, having brought us this far, had chosen our pick-up spot for us.

Rich reached for the SCR while Charlie and I got out, looking around to see if we were alone. Immediately we had our answer: not everyone had gone home. The noise of the car had attracted the attention of two uniformed men with rifles slung over their shoulders who had stepped out from the far side of one of the buildings. Worse yet, they were looking directly at us.

Merde!

Charlie sized things up and turned slowly toward us. "These guys are probably local police—they're definitely not military. Maybe they just mooched in on the picnic and are hanging around to make sure the fire goes out. I'll go over." It was reassuring, but only slightly.

"Don't do anything stupid, OK?" Rich murmured, I assumed to me. "Charlie, go talk to them. We're going to get our guns. If they go to their weapons, I'll take them both down. But let's act loose. Got it?"

"Yeah, fine," I said, trying to sound as calm as he did. I stretched a little for effect and then leaned against the side of our dead vehicle, face turned toward the rear. Charlie walked toward the policemen, who now where slowly coming our way. Rich stepped idly around to the car's trunk, keeping an eye on the two men. He slipped a hand inside his jacket, loosening his knife in its underarm sheath. I shivered. My gun and my knife both were in the back of the car; if the shooting started, I'd have to try to dig them out in the fray, which seemed preposterous.

As I watched from the side of the car, one of the policemen hopped his bike and pedaled unhurriedly our way. He was doing lazy side-to-side turns as he moved our way. His buddy stayed just behind, still watching his partner. Rich said softly, "OK, heads up. Stay close to the car. Talk to him, Charlie."

When the bike cop reached us, Charlie greeted him in typical fashion, smiling and speaking with a raised voice. Bike cop replied with a stream of chatter that sounded angry. I saw Rich slip his SCR into his outer trouser pocket, switched on with the volume down— ready to call for help.

Charlie stepped back to the car and said in a low voice, "Rich, this guy doesn't believe me. He thinks we are the wanted people, and he's getting ready to do something stupid. I told him he was wrong and that I'd show him our IDs. So, I'm gonna turn to you, you're gonna pull out some papers and hold them out to me. When I turn to give them to him and he goes for them, I'll duck and you take him. OK?"

Charlie pointed towards Rich, talking and urging the policeman towards the car. Whatever the hell he said was beyond me, but it seemed to be working. Rich pulled a sheaf of papers from his knapsack and held them out to Charlie. The policeman got off his bike, and walked over slowly. Rich then put the papers on the hood of the car, saying in English and broken Russian that these were the documents, the permits from the Politburo Office. The policeman leaned over the hood to examine the papers. That was the last thing he saw. He flinched only slightly as Rich's knife slid swiftly and surely between his ribs, straight into his heart. Rich gave the knife a tiny side to side as he pulled it out and re-sheathed it. Bike Cop One had died instantly.

With one arm gripping the dead man by his shirt collar, Rich held the corpse upright and continued his talking act, telling Charlie to use one of the limp arms to wave a *come over* the other cop. Leaning in, Rich pulled out his crossbow.

Bike Cop Two was one very suspicious guy. Having unslung his rifle and laid it crosswise on his handlebars, he now was pedaling over slowly, also making lazy S-curves to see us from all sides. He called out to his *compadre*. Charlie, suddenly a ventriloquist, deftly answered for the corpse and then continued his charade of talking to the dead man, pointing to the papers on the hood. When he was still some fifty feet away, Two hopped off his bike and began walking slowly toward us with his rifle pointed at the ground while yelling loudly at his buddy. He was getting no answers from his companion and now knew something was amiss, but he wasn't sure just what. He leveled his rifle at us, finger on the trigger, waving it menacingly back and forth. He wanted us to move. "Stay loose," murmured Rich.

Charlie kept up his loud monologue, first to the dead cop and then, turning his way, to Bike Cop Two. Rich had eyed Two's rifle—an ancient Enfield bolt-action piece, by its looks—and assumed it was loaded, since the breech was closed. But it hadn't been—until now. Quickly, Bike Cop Two worked the bolt and chambered a round; now I felt tension aplenty. Charlie stepped back and gestured with a smile, inviting him to see the papers. The policeman advanced slowly, perplexed.

When he was about fifteen feet of us, he must have realized his partner was dead. His expression changed, and he flinched, as if to fire. Letting the dead body drop, Rich swiveled and fired his crossbow Kentucky-style. It was a silken movement, done in a flash—and a hell of a shot. The slim, steel shank penetrated poor Bike Cop Two's head right through his left eye, drilling straight into his brain. He twisted backward and fell, firing into the air in a last reflex. I stepped over and grabbed the rifle. Then, dammit, I began to shake again, and my innards convulsed. I should have been getting used to this sort of thing by now, but I hadn't, so it seemed. What bush could I disappear behind for a minute now?

More importantly, from the echo, it was clear that the sound of the gunshot had carried for miles. *Jesus, what if others heard it?*

All we could do now was hurry to dispose of two bodies. Wasting no time, Rich yanked out the steel dart and wiped it on the policeman's coat. Next, we hefted the bodies and slung them over the seats of their bikes, fast-trotting them to a large stand of rhododendrons behind the picnic area. Wedging our way into a space behind the bushes, we dumped the bodies and bikes and tossed fallen branches and twigs over them—not a great cover, but it would have to do.

"Man, that was an unbelievable shot," I said.

Rich gave me a blank look, and then a wink: "Thanks—got real lucky. I've been practicing for years." That was all he said.

For a place where two men had just been killed minutes earlier, the meadow seemed strangely quiet now, save the soughing of wind through the pines and the haunting cry of a loon from the lake. For now, anyway, it looked like we were safe.

Rich glanced at his watch: I heard him mumble "BirdDawg time." He switched the SCR on power and spoke into the microphone.

"Birdy, Birdy, Skunk here, over."

Immediately, BirdDawg responded: "Go, Skunk."

For a few minutes, they bantered in slang, with the airmen confirming both our coordinates and that our pick-up was authorized. We were told to stay put; extraction would be within the hour.

So what now? Should we push the car out of view, or even into the lake? Should we hide until the pick-up came, crouching in bushes? We just couldn't. Hearing that BirdDawg was on the way simply had loosened the tension too much. Wearily, Rich walked over to smoking firepits, where the bony remains of two roasted pigs had been left behind, and unconcernedly pulled off a few chunks. I sliced off two slabs and began munching, too. It was still warm and quite tasty, and I needed the fuel.

I washed it and a roasted yam down with water we'd picked up when passing by the picnickers. We then remembered the food given to Charlie by the girl at the waterfall and found it still warm. Polishing it off, we then lit into to the lunch from the fellow at that airfield we'd left. The unfamiliar feeling of food in our bellies was making us hopeful and even a little cocky.

Rich had left the SCR's power on, and suddenly it began squawking.

"Skunk boys, you-all down there?"

"Skunk here," answered Rich.

"Stand by, your angels estimating your location in fifteen minutes. I repeat one-fiver minutes. Craft is gonna be a camo Helio Courier. They'll do a low-level pass over you, then over where they plan to touch down, and then they'll do a sweep-and-land. Be advised: He'll be taxiing real slow with doors open, but he ain't gonna stop. So pile your sorry asses on board as toot sweet as you can. And negativo on them flares—negative flares. Yew copy?"

"Skunk copies."

"OK, Skunk Boy, we'll be flying shotgun overhead—just in case."

"Copy that, too; thanks Birdy. Next round's on us. Skunk standing by, we out."

Now the wait. Rich looked at his watch. Then: "I'm getting my red smoke flare out and ready anyway. A little red smoke won't hurt nobody. They may need to know the wind direction and all." I wondered about the flare, since they'd told us emphatically not to fire one and they must have had good reason, but this was not the time to question Rich. He had his own ideas, and on the ground, he knew best. We scanned the sky, as croaking cranes and other birds flapped lazily along the lakeshore. Before us, a serene meadow.

Finally, faintly, we heard in the distance the familiar hum that grew into the unmistakable sound of aircraft engines. My heart leapt, and I ran to get my little bundle of possessions. From the direction of the lake, we now could see a small plane flying directly toward us while another was beginning a wide turn overhead. Our upstairs watchdog and our white knight were galloping our way.

But suddenly now, a more ominous sound also came from *behind* us. I spun to look. Excited voices were coming from the far edge of the meadow where the road we'd entered on disappeared. We could see a small swarm of humans, about twenty men on bicycles, riding our way, some wearing the same uniforms as the local cops we had just stuffed in the bushes. They sounded like angry bees as they advanced. *Merde!*

Just then, the single-engine plane whizzed over us, buzzed the length of the meadow, at treetop level, then banked sharply to sweep back towards us. The SCR squawked: "Skunk boys, get your asses down to the lake right fuckin' now. Your heavenly angels got them nasties in sight. We're gonna give 'em a scare and then grab you. Don't respond—just do it. We watching and dropping to one hundred feet, locked and loaded."

As BirdDawg spoke, the small plane circled once more and headed directly for the crowd, so low that several of them jumped off their bikes in flight. A few of them fired rifles up at the plane.

Once past them, the pilot went into a climb, rolled over on a wing, then turned and aimed his nose at the shooters. A white streak whooshed from a wingtip, and then a rocket exploded in the midst of the bikes, raining bicycle and body parts along the meadow floor. Through the smoke, I watched something fly straight up, then flip over like a rag doll and land hard in the grass.

We sprinted towards the lakeside landing area; I was huffing and puffing, but not Rich or Charlie. Once more, the little plane turned, and this time, the pilot dropped his flaps, slowing almost to a standstill as he touched down but kept rolling. A side door opened and a camouflaged figure jumped out. Trotting alongside the craft, he was waving at us frantically to climb aboard. As we ran, I saw Rich rip the igniting tape off his flare and tossed it as far as he could, the red smoke billowing. His idea of a fitting farewell to Red China, I guessed.

We scrambled on all fours into the tiny cabin and flopped down as the doors were slammed and locked. As the engine revved up to full, our camouflaged man jumped in the right seat, and I suddenly felt the plane lift clear, climbing at a scary angle and then banking away. We were up and—I hoped—out.

I had made it aboard with one souvenir, the rifle dropped by Bike Cop Two. It was not an Enfield, as I originally thought, but a short-barreled Mauser of World War II vintage, stamped "Mauser, Oberndorf." It looked like a museum piece. (Why I saved it is a mystery to me now, but all these years later, I still have it.)

We'd leveled off a little but were still climbing when I was startled to see something outside my cabin window. It was a mean-looking twin-engine plane, painted in green and black camouflage designs, with no markings. It inched closer until we were flying nearly wingtip-to-wingtip. I saw the co-pilot wave.

"Skunk Boys," the SCR blared, "this is your pal BirdDawg. We had you covered down there. And now yer heavenly angel there is flying yer lucky asses back home. See you on the ground."

A LIFT FROM BIRDDAWG

We looked at each other and grinned exhaustedly. There was not much else to say, though "Hallelujah" came to mind.

The shotgun plane drifted away, banking slowly into a climbing turn; the next minute, it was gone. Our co-pilot, one Master Sergeant Phil Hawkins, told us that we'd be flying for the next two hours, crossing into Thailand and landing near Chiang Mai, a little over 300 miles away. Below us was a range of craggy mountains covered with scrub pines and small lakes. Slowly, thin clouds became solid, leaving us in near-darkness. In the silent dimness, I relaxed for the first time in days, only to realize with my deep breaths that the three of us reeked, somewhat worse than barnyard offal. This plane would need fumigation.

On board was fresh coffee in thermos jugs and a small cooler filled with cold drinks and snacks. I let the coffee wet my parched throat, knowing sleep was coming on hard anyway. Indeed, the engine's drone and thrumming within the cabin was all it took: my exhausted body gave out. I checked my watch and sank back into a semi-conscious state, my mind floating freely. In my fog, I wondered if the padré had made it. And what about the rest of that bunch—the padré's woman, the two wounded men, Gigi?

Oh, yes—Gigi. No longer panicked at every glance or sound, I finally could come to terms with how manipulated I'd been. That odd attraction she'd had for me—was it real or all just part of her job? Did she truly *want* to be in my bed, or was getting me dropped into China all that she really cared about?

Desperate for a shred of self-respect, I had to believe that she felt something for me—maybe not love, exactly, but some sort of genuine attraction. *Surely,* I let myself think, *she'll be anxious to hear that I made it out alive.* But it was all too easy to imagine that she wouldn't. Slowly, I began to accept that I'd been played for a first-class fool, taken in by a hank of hair, a splash of perfume, and pair of slim ankles. I hated to think that she'd been toying with me—working at my vulnerabilities, laughing to herself that I was easy, that I could be had for next to nothing. But it would be foolish to deny it. *Damn her.*

And then there were all the new questions—about who Gigi really *was*. Could there be any truth at all in the portrait of an attractive-but-married woman working for a university research program and messing around on the side with a charming flyboy? Or was all that part of a charade as well? The Soviets had squadrons of stunning female operatives—"swallows," they were called—who would do anything to collect information or carry out an assignment. Was Gigi an American swallow? I hated to think so, but she did fit the bill. I, the swallow's mark, knew that firsthand.

CHAPTER 16

Thailand, Once Again

If you don't know where you're going, you ain't gonna get there.
—*Yogi Berra, 1925–*

I AWOKE WITH NO IDEA HOW LONG WE'D BEEN FLYING. JUST AS I WAS GETting oriented, I felt the plane tip down; we were descending. I'd gotten cramped and stiff in my small seat; I needed to stretch and shake out the kinks in my legs. The others seemed to be asleep still—Rich, his campaign hat over his eyes, and Charlie, who had changed to a baseball cap with the USC logo on its prow.

From the cockpit area, I could hear radio squawks, static, and chatter. Hawkins and the ground station were exchanging information about weather and receiving landing instructions. Finally, the co-pilot swiveled around and loudly over the engine noise said: "Get ready, folks, this bird is fixing to land."

Just ahead, the airport's string of white lights rippled down the center, giving the pilot a guideline. Once Hawkins had the plane lined up, I heard him on the radio: "Tower, Courier One-Nine has the runway, kill the rabbit and whereat you want us?"

"Courier One-Nine contact ground; out ."

"Ground, Courier One-Nine here, where you want us?"

"One-Nine, Ground, continue toward runway end. Exit Poppa and follow Sparkle Plenty. Ground out."

"One-Nine is a big Roger. Wheels on the terra firma...out."

DR. JOHN...ON ASSIGNMENT

The long runway accommodated huge transport craft, so we actually needed less than a third of the landing distance to bump down and stop. Sparkle Plenty turned out to be a small Jeep with bright yellow flashers and the standard lighted FOLLOW ME sign on its tail. We were led into a large empty hangar and directed to cut our engine. Someone on the outside opened our doors as hollow-sounding footsteps approached. I got up, loosened cramped joints, eased stiff muscles. One by one, we quietly climbed out.

Waiting for us was a cheery, smiling lady officer, clipboard in hand and holding a sheaf of papers. She gave us a big smile and a quick "Welcome back."

Turning to me, she said, "Greetings, Doctor, I'm Lieutenant Jane Witherspoon. *Sawadee* and welcome to our Air Force facility. General Cox sends his personal welcome and apologizes for not being here. He's meeting with visitors from Washington, but he asked me to see to your comfort."

I smiled.

Behind me, Hawkins and his co-pilot were pulling their paperwork and gear from the plane while Rich and Charlie, carrying only their equipment from our trip, had already begun to walk toward a lighted door in the wall as I stood listening to Lt. Witherspoon. Wanting to catch them before it was too late, I broke into a stiff, achy run.

"Hey, guys—I just want to thank you from the bottom of my heart for getting us the hell out of there. So, I, uh—I just want to thank you." It sounded a bit shallow, but I meant it, and that must have registered. I had one more thing to add. "And next time you invite me on a trip, I'm saying, 'No.'" They smiled.

"Good luck, Doc," Rich said, shaking my hand. "And thanks for going with us." Charlie gave me a goodbye nod of the head, and they both turned and walked on, two seasoned professionals in a line of work as important as it was harrowing. I watched them for a moment and then turned back to Lt. Jane Witherspoon.

--•--

THAILAND, ONCE AGAIN

SHE WAS DOWNRIGHT CUTE, A Doris Day lookalike with cornflower-blue eyes. Her face glowed with a healthy tan, but her open collar suggested she was fish-belly white elsewhere. In freshly laundered Air Force fatigues, she gave the impression of what she was: a serious Air Force officer. Sure, I'd just spent four days crawling across China, afraid at every turn that I might end up with a bullet in the head or be left to rot in the dark recesses of a communist-state machine. But eyeing perky Lt. Witherspoon and her clipboard gave me a new burst of energy.

Fine, what next?

"Doctor, we have quarters ready for you. There's fresh linen, a set of fatigues, and other items for you. After you shower and change, you should be free for dinner." Her nose may have crinkled just a trifle as she said shower, which I took to mean that I really stank. "And when you're ready, you can either eat in your quarters, or I'll be happy to show you to the Officer's Mess. Tomorrow afternoon, the base security officer will need to meet with you. If you have no questions, then please come with me." I grabbed what was left of my kit, along with my souvenir rifle, and slipped into the passenger seat of her Jeep.

This was a huge base with Jeeps, vans, trucks, and motorbikes zipping in all directions. But the lieutenant drove aggressively, and in minutes we were turning into a quieter section of the base. Sequestered among huge palms and other trees was a cluster of cottages, and small signs announced that this was housing for officers and senior NCOs. Each dwelling had a driveway and portico, and floating above the manicured lawns were flaming red blooms on large flamboyant trees. Something very fragrant—possibly jasmine—wafted through the coolness of the shade. It reminded me how badly I stank.

Pulling up in a driveway, Lt. Witherspoon led me indoors, and flipped on lights. I could hear air-conditioning humming. All was clean and neat—and finally, blessed coolness. I fairly itched for a shower.

The lieutenant showed me the kitchen where a large refrigerator was stocked with food and soft drinks. In the freezer, a variety of TV dinners were stacked. A small bar in one corner held unopened bottles of bourbon, gin, Scotch, and other booze. I popped a cold beer from the fridge and pulled deeply. The lieutenant grinned, then continued with a quick tour of the rest of the house. It was nothing fancy—GI housing never is—but compared to my last few weeks, it was palatial.

"Here's my card," she said, holding it out for me. "If you need anything, just pick up the phone and ask for me. Any questions? No? OK, then"—big, sunny smile—"call me when you're ready."

In the first bedroom was a king-size bed, neatly made. On the cotton blanket cover, an Air Force logo—nice touch. How could a guest not remember that the Air Force had accommodated him or her in luxe quarters way out here in no-man's land? Neatly stacked on the bureau were fatigues, shirts, pants, T-shirts, GI boxer shorts, and socks—everything I should need, and almost all in my size, too. (By now I was merely amused that everyone knew so much about me—my sizes, for instance, right down to my socks—men's large.) In the bathroom were towels, washrags, and a carefully selected array of necessaries. Behind a glass enclosure, a large tiled shower with plenty of hot water, waiting just for me.

I showered, shaved, and immediately felt my well-being restored. My fatigue boots weren't new-looking anymore but were still in great shape, so I took a wet towel and wiped off the dust and dirt of China, saying a quiet "Hallelujah" as I did. The rest of my old clothes went into a garbage bag, dumped on the back porch.

I began to get things organized. From my kit, I retrieved my Leica camera, my rolls of film, and what was left of my surgical equipment. The kit and equipment would stay here, but the camera and unused film went with me. I had twelve rolls of exposed but unmarked film for Mel Grosvenor— and his editors at the Geographic would have to study the slides, read my notes, and identify the locations.

In one corner of the bedroom was a standard desk with stationery in the top drawer. I pulled out a folder, found some stationery and envelopes. The letterhead read:

AIR FORCE SYSTEMS COMMAND
Andrews Air Force Base, Washington, DC.

Huh? So this place actually belonged to AFSC? One never quite knew what the military was up to at times. I grabbed some sheets of paper, picked up the phone, and got connected again to the lady lieutenant.

"Thanks for the Dial soap and all the clothes," I said.

With a coy chuckle, she answered, "Glad you liked them; the Sergeant-Major picked them out for you. They fit OK?"

"Just fine, thanks."

"Need anything else?"

My answer could well have been Yes...but that seemed terribly inappropriate. And I had more on my mind.

"Actually, I do need some help, lieutenant. Do you think I could borrow a typewriter? Then I need to send a small package to the States. Is that possible?"

"No problem, Doctor," she said. "I'll have a messenger pick you up. How do you want to do this, food or mail first? Your choice."

I was hungry: food first. A messenger squealed up in a Jeep and drove me to the officers' club—a first-class set-up, considering it was so far from home. Displayed on the walls were huge military insignia, plaques, and logos. Underfoot was highly polished parquet flooring, and everywhere there was the aroma of cooking, mixed with cigar smoke.

No one gave Lieutenant Jane or me a second look. Over my cheeseburger and her soup, I explained that I had to send a package of film to the magazine in Washington. No comment; she kept munching.

"I also wonder if you know anything about a Swiss plane that would have arrived here early in the morning five days ago, bringing a fellow with a bad chest infection." She looked at me blankly and said she hadn't heard anything but would check.

I decided to hold off on any other matters; I was tired and I needed sleep. We chatted idly, and then finished up. This was to be another night in the jungles of Outer East Nowhere.

-- • --

THE NEXT MORNING, I WAS picked up and taken to breakfast by Lt. Witherspoon.

"OK," she said once we'd started, delicately dabbing the corners of her cupid bow while at the same time smudging her lipstick, "I have the following information for you: We do, in fact, have a recently arrived wounded civilian in the surgical ward. He was flown here as an emergency and was operated upon by Major Fred Loupe, our chief of surgery. Now he's in the intensive care ward. I don't know any more than that. The Major said he'd be happy to discuss the case with you this morning after rounds. I'll take you to his office now, OK?"

"Yep, fine."

Not surprisingly, the military hospital was your standard, Government Issue Hundred-Bedder. In typical World War II military style, it was all on one floor, which was economical in that there would never be a problem with elevator breakdowns in distant lands. We were directed towards the Surgical Division in the rear, near loading docks and beyond the outpatient clinics. The place had clean halls and smelled of disinfectants, an aroma I love. The floors sparkled with fresh waxing.

Major Fred Loupe's office was tucked behind a set of counters where clacking typewriters protected him from the mainstream medical staff. He'd been expecting us.

"Dr. Sundukian, I've heard about you from our buddies at Andrews. You're their attending, I understand?"

"Yes sir, that's right."

"And you trained under Brian Blades ?"

"Right again."

"Well, I guess that explains all the instructions that came in with this poor fellow. He went straight into the OR, and we sucked out his pharynx and 'scoped him—with no anesthesia. You can't imagine the crap we pulled out of his trachea and bronchi. That operating room still stinks. In the middle of the bronchoscopy, one of our nurses ran out in the hall and barfed. But we got him all sucked out and washed off. Finally we tubed him and hooked him to a ventilator—he's on it now. We loaded him with V-cillin and Strep and he's looking better, so he just may make it. The lung's looking much clearer. Let me show you his films."

Lighting the view boxes, Loupe flipped up a series of X-rays so that I could compare his films upon arrival with those from that morning. There was visible improvement and some clearing of the lung tissue—not bad for a half-dead guy. Along with two chest tubes (one placed high to vent air, the other lower to drain pus and blood), I also saw scattered fragments of something opaque—metallic fragments, overlying a section of busted rib. Loupe and I both knew those fragments were a mix of rib and slug fragments—remnants of that very same round that had punctured the padré's lung abscess and probably saved his life—but Loupe hadn't mentioned them, knowing that they might require answers to questions that were not to be asked.

Surprisingly, it looked as though this poor guy might just make it. It was certainly one for the books, a real teaching case. And because few would believe me, I asked Loupe to make copies of the films and get them to me. He said he would, adding, "His wife is here, too. Base admin has arranged for her to stay with him while he recuperates for a while—unless the spooks take over. They sometimes slip these guys out of here early. But if they don't, and he continues to improve as he has, he should be out of here in a month or so."

I felt good about that prospect: the padré was the main reason we'd had to hike out of China, and he was here and doing well. Fair enough.

I thanked Loupe for his courtesy and asked him to drop me a note and tell me how the guy made out. It isn't often that a morbidly ill patient gets better after being shot, but that was exactly what had happened here, and it struck me as something that should be written up in *The Journal of Thoracic Surgery*. I had one more question for the Major.

"Say, you wouldn't know anything about the other persons who came in with him, would you?"

"Sorry, I don't," he said. "There was one lady who seemed to be in charge of the bunch. She met with the General briefly, and my understanding was that she flew out on the trash run the next day."

Gigi was gone.

-- • --

My first priority had been to check on my patient, and that had been done. Now I had to get to Bangkok, pick up my visa, and from there, onward to Moscow. All that was keeping me here was this pending appointment with the Security Officer, which I knew probably meant "Intelligence Officer."

Hadn't these folks had enough of me already?

CHAPTER 17

The Security Officer

Seeking to know is too often learning to doubt.
—Antoinette Deshouliers, 1618–1684

MAJOR CHARLES STOCKWELL WAS A SANDY-HAIRED, PIPE-SMOKING chap— slightly balding and with a paunch; he had an overall rumpled appearance. His horn-rimmed glasses gave him a look somewhere between owlish and sleepy.

I'd been ushered into his office. After introductions, he slid a clipboard off his desk. As he ruffled through some sheets his eyebrows rose questioningly, pretending to see what was in front of him for the first time. *Liar,* I thought. *He's been over them more than once. Corners don't get curled on papers that have only been lying flat, as in not being pored over.*

"Ah, I see here, Doctor, that you're on your way to Russia. Is that so?"

He damn well knows I am. Is he trying to establish some kind of rapport?

"Yes sir, I hope to be. I was on my way to the Soviet Union but just stopped by to visit with a Dr. Dooley in northern Laos—you know him? Anyway, I'm sure you have all my information right there on your clipboard."

"Yes, yes, I guess so." He glanced unconvincingly at his clipboard notes again. From his twang, I made him out to be from North Carolina, but his speech was inlaid with somber, professorial overtones—I was reminded of a highly educated racecar driver. So he was probably a clinical psychologist, but was he Base Security, too? Nah. He might have been an MP once and then gone on for more training, but my guess was that he really was from the intelligence people. It seemed pretty obvious.

He started with gentle probing questions, under the guise of a clinician gathering information. If he thought he was fooling me, he wasn't. I knew what he was doing.

"Most unusual going to the Soviet Union in this day and age, wouldn't you agree? Some relatives there, yes?"

"Nope, not that I know of. My genes come from those hills—the Caucasus—so I obviously do have some somewhere down there, but no recent contacts."

"Yes, yes, I see. So you're just going to visit?"

OK, enough! No more games.

"Look, Major, let's cut this silly crap. I'm sure you know all about what I'm doing and why. My dad got an invitation from Anastas I. Mikoyan, and I'm going in his stead—it's all been arranged. State and others know all the details better than I. While I'm there, I hope to visit some medical institutions and just plain look around. So what do you really want to know in *addition* to all that?"

This sort of response was not expected. Stockwell had taken me for military, probably because of my attire, but clearly I wasn't cowed by his rank at all. Surprise registered on his face.

"Why, yes, of course, Doctor. I do have a notation here that you have medical institutions to visit and meetings with Mr. Mikoyan in Moscow. I, ah...*we* just hope it will be possible for you to take some notes on the interesting people you meet—names, descriptions, addresses, that sort of thing. Any events and conversations which seem unusual or interesting. Something along the lines of what we're having just now. Serious discussions. And I also have some names for you; possible contacts in Moscow. First, of course, our Ambassador, Mr. Llewellyn Thompson, will be hoping to meet with you and offer assistance if you should need it. Plan to visit the embassy as soon as possible after you check in to your hotel."

His tone dropped some of its formality now, and he sat back in chair and looked directly at me.

THE SECURITY OFFICER

"So, just a word or two about landing formalities. It's going to be hot when you land at Sheremetyevo, and you'll be tired. You don't have a diplomatic passport, so you'll have to wait in line with all the other foreign *shlumphs*—and you may be the only Westerner, so you'll be an object of curiosity. The uniformed man who checks your passport will look through it several times, make eye contact with you, and try to make you nervous. So just smile at him—it's not what they expect. Anxiety and fear are the usual responses from people in line. If *you* smile at them, it throws them off. Some will even smile back reflexively, before they realize it.

"This customs officer is being watched by a senior man lurking nearby in civilian clothes. This overseer, probably KGB, will have his eyes on you. So, at some point during the passport check, pull out your letter from Mikoyan and nonchalantly ask in English if someone is here to meet you. That'll get action pronto. The passport guy probably can't read English well, but he'll spot the letterhead and immediately the KGB guy will move in. Most likely, you'll be taken into an important visitors area and given tea. Then another government representative will materialize with a car and driver. Whatever ministry finally handles you will be anxious to make you comfortable in case Mikoyan asks, and so they use the National or the Ukraina Hotel for lodging official guests.

"Of course, your room will be, you know, wired—that is, they sometimes do like to listen. Maybe you do sleep-talking, say, or even a little pillow-talking. You never know. It goes without saying you won't be taking anyone to your room, would you now?"

I could have laughed just then to play along. I didn't.

Stockwell glanced again at his notes. "Anyway, the old gals at the floor desk will be watching you like a hawk...regular harridans they are. And the KGB will search your room, of course. So leave what you want them to see in plain sight. What you want to hide, just leave with the Ambassador—your camera and film, definitely. Maybe your notebook, too. We'd be so very grateful for any information you could pass along. Did I say that already? Copy your notebook possibly. Yes," he nodded while shuffling his notes again, "it would be nice if we could do that."

I didn't respond.

He went on. "OK, your hosts will provide you with a guide—usually a man, but maybe one of their little swallows. They'll be introduced to you as an Intourist guide—at least that's what their badges will say. But they'll be keeping an eye on you, making sure you don't do anything silly, and also to keep you from what they don't want you to see or hear. Do you speak Russian, Doctor?"

"Oh, one or two words, maybe," I said. "But I do speak Armenian."

"You do? How interesting. Well, you won't want to speak any Russian or Armenian to these folks, because then they won't talk around you, fearing that you'll overhear and understand them. Makes for awkward situations."

He pursed his lips, sipped some water. "The guides are chosen for these tasks because they speak good English. Typically, they're trained in Tashkent at the main language school, much like ours in Monterey. Funny thing is, a lot of them have a Chicago accent. Quite a few Red sympathizers slipped over there from Chicago and ended up teaching English to spies and secret police, so the students often sound like they're from Chicago—you know, wide 'a's,' that sort of thing. We can spot them easily when they hire on at our embassy; it's really kind of funny. So just smile, be pleasant, and let them herd you around. You can tell them what you wish to do, and be firm. But expect half of what you want to be canceled at the last minute without explanation. So: Any questions?"

"Nope," I said, restlessly. "Just curious, though: why all the concern about me?"

"Well, Doctor, frankly, not many visitors are allowed into the Soviet Union these days, at least from our side. To have someone *invite* you in makes you a rare bird. And we want to make sure nothing happens to our bird."

He smiled and leaned forward, then sat up sharply. "Oh, by the way, speaking of birds, let me tell you about the feather trick—to know when your room has been searched." He proceeded to show me. "First you take a tiny feather…"

—-•--

BACK IN MY QUARTERS, I got my notes, baggage, and photo supplies in order and was getting itchy to leave. I had asked about getting to Bangkok and was told that I could hop a ride on one of the milk runs that afternoon. Once in Bangkok, I'd check in at the Erawan Princess Hotel, get my visa from the Soviet Embassy, and pick up my Aeroflot tickets from a Thai branch of Intourist, the "travel agency" that everybody knew was KGB. (I'd be taking one of the twice-weekly flights from New Delhi to Moscow, but arranging permission hadn't been easy. Initially, Intourist had asked more hard questions about who I was and what I wanted, so I had my travel agent back in Saigon send them a wirephoto of the Mikoyan letter through Novosti, the Russian press agency. Suddenly all things Russian became possible.)

So, in just a few days, I'd be in Moscow, launching the last phase of my unusual odyssey—soon my flight from reality would come to an end. It was about time: The discovery that American goodwill wasn't exactly appreciated abroad had long since sunk in. I now knew that most folks in this world didn't really give a damn about Americans doing good unto others, but this fact was unacceptable to the weavers of hairshirts, the do-gooders. I had now become a cynic and a defector from their ranks. *Poor fools.*

Suddenly, Murphy's Law kicked in. The cargo plane on which I was supposed to fly out had blown a piston mid-flight and barely made it in on one engine. It was an old, war-weary, twin-engine C-47, and base mechanics would need to dismantle the engine to find the problem. But, I was told, I could ride a small shuttle plane when it flew the following day to Bangkok for parts. Would that be to my liking? Yes, indeed. But for the next 24 hours, I had heels to cool.

The news traveled quickly. Within half an hour, Lieutenant Jane Witherspoon, my minder, called to confirm the bad news but offered to lighten my mood.

"As long as you have to hang over another night, we should do something nice," she said. "So how would you like some real Thai food tonight, Doctor? We, well, *I,* want you to leave us with a smile on your face. Does this interest you?"

"Sounds good to me, but how's it differ from what I've been eating?

"Well, it's not going to be military cooking. This will be a bit zingier, maybe spicier than Vietnamese, Cambodian or Lao food," she said.

I wasn't exactly a connoisseur; it all sounded like Chinese cooking to me, with local variations. But it was a nice gesture and sounded interesting—and there wasn't much *else* to do. So we agreed: After Miss Jane finished her daily martial-arts workout, she'd pick me up around six.

And indeed, right at six, the Jeep wheeled up, a freshly showered young lieutenant smiling behind the wheel. Her hair had been braided like a German *fraulein,* and she wore fatigues—but pressed and laundered ones, so in a sense she *was* dressed up. I had slipped into my chinos and a clean safari jacket.

With a roar, we headed off. Once we were off the base, the road became far bumpier and more rutted than I'd expected, but it didn't faze Lieutenant Witherspoon in the least. We rode through forests of teak and bamboo, leading toward low hills in the near distance. As we sped along, we squished through scattered mounds of water-buffalo droppings, and at one such spot, Lieutenant Jane Witherspoon stopped the Jeep and pointed ahead. Butterflies are attracted to cattle droppings, she told me, especially at this time of the year, and the air ahead of us was thick with them. In the broken light of early evening under the jungle canopy, the bright patches of fluttering butterflies made an eerie, glowing sight. Amazing.

We scattered them as we passed, and after another fifteen minutes or so, I heard the roaring sounds of falling water as the road entered a clearing beside a magnificent waterfall. Next to it, tucked into trees but partly cantilevered over a misty pool, was a curved veranda attached to a cozy-looking restaurant. We had a breathtaking view of waterfall and jungle. Unbelievably, there were orchids dangling from branches overhanging the pool and from trees on either side of the waterfall, as though someone had planted them there. Alongside them were clusters of bromeliads in flaming reds. This spot could have been from a movie, and fortunately, I had my little Nikon SP and some fast film at the ready. I ran off a few frames. Mel would wax melodic when he saw them—he'd probably want to go there.

As I clicked away, darkness began creeping in; by the time we got inside the restaurant, the only light was from paper lanterns strung overhead. Somewhere I heard sounds of a sputtering, popping outdoor grill. I could smell it, too: in the air was the familiar mix of smoke, ginger, and garlic. Amazingly, I spotted a brightly lit bar in a corner, stocked with first-class labels: Tanqueray, Bombay Gin, fine single-malt Scotches, and even bourbon, a rarity in Asia.

As soon as we were seen, there was much bowing and clasping of hands, and we were taken to a table on the veranda; clearly my companion was well known here. At her insistence, I let her order, and within minutes, to my surprise, ice-cold gin-and-tonics appeared before us—with Schweppes bottled tonic, no less.

Enjoy it while you can, silly boy, said my snotty inner voice.

I did. First came appetizers: grilled things on skewers and huge river prawns. Then, in turn, dishes with rice, small grilled fish, and chunks of spicy, grilled meat. Slathered over this all, huge dollops of sour cream, which, Lieutenant Jane Witherspoon told me, served to cut the peppery aftertaste.

It was a sparkling, sensational moment, eating exotic tidbits and drinking well-mixed liquors under lanterns at the base of a waterfall. Lady Jane was more relaxed now—less military and more feminine. And at the moment, quite smiley and friendly. We chatted about me and my background, and then gradually the conversation shifted to her.

I asked about her hometown and her parents, and she glanced down at her plate. She told me that she'd gone into the military for the best of reasons, the highest of ideals. A sociologist by training, she'd worked and done counseling among the poor in Atlanta. After joining the military and a short stint at an airbase in Georgia, she met a flyboy, an Air Force pilot, and she became part of his life. One day, with no prior warning, he was transferred to an unnamed base in Southeast Asia. So, after a short while—and a little chicanery and manipulation—she managed to get transferred, too. To his base.

Then one clear, sunny day a year ago, her hope for the future went out on a routine flight. The plane blew up in mid-air. End of that story.

She was handling it well, she said. But there was mistiness, a sadness in her eyes. After all, there had been no solid commitment. So, she would eventually get back to the States and start life all over. But for now, her tour had seven months to go.

To her relief—or so I thought—I steered our conversation to more trivial matters: the pilots, their missions, the reason that this base had been carved out of absolute nowhere. The time passed quietly, and by the time drinks and dinner were done, we were feeling very mellow. When the after-dinner drinks arrived, we—actually she—became totally relaxed. And I mean totally. Her shoes were off now, and her feet tucked coquettishly underneath her in her rattan chair. The braids had let go of a few loose hairs that caught the lantern-light.

What she missed most, she began to tell me, was the comfort and security of the man she'd loved, trusted, and had planned to marry. Now he was gone—just like that, her life had changed. And so it slowly came out that what she missed most was being held, *just held*. She hadn't been held since he died, she said, and she missed *that* more than sex; her voice trailed off. Did I understand?

I assured her I did. Certainly as a doctor, I could sense pain in others, I was able to commiserate, to comfort. It was part of my calling.

Quietly, she stared into her drink, still misty-eyed, with an occasional sniffle. The evening was taking a maudlin turn, and I felt powerless to rescue it. So the waiter did it for me, bringing our check. Sitting up, Jane insisted on paying: it was all arranged in advance, and after all, I was a guest of the Base Command, which had an account here. I accepted with thanks.

We drove back in silence to the compound under a half moon leading us at treetop height. The base itself was quiet at this late hour; it was nearly midnight. Jane slid the Jeep quietly up her driveway and parked under a carport. I was invited in for after-after-dinner drinks, she explained. OK, I'd have one.

She slipped off her shoes at the door and invited me to do the same. "It's oriental," she said. *Well, it's certainly more comfortable,* I figured. As we padded in silently, I realized that I was tired and felt anxious to get back to my quarters.

Jane, on the other hand, was acting nervous and tense. Smiling, but with a puckered brow, she made coffee, pouring it into small, rice-pattern teacups. We sat quietly and sipped, and as I glanced around aimlessly, I couldn't help but feel her staring at me, and a bit too intently for my comfort. A little voice began urging me to get the hell out as soon as possible, but as I sat, unmoving, that voice began to mock me. *You are so silly, Doctor—you should check this gal out! She may seem bashful, but man, she's been giving you strong signals. Wise up, you idiot!*

I cleared my throat and stood up. "Guess I better get going," I said, in as John Wayne-ly a manner as I could.

She rose, padded over to me, took me lightly by the arm, and led me to the door. She then stood up on tiptoe for what started as a gentle goodnight peck. But once our lips had touched, the two hands she'd clamped on my shoulders to steady herself slid down around my waist, and the little peck turned into a slam-bang kiss.

"Please, John, just hold me for a minute. I don't bite."

Well, I *had* been holding her, but she was up against me like my shadow. In fact, at this moment, I'd have to struggle to get loose. Clearly she had no intention of letting go, and I had no intention of getting violent.

Oh shit. I gave up. *Kamerad!*

-- • --

A COUPLE OF HOURS LATER, Lady Jane released me. She even drove me back to my quarters. We didn't say much—what was there to say? I glanced over once. She was smiling slyly.

A military patrol Jeep, carrying two men and a mean-looking German shepherd, approached us. In the light of our headlights as we purred past each other, I couldn't help noticing the huge smirks on their faces.

It was high time to leave.

CHAPTER 18

Back in Bangkok

Make me chaste and continent, but not just yet.
—Saint Augustine 354-430

THE BASE'S BEECH COURIER PLANE LANDED EARLY IN THE MORNING ON the military side of the Bangkok airport. I jumped off and caught a ride with an airline crew headed downtown.

At the Erawan Princess Hotel, I got squared away, and then took to the items on my to-do list in rapid succession: I visited Jim Thompson; I bought some trinkets, a few pieces of lacquerware, and a set of bronzy-looking cutlery with horn handles; and finally I dropped in at the Soviet Consulate, where my passport had been taken for stamping. By now it was nearly noon.

"Pulees return one hour, doktor, Dzhon. You Armen? You have relations in USSR?"

"Maybe, I'm not sure. No one I know of offhand. Why?"

No answer, big grin, "Pulees return one hour."

I returned in one hour, and goddamit, a sign in several languages hung on the door: Closed for Lunch. Tourist Passports, Return 4 PM.

At four o'clock, I walked in. The smell of something spicy still hung in the air. I was greeted with a big smile from a thick-set manager-type, his central incisor of steel sparkling at me behind his broad Slavic grin. "You know Mikoyan?" he asked quietly, eyebrows raised. I figured he was impressed.

"Not personally. He's an old classmate of my father's." That had him stumped. He smiled again. *"Kharasho."* [Russian for OK]

And that was that. I finally had a passport and visa to the Soviet Workers' Paradise, good for six weeks from the date of my arrival. That would be plenty of time.

Back at my hotel, I checked for messages…none. Honestly, I didn't really expect any, but given what had happened the last time I was in Bangkok, I couldn't be blamed for wondering who might show up. But not this time. For once, I was totally alone in this noisy, smelly madhouse of a city.

My flight left for New Delhi the next morning—a Pan Am 707 with an all-American crew. Clean, cool, and comfortable. I was in first class, up front and next to a window. A sweat-drenched Indian fellow took the seat next to me, draped in expensive fabrics and reeking of expensive perfume and curry. We nodded to one another and after that said nothing.

CHAPTER 19

New Delhi

The Devil's boots don't creak.
—Scottish proverb

Arriving at the New Delhi airport on a hot August day in 1959 was entering bedlam—noise, people, and commotion everywhere. It seemed that every variety of human being on the planet was jammed into this one blistering-hot airport. A Pan Am station rep helped me clear customs, and I stopped at the Aeroflot counter to confirm my reservation to Moscow two days hence. Piece of cake so far, despite the noise, heat, and stench.

I hopped into a vehicle of sorts—roomy and patterned after a London taxi, but strangely lopsided, riding at a tilt. We lurched off immediately at full speed. It was a wild ride and finally, I was delivered to the front entrance of the Ashoka Hotel, where an immense Punjabi with a mammoth mustache stood guard. He smiled broadly, *salaamed,* and bade me enter. Check-in formalities were simple: passport please, to register only, *Sahib,* then quickly up to my room. Once my two light bags were neatly placed on luggage racks, I dismissed the houseboys and collapsed in a chair. I was a bit done in.

The room was cool and beautifully appointed; a huge provender of fruit lay on the table, next to a bottle of water on ice and a huge vase of flowers. My first thought was that it was somehow Pan Am's doing, but to my shock, a card with the flowers simply said "G."

G? Oh my Gawd!

So G *did* know where and what I did at any moment. I was both fascinated and scared; just what was going on behind my back? Frankly, though, that it was Gigi did something for my ego, too.

Recalling that the desk clerk had invited me to be the hotel's guest at the bar, I washed up and took the lift down to investigate. I'd never had a Pink Gin before, but the barkeep assured me that it prevented malaria, owing to the high concentration of quinine in the Schweppes tonic. "Only thing to drink, *sahib*," he said, bobbing his head sideways deferentially. I had two in rapid succession—strong, but strong was just what I needed.

Fortified, I wandered around the lobby and chanced to notice an ornate, gilded announcement board. Listed on it in lavish script were several parties, including a diplomatic reception hosted by "His Excellency, Dr. Ahmed Benabud, Ambassador E & P, of the Kingdom of Morocco."

Hell's fire—Ben? I knew him from Washington days. He'd attended Case Western as a young man and was entirely at ease among Americans, which added a certain panache. He'd become highly regarded by his King and similarly high in the pecking order of Morocco. While he was ambassador to the U.S., I'd been to several receptions at his embassy. I'd even operated on him once: he'd had a small mole on his back which I removed right in my office; Walter Reed had been too "busy" at the time.

I wondered: should I just barge into a reception to which I was not invited? *Hell, why not?* I hurried back to my room, slipped on a blue blazer and necktie, and then made my way back down to the posh, jostling crowd in the receiving line.

Right there at the head of the line was Ben, wearing his standard Savile Row suit, his deep, booming voice greeting each person by name. Finally, it was my turn. He looked up, saw me; a blank look for just a tiny second, then the huge smile, "Dr. Sundukian, how very nice to see you, so glad you could join us, may I present…" and with just the tiniest sideways nod of his head, he directed me to a nearby corner of the room. I slipped over there and waited, and shortly Ben showed up.

"John," he said with a huge, questioning smile, as he grabbed me by the elbow, "I can't tell you how glad I am to see you—but what brings you to this hellhole?"

"Well, it's a long story, and you're busy with your guests, Ben. Sorry to have barged in like this, but I saw your name on the board and had to say hello. So here I am."

He stopped a passing waiter and requisitioned two large glasses filled with ice and something tan-colored, thrusting one into my hand and quaffing half of the other in one gulp. *Huh—still no Islamic abstinence for him*, I thought. I had to chuckle.

"OK, John," he said. "After you hit the buffet table, wait in the bar, and I'll meet you in about an hour. By the way, try those huge prawns—I picked them out myself early this morning in the market. Delicious."

I made my way to a row of long tables groaning with food, next to a fully stocked bar for anyone in need of their daily medications. I filled a plate and decided I needed another helping of quinine, tempered with gin. It was a grand affair.

For the next half hour, I hobnobbed with diplomats, wives, and assorted women of high social rank—quite a few alone and some remarkably friendly. All were decked in their finest: lots of gold, pearls, huge gemstones, and a few obscenely large diamonds. Dazzled, but with tired feet, I headed to the bar to wait for Ben.

He came along shortly and slid in beside me. "OK, tell me everything," he ordered, and I did. True, I omitted some steamy details about G, but otherwise I gave him a thorough report of my sojourn to date—enough, I hoped, to satisfy his curiosity.

He looked at me gravely. "Do you have any idea what you're getting into, John?"

"Yep, kind of. I've been given the tourist briefing by our Embassy people, so I guess that should cover most of my problems, right?"

"Wrong," said Ahmed, now speaking as the worldly-wise pol. "Let me tell you right now, there will be some attempt to get you in an embarrassing situation while you're there. In addition to the fact that you are an American, they don't like you to start with. You're still a goddamn *ferengi*—an outsider—and you might see something they don't want you to see. That scares the hell out of them. So be careful, my friend. And stay away from those Russian women, too, no matter how pretty, how lovely, how anything: remember, any woman that approaches you is doing it for the KGB, not because she thinks you have a big pecker—no matter what you might think. And still no matter what, she *doesn't go to your room with you.* Understood? And don't change money in the streets, don't buy anything from any street person, and always tell your guide even if you're just going to the bathroom."

Jesus, I thought. *Why the hell would anyone in Moscow care about one slightly frazzled, disenchanted doctor who could not possibly be a threat to anybody? I just want to get into and out of Russia, see Mikoyan, visit some hospitals, and that was that. Of course, I have rolls of film to shoot for Mel Grosvenor, but taking photos is second nature for me. I'll just use my small, inconspicuous Nikon rangefinder camera. I could do anything I wanted with that beauty. And I'll act just like any other tourist from the outside—like the Germans and East Europeans with Leicas and Exaktas draped around their necks, or the wealthier ones with Japanese equipment.*

Ben finally finished with my "briefing."

"So now here's the last thing I have for you." He fished out his calling card, with lots of raised gold and black printing. On its reverse, he wrote a number. "Our embassy in Moscow," he said. "If you ever need anything faster than your embassy can provide, call this number and ask for..." He had printed a name: Osman Ouedthaleb. "Tell him Ben in Delhi told you to call. Tell him what you need and it will be done, I promise. Keep the card in your wallet, not your passport."

I slipped it in my wallet and thanked him.

"Anything for my friend," he said. "Now my friend, you and I have to attend the *finale* of my reception. After these cows and others leave," he said, nodding toward some hefty matrons, "I'm having a small *kef* at the Embassy, and my hostess is a charming little French Algerian visiting the city, along with the crew of the Pan-American flight that just landed. That was your crew, no?"

I didn't know, it could have been.

NEW DELHI

"I have a reception like this every two months or so. The Pan Am station manager and his crews are always my guests," he said with a sly smile. "This way I never have a seating problem when I travel." Clever, this Ben.

With assurances that he'd have me back to the hotel early, I rode with him to his ornate, French Colonial embassy, which doubled as home and pad for the bachelor Dr. Ahmed Benabud. The social event turned out to be a swim party at the Olympic-size pool in back. Small tents, tables awash with candles, and chairs of various sizes and shapes were situated artfully around the pool. I was given a pair of trunks and promptly got into the pool.

The party had started slowly, but gradually got into full swing. Ben had tunes from Benny Goodman and Glenn Miller playing, and everyone was getting mellow. I was introduced around, met several lovely young stewardesses being watched over carefully by their grizzled Pan Am captains, and at some point chased a shapely one underwater at least half the length of the pool before running out of air, by which time she'd squirted clean away. Probably just as well.

--•--

THE NEXT MORNING AT MY hotel, I fidgeted around, packing and repacking, waiting to leave for my flight. I went down to the lobby for the English daily paper, some magazines, and a light lunch. Finally, the car and driver to the airport showed.

At the Aeroflot desk, Indian and Russian clerks were checking passports, tickets, and documents at an achingly slow pace. Off to the side of the counter, leaning against the wall, was a faceless man in a gray rumpled suit. He appeared to be looking over the passenger list, a cigarette dangling from his mouth. From time to time, he glanced down at his list and made a notation. Ashes fell unnoticed. He never made eye contact, though he'd glanced at me once, and I tried staring at him. Nothing.

Surprisingly, I cleared the ticket check-in without incident—my tickets, visa, and everything were in order. No problem, no questions. I laughed inwardly; after all the warnings, I'd *expected* difficulties.

Instead, I cleared passport control without a hitch and made my way into the waiting area with the motley horde of humanity headed to the Soviet Union.

－－•－－

At some point after our Tu-104 had taken off, I fell asleep, and became totally oblivious to where I was. I felt a hand shaking me gently, and awoke to find a beaming chubby gray stewardess handing me a tray—lunch, she said proudly. And what a lunch it was. Soup, salad, some sort of beef bourguignon, what looked like a crepe filled with cheese and jam, a small pony of vodka, water, and more. I just couldn't eat it all but settled for soup, salad, and water. I tucked the vodka in my camera bag...and then, on a whim, pulled out the Nikon. We were flying over some beautiful mountain ranges, and I wanted some frames of this.

Well, one would have thought I was raping the Queen: a steward and stewardess hustled up the aisle and began pointing fingers at me, shaking their heads and proclaiming *Nyets* loudly. I did not understand. Finally, a fellow traveler filled me in: no photography from the air over the Soviet Union.

Thinking quickly, I declared that this was not the Soviet Union we were flying over yet, but rather the Pamirs—not a part of Russia. I was bluffing, actually, but I said it so forcefully, that after it was translated, the sullen crew left me alone. I took some shots, glanced around, then put my camera back. (I was to learn later that photography was taboo no matter what the circumstances—banned from airplane windows of any Soviet airliner.)

I imagined that this had not gone unnoticed. I wondered who would squeal first.

CHAPTER 20

Sheremetyevo International Airport
(Moscow, August, 1959)

*Never trust anyone who smiles and frowns at
the same time. They have twisted minds.*
—Margaret Devletian Keshishian, 1967

THE HUGE TUPOLEV 104 TURBOJET SLAMMED DOWN ON THE RUNWAY, its brakes stuttering as it groaned to a halt. Welcome to Moscow. A Jeep-like vehicle raced towards us, and then maneuvering adroitly, cut in front of us. Flashing a yellow light, it led us to a separate unloading area marked C-41 in Roman letters and numerals. Several low-slung buses were waiting for us, blue fumes pouring from their exhausts. My fellow passengers and I were more than ready to get off. I was tired, grungy, and convinced that the world outside America did not use deodorant. The Indians had a strange personal odor of curry and garlic, so I was ready for the diesel fumes of Moscow. My nagging inner voice asked for the thousandth time, *what in God's name was I was doing here?*

One particularly ugly passenger had been eying me malevolently from the moment I boarded the plane and occasionally swiveling her scrawny neck to glare at me, probably due to my hassle with the crew for photographing the mountains between India and Russia. I had maintained that we were over India. She insisted that all photos were forbidden from any Soviet airliner and threatened to report me. I advised her that I had noted her full name and that of the crew. I was a guest of her government and would be met at the airport by high party officials. It was a bluff, of course, but it damn sure quieted everyone, at least for the moment.

I grabbed my BOAC bag, and made for the exit. The pilot stood there smiling genially, bidding departing passengers goodbye. He was an Asian from one of the Republics. Since all international pilots had to speak the international language, I chanced some English: "Nice ride, skipper," and with a smile, *"Kharashoh!"* He blinked in surprise, and broke into a broad smile. His stainless steel incisor winked back at me.

All passengers trooped slowly into the Passport Control and Customs area, joining a long line of mixed breeds shuffling forward, including many Africans in native dress, Germans, Indians, Pakistanis, Italians, and a few Armenians. Their dialect was a different from Turkish Armenian, but nevertheless clearly understandable. Watching those ahead of me, I saw that this was going to take time.

Hell with this, I thought. We Americans are sometimes foolhardy, but resourceful. I remembered my briefing and looked around for the Soviet overseer. Sure enough, he was there, just where I expected, leaning leisurely against a Passport Control booth appearing to notice nothing. I crooked a finger and beckoned him. Stony face and stony stare. I beckoned again. He frowned with annoyance. He was not one to be beckoned. I'd earlier fished out my "importants" in preparation: my letter in English from Soviet Foreign Trade Minister Anastas Mikoyan, which I'd had copied in Russian before leaving Saigon. I displayed letter and passport, making sure stone face could see the Commissariat stamp of approval, and with the other hand, pointed to the letter. It certainly got his attention. He looked at me for a few seconds, then with a *nichevo* shrug, tossed his cigarette and slouched over.

Looking first at my passport, he asked the obvious question, *"Amerikansky?"*

"Da." I followed that with *"Armeniansky*: Mikoyan," thrusting letter and passport at him. He read the letter twice, flipped open my passport and studied the stamps and markings.

His eyebrows shot up looking at me closely; he said something like *"pa-Russkie?"*

"Nyet," seemed safe.

"*Amerikansky,*" I said, hoping for a reaction.

"Pliss to take seat, yes? Pliss have sam tea, yes?" They should have been expecting me, but apparently they weren't. Stony now had a change in expression: worry. Using sign language, I asked if I was to leave the line and was directed to a desk. Phones and busy militia were all going at the same time. Stony started talking to a soldier with blue shoulder markings, gray soulless eyes and pimply skin, who looked me over and said nothing. The magic words "*Amerikansky* "and "Mikoyan" went back and forth. Suddenly a senior officer appeared. From the sudden change in everyone's manners, this guy had status.

"Ah good afternoon, Sir, welcome to the Soviet Socialist Republics and Moscow. You had nice trip, no? Pliss to come with me." He led me to a glass-enclosed, cool reception room full of stale cigarette smoke, musty cooking smells, and dark heavy furniture. "Pliss to take tea, yes?"

"Yes, I'd love some tea." He extracted a tray of cheese, dark bread, some bottled water, and baklava, that sweet delicious pastry, from a fridge. Eyebrows furrowed, he sat at a desk and began dialing on a very contemporary handset. With my passport and letters in hand he began an animated conversation with someone repeating my name and Mikoyan's, listening for long pauses and smoking. I sipped and munched. Stony's body language suggested frustration, and his voice became hard and low, as though grinding out his meaning.

It was time for my next act. I walked over, smiling enough to make him worry. "You speak English, yes?"

"Sam...leetle."

"Please ask the Ministry why I have not been met by your officials. And when do I meet Mr. Mikoyan?"

"Wull, you see, Doktor, you must pliss to understand, Mr. Mikoyan is not in Moscow and his office has no information of you. I have told them of his letter to you, that you are his guest, and they are sending a limousine for you. So pliss to have sam more tea. You like cigarette? American brand?"

"No thanks."

"I am arranging passport clearance and your baggage wull be bring here. His office very sorry. They will contact Minister Mikoyan immediately. In meantime, pliss to wait." He forced a smile. The poor son of a bitch was caught in the middle. I plopped down and looked around. Lenin's picture hung on one wall and the place stank of strong tobacco. I'd hoped for a quick, pleasant reception and a majestic ride to a fancy hotel. No dice. I decided to tickle the system again. I fished out my Nikon range finder, loaded with a roll of high speed Ektachrome with about half a roll left. I shot some frames of the room, then finished the roll taking pictures of airplanes and people outside. My baggage arrived and my handler returned with my passport, several sheets of paper folded lengthwise stapled to its back cover.

Money, I'd need money. You can't buy rubles outside of Russia, so I pulled out some American Express travelers' checks to be cashed. "Moment," he said, with the Germanic inflection. I chose a few hundred dollar checks, signed and handed them over. He soon returned with a wad of crisp notes and coins, which I pocketed without counting.

"Save this in passport," he said, handing me a voucher confirming legal exchange of money. Suddenly the door burst open. In bounded a sweaty man who reminded me of Jackie Gleason: ruddy face, straw hat, ill-fitting brown suit, rumpled shirt, and wide blue tie. Not quite on a par with our own State Department dandies. He directed a torrent of information at me in fairly recognizable English. Unfortunately Mikoyan had been called away on state business for Chairman Nikita Khrushchev and he would be in Geneva all week, but he'd directed that whatever I wanted should be granted. Was my father planning to join me?

"No" I said, "My father wrote to Mikoyan regretting." That seemed to satisfy him.

"Pliss to come to our car. Where do you wish to go first?"

I had hotel reservations at the Ukraina and wanted to go there and get cleaned up and then report to my embassy. I told him that I hoped to visit some of the Medical Centers during my short visit here.

"Fine, fine. We have excellent hotels here, the National is presently filled, but Ukraina is excellent choice. You wull be guest of our Ministry, Mikoyan's orders."

I was a hybrid guest. Half official, half private. I'd paid for some vouchers up front. As we piled into a huge Chaika limousine with a flying bird logo on the grill, I thanked the customs agent and gave him a powerful handshake and my business card. He was happy to wave me off.

--•--

TRAFFIC SIGNALS BE DAMNED. WE sped to the Ukraina Hotel. I was expected and assigned quickly to room 2206....*dvatsat, dva, nul, shest.* Easy to remember.

Jackie Gleason took me up to my room, barked at the old babushka at the hall desk, who leaped up and lumbered ahead to open the door with her master key on a fat chain.

It was a large, very clean room with a view of the river and city. There was a large bathroom reeking of a powerfully clean smell, something like Pine Oil and Clorox mixed together, not unpleasant for an old hospital hound like me. An elderly man brought up my baggage and I moved to hand him a ruble, but Jackie Gleason held out a restraining hand. Right, no tips, I remembered. Next Jackie walked over to my table, grabbed a bottle of water and poured two glasses. We toasted each other. This was laughable: a Russian never toasts with water. There was wine, vodka and liqueur on the side table, but no, it was to be water.

"Welcome, Doktor," he said with mock gravity. I wished he'd leave.

His card in Cyrillic and English identified him as Professor Ivan Benediktov, Ministry of Health. He read from a sheet of yellow paper. "You wull have two guides from the Ministry now coming from Intourist, they to be with you all times. They wull be Marina Puchkova, she speak good English, very nice lady. You like nice ladies, yes?"

"Yes, of course."

"And also you will have Mr. Malik Nazarov. Whatever you wish, they wull arrange for you...pliss. They take you to dinner this evening. And Mr. Mikoyan says pliss to accept our apologies," he wiped a sweaty brow. "But State matters require him to be in Geneva, and world matters regretfully come first." It sounded like a dodge, but I really didn't care. I'd hang around for a few days and then leave.

"Now, here is telephone number for your embassy: 52001. Also phones for Puchkova and Nazarov, at Ministry offices, is 9-2-2384. Here is telephone, you dial like this," he said, spinning in the embassy numbers.

A heavily accented female voice announced, "American embassy." I asked to speak to the ambassador's secretary.

"He is busy, who is calling?" As I started to explain, the professor grabbed the phone and spoke a few words crisply and firmly in Russian, then with a proud smile, he handed me the receiver. "Sorry," he said, "she did not understand."

The secretary confirmed the ambassador was expecting me. "Could you drop over for a drink at about 5:30? An embassy car will be waiting for you in front at about 5:20." I turned and thanked the professor. He smiled a genuine smile that suggested all had gone well. He was probably happy to get the hell out.

Time to get on my diplomatic face and clothes. I freshened up and went out to find a veteran Chevy idling. The driver was an American Marine, judging by his haircut, and a man of few words. In a few minutes we were at Spaso House, wheeling sharply through an arched gateway flanked by two lounging Russian guards, who gave us the stony once-over. Inside the compound, I saw a Marine in dress blues, a signal that brass was around.

The building was not impressive. It looked old, tired, worn out, and generally shabby. The walls were faded, earth-colored California stucco with many cracks. At the very least, it needed new paint. Inside and without ceremony, the Ambassador's frazzled secretary glanced at her wristwatch and whisked me into his office. Clearly, she was working late. She knocked and showed me in.

"Oh, there you are, Doctor, come right in. I'm Llewellyn Thompson. Been expecting you." He pointed to a chair next to his desk. "May I offer you a drink?"

"Good to meet you. What do you suggest, sir?"

"We have to go over a few matters with you. Maybe coffee would be a good idea." Within minutes, we had coffee and Graham crackers. "I'm waiting for Chip Kitchen to join us. Chip is our Political Military man and needs to meet with you, then we'll all go into the bubble and have a short pow-wow."

Thompson impressed me as a quiet man. He had a calm, confident manner and steely eyes. His dress reflected his status as an Ivy League type; button down shirt, preppie tie, gray slacks, blue blazer and penny loafers. His hair was carefully groomed.

I was slightly in awe of Thompson, aware of his reputation as a hard bargainer with the Russkies. I knew that one had to be both firm and shrewd to deal with some of these slippery Slavs and I was convinced that not much got by this man. But at this particular moment, he was a gracious, charming host and any uneasiness began to fade. While we chatted, he discreetly put his hand to his mouth to suppress a belch. Not uncommon to many folks after a meal, but I noticed a large bottle of antacid tablets on his desk next to some milk and cookies. I realized that this very important diplomat had some form of dyspepsia. Milk and cookies stop that gnawing sensation, albeit temporarily. Whether it was an ulcer, esophagitis or gastritis, it was *prima facie* evidence of occupational stress. To toil in an unfriendly country, whose every diplomatic move was wreathed in secrecy, where nothing could be taken for granted, was taking its toll on this man. He was our point man sent to scout the enemy, not just for one mission, but every day, day after day.

Were there other tell-tale signs? Deep wrinkles were etched across his forehead with several deep grooves between his eyebrows and around both eyes. My clinical mind told me that this poor guy would pay a price at some point in the future as the ulcer symptoms took their toll. Surgery had its pressures too; but given a choice, I'd take the operating room every time.

He made it clear that like most highly visible diplomats, he was a history buff. History was the timeless resource which often provides precedents when complex situations arose. Ambassador Thompson said, "Most folks think an assignment to Moscow is a punishment of sorts. A punishment for some, a challenge for others. For us Foreign Service guys, it's a hell of a challenge, especially in this atmosphere of total paranoia."

Looking at his watch, he asked his secretary to call the hotel and advise my "bodyguards" from Intourist that I'd be late. Muscovites dine late.

While I was waiting, he asked her to have my passport stamped with a notation that I'd visited the embassy, and just for good measure, to add an extender to handle more visa stamps.

— · —

WITHIN MINUTES, CHIP KITCHEN ARRIVED, still sweaty from a workout. Thompson waved us all toward the "bubble." We shuffled down an antiquated hall to a huge plastic room placed in the middle of an ancient conference room. It really wasn't a bubble at all, more like a huge square plastic box mounted on support legs. Amazing! Kitchen punched a code into a keypad and we climbed into a cool, air-conditioned room. The sides, roof and floor were all transparent plastic! No place to hide listening devices, sound vibrations pickups, nothing. Even so, it was swept electronically several times daily. The "bubble," I learned, was our answer to the snoops of the Seventh Chief Directorate of the KGB, the Russian spy agency.

Kitchen started with a warning to me: "They, the snoops, all buzz in and out of headquarters over on Dzerzhinsky Square, so stay away from there. You might look funny to them and pique their curiosity. They might hassle or detain you, so just avoid that area unless you're in a crowd, understand?" I did.

"By the way, there may be more non-Russian bad-asses in their intelligence services than Russian. For instance, their leader Dzerzhinsky was a Polack. Felix was his first name. He became one of the most feared men in the whole Soviet empire. The snoops from that directorate are all slicksters. They've riddled our embassy with listening devices, tapped all phone lines and co-opted all Russian employees." Kitchen told me that our embassy, in fact, had been bugged continuously since 1933! Some guy named Andreichin, a Bulgarian troublemaker, had whispered this information to Ambassador Averill Harriman at the embassy pissoir during a reception. Harriman was so upset with this unwanted information he almost soiled himself.

"Of course, we've tried to find all these taps and bugs, but it's damn near hopeless. So we have this bubble. And I'm happy to say, the goddamn thing hasn't been pierced yet." He went on, "The KGB wants to know, needs to know what Americans are up to. An unsure society is wracked with paranoia. So they keep pecking away at us trying to get information." At the outset, we had countered the KGB snoopers quietly with this bubble. No one is allowed in except Americans with clearance, with no exceptions, including the cleaning crew and technicians who did the daily electronic sweep, even though it was a virtual impossibility to bug the bubble. In this sacrosanct creation, the ambassador and his staff could safely discuss and conduct classified business. While Kitchen had explained all this to me, the ambassador was leafing thru some notes and correspondence.

Thompson, known to his intimates as Tommy, did no sensitive business outside the bubble. Once in, there was no direct contact with the outside world except for ventilation. All phones were tapped and all Russian personnel were considered informers, willingly or not. The Soviets had ways of handling recalcitrant employees, and some of those ways could be unpleasant.

We sat inside the plastic cube with only coffee and legal pads. Thompson had a fairly comprehensive file on me and knew my background. What puzzled him was why I came to visit Moscow from Saigon. I told the story from the beginning, about the letter from my dad and his distrust of Mikoyan, which led to his decision to send me in his stead. They listened without comment.

Dad had once been titular head of the Dashnaks, the Armenian Revolutionary Party, not loved by Moscow, nor the Turks for that matter, but admired by State. Thompson knew how Dashnaks dealt with certain troubling matters and people, and it wasn't much of a stretch for him to be aware of how Stalinists behaved, Mikoyan in particular.

"How much do you know about Mikoyan?" asked Thompson.

"Not too much," I said, "except that he's a fellow Armenian."

"Being an Armenian means nothing to that guy," said the ambassador. "He's a tough son of a bitch, an incredible survivor, and right now he's in the midst of some internal trouble, again. He sided with Khrushchev in bringing to light Stalin's reign of terror. Mikoyan knows where the bones are buried, and he may be in danger from those 'loyal' to Stalin who are at risk of exposure. No revelations at this time would be good for Russia's image, so it's best to let things lie quietly. For the present, we keep up with the Soviet's complex dealings with their subscriber countries and the activities of their KGB."

"One bit of history haunted the Russian hierarchy," said Kitchen. "Western analysts were quick to exploit any flaws in Russian ideology. Back in the early days of 1920's Communism, the head of the International Red Cross, a tough Irishman named Colonel Edward A. Ryan, described the Soviet Republic as: '...a social adventure become a ghastly failure.' Condemnation from the head of a world famous organization drove the Soviet hierarchy and their American sympathizers into a rage."

Kitchen explained, "Remarks like that heightened Soviet paranoia and have made them more secretive and suspicious of outsiders. They try to play up the idealisms and glories of their great country, but the bastards are gonna have the whole house of cards come crashing down around them at some point down the line," predicted Kitchen. "The cards are listing dangerously."

Thompson chimed in now, "Both Stalin and Mikoyan were from Georgia and both were involved in party matters at an early age, destined to rise to powerful positions. Like Stalin, Mikoyan had chosen the cloth; he started out as a seminarian. He became a revolutionary, got into immediate trouble, was arrested and sentenced to death. Somehow, the story goes, there was a mix-up and Mikoyan wasn't taken out and hung. This guy has led a charmed life and still does. No one else ever disobeyed Stalin and survived. No one who was willingly separated from Stalin survived. Trotsky and many others are cases in point. Mikoyan has damning knowledge of Stalin's atrocities, his cruelty to his wife Nadezhda, who killed herself, and to his closest friend, Sergei Ordzhonikidze, who shot himself."

Thompson and Kitchen had been ping-ponging information at me. "Chip, why don't you finish briefing the doctor."

The ambassador rose and excused himself, but stopped mid-step. "By the way, Doctor, I know about your *National Geographic* credentials that Mel Grosvenor arranged for you, but it would be best to put them away until you're safely out of here. Under no condition show them to anyone. We'd have to go through all kinds of shenanigans with the Ministry of Information if they learn that you're an accredited photojournalist. Just pretend you're a tourist and snap away at Lenin's Tomb, St. Basil's, the crowds at the Kremlin, and the Exposition. That sort of thing is smiled upon. Journalists are not. We don't want to give them any excuses to make trouble for you. Got it?" I nodded.

"Good." He left.

"Here's some more to mull over, Doctor," said Kitchen, handing me a sheaf of glossy black and white photos. "In the picture of Stalin's famous meeting at that Yalta resort, you'll see a sharp-nosed little guy with a Pistol Pete mustache hovering in the background. That's Anastas Mikoyan," he chuckled, pointing at the diminutive figure just behind Stalin. "Roosevelt went home full of friendly thoughts about our Russian allies. He told his cabinet and his administration that it was time for America to get on better terms with the Soviets. The commie sympathizers in Washington ate it up. But the Soviets had used force and intimidation after World War II to grab what they wanted in Germany, and while pretending friendship, the Russkies embarked on an espionage program of unprecedented vigor. They wanted to know about everything we did. They flooded America with spies in every conceivable guise, enlisting disaffected Russian émigrés in New York City and Brighton Beach. In short they started the Cold War." He shifted. "Today, though, the Russians are catching on. Stories of Soviet secret police carrying out senseless killings, torturing innocent people in prisons, and mass executions of the Polish militia have filtered through to the masses. And, of course, you can bet we help to disseminate bad news whenever we can. So, be advised that the Soviets might take your presence here as a grand opportunity to somehow discredit you and America in the eyes of the world. You're here on a very high-level invitation and they may be looking for a way to set you up."

Kitchen had my daily schedule all laid out "As you know, Doctor, Moscow is full of Americans just now. Dr. Michael DeBakey is here, a Dr. Ravitch from Johns Hopkins and some nurse from New York. They are all hoping to get their hands on an improved surgical stapler just announced by a famous Russian surgeon, Dr. Androsov. They stand a fat chance of getting to him because Androsov is a bit stand-offish. You, of all, may have a good meet with him because he's on your schedule, so take advantage of that if you have any interest in staplers."

"And," he went on, "Vice President Nixon just left Moscow, so the diplomatic missions have recently stopped those parties. In addition to that, right now we have a whole bunch of Americans at the Exposition here, and it's crammed with Russians asking questions, grabbing everything not nailed down. The Polaroid people are taking snapshots for one and all with their new instant camera. The Russian visitors can't get enough of those instant snaps, unheard of in Russia. The Polaroid techs snap photos as fast as they can, yank the film out, peel off the picture, and hand them out in souvenir folders. The Soviets would really go nuts if they knew we are processing the discarded paper negatives. You never know what interesting faces might show up in those negs. Exposure to the fancy displays at the American exposition is a two-headed sword for the Party leaders. Russians citizens should not know too much about the outside world. It might make them restless, so the guys and gals from the Seventh Chief Directorate of the KGB keep a watchful eye on all Americans, day and night."

Kitchen described the KGB and all its directorates. "The Soviets are so paranoid, they have the equivalents of both our FBI and CIA working together in various directorates, plus an entirely separate military intelligence outfit. These guys don't always get along with each other. They carry out assassinations, called wet jobs or black jobs. We probably do, too. The Seventh Chief Directorate will do anything to get into our files, our phones, even going so far as to prey on the loneliness of our military men. For example, some little gal will walk by the embassy day after day, wiggling and smiling sweetly at the guards, and finally one day, she crooks her little finger. The Soviet Militia men ignore her and hope that some Marine will get suckered in. Once he goes for the bait, we can be compromised. That's what we worry about."

"We have a big shot named Pyke Johnson from the American Automotive Safety Foundation here who's driving the Russkies nuts too, because they're convinced he's CIA and they don't have any information on him. If necessary, he'll get roped into an incident, and that applies to you too, Doc."

Kitchen continued: "Mikoyan visited Washington last January and got into a shouting match with your father. He was part of the Soviet 'soften-up-the- Americans' ploy of 1959. He had been invited to speak at the National Press Club, and your father got up in the middle of Mikoyan's address and lambasted him in Armenian, calling him a crook, a *khatchakogh,* someone who would steal a cross from the altar, which is as heavy an insult as one Armenian can sling at another. Mikoyan had left the seminary to become a Communist. And worse yet, he was a confidante of Stalin's. Trouble was, few of the reporters had any idea of what the hell was going on. The whole scene was bedlam and the Club president finally gaveled everybody to silence. Reporters were scurrying around pleading for a translation, and your Dad gave them his interpretation. The *Washington Post* carried it.

"Meanwhile," Kitchen said, "something is going on inside the Kremlin currently. Our sources say that Mikoyan is toting an automatic in his belt and his bodyguards are on high alert. Something is hatching, a coup, a sudden heart attack, a sudden poisoning? Our sources tell us that paranoia is brimming at higher than normal levels just now and we're not sure why." He stopped now and I realized I was hungry, exhausted, and desperately trying to focus. A smiling, bookish man entered the room and took a seat at the far end of the table.

"Hi, Alex," Kitchen said. "Meet Dr. Sundukian." We shook hands.

"I'm just finishing up with the doctor, then you can have a go."

He went on. "They call this the cold war, with each side trying to derail the other in every way possible, no holds barred. Bottom line is, Doctor, watch your topknot. You'll certainly be watched, followed, escorted everywhere, and shown what they want you to see. We've changed part of the schedule slightly, so you'll be with one of our doctors at Sklifasovsky Institute part of the time."

Several things were becoming clear. Moscow was an unhappy political environment with a lot of discord between the Soviets and the United States that I didn't understand. Probably just as well. I did know that wily Mikoyan had gotten involved in important trade negotiations with American manufacturers hoping to bring the 20th century to his backward country. Washing machines, soda fountains, all kinds of gadgets. Dr. Armand Hammer, a physician entrepreneur, was helping him. What was not known was whether Hammer cooperated with American intelligence services, too.

I turned to Alex Adams, a slight man of medium height who appeared fit. He looked at me with clear blue eyes, the hallmark of a no-bullshitter. Kitchen stood up and excused himself. "From now on, Alex takes over," he said as he exited the bubble. "I'll be seeing more of you later."

— - • - —

ADAMS AND I CHATTED FOR a few minutes. He knew Washington well and had attended Harvard, where he learned Russian, which came in mighty handy at the Embassy. As Cultural Attaché, he would be coordinating my schedule, which had been carefully planned. Basically, I was to make hospital rounds with my Russian escorts and the embassy physician, Jim Street. The escorts would arrange transportation, take me to the American Exposition, shopping at GUM, *Swan Lake* at the Bolshoi, dinners at Aragvi, at Ararat and Bazdrushnik's Chai Khana. Dr. Street would introduce me to the various physicians, surgeons, and scientists at the M.V. Sklifasovsky Institute, Wishnevsky Institute, First Surgical Institute, and Center for Thoracic Surgery. It was a helluva itinerary and I was pleased.

CHAPTER 21

Sklifasovsky Institute

*Think on the sacred dictates of thy faith, and
let that arm thy virtue to perform...*
—Nicholas Rowe, 1674–1718, Tamerlane

THE INSTITUTE WAS NAMED AFTER A LEGENDARY BACK COUNTRY PHYSICIAN who had given his life to improve health care for the poor, the undernourished, and diseased of that early time. I met Professor P.I. Androsov, Chief of Surgery, who trained under S.S. Yudin, the surgeon who had devised a technique to replace acid-scarred esophagi, the tube carrying food from mouth to stomach, in children and adults. Poor Russian families often keep a bottle of corrosive acid to clear frost off of isinglass windows, and unsuspecting children drink the clear liquid. Their esophagus is usually burned, some fatally, but for those who survive, swallowing and nutrition become a problem. Yudin and his assistants devised a way to replace the esophagus by borrowing a segment of bowel to insert between stomach and throat. Androsov and his team did two or three of these operations every day from a huge backlog of patients. I watched him as he reviewed X-ray films, patients, and selected the appropriate procedure. Androsov was an impressive and delightful man. He had a broad Slavic face, prominent cheekbones, a massive jaw, and squinty almond eyes softened with a boyish grin and a charming manner. He spoke little English, but Jim Street and Nazarov interpreted. Like many Russians, he had that winking steel central incisor which at times was hypnotically disconcerting.

I was introduced as "the Armenian professor from America," which totally confused everyone. After rounds, Androsov and his team began readying patients for surgery. It was all done under local anesthesia, with Novocain injected into the tissues at least an hour before the actual operation.

Unbelievably, before they started their arduous operating day, Androsov and his senior team members first chowed down on hefty helpings of cheese, blintzes, black bread, sliced tomatoes, and huge bunches of dill, washed all this down with tumblers of Polish vodka, and then finally rinsed it down with scalding tea from the table-side samovar.

I went along with everything but the vodka. Their bulbous noses and cheeks showed fine red capillaries under the skin, which told me liver trouble was ahead for them.

— - • - —

SURGEONS ARE CREATURES OF HABIT. A given operation is done the same way every time, unless an unforeseen situation arises, but rarely do they change a successful routine except to improve it. This way the team becomes familiar with the surgeon's technique and the operation becomes a smooth symphony of movements. Instrument nurse, assistants, circulating nurse, and anesthesiologist all work together, each has a role, and each knows what to do at the next step. There are few wasted motions, thus the patient and team spend less time in surgery: a plus for all.

Androsov led me into his operating room with a wave of his arm and introduced me as a famous *Amerikanski* surgeon to the line of nurses, who bobbed respectfully. Some were young and slender, some aging babushkas. All wore bedroom slippers or flip-flops, a white wrap around their head and surgical masks. But alas, the masks stopped at their noses, which hung out uncovered. At my hospital it would be grounds for summary execution. All surgical masks should cover the nose to prevent contamination of the patient's open incision.

But one nurse stood apart from the others. A thin strand of pearls encircled her neck just under her operating room smock. *Strange,* I thought. *Who the hell was she?* Nurses are not allowed to wear anything beyond OR smocks.

It turned out that she was Androsov's first assistant, but being a woman doctor, she was not welcome to join the vodka routine. I watched as she got things ready for her boss and the "visiting genius."

After quick formal introductions, Androsov took me over to the X-ray view boxes. The collegial hilarity and vodka toasts to our respective institutions had ended and it was now show-time for the serious business at hand.

Androsov used a short pointer to describe the X-ray studies of the patient *du jour*, a twenty-six-year-old woman who had burned her gizzard gulping acid as a child. She had been able to drink liquids until her teens, but had then required an operation, which created a subcutaneous tunnel over her chest from the upper esophagus to the midportion of the stomach to enable her to take nourishment. Androsov pointed out that these tragic acid-burned victims had very little body fat from potatoes and other starches. In that regard, they were healthy, after a fashion, with very low cholesterol levels and very little arterial disease. Their food intake was limited to ground meats and nourishing soups containing soluble carbohydrates, an extremely healthy diet that could not be continued.

Androsov showed me the X-ray films where the esophagus had closed off and where the new tunnel carried food to the stomach. Then he showed me where these tunnels had developed small perforations draining food and liquids to the outside that become infected and can be fatal. Antibiotics were not plentiful, nor always effective, so it had fallen to Yudin to develop his ingenious bypass operation to manage these situations.

Androsov's assistant brought the patient's chart for me to examine: total proteins were low; albumen levels borderline; hemoglobin borderline; creatinine levels slightly elevated; not healthy findings. I had no explanation for that creatinine level, maybe renal problems beyond my expertise. This patient had been selected and approved for bypass by her regional surgical consultant and sent to Sklifasovsky. She had endured a ten-day period of high nutrition IVs, nothing by mouth, compresses daily to the sinus areas which started at mid-chest level and burrowed under one breast before exiting through the skin. Then she was prepped with a series of enemas and cathartics to cleanse the bowel, a segment of which would replace the esophagus.

I was introduced to this woman in the preoperative staging area. She wore a thin white smock and pale blue bikini shorts. She had the svelte figure, pale pasty complexion, and long, thin limbs of a starving person, but also long blonde hair bound in a chignon and well-developed breasts. Some modern women strive for this look, but in her case, it was an indication of an abnormal nutritional state.

The first stage of the operation was to isolate a segment of colon, slip it behind the sternum and up into the left side of the neck where it would be left for two weeks. During this time the colon segment, its blood supply intact, but needing to be "accepted" in its new location, was left in situ to calm itself and gradually develop tiny vascular capillaries assuring its acceptance by its new neighbors. The lower portion of that colon would be stitched into the stomach. Two weeks later, the upper portion of the colon would be hooked up to the now divided esophagus in the neck and within another ten days, the patient started on a soft diet.

I was anxious to see Androsov at work. My minders, Nazarov and company, were not allowed in. They cooled their heels back in the hallway where the patient's family waited.

"Ready?"

"Ready," came the response all around. Androsov squirted more Novocaine, and then slowly made a high left rectus incision with a hockey stick curve up and to the left, just over the stomach. Androsov inserted abdominal retractors to widen the opening, then in a series of quick, well-practiced moves, selected a segment of large bowel, all the while growling orders under his breath. His assistant had quick fingers and was with him all the way. She anticipated his moves and was clearly fully capable of doing this operation herself in case old Androsov tumbled over dead during an operation, always a possibility.

In less than an hour, the team had taken a length of colon, divided and isolated it, restored the colon's continuity, and then through a left neck incision, gently pulled one end of the isolated segment of colon into the neck incision and tacked it down. The lower end of this segment was now sewn into the stomach, which had been tacked to the abdominal wall ten years earlier and had to be taken down. It was a tedious, ten-minute dissection, accompanied by Russian curses, but they plowed on, curses and all, and all the while, the patient was awake.

In a short time, the lower end of the colon segment was sewn to the stomach. At this point, Androsov grunted in satisfaction, stripped off his gloves rather dramatically, tossed them at his scrub nurse, and pointing to me, led us out. I'd made mental notes of the steps in the operation, and later committed them to paper. Androsov gave me a copy of Yudin's original article as a souvenir. In two weeks, he said, he'd open the neck incision and join that segment to the esophagus. In thirty days she would go home a happy woman. He would do several more cases today if I wished to scrub in? I graciously declined, thanking him profusely and congratulating him and his assistants on a nicely done procedure.

"By the way," I remarked, I had not been introduced to his assistant.

"Oh yes, sorry. An oversight," he said. "She is excellent assistant and someday might become a fine surgeon, with more training, of course. She is Ekaterina Smolenskova. We call her Katy," he smiled a bit wolfishly.

Next, we toured the Institute, Jim Street interpreting and my watchdogs trailing in awe. I was shown the Emergency Room where DOAs were quickly hooked up to blood collection bottles containing anticoagulants and drained of their blood. The blood was quickly tested (*for what?*), and if okay, used for blood replacement during surgery, for accident victims, or whatever. I was stunned, "You mean you use cadaver blood?"

"Of course, why it should be wasted? It is in keeping with our policy of everything for the State, the State for all of us. If a patient needs blood, we here at Sklifasovsky have ample blood to supply our institution and other institutions as well. The Cardiac Center is especially wasteful of blood. Many times we have prevented a disaster for those clumsy amateurs," he blurted out.

Funny these Russians, I thought. One minute very proud of all things Russian, then in the next minute, slamming their colleagues as clumsy. Hard to figure. But that was the Russian mystique, as fickle as a debutante and not as attractive. I was taken to a conference room where photos of great doctors hung on all four walls, including a smiling Michael E. DeBakey in a freshly hung frame. "Oh yes, we have great admiration for your Dr. DeBakey. He is an American hero."

It was getting late, so we made a quick run to the First Surgical Institute, where I met Dr. Avedis Samuelian, a Russianized fellow Armenian. We made arrangements for me to witness research procedures the next day. It had been a long day and I was tired. I asked Jim how we could end this marathon.

"Easy," he said. He asked my watchdogs to return me to the hotel for a rest. He had things to do at the Embassy. I was told we had dinner reservations at the Ararat, the finest Armenian restaurant in Moscow. I was becoming uneasy that the Armenian factor was becoming more important than it should be. I was an American with Armenian parents here because of my father and his interaction with Anastas Mikoyan. Where the hell was Anastas? *Nyet* in Moscow.

I went back to my room at the Ukraina and flopped onto the hard bed for a few minutes. My feet and back hurt. After I gulped down a liter of bottled water, I felt immediately rehydrated and slowly regained some sense of well-being.

It had been a confusing day of rounds, visits, forgotten names, smiles, handshakes, and business cards. I'd run out of my own cards and resorted to scribbling on the backs of other people's. The card exchange was mostly ceremonial anyway and rarely led to anything.

Glancing at my bureau, I checked the tiny gray feather that I had slipped on the edge of the bureau drawer while gently closing it. Opening it would dislodge the feather. I'd made a tiny scratch marking the feather location, just in case whoever peeked got clever and wanted to replace it. Now the feather lay on the floor, where it had lightly floated, when some nosy son-of-a-bitch had slid the drawer open. It also meant that the cleaning woman hadn't done a good job cleaning.

Nothing seemed to have been moved. My stuff was still in the jumbled mess I'd left it in: cameras, lenses, notebooks, underwear, and socks. I had to assume that everything had been searched, but so what? *I had nothing to hide.*

I decided to rig a camera, turning the self-timer lever down a click and securing it with gaffer tape to the drawer frame. Anyone opening it would pull the tape loose, and the delayed timer lever with only one click engaged completed the circuit. Sure enough, the next day someone snooped, got snapped and stupidly taped the loosened camera back without resetting the timer. I dismantled the unit and hid the film, planning to look at the face later.

After resting, I went with my minders to the Ararat Restaurant, at 14 Neclinnaia Street, for roast lamb, pilaf, *cherbriki,* Armenian meat, and *Algeshat,* a sweet Armenian wine. The moment we entered this restaurant, it smelled like my mother's kitchen and I had an instant, vivid flashback of Mother cooking pilaf and screeching inanities at Minny, her devoted cook. They never agreed on how to cook anything, but it was always delicious.

It took a moment to get acclimated inside the dark, noisy restaurant. A thick pall of blue cigarette smoke hung over the dining area, with everyone talking and gesturing at once, normal behavior for those from the Caucasus. All eyes were on the foreigner as we made our way to our reserved table. My clothes gave me away as non-Russian. I overheard remarks from diners as we passed tables. One woman was telling her companion, in Armenian, that I looked like an Italian. She'd heard Italians were hung like horses and she loved horses. Her companion grunted that she was an old nag which only a horse might consider screwing. The table roared with laughter.

In Russian, Malik told the waiter that I was an important guest of the government. I decided to throw something into the fan. Using my best radio announcer's voice, I asked the waiter in a clear ringing voice: "*Hairen gekhosis?*" Do you speak Armenian? His eyebrows went up, a huge grin," *E, anshust!* But of course!..."

Malik blurted out in shock, "Please, Doktor, stop! It will be disruptive for the diners. It is not proper." He was horrified.

Heads had swiveled and I smiled and made eye contact. Marina, too, was shaken and did not want attention now.

"Doctor Dzhon... I am suggesting we should order sam fud, yes?"

"Sure."

"I am recommending salad, *shashlik* and pilaf...is okay?"

"Sure."

"First we make toast. You prefer Russian vodka or good red *Kavkaz* wine?"

Wine from the Kavkaz, which meant a great Georgian red. "Whatever you suggest," I responded.

"I am suggesting vodka, then red wine with our dinner."

"Fine."

She smiled, a sign that things were quickly going better. She signaled to the hovering waiter and ordered rapid fire. Within minutes, we had a carafe of wicked looking vodka, some small plates of hummus, a puree of fish roe, and a lovely tin of fresh gray, pearlescent caviar, the greatest of delicacies, served with a huge sprig of dill weed and large slabs of black bread. I asked for water, too.

Marina had dressed quite nicely for the occasion. She wasn't a natural blonde, but her hair looked good fixed in a Marilyn Monroe style. She was quite fetching in a form-fitting black dress with a black silk shawl around her shoulders. Her position as interpreter clearly gave her access to American and European fashion magazines. Malik wore a clean shirt and tie with a rumpled suit. He was unshaven, which was apparently acceptable.

I was mystified by a toast to "our mission," but accepted a *de rigueur* toast on behalf of my government. The caviar was absolutely the most delicious stuff on this planet, perfectly smeared on tender black bread with chopped eggs and diced onions, and washed down with a crystal clear, fiery vodka. Malik dispensed with formalities and dug a spoon into it, gulping down a huge amount, all in one smooth motion. I followed suit.

"From our Caspian Sea," he said. "Is good, huh?"

"*Shad hamov*," I replied. Very tasty. Malik flinched and shriveled into his seat. "Please, Doktor, again you are forgetting where you are. This is public place. People listening!"

"No Malik, you are forgetting who you are! But I will try not to let it happen again." Malik relaxed. I could hear Kavkaz dialect all around me among the Armenian diners. I swiveled my head and slowly looked around. Most of them were smiling good-naturedly. They'd figured me out. I winked and smiled back. All was *kharashoh*...okay.

Then in short order, dinner came. Mother would have smiled; it was a clone of her cooking. The kebabs were borne in triumphantly by a prancing chef waving long flaming skewers. Once at the table, our waiter held the skewers point down firmly on my dish. I quickly wrapped a piece of flat bread around the meat and slid it down onto my plate. The waiter smiled and nodded, acknowledging *this guy is one of us. He knows how to handle shashlik.*

Along with the caviar, they brought out a platter of *ichli kefte*, which I alone cared to eat. It is raw lamb, ground and mixed with bulgur, chopped onion and parsley, and then squeezed into small lumps. We had a full, three-course dinner, finishing with baklava, strong bitter coffee served in dainty demitasse cups, and finally some powerful Armenian brandy labeled, *Tresht Ararat*. I'd had wine, so I tossed the remainder of my snifter neatly over my shoulder into a potted plant.

I wanted a souvenir of this evening, so I'd tucked my Nikon SP loaded with fast film into my jacket pocket. During coffee, I slid the Nikon out and started taking pictures. Disaster struck. Suddenly, a drunken woman rose from the back of the room and began screeching in Russian that I was a spy taking photographs of all the fine soldiers seated here. The police should be called!

Malik nearly soiled himself: "Pliss Doktor, put away this camera. Is not permitted to take photographs of Soviet citizens without permission from the authorities."

"I'm getting tired of this," I yammered back. "I don't have to ask anyone's permission to do anything. If someone doesn't shut up that old babushka, I'm going to complain to Mikoyan's office. I am an American citizen, not a Muscovite frightened of his own shadow. And shame on you for not standing up to defend me. You should have told her I was an Armenian guest from America."

I was partly bluffing, but I wasn't going to skulk out with my tail between my legs. I stood and gestured to the door in a clear signal to all. "We're leaving." I'd shot ten frames inside the restaurant, some of which I hoped were usable. It's a chance you take with rapid fire, no set-up pictures. But I'd practiced many times, so some should come out.

The following night we dined at the Aragvi, a Georgian restaurant, and I had to admit that it was far better in every respect. The joint was jumping, in contrast to the Ararat's tense and gloomy atmosphere.

At the Aragvi, there was loud music, laughter, and lots of cigarette smoke. On the dance floor, a troupe of flashy gals and mustachioed men were doing a wild, jumping Cossack dance. Surprisingly, they were hopping around to the tunes of Khachaturian's "Sabre Dance." The music certainly fitted with the jumping, skirling of flutes, clashing of cymbals, twirling of sabers, banging of drums, and well-developed women twirling scarves and stomping their feet. One grizzled man in a huge sheepskin was doing tricks with some very long knives. This place had ambience!

Permeating the atmosphere were the great aromas of garlic, cooked meat, smoke, and a touch of sweat. The food, like most Caucasian food, was very similar to that of the neighboring Armenians: lots of kebabs, rice, and stuffed things like peppers, aubergines, squash, and something I'd forgotten existed, *media dolma!* Stuffed baked mussels in a Georgian restaurant? Wow!

The owner was a Turk whose family was from Bolice, a suburb of Constantinople, and these *dolmas* were a delicacy at his home, so he served it on the menu. He came over to greet Malik and shake my hand.

"Wulkom, Doktor. Wulkom to our restaurant. You are our guest, a fellow countryman from Kavkaz!" He clapped his hands and waiters galloped over from all directions. In another language, he ordered a long list, rapid fire. Soon, bottles of Georgian red wine appeared, were opened and poured. Never have I seen or tasted such beautiful deep purple wines with such body and delightful aroma. Between whirling dancers, stomping boots, flashing knives, shrieking flutes, and great wine, I was having a marvelous time. I asked permission to photograph the dancers. "Not a problem," said the smiling Turk.

I fired away, and for good measure, I propped Marina against a pillar, turned her forty-five degrees to her left, asked her to turn her head slowly towards me, duck her chin, look wide-eyed, and smile. She joined in the game, grinning and tossing her head, as I posed her with the grizzled old guy and the Cossack dancers. I shot three rolls of film without a peep from anyone. Marina took directions perfectly. She knew how and when to smile and show some leg. I promised to send her some prints.

I rose the next morning thinking that another day had passed with still no word from Mikoyan. This was to be our day at the Research Institute. It called for an early breakfast in the hotel lobby, where I unexpectedly found Alex Adams.

Adams was Boston-Harvard in every fiber of his appearance. He wore a single-breasted, tan poplin jacket, gray slacks, blue shirt and bow tie, with round eyeglasses. He was reading a Russian newspaper with the name in heavy Cyrillic: *Izvestia*.

Okay, I thought, *Al reads Russian*. It occurred to me that if Alex was most likely being watched, he was sending his observers a message. *Yes, I can read your papers and speak your language.* The Soviets would not quite understand Alex Adams, so they would watch him. I'd been told it often required up to twenty agents, plus cars, radios, and more, just to follow one man. I wondered how many were watching now.

He waved me over. "Good morning, Doctor, how are things going? Everything okay?"

I filled him in on the two dinners, the hospital visits, and various discussions. I told him of my feather and taped camera trick, and how it had trapped someone.

"Yeah, I heard some of this from Jim Street. Seems you are highly regarded by the Russians as a disciple of the famous American surgeons, Brian Blades and Michael DeBakey. Please join me for coffee. I have information for you."

We entered the hard cash restaurant, where only hard currency was accepted, which kept out most of the *hoi polloi*. I helped myself to eggs, cheese, a slab of some unidentified meat, sweet rolls, and strong, bitter coffee. Alex's scowl scared away two other diners who had intended to share our table, Moscow-style. Visitors of all makes and models milled around the buffet tables: Asians, Europeans, Africans and turbaned Indians, even a few Japanese carrying miniature Nippon flags.

Alex leaned forward, sipping his coffee, a sugar cube clamped in his front teeth.

"I thought they did that only with tea," I mumbled.

"Yeah, but it works with coffee, too."

Clearly, Adams was his own man and did what he thought was right for him and for his embassy. Wonder if that ever got him in trouble?

"Listen, Doctor," he said. "Tomorrow after work, at six o'clock, the ambassador is having a cocktail party at Spaso House and you should be there. There'll be folks from the Soviet Foreign Ministry there, and one of them will tell you that Mikoyan is still in Geneva, where, unfortunately, he's contracted a bad case of bronchitis and is confined to bed. If he doesn't improve, they'll fly him to the Almond Clinic in the States."

"This is their way of saying you won't be seeing him and they're looking for a way to send your bothersome ass home. So let's plan on you leaving within the next three days, since there's really no reason for you to hang around. Go ahead and visit the clinics tomorrow, meanwhile, I'll speak to the airlines about your return flight to DC. Let's figure you'll be at the embassy party tomorrow after your tour of the Exposition, and then the next day, fly out, okay?"

"Okay." I was unsettled at the thought of going back and felt myself beginning to dread the return. I'd have to deal with my absent practice and a whole host of things that lurked in the back of my mind and came in and out of focus, usually at the wrong times.

"By the way," said Alex. "Besides the Dashnaks, know who does the termite trick?"

"Termite trick?"

"Yeah, burrow into the Russian woodwork."

I drew a blank.

He explained. "Russia has a large Jewish population, most of which is loyal to Israel. Russian Jews are in a unique position to work in all branches of Soviet government and academia and are well-respected. At the same time, they are carefully accessed by the Mossad, Israel's intelligence service. Nice guys when they want to be, but very tough cookies." Alex glanced at his watch, "Gotta go." He turned and called for the check in Russian, but I insisted that this was on me. I told him I'd be meeting my Soviet minders shortly and ordered another coffee. Alex left and within minutes my team showed up none the worse for the previous night's activities. Marina looked downright perky and Malik was his usual dour self.

"Good morning to you," I said. They ordered sweet rolls from a disinterested waiter, who added it to the tab. *Good, now I'd let my keepers pay.*

"This is clinic day, yes, Doktor?"

"Yes, indeed." I was looking forward to this session at the Research Institute with Dr. Avedis "Harold" Samuelian, who had trained with Professor Androsov using the stapling devices now being developed by Soviet instrument engineers. Samuelian, I knew, was perfecting the use of staplers for surgical operations. It was a bold step forward to staple off a main artery and divide it, trusting that those tiny staples would hold the artery ends shut. That would entail resisting the pounding pressure of a column of blood with at least 120 to 130 mm of mercury behind it. Formidable, and in some cases very chancy. My old boss, Dr. Blades, felt more comfortable using sutures and ties. He mistrusted the stapler as some newfangled gadget and suggested strongly that I not waste my time with it. I assured him that progress was our watchword, no? At times like that, Blades would grunt and turn away. He knew I was right. But I'd failed to impress him that each and every staple in the line of staples laid down had the responsibility for handling only about ten millimeters of mercury pressure;

"about the force of a little boy peeing on your finger." He considered that statement briefly, then without comment dismissed me.

This current Russian device was an ingenious gadget that looked somewhat like a delicate Stillson wrench, open jaws on one side to slide onto something: lung, stomach, aorta, bronchus, whatever, could be slipped into the jaws. Squeeze the handles, lock them shut, fire the staples, and the job was done. In the case of a lung, it could quickly lop off a tumor-bearing area. In the case of a bronchus, ordinarily tediously cut and stitched shut, it saved some fifteen minutes of operating time. And what with all the tobacco smoking and lung cancers in Russia, it was a time saver, no question. With this in mind I was ready for Dr. Samuelian.

At the Research Institute, we were again courteously met and shown around. On this particular day, the operative procedure was a gastrectomy on a huge dog. I was asked if I'd like to scrub in as first assistant.

"Sure." I said. *Why not?* This would be a great opportunity for me to use this stapling device and learn its workings. Samuelian, a first rate surgeon, was a bull of a man with close-cropped gray hair, blue eyes, dimples in a broad face, well-muscled arms, and large hands with slim fingers. He was a concert pianist as well.

I changed into the standard OR smock, scrubbed, and went in. The abdomen had already been opened and the stomach lifted out with Babcock clamps. One clamp was just north of the pylorus along the lesser curvature and the other was on the fundus. Samuelian snipped and tied a few things, but my gaze was on the instrument on the table. It was a satin finish, metal linear stapler, not the right-angled job used on bronchi. Clearly it was brand new and had some slight resemblance to the old Von Petz device. I waited and explanations were not long in coming.

Dr. Samuelian: "You see, Doktor, in this country we have too many fat people eating too much potato starch, too much bread, and drinking too much vodka. They are getting too much weight on their bodies. This is unhealthy on the body, the hip joints, their feet and ankles. But many will not stop eating. So I have this idea, that I can make the stomach smaller, then attach a piece of bowel to it, and bypass it. Let me show you." With the linear stapler, he stapled off a section of stomach so that the esophagus drained into what was now a small blind pouch of stomach. He then took a divided segment of jejunum, the portion beyond the duodenum, and stitched it into that pouch, then took the lower portion of the divided end and rejoined it to the side of the jejunum just below where it had been divided. All was in continuity again. Ingenious. The rest of the stomach emptied normally through the duodenum, but the pouched off area emptied through its new exit. Surgeons would understand.

He went on: "Now, after eating a small meal, the patients feel full and no longer hungry." After discharge, they were allowed to eat anything, but their appetite was easily sated. He felt that this new stapler was the answer to better gastric operations. My reaction was that he was prescient, brilliant and absolutely correct. I also saw a future for this instrument in lung surgery. It could help lop out a tumor or nodule in nothing flat, but I suspected that Blades would not be happy. It suggested the beginning of the end for certain instances of cut and tie surgery.

For the rest of the session, we studied the instrument. Samuelian showed me how to strip, clean, load and apply staples in different ways, and even how to diagnose and fix a jammed stapler and replace parts. By the end of our session I was proficient with this neat device.

A new idea, he casually revealed, was the preloaded replaceable staple cartridge, similar to ammunition clips. Samuelian got the idea while in the military. He hoped to have it operational by the year's end, and proclaimed proudly and conspiratorially, that he would send me cartridges from the first clinical production. I'd need a stapler first, I reminded him. He winked. Enough said.

Loaded down with articles, papers and technical drawings by the Soviet instrument industry, I left. It had been a productive day, one that had made me a stapler expert and had my Soviet watchdogs staggering with exhaustion. The smells of animal feces and disinfectant solutions at the animal research lab were too much for them. Clearly, this was a miserable assignment on all counts. My keepers had gone off somewhere in the Institute to drink coffee, but returned just as I was ready to leave. I'd had a good experience and the possibilities of what could be done with staplers had recharged me. I had two hours to take notes, label film, rinse out socks and underwear, and to catch a quick nap before the embassy affair. But first I checked my feather trick.

Yep, another feather had flown the coop. The tape was cleverly reattached to the camera, but they were ignorant of the fact that the camera had to be reset with the timer. So you flunk the exam, KGB or whoever. Someone was being nosy, but why? I had nothing to hide. I had left only a camera and film out in plain sight.

I got ready for the party. My minders were waiting in the lobby to make sure I had a ride with the embassy driver. I walked past them with a nod, "See ya later."

I headed for the idling embassy car idling in front. It was the same old Chevy, but a new driver, a trim, young black man, obviously military.

"Marine?" I asked as I climbed in.

"Yes, sir, Lance Corporal Herman McCorkle, sir."

"Hi, I'm Dr. Sundukian."

"Yes sir, I recognized you from your photograph, sir."

"Uh-huh," I said to myself. Watchdogs check up front, and my driver knows me from a photo.

"Where you from, Corporal?"

"Terrell, Texas, sir, you know it?"

"Heard of it. What's there?"

"Well, biggest thing there is the State Nut house and a new Medical office building downtown. Not much around there 'cept cattle ranches, sir."

"Miss it?"

"Sometimes sir, but foreign posts keep us busy, so I don't get too much time to miss anything. I miss my mother's cooking, but I get to go home every six months from this assignment, so it's not too bad."

"You speak Russian?"

"Heh, heh, no sir, I don't. Have enough trouble understanding all the different Americans visiting the Embassy, sir."

I understood. But being a Marine was one sure way to get out of Terrell, Texas. *Semper Fi,* I thought.

McCorkle slowly drove the old Chevy to our dreary looking embassy, ignoring the suicidal Moscow cab drivers. We drove through the gates and pulled up in front. A number of visitors were ahead of me.

Giggles and chattering surrounded me as I was ushered into the embassy and down a musty hallway. The uneven flooring made me wonder if this place had once been a log cabin and had been rebuilt. The large planks, polished by years of use, were still uneven, so the floors all undulated slightly from one level to another, giving the effect of being at sea.

There was a buzz from a larger room just to my left. I saw the ambassador engaged in a deep and serious conversation with several worried-looking Americans. Off to one side were Kitchen and Adams. They came over. "Hey Doc, nice to see you. Everything going okay?"

Before I could answer, they took me by the elbow and led me to the bar to join them for a drink.

"What's your pleasure?"

Something light, I thought, and asked for a gin tonic. The bartender was a Marine pressed into bar duty. "Coming right up. Please help yourself to the chips and cheese, sir."

Kitchen led me to the men from the Polaroid Corporation; they'd shipped in several large crates of cameras and instant film for the Exposition, but Soviet officials had refused to release them pending payment of some exorbitant duty fees, despite earlier assurances to the contrary. A call from the ambassador to Mikoyan's Ministry of Trade had cleared up matters, but the crates were still locked up. Polaroid and Kitchen feared that the Russkies were trying to see if they could steal secret instant film processing techniques. Polaroid was not releasing the new color film yet.

"The Soviets assured us everything would be out of bond and customs by morning," said Kitchen. "This sort of stuff goes on all the time, Doc, just to keep us angry and off balance. It's a form of war, a cold war, to piss us off. Short term, they succeed, but not in the long run. They'll be the ultimate losers, but they're too fucking dumb to look that far down the road and understand. As soon as the everyday folks see what's out there, there's gonna be trouble. Once you let them off the Collective, they don't wanna go back. When their athletes, dancers, and officials see what goes on in the outside world, some of them plot ways to sneak out. It's already started with their best hockey players. Last week, two of them stayed behind in Canada. And of course, we've had defections of several high Soviet officials who got bundled up and flown out before anyone missed them. Yes sir, it's a cold, cold war, and Ivan is going to be the eventual loser."

We moved around the room with Kitchen introducing me. More guests entered and Ambassador Thompson greeted them in a sort of haphazard receiving line. I gradually became aware that there were few women present at this business event and certainly no wives. Mr. John Bell, a visiting State Department something or other, was calmly sipping bourbon while speaking Spanish with a consul from the Spanish Embassy.

In another small group, a short chunky man with beetle brows and a deep belly laugh stood chatting with aides and admiring guests surrounding him. He was Aram Khachaturian, the famous composer and conductor. I gawked as an aide translated my compliments. With a huge smile, he grasped me in a bear hug and asked me to say my name in Armenian. When I did, he exploded into laughter, and in guttural Kavkas dialect, told me that he was so proud to meet me, the famous doctor from America! "You are one of us!" he said. Then he mumbled something to his aide who advised me that Mr. Khachaturian was sending me an album of his compositions performed by the Moscow State Symphony under his direction. "You like *Gayne Ballet Suite*?" Khachaturian asked me in Armenian.

"*Anshusst!*" Of course.

"*Dobre, dobre,*" he replied in Russian. He said he hoped I would enjoy the album that would be sent to the embassy with his compliments. I thanked him again. This encounter was a wholly unexpected ray of sunshine in this dreary city.

In another group, Ed Sullivan, the journalist and TV show host, was chatting and laughing with several officials from the American

Exposition. All were slugging down great quantities of vodka and munchies at the bar. Sullivan's appearance in Moscow was a mystery, but Kitchen assured me it only had to do with the Exposition.

Three very attractive ladies with Sullivan were introduced as representatives of leading American cosmetic firms. I was introduced to a stunning redhead, Miss Cushing, who specialized in the latest women's clothing innovation, pantyhose. Her company was giving away thousands of pantyhose in all shapes and sizes to all women at the Exposition.

At their Exposition booths, cosmetics experts demonstrated the latest in makeup, hair, nail polish and those things designed to make Russian women wistful with envy. It was another form of psychological warfare and provocation to make the locals unhappy with their lot, and the canny Soviets expressed their displeasure by holding back the Polaroid crates.

I stole a look at my watch, nearly eight. By now, the place had filled with more guests and voices risen a decibel or two; the bar was crowded with thirsty patrons. A few Russian cigarettes were stinking up the place and I decided to get out. Out of the corner of my eye I spied my watchdogs, Malik and Marina, self-consciously keeping to themselves, but not too far from the open bar, their glasses full. Malik held a plate of food. Otherwise they were all alone. They stuck out like cops on duty, and in this town, everyone avoids cops.

To my surprise, I ran into Professor Androsov, his colleague Professor Popov, and the stunning Dr. Katy Smolenskova smiling at me as they went through the receiving line. As they left, the ambassador clinked his glass for attention and declared that it was a great honor to receive two such distinguished greats of Soviet Medicine at the embassy. He pointed to Androsov and Popov. Katy stood aside, beaming.

"No," said Androsov, loudly, "we come only to visit your famous surgeon, John Sundukian." I felt myself blushing.

He offered a toast. So I grabbed another drink to raise my glass in acknowledgment. The room was quiet. It was my turn.

"I raise my glass to honor Professors Androsov, Popov, S.S. Yudin, and this very fine surgeon, Dr. Ekaterina Smolenskova. These surgeons have developed surgical techniques in their clinics which have greatly helped mankind. If only our politicians could work together as closely as my medical colleagues, I'm sure we would have a happier and safer world. Please raise your glasses and join me in my toast. *Tovarishes*," I said, and took a quick sip.

"Hear, hear," I heard.

"*Nazdrovia*," I also heard. A few clapped. Just then something clapped my shoulder, hard. I turned to find Alex Adams.

"Doctor, you always think that quickly on your feet? That toast was as slick as our Secretary could have done."

Inwardly, I smiled with pride.

Ambassador Thompson was regarding me with a quizzical smile and a raised eyebrow. As I made eye contact, he winked and gave an ever-so-slight "well done" nod. Standing to one side was a beaming Dr. Katy. She was wearing a simple, black dress ending just below her knees, black stockings and stylish shoes with small spiky heels and pointy toes. Draped fashionably around her shoulders was a black lace scarf, and around her neck was the string of pearls. Her hair was pulled back into a chignon and small pearls glistened on her ears. She filled out her dress nicely, something I'd missed earlier in operating room scrubs. Her bright red nails suggested that she read the European fashion magazines.

"Well, Dr. Katy," I said, my voice low, but trying to cut through the din of voices, "you certainly look different with clothes on." She blushed.

"But Doctor John, what is the meaning of your remark?" She was half serious, but smiling, so I told her that I'd only seen her in scrub clothes and she got the picture.

"Thank you, sir, I'm glad you approve. I make my own clothes, you see."

"You made this dress?"

"Yes, of course. You like?"

"Very nice," I said.

"Professor Androsov brings me magazines when he goes to Europe to lecture," she explained, "so I have opportunity to study fashions."

Then she became serious. "Please, Doctor John, I must speak with you privately. Do you have a moment?"

"You speak excellent English," I said. "Where did you learn?"

"In school, and also I teach myself. I listen to BBC," she said.

"Is that okay here?"

"Maybe yes, maybe no, I don't care. Dr. Popov brought me small German transistor radio, so I listen and learn. But I must talk with you. Please to have drink with me, yes? *Shampanski?*"

"Okay." I led her to the bar.

"You guys serve *Shampanski* here?" I asked the Marine.

"That we do, sir, coming up." *Shampanski* was a Russian form of freshly made champagne from Georgia and a great favorite. It tasted like sweet soda pop or very thin champagne.

"Yes, Dr. Katy, what is this urgent matter?" By now we were off in a corner. Across the way my keepers had taken notice, but made no move to join us. She began emotionally, her words tumbling out. "Doctor John, please, you must help me to come to America. I want to go study in your hospitals, your university centers to learn more surgery. I want to learn more pediatric surgery in Philadelphia. I know of their great training programs, their great professors. You see, I am a woman, and there is no future for me here. I will always be an assistant, and more is required if I wish to remain in Androsov's clinic." With that she stammered and turned red. "But I want far more. I want to be good pediatric surgeon. For our children. Please. I have my dossier and background and information in a large envelope and I want you to please take it and somehow you will arrange it for me, Yes? Oh please, Doctor John, you are my only hope."

What the hell! I thought, my mind racing. There had been other visiting surgeons passing through here. Had she hit on any of them, or was I being set up? Hard to tell. She seemed so earnest, sincere. I wasn't quite sure what my next step should be, so I punted.

"Let me have your résumé. I'll look it over, review it and see what I can do or suggest," I said. "I can't promise you anything. But let's assume you can get a surgical posting; will your government allow you to leave?"

"Yes, they wull, if I assure them it's for the good of the state, for our children. There is so much to be done for our children which we cannot do because we don't have the training."

I interrupted her. "How about Androsov? Will he let you go, would he approve?"

"Yes, I think so," she said looking down. "I think I can convince him it would be good for us all. So, you will hulp?" She was getting energized, heated up. Her beet-red face told me that a deeply imbedded emotion was erupting. She was blushing furiously. More going on here than meets the eye.

"Doctor John, I thank you and bless you. I hug you, I embrace you, I give you the fullness of my heart!"

I was concerned she was getting overly excited. I held up my hand. "Slow down." She understood and gave a tiny bob of her head.

Clearly she was excited about her prospects. Frankly, I hadn't the foggiest idea how to proceed, but I'd give it a shot when I got to the States and told her that flat out.

She grasped my hand again. "Thank you for listening. Please do what you can. I can only hope and pray to God for your success."

Man, that was a heavy load to bear. But I promised her that I'd find out what was available.

She went back to her two colleagues who were getting a free buzz at the embassy bar. Unbeknownst to me at the time, Alex Adams was watching all this from across the room, that nosy son of a bitch. He came over. "All finished, Doctor? I saw you chatting up Androsov's girlfriend. Nice-looking lady, eh?"

"Girlfriend?" I blurted out.

"Yeah, probably," he said. "You don't work with him unless... She probably has to put out, like it or not. There are a lot of women doctors in Russia these days since the great patriotic war. Most men went into the military as soldiers, so fewer men were left to study medicine. The male doctors either got wiped out during the war or sent to far-off clinics and this opened up the field for women to get ahead in Medicine. The good ones moved up the line quickly, especially the lookers. Androsov is a hell of a fine surgeon, but he likes his women and his vodka, make no mistake. It's a male thing in Moscow. It's well known in their circle that these gals gotta put out or no job, and as one of the top professors, he can pick and choose. He only takes on the best, in every way. And she is the best-looking one around, never mind she's a damned good surgeon in her own right."

"You're putting me on, his girlfriend?"

"I shit thee not. That's how things go here. Think how disappointed her husband must be."

"Husband, too?"

"Yep. Real can of worms, that case. I'd stay clear, if I were you," he said.

Too late, I thought. I'd already agreed to look over her CV, and I'd keep my word.

It was Alex's turn to squire me around the room, introducing me to a squadron of diplomatic people from various embassies. And, hello, I met a cute little number from the UK, one Penelope Updike from Exbury in the south of England. She worked with the British Embassy as a fashion consultant on loan to the Soviet Ministry, she explained, hoping to bring their fashions into the twentieth century. "Styles for both men and women," she added quickly. "They're so dreadfully drab, don't you think, Doctor?"

"Well, yes, some are." It looked like she was clad in something very high style, more French than British, because she was wrapped in a gauzy, black cocktail dress, with a sash wrapped around and tied in front, creating a spectacular display of deeply tanned cleavage. Oh my! As I followed Alex to the food, I hoped to see Miss Penelope again later.

Alex seemed to know everyone well, producing smiles all around. In the next room was a huge buffet table set up by in-house personnel. The embassy number two didn't trust Russians to produce decent food, so the embassy distaff handled it all, except for the booze. I filled up on hot dogs, caviar and finger food, and washed it down with a Danish Copenhagen beer. Alex was munching on a huge serving of lasagna and mumbled, "Doc, in a few minutes, follow me. We gotta go blow bubbles."

Minutes later, I nonchalantly wandered down the hall after him. My keepers were having a grand old time chatting, eating, and drinking. They'd engaged Androsov and Katy in conversation, probably talking about their current visitor, me. But they'd lost interest in what I was doing, after all, I wasn't going anywhere, and they had better things to do than dog my every step. The place was in full swing.

The bubble was pleasantly cool, quiet, and devoid of smoke. I hadn't realized what a relief it was just to get out of the noise. I'd begun to enjoy myself, alternating a large tumbler of strong Georgian red wine with Danish beer, and now I'd started working on a vodka concoction slipped to me by a Gyrene friend at the bar. I was getting mellow.

Alex sat down wearily. "Having a good time here, Doctor? You ready to leave?"

"Yeah, I think so. It's been a whirlwind and I'm getting tuckered out. Frankly, it'll be a relief to start back home. But I got a mess to sort out when I get there." He let me talk. I explained my problems on the home front; my practice and the nagging thought that I wasn't quite sure that I wanted to be a surgeon for the rest of my life. He listened patiently, nodding at the right times. Alex was a good listener; he'd been trained well at his agency. To my surprise, he was familiar with my background, knew about my family and my academic connections.

I was shocked. "How come you know so much?"

"It's what I do. It's my business to know all things about our visitors. Your dad hung a good one on Nasty, and he's probably still smarting, so when we learned you were coming, you became a potential liability here in Moscow. Something untoward might happen to you. For example, things like street muggings happen to nosy reporters when they publish something explicit. So it's my job to know all about John Sundukian and to make sure nothing happens to you while you're here. If you think you had people keeping an eye on you, we had our people keeping an eye on you and them. And that's not easy here, believe me, but we're fortunate in that we have some underground Armenian Dashnaks in our camp. As locals, they blend into the scenery. We'd stick out like sore thumbs."

I was stunned. He knew about my *National Geographic* connection; they'd confirmed with Mel Grosvenor's office. *Surprising and a little scary.*

Alex arrived at his next point. "Your KLM flight out tomorrow has been canceled. You'll hear about it when you get back to your hotel. Their new Boeing jet flipped a turbine blade or something in flight and it came in on three engines. Repairs are under way, and if they don't need a new engine, you should be out by in day or two. Listen, when you get the news, act surprised and disappointed, and make a show of having to go back to the Embassy, American Express, and KLM to make other arrangements, okay? Act upset. It's all for show, just in case.

"You'll be on the next KLM flight out, which will be a turnaround flight; nobody flies here until they get this repaired bird back. But if a backlog develops, or the repairs are mucked up, they'll fly a prop plane from Amsterdam to lift out the stranded folks. We'll just wait and see."

"So tomorrow, go into your act, and while you're at it, pack up your camera gear and film and drop it by my office when you come over. It's a smart thing to do. I'll send it to Washington in the courier bag. Never know when passport control or customs might want to check your baggage just for the hell of it. Chances are they won't, but just as a precaution, okay?"

He had more to explain. "When you get to Washington and back in gear, you'll be contacted by the State people, who'll want a piece of you to go over tons of things. Debriefing you from day one in Saigon to your various little capers up in Laos. You've become an object of curiosity for the folks in DC. Some of the alphabet agencies want a go at you too, so get ready for some boring sessions with them. It'll be tiresome, but go along with them. It could be interesting and might even add a positive wrinkle in your career."

I had to chuckle at this. My career was already wrinkled and sometimes those wrinkles don't get straightened out. I hoped to do more doctoring and traveling in the future.

Alex and I exited the bubble and eased back into the smoky crowded reception. It now required two men behind the bar to keep up with the freeloaders. I slid from one group to another, smiling, making small talk, collecting and dispensing business cards. I was having a terrible time with names. I looked around. Miss Penelope had apparently flown the coop and so had Androsov and company. Things were slowing down. The ambassador was also long gone. Time for me to leave.

I was heading for the hallway when Penelope's perky cleavage popped into view. She had reapplied her lipstick and wafted a light touch of perfume. I asked her about the Expo and she invited me to attend a show the next day.

"Absolutely. Nothing would please me more." I made a point of asking for her business card, probably pointless since I'd be leaving shortly. It had London titles and phone numbers, which I stored away. I assured her that I'd try to see the show at all costs. Reluctantly, I left and took a suicidal taxi ride back to the Ukraina hotel.

— - • - —

MESSAGES FROM KLM AND DR. Smolenskova were waiting for me at the reception desk. The desk said that copies of these messages were left with the floor warden. Before getting in bed, I got film and camera gear together and packed them in my small camera bag. I kept back one camera, the Nikon SP, and five rolls of film. The rest would go back by embassy courier to *National Geographic* to await my return.

Next morning, KLM was very apologetic about the flight. A bird, they said, had gotten sucked into the engine during flight requiring engine shutdown, but hopefully repairs would be made in twenty-four hours or less. And most probably the DC6 that was bringing cargo and replacement parts could accommodate some passengers for the return flight. They would be in touch.

Camera and film were left at the Embassy, and with my keepers in tow, I announced that I would like to eat lunch and then tour the Exposition. Before leaving the embassy, I asked a secretary to contact Dr. Smolenskova and advise her that I'd call later that afternoon about her envelope. It was now just noon. As I look back on the day's events, the timing was important.

For lunch, my keepers decided I should visit the GUM department store across from the Kremlin. It was a huge place, fountains, archways, and a festive shopping crowd. Near a booming champagne and food bar, we found a table and selected from the standard fare. Plates of salads, cheese, and cooked meats were all laid out in a display case. As an appetizer, Malik had brought over a large blue tin of Caspian caviar to go with the soda-pop champagne. It was great.

We wandered around the GUM display areas and I did the tourist gawk, taking advantage of some great photo opportunities. There were tourists from other Soviet possessions also gawking. I wondered what they'd do if they ever saw Washington DC or New York City. I love hats and picked up a mink *shapkha* and two sheepskin hats from Tajikistan.

Off we went to the Exposition. My first impression was a combination of a zoo and the Oklahoma State Fair, full of excited Russian children and their parents taking all the freebies the Americans had to offer. Cosmeticians had snared some local women who were getting their hair permed for free! Others were getting professional hair dyeing, while some had their nails done. The latest dress fashions were being shown by lovely American models. I recognized redheaded Miss Cushing, who was handing out sample pantyhose to astounded Muscovites and foreign tourists. Hot dog and corny-dog stands were in full swing, to the delight of all. The food was washed down with good old-fashioned lemonade, all courtesy of the US of A.

The Russians had not taken this assault on their backwardness kindly. Wracked with the anger which accompanies jealousy, they'd inserted men and women lackeys into the crowd to harangue us for being so materialistic. The onlookers ignored them. I grabbed a corny-dog and wandered over to a roadside bench. It was about 3 p.m.

At that particular moment in time my keepers were watching the stage, spellbound at the Polaroid people.

I took a steaming bite of corny-dog and cooled it with a gulp of lemonade. Suddenly, a beat-up laundry van stopped directly in front of me; its rear doors flew open and two men in scruffy workmen's garb jumped out, grabbed me, dragged me to the van, tossed me inside and told me in loud, clear Armenian to shut up and be still.

"Shut up and be still," they kept repeating. *I damn well understood that, but why?*

I struggled against the two men, but it was useless. These men were powerful and they pinned me firmly to the floorboards with their big feet, face down. We roared off bumping and swerving, my head bouncing off the boards, and being jammed back down with those huge feet.

The van was filthy and stank of rotting cabbage and onions. I was damn near suffocating from the stinky jute bags over my face.

Nobody paid any attention to the crappy looking van with two shabby workmen in back and an equally shabby pair up front. Most vans in Moscow looked just like this one. They seldom drew attention from anyone.

It dawned on me that I'd been abducted. The remaining lucid part of my mind wondered, *why me?*

I could swivel my head only slightly, but I was able to look up. What I saw were ordinary, unshaven workmen in leather caps and dirty, canvas jackets, with lined faces, hard jaws and eyes squinted against the afternoon sun. They ignored me, intent at the moment on the traffic around them as we roared steadily along.

It seemed that I was in for a long ride. It was too noisy to talk. I guessed, whoever they were, they were not going to kill me, at least not yet. We stopped several times, probably for traffic lights. At each stop the feet pressed down on me firmly with a clear message: be still and stay quiet. I had no choice. I obeyed.

Minutes later, we were traveling fast on a smooth highway, not fast enough to draw attention. After about forty-five minutes, we pulled off on a rough bumpy road and bounced along for another half hour. I could only guess at the times. Finally we came to a halt. The door was yanked open and I was led out, a firm hand on each arm, but I could smell fresh air and the wonderful, clean smell of pines.

We had driven into a dark copse of pines somewhere in the countryside. Behind me was a long curving driveway along which we'd driven; before us, a good-sized log cabin. The whole place was cleverly screened from the roadway by the driveway curve. As soon as we exited, the van was driven around back.

"This way, Doctor, please." Now I could easily survey my captors. Four grinning men who didn't quite look like workmen. One opened the door and waved me in. They spoke English to me, but earlier it had been Armenian.

"Take a seat, Doctor. Would you like Coca Cola, some water or tea? What is your pleasure?" The accented English calmed me and piqued my curiosity.

"Coke," I said. The oldest of the group opened a small ancient refrigerator, extracted several bottles, snapped a cap and handed me a frosty Coke. It was delicious. I swirled the dust and grime out of my mouth, swallowed Coke, and burped. They chuckled. It was obvious they were friendlies, but despite the smiles, no one spoke.

"Now, Doctor, please to go wash your hands and face. In back is washplace."

I did. The towels were brand new, in pale ecru with initials embroidered along the edges. "You need lavatory, Doctor?" asked the older man, obviously the leader. "Is also out behind building."

I grunted. "Not yet, thank you."

"So, you wonder what is happening to you, yes? Who are we, yes? Be assured we are not going to kill you. We have just taken you into what we must call protective custody. Yes?" He waited. I said nothing.

"I explain." Caps off and collars loosened, they appeared to be in their mid-thirties, in fine shape and well muscled. The apparent leader looked and acted older. They each went to the sink and washed up. Workmen they weren't.

"First we introduce ourselves. I am Ari Shapira, my friend here is Yervant Kocharian, that handsome dog there is Levi Biben and the one who needs a shave is Hovsep Sundugian. So now you know we are two Jews, two Armenians, and very good friends. We do things in Moscow together, alone, or sometimes with others. Most of our work is so awful, no one else would do it, so we are ignored, especially by the authorities who want nothing to do with such *nyet kulturnik* types.

Sometimes we deliver cabbage, goats, sheep, chickens, and venison to the Embassies. We remove garbage or even shit from stables. And sometimes we remove dead Russians to feed the river carp. We do whatever is necessary." A statement, not a question.

"So, we drink, play cards, go fishing, and fuck nice Embassy women. We have good time when we can. We never know how the dice will roll." Ari looked around at the grinning faces. One man stood next to the small doorway window looking down the driveway. "We are friends to your embassy, and so please listen. Oh yes, I am to tell you, your friend Alex says for you to stay loose. Does this make sense to you?"

It did. What made me tense were the weapons I saw tucked in each waistband, muzzles down, handles up. One man had a suspicious bulge at the back of his jacket.

For the next few minutes they told me the most bizarre tale I'd ever heard. If it weren't so damn plausible, I'd swear it was made up, but it all made horrible sense. And if they were right, I was overjoyed to be here with these men.

They said I couldn't go back to my hotel room or I'd be arrested immediately and tossed in some dark Moscow jail and not be allowed to talk to anyone, not even embassy representatives. A woman had been found in my hotel room badly beaten, her face a mess, her clothes torn, her panties off and papers scattered all over the room. There had been a fight and she had been the loser. The bed, the floor, and bathroom were bloody; someone had used the toilet and the assailant was gone. The woman was alive, unconscious, and been taken to a hospital. I was the most obvious suspect.

Who could have gotten into my room? Who was she and how did she get in?

I later learned that Ari had a contact who worked in security for the hotel who had notified the team. Ari had many contacts in many places and he was also part of a team keeping a silent watch on me in Moscow, probably at the behest of our embassy. But who were these guys?

My goings and comings had been under constant surveillance, for my own good, they said. I remembered what they'd told me at the embassy. Not only were the Russkies watching me, but our men were watching the Russkies and me, too. Score one for Alex and his guys.

It turned out the man was a member of Ari's Mossad network, which had insinuated itself deeply into Moscow. He'd learned from the twenty-second floor warden, in his capacity as hotel security, that some woman had stepped off the elevator, identified herself as Dr. Ekaterina Smolenskova, and explained that she had an appointment with me at noon to deliver some scientific material. I was expected momentarily, so she asked to wait in my room.

The old babushka warden had been dubious at first, but the woman persisted, saying she carried some important documents from Professor Androsov for the doctor. Reluctantly, the old woman let her in, but left the door open. It was the American doctor's room and the woman sat reading the morning *Isvestia*. She saw no problems with this situation. Later, the devastated old woman tearily told the authorities that it had been against her better judgment. She was told to stop wailing and answer questions.

Ari was quickly notified by the hotel asset, and since it smelled like a setup, he took immediate action. The best option was to grab the doctor, take him to the hideout, and work out the other details later.

In the meantime, the inside Mossad man had done more snooping. It seemed that some man had followed Smolenskova and had been observed riding up an adjacent elevator car. He reasoned that the man had gotten off a floor above or below and walked to the twenty-second floor.

The man could either be her husband, jealous of the professor and suspicious of another tryst with the visiting doctor, or less likely, the professor, who was in the operating room at that time of day, or the best possibility, Russian KGB looking for a reason to embarrass the American doctor and have him arrested. They could possibly try him in court and have him unceremoniously tossed out, branding Americans as rapists and hoodlums, disrupting the exposition, embarrassing the Americans, and destroying the doctor.

But the Mossad man told Ari that the individual had been severely gouged before he left. In fighting off her assailant, Smolenskova had clawed someone, and had ribbons of skin under her broken fingernails. He also learned from the hospital that she had not been raped, although it had been made to appear that way. It smelled like a setup. A scratched face might be located. And if it wasn't the husband, then it was the KGB. They did this sort of thing with ease. But whoever was responsible would not be found, guaranteed.

Now the group considered how to get the doctor out of Russia, now that they'd stalled the setup? The KGB has eyes and ears everywhere, so it had to be fast. Ari and his team explained that I'd have to sit tight for the next few days. I'd be safe here under their constant protection for the time being and there was an escape route in case of danger. I would be told that route only if it became necessary.

The hideout had food and water and was very secure. The property on which this log cabin was tucked once belonged to the Italian Diplomatic Mission. But the Soviets, still displeased with Mussolini's collaboration with fascist Germany, had converted some adjacent land into a huge landfill, and declared it a garbage dump for the diplomatic corps.

The smell of rotting things eventually offended sensitive Italian noses, especially in the kitchen, until the senior chef screamed, "*Basta!* Enough!" and threatened to quit. The ambassador moved his beautiful Italian rococo buildings brick by brick to another location. The abandoned area had become a sort of no man's land, an ideal, hidden location.

"This lane leads through the woods for a kilometer to the dump. My colleagues and I," said Ari, "are a small group of diplomatic garbage collectors. We travel to all the embassies and no one bothers us. We pick up the remains of big diplomatic receptions, garbage that no other trash collectors will touch, and take it all to the landfill. Sometimes unexpected treasures are found," he grinned owlishly, "like half-finished tins of fresh caviar, half-empty bottles of vodka and other fine liqueurs and drink. Sometimes even fancy clothing and shoes. We never know what will show up. We look for important papers, documents, letters, things along those lines too, for which we have special rag pickers trained to do quick studies on them. A very nice setup, no? And like all Muscovites, we sell what we don't want on the black market to ready buyers. The police know what we do, but we pay them to look the other way. It's the perfect cover for us."

Ari continued, "Our hotel colleague has entered your cordoned-off room in the hotel and removed your possessions, ostensibly to turn them over to the authorities. However, they will be conveniently misplaced."

Fortunately I had my passport and small camera with me, plus some film. Ari asked me to hand over the passport.

"Why?"

"We must prepare an exit visa to stamp your passport when we exit you. My friends include some of the most gifted forgers in Europe. They will make such a visa stamp for us immediately. You may need to prove that you exited legally later. Just hand it over and trust us."

I did.

After my Coke and a quick wash-up, I went around back to pee in the bushes and spied an outhouse about fifty feet out in the pines.

Extending as far back as the eye could see was a dense ring of trees. It was a very deep forest with a thick carpet of pine needles, which cushioned footsteps and bird sounds. I recognized a cluster of mountain laurel and some native azaleas. A narrow path led to the edge of the wood, and then disappeared as it wound deeper into the forest. No phones or electric wires that I could see. At the moment I felt safe.

I returned to the cabin where I was handed a mug of freshly brewed dark tea by Ari. It was about four in the afternoon and I was tired. The tea was strong and delicious and restored my flagging spirits. I was sipping it local style, holding a cube of sugar clenched in my teeth, when suddenly the air was shattered by a doorbell mounted just over the doorjamb. Ari moved quickly to the window, sighting down the lane through small field glasses.

"Is okay," he said, "my colleagues." The familiar van pulled up, and four men piled out. The fourth man looked familiar. For a moment I couldn't believe my eyes; one of the workmen was Alex from the Embassy!

But it certainly didn't look like him. He looked like the others in a soiled leather cap, a worn leather jacket, a rumpled shirt, rumpled corduroy trousers, and old scuffed boots. Even his hands were dirty. He walked with a slight limp to the cabin, and slouched against the doorway grinning hugely at me.

"Hello, Doctor, welcome."

"How the hell did you get here?"

"Same way you did, amigo, "he quipped, "I got abducted off the street in broad daylight."

"Where'd you get that outfit?" I laughed. He looked like a real bum.

"From Hollywood, Central Casting," he chuckled. Obviously, he wasn't telling.

"Okay, Doctor, let's get serious." He waved us in, the others grinned too; they knew him well. We all went in and sat down to hot tea and biscotti. One man took a position at the window watching the winding lane.

"Here's some information about Smolenskova. From police reports and information from our 'security' friend at the hotel, somebody followed her into your room. What happened next is not clear, but she ended up unconscious on the floor, with severe bruises on her face and body, her clothes torn and in disarray. The bed had not been used or touched. Now get this. They questioned her husband. He had no scratches on his face and he stated that he went up to your room at about two in the afternoon, thinking to catch you and his wife in bed! Instead, he found her unconscious on the floor. The door was ajar, so he just walked in. He was shocked. He admitted that he had removed her French panties and tossed them on the bed."

French panties? Alex went on, "Smolenskova's husband told the police that for some time he had suspected his wife of loose morals. She wore those French panties only for certain occasions. When she told her husband she was going to visit the doctor the next day to present her résumé and credentials, he watched her slip on black lace panties and he assumed she was planning to fuck him. Sexual power.

If she could fuck him, maybe he would help her get to America." This was primal thinking that I understood.

It was almost certainly the KGB who had beaten her. When the old babushka finally showed up and saw the fallen Ekaterina, she began screaming hysterically. Smolenskova was taken to a hospital, treated for minor bruises, and recovered, but refused to talk to anyone. She was in shock and claimed to remember nothing. Reluctantly, the police allowed her to go home, but gave her a day to prepare to answer questions. Meanwhile the police are looking for you, Doctor. So you see," he emphasized, "you are not out of the woods, yet." He chuckled, shaking his head at his dreadful pun.

"You gotta stay loose but tight, Doctor, right here until we get can get you out. And we will."

Yeah, but how were these outlaws, these Robin Hoods of the Moscow Diplomatic garbage dump, planning to do it?

Levi kept a constant eye on the road and my Armenian buddies continued their tea slurping, missing nothing.

"Now Doctor," said Alex, The ambassador wants nothing to do with what we do and what he doesn't know, he can deny any knowledge of."

Plausible deniability.

Alex drank his tea and continued, "Hang in there and trust us, do what you're told and we'll have you on your way shortly. It isn't the first time we've done this. It'll go just fine."

I had no choice.

"Here's the drill," Alex continued, removing his greasy hat. He spoke directly to me. "KLM is sending in a DC-6 with engine parts, mechanics, spare crew, and a few important passengers and cargo that can't wait for the next regular jet flight. Among them will be another spare flight crew plus stewards dead-heading in to relieve the present stranded crew. That stranded crew will fly out when the DC-6 flies out. The relief crew stays here until the mechanics fix the busted jet engine." He glanced at his wristwatch. You are going to become part of that crew and fly out with them. How's that sound?"

I shrugged.

"The Dutch embassy is holding a small informal reception for the stranded jet crew and the passengers tomorrow night. This is their way of saying: 'Sorry for the mess and delay, so please have some smoked eel, pickled herring, cheese, and caviar, and of course, real champagne.' We'll get you out on the DC-6 tomorrow or the next day."

And for some reason I was reassured. I thought it would work.

"You'll replace the flight engineer. You know enough about flying terms and the proper buzzwords. The engineer will become a passenger and board with the other passengers. We'll sneak you into the Dutch embassy the night before and put you in the crewmember's uniform. We have one crewmember who looks about your size and build. His passport will be altered with your picture, courtesy of Polaroid and our forgers. There may be watchers at the hotel. Russians believe that criminals return to the scene of the crime. That could be the case, so we'll have you stay with the Dutch. No sense taking chances that you might be recognized at the hotel."

I opted for the second choice too. Made more sense. We decided that I'd enter the Dutch embassy during the party, but not mix with the guests. A complete KLM flight engineer's uniform would be held in a guest room there for me. The regular flight engineer would change into civvies, become part of the passenger group at the reception and leave with the others. On the day of the flight, he'd put on a spare uniform, drive to the embassy, switch clothes with me, and board later with the regular passengers flying out in the DC-6.

It sounded well planned. By prearrangement, the captain and his crew would stop by the embassy in the morning, en route to the airport, make the switch and off we'd go. It should work. But there was always the potential for a total fuckup.

The plan was in place now and it was time to move out. The group left the log cabin.

"Check you later, Doctor," and Alex was gone.

— - • — —

ON THE AFTERNOON OF THE party at the Royal Dutch Embassy, I sat pondering my status and my future. I shuddered to think that a woman lay beaten, bare and unconscious on the floor of my room, and the local cops were hunting me.

Alex had cleared the switch with Piet Vandevanter, who was happy to help out. To be totally secure, only a trusted few Dutch personnel were in the know. Russian staff workers knew nothing and would be told nothing. The captain and crew were told that a Dutch citizen was being framed and needed to be exfiltrated. They would all act normal, joking en route to the airport, and I, the fake flight engineer would laugh with them in English.

Ari had returned to the cabin, relieved the watch, and lighted one of his smelly Turkish cigarettes. Latakia tobacco, he bragged, dreadfully strong, but much desired in Moscow. As we sipped strong Russian tea, I stretched out in a comfortable orange, muslin Scandinavian rocker, a discard from the Swedish Embassy

Events had been going too fast for me, and my thoughts were jumbled. I needed to get a fresh perspective on my present status, but I didn't have a chance. We both heard the warning clang of the doorbell simultaneously. Ari looked at his watch.

"Is wrong time for our friends. Quick, follow me, say nothing, do what I say. Now!"

We hurried out through the creaky back door, careful not to let it slam, and scurried about two hundred feet along the lane into the woods, Ari in the lead. As we passed a huge pine, he darted to his left; I followed close on his heels. Graceful as a deer now, he wove his way past birches, alders, some scruffy oaks and pines. Ahead was a massive tree fall. We were now far behind the house and deep in the woods, where several massive oak trunks had fallen in a crisscross pattern. Their roots formed a triangular base with a narrow opening to its center. Ari darted into the opening of the triangle and I followed. Cleverly concealing an inner space were several planks to which branches, shrubbery, and clumps of dirt had been artfully attached, a nice example of field camouflage.

Ari swung the planks aside and stepped into the center space onto a level, dirt floor. A standing man could peer through the tangle of branches and have a clear picture, and for a better, unrestricted view of front and sides of the log cabin, the road and surrounding area, a small plank platform rested on two firm logs. Ari stayed glued to his field glasses.

"Is bad," he said. He put down the glasses, reached down into the dark area beside the platform, and lifted out a covered golf bag. Flipping open the top, he pulled out and quickly unwrapped a tight oilskin bundle and another soft moleskin wrap with parts of a wicked-looking rifle and a long thin box.

"Dragunov," grunted Ari, patting the rifle. It had a telescope, which he quickly mounted. Once assembled, barrel, stock and sights, he slid it through the clearing in the branches, rested the barrel on a small beanbag, slid his elbow through the strap, and then carefully sighted through the telescope. Satisfied, he adjusted the focus slightly, worked the bolt manually, ejecting and inserting unfired rounds.

"Just checking," he grunted again. "Should be easy, two hundred meter shot," he whispered. "If Russians must be shot, then better with their own rifle. Good as Galil." It was a long slim rifle, with a short stock, and Ari had handled it with the ease of familiarity.

He pointed, "Take glasses, Doctor, and look." I looked. A small car had pulled up to the cabin. Two men climbed out and were talking animatedly to each other. They spent a few minutes looking around. Then, as if on cue, one headed for the front door while the other circled to the back. They had drawn their automatic pistols.

Ari was watching. "Plain clothes, KGB," he grunted. "KGB never come here, only local police. These men clever, well trained. But stupid. Wonder how they know to come here? Is bad."

I watched them enter. A few minutes later, they emerged from the front and walked slowly to their car. They lit cigarettes and again started talking rapidly, their heads and eyes darting all around. One of them picked up a bulky hand radio.

Ari assumed the sharpshooter's crouch, ever ready, his finger caressing the trigger, but not tightening. Under his breath he said, "They know somebody has been here and left, and they know they may be being watched. But they don't know who. They may be looking for you, Doctor, and they're deciding what to do. We cannot take that chance, cannot let them radio for advice. Is too bad for them." His words were drowned out by two rapid shots from his rifle. In the blink of an eye, Ari had fired twice, chambering and firing the second shot so quickly that I barely heard the click-clack. I watched through the glasses as both men dropped in their tracks, lying grotesquely lifeless like two human dolls. One moved slightly.

I was numb. I realized what had happened, but I hadn't been ready for it. Ari had acted fast. Clearly no stranger to violence, Ari had just killed two men, most likely Soviet agents. He leaned over and retrieved two spent brass cartridges and pocketed them. "If they find this place and look hard, they won't find any brass shells." That was his only comment.

I stood there slack jawed. Ari slipped out and I was close behind. He ran up to the first man. He looked dead but was still flapping an arm. Ari delivered two headshots with his hand weapon. And two shots to the other dead agent. "Always make sure a dead man stays dead," he said.

"Now, we must be quick, we have work to do, and you will help." First he took their hand radios, threw them into the car. Next he pulled out their wallets, examined their contents, nodded his head, and tossed them in with the radios. "Yes, these are Komitet men," he growled. Then together, at Ari's direction, we lifted them one at a time and stuffed them both into the back of their car and slammed the door shut.

Ari ran to the edge of the woods and brought back two leafy branches, a handful of dirt, and the golf bag containing the rifle. He scattered dirt where the men had lain. He picked up several small, bloody fragments of their skulls and put them in the car. He began brushing the dirt randomly over the entire area using the leafy branches, covering the bloody spots.

"Now, he said, you and I will piss all over this spot where these men fell."

"Huh?"

"Confuses the dogs. They howl, but they have no blood trail to follow and strong piss confuses them." We both peed randomly in that area. Then he jogged back to the cabin returning with his jacket, my things, and a small, squishy bag that he tossed to me.

"Here, Doc, run to edge of this woods and throw handfuls of this embassy party beef and lamb chunks into the woods as far as you can and make sure you surround the woods around cabin. You understand? Then throw more into the woods around the shooting place."

As I tossed out the meat, I envisioned the dogs yelping and running in circles, despite their training.

"Let's go," Ari barked.

"What happens to these men? And what happens when they don't report in?"

"Doctor, these men are going to disappear. No one will know what happens to them, not in this century. You'll see. Get in car."

I jumped into the front seat. I had only my camera, film and the papers I'd had with me when I was snatched. Anybody's guess where my other stuff was. The car reeked of tobacco. A worn notebook lay on the seat; Ari flipped it open and leafed through the pages and read.

"Yes, these men looking for you. We go." He started the engine.

"You remember," he said, "I told you this road led to garbage dump, yes?"

"Yes," I said.

"Is also back way to American *dacha* where we rarely go. Beyond the dump two more kilometers, we come to this huge reservoir, is *Kiyazminskoye vodoichranilishche*. You like name?"

"I can't even say it."

"Very few *Amerikanskis* can; your friend Alex, he says it like old time Muscovite. He smiled. "Dirty water reservoir is for swimming, fishing, and some goes to the citizens of Moskva. One small area is reserved final resting place for vehicles we remove from prying eyes. This car joins them." He drove slowly, but steadily in this unmarked, battered, dirty car, a car chosen not to draw anyone's attention.

According to Ari, these dead men had been searching everywhere for me and he had knocked off two men to save me. My jumbled thoughts quickly crystallized. Two facts were suddenly evident: Clearly the Soviets wanted to find me, and conversely, someone was keenly interested in keeping me out of Soviet clutches. If I had to guess, it was our embassy and probably our CIA people. These friends would keep me from the Russkie clutches. I cheered them on, because the alternative was not a pleasant thought. I snapped a couple of frames with my Nikon SP. *What's to lose?*

The garbage dump came up on our left. Huge rotting mounds were strewn across acres of land. I could see men and women poking long sticks into clumps, occasionally tossing something into shoulder bags. We continued ahead, off the road, over a rough cleared area and onto a narrower dirt road. We approached and began circling a huge, tranquil lake, sparkling in bright sunshine. Hundreds of sea gulls were wheeling and dipping over this lovely natural lake, its deep blue water reflecting clear, blue skies, and surrounded by green forest.

Without warning, Ari angled the car toward the water, slowing as he approached its edge, and braked to a halt. "Step out, Doctor."

I got out. He pulled the hand brake, opened the trunk and found a jack handle. Removing a necktie from the nearest dead man, he lashed the steering wheel firmly to the automatic gearshift handle, depressed the accelerator pedal with the jack handle, and jammed it against the center console. He released the brake, slipped the car into gear, and deftly jumped aside to watch the car make its funereal run to the water. Aided by the steep downslope, it roared headlong into the water, and amid a cloud of bubbles and steam, and sank quickly into murky, blue depths. The rifle and golf bag went with them.

"Goodbye KGB men. You did your duty; I did mine."

Ari glanced up. "Too deep for helicopter to see." He slipped his jacket on. "Come, we go the top of the road and wait for our friends."

"How will they know we're here?"

"I left glass of water on table."

By now it was twilight and almost six in the evening. Shadows slowly fade and the world smooths over. Our water glass had been a clear message. A small van driven by the two Armenians drove up minutes after we reached the fork. We climbed aboard and were silently driven back to the log cabin. I continued to be amazed at the silent teamwork. At the cabin, Ari told me that the remaining Israeli of the foursome was on a small embassy detail stuffing garbage into large bags for later pickup. We sat and enjoyed hot tea and biscotti. I wondered why they felt safe here. Weren't people looking for us? If they weren't worried, well dammit, I was. I took note that this cadre of four rarely drank alcohol. It made sense. Here in this vodka-swilling nation, they had to be alert at all times.

All was on schedule, advised Ari. I would be driven to the Dutch embassy in the van at about a quarter to seven, when the reception would be well under way. The crew, pilots, passengers, embassy staff would all be happily quaffing booze and nibbling food.

I would be let off at a rear entrance and led directly to a guest room in the ambassador's private wing. I would change my clothing and persona and spend the rest of the night waiting for my early morning pickup for the DC-6 departure.

I climbed in the back of the van. Ari said goodbye, short and sweet with a firm hand squeeze. "Good luck, American. Tell Alex where you are. Ciao."

The driver was Israeli number two. One of the Armenians rode up front and the other beside me. Ari remained behind to make certain the KGB men had not reported their last position. He'd be picked up later. "Not to worry, Doctor," he had smiled earlier. "There are many hiding places in these woods and I know them all."

We drove through the Dutch embassy gates. The guards recognized the garbage van and driver and waved as we drove around to the rear of the embassy where garbage had been stacked in huge burlap bags in a maze of cars, trash, boxes, and litter. Light streamed from an open door and a man stood silhouetted in the backlighting, waiting. As I got out I heard a few words, "*Asvadz* and then *yev kisher pari*," an Armenian murmured quietly from inside the van. I recognized the traditional invocation of God's blessing for a departing colleague, "Godspeed and goodnight."

As I walked up to the open door, the workman quickly climbed into the seat I'd vacated. Four men in, four men out. The van barely slowed as it moved toward the discarded boxes. They took a token few boxes and left. I entered the embassy. Someone waiting in the shadows stepped forward and closed the door.

"Hello, Doctor, Piet here." I remembered Piet Vandevanter from the embassy party, Alex's counterpart at the Dutch embassy. "Come right this way, please." We went down a hallway into a very nice, large, well-lit guest room. A marble bathroom with large mirrors, a tub and shower with huge fluffy towels.

I needed a shower, a shave and clean clothes. Piet entered the room with me, locking the door behind him. After I'd cleaned up, Piet smiled and walked to a closet. "Here's your change of clothing, Doctor."

Looking in the mirror, I saw myself transformed into a neat, white-shirted flight crew member. The uniform bore the KLM logo, "Willem Ostends, Flt. Engineer," and two rings around the sleeve. I raised my eyebrows questioningly.

"You are a flight engineer. Here are your credentials," said Piet. "Your new passport." I opened a well-used Dutch passport and glanced inside. Unbelievable! There I was. My Polaroid picture smiled at me just as though it had always been there. My pockets held some change, restaurant receipts, a book of matches from an Indonesian restaurant, and tissues.

"Where's my real passport?" I asked, slightly alarmed.

"Not to worry. You'll get it and your things from your hotel room in Schiphol. Your own passport was sent ahead by diplomatic courier to have the proper exit visa stamped in it by our very clever forgers to make it a legal departure.

"Amsterdam and Israel have some of the world's most skillful forgers, many of them are engravers and diamond cutters. They do expert work. The Soviets keep changing the design of the exit stamp, the ink color, even adding a tiny mark in one corner, so Alex and I send people a day in advance to see what the current exit stamp looks like. Then we show the forgers and presto, they create a current, new stamp.

"You will be awakened at four in the morning. You shave and dress and be ready to move, okay?"

"Yeah, sure, okay."

"This relief crew of the DC-6 will be driving from their hotel to Sheremetyevo and en route, they'll tell the driver to stop by the embassy to pick up some forms. They'll pull into the back of the embassy here, the captain will speak to the flight engineer, telling him to go in and get the papers quickly. The engineer will jump out, walk in, and go directly to your room. You go out and climb in the car and hand the captain the papers, which I have here for you. The crew will have been told that a switch would be made. The only problem might be at the airport. When flight crews arrive at Sheremetyevo, they all they walk directly to the crew entrance, their passports out, led by the captain. Their baggage is trundled along with them. One or two will hold up packages to show the Customs chaps: vodka, dolls, and caviar. One by one, the passports get stamped and they walk to a waiting bus. You will be the third man in line, two places behind the captain, first officer, then you, Flight Engineer Ostends, then the men and women stewards. Got it?"

"Got it."

"Good. I'll bring you a few snacks and there are magazines here to read. I think the bed is comfortable." He smiled wolfishly. "Hot coffee in the morning. Should not be a problem. We have done this before."

I nibbled on some excellent Dutch cheese, crackers, fruit, and a small meat pie, washed down with sparkling water and turned in. I was anxious to get the hell out of here. The next thing I knew, Piet was shaking me at ten minutes after four. It was pitch black outside my window.

"Doctor John, please get up. Drink your coffee and get ready. They will be here at five sharp. They have flight clearance to depart at 08:45."

I was shaved and dressed in a flash and had another great cup of coffee. I was never readier. *A flight engineer, what next?*

We saw the van headlights at the same time. Piet walked me down the hallway where we waited. A car pulled up, its doors slid open and someone jumped out and ran up to the door. Piet conversed with him in Dutch. Piet signaled me to move out. I grabbed the briefcase and the sheaf of papers.

"Thank you and goodbye," I said. My heart was pounding madly and I had that familiar tightness inside, but I sauntered out and climbed into the van as though it was the most natural thing to do. It all seemed unreal, but here I was, handing some papers over to the KLM captain who leafed through them, grunted, and told the driver to move on.

It was show time in Moscow and just like a synchronized ballet, we did the exit routine. In single file, we trooped up to passport control where I held out my passport and smiled. The chap never even looked at me, robot-like stamping our passports until we were all finished. We moved ahead to the waiting crew bus, and boarded, the women chattering as most young women do. Slowly, the bus moved out on the airstrip along a yellow line. It was still dark, with a slight ground fog. Flashing yellow vehicle lights whizzed by.

I glanced at my watch, we had left the embassy at about five, it was now after six and should be sunrise soon. Ahead of us, I saw the big DC-6 loom up in the darkness, service lights and vehicles around it. I could make out the KLM logo painted on its side. A red strobe was blinking on top and under the fuselage of this huge piston prop aircraft.

We all climbed out and in another procession, climbed the forward ladder. Ground electric supply was plugged in so we had electricity and power. The captain moved leisurely into the cockpit, removed his jacket, and hung it on a wall hook. The co-pilot and I did the same. After fiddling with some settings, the captain looked over at me: "Willem," he said, "go with Jorgen here and do the walk-around." Jorgen was, in fact, the actual flight engineer; he'd been masquerading as a steward when we filed through passport control. The captain never changed his expression, but he slowly winked one blue eye at me.

We went down the front ladder and did the walk-around. Jorgen would look up, I'd look up. Anyone observing us would have seen two crewmembers checking flaps, kicking wheels, and looking for oil leaks. Jorgen had a powerful flashlight, so we took our time checking and rechecking. Finally we clambered back aboard. Jorgen told the captain that all was okay.

By this time captain and co-pilot were busy with clipboards, controls, and setting radio frequencies. Jorgen pointed to the jump seat just behind the captain and I sat. He climbed into his flight engineer's seat, pulled down his small work desk and went right to work. He got busy and started making calculations into a small computer. Headphones were crackling, cockpit speakers buzzing. In the back of the craft I could hear the crew bustling about. This bird was ready to fly and I couldn't be happier.

A blonde stewardess knocked and came in with coffee, rolls, juice, and napkins neatly arranged on a tray. She poured coffee for the captain, smiled and left. We helped ourselves to warm croissants, marvelous coffee, and fresh fruit. Man, this was great! I began to relax.

Looking out the cockpit window, I saw cargo being loaded, and finally, a bus pulled up with passengers who had priority departure clearance with KLM because this aircraft was a Combi that carried both cargo and passengers. We were fueled and ready to fly. I heard ground control confirm taxi times. My pulse raced. We were finally ending this mad caper, "Operation Goodbye Ivan." The four huge Pratt & Whitney engines roared into life. The engineer and co-pilot went through a lengthy pre-take-off checklist, made last-minute adjustments, and started flipping overhead switches. I heard them call out "Flaps 20," as we slowly lumbered towards the runway.

"KLM—departure clearance approved. Contact tower one one four decimal two."

"Roger ground, contact tower." The co-pilot flipped to the tower frequency and did the radio checks. We wheeled slowly to the designated runway as the sun rose in the east.

The craft was now shuddering like a hooded hawk; it was ready to fly. We were aimed down the center stripe of a long runway. I had hoped the sun would rise and smile on me, because for the moment, I felt like a released prisoner.

"KLM special, is cleared for immediate takeoff, runway one eight. Goodbye, good luck."

"KLM special is rolling. *Spasiba*, tower."

The take-off was routine. Both captain and co-pilot eased back gently on the yoke, and, miraculously, the nose gradually lifted and the huge plane was flying. Magically, all became quiet except for the reassuring roar of the mighty engines. We were up, but still in Soviet airspace. I relaxed a bit and settled back in my seat. The throbbing engines were at maximum power, props at maximum climb setting, and we were slanting up into the brightening sky like a free bird. A sense of relief spread over me like a soothing wave. As radio transmissions between aircraft and Moscow Center continued, I began to nod off to the hypnotic droning of the engines. Within an hour after takeoff, the captain announced matter-of-factly, that we had left Soviet airspace. Next stop, Amsterdam.

CHAPTER 22

Amsterdam

August, 1959

Courage is the art of being the only one who knows you're scared to death.
—Harold Wilson, 1916–1995

WITH A FINAL ROAR AND SPUTTER, THE MIGHTY PRATT & WHITNEY engines and their long three-bladed props stopped spinning, one by one clacking to a halt. Ground power was snapped in, lights blinked back on, and ventilating fans purred. It moved stuffy Russian air out and fresh air in. I was out of Russia. After all the careful planning, I assumed I would be met in Amsterdam.

Customs officials streamed aboard through the opened passenger hatches to check passports; it was simpler to do it on board than at their usual passport check site. At some point, my false passport had to be exchanged for the real one. For appearance's sake, KLM company reps had to come on board with customs to check with passengers for connecting flights.

With the hatches open, fresh countryside air streamed in along with lots of chatter in Dutch. Willem told me to stay in my seat. When all the passengers were off, we'd be towed to the freight unloading terminal. We had cargo to unload from the wounded jet in Moscow.

At the freight terminal, our captain finished his paperwork and told the crew to get ready to deplane. A great shuffling of feet, bags, packages, mixed with light bantering, while we waited respectfully for the captain to lead us out. No one paid any attention to me, which was reassuring. I was still the phony flight engineer.

We trooped down the forward steps and into a KLM van which sped us to the operations offices where more forms were signed. Entering the office, I noticed a civilian seated in a straight-backed chair against the far wall, pipe in mouth, half-glasses barely hanging on an aquiline nose, reading an English language paper. He rose languidly and walked slowly towards me.

"Doctor?" Before I could answer, "I'm Henry Strohmeyer, a friend of Alex's. He asked me to meet you and help get things in order here. Passport, customs, that sort of thing."

"Yes, I'm Dr. Sundukian, thanks for meeting me. I'm not sure what to do next."

"That's quite all right. Come this way and we'll get things sorted out." His business card introduced him as:

HENRY C. STROHMEYER
Cultural Attache,
Embassy Of The United States Of America

It had the great seal, addresses and phone numbers in raised print and looked legitimate enough. I'd become aware that *all* these guys were intelligence, no matter what they called themselves. It was part of the game. They all came out of the same mold and only the labels differed.

Strohmeyer led me to a spare office, containing, to my amazement, my things from Moscow all neatly laid out on a desk. They'd been sent on my plane with passenger luggage right under the noses of the Soviets.

So I changed back into clothes I'd left at the Dutch embassy in Moscow. The genuine flight crewmember showed up for the flight with other passengers and my stuff was in his small luggage bag. He had a genuine passport, tickets and exit visa, which showed he'd been in Moscow for several months. He flew out with the others. And now, here were my things! I shouldn't have been surprised. He smilingly returned my original passport "adjusted" to show I had exited the Soviet Union properly.

Strohmeyer explained, "BVD, Dutch National Security Service, did this little job for us. They occasionally assist us and we reciprocate.

Their master forgers worked all night perfecting your exit stamp. It even fooled the Dutch passport men who see exit visas almost every day and are quick to spot fakes. You might say your exit stamp was a *genuine* fake!"

Strohmeyer offered me water, tea, coffee, plates of fruit, and pastries. He was slim, of medium height, and had broad shoulders encased in a neatly pressed gabardine suit a white shirt, striped tie, and laced cordovan shoes. He was in his late thirties or early forties and in good physical shape with an athlete's build. He had a fighter's nose, broken at the bridge and now a bit off center.

"Now, Doctor, we have a few things to go over. The Soviets must be very unhappy right now. Two of their agents are missing and one of their doctors was mauled in your hotel room. Every possible port, airfield, bus, and train station back there is being watched. Amsterdam may also be under surveillance, so we need to put you on ice for a while. Too many people with poisoned umbrella tips, hit and run drivers, bicycle men with silenced weapons, or teams of kidnappers. They may slack off after several weeks when they realize you left Russia.

"One piece bit of news, though, should interest you. One of the reasons Mikoyan couldn't meet you is because he's involved some in high-level Soviet scheming. Khrushchev recently sent Mikoyan to Cuba to cozy up with Castro. Our sources tell us that the Russkies hope to set up huge military bases there. You can guess how we feel about that.

"We have eyes in Cuba who tell us Mikoyan probably had no intention of seeing you in Moscow. The pressure may be off you soon, since a more important situation directs Ivan's attention elsewhere. Maybe you've just been a temporary annoyance, so they may reduce the intensity of the hunt."

I was not at all ready for what came next.

"We want you to take a short vacation to get you out of circulation until we decide when to bring you home. First, you go to a safe house on the outskirts of Amsterdam and change clothes. Then our next stop will be to one of our special canal barges."

I was absorbing these sudden developments as I changed into my chinos, shirt, and blazer, and grabbed my passport and wallet.

"Any chance I can call home?"

"Best not to. We've explained to your medical people that you've had a flu in Moscow and are recuperating. Let's be on our way."

We climbed into a small Simca five-seater and wheeled through winding back streets, crossing canals, passing parks full of bench sleepers, and weaving through herds of bicycles. Finally, we sped onto a fast roadway along the top of a levee, as odd names, like *Huidekueper* and *Kloppstrasse*, flashed by. Strohmeyer and I sat in the back, as our skillful, silent driver cruised knowingly through mazes of streets and thoroughfares.

After twenty minutes, we drove into a small middle-class residential community. In the distance, I caught a glimpse of green and a wide expanse of water, otherwise, the scenery consisted of row upon row of matchbox houses, each with red tile roofs and flowering shrubs. We wheeled to the rear of the first row of houses, down an alley, and entered a garage, its door opening as we arrived, and just as quickly, it closed behind us. Without comment, I followed Strohmeyer into the house, while our driver preceded us unlocking the door. It was a sterile place, a house but not a home.

Strohmeyer led me to a first-floor master bedroom where clothes were laid out on the bed. Strohmeyer pointed, "Get into those, Doc." I put on faded tan corduroy trousers, a worn blue flannel shirt, a sweater and seaman's wool cap. There was a pair of scuffed white tennis shoes in my size. I shoved my good clothes into a ditty bag. Strohmeyer changed into similar nautical garb.

Our driver had made a quick pot of espresso for himself, and Strohmeyer and I quaffed a Coke from the refrigerator. Strohmeyer grabbed his ditty bag and led the way directly through a passage from this house into the house next door, through it, to the house beyond it, and then through that house's kitchen into a garage. We climbed into a small lorry and tossed our stuff in the back. Our tall, silent driver wore a flat cap and Cartier sunglasses. He had large hands and a tight mouth and during the entire time he said nothing. I thought I saw a bulge in his waistband and guessed he was one of Strohmeyer's local men who knew this town well.

I was reduced to the role of amazed observer. Whatever happened from here on out would now be my new realm of perfectly normal.

After a half hour of motoring through back roads, we pulled up to a dock area on one of Holland's numerous and unmarked canals. And there before us tied up at that dock was the *Estrellita*, a long, fat, green-and-black painted house barge, floating in calm waters as though waiting for us.

We crossed the gangway and stepped on board. "*Wilkommen an boord*," said Strohmeyer, smiling and speaking Dutch. We entered a narrow passageway to the cabin area amidships and stepped into a nice, small office that smelled warm and friendly, with polished furniture, gleaming brass fixtures, gimbaled lamps on the walls, and even a Persian carpet on the deck.

"Okay, Doctor, pull out your passport." He opened it to the first page, and penciled in a row of numerals in very fine script. "This is an emergency number. Use it, if necessary, anywhere in the world, if you want to talk with one of us. If you need to contact me, say *Operator, this is Kodak, please put me in touch with...* If you sense danger, say *Operator, this is Ektachrome*; she'll find us, got it?"

"*Kodak, Ektachrome.*" I got it. Clever. Kodak was regular speed film, Ektachrome is faster.

"Good, now let me explain the setup. We are on what appears to be a lovely old canal barge for passengers or freight. It is a hundred and fifty feet long, and the wide beam standard on these canals. But under her skirts, she hides a powerful engine and is home for a US Naval electronic surveillance unit installed in the forward cabin section, the foc'sle. We've stashed a massive bank of powerful radio equipment manned by our Navy electronic technicians and capable of eavesdropping on radio waves, everything from ordinary phone conversations to ship-to-shore phones. We monitor Soviet Navy and military traffic and sometimes relay for Voice of America transmissions when Soviet jamming gets too heavy. This close to Radio Moscow transmitters, we can blast right through their jammers. For all intents and purposes, this fat old barge just travels quietly up and down Dutch canals carrying freight, and once in a while ducks into France and Germany to pick up more freight. It has no fixed schedule so it proves to be a wonderful cover. We sometimes ship flower bulbs or vegetables to maintain a semblance of legitimacy. Our people here manage travels and logistics and are in constant contact with the captain when needed."

Strohmeyer continued, "The captain, his wife, and one mate are Dutch, carefully vetted and totally loyal. They've worked with BVD and us for years. We have five Navy techs aboard who rotate duty on the equipment and rotate to shore every three weeks. One man is always on duty for an automatic monitoring system with important intercepts recorded on tapes. Voice transmissions with specific words and numbers on the intercepts automatically trigger the equipment. The entire recorded material is forwarded to us in Luxembourg and Washington. Every thirty days, visiting specialists carry out spot analyses of the tapes on board. If our trained techs hear something unusual, or if the trigger is pulled by a specific intercept, they have two choices: contact us immediately and send over a secure transmission, or hold on to it."

"You should be aware," he concluded, "one of the monitors is Eva, a woman from our Paris office, who's a whiz at deciphering codes and transmissions. She's recognized several important intercepts and provided priceless bargaining chips, which in turn actually helped shape our foreign policy. She's also a fashion junkie, a darling of the fashion houses who considers barge duty beneath her station and barge food inedible. She speaks and understands an incredible number of languages. She only stays for a day or so then jets back to Paris. She can be a royal pain in the ass, but we have no reason to suspect her loyalty or her ability to keep her mouth shut. But we do keep tabs on her. Part of the drill." He shrugged.

The barge had staterooms in the forward cabin section, each with a private bath, a fridge, deck chairs, a lounging room, lots of reading material, a television monitor, and music cassettes. It held exercise equipment and bicycles for use on ashore. "Use caution. Don't stray far from the boat and use this when you're ashore." He handed me another passport in the name of William Guiberson from New York City.

On deck, I met Captain Hendrik Korbel, a chubby, white-whiskered Dutchman of medium height. His bushy eyebrows tried to hide deeply set twinkly, but sharp, blue eyes. A battered officer's cap crowned his craggy face and a pipe was stuck in his friendly smile. His wife, Henrietta, was a slim and attractive boat *Frau,* who doubled as ship's cook and engineer. She held an engineer's license for diesel and gasoline engines and still had lovely, manicured fingernails.

Eugene, the deck mate, did odds and ends while underway and handled lines and supplies and all other chores when berthed. Strohmeyer said he was a BVD man needed to assist us because of "unnamed concerns."

The Navy men appeared to be polite eggheads who kept to themselves. They were not rude, just distant, but they were *our* sailors and their presence was comforting to me.

"How long do I stay out of sight?"

"I think a month ought to do it. We'll stay in touch with you by radio. I'll call at least twice a week and keep you up to date on world events. Don't worry; if you don't hear from me on schedule, it doesn't mean you've been forgotten. We consider you important cargo. You may have a visitor or two fly over from Washington at some point during this trip. They will need to debrief you while events are fairly fresh."

I thought I was in hiding.

"One last thing. When you reach a place called Velsen, the barge ties up for a few days to replenish food, fuel and other supplies. Take a bike into the local town and contact me by phone. Quite a few tour barges tie up there, so there are lots of kiosks, shops, and tobacconists, several with phone booths outside. Shouldn't be a problem. Try to call during waking hours. I hate to be wakened in the middle of the night." He chuckled. "If nothing is available, ask the Navy guys to make the call and patch you in. They know the drill."

This made wonder if he was based locally, because then my call would be during *his* waking hours, but on the other hand, if he wasn't, where was he based?

"Will I have any problem getting a bike?" I asked.

"No, the captain knows you'll use a ship's bike occasionally for exercise when tied up to a dock. Listen to his advice about the local area. Generally, you'll be far away from large communities, but you never know. Don't make yourself overly visible. Dirty Levis and rumpled shirts will help keep you incognito. There may be other barges passing or tied up at docks along the way, and that means chatter and visits back and forth. You might just act like one of the crew. Listen to the BBC and play things by ear. Act like you belong."

Strohmeyer's voice dropped. "From time to time you'll see clotheslines triced up on deck. They do hold clothes, but the posts and lines also act as an elaborate antenna system. In fact, by pushing a button, the clothesline posts extend up to form a transmitting and receiving antenna. And those life preservers mounted on the bulkheads aren't what they appear to be either. Two of them can extend and tilt to prearranged angles to serve as parabolic dishes, for transmitting to or receiving from satellites. They're also used to communicate with our ships at sea, aircraft circling overhead, or our snooping submarines.

He smiled. "So, please don't hang any clothes out to dry on those lines. Give your laundry to Eugene and he'll handle it."

Things were getting curiouser and curiouser. My stateroom was a surprise. The inside of this old scow had been made homey and comfortable with wood paneling, gleaming brass fixtures, and earth tone damask drapes, much nicer than the usual sterile, functionary Navy interiors. The room included a comfortable bunk placed against one bulkhead with a side table and lamps, and opposite it were a small locker and a private head with shower and washbasin. We had plenty of fresh water available due to an onboard distillation plant. Luxurious fluffy towels and a terrycloth robe were stowed on shelves.

My clothes fitted easily into the small locker. There was also a small desk with pads of lined paper, pencils, and pens. Two portholes on the starboard side were covered with thin gauzy curtains that let in the light but blocked surveillance. An overseas Zenith radio was plugged in next to my bunk. Food was prepared for all onboard in the same galley. I was to dine with the captain and crew, while the Navy men messed up forward in their own quarters.

After several days, I adjusted to barge life. The huge engines drummed quietly with just the faintest tremble through the hull. At times I heard the ripple of waves as our barge pushed her broad bow through still canal waters and occasionally the outraged squawk of a heron startled by our sudden appearance as we silently rounded a bend in the canal. I had time to make notes, clean camera gear, shoot scenery, and contemplate. I also had BBC and the Armed Forces radio network available to keep me company, although the events reported didn't always jibe with each other. Even though I realized this situation was for my safety, I knew I'd soon be chafing.

During quiet moments, I thought back to my capers in Saigon with Antoine and Gigi. I wondered where they were and what they were doing. Did they miss me? Hard to tell. I might never know if I'd been taken in by a sultry temptress or if she'd really been fond of me.

I recalled the hairy aerial battle, the gunship adventure with Antoine in the Beaver and the perilous escape from the baddies. Then that unbelievable snatch and grab mission in China and almost being left behind in Yunnan province. Our rescue team. Sent from heaven. I wondered how the Hound-Dawgs were getting along? Would anyone hearing these tales ever believe me? Even now *I* had trouble believing them myself. I thought I had the pictures to back it up. One battered camera may have caught some exposures. I couldn't remember because on some occasions shooting pictures had been the last thing on my mind. It would all depend on what the slides showed and I'd just have to wait and see. Mel already had some film, but I had some other precious rolls to protect. That was something to look forward to.

And what about my patient, the missionary, and his Mei Ling? And tender little Miss Witherspoon? Had she really cared to listen to my rambling recitation of hopes or had she merely been filling an assignment? She, too, had needed a sympathetic ear, but that episode was just a small bump in the road. I had many platters of food for thought, with a few pangs of guilt and concern. My conscience would be never be completely cleansed, but I was determined to face the future with some baggage and take whatever came along.

We next tied up at a drab, uninteresting place called Westlanderen. I decided to go ashore, breathe some fresh country air and look for a kiosk. I wanted to look for newspapers and try to phone the States. I'd have to lie about where I was, but I just needed to hear a friendly, familiar voice.

Earlier that afternoon, just after we tied up, our Paris communications expert had shown up and sashayed aboard. She was everything Strohmeyer had said. Eva, pronounced a*y-va*, if you please, was slim, attractive, and dressed in a safari outfit, complete with shiny tan boots, an expensive Hermès scarf, and dark glasses. She pouted her full lips, sparkled from touches of gold spangles as she moved, and at every step, she gave off whiffs of expensive perfume. Over one shoulder, she'd slung a light overnight bag.

"Pleased to meet you, Doctor, I heard you were here."

What? I was supposed to be William Guiberson! If she knew who I was, then everybody did.

I smiled enigmatically, "Pleased to meet you." I excused myself and went ashore.

I'd picked out a sturdy bike with a soft, comfortable, crotch-sparing seat, fully inflated tires, and a fancy geared transmission. I wore a thick sailor's shirt, windbreaker, chinos, and tennis shoes. Not exactly local, but not outlandish. I pumped easily along a narrow dirt road that skirted a marsh, where a large windmill loomed off in the distance. The chatter of frogs, crickets, and birds escorted me. I pedaled to a village looking for a kiosk, and saw one with several enclosed phone booths. I noticed another bicycle from the *Estrellita*.

Nonchalantly, I pedaled closer and spied Eva. How had she somehow gotten there ahead of me? She was talking and gesticulating with one arm while screeching into the mouthpiece. I'm no language expert, but I recognize Russian when I hear it! I quickly pedaled away, circled, and came back to the kiosk area from the opposite direction. Maybe that's what she'd done. Clearly she knew this area well.

Eva was just exiting the kiosk when she saw me and smiled. "Hello. What brings *you* here?"

"Looking for a newspaper. I see the phone booths. Any problem making an overseas call?"

"It's quite easy. Just ring the operator and she can make the connection for you. I just spoke to Paris."

"Thanks." *Paris? Why speak Russian to someone in Paris? Had she lied?*

I placed my call and got through to Mel at *National Geographic*. He was in an editors' meeting but Karen interrupted his meeting. "Great hearing from you, John! We got a great connection here."

"Mel, did you get my stuff, did they come out?"

"Yeah, John, you got some terrific shots for the Laos story, just great, fellah. Good thing you bracketed and gave us a choice of usable shots from Dooley's place. Definitely keepers, John. Your other stuff will be just fine for stories we're lining up for later. You know, the Southeast Asia stuff Garrett is hopped up on. By the way, just where the hell are you and when do you get back? I need to talk to you about captions and about Short. He's not well, you know. We're gonna publish some of your stuff in the January issue; did I already tell you?"

"Real soon, Mel." *Where was I and when was I getting back?* I couldn't tell him, and I hated to do it, but I spun the dial a quarter turn, crumpled a sheet of paper in the mouthpiece and hung up. He would assume the connection had gone bad. I was in no position to answer questions.

I didn't have a chance to chat with the captain when I got back on board, but I scribbled some notes about my incident ashore. I'd found a news-stand kiosk, bought an Amsterdam paper, a week old *International Herald Tribune*, and several bars of fine chocolate. I had a clear memory of Eva.

It was a fancy dinner that night, featuring a Dutch-style bouillabaisse of cockles, mussels, clams, crab and ocean fish mixed with hunks of potato and onion, with side dishes of dumplings, red cabbage, and white asparagus, cold crackling Rhine wine, coffee and a torte bisch for dessert.

Henrietta had set out a delicate wildflower centerpiece, candles in low silver holders, and her best china and silver set off by crisply starched serviettes. Eva looked showy in a deeply cut black cocktail dress, high heels, and long dangly earrings.

The *Herald Tribune's* lead article prompted a spirited discussion of problems among Holland and Indonesia and Timor, but nothing was settled. The talk continued through dessert and coffee and I was getting slightly bored. Eva seemed to have answers to everything and dismissed anything to the contrary with an imperious wave. I was beginning not to like her. I excused myself, went to my quarters, turned on Armed Forces jazz, and turned in.

The next day early we shoved off for Velsen. Eva was leaving us there. She had spent the better part of two days in the foc'sle buried in mounds of paper and audio tapes working with the Navy men. She wore a clingy turtleneck shirt, jeans and dark glasses, her hair pulled back in a ponytail. We saw little of her except at meal times, which suited me, since she had become an unmitigated pain in the ass.

We arrived at Velsen late the next afternoon and tied up at a long wharf parallel to the road. One of the few level ocean cuts was directly ahead where the port was at just above sea level in this below sea level land. The dikes behind the port kept water from overflowing into the lands behind it, probably because clever engineers had worked out the tides. And here, mercifully, ocean breezes dissipated the foul diesel fumes from our exhausts.

There were no other barges on our side of the ocean cut, but to the north, several large freight barges and one small cutter-size freighter were berthed, and judging from the flapping laundry snapped to deck lines, they'd been there for a while. Velsen seemed larger than the other small villages and towns we'd passed. It fairly buzzed with activity. Barges, coastal freighters and small boats chugged slowly both ways, in and out of harbor. Dozens of motor scooters zipped along harbor roads. I decided to go ashore!

I pedaled a bike to the main harbor docks. There was a great hustle and bustle of goods being loaded and off-loaded. I saw cases of canned fish and eels from a local fish house being hoisted aboard the small freighters. The fish presence was clearly identifiable by wheeling hordes of gulls. Being ashore was a relief after days of nothing but marsh, water, and squawking marsh birds. A light chop was moving in from the ocean bringing a tangy mist, and the ever-present gulls wheeled loudly overhead. They dived and fought mid-air to grab a cleaned fish carcass that was tossed from the packing house at the harbor's end.

After a pleasant afternoon, I stopped at a bench and pulled out a bottle of Amstel that erupted foam when I popped the cap. I took a huge swallow and opened package of large cashews that I munched, watching some slow-moving dark clouds and a cold wind presage deteriorating weather.

Hey, what the hell's that? I saw something off to my left and did a fast double-take. On the outboard side of a decrepit trawler, two men clad in black wet suits and masks were easing down a rope ladder and into the water in broad daylight. Each had a small back tank and knapsack slung over their shoulders. Silently, sinuously and without a ripple they slid below the surface and disappeared from view. I blinked and they were gone! Not even bubbles in the canal. This smelled like trouble. In the approaching dusk, I checked for a flag on their ship, but saw only dim lights from the bridge. No other signs of life, and then suddenly, I spotted someone hauling up the rope ladder. My neck-hairs were tingling. I had to act fast. I pedaled back hastily to the *Estrellita*. I was riding south and if I'd guessed right these guys were outboard of me in the canal as we both made for the barge. It was a race, and I thought I had the edge, but no time to waste.

I leaped back aboard and found Eugene and told him breathlessly what I'd seen. He showed concern and asked me to describe once again what I'd seen, earlier at our last stop—the Eva incident—and just now at the harbor. Frowning, I watched him come to a decision as he walked into the Navy quarters. It was now almost ten minutes since I first saw the black-clad men. Those swimmers would be reaching us by now.

The Navy doors burst open. Three sailors and Eugene emerged wearing black gear, masks, and tanks. They carried weapons: one had a spear; another a hollow tube with a bulge at the rear, the last two carried short muzzled black shotguns. Without a word they nodded to each other. The lead man pointed down and one by one, they slipped overboard between portside hull and the end pole to which we were tied. Two minutes later, I heard, or rather, *felt* two sharp "thunk-thunks" under the hull, then nothing. By this time I'd moved up to the prow, looking overboard and waiting.

I could only guess what might be happening under the hull. The men from that seedy small ship had to be Soviet military, probably Spetsnaz commandos. That dirty old trawler was obviously not just a trawler, seedy just for show. It dawned on me that the Soviets had planned this little operation to rid them of the pesky barge which, among other things, was beaming Voice of America past their jammer. I thought of Eva in the phone booth, speaking Russian, and in a nanosecond, I worked it all out. The bitch had fingered us, me especially. I was the doctor who had flown their coop! She must've out given our approximate arrival time to an offshore Soviet trawler and they'd made us. Damn!

Looking over the side, I saw dark blood spiraling slowly upward, followed shortly by our men, who popped up, one by one. They towed two very dead commandos whose suits were shredded. Each body displayed a gaping hole from which blood and seawater continued to ooze. They looked like the men I'd seen slide down the trawler ladder.

Our sailors swiftly lashed two lines to each dead man and then to the dock mooring post to keep them submerged. One of our men had brought aboard a small square black object, handling it gingerly. They left the bodies tied, climbed aboard, cleaned up, and changed into dungarees and T-shirts. They were quiet and began talking in low tones. I had the feeling they were planning something as they gradually became more talkative and intense.

"Limpet," said the tall sailor, pointing to the box. I stared at it. It had a timer knob, which had been spun around to a forty-five minute setting. Carefully, they set it up on a table, toweled it off and eyed it from all angles. Talking amongst themselves, they nodded assent. I heard them mention RDX and timer.

"OK, here's what we do," they said. I listened.

"First get the camera, then bring up Naval Ordnance on a secure frequency. I'll talk to them from out here with the portable unit."

"Aye, aye, sir." So one of these undercover guys was an officer. They took several pictures. I produced my camera, too.

"I need a photo for my scrapbook."

"Sure, go ahead, Doc. It's not gonna *be* after tonight."

I made exposures from all angles. In the meantime, following instructions from the ordnance expert via radio, the Navy guys, using a tool kit, tenderly took the limpet apart. They described the unit to him, the writing on the sides, and the inside thoroughly. I realized the man at the other end knew the device well and gave instructions on what to do, step by step. They began by disconnecting wires from the timer; it seemed so easy. It had not been booby-trapped, so there was no blast, and then after a few minutes of work, all wires lay bare and isolated. Clearly this gadget was now harmless and safe. When the ordnance expert had finished with the dismantling instructions, I overheard other instructions that were carefully written down, double checked, and then signed off. The Navy guys seemed more relaxed and breathing easier.

Eugene joined them and now some animated chattering started. They examined the limpet from all sides and glanced at their wrist chronometers. Eugene led the discussion emphasizing his remarks with a pointed index finger. Heads nodded; all agreed. The limpet and its parts were taken into the Navy's quarters.

In quick succession, they donned foul weather gear and lowered a small motor dory overboard. By now, the weather was turning sour. Dark clouds scurried in from the ocean bringing sheets of stinging rain. The two dead commandos were still tied and submerged below the hull. The sailors attached long lines firmly around the carcasses, and lashed two small anchors to the line ends. They hauled everything, bodies, lines, and anchors inboard the dory, covered it all with a tarpaulin, and headed to the cut and out to sea. The Russkie commandos would shortly be fish food.

Eugene and a sailor went to work on the limpet, grunting until they were satisfied. Finally, it was wrapped in thin cotton toweling, covered with tissue-thin oilskin and the whole package tied smartly before they retreated to the cabin. Eugene emerged wearing a pea jacket and carrying a large box of fancy wrapped chocolates, which he now stuffed into a large designer shopping bag, atop this a fancy clear plastic-wrapped basket of fresh fruit. The shopping bag fit snugly in the handlebar basket as Eugene set off on his bike.

Eva had disappeared. Henrietta told us that she had dashed into the galley to say that her car had arrived, kissed her goodbye, and dashed off. *Goodbye tovarish Eva.* We'd catch you later, I was sure.

Time now for me to do the Ektachrome call. I biked into Velsen, found an empty phone booth, and placed the call. There was a great deal of background chatter, noise and static on the line. The voice sounded very distant. "This is Ektachrome, that you?"

"Yeah, no names, please."

"You heard anything about my, er, hotel?"

"I think so. Elevator problem in the basement?"

"Yeah, and our canary just flew off."

"We know about the canary. Go back to your hotel and call me on your other line in about half an hour. Let me get some things in order."

I hopped back on my bike and did a fast pump back to the barge.

The motor dory had returned and been hauled back up on its davits. From all appearances it was back to business as usual. Lights were on in the cabins and I smelled food cooking in the galley.

But why had we been targeted for a hit? Two obvious reasons: the Soviets had tired of this pesky floating electronic flea in their hide and decided to just blow it up. With me aboard, they could kill two birds with one stone. They knew all of it from Eva, no question. Strohmeyer had implied that they were playing her like a fish on a line, trying to catch a bigger fish.

I tapped on the Navy door.

"Hi, Doctor, I'm Lieutenant Clint Fikes, come on in. Coffee?"

"Yeah, thanks. I'm..."

"I know who you are. We were briefed on you earlier," a wry smile. "This cruise been exciting enough for you?" He poured out two mugs of strong coffee.

"Today it has. What went on down there, or can you say?"

"I can tell you. We really owe you for alerting us to those guys. You gave us the jump on 'em. They were Soviet commandos, most likely Spetsnaz, getting ready to slip a limpet on our hull. It was set to blow when we were in our bunks, we'd all be asleep except for the man on watch. I'm sure we'd have been seriously holed and sunk with the loss of all hands, including you.

That was sobering. "What went on below?"

"Pretty much what you'd expect. We dropped overboard on the dark side of the canal. We were in the dark and they had no idea we were there. We ambushed 'em. Not looking for us; big mistake on their part. In fact, one man had a small flashlight shining on the hull, so we spotted them fastening the limpet onto our wooden hull. When you have a steel-hulled target, it's done with magnets, but this one's wood and they didn't dare use nails and hammers, too noisy. They were so busy concentrating on hand-screwing in the hooks, they forgot to look around. We jumped them and they didn't have much chance to react. We can't take prisoners on this mission. They never knew what hit 'em. I blew one away with my shark gun, the long pipe with the bulge. Clancy got the other one with his short-barreled shark blaster."

"Do you suppose these guys will be missed?"

"Yep, more'n likely. But in these games, nobody looks too hard. The Commies won't admit to anything. Will they suspect? Sure. Will they do anything? Nah, I doubt it. Not much they can do. We'll be moving out shortly, right after evening chow.

"Where did Eugene go with his package?"

"He had a delivery to make. I have no idea where he went." He fell silent and drank his coffee.

"Lieutenant, I was told to ask for a secure connection to Ektachrome, can we do that now?"

"Sure thing. Come on back." We entered a small closet-like area, packed with electronic gear from deck to overhead. It was warm and everything to my ears made a friendly hum. Dials and tiny lights blinked and flickered while tiny bulkhead fans struggled to keep the place cool. Clint walked over to a unit, spun to a frequency, and spoke into the mike.

"Sampan to Hometown, over."

"Hometown reads Sampan fiver by..."

"Sampan to Homey, small fry needs contact Ektachrome with patch, can do now?"

"Wait one."

"OK Sampan, have small fry stand by, patching Ektachrome, over." Clint motioned me to the mike.

"Hi this is me...hope I'm on time."

"Strohmeyer here. This to both of you. We have a clear, safe line and we're scrambled, too, so no one else is with us. We know about your little escapade. Our best advice is that you folks get underway as soon as the BVD man gets back. I want you, Doctor, to be ready to move out at the next stopping point. Have your gear ready and take it with you. One of our men will be waiting on shore in a blue windbreaker and baseball cap there. He'll ask if you have any Kodachrome. You'll say sorry, I only have Ektachrome. Keep it simple, got it? I'll catch up with you later."

"I got it."

"Now let me speak to the lieutenant." Clint got back on mike.

"Clint, you guys monitor the sparrow?"

"Yes sir, affirmative on that. We got her on tape, plus the tone signals for the number she dialed."

"Great, we're gonna run them all down now. Clip her wings once and for all. We've got enough on that whole ring now. They're all tied to a bigger cell in Paris and they don't know each other, but we do. This last episode with you guys was too close. Time to reel them all in. I'll need those tapes; hand them over to the doctor to bring with him, and just to be safe, send us a copy by burst on the fast channel."

"Aye, aye, sir, Roger that. Anything further?"

"Yeah, tell the captain to head for our landing spot near Haarlem to quick drop the doctor, then you guys keep going. Keep two tapes running for the next forty-eight hours. I suspect there'll be lots of radio activity between Murmansk and the trawlers. We'll check with you later. Out."

Henrietta had prepared a fricassee of pork with red cabbage, fresh salad with garlic butter on toast, and rice pudding for dessert. She was waiting for the captain to announce dinner. The captain was in the engine compartment checking equipment and preparing to get underway, when Eugene finally returned wearing a satisfied smile, but saying nothing.

"Wash up please," commanded Henrietta. "Tonight our Navy guests dine with us and we mustn't be much longer; we get underway shortly."

A huge crock of pork was placed in the middle of the spacious galley table, with large bowls of cabbage and salad beside it. There was a dish of small, roasted potatoes and hot, baked rolls with fresh, whipped butter. Henrietta served all hands generous portions. Wine was offered to me, the guest, but none for the Navy and the captain. We all were uncommonly silent. We'd dodged a bullet, but it was odd to eat in silence. We were unconsciously wolfing our food in response to an unspoken need for haste. I think the captain wanted to get the hell away from here. Only Eugene seemed totally relaxed.

The Navy men finished first, thanked Henrietta, and went forward. The captain and Eugene left next. In a moment, the main engines started up and thrummed into life; it was well dark now. The Navy men and Eugene untied the barge, and we quietly shoved off. Slowly, we motored up to the cut, made a half circle, and then headed back the way we'd come. The barge continued quietly along the winding canal back towards Amsterdam for at least thirty minutes with the engines purring powerfully.

I wasn't able to sleep. There had been far too much excitement and I was still wired. I had the feeling that I'd become a lightning rod for trouble. Every place I visited ended in some unexpected, violent activity. I've never subscribed to coincidence, but I was beginning to get a message, "Yankee go home!"

A sudden dull boom in the distance sent me darting to the rail. Way off on the horizon, from the direction of Velsen, a bright ball of flame lit up the night sky. As the crow flies, we were not too far from Velsen, but canal wise, we were now maybe an hour distant. Eugene joined me at the rail. He said nothing, but stood looking at the lit sky.

"What the hell was that?" I asked.

"It sounded like an explosion," he smiled, turning to me. "I had a box of chocolates delivered from Eva to the trawler this afternoon. You see, Doctor, two can play this game."

"I see," I said, staring at the flames shooting skyward.

After another hour, the engines slowed and I felt the barge veering towards the shoreline. In the far distance on the port side were some dim fluorescent lights, probably the specified docks near Haarlem. I had my gear beside me on deck.

The engines were on idle as we glided into a long parallel dock along the portside bank. As the captain powered into reverse, we stopped inches from dockside. The dim lights illuminated some abandoned shacks.

"Up you go, Doctor," said Eugene. At the last minute, Clint shoved a mailing envelope into my ditty bag and slapped me on the back. "Good trip, Doctor, and good luck. Nice having you aboard."

I stepped on the dock and looked around. The place was deserted and clearly the shacks were abandoned. The *Estrellita* was already easing off towards mid-channel.

I was alone. Where was Mr. Baseball Cap?

My feet crunched along the gravel leading away from the dock as I headed toward a shack. I'd stuck my automatic in my belt, just in case. Two greenish fluorescent lamps high on thin metal posts made a weak, garish pool of light. Standing in it was my contact, wearing a blue windbreaker and Yankees baseball cap.

"Hey, you got any Kodachrome film?"

"Nope, only Ektachrome," and I added needlessly, "Kodachrome's no good in the dark."

"Yeah fine, Doc, I dint know you wuz a wiseass, too. I'm Chief Bos'n Enright, from the *Forrestal*. The helo dropped me to wait on you, since you wuz late and they took off. They'll be right back after another wide circle and then the helo is gonna lift us two back on board the carrier."

He mouthed into a hand-held SCR, "Yankee here, we got Ektachrome, make the pickup."

"Roger, boats, on our way."

Thundering out of the gloom came a huge chopper, its powerful searchlight illuminating the landing site. Coming closer, it swooped down to land scattering dust, dirt, and loose trash in all directions. Its rotors were flattened, but still spinning, at just below takeoff rpms.

"Okay, Doc. Let's go."

The Chief Bos'n took my bag with one hand and rushed me to the waiting helo. A helmeted crewmember helped me aboard, strapped me in a seat and handed me a helmet, "Put this on now, sir." Enright climbed in right behind me. The hatch slammed and we lurched up and forward, nose tilted down slightly, as we whirred off across the water. I gathered this was one of the Navy's huge Sikorsky Sea Stallions. It never ceased to amaze me how something this huge could fly.

My earphones crackled. "Welcome aboard, Doctor. We estimate wheels down in about thirty-plus minutes, sir. Make sure you're secure, and the Chief back there should have a thermos of coffee." I gave a thumbs-up and click-clicked my transmitter button. A thermos appeared as if from nowhere. It was now nearly three in the morning, and once again the excitement of the unknown set in.

We landed on a huge aircraft carrier displaying huge black numerals on its tower, black on gray, "59" painted on a massive off center tower rising from middeck. This was the USS *Forrestal, CVA 59*. The helo blades were still blowing a fierce downdraft, while the ship rushed through the waves making her own wind currents; a cacophony of engine sounds roared around me. I was out of one frying pan and now here.

AMSTERDAM

Helmeted men greeted me, "Welcome aboard, sir. Please come this way." They directed me to the mid-island tower. There was a great amount of noise and activity on this monstrous ship. I was guided in through the island hatchway, and assisted up narrow steel ladders to this very comfortable stateroom. My quarters aboard ship were obviously a VIP stateroom. I was tired, but exhilarated to be out of Russia and off the barge. The Russkies would have a hellish hard time finding me here, which was a welcome relief. I had no idea how anxious I must have been, because I suddenly felt totally relaxed.

I looked around my cushy quarters. Not many civilians were this lucky to ride like this in a ship of the line. Wow! Would anyone believe me? I grabbed my Nikon.

From my cabin porthole, I watched sunrise breaking over the distant horizon. Miles of water lay between us and those first rosy rays of sunshine. I could feel warmth on my porthole with these first welcoming rays. It was great to be alive, slashing through the ocean to some unnamed destination. Something new and different, but I wasn't sure just where the hell we were. Logically, it had to be the Atlantic.

A young ensign appeared at my doorway and told me I'd be breakfasting with Mr. Strohmeyer and the ship's captain shortly. I had time to freshen up and shave.

Strohmeyer, huh?

Taking the hint, I shaved and rinsed off in a hot shower with blasting water pressure and was ready when the ensign tapped on my door.

White-jacketed steward's mates were setting covered pewter dishes on crisp white tablecloths as I was shown to my seat. Strohmeyer smiled a sleepy smile as he introduced me to Captain Bobby Crichton, a handsome, John Wayne–like four-striper, whose Annapolis ring stood out against his tanned skin.

"Make yourself comfortable, Doctor. Strohmeyer, here, tells me that you've had an exciting few days."

I had no idea how much he knew, so I just smiled and mumbled, "Yes sir, it's been very interesting, and thank you, Captain, for the very nice quarters."

I looked around the room slightly wide-eyed. Pretty fancy trappings for a ship: dark paneling, gleaming brass, and highly polished furniture. This flag mess was just like an executive suite in a big corporation. They served freshly squeezed orange juice, scrambled eggs with sausage, toast with real Seville marmalade and strong coffee. This setting would please a king. No question, the Navy knew how to live at sea. I hoped the crew had it half as good. Imagine having clean, fresh sheets and towels daily. Nothing like my old LST 466. Imagine eating in elegant dining quarters, a holdover from early British naval traditions cleverly retained by the upstart American Navy. If I ever went back into military service, it would again be the United States Navy.

I was demolishing eggs and sausage, when a courier hurried in to whisper to the Captain who then rose precipitously, took one last gulp of coffee, and excused himself, saying, "COD coming in with people from Main Navy. I need to be on deck."

It was an unannounced visit by the SecNav and several admirals. Strohmeyer had told me he thought we'd be on our way back to the States in a few days. But I had no idea where we were. We were underway, not flank speed, but turning some pretty good knots and I knew we weren't making circles. I asked about our location and destination.

"Well as I understand it, Doctor, the big brass are here from London for a short stay, and then they fly off to our base in Rota. We swing west and steam towards Norfolk, which is almost at the same latitude. This ship is returning from the Med for a crew change and some new equipment. They'll add some aircraft, and back it goes. At some point you and I will take off from this carrier for Andrews Air Force Base, and you go home for a short visit."

This set my mind reeling. *Home,* I understood. The *short visit* I didn't. But for now I was a guest aboard this mighty carrier, with crew of 4,000-plus and planes thundering on and off.

--•--

THAT AFTERNOON, IN A NOD to British Naval tradition, Strohmeyer and I followed the custom of receiving high tea in my quarters. Our Navy steward served fresh baked pastries along with delicious Oolong tea or a damn fine Arabica bean coffee for all hands at all times.

"Well, Doctor, here we go again. What d'you think of all your escapades since you left Washington to teach surgery in Saigon?"

My escapades? I had no idea how to answer him. I'd started out to do good things for mankind, then at some point, became aware that no matter what I did, it would only scratch the surface. Frankly, I didn't enjoy that experience as much as I'd expected. So I told Strohmeyer just that. He was nodding as I recited my thoughts.

"Doctor, you're an activist with fine ideals, who's been disheartened by some tough experiences. You risk slowly becoming a cynic. Someone once said that a cynic is the last refuge of an idealist. Do you see yourself there now? Were you an idealist? Many in our line of work sour into old cynics, disbelieving in our fellow man."

This was getting too philosophical for me. I shook my head in frustration and decided to counter.

"Whoa. Where are we going with this? What's your profession, Mr. Strohmeyer?"

"My profession, if you want to call it that, is that of a gatherer of information. You see, I'm an officer of the Central Intelligence Agency working in Europe. And for your information, the Agency has been watching and working with you ever since you left Washington."

So that was it. "Why me?"

"Because we think you're an individual who can carry out a mission with an ingenious combination of instinct and on-the-fly creativity. It's an uncommon attribute. We seek it out, among other traits, when considering someone to work with us."

Was this working up to a pitch?

"Let me go on," he said. "I've been tasked to see if you would consider working with us."

"Consider?"

"Yes, consider working with us. Not full time, but from time to time, on an *as needed* basis. To see if you have the capability or interest in working on some of our special projects for which we think you are ideally suited. You would *not* become one of our agents, but you would eventually become what we refer to as a controlled asset. For this, you would, of course, be rewarded handsomely with an arrangement, and much of it would be tax free," he said in a lower voice.

"Tax free?"

"Yeah, some of your salary would be in cash, and the rest deposited in your bank as payment for consulting fees. The payor is a perfectly legal organization, usually one of our proprietaries. I'm authorized to deposit an amount reflecting what you'd expect to earn from your profession, plus a twenty percent bump. You'll also get benefits like club memberships, attendance at professional meetings and social events, and it's all on the house, so to speak.

"First we'll need to work with you on developing certain skills. We'd like to send you to a training center near Williamsburg, Virginia, to a place we call the Farm, for brief courses in covert work, like reading someone's mail. That course is jocularly called *flaps and seals*. And there are surveillance techniques and tactics to learn, some courses in enemy psychology, and rudimentary weapons skills. We may ask you to audit some language classes and then do some field work."

What he was really saying was: *We're planning a mission and we have you in mind to help us as soon as our plans and details are in order. I can't say more at this time, but your photography cover and medical talents may come in handy at the appropriate time.*

I let it sink in. I wondered if these guys made any real difference in what went on in the world. "I understand, but first things first, Mr. Strohmeyer. I have to work this into my concept of being a doctor, of restoring my practice and my life. I just can't jump into this new world overnight!"

"Fine. Take all the time you need. By the time we land at Andrews, you should have some thoughts, hopefully favorable to us. As for your practice, it won't be a problem. You'll still receive referrals from certain government agencies and their affiliates. You will be asked to see a few outside patients for consultation. This will maintain your façade and you'll charge your standard fees. So consider it a given that you won't have any financial worries for the foreseeable future."

"As far as returning to the academic world, Dr. Parks has received glowing reports of your overseas medical work in Saigon. And of course," with a slight lowering of his voice, "there's been no mention of your other friends, or your other good works. We'll keep it all between us." Strohmeyer was applying a smidgeon of pressure. He went on, "One of our proprietaries has made an anonymous donation of one million dollars to the medical school in your name, which should cement your position with Parks, the university, and the whole medical school board. You should have no problem maintaining your academic standing and hospital privileges."

"Finally, during the background check, we spoke to your friend Frank Short at *National Geographic* to confirm that your Laos photos will be used and that Mel Grosvenor is, in fact, really pleased with your work. And further, that he, Grosvenor, is anxious for you to get some photos for a story on the River Nile."

The River Nile? Now that came out of left field and I wasn't biting, not yet. I smiled. "Gosh, that sounds interesting; guess I better talk with Mel first."

It was a lot to digest in a short time, but I suspected that I knew my answer already.

CHAPTER 23

Washington DC
(Fall and Winter, 1959)

I don't want to see the uncut version of anything.
—John Kerr, 1923–

Thomas Wolfe once wrote something to the effect that you can never go home again. But actually you *can*. It just that things aren't always the way you remember them. I hadn't been away all that long, in fact it seemed as though I'd only been gone for a long weekend. Other memories made me feel like I'd been away forever. First off, I had to get my priorities in order.

The CARE organization, delighted with the success of their first team to promote good will and provide medical skills to the people of Vietnam, had scheduled talks, appearances and events to trumpet this achievement. I was often designated the featured speaker. At these fund-raising events attended by the *glitterati* and social *liberati* of the Washington social demi-world, money was poured into CARE's coffers, and many directed that certain funds be directed to Tom Dooley's isolated hospital in a far-off place called Laos.

Invitations were eagerly sought for these events, and now as a featured speaker and provincial shill for CARE, I was eagerly welcomed. All I had to do was show up, smile, kiss-kiss cheeks, and join the gossipy chatter. Nubile young ladies fluttered their eyelids at me as I mixed with the attendees after my presentations. One breathless girl told me I was like a great white hunter returning in triumph from a faraway part of the world; to her, a very desirable catch.

My appearances also generated unanticipated invitations to dinners and meetings at ladies' club socials. On one notable occasion, I accepted a large check for CARE from a well-funded labor union. By now, CARE considered me a hot P.R. property.

I carefully screened the invites, selecting the Georgetown salons which served the best food, wine, and company. There was always delightfully light dinner chatter in which I tried to participate with the fine folks who were heavy contributors to CARE. I knew that my presence only reflected my temporary notoriety, but I smiled and everyone was happy. Among other notable firsts, CARE had set up worthwhile child health programs in Poland and Afghanistan. They hinted that my appearance in those countries would be useful from a humanitarian aspect, and for public relations too. I agreed to consider future visits to those countries, thinking also of the great photo opportunities there.

I became convinced that developing world politicians will do anything to obtain and keep power, and if cavalier Americans want to send money, medicines, food, and social workers to do all manner of good things for the foreign poor, fine. The politicos would take credit and stay in power.

How did I know all this? Dealing with their high level officials, I saw first hand that their main concern was how to become involved in high profile projects: can America build us a hospital, get us new equipment, train more doctors?

During my travels I'd seen unused U.S. equipment stacked in dusty storerooms because no one in a foreign Ministry of Health knew or cared to learn how to set it up or use it. When ministers were photographed receiving these crates from America, it made a big local public relations splash, but nothing more. It was part of an international con game and our country succumbed to their blandishments like a low-priced hooker.

After I was back, CARE received word that a biopsy from Dr. Tom Dooley's axillary lymph nodes revealed a very bad actor. Cancer cells from a forearm melanoma had crawled into them, an indicator of a rapid and bad outcome of malignant melanoma. A visiting surgeon had noticed an unnatural stiffness in Dooley's arm and shoulder movements as he played Chopin on his zinc-lined piano. After palpating some hard nodes, the surgeon took a biopsy, pickled it in formaldehyde and flew it to New York. Microscopic sections confirmed the presence of metastatic melanoma. Dooley returned to America for therapy but died within months, despite intense chemotherapy. He had gone into a frenzy of writing, speaking, and visiting religious refuges. His books were published documenting his legacy of help for the underprivileged.

As Strohmeyer had predicted, my patient referrals and medical activities began to increase, so much that I couldn't care properly for my increasing patient load. I teamed up with another surgeon, a long-time close friend, to combine our efforts and talents. This proved fortuitous as it finally freed up some spare time.

Things went smoothly, and one day, a few months after returning to the fold, my beloved chief, Brian Blades, spotted me on rounds at the George Washington University Hospital. He crooked a finger, led me into his inner office, and shut the door. He instructed his long-time secretary to keep everyone out. He pointed a gnarled finger to the visitor's chair and told me to sit.

Blades, a native son of Kansas, was very direct when he had something important to say. Called Blackie by his intimates, Blades was a descendant of dark-skinned Irishmen whose ancestors had floated ashore following the disastrous drubbing of the Spanish Armada in the late 1500s. Eventually some Blades had come to America where a few had settled on the Maryland Eastern Shore, then later moved out to what eventually became Kansas. Blades had coal black hair, a rugged dark complexion, played college football, ended with a limp, finished medical school, and then trained under famed surgeon Evarts Graham in St. Louis. He resembled at times a pensive Clark Gable: same height, black hair, deep basso voice, and suave manners. Blades projected a commanding personality as a natural leader, and most of the time he was an irresistible smoothie. On the other hand, I had watched surgeons turn into Jell-O after one of his crisp tongue-lashings.

Lighting an unfiltered cigarette, Blades blew a plume of smoke at the ceiling, flicked an ash on the carpet, and dropped a bombshell.

"John, goddamit, I wanna talk to you."

"Yessir, what is it?" I'd taken a seat in front of his desk, which was the altar of the almighty. Behind him hung photographs of surgical greats. On his desk, his beloved "jukebox" into which he bellowed reports, letters, and memos.

"You know, John, I've always been fond of you."

"Nice to know, sir." I was amazed, but very wary.

"Don't be a smart ass...you remind me of me when I was coming along."

"My sympathies, sir."

"Hah!" he snorted, then gave me his famous glare, "You've got good hands too."

"Thanks, that's nice to hear coming from you, sir. You got slick hands too."

Grunt.

"Well, one last thing I ask of you. I'm getting along in years and my friends are dropping off...sad times for us old guys. Didja know I'm going to step down and move over to the VA?" It was not a question, rather a statement. "They set up a cushy job for me, Surgeon in Chief of the VA. Actually," he snickered, "I talked Paul Magnuson into it years ago, just in case they dumped me at GW. And they're getting ready to dump me, so I'm gonna walk out first." This was surprising news; it had never occurred to me that he would ever step down.

"But I want you to keep in touch after I've moved. I may get lonesome over there, so I want you to call me from time to time, come by and shoot the breeze, drink my coffee. Promise? Is that a deal?"

"Absolutely sir, I'll stay in touch with you. You know, sir, at times I hated that you tested me, but deep down, I knew you were always looking out for me."

After moving to the Veterans Administration, he said, looking me straight in the eye, he would be sending all patient referrals to me. I was the only chest surgeon that he'd trained who *thought* exactly like him. But there was an important condition: I could not breathe a word of this to anyone. He'd only be across town in the VA hospital, so we could remain in touch. That was somehow comforting.

I had moved most of my practice from George Washington Hospital to the Washington Hospital Center, a larger hospital where it was easier to get operations scheduled and without the pomp of the long white jacketeers at GW. In short, I had better control of my time.

I needed hours of free, non-medical time to attend to non-medical pursuits. A raft of slides and photos waited identification in *National Geographic*'s editorial offices. These carefully culled slides had been selected for the Laos story scheduled for the following January.

Mel was delighted with the picture choices, and pawed through the slides again and again to make sure his people hadn't missed anything. Mel tended to excesses at times and crowed, to any who would listen, about my newfound photographic prowess under his tutelage. Grosvenor was a delightfully eccentric individual; a loveable, suave, sometimes oblivious, but very shrewd visionary. He often bounced ideas off me, knowing I was no sycophant. Our friendship led me to new heights, new experiences, and eventually to a great disappointment.

After approving the quality of the slides I'd sent back to the magazine, Mel decreed that henceforth *National Geographic* would keep me outfitted with cameras, lenses, film and necessary supplies, that everyone was to regard me as his personal medical consultant, without portfolio. This did not set well with everyone, least of all with a mean spirited administrator in the film division. Her anger at my lofty status was palpable and transparent, more so because I feigned ignorance and always smilingly complimented her on the efficiency of her department. Despite her opposition, my cameras and light travel gear were always checked over by the photo techs, and at the ready.

My talents were promptly put to use as many of the senior editors at Mel's shop called on me for medical advice and services. And once in a while, they used my pictures.

Back at the hospital on a regular schedule, I climbed back on my daily treadmill: get up early; quick bite; make rounds on post-op patients; meet new patients and their families; see patients for the next day's operations, then head to the operating room. On days with more than one operation, I started the first case with one team and as the operation was nearing completion, moved over to the adjoining room where another patient had been readied by my second team. My assistants closed the first case while I jinked over to the next room and started that case with the next team. I rarely took time for lunch, at the most, a diet cola and sandwich snatched from an unguarded diet cart on the wards.

Just before Thanksgiving I received a phone call from General Archie S. Koffman, a fervent Bostonian and head of Andrews Air Force Base Hospital. Archie never called unless he wanted something, otherwise his assistant, Dotty Tronka, the real boss of the hospital, called.

"When can you get back on schedule here, Jawn?" I could hear the liquid chomping and slurping on his ever-present cigar as he spoke, and then a loud *poof,* as he blew a plume of pure Cuban smoke into a hazy blue cloud.

I was their senior surgical attending and consultant. Without my attendance and training of their surgical fellows, Archie would have no surgical training program, and his residents would receive no board credit for their time at his hospital. Worse yet, complex surgical cases would be shunted from Andrews to hated rival Walter Reed Hospital, an intolerable prospect for Archie, because playing second fiddle to Reed meant losing yards of face.

"Jawn, in addition to the consultation fee, I promise you front row seats for all air shows and a reserved parking sticker, plus chopper rides any time you want, and you can race my car against Curt LeMay on the runways. Lastly, I can make it happen that you can fly your plane to Andrews, land and have hangar space when you come out here; howzat grab you?" I couldn't turn an offer like that down. Especially chopper rides.

"OK Archie, you're on." I agreed to return to my weekly visits to Andrews. I loved flying and the sound of those huge jets blasting off.

The paltry consultation fee was laughable, but how many lucky civilians got to ride military choppers for free? Eventually I had many hours of stick time on the big Sikorsky CH 53s duly recorded in my log book by instructor pilots.

A few weeks later, on a routine visit to Andrews, Dottie Tronka asked me to please stop by General Koffman's office before starting my rounds. I was to meet two visiting Air Force generals, Walter Thatcher, the White House physician, and Jim Kernigan, one of the ranking Air Force surgical hierarchy.

Archie had suggested my name to Thatcher to be his consultant at the White House, mostly because I'd been asked to review a set of X-ray films on a Mr. X. The envelope was marked Confidential/White House Medical Office, in red ink. Mr. X was undoubtedly the President.

Thatcher had sent the films to Archie for his look-see rather than to Walter Reed. And at Archie's request, I'd given them the quick once-over and concluded that the lung lesion seen in those films was probably benign. According to his X-ray records, that lesion had been there for years. This was a dangerous position for a chest surgeon to take. I was told that the patient had spent considerable time in the California desert country.

When in doubt about a lesion, we always resected them. But I'd learned much about these things from Blades. He had an uncanny knack for accurate spotting of benign lesions, and coached me well. At that moment Thatcher swore us to secrecy, told us it *was* the president, and that information from the films must be kept a graveyard secret for obvious reasons. That was no problem.

Kernigan, not to be outdone by General Thatcher, decided then and there to appoint me as National Surgical Consultant for the Air Force. I was certain Archie had arranged all this. With his delightfully scheming mind, Archie kept Andrews in the running as the top Air Force hospital in the East. Good for Archie, and very heady news for me. Within two weeks, I had new ID cards reflecting my loftier levels of security clearance.

Once again, my calendar and schedule were rearranged and now I penciled in a visit to the White House Medical office once a month to review films on *Mr. X*. I signed papers to the effect that I would not discuss any aspects of my visits. *Mr. X's films* were repeated at six-month intervals and happily, they remained unchanged.

These new consultation visits were followed by lunch at the White House mess. As Navy stewards fussed over us, I, outwardly Mr. Cool, was inwardly as giddy as a teenager at the prom. Thatcher pointed out some famous faces as we munched on huge hamburgers. No question, the Navy Mess did things with class; shiny crystal, bone china, and crisp linen serviettes. On my first visit, Thatcher jammed something into my jacket pocket as we left. Later I lifted out several books of paper matches with the presidential seal emblazoned on their covers.

--•--

I HADN'T FORGOTTEN MY NEWFOUND allegiance to the organization behind Strohmeyer. Mel had never said a word to me about his link to the agency and I never asked. But he had to know I was doing things for Strohmeyer's bunch. After all, they'd asked him to set up the photo capers for me, hadn't they? As I'd hoped, things began to percolate. Within the next few weeks, a number of situations came along.

For one, our local medical society wanted a radio voice to explain social policies on current health problems to a curious public. They needed someone with prior radio experience who could deliver with authority, but there was nothing in the budget for a professional announcer. Publicist Lou Brott knew of my radio experience from Hal Stepler, a top local announcer and my tutor at GW night school. He knew about my stand-ins for Steve Allison, an ailing local late-night radio personality, and other public service appearances. As an expert on the medical ills of smoking, I had credibility. Lou persuaded me to do spots and radio work as a public service feature, a further affirmation of my good will for mankind. I jumped at Lou's offer.

For me, a live mike is like a magician's wand. I become a totally different character: I turn into a ham. I became *Dr. Jack Cartwright*, thus deflecting any suggestion of self-aggrandizement from medical colleagues. With Lou Brott as straight man, I commented on the ills of smoking and other timely medical topics on WRC, the local NBC station. Later, when I filled in on the evening radio shows, I used my own real name. I interviewed high profile guests ranging from mountaineers to journalists. These were public service stints so I didn't need an Actor's Guild card. This all resulted in some network feelers and even a job offer from NBC, but radio and television were not for me.

The Medical Society decided to go a huge step further, and the Medical Society of the District of Columbia convened a major *Anti-Smoking* conference at Medical Society headquarters. At the conference, major airlines announced the beginnings of the "no smoking" rule on passenger aircraft, and in recognition of their momentous decision, we presented each airline with spectacular framed citations replete with gold seals and multicolored ribbons, worthy of public display.

Possibly as a result of this meeting, coupled with my record of research in lung cancer, smoking, and public appearances, I was invited to become a consultant for both NASA and the FAA. Then through some convoluted networking, I was asked to accept the vacant position of Medical Director of Pan African Airlines. There were no conflicts with my other positions and the requirements were few. Apart from an occasional medical matter, I had merely lent my name to the firm stationery. But now as an airline official, I had legitimate reasons for travel. The parent company provided a generous honorarium and many benefits from the holding company, Dispatch Services, based at Miami International Airport.

Strohmeyer was bang on target about intense debriefing. After disbelieving specialists at the State Department reviewed my experiences in Laos and China, more specialists gave me a good going over. It was all the same: "How did you manage to do this? How did you get from here to here? What did you see? *What? Are you certain?* Did you get photos of these areas? You did? Who has them?"

"*National Geographic.*"

"We have a great interest in seeing those photographs and we'd like very much to review them with you. When can you make them available for us?" I explained that *National Geographic* had them in their possession. That was a problem. They'd contact me when they had them in hand.

"Understand," they said, "your captioning this information was vital to National Security needs."

"Sure," was my standard, safe response.

Again, the same line of questioning. What make of car did you steal? Did it have a radio? Were the characters on the dash in Chinese, Russian, or English? I had to admit that by their repeated nagging questioning, my inquisitors helped me to recall events which I'd totally put aside, not forgotten, but shunted to a dark recess of my mind. From long practice they knew how to retrieve this information from those hiding spots and were experienced in how to wring out the last bits of memory.

"Why don't you guys talk to the others in our group? They should have some of this information."

"We have."

"Oh."

One day, two new patients appeared at my office. They'd made an office appointment to be seen together as last patients of the day. Such a request is most unusual, outside of married couples with serious problems.

Both were trim, in their early thirties, neatly groomed, and in business attire; one in a light gray Glen Urquhart plaid, the other in blazer and gray slacks. Both wore button down, blue Oxford shirts, standard repp ties, and highly polished, laced shoes. They could have been lawyers or sales representatives, except that their IDs encased in red carnets made them officers of the Central Intelligence Agency. One carried a small, worn leather briefcase from which he extracted a plain sheet of paper in standard Courier font, no letterhead, and no identifying marks, exacting my pledge not to discuss this meeting with anyone. I signed.

The senior of the two, "Jack Taylor," confirmed most of what Strohmeyer had told me on the trip back to Washington. That if we all agreed, I would begin training sessions with their company specialists and at some unannounced point, I'd be required to take a "lie-detector" test.

"Any problems with that?"

"Nope."

I'd been expecting the polygraph test, standard for new hired hands. The FBI would also conduct a background check which would take weeks. I'd be contacted when they were complete. In the meantime, I should continue my daily routine, and keep in mind that I might *not* hear from them, so don't hold my breath. As they were preparing to leave, Taylor extracted another sheet of paper from his briefcase. Again, another plain sheet of paper with typing.

"Doctor, I was asked to hand this to you personally. It was forwarded from one of our brother agencies."

There it was again, the eerie knowledge that someone always knew where I was and what I was doing.

Unconfirmed reports from xxxx in Saigon indicate one François Sully and one Giselle Prudhomme involved in an aircraft accident; both reported as fatalities. No further details available.

I was stunned. There was no date or other information. I searched their blank faces. If they knew anything, they weren't saying. That report had no meaning for them, though for me it was an emotional hammer blow. François and Gigi dead? *It couldn't be, dammit! Gigi and François both?*

When they saw my reaction, they broke off questioning. "This is obviously not a good time. We'll schedule another visit next week." They left.

I tried to visualize a scenario of how it could have happened. Obviously, they must have been flying together, but who was the pilot? No mention of him. It was almost certainly Antoine. So many questions and it was all so far away. How could I get any sensible answers? The distance, the time zone, and who to contact?

I got on the phone to the CARE office in Saigon. No one knew anything, but they'd call their Michelin contacts and ask Antoine, if they could find him, and get back to me. Next, I called the American Embassy, where no one knew anything. Sorry, please call later.

I searched my mind for some person, some point of contact, but nothing clicked.

I pictured Gigi, as I had known her, smiling, frowning, coy, and chatting. It was hard to accept that she'd been killed. Until I was given incontrovertible proof of her demise, I wanted to consider her missing. Gigi *dead* was not acceptable. I returned to my everyday life as a surgeon, but my mind seethed. Someone had to know what went down, literally, in the jungle.

-- • --

AS A SPIN-OFF TO MY Air Force consulting appointment, Jack Schaefer, the FAA Administrator, quietly appointed me to his panel of medical/pilot specialists along with doctor and former Navy fighter pilot Carl Almond. We became the new Thoracic and Vascular surgical mavens. But there was a catch. I had to be a rated pilot, multiengine and instrument rated.

Well, a fully trained and rated multiengine pilot I was not, so the FAA sent me to Woodbridge Airport in nearby Virginia and into the tender care of Charley Bain and Riess Brown to get rated.

Hah! They were two of the toughest, meanest, but basically nicest and slickest instructors anyone could wish for. As former military pilots, they regarded me as a freak. I'd had no real flight training. I couldn't even start the Piper 140 trainer. French pilots in Vietnam had taught me to fly?

"Are you kidding, Doctor?" No, I confessed and told them about my experiences in the Beaver and the Otter in Laos. They were now convinced that I was a liar as well! Charley Bain contacted Pete Campbell, the FAA's man for all reasons, for verification. It was the truth, said Campbell. And now my flight training started in earnest.

Brownie was from Virginia tidewater country; he mumbled and ate most of his words. "How the hell would any sane man let you handle those goddam planes, when you don't even know how to set up a Piper for takeoff? Those goddam French must be nuts!" he railed.

"Get in the left seat, Doc. We're gonna let you take off." He got the Piper cranked up, told me how to set trim tabs and power for take-off, and we did. This was my introduction into *his* flight-training program. A take-off, a slow angle climb to five thousand feet, then level off. We tooled along at level flight for about five minutes and did some S curves. I was nervous.

"Want to fly 'er some, Doc?"

"Sure."

Under his guidance we flew straight and level for a few more minutes. I was getting the feel of the Piper. Easy so far. Then with a wicked grin, Brownie said he was taking over and pulled the Piper straight up into a gorgeous blue Virginia sky, *and into a climbing stall.* The little trainer shuddered to a mid-air halt, and fell away into a sickening downward spiral. *Shit!*

To my unbelieving ears, Brownie yelled, "You got it!" That meant I had to get us out of it and there was no way. I reacted in an instant.

"The hell I do," I yelled back. "I got nothing, you do!" I folded my arms. "You got us into this, now you get us out. I can't."

I crossed my arms across my chest and closed my eyelids tightly to blot out the dreadful, fast spinning. Brownie got the message, but the sadistic bastard let the plane spin down another three thousand feet, which seemed like forever, before pulling it out.

We had some choice words back on the ground. My face was ashen and I was close to vomiting, but choked it back. That day was my inauspicious start of a lengthy flight curriculum from which I graduated *sine cum laude,* and eventually ended up with a Commercial ticket, single and multi engine ratings and IFR, and instrument flight qualification. Charley Bain, Brownie, and I eventually became fast friends, but it was rough going for a while. I used Woodbridge airport for a home base until some developers took it over.

— - • - —

THEN TWO EVENTS JUMPED UP in rapid succession. It started with a call from Jack Taylor, the gray-suited chap who'd been in my office two weeks earlier, asking me to meet the following day at Howard Johnson's in Rosslyn.

WASHINGTON DC

It was a beautiful October day. Georgetown University basked in bright sunlight just across the Potomac. On the river, shells were sculling, noontime joggers were out in full force, and the dining room was filling with employees from local firms. This time Jack was alone. After the preliminaries, he said that my paperwork was moving along.

"Have you heard from a Dr. George P. Bedrosian? You will. You've been listed as a consultant for the Agency's medical outpatient department, so they'll be sending you problem cases, mostly lung stuff. George will get with you and work out the details. As is sometimes the case," said Jack, "a sudden requirement had come along which might require your assistance." A waiter appeared and we switched to the menu and drinks. I was sliding into the behavior of the sneakies.

Jack lowered his voice and resumed his guarded pitch. "In your new position as chief doc for Pan African Airlines, a wholly owned subsidiary of *his* company, you are now in a position to travel to International Aviation related meetings anywhere in the world, correct?"

"Yes, I guess so."

"Here is our requirement: you are the *most suitable* person to attend the annual meeting of the International Society of Aviation Medicine in Beirut."

"Beirut?"

"Yeah, Beirut. The meeting takes place in about three weeks. Can you prepare a scientific paper to present at that meeting? We'll put you on the program."

"Yeah, I guess so, but why me? What is so important in Beirut that I need to go there on short notice?" Taylor took a bite of his huge hamburger and smiled indulgently at me.

"There will be two very important members of the visiting Soviet delegation there. We want you to contact them and establish a friendly relationship. If they mention the word "defect," refer them to the Embassy. Tell them you are not into politics, only medicine. You never know, Doc, when someone is for real or trying to set you up. You see, if you fall for what might be a 'dangle' on their part, you get tackled in the end-zone, and we lose the game. Exchange business cards, invite them to join you for drinks, and be a pleasant American with lots of loose change, to use as you wish. Be your charming self, cozy up to them. Make them *want* something from you, and believe me, the moment they realize you're a free spender, they'll ask you for favors. Whatever it is, say yes, we'll work it out with your on-site contact and it will be engineered without any fuss. Just stay the fuck out of any political discussion. And that business in Moscow? It's over with. Again trust me. We know. You're safe from that episode."

How they knew would be interesting to hear, but for damn sure they weren't telling. I suspect the husband got blamed for that whole mess. Not my concern.

By now, I was curious. *Beirut?* Of course I was in.

"How do you know the Russkies will want something from me? They don't even know me. This all sounds ridiculous."

"Doctor, in this game, you listen and learn. Trust me, I don't make suggestions without a high probability of being correct. *Someone* in our company is more than halfway certain of the probabilities. This is not the first time we've dealt with Soviets attending meetings," he said quietly and firmly. "Hear me out. We believe one of the scientists has a diabetic father who is in constant need of American medicine. He may ask you to arrange to send him some insulin. He does it at every meeting he attends. We *want* him to ask you for it. You will say yes, what strength do you need? We need to bond with him, because it's really his wife we are interested in. She's a high-level molecular biologist, and our scientists are curious about what molecules she's working with. Your concern will be making friends with our two Russian scientists. It helps us in the long term, whatever the eventual scenario. It sounds simple, but you never know what to expect. We think you are the ideal man for this particular project."

He went on in the same quiet voice: "The other guy is a decent, slightly absent-minded, space scientist, who will want to chat with you about space physiology. We're betting that he'll seek you out after you present your paper on busted lungs. Your presentation will be our 'dangle' and he may nibble. Basically, we want these men to have a friendly mindset whenever your name or 'America' pops up, rather than knee jerk anti-American thoughts. You can help us."

Jack smiled. "Can you present a paper on a topic related to Aviation Medicine? Busted lungs or something along those lines?"

In fact I could. I offered a paper co-written with Colonel Fuller Cox, *Lung Collapse at Altitude in Air Force Pilots,* that had been accepted for publication in *Aviation Medicine.* An important topic. We concluded that an operation on the ruptured lung, repairing the defect, like permanently patching a blown inner tube, was far better than grounding the pilot. Grounding had been Air Force policy until our revolutionary concept was accepted. After the operation and a satisfactory pressure tank test of his lungs, the pilot could be back flying within six months.

"Great."

I realized *he already knew.* He'd mentioned busted lungs, the son of a bitch. He'd known all along.

"Now, as I mentioned," Jack went on, "two Soviet delegates will gravitate to you. Your name will appear on the program as a speaker. They've been briefed by their people to contact you and pick your brains for information dealing with flight and space medicine, so this is a great opportunity for us to cement two contacts." He showed me a list of Soviet delegates attending the Beirut meeting with two highlighted names: Lev Peruzian, Professor of Aviation Medicine, USSR Academy of Medicine, and Armen A. Gurjian, Director of the Commission on Exploration of Outer Space, USSR Academy of Science.

Both were Armenians. The ethnic card dealt once more. Jesus, these Soviet Armenians had penetrated deeper than the Mossad and the Hasidic Jews. My ancestors, like all surviving minorities, had traveled a long hard road, and now I'd be seeing more brethren from a foreign land.

"Here are some details." He laid out dates, times and places for a short stay, ten days at the most. Reservations had been made for me at the Phoenicia Hotel in downtown Beirut. I would have a few weeks to get ready.

Covering my hospital duties should be no problem as I had a partner now. Jack told me it would all be arranged, and lecture slides would be made for me, with an extra set to be sent ahead, just in case. These guys thought of everything.

－－●－－

I WAS BRIEFED AGAIN SEVERAL times before my departure date. I would fly PanAm to London, overnight at Brown's Hotel in Mayfair, and then take BOAC direct to Beirut. At Brown's, I'd be contacted by Alec Breslow, an administrator for the Company who would be attending this meetings as Team Control. He was a clinical psychologist and my *go-to man* in case of a sudden change of plans.

I reviewed the photos and brief bios of the Soviet delegation. The leader was Dr. Oleg Gazenko, director of their Biomedical Institute. He was crusty and fond of his vodka and his wife was a practicing pediatrician. Both were Party members. I found my targets: Peruzian and Gurjian. My first responsibility was to rendezvous with those two Russo-Armenians and guarantee future smiles when they heard "America," rather than a knee jerk *nyet*. On the list of *our* attendees, a name jumped out: Dr. Robert Yablonski, an FAA accident investigator and psychiatrist whom I'd met at our panelists' meeting. He just looked at me and grunted! Another panelist later pulled me aside, "Listen, Dr. Sundukian, don't let Yablonski bother you. You see," he whispered, "he's married to a woman he *delivered*, years ago."

"Huh? Say that again."

"You heard me correctly. He delivered a girl baby, kept in touch with her family, and then years later, divorced his wife and married the girl. It's complicated. She's cute, he's weird, and they get along fine. But he's quite paranoid of anyone who might represent a sexual threat."

"Okay, thanks. I'll keep that in mind."

CHAPTER 24

London, Brown's Hotel, Mayfair

We never know, believe me, when we have succeeded.
—*Miguel de Unamuno, 1864–1936*

It was two in the morning by my body clock when the cabbie dropped me off at Brown's Hotel. I was jet-laggy, but the registration was smooth, all arrangements made in advance by the FAA, I assumed by Strohmeyer. The porter and I rode up a silent elevator to my room. Everything was first class in this place: flowers, a bottle of wine, a terrycloth robe, and a huge bed. Impressive. I thanked the porter and tipped him too much. A note held the message: 1837, 5:30, Breslow. Probably the restaurant for dinner with my contact.

The maitre d' showed me to a table where a man stood smiling, his hand extended. "Dr. Sundukian? I'm Breslow."

I recognized his bearded face and horn-rimmed glasses from the photo I'd been shown in Washington. Breslow was cordial, unassuming, and looked a typical intellectual with a sleepy exterior, but eyes that missed nothing. He would blend in anywhere in his chinos, blue blazer, button down shirt, subdued tie and cordovan shoes. Nothing to make one take a second glance. It was a very low key meeting. Tanqueray tonic for me, Scotch rocks for him, a Dover sole and lamb chops.

He recognized me from my photo. After pro forma pleasantries, he reviewed our individual roles. He would be the *go to man* in any situation and I was not to be a *cowboy*, but stick to my protocol.

He confirmed that I'd been selected because of my expertise in aviation medicine and experience in dealing with foreign nationals. Little things all add up to make a man of possible use. All I had to do, he reminded me, was to chat up the two Armenian delegates, buy them drinks, dinner, whatever, and leave a good impression. He handed me a small box marked *Copenhaver, Washington*, containing a supply of nicely engraved business cards. Classy. Then he passed over a sheaf of American Express traveler's checks, an envelope containing a thick wad of crisp hundred dollar bills, and a narrow slip of paper with telephone numbers. "I'll be staying at the Phoenicia, with you and most of the other delegates. Here is my phone number at the hotel. I'm registered and someone occupies my room under my name. Any problems, call that number first. If anything goes wrong, call the other numbers in sequence. The call will be answered, "Hello," and you say *this is Doctor John, I need help.*" Then you'll be given some options. I'll be around the meeting areas and know your whereabouts. It should be a good time."

I checked my BOAC flight schedule with him; we were both flying first class out of Heathrow on the morning flight eastward. We would not acknowledge each other's presence. We would arrive in Beirut and check in at the Phoenicia Hotel. Again, I was not to contact him except by phone under some unforeseen circumstance. He handed me a copy of the meeting agenda; this was Saturday, registration was on Sunday, and I was slated to speak at ten a.m. on Tuesday. I had twenty minutes allotted for my presentation and ten for questions.

Back in my luxury suite I got ready for bed, wondering who had decided that I was an aviation medicine expert. Just as I was dozing off, it dawned on me...my Andrews connection, my paper submission, and my appointment to the FAA panel. It was all a matter of accessible record. Somebody out there had put two and two together, and now I was an Aviation Medicine expert. What next?

CHAPTER 25

Beirut, Lebanon

*Advice is seldom welcome, and those who want
it the most appreciate it the least.*
—*Lord Philip Chesterfield, 1694–1773*

All went well in Beirut, almost. I met the two Russian scientists as the conference began. As predicted, Peruzian requested a large supply of diabetes medicine for his father, but it was clear to me that it was for him. He had that chubby look of a type II diabetic. Peruzian was a smiling, swarthy man in a badly rumpled suit, with a beard that suggested lowland Armenian origins. His bio indicated that he was a highly respected research scientist out of favor with Party officials because of his disregard for Party guidelines. He was genial and we got along famously. He rued the day his grandfather had not departed for New York with his brothers and lamented his miserable status in the Soviet research hierarchy because of Party politics. He amazed me by confessing that when his superiors used him to ferret out the latest American research projects, things went better for him.

"Thank God for you Americans," he said. "Without you, our research would be nothing, *nothing*. We need you to do the work, then our people steal it and we go on from there." He said this in Armenian, in an abysmal local dialect, difficult for an outside Armenian to understand. We agreed to keep in touch and meet at the Las Vegas meeting the following year. Hell, I had no idea that there was such a meeting next year. Yes, of course, I would be happy to send over any medicines he needed. We planned to meet for dinner.

It was the same with Gurjian. He was short, stocky, and reminded me of Inspector Poirot. Not much over five and a half feet and shy at first, he warmed up when he saw that Peruzian and I were on good terms. I gave him my crisp clean Copenhaver card on fine vellum and received his quickie print card with English on front and Cyrillic on the reverse. He asked if he could join Peruzian and me in Las Vegas next year. Sure. Smiles all around.

As I stopped in the gift shop for a copy of the *International Herald Tribune*, Breslow was buying a copy too. I folded my paper, and without looking his way, pantomimed putting a phone to my ear. Ten minutes later, he called my room. I passed on the information about Peruzian's relatives in New York, the Las Vegas conference, and our dinner plans.

"Fine," was all he said.

At five o'clock, I met Peruzian and Gurjian at the Phoenicia bar for drinks. We were shown to a table next to a glass side wall of a swimming pool. Underwater swimmers slid by waving and blowing bubbles. Peruzian loved it. He waved back with a gleeful cackle, while quickly downing his first vodka neat. Gurjian seemed bewildered. He wondered what kept the glass from breaking and began to discuss water weight and pressures, typical scientist talk. Peruzian told him to drink up and relax, snagging a waiter for another round. I wisely decided that one drink was enough for me.

As I ordered another round, our waiter asked in a low voice if we were enjoying the scenery. "Yes, of course," we replied. "Then please wait a moment, my friend would like to speak with you." On cue, a young chap appeared at our table and took an uninvited seat.

"Gentlemen," he said quickly, "for twenty dollars American, several naked women will swim by and wave to you. For fifty dollars I can have many women of different sizes for you to enjoy." I glanced at Peruzian, who grinned widely in anticipation. Gurjian appeared not to understand. I raised my eyebrows at Peruzian and he nodded vigorously. I gave the man a twenty.

BEIRUT, LEBANON

"Let's see the merchandise first, hajji," I said, "then we'll decide about the others."

"Sir," he said haughtily, "I am Christian, not Muslim."

Taking my twenty, he left. Five minutes later, a voluptuous, dark-haired young lady lazed by the window, waving and smiling, her long hair trailing. She was totally naked except for a fish tail, which did not quite cover her groin. She smiled invitingly, flipped over and swam back and forth a few times, and then wiggled away. Our table was ready so we passed on the rest of the show.

We were seated in the center of the dining room amid other attendees. Table hopping was in full swing, which played havoc for the waiters. I opted for Damascus *Shish Kebab,* with rice and *patlejan,* grilled eggplant. Something told me that seltzer water was safer than wine tonight. As I expected, Peruzian ordered like a man at his last meal and called for two bottles of expensive French Burgundy. What the hell, he'd done this before and knew that rich Americans always picked up restaurant checks. The lamb tasted like Brooklyn mutton, but was edible. After heavy desserts and espresso for my guests, dinner was finished.

Peruzian invited me to the Soviet quarters for more after-dinner conviviality. I got the message: more drinking. As their newfound friend I could not refuse, so with silent reservations, I went along to their suites.

As delegation head, Oleg Gazenko occupied a large suite. When we entered, the party was in full swing. Wild music blared from somewhere. I heard Russian, English, and French chatter from the group. Peruzian and Gurjian first led me to a side room where several cases of liquor were stashed. Reaching into one case, Peruzian presented me with two bottles of Ararat Cognac, very potent stuff from the highlands of Armenia. He also gave me a replica of an ancient gravestone and a photo atlas of Armenia, plus some music records, and placed it all in a large blue and white Aeroflot bag inscribed with my name in large letters. I thanked them warmly. These were the only gifts enslaved ones could afford, part of the propaganda *systema* everyone understood.

Back in the main salon, I was introduced to Gazenko and a swarm of Soviet delegates whose names I could not pronounce. Fortunately, we exchanged cards, so I had names to which I might attach faces. We made our way to the crowded hors d'oeuvres table where huge open tins of fresh caviar were flanked by baskets of pita bread, platters of fish, olives, and dill weed. A savage throng gleefully spooned gobs of caviar, followed with great quaffs of Stolichnaya vodka.

Sounds of excitement and ribaldry came from the master bedroom. Through the doorway, I watched a woman vault high into the air from a large bed and do a forward flip, falling awkwardly, and bouncing even more awkwardly to the floor with a sickening thud. She lay there ignored. A stocky man took her place doing an unsteady dance, twirling drunkenly and waving a soiled hanky. Cackling and laughing, he bounced up and down using the bed as a trampoline. Every third or fourth bounce, he did a complete forward flip. The crowd roared lustily. Egged on, he managed one last flip, landing miraculously on his feet, but his crimson face attested to too much vodka. He collapsed on the bed and lapsed into coma-like stertorous snoring, while onlookers clapped with glee.

Wild, tribal music blared from a bedside turntable. I kicked the electric cord to cut the music, but the savage, wailing Kavkaz music had gotten their blood up. A woman with almond eyes raised her plump arms, stamped her feet, pirouetted, and staggered, finally sprawling on the carpet and revealing bright red underwear to match her bright red boots. She was a leading Uzbeki scientist who liked her grape. The revelers were at it until all the food and drink was gone. Gazenko, their team leader and gracious host, stayed sober and alert. Sometime after midnight, I made my way to my room, reeking of vodka, caviar, and tobacco smoke.

CHAPTER 26

Doctor, We Have a Problem

You always pass failure on the route to success.
—Mickey Rooney, 1920–

SEVEN THE NEXT MORNING, WHILE I WAS STILL SLEEPING OFF THE PREvious night's revelry, the bedside phone shrilled loudly. It was Breslow.

"Doctor, please get dressed and come up to room seven ten now. We have a problem. I'll explain when you get here."

Surgeons know the knack of quick dress. I was at his door in less than ten minutes. It was ajar.

"Come in," croaked Breslow. "We have a bitch of a problem from last night, and don't want an international incident. You may be the guy who can get us out of this goddam mess, but it'll cut your visit to Beirut."

I was bewildered.

"What the hell are you talking about?" Unusual capers seemed to flow my way. Moscow had introduced me to some fun and games and it was sheer luck that our Russian exit had worked. Now something else was cooking. Breslow pushed some black coffee at me to jump-start my brain.

"Last night," he said, "one of our delegation, Dr. Semerjian, a biomedical man, from our hush-hush laboratories in New Mexico, took a local gal from reception out for dinner and drinks and she claims that, at some point during the evening, he proposed marriage.

She went home and proudly announced it to her family. The whole goddam clan is down in the lobby demanding to see him. The stupid son of a bitch is hiding in his room and the father announced loudly that if he doesn't come down soon, they will go up and get him. Hotel security is holding them back." Breslow was agitated.

"John, you gotta go down and stall the family until I can shuffle this idiot out to the airport and get him on the first MEA flight to Paris. *You'll* have to go with him, too, if it works out. And don't let him out of your sight until someone meets you both in Paris. From there, he's got to get to Sweden with no more delay. The silly bastard has fucked things up badly. We just have to exfil him now. You should know that this idiot is a true genius in his field, doesn't usually drink, and is married with children. The receptionist met him in the lobby yesterday and accepted his invitation for dinner. They ended up heavy petting in his room, but he swore he didn't screw her. He didn't drag her to his room, either. She was a little high, but he assures me that he was in control. She opened her blouse and let him play with her knockers; then he moved his hands up her skirt and pulled down her tiny panties, but she kept her legs crossed and was confused about what she wanted. He decided he'd had enough when she got scared and started whimpering. He has no recollection of proposing to her. He thanked her for the evening. She got herself together, he walked her down to the lobby, and watched her drive off in her little car. End of story. I've gone over this with him several times and he may be telling the truth. When she got home, she told her family that she had a marriage proposal from an American scientist. The shit hit the family fan."

I waited for more.

"Here's where you fit in. She's Christian, not Muslim, and her family is from Antilias. You know where that is?"

"No."

"It's a little town just up the coast where the *pure* Holy See of the Armenian Orthodox Church is located. Everyone in those parts respects Armenians, so you go down to the lobby and exert your ethnic charm and influence on the family. I don't care what you tell them, but there was no marriage proposal. This is all a great misunderstanding. Do what it takes to make things right, then bow out. Got it?"

So my task was to get them quieted and on their way back to Antilias.

"Semerjian is a world-famous human bioengineer. He's only stopped here en route to Sweden to hash over research with some colleagues. He's *carrying with him* a fighter pilot's helmet that's asymmetrically loaded in a fatally flawed design. When a fighter pilot pulls out of a steep dive, the high G forces at the pull up point can yank the head violently enough to the overloaded side to cause neck fractures. We gotta get him and the helmet to Sweden and you've got to ride shotgun with him. We have no other choice."

He didn't wait for my answer. "Talk to the family and offer them money. You don't want to insult them, but money talks. I trust your judgment, you have carte blanche on that assessment." He handed over another of his fat envelopes, "There's ten grand in here, which should be enough to soothe over any imagined insult."

What could I say? I had to help get this sorry mess straightened out.

"Okay, I'll give it a go."

"Our helpers will stuff Romeo into a dirty-linen hamper, whisk him down the service elevator to the loading dock, into a waiting van, and off to the airport. He's already agreed. I pick you up and my helpers will get you both aboard the early MEA flight. In Paris, others will take over. You fly back to Washington. I'll read your presentation, giving some excuse for your absence. In our scale of priorities, that helmet means more to us than your presentation. As for the Russkies, you've certainly done everything we could wish for. I'll send a note of thanks for the cognac and to please keep in touch. I guarantee that you'll be hearing from your new best friends."

"We have a problem. I'll get right on it," I replied.

"Fine. When you've finished with the family, get your bags and go directly to the loading dock to a white van with Middle East Airlines on its side. Dr. Jacques Nassif, their Medical Director, is a good friend and also on our payroll. He'll get us all to the plane."

It went down smoother than I anticipated.

Stepping out of the elevator, I saw the family seated in the lobby. It was a scene right out of Hollywood, starting with the patriarch, a short wiry man with puffy eyes, hunched eyebrows, and a beaked nose over a Pistol Pete mustache that arched across his thin, compressed lips. His oily face was unshaven, and his scrawny neck skin hung like loose turkey wattles. He wore a buttoned collar, a worn jacket, old trousers, and *babouches* on his huge, stockinged feet. He sat stiffly erect, with his arms crossed defiantly and jaw jutting. His dumpy wife sat beside him, a bandana tied under her chin. She was obviously uncomfortable in a fine hotel and her anxious eyes darted furtively towards the entrance. Seated next to her, were two swarthy young men in workday clothes and two attractive, fashionably dressed young ladies in stiletto heels. Nearby, hotel security men stood planted, watching.

I addressed the elder gentleman. I was here to apologize for the unfortunate events of the previous evening and hoped the family was not offended.

"Who are you and what business is this of yours?" he demanded.

I pronounced my name with an Americanized pronunciation of Sundukian, and explained that I was a physician with the Aerospace meeting and mumbled a few placating words. This made no impression on him.

"If you know where this famous scientist is," he said in heavily accented English, "please bring him down immediately to meet me."

I explained that this was not possible since he had left to attend a meeting in another country. Then I took the leap. I said that I realized he and his family had gone to a great deal of trouble to come here all the way from Antilias, when he interrupted me.

"What did you say your name was?"

I repeated my name, reaching into my jacket pocket to extract a business card, at the same time allowing him to see a thick wad of American dollars in my bulging wallet.

"And your name, sir?" I asked.

"I am Nejib Harmouny," a glare and silence.

"My pleasure to make your acquaintance, sir. I know this has been very inconvenient for you, and if you would permit me, I would like to reimburse you for transportation costs and any time lost from your work and, of course, from that of your family members here." I smiled innocently, reached into my wallet, and extracted five crisp American hundred dollar bills and held them out like a hand of cards. He reached for them like a man entranced. After counting the money carefully, he softened. There was a brief family discussion, the clasped money being stroked as he spoke. He turned back to me.

"Please tell your famous scientist that he has not properly presented himself to request my daughter's hand."

"*Gele*," he said to his troupe, and without a backward glance, they rose and filed out. At the doorway, the old man turned toward me. "*Shad shenoragalem*," he said earnestly, patting his breast pocket where the money was stashed. It meant *thanks* in Armenian. I was giddy with relief.

I lugged my bags to a van at the loading dock and climbed into a get-away van for the third time. The driver drove straight to the airport, veered off on a side road past a waving guard and around to the MEA hangars, and parked. I glanced at the bulging linen hamper at the back. A very rumpled man climbed out carrying a small briefcase in one hand and a bowling ball bag in the other. The all-important helmet. I smiled at him and Breslow hurried over.

"John, I'd like you to meet Professor Hrant Semerjian; Professor, Doctor Sundukian." I was looking at a defiant, confused, and sleepy professor.

"Gawddammit," he said in a heavy Bostonian accent. "I didn't do a gawddam thing wrong except have a drink with a sappy woman." Breslow led him aside and I backed away. We boarded the MEA Comet jet destined for Le Bourget field in Paris. Breslow made sure we were seated in first-class and then departed. The professor ordered a glass of champagne from the Lebanese stewardess, quaffed it all at once, gave me a withering look, turned his face to the bulkhead and closed his eyes, the precious bowling ball bag secure between his ankles. Screw him. Some guys don't know how to say thanks.

We cruised towards Europe at thirty thousand feet and I had time to muse. No pictures for Mel on this trip and I'd hoped to see the famous Maronite church, some ancient ruins, the waterfront teeming with tourists, and the famous gambling casinos. I'd barely gotten there before being pressed into watchdog duty. So far, this new career was challenging and confusing, but interesting enough to go along with for a while. What the hell, I was doing clinical surgery, teaching at the medical school, consulting for government and private agencies, giving learned opinions, writing papers, *and* photographing for a famous magazine.

My new connection with the Agency left me with a lot of questions. I wasn't an agent, but I *was* an asset of sorts, useful to them as a photographer and physician. So far, they'd asked very little and they certainly were more than generous. Less a pact with the Devil and more of a great opportunity to be a patriot.

As the plane ploughed along smoothly, my mind slid over to an image of Gigi. I had trouble accepting that she was gone and considered that it might have been a way for her to go into hiding. But if that were true, why was François Sully reported missing? Had it been an orchestrated disappearance? I imagined possible scenarios. It could have been a sudden disaster, where facts would be murky and answers nearly impossible to confirm or deny. Wasn't Gigi a master of deception, trained to lie, seduce, and manipulate? What if Gigi was *not* dead, but hiding? I decided to investigate further exactly when and where the plane went down before I dozed off and awoke in Paris.

CHAPTER 27

Washington, and The Beat Goes On

Success has always been a great liar.
—Nietzsche, 1844–1900

I HAD BEEN TO BEIRUT AND ARRIVED BACK IN DC, BUT I FELT ROBBED TO go that far without a peek at any interesting sites. I did successfully get close to the Soviet scientists and I felt proud of my contribution. After all, few surgeons are selected for this type of assignment to assist the government. But thanks to that cretin Semerjian, my medical paper was presented by Breslow. Small matter: the Air Force had already implemented my suggestions.

So it was back to the salt mines: the office, the operating rooms, receptions, consulting with patients, and attending countless meetings. The challenge was gone. I realized that this desire for excitement was like playing with the tiger's tail. I missed the adrenaline rush and was looking for trouble, not the way an organized mind should be working. I should be focused on my chosen profession, doing surgical good for others and getting my life in order. Still, I wanted to grab that tiger's tail and give it a hard twist, and then see if I could dodge its nasty swipe.

Happily, Mel Grosvenor had seen my Laos photos and loved them. They would be published in his January issue. I never realized how fortunate I was to be involved in so many activities and still be practicing medicine. I was a fast moving train switching tracks as needed. Mel was actively abetting my future in photography while keeping alive a cover, and I was still a medical man.

I'd been back for several weeks and in my daily schedule, but strangely, no word from Strohmeyer. But then I wasn't the only trained seal in his circus troupe. I was signing charts at my desk, when my inside phone rang. "Hello Doctor, Strohmeyer here."

"Hi, long time, no hear."

"I just got caught up on your Beirut lecture trip. Fine job. Time to get you on to some graduate work." We set up a lunch at the Jefferson Hotel for the following week.

In a back corner table at the Jefferson, Strohmeyer told me about the courses and classes I would attend for my low level training. My instructors were called Sasha, Jarbig, and Becky. We would meet in safe houses, basically motels, apartment houses, condominiums, and go occasionally on weekend visits to the "Farm."

I took an unannounced lie detector test at an early meeting with Becky and a crew of two in an upscale condominium in nearby Alexandria. The space was sterile, clean, and devoid of personality. I knew the underlying principles involving lie detectors: they ask you a question whose answer they know, and then watch the needle record your response. Once they have a baseline of truthful responses, they know when you're lying.

The stone-faced operator tossed nosy questions and I answered as truthfully as possible. There was no change in the intonation of his voice or expression as I answered that I had not engaged in homosexual acts, that I had messed around with married women, had never been arrested or imprisoned, and I had no medical problems nor had I used drugs. I assume I passed.

Becky reviewed with me responses in certain situations. She would select a social, business, and/or embarrassing situation, like *robbing a cash register!* What do you say when caught in a robbery? I had never contemplated how to explain to that to the police. She suggested several alternative responses.

Outwardly, Becky appeared to be a modern business executive, and spoke very precise English with a tinge of a middle European accent. She was mid forties, conservatively dressed and physically fit. She wore a slim wristwatch, no rings, and pearl earrings. Probably a clinical psychologist, and she was hard to read.

"Why all the mind games?" I finally asked, as the sessions became repetitive. I was tiring of struggling to come up with answers while she sat there smiling, trying to confuse me.

"John, after we review your responses often enough, you'll be able to respond quickly without hesitation, almost reflexively, and you will seem truthful. A safe response buys time. If we go over these situations often enough, you can explain logically why you are hiding in a closet when the husband opens the door." Our sessions were completed a couple of weeks later.

My next meetings were with Sasha, who reviewed rudimentary rules of behavior in the field, calling it "tradecraft." He demonstrated how to poke at a discarded newspaper in a trashbin while making a small chalk mark on the inside; how to pocket a small package lying on a perfume counter in a major department store while fussing with samples. I learned to exclaim when the kiosk vendor has sold out of my newspaper, thereby passing a message. I had to distract a viewer, by buying lingerie without fluster when a smirking sales lady asked for size, color, and panty cut. He gave me these tasks, some real, some not, just to monitor my behavior. I suspected that I was observed most of the time.

My greatest surprise came working with Chuck Kelly, a retired master locksmith and former Midwest police captain. After several sessions, Chuck declared me a natural lock picker and gave me a set of picks as a graduation gift. He warned, "If you haven't popped a tumbler in thirty seconds, get the hell out fast. You may get caught. In some states it's illegal to own picks and big trouble if they're found on you."

The Company Farm in Virginia was interesting. I was one of several low level observers, each with a badge and number, who attended classes and joined exercises. A course called *Flaps and Seals* covered reading someone else's mail, opening various sized packages, and demonstrations of how to steam open letters and reseal them. The instructors showed us ingenious ways to open letters, packages and even wax sealed envelopes. One way is to slip two knitting needles under the flap of an envelope, tap the envelope sharply, "trap" the letter, then roll it up like a shade and presto, out comes the letter, the envelope remains intact. Just as easily, roll it up tightly and slide it back in. I was able to do that with effort, but performing the other tricky openings was not within my range of abilities. I had no future in that line.

After lunch, there was a session on dressing to be inconspicuous in a crowd by changing hairstyle or shoes, removing a jacket, or altering facial appearance using dental wadding between cheek and gums.

The next day there were lectures on the rudiments of surveillance: how to tell that *you* were being watched, how to shake it, and how to get away. My lone field project dealt with surveillance. I was assigned to an instructor who resembled a ferret. He was short, with a tiny mustache and a disarming stoop. A forgettable face in rumpled jeans and denim jacket. He spoke in the low voice of a patient college professor. You'd not look twice at this guy for any reason. For this session, we drove to a nearby town to become hunter and hunted.

My instructor and I picked a street corner as a point of reference. I was to give him a head start. He would walk away from me in full view, after crossing the intersection, and continue down the street. As soon as he had crossed that street, I was to try to follow him as he walked around and returned to our starting point. Sounded easy. If I lost him, in half an hour I was to return to the starting point.

Good plan, but as I looked both ways to cross the street, his figure bobbing down the street had vanished. I walked to where I'd last seen him and looked around. No sign of him. Baffled, I stared in store windows at reflections, but of course this move was all wrong. Don't look in windows, they cautioned, that's only in movies. Searching several blocks further, I felt a slight tug at my arm. "Hi Mister, can you spare a dollar?" The goddam ferret instructor was there beside me grinning, his mustache quivering. He'd donned horn-rimmed glasses and an Irish walking hat, and he'd changed his gait, hobbling along the crowded sidewalk with a collapsible cane, *almost parallel to me from the moment I'd crossed the street.* Easy for him, mortifying for me. It was crystal clear that I was not destined for this type spook tradecraft.

On my last day, we were taken to a mock setup of Saigon's river, the Mekong, located smack-dab in the middle of the vast acreage of the Farm. Their engineers had rerouted a natural stream in order to provide an amazingly accurate rendition of that waterway. There were even some small river craft bobbing at a dock. I had a momentary flashback of driving Antoine's speedboat, as he and Gigi hooted and hollered on skis behind me. It was unsettling that my mind found excuses to flip to Gigi's smiling image in flashbacks. I had to get those memories behind me, but damn, it was slow going. I think I missed her more than I cared to admit, causing more than a few sleepless nights.

The final event at the Farm, or Disneyland South as it was known, was a quick stop at a mockup of a Central European city. At a dummy international airline counter, we were harangued by a foreign ticket counter crew. We had no advance knowledge of this session. The trainers sprang it on us as a taste of foreign frustration.

The bogus ticket agents were Farm faculty from Eastern Europe. Our job was to check in for a flight with dummy tickets, passports, and visas. At the check-in counter, we were to demonstrate persistence in demanding passage, seat assignment, and anything else. When my turn came, the agent was an unpleasant, bored, overweight woman, with a pencil behind one ear and hair askew, exhaling heavy garlic and a bad attitude. She grabbed my passport, thumbed through it, snorted and tossed it back at me announcing loudly that I had overstayed my visa. "Please step aside," she said. She would consult her supervisor after the other passengers behind me were processed. "Anyway," she said, "my tickets would no longer be valid for a flight I could not be on, and therefore no longer existed. Next!" she announced, dismissing me.

"Just wait a goddam minute," I said, banging my fists on the counter, my voice raised to an outraged bellow. "Maybe you can't read English. Where is your supervisor, Madam? *I* want to speak to her *now*. These tickets are first class; my visa is perfectly in order. You are trying to

extort money from me. I am an American citizen!" I was shouting for effect, pretending outrage. Everyone was hushed, pretending not to hear the crazy American losing his composure. It worked. A male "supervisor" in an immaculate suit glided over.

"Is there a problem sir?" he said, smoothly.

"You're damn right there is," I went over it all. He took the documents and carefully examined my bogus visa and tickets. After some head shaking, lip pursing, and pretending to look at schedules, a huge smile. "A thousand pardons sir, you see, our schedules are misprinted." He announced that all was in order and he was sorry for the inconvenience. My fake passport and fake tickets were stamped and given his blessing. I walked out without a glance at the others. Outside, my "guide" and some others were guffawing.

"Great job, John! You turned the tables! Those are our language instructors who take turns being pricks at the desk for fun. You just shook up our chief German language instructor. Tell me, did you really lose it in there, or was it just an act?" I smiled broadly. "What do you think?" Raise enough hell and they either call the guards or give in—anything to shut you up. I was finished training.

--•--

A WEEK LATER, I GOT the phone call that I'd been expecting ever since the conversation with Strohmeyer had hinted of things to come.

"Well Doctor, how's your schedule for the next two weeks?" We set up lunch for the following week, and met once again at the Jefferson Hotel. "I've got work for you. Take it home and go over it fairly soon. Should take you no more than a few days and we'll meet again." He passed over a bulging brown accordion folder, its flap secured with a thick rubber band.

CHAPTER 28

Clearmont Mews, McLean

Do what you can with where you are with what you have.
—Teddy Roosevelt, 1858–1919

B ACK HOME AGAIN, I SET UP AN OFFICE IN MY DIGS IN MCLEAN, WHICH I called *The Mews,* and signed up for electricity, gas, and new phone numbers. Strohmeyer had added a new wrinkle to my life that re-energized me. The three-ring binder he had given me contained a biography of Gamal Abdel Nasser, ruler of Egypt! It also included a chapter on Diabetes from a medical treatise, a small folder on the history of Egypt, maps of Cairo, a thin sheaf of eight-by-ten black-and-white glossies, a batch of sheets marked "Gezira Sporting Club," a list of restaurants and a thick wad of Xeroxed sheets entitled NAMRU 3. A small separate folder was titled Arsen Khorvudachi. How much of this mass of information could I possibly retain?

It would have to wait, because the next day I received an urgent page at the hospital. Worrying that something was wrong with a patient, I grabbed a hall phone.

"Hey Doc, Sam Kupak here."

"Hi Sam, what's up?"

"We got a problem, need your help. Hold on, Mel's coming on."

Mel told me in an anguished gravelly voice that one of their top men was bleeding to death in a hospital in Switzerland. He wanted me to get over there.

"If you can save this guy, John, I'll give you the world, and that's a promise. Whatever you need to get my man back, just say the word." Mel was pleading.

I agreed to come over. I checked my patient first, hopped over to the 17th Street building, parked next to Mel's limo and zipped up to Kupak's office. Sam's usually taciturn face looked worried.

"Thanks so much for coming over, Doc. Pete Jahnke, our chief Lab man, is in a hospital in Switzerland. Milt Lincoln is there with him, says Pete's in a hospital bleeding from his gut and they're gonna cut out his stomach tomorrow. Pete's afraid he's gonna die there. He wants to come home. Christ, Doc, any chance you can bring him home? Like Mel says, whatever you need, just say the word."

"Give me a minute to think, Sam." I was back in the spin again, where one goof and it could all go wrong. True in surgery and true in this crazy, new world I had slid into. It can lead to a deadly spin, crash and burn. I'd have to get over to Switzerland for Mel, Kupak and Geographic. Of course I'd do it. And I'd let Strohmeyer know what was afoot.

Within the hour, I'd contacted the Chief of Surgery, Professor Jorgen Schiff, at the Cantonspital in Fribourg, where our patient Pete lay slowly bleeding. Schiff was courteous as only a European can be and explained the medical situation as he saw it. Pete had an acute gastric bleed not responding to accepted therapy. They'd tried everything, including ice water lavage, and were now seriously leaning toward total gastrectomy. It seemed a bit drastic to me. If we could tide him over, then there might be other measures we could take and maybe I could get him back to Washington. After all, I was a battle hardened extractor of the sick and dying!

After a polite discussion of all aspects of the case, the surgeon agreed to hold off until I flew over and reviewed the case with him. He looked forward to meeting me tomorrow. I'd be on the next Swissair flight out of Washington tonight, I advised, looking meaningfully at Sam as I spoke. Sam nodded and picked up his phone.

Kupak's travel people arranged a first class seat on Swissair for the evening flight. I asked for a wad of American cash plus traveler's checks, a Geographic charge card, and an employee ID card in case people asked questions, and lastly, a hotel room for me in Fribourg. I called an anxious Mel to report my plans.

"Perfect, John," was his relieved response.

In the next hour, I handed my hospital cases over to my partner and rescheduled another elective surgery for the following week. Mel's driver followed me to my McLean digs, where I located my passport, grabbed a shaving kit, clothes, my London Fog coat and tossed them into an overnight bag. I was off.

The Swissair jet landed in Geneva early the next morning. After deplaning and clearing passport control, I rented an Avis Ford, complete with a compact little road map. Fribourg was only sixty miles away, around the lake. The weather was crisp, clear and sunny and I passed some lovely, small farms as I circled the lake. I decided to check in at the hotel first. The concierge had selected a corner suite opening onto a flowering garden.

The Cantonspital personnel were extremely hospitable and the facility had a wonderful, old world charm. I was treated as a visiting dignitary. Fresh-faced, student nurses blushed and older ones smiled, some bobbed their heads. They wore crisp uniforms, lovely little cupcake hats, so unlike the rumpled scrubs I saw at home.

While Schiff was in surgery, I was served hot tea and an obscenely large slab of pastry slathered with whipped cream. I sat in his consulting room leafing through a copy of *Der Spiegel*. Great pics, but the German text was beyond me. In the washroom, I caught a movement behind me in the mirror. There was a man waiting beside the exit, a broom in his scrawny weathered hands. His dark, troubled eyes were darting back and forth. His eyebrows were raised and the corners of his mouth drooped. Strange chap. I turned, but he was gone. Down the hall, I passed an office entryway where the man stood waiting.

"*Hsst* sir, do you have a moment?" His English was heavy with French intonations. "Please sir, I know you are the American Professor come to see your patient. Praise Allah, sir, that you have arrived. And please God, do not let this man be operated on here or he will surely die."

Somehow, I wasn't surprised to hear that, because for no sound scientific reason, I had the same feeling.

"Why?"

"Because, Excellency, no one survives from bleeding so much, then loses more blood on the operating table when Dr. Schiff operates. Very bad situation, sir. I have been in operating rooms all my life. Please, you must trust me."

Who was this guy? He looked older than fifty, with a thin mustache, hollow cheeks, and a package of cigarettes tucked in his breast pocket explaining his olive-gray skin. He wore a white scrub ensemble with a round, white hat perched on his head, dirty tennis shoes and stitched on his pocket: *A. Gholemienne, Diener*. He was the orderly who cleans the operating rooms. He probably knew what went on in the operating rooms *and* the hospital. This then, was a man to heed. Men like him were front line troops. His name was French, probably an Algerian refugee.

"You Algerian?"

"Yes, Moroccan, too." He smiled, showing crooked, yellowed teeth. "My father was French Foreign Legion in Algeria. He met my mother in Morocco. She was from a fine family. They fled to Switzerland. Her family would have killed him for even looking at my mother."

I cut right to the point. "Why do you think this man going to die?"

"He has lost much blood, his bowels are black, his pressure is low and he is pale, like a person with the look of death." At that moment, I heard a door slam up the hall.

"Shht, say no more." Professor Schiff was marching down the hall with an anxious look, sweaty scrub suit and mask dangling. My host saw me, smiled, and pumped my outstretched hand vigorously. He seemed relieved to see me and spoke of our patient in old-fashioned surgical clichés. I began to realize that he was a surgeon competent in minor surgeries, but not a total gastrectomy. There has to be some fancy rearranging of the gut after hacking out a stomach, and I sensed that this was neither the right hospital nor the right surgeon.

As we reviewed Jahnke's films and chart, I made up my mind what had to be done even before seeing him. As Schiff spoke of hematocrits, white counts and other important numbers, I searched the chart for blood ammonia levels. Not ordered, probably not even considered. I learned they didn't do blood ammonia levels in this Cantonspital. *Merde*! Gut bleeders get dangerously high blood ammonia levels. This further convinced me that I had to get this man home, but how?

My brain zipped through scenarios. Another extraction, like China. The ammonia levels were probably elevated. I knew from bitter experience that people who've bled and have black stools require antibiotics to prevent high blood ammonias or end up with ammoniacal cerebral intoxication. I'd have to do something fast or this patient faced mental deterioration.

"Professor Schiff, shall we visit the patient?" He nodded. A grand sweep of a pudgy arm and we paraded down the hall into the Intensive Care ward, now in the company of several nurses. I spotted Jahnke, and sweet Jesus, his face was as white as his pillow and his eyes slightly yellow. From one nostril, dangled a thin string and from the other a red rubber tube led to a bottle on the floor. Early surgeons used a string to spot the gut bleeder site. Once the string was in the stomach, any bleeding would leave a red blotch on it and it was a simple matter to determine the bleeding site.

Schiff gently removed the string; four inches of its lower end were dark red, not bright red. He'd stopped bleeding! Dark blood was old blood; red blood meant active bleeding. Good. I could get him out. I formulated a plan.

"How you doing Pete?"

"Shit, Doc, sure glad to see you. 'Fraid I wuz gonna die here. Please, do something. Get me the hell outta here, so I can go home and die with my family."

"Pete, you're not going to die. You're going to be fine. We're going home. Just relax and be patient."

A weak smile…"Okay, Doc, God bless you."

I checked his weak pulse and low pressure and checked his IVs. He was getting some Lactated Ringer's, but needed at least a unit of blood.

I located Milt Lincoln, the other Geographic technician who had come over with Pete to attend a Ciba photography conference on dye transfers and explained to him and Professor Schiff that Pete wanted to be with his family and asked for their help. I was prepared to assume responsibility for him and take him home. Schiff understood and seemed relieved.

Pete's blood count showed that he was about a quart low. I ordered two units to be given, stat, and asked Schiff to have 500 ccs of Neomycin in saline squirted down his gastric tube to knock out gut bacteria, reduce his blood ammonia, and improve his chances of survival. He was given an enema to clear his colon of old blood, which was a serious source of ammonia. All this was done promptly with the Algerian orderly overseeing everything.

Things were falling into place. Schiff called Swissair, explained the circumstances of a physician flying a sick patient home, and reserved four first class seats. We had a golden period now. The next thirty-six hours would be critical if Jahnke were to survive. I needed to get him to a US hospital and had George Washington in mind. Lincoln paid for the plane tickets and arranged for an ambulance standing by out front. We'd head for Geneva in time to catch the westbound flight. I also ordered a small carrying pack with two units of blood, four units of fluid to for keep an IV open; some Benadryl, Scopolamine and a dozen other meds I hoped not to use.

Next I called Kupak and told him the plan was to fly Geneva-London, London-DC. Lincoln would keep in touch with his office and advise our flight number and arrival times. I wanted a limo planeside when we arrived at DC. Then I contacted Maury Levinson at GW Hospital and explained the situation. Levinson, a seasoned gastroenterologist, listened and then grunted.

"Jeez man, you don't want that mess on your hands. If you gotta come to the States with him, why not drop him off at Mass General?" We exchanged some choice words. "Listen up, Maury. I need this poor bastard in good hands and I thought that would be you!" I explained what had to be done and how I would hold him personally responsible if anything went wrong.

"Okay, I'll see the guy when he's admitted," he grunted. "Good luck."

Over the next few hours we packed our patient, fluids and meds, blood units on ice, and got ready to move out. The ambulance bumped us to Geneva in record time and Swiss Air assisted us into three seats. The fourth seat held the blood and meds.

Miraculously, Jahnke's color had improved, probably due to a combination of the blood and excitement. Our 747 left right on schedule. There were a few curious glances as passengers boarded, but the Swiss are ever polite and no one said a word. We landed at DC twenty minutes late due to head winds and were cleared by Customs and Passport Control as a medical emergency. The waiting Geographic limo sped us to GW hospital where Jahnke was immediately admitted. A flurry of nurses, interns, residents and Maury Levinson took over.

A few days later, Maury called me. "Jahnke's doing quite well. Thought you should know," he started. "This guy has Bromism."

"Bromism? What the hell is that?"

"Yeah, Bromism. Something you don't often see in the occasional boozer. These guys were being wined and dined every night by the Swiss, way off their normal feed patterns, especially with the fancy booze. They went to bed with food in their gut and woke up with a hangover and sour gut. Retained food all night can make you powerful sick, and alcohol makes it worse. They must have felt like shit every morning. So Jahnke took some bromide tablets with seltzer water from the pharmacy and ended up with acute bleeding gastritis. You were right, he had elevated serum ammonias, but once he stopped taking the bromide, his bleeding backed off, and bottom line, we all got lucky. Nice touch giving him Neomycin." He let out a gravelly chuckle. "He's gonna make it, after another week here. In the meantime, he's stopped smoking, too. Thanks, it was an interesting case." Maury, man of few words, was a lion in his field.

Shortly after that episode, Grosvenor's secretary called to request a visit in his office two days hence at ten in the morning. She indicated that it was important. So at the appointed time, I made my way to Mel's office, passing pleasant smiles as I strode by. I knocked and entered the lair of the lion. There stood a smiling Mel and beside him a small cluster of Geographic All Stars: Mel Payne, Ted Vosburgh, Frank Short, and Bill Garrett, among others. To my complete surprise, this was a presentation ceremony for me. A beaming Mel gave me a bear hug, gushed some nice things about me, and told me I was an honored member of his group, since I'd recently saved their top photo man from a horrible death overseas. Then he presented me with a beautifully inscribed and framed proclamation that I was now a Life Member of the Society. I'd never have to pay for another magazine subscription! I felt like I'd received the Medal of Honor as Mel loudly proclaimed that from that day forth I could do no wrong in his empire and the assembled group nodded dumbly. We all retired to his private dining room to enjoy wine and cheese. I was in a daze and felt dizzy with happiness and pride. I was aware that my cup truly runneth over.

This cemented me in Mel's circle, and it was hard to return to earth and my humdrum work, but return I did. It's that way with driven people. For this extraction, I'd been gone a week and no one, no one, in and out of the hospital had missed me or had even noticed my absence. With my professional life now on an even keel, I began mixing squash, advanced flight training, conferences and consultations along with my scheduled operations. No predictable forty-hour weeks for me; it was either more or less. My personal life was a shambles, but I felt like there was time enough for that later. Someday the right lady would pop up and by that time I'd be ready. What I really wanted was to be a surgeon who could mix interests and career.

Sometimes I thought of Gigi, but to keep loneliness, that scourge of bachelors, at bay, I accepted invitations to neighborhood parties in the Mews. The local hostesses spotted me as fresh meat, a possible fill-in for dinner parties that I wasn't yet in a position to reciprocate, but it was a great way to socialize, nibble on someone else's food and play word games with neighbors.

My physician friends occasionally dropped by for drinks and a pizza. One of these was a particularly attractive Brazilian plastic surgeon, Dr. Katerina Pereira, who was rotating through DC for additional training. Sometimes, Bill Garrett and his photography friends visited my Mews digs. On those occasions, I made Clams Casino and chilled some bottles of white wine and beer. On weekends, I invited some of the hospital residents to come for dinner just to get a taste of freedom. I prepared *shish kebabs*, rice and salad for them, served buffet style, with beer and jug wine to wash it down. I consider my lamb dishes a gift to mankind.

And I finally got around to doing my bulging homework folder from Strohmeyer.

CHAPTER 29

Cairo, Egypt

It is hard to know that a man is telling the truth when you know that you would lie if you were in his place.
—Henry Mencken, 1880–1930

I'D PUT OFF OPENING STROHMEYER'S FOLDER LONG ENOUGH. I SET ASIDE the weekend to do nothing but read those files and then call him. But quite unexpectedly, I received a dinner invitation from Mel Grosvenor for a gathering of the Explorer's Club to be his guest at an exclusive grouping of world-class nomads. I put away the files and pulled out my blazer, Brooks Brothers button down, blue and gold striped repp tie, gray slacks, and black Italian loafers, the uniform for most affairs in Washington.

The Explorers had assembled in the exquisitely decorated Warne Lounge on the second floor of the Cosmos Club for cocktails. Mel stood smiling amidst a crowd of admirers, his face alive with expression, eyebrows lifting and lowering with each sentence, waving his gnarled finger for emphasis. The audience was in his grasp. This benevolent king knew that his every wish was a command in his realm: The National Geographic Society, respected by governments the world over. Turning from one listener to another, his big bony hands gesticulating like an orchestra conductor, Mel told a joke and they all guffawed. He spotted me and waved me over.

"John, come meet my friends."

In rapid succession, I was introduced to the Director of the National Park Service, a Supreme Court Justice, the Director of the

CAIRO, EGYPT

Geological Survey, an Ambassador from Sweden, an Arctic Explorer, a hilarious treasure hunter from Bermuda, a Spanish Galleon gold finder, and lastly a slender mountain man, head of Mel's book service.

Bill Garrett had told me about the gold finder, Kip Hagner. This was the man who had discovered the wrecks of the Spanish Plate Fleet of 1715 off the east coast of Florida close to Sebastian Inlet, near Melbourne. Kip and I hit it off. He asked about my Navy service and my interest in small craft; he had a workboat, he said, and before the evening was over, Kip extracted a gleaming coin from an inner pocket, a reproduction of a gold *escudo*. "Come visit me in Florida and I'll take you to underwater wrecks, where you scrape away coral and sand and find lotsa gold coins. Keep all you find. How's that sound?" Unbelievable! I was now anxious to see those gold-laden wrecks.

The Explorer's dinner was a grand affair, prime rib and all the trimmings. Mel introduced me in glowing terms as his consulting physician for the Society without portfolio. I felt their quick curious glances. As the evening wore on, I listened to their tales of adventure and travel and wondered, *dear Lord, can all this be true? Is this only for wealthy adventurers?* I wondered whether I would ever accomplish all the things I hoped to do before I died. I finally admitted to myself that that *was* my intention; I'd decided by now that I wanted to be more and do more than just be a surgeon. With that final confession to myself, I was able to erase my anxieties.

As dinner came to an end, Mel beckoned me to his side. Mel leaned over conspiratorily, and in a brandy-laced whisper, "Say John, has Braden or Kupak talked to you about getting Cairo pictures?"

I was taken aback. "No, Mel. Am I going to Egypt?"

Mel became flushed slightly when he realized that he'd talked out of turn. Napoleon brandy will do that to you. "John, I understood you were going to visit the Navy Research Unit in Cairo and thought you could help us get some specific photo shots for us. Can you?" He stopped and scratched his head; "But I guess you better first check with Braden and Kupak will know what it's all about. Then come see me, okay?"

"Yeah, sure Mel. Thanks for a great evening."

All the dinner guests left, smiling, back slapping, and shaking hands. I headed for the George Washington Parkway, the fastest route to McLean. Now I was totally confused! What the hell was this Egypt trip? I'd seen a file labeled NAMRU 3, the medical research facility in Cairo. Clearly, I had to go to ground all weekend, digest the contents of that folder and get back to Strohmeyer. I disconnected the phone, hid my car in the garage, and opened the NAMRU 3 folder first.

<u>NAMRU 3:</u> US Naval Medical Research Unit #3, Cairo, Egypt

"An advanced infectious diseases laboratory for study of bacterial and other diseases in Egypt and Nile waters in particular. Staffed by Naval and epidemiological specialists studying environmental factors in disease transmission. Several laboratories specific for accurate identification of materials, toxins and chemical agents. Civilian personnel recruited from universities and institutions in CONUS for temporary and/or long term duty. Excellent relations with Egyptian authorities who allow NAMRU a great deal of leeway in accomplishing their mission. Personnel live in compounds or private residences depending on circumstances. NAMRU 3 is independent of our Embassy but cooperates as necessary. Sites also at Helwan, Abu Homos and Benha."

Basically, it described a Navy Research Unit in Cairo studying everything from bugs to river flukes, viruses and more. The next folder was a biography of Gamal Abdel Nasser, President of Egypt, with his medical history highlighted for my attention.

<u>Gamal Abdel Nasser:</u> b. 1/15/18.

"Former military officer overthrew King Farouk in 1952, and Muhammed Naguib in 1954, is current Egyptian strongman. As youth, opposed British rule, became fervent revolutionary and nationalist. Became president in 1954. New constitution created under his hand. Later joined with Syria as trade partner, and with Yemen (Sana) to form United Arab Republic. This alliance collapsed 1961 for political and financial reasons.

Was instrumental in negotiating funds from USSR for construction new Aswan High dam after requests rebuffed by US for unwillingness to collaborate on other issues. Amount estimated at one billion hard [USD] dollars."

Nasser was reported to be a severe diabetic with heavy insulin dependence, and thought to have advanced kidney disease with early retinal involvement. He was believed to be hypertensive and a heavy smoker, who was lax in caring for himself and did not adhere to a diet. Nasser required large doses of insulin by injection, overseen by Swiss physicians flown in from Geneva, at Egypt's expense. The first Swiss doctor was competent, expensive and kept excellent records. But he retired due to a debilitating stroke, and the new physician's files showed sloppy record keeping and were therefore an information dead end. His attractive but dimwitted office nurse was also a fruitless information source, so it was decided that useful and correct information would only be obtained from a sample of Nasser's own urine. *But how was this mission to be accomplished?*

It was known from previous lab tests that Nasser's kidneys showed deteriorating renal glomeruli, the kidneys' final filter for the body, the interface between blood and the outside world. As blood whizzed through these tiny vascular globules covered by a thin membrane, tiny drops of urine eased out and drained into the bladder. In healthy people, it was light yellow and clear, but in a sick patient, it could be cloudy, frothy, smelly, or even frighteningly bloody. Without a sample we'd have no idea of the patient's status. His kidneys were in the early stages of a downhill spiral leading to kidney shutdown or deadly uremic poisoning. Few recovered without quick medical intervention and US medical advisers felt the ability of the Egyptian doctors to manage this was suspect. Kidney trouble in diabetics coexisted with coronary artery disease, including involvement of leg arteries and the carotid arteries leading to the brain. President Nasser might require treatment, might or might not respond, and might not be long for this world.

Another file included information on failed assassination attempts by the Islamic Brotherhood. Somehow, *we had to access his medical files* to see if there was any more recent information, and we had to get some urine to see for ourselves. Who would want to know this and why? Nasser was a source of stability in the Middle East. But did our country want him to stay alive or croak? It seemed we needed a good estimate of *when* he might pop off, provided of course that the Islamic Brotherhood didn't *off* him first. Interesting situation.

Next, I thumbed through a folder labeled <u>Gezira Sporting Club</u>, crammed with floor plans of the Club, from dining rooms to washrooms, and a Xeroxed copy of a club membership card. Photos of the Lido exit and of the washroom stalls and urinals. A Cairo map showed El Zamalik, home of the Sporting Club, which is an island in the middle of the Nile, closer to the far shore than to the Corniche side. On the near shore, the Nile Hilton was marked in red. The Club had its origins in the British Raj. British debutantes looking for a husband would pop out to Cairo for the mating season, hoping to seduce and marry an officer to escape a life of tedium in England. The Gezira Club was one of their favorite hunting grounds. Russians had used the grounds of Gezira Sporting Club to train Egyptian helicopter pilots and a number of fatalities had occurred during chopper exercises.

Someone banged on the front door. I peeked through the dining room window...rats! It was the plastic surgeon fellow, Dr. Pereira, her magnificent body fetchingly displayed in a pink T-shirt and tight designer jeans.

"Open the door, Jown," she blasted, through the open kitchen window. "I know you're there."

I opened the door, "Whatcha want?" I growled.

"Jown," she cooed, "I have came out to go to swimming with you!"

"I've got no time for swimming just now. You've come at a bad time. Why didn't you call first?"

"I did," she replied. "They said you phone ees no working, so I just drive out. Ees okay, no?"

"No, is not okay."

"*Well*," she stamped a foot, "*you are a first class sheet, Jown*! The nice people down the street told me you were home, and invite us to swimming pool party. I told them yes, of course. SO, I AM GOING

CAIRO, EGYPT

SWIMMING IN THEIR GODDAM POOL." Tossing her long, unbelievably blonde hair, she swung around. "I wish to use your bathroom to change...ees okay?"

"Yeah sure." I was chastened, but still had no desire to go swimming.

From the boot of her little BMW she pulled out a Vuitton sport bag. Someone in her family had lots of money because no graduate student could afford her clothes, looks and cars and study in a foreign country without lots of disposable money. She must have zeroed in on me because I was unattached. She banged into the guest bathroom, emerging a few minutes later clad in a long thin white bathrobe with a deadly Brazilian bikini clearly visible underneath. She was almost falling out of the bikini top and barely wearing a *fila* thong bottom. *Fila*, Brazilian for dental floss! With difficulty I went back to the map of Zamalik, fighting a fleeting mental image of Katerina's tawny skin sliding through the swimming pool.

Looking at these files it was clear someone wanted me to go to Egypt, take photos, do something with NAMRU 3, and collect a sample of Nasser's urine to confirm his critical renal status, and that was the pisser. I'd know more after I got with Strohmeyer. I went to the kitchen for a beer, passing a strewn pink T-shirt, a filmy pink bra, the briefest matching thong, Levis and loafers. Make-up and perfume spilled across the sinktop. Some gal.

I went back to work. A file marked "Hovsep Barsigian" included pages of names, photos, and background summaries. Barsigian was an Armenian name, *the ethnic card popping up again.* Hovsep meant Joseph. Barsigian meant that he was a Barsig, originally Persian or son of a Persian. A grainy photo revealed a beaten man with drawn features, a mustache, rimless glasses, puffy eyes with dark pouches, acned skin, and a Basra bite on his cheek.

<u>Hovsep Barsigian</u>, *55, Egyptian of Armenian descent.*

"Family once owned automobile battery manufacturing plant. Plant and all assets nationalized by Nasser, no compensation for confiscated assets. Family dispossessed of all holdings. Bears anger, bitterness and resentful of present status.

Current employment: Washroom attendant, Gezira Sporting Club." *The plot thickens*, thought I. "Family: Wife, three children; two boys, ages 12 and 14, one daughter age 10. Has relatives in Fresno, California. Mother-in-law lives with Barsigian. Modest home near Heliopolis close to trash pickers community. Owns a small Fiat."

Hrant Guiragossian: Owner of boutique shop Nile Hilton.

"Excellent reputation as honest dealer, but has been known to sell items removed from ancient tombs, some suspected fake." *That meant he was a fence.* "Great stopping place for tourists. Tour managers receive kickback for bringing tourist groups. Active in local Dashnak activities. Was once Egyptian international weight lifting champion. Resembles George Atlas; remains man of immense strength. Occasionally lifts and moves Volkswagen cars illegally parked in driveway of Hilton. Great favorite of hotel employees, tourists and wives of high government officials. Though anti-Nasser in philosophy, not harassed nor subjected to extortions and given wide berth by security officials."

Arsen Khorvudachi: Younger son of famed Egyptian philanthropists.

"Has mansions in Zamalik, Alexandria and Lake Lugano, Switzerland named Villa Cristi Lamenti. Ski lodge in Lech, Austria. Lake home reportedly used during collaboration with German generals plotting Hitler's assassination. Properties originally part of elder Dragviz estates. For years of devoted service to generations of Egyptian rulers, Dragviz given title of both Pasha and Bey by Egyptians. Political and financial assistance making possible Suez Canal, Egyptian railroad system and introduction of European culture into Egypt placed him and descendants in high esteem in Egyptian hierarchy. Homes contain rare old master paintings, Pre-Columbian pottery, sculpture, tapestries and furniture; Lugano mansion has

CAIRO, EGYPT

greenhouses for orchids; Alexandria mansion overlooks bay where battles took place and is a repository of artifacts from ancient Roman Temples destroyed and toppled into waters. Being recovered by grant from family for later reconstruction. Family owns shipping lines, private fleet of aircraft and has wealth rivaling de Rothschilds. Religion not known. Said to be Christian, but elder Dragviz affected Fez in all public appearances. Arsen Khorvudachi very modern, decidedly pro-American and fervent admirer National Geographic Society and has offered use of his guest quarters to Dr. Grosvenor and advisors. Married to Karen Bourget Stenuit, wealthy Belgian heiress; father principal holder *Union Miniere*. Belgian Congo copper, tin mines. Said to be charming, glamorous, kind. Entertains lavishly; wears latest Parisian fashions. One daughter, Sophia, attending school in Switzerland. Devoted couple, travel frequently; divides time in family estates."

— • —

I WOKE WITH A START: the clock read *2 a.m.* Jesus, I'd fallen asleep. I got up and stumbled in to my bedroom where a miniscule pink thong was artfully placed on my pillow with a note: *"Querida mio, you are so cute when you sleep I don't want to wake you, so I leave this for next time. I party with your neighbors until midnight. Anyway, I have to work tomorrow. Next time you take me out, you don't be so grumpy. So I come to see you again soon. con amor...K"*.

— • —

THE NEXT DAY I PLACED calls to Strohmeyer and Mel, and then made quick hospital rounds. I was bailing out early to go to a cookout in Leesburg hosted by a fancy, but friendly socialite family I'd met at one of my lectures. Leesburg was only a short drive and the weather was beautiful. After chatting with a few guests, I grabbed a glass of chardonnay, a plateful of barbecued ribs, and found a seat in the sunroom. A pile of recent magazines lay stacked on a small table before me and something caught my eye. In a group photo of smiling ladies, there was Gigi! *It looked like Gigi, alive and well. Could she have survived?! Was it possible that she could be alive and in Washington?* The woman in the photo looked High Society and high fashion. I ripped out the magazine page and stuffed it in a pocket. My search for the truth about Gigi was on.

−− • −−

ON MONDAY AFTER ROUNDS, I went over to Mel's office and was ushered in immediately. Mel broke into a wide grin, "John! Here's where we are: basically, for our Egypt country story, we want photos from all over. As many people shots as you can get. Activities that take place within a few miles of either side of the river. That's the only green area of Egypt...the rest is brown desert. Ya got it?"

I nodded, but not yet with complete understanding. We pored over a map of Egypt. I could see the Nile surrounds marked with green shading and brown desert outside the green.

"We have to show the contrast between modern Cairo and old Cairo. Get your camera and tripod on top of that old tower on Zamalik; we've cleared it with the Egyptians. You need both the foreground and those Makkatam hills way in the back in focus. Kupak says you'll need a long lens, fast film, a tight F-stop and maybe a polarizing filter. You can play around with all combinations, and don't spare the film. The city and river can be full of smog for days, so you gotta wait until the haze clears to get some usable photos, so be patient and alert. When the stuff clears, move fast to get the shots, because it can come right back again, especially this time of the year. You better take two cameras to the tower—Kodachrome in one, Ektachrome in the other."

I let this sink in. Kupak was absolutely right: Mel knew his stuff.

"While you're up there," continued Mel, "we want some shots of the famous Gezira club, and then get some shots from ground level of the club house interiors and gardens."

Mel left and Braden, who had been listening and making notes said, "At some point, John, we want you to visit NAMRU 3 and get some shots there, too. We must show readers that we're involved in

Egyptian health matters. Our editors gave us a list of photos they need, both for the magazine and a book. Okay with you?"

"Okay." I was flattered that I was being treated as a photographer, although being a doctor probably still provided my greater entrée. Braden went over angles, views, objects and other technical advice in his deep West Virginia drawl and gave me a list of equipment including film, cameras and lenses that had already been assembled to be cleared by customs for my exit and return. Make no mistake, Mel's bunch was professional.

"When does all this happen?"

"You give us the dates and we'll prepare your travel itinerary, accommodations and a fund advance. You do the camera work; we take care of getting you there. Mel wants you to travel first class."

-- • --

STROHMEYER HAD RESERVED THE WILSON Room, on the private floor of the Cosmos Club, for our afternoon meeting. At the appointed time, I tapped on the door and entered. Strohmeyer was seated at the table head in his Brooks Brothers uniform. Beside him, a civilian lady and two uniformed personnel. One was a female naval officer, a two and a half striper, Lieutenant Commander with a Medical Service Corps oak leaf above the gold stripes. The other, a Marine sergeant, with a load of stripes and medals on his immaculately pressed uniform. Okay, now my agenda was going to surface.

"Come in, Doctor." Strohmeyer rose to shake my hand. "This is Commander Gwendolyn Truitt, Master Sergeant Brent Arnett, and my assistant, Mrs. Hermione Goodwin. I smiled, shook hands and sat.

"Coffee?"

"Yes, thanks."

"Okay, Doctor, let's get right down to business. First off, my understanding is that you willingly undertake our request to participate in a mission, code named *Cheops*. We pronounce it Chops. I have to tell you that my organization will deny any connection with you. You will have no protection beyond that of any average American citizen, but you will be accredited to the National Geographic Society as a photographer on assignment. You will carry be the usual number of *dago dazzlers* signed by Dr. Melvin Payne and Dr. Grosvenor. If you get into any kind of trouble, you're on your own as a *National Geographic* photographer. We won't know you and cannot interfere in any action that arises as a consequence of anything which takes place. But we can and will be observing you through other channels. We'll deny that you're a controlled asset, which you are. Got it so far?"

I nodded dumbly. *Get on with it.* "Your reimbursement will be as per our usual arrangements. If you have any second thoughts, the sooner we hear them the better. Still on board?"

Again, I nodded.

"You need to know the task we have for you is a very important and delicate one. It will tax your ingenuity, and will be enormously important to our country in assessing a foreign policy posture. You may never know the results, and no one else will ever know that you were involved. That's how it is in our line of business."

I remained silent.

"Here's the task: "You're going to Cairo to get photographs for Mel Grosvenor. It's a neat cover. You know enough photography so that no one will be suspicious. But, your main job will be to *get us a sample of Gamal Abdel Nasser's urine!*"

Huh?

I stared straight ahead at Strohmeyer. *As I suspected, I was going to Egypt to collect pee from Nasser. But how? Was he crazy?*

"Quite simply, Doctor, we have arranged with the washroom attendant to place some of Nasser's urine into two empty film canisters and hand them over to you. You give them to the sergeant; he takes them to NAMRU 3 for analysis; and that information gets passed on to us. Simple enough, right?"

I said nothing. Strohmeyer assumed I got it, understood. It sounded simple enough. It must have been rigged up with the washroom attendant. So why did they need me?

Strohmeyer continued, "I'll spell out some details." He began reading from notes. "Sergeant Arnett is assigned to NAMRU 3 as part of the Navy detail. He speaks Arabic fluently, his mother is an

Egyptian national, and his father was a Marine stationed there. He was born in Camp Lejeune and learned the local patois at his mother's knee. Dressed in local garb, he is transformed into a Cairo native. He will be your constant escort, *and* your link to NAMRU 3. It will be a double cover for you, taking photos of NAMRU 3 for *Geographic* and arranging to collect the specimen."

"Commander Truitt is in charge of a laboratory at NAMRU 3. She can explain what she does with the urine sample."

I thought I knew, but to be polite, I listened over coffee.

"As you know, brittle diabetics have to be on tight dietary regimes, check their urine for spillage and ketones. Nasser has bodyguards at all times. At some point each day, a bodyguard checks his urine, a Litmus paper dip and maybe a quick ketone and sugar check. At our lab, we'll do a complete analysis of everything in Nasser's urine, including flame photo-spectroscopy to identify all chemicals present. We can identify his medications, the amount he takes and even the manufacturer. Once that part's done, we spin down the urine, collect the residue and examine for cells, casts and whatever else shows up under the microscope. The type and number of renal cells will give us strong insight to the health of his kidneys. This data will help us put together a pretty accurate estimate of his current health.

"The planners higher up the food chain want a reasonable estimate on how long this ailing guy is going to be around. There is some concern that the Islamic Brotherhood is trying to kill him, so it's actually a question of what gets him first. Once you get the sample for us, your job is done." Strohmeyer pulled out more notes and went on, "Barsigian, the washroom attendant at the Gezira club, has been approached by Guiragossian, who works for us on occasion. Barsigian has family in Fresno, and we're sending him and his family for a visit, *with no return*. All we want him to do for us is open a small valve from the urinal drain line from the washroom the next time Nasser's at the Club, and collect some urine."

"You must find a way to get in there as soon as Nasser leaves. Barsigian will hand you two urine-filled canisters. You put them in your camera bag and when you and Arnett get the urine to NAMRU 3, your job is done. Barsigian might screw the delivery and compromise the mission because he's terrified of the whole project.

"There would be no reason for Arnett to be there in the first place, and no way Barsigian can keep that urine sample fresh long enough to be analyzed reliably, especially in Cairo heat. With you, a bona fide photographer on assignment for *National Geographic* there and a temporary club member, we've got a greater chance that the project will go as planned. You may have to improvise as you go along. These are the basic guidelines. We'll be watching and be in touch. Okay?"

"Yep."

Strohmeyer added other details. "You'll be housed at the Nile Hilton for the first week. Check in and find Guiragossian. He should be in his lobby boutique. Tell him you're looking for a small statue of *Cheops*. That identifies you as a visiting photographer friend of Barsigian. As far as Guiragossian knows, Barsigian is a fellow Armenian who has a beef with the government, and is planning to visit relatives in California."

Commander Truitt excused herself, leaving Strohmeyer, Mrs. Goodwin, and the sergeant.

Strohmeyer said, "The next time you see the sergeant will be in Cairo. He'll make contact with you, and the word is *Cheops*. Mrs. Goodwin will take any calls from you, and if I'm not available, she'll take action for me. Just call *National Geographic* in Washington, ask the operator for Mrs. Goodwin, and her extension will ring at Langley. Anyone listening will consider it normal for you to call *National Geographic*. We'll stick to the conversation patterns we used in Amsterdam."

Strohmeyer rose, thanked the sergeant for coming over on such short notice and led him out. Strohmeyer's file contained letters of introduction from Mel Payne and Dr. Grosvenor, sporting gold seals overlying green, blue and yellow ribbons or huge red wax seals atop their ribbons. These imposing-looking documents are widely known as Dago Dazzlers, a well-established Geographic method of impressing foreign governments. The documents are often framed and hung on an office wall. The file also included letters from the

Egyptian Ministry of Tourism, the Ministry of the Interior, the Director of the Cairo Museum, the Hilton Hotel, the Manager of the Tower and a heavy vellum letter bearing a royal crest of sorts from Arsen Khorvudachi inviting Dr. John Sundukian to their home.

I considered my current daily schedules and agreed to leave in ten days. I met with Bud Wisherd's team to check out my equipment. He'd opted for lightness, simplicity, and user familiarity. He knew I preferred the Nikon SLR camera and either the Nikon SP or the Leica M4, and chose the newest, smallest, and lightest cameras. A tripod and shutter release cable were an absolute necessity for scenery. Bud left nothing to chance. We went over all possible outcomes, and added a small folding Polaroid camera for instant printouts to quickly evaluate light and composition. Satisfied that I could handle the assignment, Bud waved me out.

Before leaving, I contacted a lawyer who was a former patient. We'd seen a tumor on his lung X-ray, and within the week, I resected it. Six weeks later, he was back at work, a grateful patient and friend. Now he had risen to managing partner of a prestigious Washington law firm. Plainly and simply, I asked his help investigating Gigi. I gave him the magazine page with her photo and filled him in on the background material. He made notes, refused a retainer, and assured me that all the information would be ready for me by the time I returned from Egypt. His firm had folks who did that sort of thing. The report would have information on her early years, schooling, activities, boy friends, lovers, and husbands. I added that she was reputedly married, wealthy, and a society figure, but also had another life as a political consultant for a major American university. I reminded him that without a retainer, I could not legally be his client, so we settled on one dollar.

CHAPTER 30

Cairo on the Nile

THE TWA FLIGHT STOPPED IN ZURICH FOR REFUELING AND A PLANE change. I stayed overnight at a most civilized airport hotel where the Swiss chef was an unlikely convert to Indonesian cuisine, and he produced a dinner that was unbelievably peppery, tasty and filling.

Early the next morning we left for Cairo. I was met by someone from the ministry. "Willcom, Dr. Sundukyan," said the Ministry fellow, handing me a card that read:

MOHAMMED HUSSEIN ZAKI
Assistant Director,
Foreign Press Representatives, Ministry of Interior

The card was embossed with a gold two-headed bird, a government address on Adli Street and phone numbers. I responded with my card in exchange. He smiled weakly and offered me a flaccid handshake. "Please come right this way, Doctor. We were expecting you. The Minister's apologies; he had to inspect a new find in Saqqara."

As we passed through Passport Control, I observed slovenly, black-bereted soldiers, rifles slung over their shoulders, wearing rumpled baggy uniforms, droopy walrus mustaches, and slouching around aimlessly.

CAIRO ON THE NILE

My baggage was waved through at the Adouane counter after rapid exchanges in Arabic and a Cheops tour guide chap materialized at my side. I did a double take! It was Sergeant Arnett winking at me with absolutely no change of expression.

"So, Doctor," said Zaki, "welcome to Cairo. Please call if you have any problems. Your photography permissions are in order. Is this chap your travel guide?"

"Yes," I said, showing him my itinerary indicating Cheops Travel.

"Fine, verra good then, Doctor." There was a rapid exchange of Arabic between Arnett and Zaki with much smiling, bowing, and hands placed over their hearts. Arnett had grabbed a *hamal* to carry my bags to his travel company limousine, an old but serviceable looking Chrysler. "Stick close to me," said Arnett out of the corner of his mouth.

The airport in Heliopolis was a complete bedlam of heat and noise; passengers hurrying to catch flights, lost children screaming, women wrapped from head to toe in colorful sheeting, and hustlers shouting out taxi offers in passable English.

"Right this way sir," Arnett pushed aside the other drivers grabbing at my elbows. "Stay close, sir. We're doing fine." Within minutes Arnett got us loaded and on our way to Cairo city. *Here we go*, I thought.

-- • --

THE NILE HILTON IS A favorite lodging and watering hole for international travelers. It sits perched on the Corniche with tour boats docked in front overlooking the river. Arnett pulled directly to the front entrance of the hotel and had my baggage unloaded by the bellman.

It dawned on me that Sergeant Arnett had been carefully chosen as my minder. He was ideal, given his fluency in the native patois and knowledge of the city. I was reassured to think he might also be keeping an eye on me for Strohmeyer. No sense taking chances with an amateur doctor in a tough business.

My reservation forms, letters from Egyptian ministries, my passport and health card were flashed in rapid succession and Arnett rejected the room assigned me out of hand.

In loud English, mostly for my benefit, Arnett said to them that I was to have been assigned a suite overlooking the river on a top floor and I saw a few bills laid atop the counter, followed by something like profuse apologies from the desk clerk, who quickly corrected the problem.

Arnett's brazen performance disarmed them and the display of letters from the various Egyptian ministries warned of trouble if I complained.

I was shown to a fifth floor corner suite overlooking the Nile River. Off to the left and across the river was the Cairo tower with a revolving restaurant on the top. Arnett pointed out different sites and identified them on my city map.

I got unpacked, cleaned up and changed into a safari jacket and slacks and grabbed a camera. We found a table at the hotel's outdoor dining area and ordered soup, gyro sandwiches, and bottled beer.

I heard a babble of voices, some Yankees, some Germans, and other languages I couldn't identify. Arnett thought we should make a quick tour of Zamalik after lunch, just to get the lay of the land. I spotted Guiragossian's boutique on my way through the lobby. Inside, a large man with immense shoulders wearing a Fez was chatting animatedly with a small group of American tourists. I could tell they were charmed. He excused himself and came over, smiling, "Good afternoon, gentlemen, how may I be of service?" I told him I was in Cairo to do some photography for a magazine and wondered if he had a small statuette of Cheops. Guiragossian never blinked.

"Cheops?" He said. "I may have one or two available. Did you want a copy or an original?"

"I'd like to see what you have."

"Will you be staying long, sir?"

"About ten days."

"In that case, I shall have one or two for your inspection before the week is out. Please make yourself at home; I must return to the ladies."

When we reached the sidewalk, Arnett said: "A cool customer, that one."

"How do you figure?"

"He never blinked when you said Cheops. As soon as the ladies leave, he'll pick up the phone and the Gezira washroom attendant will know the game is on."

"I guess you're right."

—--•--—

IT WAS EARLY AFTERNOON AND time to establish the daily behavior pattern of a photographer on assignment. I made a plan of lenses, film, routes, times of sunrise, sunset, scenes to photograph, names of persons to contact, interview and photograph, including the name Khorvudachi underlined, tore off the sheet and left it conspicuously on my hotel desk under an ashtray with change in it. In case any snoopers knocked it over, I would know, because only a thin film of underarm deodorant held two US half dollar coins together.

I took my single lens reflex camera, a zoom lens, lots of film and a hand-held light meter. At the front desk, Arnett harangued the desk clerks to retrieve my passport, and after an argument, withdrew some paper money from the huge wad he carried, and got my passport back.

Arnett was parked in the Hilton lot, and at his insistence, I climbed in the back like a tourist, and we set out. We planned to pass by various hotels, scout for photographic vantage points, checking for light angles, shadows, composition, visit the Tower on Zamalik, drive by the Gezira Sporting Club, and finally, drive by the Khorvudachi estate.

Traffic was a nightmare of maniacal drivers swerving in and out of lanes, with the occasional slow donkey cart clogging up lanes. Furious drivers blasted their horns, shouted and cursed, and frequently waved the expected obscene finger. Truly frightening were the people clinging to the outside of diesel buses as they lurched along the streets, spewing huge clouds of blue-black fumes.

Arnett got us across the Qasr el Nil Bridge with some nifty maneuvering and once across the bridge, he jinked right, passed in front of the Borg Hotel and swung left to the Cairo Tower. I pulled out my photography permits from the ministry and entered the lobby. The lobby reminded me of a seedy Miami Beach hotel that stank of cigarettes and cooking grease. The guards stood smoking, unaffected.

Arnett pointed to me and showed my documents to some pitifully confused ticket takers. The senior one shrugged and pointed to the elevators. We boarded the service elevator. "They can barely read," Arnett said. We rattled up for several minutes before the door slid open and we stepped out onto a fairly wide ledge with a high safety railing and a dizzying view of the surrounding area. I thought I could see the Mediterranean to the north, but it was a mirage. Overhead and behind us we heard noisy clanking sounds from the gears underneath the slowly circulating restaurant. I decided not to eat there.

Looking out over the balcony, I identified the Gezira Club to the north, a huge transmitting tower to the northwest, and far to the east, the tomb City of the Dead in the Makkatam hills, and barely visible in the distance, some remains of the old Cairo wall.

I needed some quick reads of available light and lens views of the surrounds. After a great deal of head shaking and finger waving, Arnett once again slid over a small wad of paper money to the resistant guard, and that solved the problem. I checked the setup. My hand-held light meter indicated that plenty of light was available, but the blue haze was not helpful. I wouldn't get clear definition to shoot through it, so I tried shifting pale orange or dark yellow filters and even a polarizing filter to block the blue haze. They worked to some degree, but I needed clear skies. Arnett had asked the guard about the hazy atmosphere and learned that some French photographers had waited weeks for clearing weather. The morning that a sudden breeze blew the haze away, they had overslept and missed the opportunity. They just packed up and left. The watchword was to be ready to get to the tower on short notice and that was going to be a challenge.

I decided a fifty millimeter lens would handle the nearby scenes and a two hundred millimeter lens would work fine for distant shots. I was aiming to get both foreground and background in focus simultaneously by using a very small aperture with a tripod, cable release, slow shutter speed, and Kodachrome film. I also set up another camera loaded with faster Ektachrome. Kodachrome gave the deep color saturation and density engravers and editors like to work with. Ektachrome tended to give bluer colors, but was also very usable. I worked out all combinations in my head, mumbling and talking to myself. Lastly, I set up the Polaroid, shot some scenes and extrapolated from fast Polaroid to the slower Kodachrome 64. Just for the hell of it, I shot two rolls each of the two Kodak brands I carried to document the crappy smog that pervaded the Cairo atmosphere most of the time.

— — • — —

OUR NEXT STOP WAS A tour of Zamalik and a courtesy stop at the Gezira Sporting Club. I wanted to get an idea of picture opportunities, I needed a pit stop, but more importantly, I wanted to speak with Barsigian. He was the key to the whole caper. It was mid-afternoon and I knew Arnett and I could use a bite.

"Where can we get some coffee, sergeant?"

"Well, sir, I hear they serve some first class mocha java at the Gezira Club, but the problem is, I can't go in. I'm your driver."

"Well you're going in, 'cause I'm not going in there alone. Once they know you're my assistant, you can come in here with me any time. *Capisce?*"

"Sounds good, sir."

We were still parked at the Tower. Arnett opened the car trunk, pulled out a small duffel bag and headed back to the Tower entrance. In minutes, out stepped a well-dressed, smiling Arnett in business attire, the picture of a successful man-about-town. Tossing the duffel bag into the trunk, we set off for the Club.

Driving back towards the Borg Hotel, we pulled off onto a narrow side road which led onto the Shari El Gezira and pulled up at the Gezira Sporting Club. At the front door, the Nubian doorman in full native regalia offered to carry my camera bag. He knew I wasn't British, and Americans rarely visited the Club. Arnett explained that we were just paying a courtesy call and I showed him my guest membership card, which satisfied him.

Inside the foyer, a smiling man, who immediately reminded me of Hercules Poirot, smiled and said, "Wilcom gentlemen, I am Saleh Sabri at your service. I am the assistant manager. How may I serve you?" He spoke excellent English with a faint British accent.

I extended my guest member card. "Would it be possible to have coffee and look around? And would you join us?"

He glanced at my card, the ministry papers, and looked up. A worry frown appeared. Papers from a ministry were always a source of concern.

"I have some requests and during coffee I'd like to explain them to you." Arnett nodded. Sabri ushered us to the Lido area. It was old world posh, with pictures, trophies, and lovely old furniture. Stuffed animal heads lined the wall, including a lion and a grinning crocodile. Next to them hung huge crossed sculling oars, two crossed muskets, and a wooden airplane propeller. Tables were generously spaced apart so as to discourage eavesdropping.

Sabri directed us to a table in a sitting area off to one side where we'd be uninterrupted.

"Is this satisfactory?" I looked around. Behind the long wall were large glass doors and the splashing sounds of a swimming pool. I assured Sabri this was just fine.

"Very well, sir, how do you take your coffee? We offer coffee *Americain*, Turkish coffee, Nestle's coffee and of course Espresso." I opted for American and Arnett seconded it. In short order, a Nubian waiter resplendent in flowing native regalia, shiny green and yellow silk bands over a cotton shirt, flowing gown, and leg drapes wheeled out a serving cart with a sparkling, antique silver service, a tray of fruits, cheeses, pastries, and coffee. Small creamers and containers held milk, sugar, and serviettes in silver rings to rival the finest British clubs. Sabri had laid it on, and I invited him to join us, pointing to a chair at the table.

"Terribly sorry, sir, but club rules don't permit me to sit with guests, but I can certainly stand with you. Is there something you wish to tell me?"

"Yes. Please. Sit the hell down." He gave me a startled look and took a chair.

I said, "Thanks." I thrust the letters prepared for me by Strohmeyer and the Ministry, my letter from the Gezira Club granting me guest membership, and finally the "dago dazzler" from *National Geographic*'s Mel Payne, announcing that I was on an assignment for them.

Sabri glanced wide-eyed from one letter to the other and was properly impressed. I told him that I would be wandering around the premises for a few days taking photographs and that it would be easier if my assistant and I were left alone. I asked him to please advise the staff."

Sabri assured me that it all would be arranged. The Club Manager, presently in Alexandria, would be away until a few days before the gala reception by the Khorvudachis next week.

My brain shrieked BINGO.

Sabri again assured me of the total cooperation of the Club. "Is there anything else?"

"Thank you, no, Mr. Sabri."

The coffee was surprisingly good. Arnett and I each had two cups and a Danish pastry while I got the lay of the place.

-- • --

I COULD EASILY GET INDOOR shots with daylight Kodachrome during the day, and would switch to tungsten and Ektachrome at night. But my role here shutter clicking would mostly be for show. Kupak wanted outdoor scenes from the tower and rooftops near the Hilton. I wasn't really at the club for photos. I was here to collect enough of Nasser's urine so that our Lab people at NAMRU 3 could inform our policy makers of his state of health. Whatever happened after that was not my business, now or later.

So I planned to make a good show of it: tramping around squinting into the view finder, pointing my lens now, and then clicking my shutter. I knew I'd be watched by club employees and others, and my every move reported to Sabri, so I'd have to maintain an innocent façade. If the Khorvudachis were having their huge event at the Club, then it was certain that Nasser's security people would be doing advance work, looking for possible sources of danger for their leader. And I, the photographer, wanted to be seen as an accepted part of the scenery, to let these security people vet me using their own methods, and try to remain inconspicuous as I came in and out of the Club brandishing my camera and carrying bag. With luck, it would all would work.

Time to start looking around. The washroom was behind the dining room. I made a mental note that we had to go outside and enter the men's dressing room through a separate entrance. The washroom was well lit and had three stalls, three standing urinals, and three wash basins. On the far right were shower stalls where squash, handball, and tennis players cleaned up after games.

A large table at the entrance contained soap, combs, and other necessities. There were huge racks of towels along the right rear wall, and sitting stools in front.

I really wanted to meet Barsigian.

Arnett was waiting outside and Sabri had left, but he must have alerted Barsigian. As I washed my hands, I saw Barsigian in the mirror, entering a side door. He picked up a hand towel and held it out. I gave him a dazzling smile and said, "*Parev, tzez,*" in everyday Armenian.

He stared at me wide-eyed, eyebrows climbing up his forehead. I've done that to other unsuspecting Armenians.

"*Took Hay-ek?*" He blurted. *Are you Armenian?* Disbelief crowding his features, his eyes bulging, a look of fear or amazement.

"*Ayo*"...*Yes.*

"*Anoones Sundukian-e.*" I told him who I was.

"*Oor deghetzi-ek?*" *From where are you?* A formal question which requires a full answer, so I answered him in English to make sure we both understood.

I'd been told he had a good command of English. I told him quietly that I was the man who'd be taking the *samples* from him at a certain time. Did he understand? For what it was worth, I also mumbled *Cheops*. Barsigian understood all right, because he suddenly changed from curious to angry when he realized that we were going on stage soon and he had to make certain his part of the show went off well.

"You Americans are crazy people!" he blurted. "What do you think you are doing here? You come here to demand this, you put my family's life in danger for this foolish thing." I held up my hand.

"*Inger* Barsigian," I said, *Friend Barsigian*, a respectful address. "Please do not forget the travel and financial arrangements. It would be a sad thing for your family if things did not go well. Imagine how disappointed you would be if they were not able to visit relatives in Fresno. So please, let's say no more. I am here to see where you will collect our sample. Remember, that's all we expect of you. Five minutes' work, and a lifetime of freedom and happiness in America for you and your family. Surely this is not too much to ask of you? Just to fill two small film canisters?" That seemed to take care of his concerns.

In Rosslyn, Sasha taught me that at times you have to hint at real threats that instill fear and regrettably, I had to do that right now to this beaten-down, terrified man who suddenly acted like a cornered rat. He was in trouble. The magnitude of what he had gotten himself into loomed large and I had to reassure him, but make it clear to him there could be no backing out on his part. Barsigian looked even more haggard now than in the photo Strohmeyer gave me. What must have seemed like a good deal at first was now giving him second thoughts.

I had no time for hesitation. I had a job to do and so did he. It was show time and by rights, it should go well. I emphasized the advantages of following through, and mentioned the severe disadvantages of not going along, a technique that I've often used to convince patients to go along with my surgical recommendations when delay could be fatal. I told Barsigian to meet me in the morning after breakfast, dried my hands, tossed him the towel, and waltzed out. Better not to give the target a chance to recover his wits. The next morning I would go over all details of what he must do.

Arnett and I dined that night at a small restaurant on the Shari Hassan Pasha just west of the Borg Hotel. It was smoky, noisy and crowded, the room filled with a mix of body odors and hashish. A short chubby woman sang, beat a tambourine and belly danced, gyrating and stamping her feet under a dim spotlight. A small group of male musicians assisted her in a traditional wailing melody, singing in mournful voices and playing the oud, flute, drum, and zither.

The shashlik was better than I expected, accompanied by a good French red. Over dinner, I explained to Arnett that the urine sample would be put in two water-fast aluminum film canisters. Tomorrow I'd hand them over to that wretch Barsigian. I didn't trust him.

The next morning Arnett and I breakfasted at the Gezira club, posh by any standards. It was a typical European breakfast of cheeses, ham, fruit, acceptable croissants, and strong coffee. A freshly shaved, lavender-scented Sabri greeted us and I invited him to join our consultations, surprised that he was at work so early. I learned that the Khorvudachis' event signaled the opening of the fall social scene, and that all invited Egyptian dignitaries would throng to the Club, including, of course, President Nasser.

Sabri said that this event was usually held at their mansion here on Zamalik, but ongoing renovation had delayed the completion, so Mrs. Khorvudachi, furious at the delay, decided that the Club site would do. The club would be closed that day in preparation for the event.

No expense would be spared. Two European orchestras were imported for the occasion, tables and serving stations would be set up everywhere, and the chefs would be working for days preparing food and pastries. Champagne had been imported. It was to be a lavish affair. And I would collect my sample!

I knew from the briefings that Nasser never handled himself with unclean hands, washing his hands before and after emptying his bladder. Four of fifteen elite bodyguards always flanked him front and back.

The pipes in the club's plumbing system were fitted with drainage spigots and spill-off valves set at various intervals, making it easy for Barsigian to hang a little bucket just beneath the spigot from the urinal to the main drain lines. After Nasser left, Barsigian would quickly fill the film canisters from the pail and hand them to me to get to Arnett for delivery to NAMRU 3, which would do the analysis immediately.

After breakfast, I started working the Leica with a wide-angle Summicron lens to give me depth of field, then backed it up with the Nikon loaded with faster Ektachrome.

I sauntered into the washroom and heard splashing from the pool. Where the hell was Barsigian? He should be here picking up wet towels. I moved to the small doorway he'd used the other day. To double-check the drainage pipe system, I needed to get in there and firm up my plans. I banged on the door. No response, so I turned the handle and walked into a long narrow passageway about forty feet long. The floors painted battleship gray. Pipes lined the walls on my right and extended towards an exit door, whose glass panes added daylight to the few weak tungsten bulbs of the hall.

Halfway down the corridor on the left was a room with a closed door. I leaned in close and overheard angry voices in Arabic. I rapped sharply and the door flung open. Barsigian stood staring at me in disbelief.

Sitting at a small desk was a very slick looking hombre, with neatly cropped hair, graying at the temples, gray eyes, olive skin, and an aquiline nose. The man snubbed out a foul cigarette and rose to face me. He was forty-something and a fit five nine, wearing an expensive suit and tie, with polished oxford shoes. I looked for a holster bulge under his arm He was not just any self-assured businessman. He smiled. "Are you the famous Dr. Sundukian?"

"Yes."

"Allow me to introduce myself. I am Colonel Ashraf Arif, at your service." He flourished a card with practiced nonchalance. I gave it a quick glance as I filched out my own with the Geographic logo. His read: Chief of Security for the Office of the President.

"You are here to do some photography, doctor?"

"Yes I am, sir. In fact, I was hoping Mr. Barsigian could show me around. I'd hate to walk into the Ladies dressing room with my cameras." Arif's eyebrows twitched and he smiled briefly.

"Of course, Doctor. Barsigian is very concerned about the upcoming Khorvudachi party. I assume you'll be attending? This area is for guests and members only, because when our president uses the washroom, no one else is allowed in except bodyguards. It was necessary to clarify some procedures."

The man smiled with his mouth but not his eyes, and warning bells sounded. I remembered what my mother had said: *Anyone who smiles with a frown is twisted in the mind.*

And now my brain was telling me that this man was *not* an Egyptian because Egyptians use three names and he was using only two. Secondly, his accent was not local, which suggested Jordanian origins. Clearly he was military, possibly one of the *Mabahes*, guards who could arrest, imprison and do any damn thing they wanted, including *losing* you to the deepest desert jail of Abu Zaabel. And his English seemed crisp, possibly trained by the Brits.

"I have seen your documents and permits, Doctor. May I see your passport please? I have to make sure *you* are you."

I extracted passport, health card, and a sheaf of papers, plus the plastic-covered Dago Dazzler, with the letter and the heavy vellum invitation from the Khorvudachis.

He rifled through them quickly and returned the whole batch of papers. "Interesting. You are a doctor, yes? Why do you do this camera business? I fail to see the connection and the reasons." His smile had hardened a trifle. And of course, I had a carefully honed answer.

"Well, Colonel, I'm a throwback to the early days of this century, when many European physicians were also musicians, composers, artists, painters, writers, and some were even skilled carvers and goldsmiths. If there had been Leicas and Nikons available then, who knows?"

Perhaps I saw grudging admiration in his expression, but that also meant he had me tagged as someone to watch. I'd be careful, of course, and do nothing to rouse suspicions.

"I see. Just a reminder to you, because our leader is attending Mrs. Khorvudachi's gala next week, you may not use your cameras, until they are first checked out by me personally. Further, you may not approach him with a camera nor be in his presence unless invited. Are we clear?"

"Haven't I been vetted by your people?"

He just glared at me. "In this part of the world, danger lurks at every corner. Many bear grudges against Mr. Nasser. The Islamic Brotherhood is full of fundamentalist fanatics who will stop at nothing to divorce us from the twentieth century. They have made several attempts to assassinate Mr. Nasser and will no doubt try again. Their leadership is in hiding in Khartoum. We know who and where they are, and we want to make sure none of them slip back into Cairo. We take no chances, trust no one, and suspect everyone."

"I do plan to photograph Mr. Nasser," I said. "I can easily use a long lens and stand at least ten feet away, Colonel. If you wish to examine my cameras and lenses, why not look at them now? Here are the two cameras I plan to use at the party."

I put the cameras on the table. First I took the Leica, rewound and removed the film, and twirled off the lens. I repeated this with the Nikon. I pulled out several cans of film, and dumped everything into a large pile. "Here you are, Colonel. With a list of camera and lens serial numbers cleared through Egyptian Customs." I finished with a flourish.

"Very good, Doctor. Please excuse me. Good day to you and Barsig, too." He rose, almost clicked his heels, and marched out the rear exit with Barsigian scurrying ahead to open the door.

What did he say? He said Barsig instead of *Barsigian*, which means son of a Persian? A normal thing for *an Iranian* to do. Arif wasn't Egyptian or Jordanian. What if Arif were himself an Islamic Brotherhood operative? Right now I planned to simply stay the course, take pictures, collect a urine sample, and with all due speed, skeedaddle.

I reloaded my bag and walked to the back exit and stepped outside as Barsigian gravely saluted the departing Arif. This back exit would play nicely into my newly emerging plan.

Barsigian returned a few minutes later. "I can't believe I allowed myself to get mixed up in this business. Colonel Arif is smart. If he finds out, I am dead. My family, too."

"*Calm down, Barsigian!*" But he was not to be stopped.

"You don't understand. I am an accountant by training. My family had a huge battery factory in Cairo that we owned it for several generations. Nasser and his people took it and nationalized it. They threw us out without payment for our seized property. Their stupid managers ran it into the ground and then came to ask us for help! But the equipment was misused and ruined. It needed to be completely overhauled and these idiot people called in German engineers to rescue them. Doctor, I know how to compute probabilities and the chances for this scheme of yours." He shook his head from side to side like a man awaiting execution.

There was something more going on here, but I couldn't fathom it. Something with Barsigian was not right. We calmly returned to his office and went over his simple chores. I also reminded him of his future in America. This seemed to snap him out of his *state*.

"Okay, Doctor, I will do your bidding. Please go away."

"First show me the pipes and the spigot for the urinal drain lines." We trudged toward the rear exit and checked the long pipes that ran parallel to the walls covered with white plaster and stenciled with Arabic and English writing. He pointed to the spigot. The handle moved easily.

"Okay, Barsigian," no longer Mr., "hook up the pail here and we're in business." For the first time, a slow smile spread over his pallid features.

Finally! I thought. The son of a bitch got it. But why the haunted look in his eyes? We tried the whole collection process, and sure enough, a stream of water spurted out of the spigot and right into the pail. Bingo! I closed the spigot as Barsigian was returning.

"It works fine," I said, and handed him the two special film canisters. "Put these in your desk drawer, and after Nasser has peed, fill them and hand them to me. I'll come in here. Understand?" A silent nod.

"Good," I said, clapping the miserable man on the shoulder. "Everything is going to work out just fine. Remember, you do your part and we'll do ours." I grabbed my camera bag and headed out. "I'm going out to take some photos," I said to the Barsig. "I'll be somewhere around all morning."

-- • --

OUT IN THE GARDENS, I took photos of azaleas, bottle brush plants, oleanders, Blue Nile lilies, and shrubs I'd never seen before. The sky changed from gray to blue, with wisps of clouds and swaying palm leaves from a light breeze.

I swung back to find Arnett was leaning against his car. "Let's head for the tower. I think I see a chance for some great photos." We zipped back to the tower, went up to our "reserved" balcony, and stepped out. Sure enough, the murky skies had cleared and for the moment, Cairo was a perfect setting. No time to lose.

I flipped open the tripod, screwed on the cameras and started using the cable release to ensure no vibrations would muzz up the shot, noting in my caption book roll 14, tower shots, the lens, and exposures. In the space of an hour, I shot six rolls of film, roughly 215 exposures. I'd gotten every possible scene from the river to the horizon, including the Makkatam hills and the City of the Dead in the background. I'd been tasked to show the present modern Cairo against the background of the old city, easily done with clear air and bright sunlight. My Polaroid instant photos extrapolated to the Kodachrome confirmed I would be bang on target.

"Let's get some more, Arnett." We headed for the hotel zone near the Corniche and in rapid succession, climbed hotel rooftops and fired away. Arnett handled the doorman *bakshish* to access rooftops. Money solves problems. It was a happy afternoon city tour, once the dirty skies had cleared. In fact, I'd completed Mel's and Kupak's request. I had only to get the film off to them ASAP.

--•--

A MESSAGE AWAITED ME AT the hotel to contact the *National Geographic* film office. I dialed and was connected to Mrs. Goodwin's office.

"Good morning, Doctor." She was on East Coast time. "Your film arrived safely last night, and was processed. The notation reads that some of the frames were overexposed, but most were usable. And I have a note from the editor requesting some frames of the visiting Smithsonian and Geographic groups who arrive in the next few days. Could you please use the Cairo Museum as the backdrop?"

"Fine," I said. "Please tell the editor I'm sending a new batch film right away." Both groups were scheduled to arrive in the next few days. And now the big gala was only five days away.

It was late in the day, either high tea time or early cocktail time depending on one's culture. On a whim, I called the Khorvudachi home and someone answered.

"Aiwa?"

I asked for Mr. or Mrs. Khorvudachi.

"Very sorry sir, they not home."

"When will they return?"

"Not home." This exchange was fruitless. Where the hell was Arnett when I needed him? I hung up.

When Arnett returned, I grabbed fresh film, rinsed off my sweaty face and we headed out to visit the Khorvudachi estate.

We drove back to Zamalik, out to the Shari Ben Hassan, up to the northern quarter, and slowed as we approached the mansion. Heavily screened by palms and shrubs, it was quite a place. Mediterranean style, with fountains in neatly planted gardens, and of all things, peacocks wandering around. I used a bell pull at the huge wrought iron doors, but no one showed up. I pulled again. Nothing. I intended to leave my *visite* card, when I saw a woman in blue jeans, tennis shoes, and a sweaty T-shirt crunching along a gravel walk, a trowel in hand. Behind her followed gardeners, pushing a barrow and dragging a huge burlap-covered plant. She looked at us in surprise. "Yes? Who are you gentlemen?" I introduced myself and my assistant.

"How nice to meet you, Doctor. I'm Karen Khorvudachi. Please come in." She led us to an awning-covered portion of the patio.

"Ali, please fetch iced tea and cold water and some biscuits." Ali dropped his barrow and scurried off.

For the next thirty minutes, we chatted with this very charming lady. She said she'd just returned from Switzerland. Between sips of tea, she explained that her garden was in ruins because of lazy gardeners while her home was being renovated by equally inept Italian renovators and gilders. She said in a lady-like fashion that things were not quite right at the moment, but hopefully would be for the gala week.

Her husband, Arsen, was in Alexandria at the moment. We would be coming to the gala, of course? We'd meet him definitely then. I assured her we were attending and told her about my assignment from *National Geographic* to take a photo of her and her husband in full ball regalia somewhere in their stately home. When would that be possible? She was flattered. We settled for a photo shoot on the morning of the event in their home. She would be making last-minute adjustments to her cocktail dress.

We'd finished our iced tea and it was time to leave. She apologized again for her work clothes, and with dignity and grace, walked us to our car. She comported herself regally, and she may well have been some kind of royal. No matter, I'd just met a very down-to-earth, very upper-class lady.

— - • - —

The Smithsonian group arrived on schedule, and unsurprisingly, Jorge D. Watson III was part of the group. Watson appeared to be a true blue blood, but was in fact Strohmeyer. We went to a corner of the hotel lobby, sat down, and after making sure we were alone, began chatting.

He listened as I explained Barsigian's strange behavior. Strohmeyer reassured me that things would go well and that someone would be speaking to Barsigian and his wife that very evening. We reviewed my activities and he seemed satisfied that I was on track.

He left for Switzerland early the next morning, and was not in the group photo which I'd arranged. He'd be in touch. He didn't say how, and I didn't ask. I had a job to do and when that was over, I was on my own.

I set up a tripod for the group photo, using a wider lens than usual, a 28mm. I did the usual "say cheese" routine to elicit smiles. The group included Miss Amanda Conant, an Egyptologist, who cracked up at my humor and introduced herself. She mentioned many mutual friends and announced that she'd be moving on from

Cairo in a few days to a large houseboat parked on the Nile, just upriver from Aswan and not far from an ancient Coptic redoubt. It was a group of old sites that were destined to be lost forever by the rising Nile River and the new Lake Nasser when the new dam was completed. She seemed anxious to get to the site.

Her specialty was tomb pottery, she said, and she had a workbench full of items to attend to, especially a batch of votive clay pots covered with fine embroidered linen, inside each a long dead ibis. She didn't say where she got them and I didn't ask. The houseboat had its own generator, radio, water filtration system, staterooms, visitors' quarters, and a full kitchen. Small boats carried them back and forth from land. I would be welcome aboard, she said, and could take some photos which might interest the *National Geographic*.

I assured her that I'd keep her kind offer in mind and made a point to keep in touch with her. I guessed she was in her early thirties, and something about the twinkly look in her eyes suggested she could be fun when the occasion warranted.

— - • - —

ON THE DAY OF THE gala, a slow excitement set in. I dressed casually in a blue blazer, white cotton shirt, pale yellow tie, cream linen trousers and Italian loafers. We drove out to the Mansion to photograph the Khorvudachis. I set up my camera in front of the fireplace and fired away, coaxing them through several rolls of film, knowing that one shot would be perfect. Their daughter, Sophia, was away, unfortunately. They'd never seen instant Polaroid prints before and were amazed by my preliminary shots. They were thrilled with the duplicate copies.

The Korvudachis were nice people, among the few wealthy people who are at ease with people around them. Karen was stunning in a frilled, black frock with touches of gold, and sparkly *peau de soie* shoes. Her hair was perfectly groomed, and she wore a light French parfum and matchless pearls gracing her perfect neck. She was a far cry from the gardener I'd met earlier.

Arsen wore a handsomely tailored dark suit. He had an aristocratic bearing, finely chiseled features, an aquiline nose, and graying hair brushed back sharply along his temples.

I told them that I planned to arrive early at the Club to check on the lighting and would see them later. But as I started to leave, Arsen courteously offered to give me a quick tour of his wing of the mansion. I was anxious to move on, but I smiled and said I'd be delighted. He led the way.

Their home was laid out like a Mexican hacienda, with large terracotta tiles and pastel, earth-toned walls. We strolled down a hallway of long oriental Kazak carpet runners in geometric figures and vivid colors that had been muted by the years. On the walls hung hunting photos. "Africa," he murmured. There were also shots of sailboats and polo horses, trappings of the very rich. In his den stood several mounted birds on stands; a Nile Ibis, a Quetzal, and an owl. Arsen was really proud of his glass-sided armoire and the objects artfully displayed inside. It held a pleasing array of things, including several Mayan pots, found in some tombs near Tikal, Guatemala, museum class pieces.

He also pointed out Chinese vases and figures, "That's a set of funerary vessels, probably Sung dynasty." There were some Roman artifacts, bowls from the Moche of Peru, carved bowls from Honduras, an ugly Olmec figure in obsidian, a gilded wooden Bodhisattva head from Angkor Wat, and Buddha statues from Burma. He was evidently proud of this collection, one that would make museum directors squirm in envy.

I was impressed by the diversity of the collection. He even had a huge woven grass basket from the Congo in which he stored walking sticks. I mumbled my thanks and stopped in the lavatory on my way out. If I wasn't mistaken, there were several paintings that looked like Renoirs. I was tempted to take a quick snapshot, but thought better of it.

Arnett and I took a quick run out to NAMRU 3, located down near Helwan in an area only he could have found. After entering the gates and identifying ourselves, we were passed in to the laboratory section. I had to make sure that an analysis was arranged for tonight. They confirmed that they could do all the necessary tests. I had no idea if the Lab was clued in on the mission. The chief asked for more samples, but I told them this was a one-shot deal.

"Fine, Doctor, it's your call. When we get the sample, we'll get to work on it stat." It was nearing show time.

CHAPTER 31

The Gezira Sporting Club
El Zamalik Island, Cairo

Nobody forgets where he buried the hatchet.
—Frank Hubbard, 1868–1930

GUNNERY SERGEANT BRENT ARNETT WAS RESPLENDENT IN A DARK SUIT, white shirt, repp tie, and GI-issued cordovan shoes. It was a comfort to know he'd be with me. We pulled up to the Gezira Club and parked in the same spot, one that was convenient to both the front entrance and back exit.

A number of police were standing around smoking, legs akimbo, berets askew, trousers ruffled and unpressed. They didn't give the impression of effective law enforcers and I suspected they would be useless for anything other than telling drivers to move along.

I took out the two cameras for the evening's shoot and stuffed plenty of film in my pockets. On a hunch, I gave Arnett a few extra rolls to hold for me, just in case.

We entered through the front door and made our way to the front desk. Sabri noticed us and waved a greeting. We were early, and he was busy moving around in high gear. We headed for the library and found two chairs. "Look Gunny," I said in a low voice. "Here's how I figure things will go." I had to air out my thoughts, bounce them off him. "Nasser will blow in late, about halfway through the evening. If things start around seven, early for Egyptians, that's about eight or eight thirty. He'll smile, take obeisance from his sycophants and charm some of the women. He'll probably drink fruit juice instead of Scotch and munch on a few goodies. He won't plan on staying long. Uncontrolled diabetics? They're thirsty, crave sweets, urinate frequently, and are often ketotic. He'll have to go while he's here, so he'll head for the washroom before leaving."

Arnett nodded.

"Doc, it's gonna happen. Your medical background sure comes in handy."

"You just saying that to make me feel better, right?" I was pleased.

"I'm a gyrene and I *feel* it; we gyrenes have a sixth sense. It keeps us alive longer."

"Hope you're right, man. Let's go check on Barsigian."

"No, Doc, let *me* go. You spook him. Wait here and I'll be right back. Stay away from the ladies." He chuckled.

Arnett returned a few minutes later. "Everything's okay. He showed me the bucket to hang over the spigot. It should go down fine. All the big guy's gotta do is take a healthy leak."

"Amen to that."

After a few minutes of eyeballing the surrounds, I decided to shmooze. We had time to kill and I'd been forewarned that no one in Egypt ever arrived on time. The Khorvudachis were standing in the foyer in a receiving line. I watched a tall, blond man fuss over the flower arrangements and give orders to the staff, even Sabri. He must be in charge, possibly a German or Swiss, and evidently good at his business.

Most of the festivities would take place at the far end of the great hall at the buffet. Egyptians enjoyed food and drink immensely, especially at galas like this where it was all free. There was a small music ensemble with two fiddlers, a guy with a huge guitar, a skinny lady with a mini harp and a tambourine fastened to her waist. A young, blonde girl was playing the oud and I wasn't sure what to expect. I tried to imagine what they kind of music they would play for this crowd.

Madame Korvudachi saw me standing with Arnett and gave us a tiny, friendly wave. Good. They knew we were here. I took some snaps using high-speed Ektachrome, which might come out grainy, but would give me some shots of the site and serve to refresh my memory later.

We eased over to the truly amazing food display. There were glazed fowls, hams, haunches of beef and all the trimmings, vegetables and salads, huge artichokes. A large bar was stacked with bottles of everything. Arnett and I opted for tall Cokes, planning to stay sharp for the evening. We filled plates with slabs of smoked salmon, a snippet of tender beef on a dainty bun, and a flaky petite pastry with cheese in the middle.

The crowd began pouring in, filling the clubrooms. I just kept moving around and smiling, shaking a hand here and there. I smiled more warmly at several classy looking *jeunes filles* with nice cleavage.

But my mind was focused on Nasser's entrance. *Where the hell was he?* Mr. Nasser had told the Korvudachis personally that he would attend. It was a waiting game.

The place was getting smoky, noisy, and giggly. I needed fresh air and opened a door. Thankfully, delightful breezes from the river swirled in to drive the thick smoke out. Occasionally, I'd hear a laugh from the crowd and several times I heard champagne flutes drop and shatter. The party wasn't into high gear yet.

I sneaked out onto the veranda, mostly to get away from the horrid strong stuff they smoke in Egypt. Happily, a breeze from the Nile wafted through the main ballroom and helped clear smoke and keep tempers and temperature down. The humidity was low, thanks be to Allah, I guess, because sweaty people are unhappy, and tonight I needed a happy environment. I wanted things to go smoothly, quickly, and to remain unnoticed as long as possible. The sound of sirens rang out, meaning Mr. Big was on his way.

I watched as a new stream of guests trooped in. Military officials, mostly Egyptian, including a high-ranking Soviet officer and his aide. I managed some good shots of them and some of the ambassadors who wore small rows of ribbons on the breast pocket of their business suits. One hefty chap wearing a huge red sash under a smoking jacket bypassed the receiving queue and headed straight for the bar.

I didn't see our Ambassador, and anyway, he had no reason to have anything to do with me. I was just a gawking tourist with a camera tonight. I spotted Colonel Arif standing just outside the Lido entrance watching Nasser's entourage arrive. After a lead car, a shiny Cadillac with darkened windows and a backup Chevy station wagon drew up. I sped over to Arif. "Evening Colonel. Would you please give your blessings to my cameras?"

I tossed him a huge friendly smile and got a frown in return. I had detached lenses from both cameras and held them out. He waved me off. He was totally uninterested in cameras and very interested in Nasser's arrival.

"Yes, Doctor, take all the bloody pictures you want, but just remember, keep your distance from Mr. Nasser." That camera clearance was all I wanted. And a urine sample. If pictures of Nasser got into the string of events, that was fine, too.

The tension and excitement in the main room was almost palpable. Everyone continued kissing cheeks, sipping champagne, and munching on delicacies, but all eyes were glued to the entrance. The musicians stopped and stared at the doorway. I supposed they were ready to swing into an Egyptian "Hail to the Chief."

And sure enough, in walked two very burly men in gray suits, mustaches, and frowns who immediately scanned the room. They gave a signal to a man outside, and within moments, in strode the great one.

He looked like a security man, himself; big, burly and beefy, with a firm mustache and an aquiline nose. Most importantly, he had the bearing of an *in charge* person. Two other bodyguards followed immediately behind him. Four, not counting Arif, plus the drivers.

The crowd was still and a few applauded politely, timidly, as though they were *afraid* to clap. Nasser strode directly to the host and hostess after his security men had gently nudged everyone aside. He wore a charming smile and I fired off some Ektachrome frames.

Two official photographers with Nasser's party fixed me with hostile, suspicious stares, but I ignored them. After a handshake and hand kissing with host and hostess, Nasser stood and chatted politely.

THE GEZIRA SPORTING CLUB

Karen was at her charming best, cocking her head as she smiled at Nasser's remarks. We were off to a great start for the evening.

Then my first moment of success! Arsen looked my way and waved for my attention.

"Doctor, please come over." Nasser turned and saw me, and smiled, too. I went over to him, cameras dangling from my shoulder. I felt all the other guests' eyes upon me and I was tickled pink.

"Excellency," said Arsen, "may I present Dr. John Sundukian visiting us from America. He is a good friend of Dr. Melville Grosvenor, head of *National Geographic*, and is here to photograph some areas of Egypt for their magazine."

"Wilcom, Doctor," said Nasser in a deep strong voice, then extended his hand. Unlike many Egyptian men, this guy gave me a firm handshake. "Wilcom to our country, to Cairo. Please give my best to Dr. Grosvenor. I remember he has a sailboat, the *Grey Mist*, no? Please remember me to him. Now what can we do to make your stay more pleasant?"

"Sir," I said in my firmest voice, that may have sneaked up an octave. "It's certainly an honor to meet you. Frankly, everyone here has been very considerate and helpful. There *is* just one small favor. Would you allow me to photograph you standing here with our hosts? It would be so helpful for our story."

"But of course, Doctor." He turned and waved Arsen and Karen to stand beside him and shooed the burly guys out of the picture. I spotted a frowning Arif standing beside the bar and pretended not to notice him.

The crowd had gradually resumed their chatting and champagne. All seemed to be going well for this gala event and I was getting pictures which damn few photographers could get. I checked available light at this spot and chose Kodachrome because K 64 gave warmer colors. Nasser was photogenic and knew how to look directly at the camera and give a great smile. I shot two rolls of the whole bunch. At the end of the shoot, I asked for "just one more," slipped on my mini flash and got some insurance shots with a light value I knew would be fail-safe to be satisfied that I'd gotten some usable frames.

I said to Nasser, "Thank you, sir. Dr. Grosvenor will be pleased to see these photos, and if I may, I'll have some prints sent to you, and to our host and hostess."

Nasser smiled again, stroked his mustache. "Well, if they come from your *National Geographic*, of course they will be excellent. Just have the photographs sent to our embassy in Washington and someone will fly them here. Now let us make a toast to our hosts."

This was all in English with an occasional explanatory word by Arsen Khorvudachi tossed in. Arsen waved to a waiter, Nasser took soda water, and the rest of us went for white wine.

Arsen raised his glass, *"To your health, Excellency."*

"And to yours," he responded. We raised our glasses, and to my surprise, everyone chanted: *"Hear, Hear,"* with some polite applause from the guests.

Was that toast prophetic?

Nasser beckoned me and led me off to one side. I was awed. Bending to my ear, he growled softly, "Tell Dr. Grosvenor to tell his friend Mr. Dulles not to be so stingy. We can still do business together to our mutual advantage. He must not force me to make another pact with the Devil. Do you follow?"

I thought I did. He meant the Russians.

"Here," he said. "Take my card and pass this on to Dulles with my comments. He will believe you then." He pulled out a gold pen, scrawled something on it in Arabic, drew a line and signed it *Nasser* in English.

Without blinking, I took it and said to him, "Would you have another card for me?" He smiled, "Of course," and handed me another card on which he also made his signature.

I had no idea how to reach Mr. Dulles, but Mel would. I pocketed the cards. Sometimes people find me open and disingenuous, I think. It worked with Nasser.

Nasser stepped away, smiling and shaking hands with guests. His four strong men made a square around him like Praetorian guards. Out of the corner of my eye, I saw Arnett taking it all in, not moving a muscle. I continued snapping random shots of possible interest. I'd just about depleted my film supply.

I turned down expensive French bubbly, sipped a soda water, and grabbed at hors d'oeuvres from passing waiters. The music ensemble had resumed playing and things were going smoothly.

—-•--

IN THE CENTER OF THE room, I spotted a very attractive lady in her early thirties chatting with a distinguished-looking man. She wore a high-fashion frock and he wore a Savile Row suit, a regular dandy. I stared, until I suddenly recognized her as Miss Conant, that plain little archaeologist! All dressed up next to her stood my erstwhile mentor, Strohmeyer. What a difference clothes make. I remembered my trainer, Sasha, telling me that active agents don't wander into foreign countries unless they were very deep undercover. I guessed Strohmeyer was not deep in anything, except conversation, but one never knew about this guy. Further, I suspected the entire Geographic study group had somehow received invitations to this grand affair. The Korvudachis were friends of Mel, after all.

I had to ignore those two just now, because I had to stay loose and wait for Nasser to make a move to the loo.

A few minutes later, Arif smoothly materialized beside Nasser; they bent heads and talked. Both glanced at their watches. Arif wanted them to leave, but Nasser seemed to be enjoying himself and wanted to stay longer. They apparently agreed on a departure time.

Okay, Excellency. Let's get the urge.

I was aware that Arnett had moved away from his observation post and had my extra film. Now Arif was nowhere to be seen, so to kill time, I took more shots and damn near used up all my film.

After Nasser used the washroom and left, we'd grab the bucket in the passageway, fill the canisters, and go out the back door directly to NAMRU 3.

Nasser glanced at his huge diamond Rolex, said something to the nearest bodyguard, and they headed in the direction of the washroom. My adrenaline was pumping.

I gave them about ten seconds and followed. Sure enough, there were two burly men standing outside the washroom, arms across their chests, coats unbuttoned, guns in waistbands. I stopped, smiled, and indicated I wanted to take a photo when Nasser came out. They looked at each other and shrugged. They knew from the upstairs receiving line that I was no threat. I took photos of them, too, and they seemed pleased.

And then it happened.

From the direction of the washroom came a muffled boom. A gunshot! Immediately, the swinging doors burst open and two inside burlies stormed out propelling a confused Nasser between them. The other two fell in front and they all barged ahead full blast shouting something in Arabic at the top of their lungs. They were clearing the way. The back two had Nasser by each arm moving him along in a well-orchestrated move. In less than a minute, I heard sirens and squealing tires, and racing engines pulling away.

I'd noticed a huge wet stain on Nasser's trouser, as though he hadn't finished emptying his bladder at the moment of the gunshot. I got one fleeting photo-shot of the scene and dashed into the washroom. Water was running in one basin, but the room was empty. I turned to the side door and ran into the passageway heading for the bucket.

Shit! Barsigian lay sprawled on the floor, squealing like a wounded pig and clutching at his shoulder. There was a huge bloodstain on his white jacket. On the floor beside him was a folded towel, but to my continuing horror, standing over him was Colonel Arif, with a foot on Barsigian's chest and a snub nosed pistol pointed at him, growling in Arabic. I had no idea what the hell was going on, but it was bad.

Arif looked up and curled his lip. He swung the pistol round aiming straight at me. "You are a stupid man, Doctor. I warned you to stay away, but you wanted to get in the way. Now I must kill you and this foolish man, too. You give me no choice."

In a flash, Barsigian's hand snaked out and yanked Arif's trouser cuff. Arif lost his balance momentarily, and Barsigian began screaming at the top of his lungs, but the party noise drowned out his screams. Arif quickly regained his balance and stamped hard on Barsigian's bloody shoulder, provoking another shriek of anguish and pain. Then he swung that little black muzzle back on me.

The cavalry arrived in the nick of time. A familiar voice boomed, "Hold it right there, you fuckin' camel driver." Arnett had entered silently from the back door and fired his .45, which made a helluva noise and blasted Arif off his feet, dropping him like a felled ox. The Colonel died instantly and lay with a neat, round third eye in his forehead. The shot had been fired close and went clean through his forehead, but the back of his skull had been completely blown out. The white walls had blood and brain splattered across them.

Barsigian was hysterical and incoherent. Arnett rushed over and cuffed him across the face, "Shut up, goddamit." Barsigian had been shot through the shoulder and to my surprise, he had a Luger hidden in the folded towel!

Arnett, the trusty Marine, figured it out immediately. "Holy shit, Doc, the whole thing was a set-up! He was gonna shoot Nasser through the towel when he handed it to him. We gotta pump some more outta this slimy little bastard." Arnett was right. Our innocent effort had spun into an assassination attempt. I mean, what harm was there in collecting a urine sample?

Arnett grabbed a terrified Barsigian and sat him up. "Listen to me, you son of a bitch, what the hell was going on here?" He kicked the dead Arif, whose blood was still oozing out over the tile floor.

A trembling Barsigian said, "Arif was trying to force me to shoot Nasser. When I refused, he shot me."

"Whose gun is this?" Arnett pointed to the towel and gun.

"I don't know. Arif's I think. He gave it to me folded in the towel. I don't know how to use it."

That had to be a lie. My bet was that Arif had shown Barsigian how, but at the moment of truth, he'd chickened out.

Arnett was doing some fast thinking, and so was I. We'd stumbled on a plot to kill Nasser, and literally shot it down. Which meant that Arif was probably an agent for the Islamic Brotherhood. It was no secret that Nasser was tagged for assassination many times, but no attempt had succeeded, and praise Allah, I guess, neither had this one.

Arif actually was the hit man in a well-crafted plan, but for some reason, he'd seconded it to Barsigian. The pressing question was what to do next. We still had some urine samples to deliver, and we had to act fast. It had only been a few minutes at most, but it seemed like hours to me.

Arnett retrieved Barsigian's weapon with the towel, put on the safety, and handed it to me. "Don't touch it, Doc, and stay right here. I'm gonna run to the kitchen and hide the sample." He grabbed the bucket, dipped in the two empty canisters, capped and sealed them, and dashed out, wiping his hands on a club towel. "I'm going to the kitchen. When the cops show up, tell them I ran out the door looking for bad guys and I'll be back. Can you handle it? We gotta get this out *now*."

"Go, I can handle it." I needed information. "Let's hear it, tell it straight." I was shaking with fear, anger, and adrenaline. I had to get some idea of what Barsigian's deal with Arif had been. I was potentially in a world of trouble. A dead high-ranking Egyptian security agent, a wounded locker room attendant, and yours truly standing here while this was all going on. The cops would arrive soon, and I needed to get my story straight.

Arif had shot Barsigian. Arnett had fired at Arif in self-defense. Would anyone believe us? Maybe. Would Barsigian corroborate it? I wasn't sure. If I had to bet, Barsigian might try using this scenario to get immunity from the cops. He'd tell all in return for protection. That wouldn't work in this part of the world. He had a shoulder wound and needed medical attention. How reliable was he?

I needed the little bastard alive. I ripped off his shirt and looked at the wound and saw a neat entry hole on one side of his chest and an exit hole in back. The slug had gone cleanly through the soft part of his trapezius muscle just under and behind his arm and done little damage. *How could Arif have been inches away from the kill zone? Barsigian must have twisted his torso, a reflex move that saved his life.* I placed clean towels over the wounds and wrapped an ace bandage tightly in a shoulder bandage arrangement. He was all right for now.

Arnett returned and said, "I stuck those two cans in the refrigerator. I told the kitchen people in Arabic not to touch them. Keeping them cool will buy us time. Urine can be stored cold overnight."

By this time, police were thundering in with pistols drawn, looking at the downed Barsigian. Several Egyptian Military officers stood slack-jawed taking it all in and some guests had been ordered out by police. My bet was that Strohmeyer was long gone. *Wonder what happened to that cute archaeologist gal?*

I used the authoritative doctor ploy, which usually worked. "Please, everyone, move back." I said. "I am a *Hakim*, a physician." This man is wounded and needs help." Military officers arrived with weapons drawn, adding to the noisy chaos.

Everyone was stunned by the sight of blood on the floor and walls, dead Arif sprawled on the floor, and a cowering attendant covered with blood and wrapped in towels. I wondered who would step forward and take over, so I continued my spiel.

"The dead man is Colonel Arif. This is a crime scene. I am a physician attending to this wounded man," I pointed at Barsigian. "Will the officer in charge please step forward and identify himself so that I can explain this situation to him."

We covered Arif with a sheet. "Don't touch anything," I warned again. "I will wait here until the police officer in charge arrives and takes over." At the same time, I pulled Barsigian into his office and sat him down.

"Okay, Barsigian, quickly, no bullshit. I want a quick explanation or I turn you over to the police as the killer," I bluffed. "What the hell was going between you and Arif?"

"He wanted me to shoot Nasser and I refused," he squeaked. "So he shot *me*." He was trembling, his face was ashen, and sweat covered his face. He'd last about one minute of questioning by police interrogators. "I saved your life, you know," I added needlessly, "Why did he ask *you* to do this?"

Slowly it came out. "We were angry with Nasser, my family and me. Arif knew we were angry and came to me one day. He had been watching us for some time. He said he could arrange for us to get our factory back, and all I had to do was shoot Nasser. He told me how to do it, tonight in the washroom when he reached for the towel. He promised that with Nasser gone, everything would return to normal. After I shot Nasser, my family and I would go to Alexandria and leave by boat for America. When things were normal again, we could come back here to our factory. We would always be protected," he sobbed, the initial shock wearing off.

"So when Nasser was shot, who was going to be blamed?"

"Some man burst in from the back entrance, shot Nasser, and escaped the same way. Arif and the guards would all say the same thing, he promised. It was so simple an explanation that Barsigian had bought it, hook line and sinker.

"You idiot," I said. "Did you believe any of that? Did you ever consider that the moment you shot Nasser, you'd immediately be shot by Arif, that he'd be a hero for saving Nasser, and you'd be a dead nothing. You would have assassinated the President and then been shot yourself. And your family eliminated, too. You are an unbelievably total idiot. When did you decide *not* to shoot Nasser? Hurry, the police are here."

"When this woman from your embassy talked to my wife and me," said Barsigian, explaining the offer that Strohmeyer's people had made.

I'd speak to Strohmeyer later about that, damn him. That tidbit had been left out of my information packet. So Barsigian, ever the fool, had decided to be a double agent. He would *not* shoot Nasser, double cross Arif, and assume we'd save his ass and get him out. For now, it was imperative that Barsigian have a plausible story.

"Listen, if you want to stay alive and become a hero, you will tell the police this: *Arif was here making arrangements for security. He knew you were unhappy about the factory seizure and told you that you must shoot Nasser or he would kill your wife, children, mother, and everyone in your family. He was the police. If you shot Nasser, they would get you and your family to America. Understand? Tell them you agreed, but changed your mind when you realized the enormity of the act.*"

The police officer in charge finally arrived. He was portly, wheezing, and appeared totally confused. Huge bands of sweat at each armpit ruined the appearance of a crisply starched uniform shirt. A bald pate and the *de rigueur* mustache completed the picture of an Egyptian Hercules Poirot. A tightly ratcheted belt held in his portly belly, where keys and a walkie-talkie dangled from his belt. He was clearly trying to make sense of the mess before him. I identified myself. He stared at the blood and scattered brains, wiped his brow, looked heavenward and sighed.

"I am Inspector Shukri in charge. Will you please tell me has taken place here?" He looked at the wounded Barsigian and at the sheet covering Arif.

"That's Colonel Arif," I said.

"This is a very serious matter, Doctor. Please sit down. I want statements from everyone. You first."

I had stated my medical presence and authority, so I gave him my story about the muffled shot, seeing Nasser pulled out by his security, seeing Arif standing over Barsigian, being threatened by Arif, and how Barsigian had saved me by yanking on Arif's pants leg, giving Arnett time to shoot Arif.

"And how did he come by this pistol, Doctor?

"Who?"

"The man who shot Arif."

"My driver, Sergeant Arnett, is an American Marine Gunnery Sergeant, stationed at our embassy. He is allowed to carry a weapon," I bluffed. "He was assigned to protect me here in Cairo, with the knowledge of your government," I threw in just for good measure. I continued, "I carry expensive cameras with me. Mr. Nasser invited me to photograph him at the reception and I would hate to have anything happen to my cameras and film." I threw that in for good measure.

"Where is Arnett now?" I pointed to Arnett standing quietly near the back.

He asked Arnett, "Are you aware that you are not permitted to carry a weapon?"

"Well sir, I am a United States Marine on assignment to guard the doctor while he visits our Naval Research Base. I was asked to drive him around the city and be of assistance. Of course, I carry a weapon, holstered and for no other reason than to protect my charge, *sir*."

Another long look.

The Inspector heard my story, Arnett's, and most of Barsigian's. He had also seen me talking and laughing with Nasser at the reception. Arif was dead, his hand clasped tightly on a gun which clearly had been fired. If *I* had planned to kill Nasser, I could have done so earlier. He must have surmised that Nasser was safe now, after an attempt had been made on his life. Thankfully, Barsigian had acted as directed, repeating to the word what I'd coached him to say.

"Doctor, I shall not detain you longer. You are free to go to your hotel. But please do not leave Cairo without my permission. I may wish to take further statements from you."

"Yes sir."

"Very good. This man Barsigian, is he well enough to leave?"

"He should be given a shot of tetanus antitoxin, a shot of penicillin, a sedative, and then be allowed to go home and rest. He acted very bravely in the face of danger, and he did save my life, Inspector."

Shukri thought that over. Nasser may have been saved by the actions of this washroom attendant. Who had been harmed? No one. An assassination had been averted. And they had killed a senior agent of some fanatic fundamentalists. With a little finesse, he could take some credit for all of this. He had enough statements and needed to make some notes.

He issued some curt orders in Arabic. Arnett whispered that he was asking for statements from the manager and some others; we were off the hook, at least for now.

He rose. "Make sure the Medical Examiner is on his way to remove this corpse. No one to touch the scene until he arrives. Then take this man, Barsigian, to Maadi, to the hospital and get him his medicines, then drive him home." Two policemen jumped to carry out the orders.

I said to Barsigian in quiet Armenian, "Don't ever change your story and everything will be all right. *Hasketzar?* Otherwise they may shoot you." He nodded without looking as they escorted him out.

If proper police work had taken place, each of us would have been taken to separate rooms for statements, questioned, and there might have been some suspicions. But the facts were right there for all to see, and the stories made sense. So, *malish*. We might have ended up in a desert prison, but what the hell, all I did was collect some urine. Was that a crime?

I had the series of frames of dead Arif and the bloody walls, Barsigian and several of the faces standing around. My Leica has a very silent shutter and using high speed Ektachrome and I shot from the hip. The photos were my "insurance" in case anything further came from this, assuming I got out.

The party was still going full blast as Arnett and I left the club. On the way out, Arnett dashed into the kitchen and retrieved the two little canisters. Instead of going to the hotel, we shot out to Helwan and delivered them to the NAMRU Laboratory. I waited in the vehicle while Arnett went inside. Minutes later he returned.

Commander Truitt had said the specimens were fine, they'd go ahead with the analysis. She asked for more samples and I told her it was not likely. It was easier that way. She had no idea of how we went about collecting it.

--•--

AT THE HOTEL, ARNETT JOINED me in the bar, where we knocked back two gin tonics. I put away a large dish of pickled capers and several handfuls of Indian cashews for good measure. We were exhausted by an event that took only a few minutes, but could have led to untold troubles. I had every intention of being long gone by the time any Coroner's hearing was initiated. I'd got the photographs from the various sites, set up and pulled off the Gezira caper. Now I needed a way back to Washington.

--•--

THE NEXT MORNING, I WAS planning to call Arnett when my bedside phone rang. It was Arsen Khorvudachi. "Good morning, Doctor." We exchanged greetings and pleasantries. Then he indicated that his driver arrive shortly and would I be good enough to join him for a late breakfast? I suspected I had no choice.

Meanwhile, I called NAMRU 3 and left a message for Arnett to meet me at the Khorvudachi residence in two hours. That should be more than enough time for whatever was in the air.

A gray Mercedes sedan was waiting in front with a driver in *tarboush* and *jalaba*. Within minutes, we'd crossed the bridge and zipped up the west side to the residence. Karen Khorvudachi was not evident.

A breakfast table was set for two on the balcony, with crisp linen and goblets of water, orange juice, and croissants. Silent Nubians poured coffee from a silver service as we smiled at each other.

"A bad business last night, Doctor." Arsen shook his head.

"Yes, wasn't it?"

"We were all shocked at the shooting."

"Yes." *Less said, the better*.

"What do you suppose really happened? What was going on in the washroom area?"

"Well, as I told the inspector, I was waiting for Mr. Nasser to come out of the washroom. I wanted some candid shots of him away from others, when I heard this muffled bang come from the washroom, like someone had dropped a heavy box. Before I could react, Nasser and the bodyguards rushed out of the washroom, with their guns drawn. I ran in to see and found Barsigian shot, lying on the floor with Colonel Arif standing over him. Arif said he was going to kill me, and if my Marine Sergeant hadn't shot him first, I might not be here." I let all that sink in.

"Yes, yes, I heard. Barsigian told the police the same story, that Arif wanted him to shoot Nasser." We sipped our coffee.

"Earlier this morning I spoke to Mr. Nasser's chief of staff. Mr. Nasser expressed his thanks for last night's affair and for handling the problem. He apologized for the disruption. It appears that Arif had been under surveillance because of some unexplained contacts with known fundamentalists, but he was not considered disloyal. But one never knows until these things happen. Shocking. For safety reasons, Mr. Nasser is staying at one of his desert retreats, but he asked me to thank you and your bodyguard. Barsigian is a minor hero since he helped save you."

I listened and said nothing. I sensed there was more coming.

"And Mr. Nasser's chief of staff asked me to pass on to you that you are free to leave Cairo any time you wish. They would be most grateful if you would keep all this business to yourself, since few guests had any idea what happened last night. The Egyptian government wishes to keep it all very quiet. No need to cause an international incident, since Arif was apparently a native of another country."

I wondered if that could be Syria or even Iran.

"So, Doctor," he continued, "at the request of the government, I am at your service for whatever you need whilst you're here. Let's proceed as though nothing happened and your return flight will be scheduled whenever you wish to leave. Just let me know your wishes and it shall be done. Is that agreeable?"

I nodded. "What about Barsigian?"

"Barsigian has been taken home to rest. He and his family will be allowed to go on holiday to visit relatives in America, I understand. He is under police protection until he leaves." That was a relief. Barsigian had stuck to his story and was also free to go.

I thanked Khorvudachi, and extended my regards to his wife. I planned to leave the next day or so. Flight choices and information would be left for me at the hotel.

Arnett's car wheezed up the driveway. It's so nice when things mesh nicely. I shook hands and promised to keep in touch.

Back at the hotel, I stopped by to see Guiragossian to tell him I was leaving. Amazing. As though nothing was amiss, he roared a welcome. He was happy to see me and had a souvenir for me, the statuette of *Cheops*, for a most reasonable price. If he could play it straight, so could I. I thanked him, forked over a few pounds and left. I hunted around for Miss Conant, but she had gone out, so Arnett and I had a coffee in the lounge. I told him I'd probably be leaving the next day or so and that everything had been swept aside, maybe under a rug. Since he was not embassy, there'd be no political officer to brief. I thanked him profusely for his quick thinking, shooting, and handling the specimens before questions were asked.

"Just what did you do with the bucket?" I asked him.

"Hell, Doctor, I tossed it far out in the bushes when nobody was looking.

I had to chuckle, "You're a good man, Sergeant."

"Thanks, sir. You can count on a Marine."

"Well, I owe you my life," I said. "I've never had a gun barrel staring me in the face before."

"*Semper Fi*," he said and walked away.

That was the last I saw of the sergeant.

--•--

MISS CONANT RETURNED MY CALL and joined me for cocktails that afternoon. She repeated the invitation to visit their huge houseboat anchored on the Nile near Qasr Ibrim, an ancient Coptic site. Since the river would rise when the new dam was completed, it was imperative to rescue some of the temples. UNESCO had given them a huge grant and teams were working to save important sites. She told me about a project at Abu Simbel, where engineers and architects planned to chop up the temple of Ramses the Second and move it to a hilltop. She could arrange for me to see that if I had any interest.

Now *that* project sounded interesting. Maybe I could talk Mel into a quick photo assignment there. And this young lady was very interesting to me, too.

I caught a flight back from Cairo to Geneva to Washington the next evening. Arsen and his driver escorted me to Heliopolis and whisked me through the formalities. One loud stamp on my passport, and I boarded my flight.

CHAPTER 32

Return to DC

I WAS BACK IN WASHINGTON ALMOST A WEEK BEFORE CALLING MEL. I STALLED because I desperately needed to attend to some necessary chores, laundry, a low tire on my Beemer, two huge piles of unopened mail.

Mel answered immediately on his private line, roared with laughter when he recognized my voice. "Glad you're back, Rover Boy. Where the hell ya been?"

I mumbled something about jet lag and fatigue, which he'd heard before. Mel told me my film had been processed, labeled, numbered and assigned to Frank Short, a senior editor, for review. At that very moment, my transparencies were laid out on a light table, along with other slides under final consideration for the article. Mel had been waiting for my call. With luck, one or two of my frames might be selected. Slides were selected on merit. In a decision between two slides of equal merit, the house slide won. That was an unspoken rule. In any event, Mel had the final word and few dared question his selections. Bill Garrett didn't always go along with Mel's choices and only grudgingly gave way. But in the end he did.

I knew Mel secretly admired Bill, and in fact, was getting ready to promote him, but that was a secret between us.

"Dammit, John, keep this under your hat, you hear? I gotta trust somebody, and I gotta be able to bounce things off you, understand?"

"Yeah, Mel. Mum's the word."

Slide selection was *merit* only. Still, I hoped. Slides that didn't make the first cut went into a giant repository known as the Egypt Work Box for a possible second look. Mel had decided the Egypt story text was far enough along for a first screening of the slides with his editor.

We met the next day at the end of my surgery schedule. It was in a fifth floor layout room in the 17th Street building. A few slides had been pulled out, printed up in black and white, and pinned to the cork wall.

Mel was wearing his charcoal gray, wide-striped Mafia suit, hand made by an exclusive Hong Kong tailor to Mel's specifications. I recognized several prints that I'd snapped from the tower on Zamalik Island looking eastward to the Makkatam Hills. The Nile River and Corniche were in sharp focus in the foreground. A helluva shot by anyone's standards. That they had been printed in B&W was a good omen. The formal portraits of Arsen and Karen Khorvaduchi also came out nicely.

No one mentioned that my shots from NAMRU 3 were not germane to the story. In fact, the Navy outfit wasn't even mentioned in the story. NAMRU's true importance had only been to cover our little Nasser caper! But the Egypt story would soon be written, photos selected, and published.

I worried that some of my other photos might have bad lighting or exposures, the sort of mistakes that pros don't make. Assignment rules were strict: stay focused, stick to your assignment, and avoid distractions. Don't make introduce bias in your photos. Leave that to the editors.

Mel shambled slowly from one view-box to the next, looking at pinned-up prints and then the slides. He'd often strike a meditative pose, right hand to his chin, left hand to his elbow, with strands of gray hair ruffled in all directions, horn-rim glasses perched high on his forehead. Shirt collar open, tie askew, sleeves rolled up, and trousers slipped down to hide his shoes, Mel squinted in deep concentration, mentally cropping and changing angles. When he made up his mind, he decreed which wall prints and frames on the view-box were to be used for the story.

Satisfied with the selections, Mel took my arm and propelled me back to his office. "Have a seat, John." Mel pored over the marked-up manuscript. "Okay, I've identified the pages where I want to use your pictures." Taking a blue pencil, Mel scrawled some gross marks in the margins, huge arrows and lines.

At length Mel looked up. "So, John. What's on your agenda these days? By the way," he said, not giving me a chance to answer, "I'm nominating you to the Geographic Board. You know we've always had a doctor on our board. You've done some great things for us at the Society and we're grateful. It's gonna take a few arm twistings, but I want someone on our Board who has common sense."

Wow! A bolt from the blue, *me,* on his Geographic Board? But I doubted it would happen. Mel's ideas and talk jumped around at times, but he had a very focused mind and handled lots of information on several tracks simultaneously. The guy was truly a genius in disguise. We finished the meeting, then had lunch in his private dining room. I was satisfied that my pictures would be used.

—-•—-

AFTER I'D BEEN HOME FOR a while, I grew concerned that I hadn't heard from Strohmeyer. No word on how things had gone with the urine sample, but Strohmeyer's silence was understandable. Or was it? For people in the intelligence business I was a commodity, an uncomfortable status that I accepted. I decided to call in to the *Geographic* and ask for Mrs. Goodwin.

"*National Geographic.*"
"Mrs. Goodwin, please."
"I'm sorry, sir, no one answers."
"Can I leave a message?"
"I'm sorry sir, there's no one there to take a message."
Damn! There was a message, "Get lost."

—-•—-

LATER THAT WEEK I WAS scheduled to visit Andrews for rounds, and assist their chief surgeon in several tough vascular operations. The first, a portacaval shunt in a general's wife, and after that, a hiatal hernia repair in a retired pilot. Getting back in the groove at Andrews would get me back on track in a hurry. Waiting for me on my desk was a note from Steve Kimler, my lawyer-patient, who had collected information on Gigi while I was away, suggesting I drop in for a visit. I called and set up an appointment for the next afternoon.

A thick folder sat on his desk and my pulse quickened when I saw it. He led us into a small conference room.

"Have a seat, Doc."

Kimler opened the folder and passed me a collection of typed sheets, letters, envelopes, and a few telefax sheets.

"How much did you know about this lady, Doctor?"

"Not much. She was in her thirties and may have been married. She said she worked for a university and our government."

"Right on some counts." He spread out the papers and photos across the table. "My hunter-gatherers did some first-rate sleuthing and put it all together for me. Let me fill you in."

He produced a small sepia tone print of two young girls holding a trophy cup.

"I've seen a photo just like that, in Saigon."

"It's your friend, Gigi, although that's not her real name. The young lady beside her is her *identical twin sister*, Mrs. Shirley Chatham, of Warrenton, Virginia. The girls were born into a diplomatic family of East Coast Brahmin blue bloods, lots of money and connections. Her father was a career diplomat and her mother was a socialite from a wealthy New Hampshire family. He's retired and they live in a condo in Arizona."

"That picture was taken at Foxcroft, a finishing school in Virginia. They were excellent students and athletes, shared many prizes. After Foxcroft, she became a debutante and spent her time at parties, trips, dances with one or two boyfriends, none too serious. Met an up-and-coming Baton Rouge stockbroker named Prudhomme and they married. It lasted two years, no children, and they separated."

Kimler went on. "With an honors degree and fluency in French, German, and Italian from living abroad, she easily qualified for our diplomatic service. She was posted to embassies in French-speaking countries. She never remarried, and in 1959, she was "seconded" to a Michigan State University team and sent to Vietnam to evaluate the political situation for the State Department. She had one close friend in Saigon named Antoine Nicolai.

"The twin sister married a banker and had a son and a daughter, both now in college. The husband went astray in business and in marriage. Ten years later, he developed a fatal blood disorder and she became a very rich widow. She took on a 'close friend,' Jason Royce. They've never married, but occasionally take long cruises and trips together. She's kept in touch with her twin while Gigi was in Saigon. Mrs. Chatham built a mansion with guesthouses and a small office building on her property. She founded the Institute for International Concerns, a think tank for college professors and retired diplomats."

He continued: "This huge conference center is now under the umbrella of the Fairlie Foundation, connected to Fairlie Farms. Three weeks ago, Mrs. Chatham readied a guesthouse and left on a trip without Royce.

"We accessed her telephone and the main house had calls to and from Saigon, especially the Seventh Day Adventist Hospital in Bangkok and the American Embassy, and several to Nice, France.

"I contacted your military buddy, Hank Peters, and spoke to him directly. He said lots of nice things about you. He remembered Nicolai, an interview by Sully, and seeing Gigi at a Saigon city club. The Michelin rubber folks told him that Nicolai flew from Saigon to one of the plantations, and then on to Nha Trang. Mrs. Prudhomme and Sully were aboard that plane with him. Nicolai never arrived at the plantation. Peters contacted his friends at Air America, and he and a Navy pilot traced the route, but saw nothing. Peters decided to go into the jungle and split his men into two groups, one heading outbound, the other inbound back to Saigon. He took six men with full jungle packs and survival equipment.

"They landed the Porter at a clearing near the halfway point and off loaded. The pilot would fly to the halfway point each day at the same time and look for them; at some point Peters and his men would return for pickup. Radio contact was with them was limited. On the second day, the inbound team found the crashed Cessna 206. By the way," Kimler said, "another name for the 206 is *undertaker's plane*; it's used to fly coffins from one city to another.

"The 206 appeared to have nosed into the jungle on a slant, its prop blades bent back, its wings snapped off, and parts of the tail section dangled from overhead branches. There was no fire, probably because the wing fuel tanks had sheared off escaping the hot engine. Peters found papers, blood, remains of a picnic basket, three empty canteens, and lots of native flip-flop prints, so he concluded that there *had* been survivors.

"Peters and his team went to the nearest village set up on stilts alongside a muddy river. Yes, they heard a plane come down in the jungle and went to investigate. It was not an army plane. Some of the men worked as rubber tree slashers for the nearby plantation and they recognized the Michelin name. The village chief sent runners and within the day a truck arrived from the plantation to remove an injured woman and man. Peters rewarded them generously with cash and cigarettes, eventually concluding that one man apparently died in the crash. The elder chief had complained of poor wages and bad treatment from Michelin."

Kimler took a swig of coffee. "Peters' team drove to the Michelin plantation, where he found Nicolai and the girl injured, but alive and stable. She'd suffered a broken ankle, ribs, and a cut on her scalp. Nicolai had a broken arm, bruises, and a twisted back. Sully's neck had broken on impact. Nicolai said they'd survived on a picnic basket without a radio, and had finished the last of their water when the villagers found them. It was sheer luck.

"As soon as he could get a plane, Peters airlifted them to his Special Forces camp for medical treatment."

"What did they do with Sully?"

"No information, I suspect they left him at the plantation for burial."

"The Special Forces medical officer went to work on the damages, casting broken bones and repairing wounds. Within a week, they were well enough to be up with assistance. Nicolai told Peters he was sure his Cessna had been sabotaged. Thirty minutes after takeoff, he began having power problems. Somehow, not enough fuel was getting to the cylinders, he was losing power and altitude. It meant his fuel line was clogged or cut. He called Saigon tower and told them he was in trouble and would make an emergency landing; the tower operator acknowledged, but forgot to pass it on.

"Nicolai is convinced that he was a marked man, but he thought the lady was an innocent bystander. He didn't know about Sully. It was decided to let Saigon think they had been killed in the crash.

"Peters flew them to the Seventh Day Adventist Hospital in Bangkok. Our Bangkok embassy arranged a new passport for Gigi. Nicolai flew to Nice and she left Bangkok with her sister. She's probably hiding out at Fairlie right now, and for some reason, is not anxious to let the world know her whereabouts."

Kimler pulled out a black and white print he had been saving for last. "This was taken a few days ago at Fairlie." It was a long lens shot of two slim ladies in shorts and halters in animated conversation beside a swimming pool, one wearing a cast.

"Mrs. Chatham had Gigi's possessions packed and shipped to her at Fairlie, and closed the Saigon house. Our Nice correspondent located Nicolai near the town of Eze where he is recuperating."

I offered to pay for the expenses incurred in his extensive investigation, but Kimler hinted with a wink that much of it had been laid off on corporate accounts. I went back to my routine, but the Saigon business was never too far from my thoughts.

CHAPTER 33

Andrews Air Force Base
Cheltenham, Maryland

At Andrews, I was back on familiar ground. An AP sergeant at the gate gave me a snappy salute and waved me through. I parked next to Archie's Jeep sitting in a spot *Reserved for Generals*.

Air Force hospitals are very much alike. Slow, silent efficiency at the front end; bustling activity back in the patient areas. I've always maintained that surgical wards are busier than medical wards, but that's my own personal bias.

At the Surgical Office, Archie's attractive secretary, Dottie Tronka, dropped by to leave a message for me, and the guys took that opportunity to flirt with her. I knew she enjoyed their attention, but she was waiting to tell me that General Koffman needed to see me as soon as I finished. He was in his office. I noticed she was wearing a small frown instead of her usual radiant smile.

Before our first surgical procedure, I made mandatory quick rounds, seeing old and new patients and answering a few questions. The first operative patient was being readied for a portacaval shunt that would reroute blocked-up gut blood around the liver back to the heart. I studied my whole day's roster and planned to be through with all procedures in time for lunch with Archie.

Archie had laid on a two-hour chopper ride for me, a practice evacuation run from the Pentagon, to Harper's Ferry, over to Mount

Weather, then back down the Potomac, turning east just south of Alexandria to Andrews. The pilot, an Air Force light-colonel, was an old patient and friend. He occasionally let me log an extra hour of chopper training. So far, I had six hours in this beast, the huge CH-53, a powerful, ponderous craft, big enough to carry Jeeps. I loved it. Flights like this one were rare for ordinary civilians. Each time the jet turbines turned over, they burned hundreds of dollars a minute of fuel that only the Air Force could afford, so I was very lucky. It was a perk given me as a consultant. If the Air Force had ever suspected that a civilian doctor had been part of unreported, unscheduled piloting times, there could have been trouble. And worse yet, taxpayers might, rightly, have been outraged. In actual fact, though, this was a training flight, and I just happened to be along and at the controls.

In any event, I'd always had Archie Koffman's big shadow protecting me, and over him, his friend Curt LeMay. When I'd added signed-in official rotary wing time to my fixed wing logbook, my fixed wing instructors hinted darkly at fraud on my part. They questioned my helo time and said the FAA might take a hard look at my logbook. To settle things, I made a fiendish deal with the helo pilot for that day's flight.

After notifying Andrews Tower of a practice emergency strange field landing, we flew the huge chopper over to tiny little Woodbridge Airport and hovered over owner and chief pilot Charley Bain's office sending thundering blasts of air onto his roof and set down smack dab in the front of his parking lot! Bain and his flight instructors poured out of the office, astonished to see the student pilot, *the Doc*, waving from the cockpit window! We reduced power and slowed, but did not stop the massive rotors. We didn't dare stop the turbines. I made damn sure they all got a good look at me before the Air Force officer in the right seat, the real pilot, lifted us up and away.

The pilot in a helo sits right seat; in fixed wing planes, left seat. Our huge, whirling main rotor scattered dust and gravel all over as we blasted up and away. I never gave them a clear explanation of how I managed that flight, but after that, they were convinced I had a connection somewhere and believed anything I told them.

I wasn't prepared for today's meeting with Archie. We never had lunch because he'd been caught in an unexpected conference, so I'd grabbed a sandwich before lifting off in the chopper. After we landed, there was another message to stop by his office before departing Andrews. Not an unusual request. I often sat and listened to him complain about his gimpy leg.

He frequently bugged me to do a bypass procedure on his clogged leg artery, but I'd held off because he wasn't in quite enough leg pain. It was too early in his symptom complex, and besides, he would be forced to retire if it didn't work out perfectly. And he wanted me to operate in a civilian hospital under a fake name. Dangerous, but it was part of our game plan, so I expected another gentle haranguing from Archie.

"Come in, Jawn." Archie was seated at his oversize desk, a smuggled Havana that I wouldn't allow him to smoke clamped unlit between his teeth. He looked worried.

Something felt wrong. "What's up, Archie?"

"Man, I'm not sure. Have you done something real bad lately?"

"Probably. What're you getting at?"

Archie pulled two Cokes out of his private fridge, handed me one, stuck his ailing leg on the coffee table, and looked me in the eye.

"We got an order from the Secretary of Defense. You are no longer our National Consultant, all IDs are canceled and you can no longer visit the base. You have any idea what the fuck's goin' on?"

I was stunned. "What?"

Archie went on, "I took matters in my own hands and I got Curt LeMay on the horn. Told him I wanna know why. He knows that without you, we can't be a fully accredited service hospital for the Air Force. We'd have to shut down our goddam training program. LeMay's flunkies raised uncommon hell, made phone calls, then threatened to go to the press, etc. Things are now partially restored to normal; you can visit as a consultant, but only visit the hospital until further notice.

"Now, Jawn, you gotta level with me. What the hell have you done, man? Only a breach of National Security would bring all this shit down on you."

I winced inwardly. "Have you talked to Jim Kernigan?" General Kernigan ran the surgical program for the Air Force and made appointments at the national level.

"Hell, yes, and he's just as befuddled as I am. He got the same information, and it was *he* who appointed you, Jawn, and *they went right over his fuckin' head!* The big question is why? Jim says in his military experience, only the CIA or the NSA have that much clout, Jawn. You messin' with any of them?"

So I lied, "Not to my knowledge, Archie."

The heat was on. Somewhere in the CIA, somebody didn't like me. No one had answered when I called Strohmeyer or tried the Geographic extension number. I was being squeezed out, silently.

I was in a daze the rest of the meeting. Archie clapped me on the back and assured me that it would get straightened out. I knew he needed me for the hospital's status, and also to do the surgery on his leg. I was his insurance against a medical discharge.

I handed over my ID cards and left. Archie promised me new ones on my next visit, but still, I felt sick, and felt the beginnings a slow burn. My mind twisted with plans of how I'd get to the bottom of this myself.

For now, I was an Air Force outcast. I retreated to my old routine for comfort. I needed information and to mull things over before taking any revenge.

The next afternoon, I played squash with Bill Garrett and let him have it twice in his butt with the hard rubber ball due to a lack of concentration. He was outraged, exploded at me, and I apologized. I bought him a few drinks and he laughed it off. Said I should treat him more respectfully, especially now that my Egypt pictures were at the engravers and going to press. That great news was the only bright spot in the strange events of that week. Things could only get better, I said to myself, then gulped down a second gin tonic.

－－•－－

I USUALLY VISITED ANDREWS ON Thursdays, a schedule that worked for everyone since we had started up my specialty, thoracic and vascular surgery, as part of their surgical program. Military pay for medical consultants was a pittance, but I didn't care about the money. The benefits mattered. Chopper flights, the right to land at Andrews, front row seats at air shows, and many other goodies that money couldn't buy. General Kernigan had informed me by letter that as a National Consultant, I enjoyed the civilian level of BG if I ever went out on an official mission. That was a lure and an ego builder. But all the benefits I cared about were in shambles along with my clearances. Clearing my name was my first priority. But *how*? Who was behind this and what precipitated it?

My first tip came when I least expected it. Someone took the time and effort to study my daily routines, which meant I'd been surveilled. A few days later, I was shopping in McLean when a stooped man wearing a weathered cap and carrying a cane nudged me.

Son of a bitch, I knew this guy!

Out of the side of his mouth, he murmured that I should take a booth at the Chinese restaurant and wait. Then he evaporated. This man was a long way from the Farm, but I did remember his ferret face. He was the CIA surveillance instructor who had taken me out on the streets of Richmond.

I took a booth at the Chinese restaurant, ordered a Tsingtao beer and waited. Five minutes later, Strohmeyer strode in and sat down. The headwaiter led us through to a curtained area with several small booths.

"Hi, Doctor."

"Henry. What the hell's going on? First, no one answered my calls, and then I got bad news from the Air Force. Now, suddenly your little man from the Farm bobs up and tells me to get over here?"

As we had passed through the curtains, Strohmeyer had told the waiter, "Cha." Our waiter now appeared with a steaming pot of black tea and a plate of appetizers.

"I owe you an explanation, Doctor," he smiled wryly. "Some of our people play rough. I have to play by our rules, at least on the surface, even though I know what goes on. You got a raw deal over a matter that makes no sense to me. I think it started after you returned from Russia."

I stared at him.

"You had contacts with the Dashnaks in Moscow, right? You were asked if you had relatives in Armenia, in the Soviet Union, and you said you probably did, but you were not aware of them and had had no contact with them, correct?"

I nodded.

"Well, JJ Singleton's counter-intelligence shop got copies of your debriefing as a matter of routine distribution, read them and tagged you as a possible Soviet mole."

I couldn't believe my ears. "You can't be serious. How do you know this?"

"Dead serious. The decision to can you was made by Singleton's shop. An edict went out to remove you from all sensitive USG positions. There's a Company doctor named Manuel Gunner who read the debriefing reports and couldn't accept the authenticity of the Mikoyan letter, or the ease with which you got around Moscow. Just a mean-spirited little turd. He decided you must be a plant, without even consulting Moscow. Singleton's people decided it all sounded fishy, and they're so goddam paranoid, they got their shrink to say you might have been an easy mark for the skilled Soviet turners. Given the paranoia of the times, it was simple to tag you as 'potential' and leave it at that. I know better. You're no mole. You messed up some of the courses at the Farm, but overall, you did fine, and you're not even the right type for the Russkies."

He went on. "Singleton suspects that the Company has been penetrated by Soviet agents and he's obsessed with the thought that our own people could be working for the USSR. Sadly, he may be right and it's driving him nuts. You got caught in the mix and you're expendable, so you've been pushed out and are one less person to worry about."

He shook his head. "At the moment, you're burned toast. When you responded that you probably had relatives in Armenia, that was truly *the wrong response*. Take my advice, Doc, drop this association with the Company and just walk away. You're a damn fine surgeon. They could make life miserable for you, in a million sticky ways. Go back to being a doctor and photographer and start chasing big-titted women."

Reluctantly, I replied. "Thanks for being honest, Henry. I hope your ass isn't in a sling over this, too. I'll consider your advice. It's just fucking unbelievable." I was reeling, I was so stung by this accusation, no, assumption of my disloyalty. "But don't be too surprised if you hear my name again."

He smiled. "Good luck. It's been fun working with you. I think you're a great guy and I hope it gets cleared up." We shook hands and he left.

I sat staring at the skewered shrimp and pondered how such an exciting opportunity with the Agency had collapsed so miserably. Me a mole? Fucking ridiculous! I'd seen combat as a deck officer on an LST, Amphibious Forces. Invasions in the Pacific Theater, no less. I was so damn patriotic that at times I had to laugh at myself.

What fucking idiots. Somebody had made a serious mistake and I was going to do something about it. I had some scheming to do. I sat there ruminating until I finally had the vague beginnings of a plan. Armenians don't always get outwardly angry, but we do get even.

--•--

MRS. GHORMLEY, MY OFFICE MANAGER, informed me that the receptionist at Dr. Bedrosian's Agency clinic told her my name did not appear on their consultants list any longer. My resolve became firmer.

I called Bedrosian's office and left a message concerning *two patients who needed surgery*. He was a doctor, and he was Greek, so I was not surprised when he went against orders and called me. One of the patients had called my office. He'd been told I was no longer with the Agency and he was upset. I went over his chest films and scheduled him at GW hospital for bronchoscopy. He had an X-ray shadow which was probably lung cancer and needed a quick lobectomy. I 'scoped him, opened his chest, and was able to get the tumor out clean.

For the next few weeks, I existed in two worlds simultaneously. One was the everyday business of being a physician, giving lectures, making rounds, and operating at the Washington Hospital Center. But my mind was constantly searching for ways to force JJ Singleton and his dwarves to reassess their unfair and egregious judgment of me.

First, I needed their attention. The Agency was as closely guarded and unapproachable as a Sultan's daughter. I needed an ally, someone who had an entrée into to that closed circuit. It had to be someone who would be sympathetic to my story and had access to people at high levels. I racked my brain. Who did I know?

Happily, my FAA position was still secure. For some reason, that connection had been overlooked. I wondered how long that status would last. I was going along unnoticed as a consultant at staff meetings and no one seemed any the wiser. I certainly had no intention of bringing up my problem.

My airline medical directorship with Pan African Airways was still in effect, so that was always a fall-back connection. The following week, I received an unexpected call from Tom Black, president of Pan African, headquartered at Miami International. I was still their Medical Director.

Tom had a medical problem and asked to see me. I told him I would fit him in whenever he got to DC. Within days, he flew his Cessna 210 to Washington National and came straight to my office. Tom had been coughing lately and his Florida chest film showed a large mass. It was an ugly-looking lesion and Tom was a two-pack-a day smoker. I knew immediately that it was a lung tumor.

His consultants in Miami had suggested an immediate biopsy and resection of the tumor, followed by radiation therapy. I agreed with that approach, and refused to come down to Miami and operate on him. He might require extended treatment after surgery, and it would be easier for him and his family to have a surgeon close to home. But Tom blurted out the burning question, "Can I be certified to fly again?"

"Yes and no," I answered evenly. "Yes, if all goes well and you're up and around quickly, as I expect you to be. But no, I will not reissue you a First Class medical license. You don't need First Class to fly that 210, and you won't be flying for Pan African again anyway, so forget that First Class ticket. When you are fully recovered, I might grant you a Second. Okay?"

Tom gave me a long, frosty stare. "You sonofabitch, you can't take away my First Class medical ticket, dammit. That's my proudest achievement, John. I'm a transport pilot; I can fly anything, and goddamit, I'm also president of an air carrier and you're our medical director! I thought you were my friend. You gotta help me. I have to fly big planes. Why do you want to take that away from me?"

I shook my head and carefully explained the problems associated with flying after lung surgery. Lung function tests, medications and FAA's proscriptions of flying on certain meds. We'd have to wait and see how things went. I told him there might a loophole. I might get him back in the air on the big planes after his surgery and treatment if he passed a rigorous examination.

Suspicion crossed his face. "How?"

"Promise, you didn't hear it from me."

"Promise."

"You know you don't have to fly big planes. That's all ego and bullshit and we both know it. But you wanna fly big planes, which requires two pilots, right? Well, I can maybe give you a Second Class ticket, which lets you fly right seat in cargo craft, so if you have a guy in the left seat with a First, what's to stop you from flying the damn plane from the right seat? Think it over."

Tom Black, a grizzled Pan Am pilot and veteran of God only knew how many hours of flying everything, even smuggled flights in and out of Cuba, broke into a crooked smile. Sneaky stuff appealed to him. It was a legal way around a problem.

His face brightened. "Oh hell, I knew you were my friend, John. Sorry I blew up. Hearing about a lung tumor is bad news. Being told I'd be grounded would be worse. I'm gonna take your advice and do what the docs tell me. What the hell, I got lotsa money and I can't take it with me, so I'm going to spend a big chunk getting well. I'll pass your fuckin' exam and I'll be flying again."

"Sure, Tom. Hang in there and go through the drill. You'll get first class care at that Miami hospital. They've got excellent chest surgeons. Get started on the treatment schedule as soon as possible."

"Okay, John, and thanks again. I'm gonna fly back to Miami as soon as I can get myself to National. Mind if I use your phone?" I nodded and he was on the phone filing his flight plan.

As he was leaving, Tom said, "By the way, Doc, our airline has a condo on Grand Bahama Island, right on the ocean. Why don't you take a few days off and use it. Be my guest. It's got maid service, a car, and a fully stocked fridge and bar. Just call my office and tell them when you want to go. You got priority."

I thanked him, tickled to have such a wonderful offer, and told him I would take him up on it soon. Fall was in the air and some sun would make life seem rosier. Once I'd hatched my plan and gotten what I wanted from Singleton's gang, I would head for the sunshine.

CHAPTER 35

A Shark Is Hatched

As days stretched into weeks, I began weighing plans and considering what action had the best chance for success. I wanted my good name cleared, no question. I started sniffing around for information, and like a shark, once I zeroed in on blood, someone was guaranteed a bad outcome. Three missions ran concurrently in my plan of attack: Fairlie Farms, JJ, and JMS. Project JJ had the greatest priority.

I had to get to a highly placed individual in the Agency who had clout, but now there was no way I could approach anyone in the Agency. I didn't exist. I was shunned like an old-time church sinner.

Who did I know with serious clout? General LeMay had interceded for me to keep my visits to Andrews alive and General Archie Koffman had gone to him on my behalf.

That was it.

I called Archie's office and was told the General was on an inspection tour in Alaska for ten days. I knew the upcountry salmon, char, and trout were the inspectorate's true mission! On his return I planned to take him into my confidence and tell him everything. All the important details of my trip to Moscow, my stint in Vietnam, my sneaking into China and getting out, my visit to the Air Force

A SHARK IS HATCHED

hospital in Thailand. I'd show him the letter from Mikoyan, my passport, my photos. Everything.

I'd give him names like Hank Peters and ask him to suggest to General LeMay that my name be cleared and I be reinstated. Archie and LeMay had a close relationship. I would offer to do the bypass operation on his leg and guarantee that it would not appear on his Air force medical files. I wouldn't tell any lies, but I might fudge things a bit for Archie in the record. I hoped he wouldn't turn this down. Now all I had to do was wait for Archie to catch his fill of Arctic char and get back.

CHAPTER 36

Dr. John Strikes Back!

WHILE I WAITED, THE DARK SIDE OF MY ANGER BEGAN TO EMERGE. I wanted to get even with that miserable shit in JJ's shop, the one who had dubbed me a mole. My reputation had been sullied, and you just don't do that and get away with it.

At the Rosslyn outpatient clinic, the other consultants and I moved in and out of various offices in connection with patient visits, filing forms and making appointments. I developed a nodding acquaintance with one of the other doctors from an office near mine. He was Clem McCurry, a South Carolina boy from Moncks Corner, a jolly, chubby Southerner. I turned to him as the first step of my plan and put in a call to his private Georgetown office.

"Hi, Doc, fancy hearin' from you."

"Why's that?" I chuckled, "Am I on your shit list?"

"Hell no, we just don't deal with surgeons much, y'unnerstan'. What can I do for you?"

"Well, Clem, I'm trying to locate a Doc in our Company named Manny Gunner. You know him?"

"Yeah, sure do. He's a strange one. Lives here in Georgetown. I got his office number right here, hold on." He gave me a Rosslyn number, which was really Langley, and his home number. "That he'p? Whatchoo want him for?"

"I want to ask him about a patient I saw for him earlier, "I lied.

"Yeah, he's around. I saw him las' night having dinner at the La Chaumiere with his wife or girl frien'. Reckon he's at work."

"Okay, Clem, thanks. And for your ears only, I just got a pink slip, so you won't be seeing me at the clinic anytime soon. Been nice."

"Sorry to hear that, Doc. These things happen over there. Crazy people we have to deal with," he let out a guffaw. "Nice talkin' to you, see you roun'."

I called Gunner's office and got a recitation of the extension number. I asked for Dr. Gunner.

"Who should I say is calling, please?"

I gave my name. "Hold please."

A minute later, "I'm very sorry, Dr. Gunner does not recognize your name. If you wish to communicate with him, he suggests you write him in care of his office. Thank you so much for calling." Click.

Write his office? That was a clever kiss-off. I had no address for him. If that silly bastard thinks he's clever, he has no idea with whom he's dealing. I called his home in Georgetown and left my name on his answering machine. That ought to get his gears turning. Then I plotted.

My office was a few blocks from the La Chaumiere, an upscale little French country-style inn. Its clientele was upper class, with a few limos always waiting at the entrance. The restaurant served excellent French food and gorgeous red wines, and best of all, they were reasonably priced.

I often lunched there on Tuesdays when they featured a garlicky fish stew and decided to lunch there the next day. I planned to speak to the owner, Gerard Lazin, whom I'd known well for years. Lazin was a superb chef, an elegant dresser and a first-class gentleman of the old school.

Lazin greeted me at the door, and after the usual pleasantries, I told Gerard I needed some information. He raised an eyebrow.

"Something I would know, *Docteur*?"

I nodded.

"Do you know a man who dined here last night, a Dr. Gunner?"

"Yes of course I know him. He dines here almost every Thursday night after his bridge lesson."

"Alone?"

"Sometimes, I can never tell. Last night he brought someone from his class. Why do you ask?"

"I need to ask him about a patient." I was purposely vague, but Gerard, always the discreet Frenchman, said nothing.

My lunch arrived and he excused himself with a wry smile. "Be careful, *Docteur*. I know where he works. Nasty people. *Bon appetit*."

Oh. He knew where Gunner worked. But most folks kept things to themselves in this town. Gerard might be curious, but he'd help me.

I'd left my name for Gunner at his office and his home, so he must be getting curious. It would be procedure for him to inform JJ that I'd tried to make contact, and to make note of the dates and times.

I was waiting at the restaurant at dinnertime the next Thursday, but Gunner never showed. Gerard saw me and said nothing. *Rats!* I needed to see this bastard before I saw Archie at Andrews.

Finally, on the following Thursday, I was seated at a side table, when I saw him enter alone. I'd never seen Gunner in person and I had no idea what to expect, but I recognized him immediately. They all dressed alike. He wore a gray suit, a blue button down shirt, a red and blue repp tie and lace-up, cordovan shoes. I made him in his late fifties, with a slight hunch to his shoulders, a pinched face, rimless glasses, and a furtive look. Gunner's eyes darted around never seeming to make contact with anything for more than a second. He had arched eyebrows, graying temples and slicked down, thinning hair. I doubted this guy could ever make a living in the real world. Working as a doctor for the spooks was a loser job.

I gave him a few minutes to order, then I rose leisurely, walked over and slid into the chair opposite him.

"Dr. Gunner? Please don't get up. My name is John Sundukian. Sound familiar?

His eyes bulged, and his jaw dropped open.

"Sit there, you sonofabitch and listen," I said, departing from my usual good manners. "You better get back over to your shop and go over my records more thoroughly, not the half-assed way you obviously did before, and come up with a clean report on me. *Understand? Let me repeat myself. You will get my records cleaned and corrected, and get my status reversed.*"

I was shooting from the hip. Threatening a CIA agent, even a medical stooge like Gunner was stupid, but I got a perverse pleasure out of watching his face. The question was, would he have me arrested or visited by spook intimidators? Maybe, but I might have him intimidated. He knew that I knew all about him, and worse, I was formidable. And very, very angry.

"There's more," I continued darkly. "Get this straight, too. In my lawyer's safe is a complete record of all my activities, of how I worked for the Company, returned, got debriefed and dumped for no good reason, along with notes about what you stupidly concluded from that debriefing. You proceeded to impugn my honor based on some flimsy bullshit. My notes contain names, dates, places, everything, in case something happens to me. More copies are sitting in a safety deposit box with instructions that in the event of anything untoward, a copy goes to my contact at the White House and one goes straight to *The New York Times*."

Gunner grabbed his drink and gulped it straight down. He started to speak, but I cut him off and leaned over him, menacing. "Keep in mind, Gunner, it's a small town. I can track you anytime as easily as I did tonight. I want my clearances back or I will destroy you. There are many ways. D'you hear me, shithead?"

He rose quickly to leave and I stood, too. I couldn't stop myself, I was so angry. Under the table, I stomped down heavily on his instep with my big, size 14 shoe. He jerked in pain and darted for the door.

"Get going," I said with disgust, and walked back to my table and sat down. Gunner limped frantically out of the restaurant.

Gerard Lazin had seen it all from the bar and sauntered over to my table, a quizzical look on his face. "What was all that, *Docteur*? Why did *Docteur* Gunner rush out like that?"

"I haven't the foggiest idea, Gerard. We were talking medical things. He's having some pain in his foot. Anyway, the drinks are on me." I smiled innocently.

Gerard wasn't fooled, he had seen a terrified Gunner flee his restaurant, but in true Gallic fashion, he shrugged and retreated to the safety of his kitchen.

Excellent, I thought. For the record, all I did was buy Gunner a drink. And there were witnesses.

I slept well that night. Before nodding off, I decided to bare my soul to General Thatcher during my next visit to his clinic in the White House. For some odd reason, that connection was still going and Thatcher could be another vector of force through his channels. I had nothing to lose. After my meeting with Gunner, I hoped that I'd tossed sand into some finely meshed gears over which few controls had ever existed. Let's see how long it took to mess up the machinery in JJ's shop.

Next morning over coffee, I reviewed my situation. At the moment, I was waiting for Archie Koffman, the influential Air Force Major General, to use his substantial contacts on my behalf. I planned to talk with General Thatcher, too, on my next visit, so just to make certain we were still on, I called Thatcher's office at the White House. A Navy corpsman confirmed that I was scheduled for a visit. *Good!* So far, I still held that position with the White House. But for how long?

I wanted to dig into the situation at Fairlie Farms, to try and trace Gigi, but I needed to take a few days off. After all this anxiety, I could use some down time. Why not visit Tom Black's Bahama condo and hit the beach? It would take a few days for things in DC to heat up, so I had time to enjoy some island sunshine.

CHAPTER 37

The Bahamas

I INVITED THE WILD AND SENSUOUS KATERINA PEREIRA TO JOIN ME FOR A weekend in the tropics. We flew over Miami to Grand Bahama Island on the extended Eastern flight. Tom Black came from his Dispatch Services office to meet me at the Miami Eastern gate. He was mildly surprised to see Dr. Pereira. I introduced them and spotted a twinkle of appreciation in Tom's eyes. During the brief layover, Tom told me he had undergone biopsy and had started on a calculated dose of radiation before undergoing his exploratory thoracotomy scheduled for the following month. I assured him that I'd keep in touch.

－－●－－

TOM'S CONDO WAS A CORPORATE titan's dream. A beautiful one-floor villa overlooking the ocean, just a few stories above a sandy beach. Several luxuriously appointed bedrooms, huge bathrooms and showers, walk-in closets, and a spacious kitchen completely equipped with the latest gadgets. The oversized refrigerators held all kinds of food and beverages, and the freezer bulged with goodies ranging from gourmet ice cream to venison. A cook came every day to prepare meals to order. The cook and a maid kept the place running, and did everything from shopping to driving.

The weather on Grand Bahama Island was marvelous, the ocean a deep cerulean blue, with white clouds and dulcet ocean breezes. One of Tom's friends, a senior island official, Judge Michel St. Stephen, invited us to his home for an "island party." We were delighted.

We drove up his long, gravel driveway and a native valet whisked away our car. There was a feeling of general madness in the air we felt the moment we stepped out onto the drive. Huge bamboo torches lit up the grounds, the swimming pool, and most of the beach, flickering over a spectacle of food, music, drinks and dancing.

Our host, Judge St. Stephen, was clad, unbelievably, in a batik sarong, with a huge chain of cowry shells and boar's teeth dangling over his unbelievably hairy chest. He was bare-chested and barefooted, a fake bone through his nose, a spear in one hand, shaking his wrist cowries and looking like a textbook cannibal smeared with enough hideous war paint to frighten anyone.

Katerina took one look and murmured, "That is one very ugly man!" We grinned at each other. Even our hostess avoided her husband as she very slowly got smashed.

It was hard to believe this man was a jurist. Someone told me he had native blood in his veins and enjoyed going native at his parties. After a quantity of rum, he'd lapse into island talk, giggle, roll his eyes and babble incomprehensibly. I was certain it was all a put-on. His wife, Lady Daphne, was just the opposite. She looked like a proper lady, fanning herself furiously as guests and servants swirled about her. She took no notice of any of them, just kept fanning and sipping rum fizzes.

Katerina was a stunner. Trouble was she knew it. Her delicious body was tucked into a long black sheath slit way up one side to show off her slim, tanned legs. She even forsook panties; the lines showed, she explained. She could be a rotten tease at times. Her dainty feet were thrust into stiletto Ferragamo sandals that click-clacked as she walked and showed off her pink pedicure. Her lively, almond-shaped green eyes stared out from underneath a mass of blonde hair in a swirl atop her head. A single strand of lustrous, white pearls circled her neck. She was an arresting sight, and as usual, drew admiring gazes. She pretended not to be aware of the attention, though I knew she reveled in it. Before we'd left the hotel, I'd warned her not to overdo it.

"Zip me up, John," she cooed.

"Baby," I implored, "wear some underwear. Try to be a lady. Don't torment all the men at the party!"

In reply, she stuck her out her tongue, spun around and wiggled her bottom at me as she headed for the door. She was saucy and unpredictable both in and out of the sack.

The evening was a total success. She dazzled the troops, smiling and sashaying her way past a mélange of wide-eyed, envious males and females. I was enjoying myself, too, and made sure we left before it got out of hand.

The next day, we spent time on the hotel's signature pink beach, sprawled in a lounge chair with a jug of cold lemonade, reading and snoozing. I did some deep thinking. Katerina lazed on a chaise covered in oil, wearing a huge floppy hat and little else. She might as well have been totally naked because the Brazilian *fila* bathing suit covered nothing. Katerina insisted that one must take advantage of the sun. It was hard to believe the languid creature sprawled beside me was in fact a brilliant, highly skilled plastic surgeon.

She wore a different eye-catching bikini each day and was totally in her element: relaxed, uninhibited, and ready to party at a moment's notice. And party we did. After a third Rum Collins, no matter where we were, she made me aware that she had needs. In public, I cringed with embarrassment, but in private, I was happy to meet them.

Booze, food, sun, and satin sheets served us well.

— — • — —

IT WAS A QUICK WEEKEND. I flew back to Washington in a much better frame of mind. While waiting for Archie to return, another name had sprung to mind: *Mel Grosvenor! Of course!*

Two days after returning to Washington, a shade browner from my Caribbean *hegira*, I walked into Mel's spacious office. He'd squeezed me in between lunch and a two o'clock slide viewing. Jacket off and shirtsleeves rolled up, Mel grinned, and pushed color proof sheets toward me. "You seen these, Jawn, from the Egypt story? Just got 'em back from the engravers. Color's just about right," he crowed. "I love 'em."

I must have appeared too somber. He gave me a double take. "What's going on? Aren't you thrilled with your pics?"

I took a deep breath and let it all out. When I'd brought him up to date on my "firing" by the Agency and poured out my anger about being dubbed a mole, he joined in me in outrage.

"Goddam it to hell, John," he scowled. "Something's wrong here. How did you find out?"

I told him.

"I don't believe this. I'm going to call..." and stopped short of a name. "I'm gonna look into it. After all the things you've done for them, something doesn't set right. My Gawd, you're as honest and patriotic a man as any I've ever known. You were in the Navy, like me. *And I am a patriot!*"

Mel, the kindest, most up-front man I'd ever known. Once a friend, always a friend.

"Let me see," he said, pursing his lips. "We're going to a dinner party Friday at a stockbroker's in Georgetown. The Director and his new wife will be there." He looked at his desk calendar. "I think I'll take the Director aside and chew on him a little. I'm willing to bet he knows nothing about this." Now that Mel had all the information, he'd go to work as only he could do. I'd bet good money that some serious questions would reach JJ's shop after Friday night.

No one liked being around JJ, because he reeked of tobacco, wheezed, gasped, coughed, and farted. To manage his emphysema, he toted a small oxygen bottle and plastic breathing tube in a sling around his neck. He was a mean-spirited guy, who, oddly enough, was an orchid specialist and worked in his greenhouse on special hybrids.

There was nothing to do in my war against Singleton and Co. but wait and see what happened from Mel's meeting with the Director.

--•--

THE BAHAMAS

According to Archie's office I was expected to continue my visits to Andrews and remain a contract physician, but now it was necessary that I log in and out each time at the guard gate. I got looks of concern from the hospital staff, and other surgeons mentioned rumors about my lifted security clearances. I had to clear my name and denounce the shitheads who'd sullied it.

I waited weeks for something to happen, for someone to call me. In the meantime, I took a few minor safety precautions. I wired up my Mews home with an alarm of sorts, a watchdog arrangement, just in case something nasty happened.

This might sound alarmist, but I wouldn't stand a chance against a pro. I hung tin cans on invisible fishing wire strung through the underbrush around my home. I'd used them in a Guatemalan jungle caper.

The first night, they jangled twice in the wee hours of the night. I used LL Bean night vision binoculars and spotted deer on the lawn the first time, but the next jangling was a mystery. *There was nothing to see.* I stayed up watching and listening, still nothing. Sleep became difficult. But with Hank Peters' weapon tucked under my pillow, I felt safer. I'd decided that if I saw anyone, I'd put a round over his head first, and shoot him if that didn't make him run.

— - • - —

By the following Wednesday, I hadn't heard from anyone and my hopes were fading. On a whim, I spread out a Virginia road map. Fairlie Farms was just a short drive from Washington Circle. I took off and easily found the main building, fronted by a circular drive. There were taxis, a few Lincoln town cars, one or two passenger cars and a security patrol Jeep, whose driver wore a sleeve patch with Fairlie superimposed on a green pine tree. I asked for directions to Mrs. Chatham's office.

"She 'specting you, sir?"

"Not sure," I lied. "My secretary may have called."

He activated his walkie-talkie. "Your name, sir?" I gave him my card. Another brief exchange. "Go right on up, sir. Her secretary will meet you."

I followed the road across a small, granite bridge spanning a fast-running brook, which emptied into a large lake. On its bank strolled Canada geese, coots, and assorted ducks. A stately Ward's heron stood impassively in the rushes, head down, waiting, and beyond him, on an overhanging branch, perched a little green heron.

I parked at an office building and presented my card to the receptionist at a desk inside.

"Is Mrs. Chatham expecting you?"

"I'm not sure," I lied again. "The guard told me to come on over. Please tell her that the doctor from Saigon is here. She'll know."

A few minutes later, a secretary emerged.

"Mrs. Chatham would be pleased to meet with you, sir."

I waited, and a slim woman strode out to greet me. She looked like a taller and slimmer version of Doris Day in beige linen slacks, a white blouse, tan cardigan, and tassled loafers. She wore the same bandeau across her hair.

"Doctor, how nice of you to visit." She came flat out and asked, "You mentioned Saigon. Did you know my sister?"

I hadn't expected such a forthright question.

"Yes, of course, Mrs. Chatham. Hasn't she told you?"

She was mum.

"We called her Gigi. I heard that she survived a plane crash, and went to Adventist in Bangkok. The pilot, Antoine Nicolai, was a good friend and I heard he survived, too. You're her closest kin. Is she here?" I reassured her. "I'm only here to pay a courtesy visit, wish your sister well."

I hoped for an honest response but she seemed pretty diffident. She pulled at her lip, considering. It was uncanny, staring at Gigi's twin, so like her, but a complete stranger.

I thought I'd finally come to terms with my fantasies about Gigi, as my memories had faded. Time, place, and distance often change circumstances. What was real in Saigon didn't seem quite the same here, but something kept me from completely severing that fine thread. I had a lingering curiosity. Who the hell was she, really?

Her sister digested all this, and led me into her lovely, Williamsburg-style home. I noticed it was done in early Colonial motif; the furniture appeared hand made, original and in beautiful condition. Her Turkomen carpets blended perfectly with the furniture and the room's warm colors. Touches of yellow here and there accentuated the light airiness of the rooms and there were bowls of wild flowers everywhere.

She waved me to a comfortable wingback chair. "The family name," she said, "was Smythe. I use my married name. Gigi's real name is Maeve, Maeve Smythe. As you know, Doctor, in her line of work, it's often necessary to use different names."

She said Maeve was recuperating in her guest quarters. Doctors estimated it would be months before she fully recovered from her injuries. It was clear that I would not see Maeve today, but she was alive and on the mend. I felt relieved.

"Mrs. Chatham, I knew your sister as Mrs. Prudhomme. Is there a Mr. Prudhomme?" *Nothing like being direct.*

She tossed her head back and chuckled. "Don't tell me you were interested in a *married* woman, Doctor?"

"Not exactly ma'am, I just wondered...if there was a Mr. Prudhomme around?

She laughed again. "No, there is no husband at the moment. It was just one of the names and situations she used. Being married helped stave off certain types, you follow?"

So it was a cover. But who was the pilot she was supposed to be married to? Guess that was all hokum too.

"Look, Doctor, why don't we do this? When she's feeling better, I'll arrange a little get-together, for old times' sake. Would that be agreeable?"

"Yes, certainly. That's very gracious of you." She sneaked a glance at her watch. Time for me to leave.

"I'm sorry to rush off like this, but I have a meeting at four. Thank you so much for coming by. It's been a pleasure to meet you." She walked me to the door. I left my card with telephone numbers in her silver salver, shook hands and left.

It had gone better than I'd expected. Her sister was downright friendly for an upper-class Virginian, once she'd sized me up.

As I backed my Beemer out, I had a fleeting glimpse of drapery movement from an upper window, just a flash of white. A shadowy figure behind translucent curtains moved quickly away. Someone had seen me. Was it Maeve? A tan Bentley convertible pulled in, driven by Jason Royce, tossing his long blond hair.

I stopped at the little lake to watch birds and review my brief meeting. Shirley Chatham looked like Gigi, now Maeve, and her mannerisms and responses, were similar. They shared the same ease of movement, a slinky sensuousness of limb. I had a momentary flashback of a slightly crazed woman dancing in front of me one dark Saigon night.

Maeve was alive. She needed time to heal her body and mind. Her reclusiveness was most likely post-traumatic withdrawal, an understandable reaction to a horrific jungle plane crash.

Haunting trauma. How many times had *I* awakened in the middle of the night with the image of Arif before me, that huge black hole in the end of his pistol staring at me, my heart racing, pulse hammering, body covered in sweat, still waiting for a big bang?

I could understand.

A Fairlie patrol car pulled alongside me. "Doctor," the friendly trooper boomed out, "Mrs. Chatham wondered whether you would mind going back up to the residence for a minute. She forgot something."

That was a surprise. "Yeah, sure. I can do that."

I knocked at the door again, and Shirley ushered me in again, gushing in her high-bred Virginia drawl. "Maeve has just awakened from her nap and was upset to learn you'd been here and left. I asked Officer Barr to see if he could catch you. Please come in."

As I walked in, the blond man stood wearing a friendly smile and held out his hand.

Late forties, maybe early fifties, he was in great shape, and from his weather-beaten aristocratic features, an outdoorsman.

"Doctor, Jason Royce. Pleased to meet you, sir. Just hearing 'bout you from Shirley, here. Understan' you know her sister." A statement, not a question.

"Yessir, nice to meet yew, too." I can slip into the local accent easily, a feature of my plastic personality. We looked each other over cautiously, like two smiling fencers.

Shirley fluttered around until a white-jacketed young man brought out a tray of drink fixings. "Can I offer you something, Doctor?" It was early afternoon and I was driving, so I settled for iced tea. Royce was already pouring his Virginia Gentleman. Then, as if on cue, in waltzed the Maeve! Her wafting "lemony" scent alerted me.

I got a mild shock. It was the Gigi I knew, all right, but she was changed. Her hair was trimmed like her sister's, but more severely, probably from hospital snipping prior to scalp stitching. A few red scars remained clearly visible.

At the sight of her, my mind went into instant overdrive; all the intense feelings and emotions popped into focus. Was this the woman I'd been deeply involved with, half a world away? I became aware, with crystal clarity, that all my gut-wrenching lust for her was gone. And the worry over her fate had lifted from my shoulders. I was relieved on both counts.

I knew this lovely creature before me, but I knew her as Gigi, many months ago in Saigon. She was different in a new setting and she was no longer playing a role.

"It's good to see you, Maeve."

"You too," she grinned and looked genuinely happy to see me.

"I heard you had an accident with Antoine. They told me you were killed. Sully, too." I said softly. "What happened?"

"I'll never be sure, John, but Antoine is certain someone was out to get him, or Sully or all three of us. Elements from the North? Who knows? We all had baggage. He's convinced that sugar was poured into the fuel tank and gummed up the carburetor. We lost power and went down. Antoine put us into a glide through some small trees, then we smacked into some muddy ground. Antoine says that mud, *karst,* saved us." She looked away and her voice quavered. "We lost

François, John. His neck was broken on impact." A quiet tear slipped down her cheek and she wiped it away. "At least he didn't suffer." Her chest heaved and I moved quickly to change tack.

She looked so fragile, I wanted to take her in my arms, but we weren't alone.

"I'm glad to see you looking so well," I jumped in. "You've trimmed your hair."

Her hand flew to her crooked blonde bob and she smiled. "I got these cuts in my scalp, and the Adventist doctors had to trim my hair to stitch it up. When I got back, Shirley decided that we should match."

She glanced at her sister, they both giggled and the tension was broken. She pointed to a cock-up splint on her left forearm, which meant a Colles' fracture of her wrist, and wiggled her fingers, "I still have some pain in my wrist, but it's gotten much better."

The rest of the conversation was lighter, easier. Maeve planned to recuperate at her sister's home and then move into one of the small cottages nearby. Eventually, she'd join the Foundation administrative faculty. She had a Master's in International Studies and wanted to get back to work. She would take this new position slowly. Things were going well. I promised to return for dinner or a conference sometime, but it was idle chatter. Everyone in that room knew that our paths would not likely cross again.

But I left happier and relieved. Seeing Maeve alive, well and in good spirits was reassuring after I'd come so close to giving up on her.

— - • - —

I TURNED MY ATTENTION BACK to my immediate priority; dealing with JJ and his bastards. On Monday, Mel left a message to call him and follow up on his crucial Friday night dinner party.

"I think I hit some tender nerves the other night, John. No names, but I've been speaking with someone who can take care of your problem."

"Yeah, Mel. How did it go?"

"Well, I took him aside and brought up your problem. I told him how you work with us, and how you'd gotten into some scrapes helping *his* friends, and that now *those* friends want to hang you. At first he got sore at me for bringing up business at a dinner party, but I reminded him how my people have always helped whenever he's asked. He asked for your name and I wrote it on my card. He stuffed it in his pocket and nodded. I told him firmly that I expected him to fix it. He promised he'd see to it personally and get back to me. I know the guy, John, we sail together. He'll do it. We just gotta wait."

Before I had a chance to answer, he added, "By the way, you better come over next week and look at the dummy proofs of the Egypt article. Your pictures fit in just fine." With that he signed off.

Having friends in high places *does* help. He was right, I *had* given my services to the Agency, so dammit, I was entitled to more than just a kiss-off. I was no fucking mole!

I focused the following weeks on surgeries, meetings and routine business, enlivened by an occasional evening or two with Katerina, the green-eyed sorceress.

She sometimes took me to Arlington bars I'd never heard of, packed with Brazilians. The drinks and food were uniquely exotic. One of those alcoholic concoctions was about all I could handle, but once in a while, after one or two of those crazy mixes of rum, coconut milk, lime juice and Gawd knew what else, Katerina would get cranked up. I had to struggle to stay alert and *functional* with her, because she became very demanding as the evenings wore on.

-- • --

THE NEXT WHITE HOUSE VISIT was unremarkable; I did a perfunctory review of the Great Patient's medical records. There had been no change in his X-rays, his situation or health. I was fully prepared to hear that I was dismissed from the whole project, since there was no hint of any medical problem, or that my clearance had been pulled. I expected the worst.

As I was leaving the clinic, a Navy corpsman ushered in a presidential staff speechwriter, Mortimer Busby. The Great One's secretary had sent him down.

Busby, a pleasant rotund Texan, was suffering from an advanced case of heartburn. I gave him two tablets of Alka-Seltzer and a gulp of Pepto-Bismol to produce instant relief and profuse thanks. I was surprised he didn't know that remedy.

"Sounds like you really know your stuff, Doc," he gushed. The corpsman grinned. "Tell you what, Ah'm gonna invite you to the next Texas barbecue as my official guest. Be sure you got those pills with you. That chili can hit yore gut hard." He got my name, shook hands and left.

-- • --

THREE WEEKS AFTER MEL'S "CHAT," and I began to fidget about hearing from the director. But I was happy to learn that my photos had been tucked nicely into the Egypt article. Mel reassured me that they were still working on my Southeast Asia pictures layout, too. Having *any* of my pictures considered for publication was an honor. I was proud.

Finally, Mrs. Ghormley got the call and booked me a ten o'clock appointment at the Mayflower Hotel with some friends of Mr. Grosvenor's, Mr. Slatkin and Mr. Casey. *This was the call I'd awaited.*

Nice names. Damn right I'd be there. But I was cautious. I suspected it would be nothing more than a *check him out* session. The Mayflower was a public place and at best it would be a grilling or a Q and A session.

At ten minutes before ten, I parked my car in the *Geographic* basement, left via the back ramp, and crossed the street to the Mayflower back entrance. In the dining room, a maitre d' ushered me to a back table.

Both men were seated with their backs to the wall, leaving me to face them. I chose to sit at the right corner just to disconcert them. They could ping-pong me if I sat facing them and I wasn't going to play their game.

But it was all smiles from the beginning. When they saw me enter, they rose to shake hands and exchange cards.

Their cards were interesting. I looked at Casey: "What's the Q stand for, Mr. Casey?"

"Quentin," he flashed a toothy smile. "It's Irish."

That sounded genuine.

Bernard L. Slatkin was an assistant counsel at the Department of Defense, pure baloney. It was the Agency. Mr. Casey's card sported a large Philadelphia law firm. I bought that.

I gave them a quick once-over. Casey was tall, gangly, and had a little gray in his sandy-red hair that scraggled around protruding ears. His long face stretched upward onto a high forehead. He wore wire-rimmed glasses, an expensive dark suit, white shirt and a conservative repp tie.

Slatkin was stocky, with deep-set black eyes and dark curly hair that was beginning to bald. He, too, wore a dark suit. They made an impressive pair.

Obviously they had worked together as Mr. Inside and Mr. Outside to settle manpower problems. My problem had been assigned to them with instructions to get it fixed, I was sure. I had the feeling they wanted the facts.

I gave them an innocent smile. "Gentlemen, what can I do for you?"

"Doctor, I understand you're a friend of Mr. Grosvenor."

I nodded. They expected an answer, but I said nothing.

Casey tried again: "Doctor, you've got some powerful friends in high places."

"I guess at some point in life, we all make some interesting connections," I said. "If you do good things for others, it's sometimes rewarding." I wanted to quit playing games. "Let's cut to the chase. We both know Mr. Grosvenor has spoken to your director about my problem. For whatever reason, JJ Singleton's shop has declared me a mole, and as a result, the CIA is fucking up my life and my career. My security clearances have been pulled and I'm probably under suspicion as a potential traitor, and this is a superb screw-up. I want it corrected immediately, because I am not now, nor ever will be anything other than a loyal American. And let me add that if it doesn't get done soon, I plan to go to the courts and the press. I am a seriously angry man."

I was close to ballistic, but reigned myself in and forced a smile.

Slatkin said smoothly, "Yes, Doctor, we've reviewed your extensive record. You've done some very good work and I think we may have found the problem."

He continued, "Do you remember being asked if you had any relatives in Soviet Armenia? You answered, probably, but you had no knowledge of them. Then you were asked if you had ever met with any persons who might have been relatives, and you said you might have, but not with any sure knowledge of that. Why didn't you just say no? Don't you think you sounded evasive, answering that way?"

So that was it. They thought I had been evasive in my answers. How stupid.

"You can't be serious."

"Well, Doctor, we are reporting to you that they considered your answers very evasive."

"Why the hell didn't they come back and ask me directly?"

"Very good point, Doctor. In retrospect, this could have been avoided if they had. But if you were a mole, that would have been a tip-off, and you'd have gone to ground."

"Do you fellows really believe that explanation?"

Casey answered. "It is a bit weak, Doctor, and we see your point. We are not in a position to believe or disbelieve an explanation. We are just here to put all the facts together. I hope things will seem a bit brighter for you. Yes, I agree they should have re-questioned you and ordered a polygraph. An oversight on someone's part. I suspect it was easier just to dump you. No offense, but you were expendable."

Slatkin shifted in his chair. "When your powerful friend interceded on your behalf, we were charged with doing a complete review of everything in your files. That is what we are doing."

Casey opened a file. "Your adventures, flitting in and out of danger zones, blithely cavorting around in the Soviet community in these times, when even legitimate reporters are harassed, evoke suspicion and a certain amount of envy from certain sources. You understand.

THE BAHAMAS

With your ethnic background and foreign contacts, you're not just some nobody. How can we best arrive at a happy outcome for all concerned?"

This guy Casey was sharp. *What the hell did I want? For starters, I wanted to be back in the fold and get my clearances back.*

"First off, I want to identify exactly who made the decision to can me, and on what basis they viewed me as a potential traitor." I was serious. "Conduct an independent review and ask some other security organization, for example, the National Security Agency or the Defense Intelligence Agency, or a private independent arbiter. This is what we doctors do when working to diagnose a problem case. We get another opinion. Subject me to a polygraph, if that's still a concern. Let's see what comes from all that." I had to be reasonable and frank. "I want to clear my name and get my clearances back."

Casey was making notes as I spelled out my wishes, but strangely, without taking his eyes off me. That takes training. He was reading me as I spouted off, and I was impressed. This guy was good. Did my irises constrict? Dilate?

Slatkin was just taking notes. I had the feeling he was listening to my voice while Casey read my facial expressions and the eyes. Both were probably searching my behavior for hints that I was hiding something. I had no illusions I'd get an immediate answer. This was a quick interview and on-the-spot character analysis. They'd complete their evaluation and report back to whoever tasked them. An independent review would have to find in my favor. That was the only scenario that made sense. I had to hope things went my way.

I had a hunch Casey believed me. But in the final analysis, knowing that a highly placed individual was concerned enough about my squawks to send this team boosted my spirits. On the other hand, maybe I was the sort of person the Agency would never understand and would always be viewed with suspicion. I just hoped someone with brains and common sense would work it out.

Casey and Slatkin stopped taking notes, but they seemed to be waiting, a form of silent questioning. *Let's see what this guy says.* They looked at me benignly. I could play that game, so I smiled back as the waiter arrived with fresh coffee.

"Well, gentlemen, you've heard my suggestions. Where are we?"

"We pretty much covered all the bases, right?" Casey asked and Slatkin nodded. "So, in light of our discussion, we'll pass on our recommendations and suggest they be acted upon as soon as possible. That pretty much wraps things up."

Slatkin added, "I wouldn't say anything about our meeting to anyone. Even those with whom you've already discussed it. It wouldn't be useful."

What the hell did that mean? Was it a threat?

"One last thing," continued Slatkin. "We were also given some bizarre information that you'd threatened an agency medical colleague? That kind of thing usually goes to internal security or to the police. Do you have any comment?"

They must have talked to Gerard. I had no comment, so I just shrugged my shoulders. That seemed to satisfy them.

Casey said, "Then we'll dismiss that information without prejudice." Sounded like a judge, which he may have been.

"Thank you for your time and candid discussion. It's been a pleasure."

We rose, shook hands and they left. The check must have been paid, so I finished my coffee. Nothing to do now but wait.

— - • - —

WAITING MADE ME HUNKER DOWN in my routine at the hospital and at home. My place was at the end of a long, tree-lined lane in a heavily wooded area. Shady in the day, spooky at night. Deer, owls, raccoons, foxes, and other critters regularly paraded by my windows. Deliverymen had trouble finding the house. The Mews in McLean is a small colony of lovely homes, spacious lawns, and narrow winding roads, situated uncomfortably close to the headquarters of the CIA. Few neighbors socialized together or knew each other well. It was a mobile population that changed often and contained few families with children. The inhabitants of my odd neighborhood might be lawyers, doctors, executives, or even spies. Who knew? They all had plausible covers and lived in houses like heavily guarded bunkers. I liked the isolation, but word got out that I was a doctor, and they didn't hesitate a damn minute to knock on my door.

I hired Rashid, a Pakistani graduate student at Northern Virginia, to help keep the place up during my frequent absences. He drove a motorcycle, made a mean lamb curry, and had a charming British accent, to boot.

A few days after my meeting with the Agency lawyers, Rashid telephoned me. He had been cleaning windows that morning and watched as a white van came slowly up my driveway then stopped. A man wearing a white hard hat and workman's clothes stepped out and looked at the phone lines which led to the house. The truck door read "C and P Telephone Company" and had Virginia plates. Rashid had opened the door and asked hardhat what he was doing. He mumbled something about checking damaged phone lines and quickly drove off. Nothing wrong with the lines. Rashid climbed each pole looking for little black boxes. Nothing.

Our comings and goings were erratic and Rashid's bike was unseen in the garage. We suspected someone was tapping my line and I hoped that my house and phones were not bugged. I wondered if someone, somewhere, was getting nosy. That suited me fine. I was clean, and always had been. Nevertheless, I stuck a feather in the drawer, a feather on the doorjamb, and fine, dark threads in the doorways, just to know if anyone was snooping while I waited.

CHAPTER 38

General Archie S. Koffman

Archie had been back at Andrews for several days before he phoned. "Hey," he gurgled into the phone. "I got some frozen fish for you."

"No kidding, Archie. That's mighty thoughtful of you. What kind?"

"Arctic char, ya heard of it?"

"Yeah, sure, first cousin to salmon, right?"

"Right, smart guy. When you coming out here again? I got it here in the hospital freezer. Brought back sixty pounds for me, and LeMay brought back enough to last him all winter. Mighty tasty and it's good for you." He didn't mention that the legal limit to bring home was forty pounds, but he probably didn't have to be concerned. I doubted that Customs ever bothered them at either end. They flew from American soil to American soil in General LeMay's plane, so why would they?

"Better for you than lox and bagels. Archie, I need to talk to you about a problem, then we'll talk about your leg, sound good?" I had to move ahead, no matter what.

"Yeah sure. Come see me early on your regular rounds day, okay?"

So I did, and when I poured out my concerns, he promised to keep his mouth shut, unless I told him otherwise. I told him about

Gunner and a massive fuck-up at the Agency, and that I fell victim to the fallout.

I reassured Archie that if he went to his buddy LeMay to ask for help, no matter what the outcome, I'd still operate on his leg, whenever he wanted. I left him considering his unlit cigar.

Not surprisingly, Archie called the next morning. I'd just finished a bronchoscopy and was washing off my face and glasses. Most of the coughed-up stuff had gone all over my protective shield and mask, but some always gets on you. When it's TB, you really have to wash up.

"Jawn, Archie."

"Good morning, General."

"Jawn, lissen up. I talked to Curt about you. He said he'd do what he could, but only because of me, Archie. Ya hear me Jawn? Don't forget it. He wants this Air Force Base Hospital to stay on top, and I told him that without you, we'd go down, and Reed would take our patients. Ya follow me?"

"Loud and clear, Archie."

"He said that half those spooks at the Agency and NSA are former military, and the ones in the highest spots used to be Generals or Admirals. He knows most of 'em personally. Ya gotta remember, Jawn, LeMay did some low-level flying over Japan that took real guts, and the big guys don't forget. They listen to Curt. Anyway, he pulled in some chits and told them it was for the good of national security and more bullshit, even though it was true, you unnerstan', Jawn, donchoo? They promised him they'd look into it and do something. That's the best I can do. Howzat grab you?"

I was elated. "Don't know how to thank you, Archie."

"Yeah well, here's how you can start. When can you do my leg?"

When did we last do an arteriogram?"

"Two years ago."

"We gotta get a new one."

"Then what?"

"Tell you what. You decide when you want the operation. I'll check you into GW as A. Koffman. We leave off the doctor and military mumbo and you can file Champus for the hospital payments.

The medical reports that would ordinarily go on your chart will come with me, and I'll hand them to you. What you do with them is your business. I don't want to know. Are we straight?"

"Yep. Figgered you'd do something honest like that."

Ten days later Archie was admitted to GW Hospital. We did an arteriogram under local anesthesia in X-ray. The radiologist slipped a needle into his right femoral artery at the groin crease. We chose to do the right leg first because it tired more easily than the left. Archie grunted when the contrast was squirted; it smarts, but when the films came out we could both see his blockage dead smack in the middle of the femoral artery. Fixing it would be a piece of cake. I'd bypass the block.

I operated on him the next day under epidural anesthesia. A generous squirt of a local anesthetic in between the vertebrae just outside the spinal canal, some sedation, and Archie began flirting with the female anesthesiologist while I waited for the nurses to paint and drape his leg. I felt more tense than usual, but I was a professional and ignored my nerves. He was just a patient needing my services.

When the superficial femoral artery develops a blockage, as Archie's had done, the blood finds a detour, in this case, the *profunda femoris* artery carries enough blood to keep the leg viable. I planned to remove a piece of his own saphenous vein from an incision in the groin and use it to help detour the block. We used warm saline containing heparin and xylocaine to stop muscle fibers from clamping down and stopping blood flow, and he got a bolus of heparin intravenously to protect him from clotting and to give us a bloodless field to work in. Rapidly, my assistants and I reversed the vein and hooked it into the upper artery, with the upper portion going into the lower artery. Using very fine 6-0 monofilament sutures, we sewed the open end of the vein to the opened artery walls, briefly let blood pump through, and moved to the lower end to repeat the process. Archie was fixed, at least for now.

He was back at his desk in a week. Except for a slight limp, he was doing well, but I knew the other leg would start cramping as soon as he got back up to speed. I'd deal with that surgery when it became necessary, too.

I wasn't too surprised when I received a phone call from Bernie Slatkin several weeks after Archie's call to General LeMay.

"Doctor? Bernie Slatkin here."

"Yessir, nice to hear from you."

"Doctor, you know the Metropolitan Club?"

"Yessir, I do."

"Can we meet for lunch sometime this week?"

"With pleasure," I responded. We arranged to meet a few days later at the tony Metropolitan Club. What he had to tell me came as no surprise.

He would not confirm that either he or Casey represented any agency of the U.S. government, but after listening to my concerns, he and Mr. Casey felt that a serious injustice had taken place. There had been some misinterpretations that had led to erroneous conclusions. My problem had been reviewed by an ombudsman in their organization. *There must have been an impartial review, and that sounded good.*

Bottom line, I'd been considered tainted because I had associated with someone suspicious in an embassy and ended up temporarily quarantined until matters could be put in order. My situation had been unfortunate, but necessary, and would have been straightened out eventually. Strong concerns that my absence would be a serious detriment to a government department had been voiced and my case considered ahead of others.

"Does that mean I've been cleared?"

Big smile. "That would be my take, Doctor."

Yahoo!

I hardly tasted the rest of the food. I was doing mental handsprings. *Whee. It sure sounded like I was gonna be normal again.*

Being restored was a funny sensation. It had no more impact on me than, say driving from DC to Virginia. No bumps in the road where signs read "Welcome to Virginia." There was no great change in the atmosphere, just one big mental sigh of relief. The defeat I'd first felt enhanced my present relief of mind and spirit. The system had worked after all, but needed a good goosing to get started.

— - • - —

ARCHIE HAD RETURNED TO WORK part-time. His appetite got back to normal, and his everpresent, unlit cigar was still firmly clamped in his teeth. But now the opposite leg was beginning to cramp slightly. His repaired leg stopped cramping, so he was walking faster and longer. He then developed opposite leg pain; the medical term is claudicating. My biggest fear was he'd get his heart pumping too hard and develop angina, not uncommon in these artery cases. I planned to counsel him and keep an eye on his case.

I was back to square one with the Air Force. It was as though nothing had happened. One by one, various agencies that had dropped me from their schedules called to reschedule visits. Interestingly, no word from the Agency outpatient clinic, which was fine since I had never fancied myself as anything other than an occasional expendable consultant. So in a sense I was clean again.

— - • - —

SUMMER WAS NEARLY GONE. It was coming up Fall in McLean. Squirrels were hiding acorns, roses bloomed again, grass needed less attention, and it was time to lay in firewood and think of the coming snow-clogged lanes. I thought of Tom Black's condo and wished for a month in the Caribbean. Maybe I'd slip down for another long weekend with Katerina. The sun brought out the best in her. Although we got along fine for a weekend, longer would be too much.

Academically and professionally, life was returning to a satisfying state. Several months had passed since the trip to Southeast Asia. Now it was just a memory that I pulled up in quiet moments. Dooley, Antoine, Gigi...all those names are etched indelibly in my mind. I'd never forget the unbelievable times I'd had with them.

For the next month, I trudged along familiar, boring paths, like a pitiful mule on a treadmill, moving, but going nowhere. My Laos photographs were published in the Geographic along with some stock photos to round out the story. I basked briefly in a secret glow of personal satisfaction. I'd accomplished something in a different field! Something outside my medical envelope. And my Egypt photos were now being readied for the public eye. Things were improving, but I was still hanging onto unfinished business regarding Gigi, now Maeve.

She would always be Gigi to me. I'd thought she had slipped into a distant memory, but she was alive and here. Did I feel the urge to see her? Her sister had mentioned a dinner, so I waited to see what came of it. I made no effort to contact her and her sister might forget. Was she the same woman who had so shocked me with her exotic seduction? Had it all been an act or was some piece of her affection genuine? If I had the chance, I wanted to ask her.

Lusting after Gigi was a thing of the past. She was history and a bittersweet memory. I didn't need a phantom Gigi, especially with Katerina flitting in and out of focus in my current life. If the dinner invitation came, I'd go and follow up on these feelings; if not, time would take care of things.

—-•—-

ONE SUNNY SATURDAY, KATERINA CALLED, sounding serious, and announced that she was driving out for a visit.

She showed up dressed casually, but expensively, in a tightly fitted blouse, a pale lavender cardigan, and wrap-around belt over designer jeans. She mentioned, extremely casually, that she was going home to Brazil for an extended Thanksgiving holiday to visit her family. She let it slip that one of the nice men she'd met at our neighborhood swim parties was stationed at the Embassy there. She suggested a farewell dinner in McLean village, so we went out for Italian, after which I said goodbye and sent Katerina home pouting, at the diplomatically correct hour of 10 p.m.

CHAPTER 39

London Calling—It's Mandy

A WEEK LATER, I WAS TOTALLY UNPREPARED FOR A TELEPHONE CALL FROM Mandy Conant in London.

"It's been a while, John. How are you?" We exchanged pleasantries and she asked about my current situation. We had last met in Cairo and she was now calling from her London base. "So, you're settled in Washington DC? Will you be there for the next fortnight?"

"Yes," I replied.

"Oh, good! Would it be possible to meet? I'm coming to Washington with my senior investigator, Dr. Oberhoffer, to visit the National Science Foundation and the people at *National Geographic*."

"Yes, of course."

"Great. I'll call before leaving to arrange a suitable place and time, okay?"

"Okay. And, Mandy? Can you stop by Harrod's and bring me a tin of Lapsang Souchong tea?"

"That's a dreadfully strong tea. You sure you want that?"

"Yes, absolutely, it's my favorite. I'll be in your debt forever," I said chuckling.

--•--

LONDON CALLING—IT'S MANDY

A WEEK LATER MANDY AND her troupe arrived in Washington. We met at the Jefferson hotel for lunch. We were off to a great start; she brought my tea! I was curious about what she might really want.

Mandy was good looking in a conservative way, like a librarian without makeup.

She had a slim appealing figure. The nice thing about her was that in a conservative way, she nevertheless held liberal views on life and matters in general. Like most smart women, she had strong opinions, and one had to be careful not to set her off in a verbal tirade. We started a polite conversation that brought to mind the party on Gezira, when suddenly, she turned the discussion to her field and asked me if I'd ever heard of an ancient Egyptian named Imhotep?

Maybe I had. I had a vague memory that he was some revered person in the same league as Hippocrates. He had something to do with pyramids and medicine, but it was sketchy. An architect doctor of sorts. I'd never given him much thought. Where was this going?

She said she had some serious thoughts and interesting photos to show me after lunch. We took our coffee to an empty table in the lobby. She hefted her large shoulderbag onto the table and pulled out two objects that looked like small clay flowerpots covered with linen cloth and embroidered all over with green birds and some kind of glyph writing.

She asked in a low voice, "You have any idea what these are?"

I hadn't a clue.

"These are clay pots. Inside each is a stuffed Nile Ibis, the sacred bird of the Egyptians. Thousands of Egyptians placed them in underground chambers as a votive offering to Imhotep. You see, Imhotep was many things, but he was best known as the father of medicine to the ancient Egyptians. Kings and Queens revered him. He was the architect of the Pyramid of Zoser; he was a priest, an architect, astronomer, even a magician, and revered by one and all."

What was she was driving at?

"You see," she went on, "everyone thinks he was buried at Saqqara near Memphis, which is just down the road from Cairo on the other side of the Nile. Archaeologists looking for his tomb have found numerous passageways under the desert there. The Brits, especially a chap named Smith and his crew, have been digging there for years, but they haven't found anything, not the tomb of Imhotep, or any other tomb. What they found were underground chambers full of pots like these, each containing a stuffed bird. Thousands of them."

"Really?" I asked, trying to sound intrigued.

"So, *we've* been looking for someone else, a different Egyptian, at a site far away from Saqqara on the shores of the Nile. And I found *one of these pots* in an underground passageway. Here, I'll show you on a map. We don't even know who we're looking for at this site, but we have unmistakable evidence that we're close to finding a tomb." Her low voice became reverential. "It could be Imhotep's. This votive offering is an Imhotep tradition! Isn't that exciting?" Her eyes glowed.

I was beginning to wonder if this sweet girl was, well, a wacko. How could they be looking for someone, but didn't know who? At first hearing, it sounded like a lot of wasted money had poured into Egypt.

I said, "Seems like if you found pots with stuffed birds in underground passageways, and they are offerings to Imhotep, then Imhotep should be buried somewhere close. Right? Did you find any other corroborating evidence?"

"Yes, we did. One of the workers showed me what might have been a midden pile, a trash dump. There were several very old skeletons. Most showed evidence of damage, fractures, arthritis, that sort of thing, and discarded pieces of clothing. There were pieces of basalt stone shaped into carving tools, yards of hemp, broken pots, and these votive pots, three of them. Two are damaged badly, one is broken, but the inside is intact. This pile had been buried deep in desert sand. But after a recent sandstorm blew the sand cover off, my man Kharpet chanced on them.

"So you see," she said conspiratorially, "these are the same bird pots as those from Saqqara, and the hieroglyphs on the embroidery confirm an offering to Imhotep. Why would offerings to him be so far away from his pyramid in Saqqara? That's what's so puzzling. One explanation is that Imhotep wanted to be buried at this unlikely site, miles away, hoping to dupe looters. He knew that graves were robbed as soon as the mighty were buried and could have tried to outfox them. How's that sound?"

Why ask me?

"I can't help you, Mandy, I know nothing about Imhotep or any of those ancients. You said *one* of these pots came from your dig site by the Nile, right? So where did the other one come from?"

"Saqqara."

"How did you manage that? They're a long way apart."

"My houseman, Kharpet, used to work at Saqqara. He was able to get a few for me to compare. Acting strictly on the basis of confirming our research findings."

I didn't believe her for one minute. They had been swiped, probably right from under the Brits' noses.

She continued with a tiny smile: "Oh, but you *can* help me. You told me that you knew Dr. Wetmore at the Smithsonian during my Cairo visit. Remember?"

"Faintly."

"Can I coax you into taking these pots to him? I have some extra bird bones found in the passageways for him, as a gift. And we could ask him what he thinks. I need to make sure they are both are the same, that both are Nile Ibis."

I was mulling this over when it suddenly dawned on me. "Wait a damn minute," I said. "How the hell did you get these things out of Egypt? I have a feeling the Egyptians wouldn't be happy about this."

Mandy showed some mettle. "Oh stop fussing," she said. "We archaeologists do this sort of thing all the time. Especially for museums."

"You sneaked them out of Egypt and into the States? You're probably guilty of a dozen Customs violations, you know that? Isn't it against the law?" I shook my head. "Okay, I'll contact a buddy of mine, Dr. George Watson, who works with Wetmore. He's a bird man. We'll see what he thinks."

We met Watson at the Smithsonian the following day. When Mandy showed him the bones and the pots, his eyebrows shot straight up. "Sweet Jesus," he moaned, "How did you get these here? These are sacred votive pots. I've read about them."

"George," I said through clenched teeth. "Unless you start blabbing about this, nobody will know anything about these pots. Please, just look at the bones and keep your voice down."

Mandy looked concerned.

Watson said, "I think these are the bones of a Sacred Nile Ibis, but let's ask Dr. Wetmore."

George phoned Dr. Wetmore from his desk and explained in hushed tones what he had before him. *Come right up*, came the answer.

Dr. Alexander Wetmore was the bird man's bird man, head of Ornithology at the Smithsonian and a highly respected authority. He had identified bones from X-rays of a prehistoric fossilized ostrich egg, inside which were fossil remains of the chick. He was that good.

Dr. Watson led us up some back stairs into Dr. Wetmore's airy office, which was cluttered with stuffed birds, tagged bird wings, and piles of birds waiting for classification. Off to one side, a huge stuffed owl on a roost stared at intruders. When Wetmore gazed at you through his rimless glasses, he bore a slight resemblance.

His office had a musty smell mixed with whiffs of formaldehyde. He asked, smiling, "What do we have here, George?" He was not a pretentious man; he could have been an Iowa farmer looking at an ear of corn.

George handed over the bones and pots.

"Yes, I see." He gave them a careful going over. No one said a word. Finally, he said, "Yes, these are Ibis all right. You say Egypt? The pots have the Ibis embroidered on their cloth covers. I'd have to say it's the Nile Ibis. I won't ask you how you got them." His eyes twinkled. "But we don't have any in our collection yet, do we, George?"

In low strangled tones, "No sir, not yet."

Mandy got the message, loud and clear.

"Well, if you folks will excuse me, I have things to get together for my trip to Panama. Going for the dickie-bird migration. I'm leaving Dr. Watson to mind the store. Nice meeting you." He rose and strode out. I noticed boxes, camping gear and camera equipment piled along the wall stenciled: *Wetmore, Smithsonian*.

We thanked them and left. Mandy left her card and a few Ibis bones on Wetmore's desk, but retained the two pots. As we said our goodbyes, Mandy thrust the two pots at him. Surprised, Watson reflexively took them.

"Keep them. They're yours," she said. "There're plenty more where they came from. I don't plan on taking them back." We left a grateful Watson and drove off.

I drove toward Chez Lilliane, a quiet restaurant on 30th Street in Georgetown. We found a table on the veranda and started with iced tea. I ordered onion soup and a Salad Nicoise for us both.

"I have another surprise," Mandy said. "On our large house boat, I have a small laboratory for chemical testing. I can also use it for developing and printing film, but only black and white. You really ought to come visit. I guarantee you won't be bored."

"Hmm. I'll take it under advisement."

The soup arrived with just the right amount of garlic and sherry mix.

She continued. "And something else happened recently, too. I saw a dead Chinese fellow washed up on a sandbar beach near the houseboat," she said, matter of factly.

"Huh?" I spilled my soup back into the bowl. "You saw what?"

"I know, it sounds strange, but I was shown this dead man on the beach, so I photographed him. He looked Asian, I thought perhaps Chinese. I knew he was dead; he'd washed up on the beach and was partly covered with sand. It hadn't been that long. He hadn't begun to swell or decompose, so it had to have been a day or two at most. I took color and black and white and brought along some prints to show you. I'm afraid no one will believe me, and somehow I thought you might."

She pulled some five by seven glossy prints from an envelope. I stared at the pictures. They showed a husky man, eyes closed, lying face up on sand. Water was lapping around him. His upper body was naked above skintight pants, probably part of a wet suit. One foot was bare; the other still had a flipper. Five prints taken at various angles. Behind the dead guy and up from the sloping beach, I could see the base of a cliff, with shadowed crevices and large blocks of stone. At the edge of the print, there appeared to be a cave opening.

The dead man had slanted eyes with a distinct epicanthic fold and high cheekbones. His well-developed torso tapered to a firm abdomen and slim waist. I looked at the first print more closely. There was a contusion on the side of his head, just anterior to and above his left ear. His head was hit hard, perhaps knocked unconscious while in the water, which suggested drowning.

This was amazing in every respect. A Chinese man washed up on a sandy beach in the Nile. What were the statistical chances of that happening?

"Okay, Mandy, starting from the top, try to remember everything about this episode. I'll make notes while you talk. Finish your soup first, the salad's already cold."

Mandy wiped her mouth, took a deep breath and started. I scribbled notes on the back of my menu. I was *debriefing* her, since no one else knew what I was about to learn.

Mandy had been in the houseboat stern workshop cleaning pottery shards from an earlier find. The windows were open to a fresh, cool breeze. She heard one of the dinghies motoring up alongside. The boat boy, Kharpet, who ran the boat and did household chores, came running in excitedly. He had something to tell the lady. "Yes, what is it?"

Kharpet was just out of his teens and not used to Americans. He blurted that he had seen a dead body washed up on the sandbar near Qasr Ibrim. It didn't look like an Egyptian who'd fallen off a caique or a small dhow, because the body was dressed strangely. It was floating there on the sandbank because the crocodiles had not found it yet.

"What was Kharpet doing at the sandbank?"

She recounted their conversation for me.

"Catching fish for dinner. Much good river perches, Madam. Cook told me not to come back without many fish in my basket."

"Did you catch many fish?"

"Yes, Madam, I did."

"And when did you see this body?"

"Today. The lower end of the sandbar curves and is always good place for fishing. I saw this body half in water and half in sand. It was not there yesterday. You are the only one I can speak with. You would know what to do."

Mandy puzzled; what could she do? Not much. But she went with Kharpet to see for herself. She was nervous. Looking at a recent death was quite different from studying a mummy, which didn't make her at all squeamish. She took two cameras and film and set off in the small boat with Kharpet.

It was a short distance. Directly northeast of the houseboat, about six miles distant, was a large sandbar, three hundred yards long and slightly elevated, even at high tide, with a few shrubs and a large boulder in the center, and tapering off on either side. At low tide, a few crocs crawled up to sun, otherwise, only birds and fishermen ever stopped there. They beached the boat and Kharpet led her to the body. Mandy had seen many bodies, but never anyone recently killed. She was struck by his crew cut, almond-shaped eyes and robust military appearance. It was stiff and blistered, so it had been more than six hours. The man wore a wetsuit, a flipper on one foot, and had scratches and bruises on his torso and arms. There were several diagonal slashes across his abdomen. She photographed everything, including a close-up of a small Chinese ideogram tattooed on his forearm, also slashed diagonally.

Not sure what to do, Mandy told Kharpet to get some men to move the body somewhere away from the crocodiles. They carried it to an abandoned Nubian home and put it in a dark room, covered with layers of eucalyptus leaves to dry out in the heat.

Mandy puzzled over this weird finding. Why would a Chinese man wash up in the middle of the Nile, far from everything? There was one other houseboat on the river, a Polish expedition, but she knew of no one else in the area. She developed the black and white film and saved the color cartridge to bring with her.

"Who else knows all this?"

"I told Dr. Dutta, but he wasn't interested. Thought the man probably fell from a river boat between Aswan and Khartoum. I haven't told anyone else."

"Why me?"

"I didn't know anyone else who'd done any exploring. And you're a doctor who must have seen dead bodies. I thought you might have some ideas."

That was flattering.

"Mind if I keep these prints?"

"Sure, I have another set and the negatives on board. I catalogue lots of pottery and tomb artifacts with photos."

Mandy left to meet the *National Geographic* research people to update them on the Egyptian expedition findings. Something in the photos had me thinking. I wanted to look at them more closely, maybe enlarge a few.

--•--

THE FOLLOWING WEEKEND, I ATTENDED a small noisy neighborhood party full of attractive ladies and smart-looking men, drinking and smoking. I convinced myself I fit right in.

I grabbed a mild gin and tonic at the bar and lazily checked out the talent. The women were dressed to the teeth, flashing gold and sparklers, but most were married or there was an attentive male nearby. There was no one for me to ogle too closely, so I went for the food. A nicely catered affair. Piles of fruit, veggies, spreads and chilled shrimp, my choicest delicacy. I quietly attacked the shrimp, hoping it went unnoticed.

I knew no one but the hosts, and the others all knew each other, which made me odd man out, so I tackled another plate of shrimp.

"I see you like shrimp."

I looked up. A chap about my size was also filling up a plate. He took a chair beside me, smiled and began gobbling shrimp. We introduced ourselves. His card read, *Shlomo Yahr, Second Secretary, Embassy of Israel.* Funny, he didn't look Jewish. He looked just like every other

East Coast preppie in Washington, right down to his blue and gold striped tie and penny loafers.

He introduced me to a slim, very attractive, strawberry blonde with striking hazel eyes named Ariana Kahan. She was a Sabra, born in Israel, and a grad student at Catholic University doing research on the Old Testament. He had just moved here recently, but not into The Mews. I assumed he meant the city or the area. He spoke perfect English, but his home was Tel Aviv. Yahr told me, with a crooked grin, that Ariana also worked as a belly dancer in an Indian restaurant near Dupont Circle for tuition money. Honest.

-- • --

THE NEXT DAY I DROVE to the House of Fortune in McLean and asked to speak to the owner, Herman Wu. He was busy in the kitchen, but saw me and came out.

Herman was short and dumpy, with a pot belly, and wore both a belt and suspenders under a huge apron. His food-stained, monogrammed felt slippers were made in Hong Kong by his cousin. His shirts were works of art; dark blue with white stripes, white collar and cuffs, made by Ascot Chang, to which he always added a florid, expensive tie. His glasses were heavy horn-rimmed, with thick, dirty lenses. He was eccentric, but a very likeable guy. We'd known each other for years.

"Whatchoo wan', Doctoo?" he said in Cantonese-tainted English. He was a Hong Konger.

I nodded to a table near the window. Herman shouted something which produced hot tea and almond cookies.

We sat a table near the window, and he produced hot tea and almond cookies. I pulled out the glossies and pointed at the dead man's tattoo.

"Herman, isn't that a Chinese ideogram?"

"How da fuck I know? Not my language any moh'," he snickered.

But he squinted carefully, shook his head as though disbelieving, and yelled something at the staff. Someone produced a magnifying glass, and he squinted some more.

"Where you see this, who this person, where this picha taken, huh?"

"I don't know. Can you answer my question?"

He squinted at me suspiciously. "You shittee me boy? This man, he b'long some tong, some how you say, club of people. He Chinese man. This character is…" and he sketched it on his napkin. The first part looked like an earthworm doubled back on itself, but the next part was not like any I'd seen in menus. It resembled the huge L symbol for the British pound, and underneath it a small cross.

"By itself mean nothing, but everyone his organization have it on arm just like this man. Yeh, he Chinese, maybe soldier. Where you get this?"

"Oh," I lied, "some doctor saw this man on a river beach in China and tried to save him. He had fallen off a boat and hit his head. I think he died. But thanks, Herman, maybe I'll come for dinner tonight. Can I pay for the tea?"

"Hell no, and Doctor, you try boosheet me an' I no believe you." He let out a course laugh. "Go 'way, come back for dinner, spend you money here," he giggled, then waddled back to his kitchen.

Herman had worked in China for the OSS, he knew how things were in McLean. This restaurant was his reward from the men in gray suits when it was time for him to get out in a hurry. Fried rice and wonton soup was his business now.

I took my pictures and left with a partial answer. But what to do with it? Mandy was right, the guy was a dead Chinese. She had stumbled onto something, but *what*? What would a Chinese military man belonging to an elite organization be doing so deep in Egypt? And what the hell business was it of mine?

The answer was that I'm intrigued when things don't make sense. I feel obliged to work out a rational explanation. And I like a challenge.

CHAPTER 40

The Chinese Photo

Mandy and her photos seized my interest. *A dead Chinese soldier in commando swim gear washed up on the banks of the Nile.* Unbelievable!

Herman Wu's identification of the tattoo in the photo convinced me that it was genuine. Why would a Chinese man be there in the first place? To open a Chinese restaurant? A worker on a river boat? More likely, he sneaked in from somewhere. From where and *how*? I had an idea.

I'd do some research in the Geographic atlas I'd swiped from Mel's office, keeping some historical facts in mind. One, the Russians had been tossed out of Egypt and Ivan was pissed at these unappreciative idiots. Two, the Chinese hated the Russians, and now had perhaps decided to teach the Egyptians a lesson. What were the Chinese up to that would embarrass the hell out of the Russians? And scare the Egyptians, too, while they were at it. I had an inkling.

-- • --

Mandy would be more attractive if she'd let her hair hang loose. I'd seen her looking relaxed with Strohmeyer in Cairo. She had worn a French creation loaned her by Karen Khorvudachi and looked terrific in it. But here, she was all business, wearing a tight bun, a severe dress and an occasional smile. What did she think about outside of archaeology? I was mildly curious.

I put on my medical detective hat to solve the dead body conundrum. Mel was holding a reception for the visiting archaeologists from Israel and Egypt in the *National Geographic*'s Explorers Hall. I received a heavy vellum card requesting the pleasure of my company, etc., and realized that I was now on the *A list*. I'd moved up a notch! It occurred to me that this meeting could become the world's biggest social gaffe, flinging Egyptian and Israeli archaeologists together, so I mentioned the potential screw-up to Bill Garrett. He snorted and said he couldn't care less, goddamit, *he hadn't been invited*.

"But *you* got invited?" He sounded incredulous.

"Yeah, what's your problem?"

"Shit, peasants like me don't get invited to nothin'. I'm not working on any of those stories, so it figgers. *Fuckem*." He slammed the phone.

-- • --

EXPLORERS HALL IS A HUGE space whose ceiling rises two stories high. Its chief feature, aside from troves of nicely displayed expedition discoveries, is a massive globe, rotating silently and apparently floating in a large pool, whose bottom sparkles with good luck coins. The hall also holds a copy of a Mayan stone carving, known as the La Venta head, uncovered deep in Mexico's jungles by famed archaeologist Matt Stirling. Ten feet high and almost as wide, it sports a fierce looking face with large sightless eyes and huge, thick lips. An enormous Guatemalan Macaw usually perches on its own special roost behind the great head, and occasionally flies around flashing its colorful feathers. The bird was unquestionably a thing of beauty and a great attraction, but it was infamous for the profanities and droppings it loosed on the unsuspecting public. For this reception, it was caged and moved.

I was delighted to see a huge mound of jumbo, chilled shrimp with an adjoining raw bar. I loaded up a plate and found a quiet spot

THE CHINESE PHOTO

where I could eat and watch the parade of guests. There were the usual research types in beards and ponytails, Bohemian long dresses and open-toed sandals, as well as professionals dressed in standard East Coast preppie. I preferred that look; women in cocktail dresses, slingbacks, fancy hairdos and splashes of gold. I eyed some exceptional cleavage and enjoyed an occasional whiff of flowery perfume.

Mel, MBG to the staff, stood near the oyster bar surrounded by well-wishers and ass-kissers. I spotted a deeply tanned, well-groomed man whom I recognized as the Egyptian Ambassador, chatting with Frank Short and Luis Zarden, both senior staff at the magazine. To my surprise, another small group included my new friend, Shlomo Yahr, and an older, balding, mustachioed man in a white turtleneck and safari jacket and an unmistakable military bearing. Everyone seemed perfectly at ease, Jews and Arabs chatting comfortably. I suspected it was because they shared a common passion for archaeology. So much for my fears.

I'd polished off my first batch of shrimp, and as I reloaded, Shlomo Yahr fell in beside me. On the lapel of his blue blazer, I noticed a tiny six-pointed star, blue on white.

"Hello, Doctor," he grinned, "what a pleasure to meet again over shrimp! I pointed you out to our ambassador, Dr. Rovner. I told him you were a famous surgeon and photographer. He would like to meet you. Will you be free to join us after the reception? He's visiting his niece who's a dancer in an Indian restaurant."

"Sure, I'd love to join you and the ambassador."

And along came Miss Conant. She'd slipped into a trim, black cocktail dress that accentuated a great figure, black stockings, a silk shawl and sparkly earrings, hardly looking like Miss Archaeology at all. With her hair done up so sophisticated, it was hard to tell her age. I guessed early thirties. She had a chameleon-like quality, changing to fit the occasion. I wondered if she could dance.

She held a plate of food and a flute of bubbly. "Hi, Doctor, I've been looking for you." Big, toothy smile. "Any luck with the photos?"

"Yeah, you were right. The tattoo was a Chinese character."

"Well, I know Egyptian hieroglyphs, and this wasn't Egyptian. What did you learn?"

"I showed the photos to a former OSS Chinese chap. He was pretty certain the body was a Chinese male and the tattoo suggested military. Members of military units often have the same tattoo, a bonding thing. I can give you the photos back after the party tonight, if you like." She nodded.

It seemed only natural to ask Mandy to join the ambassador's group, too. I had no clue as to where we were going, but the dancer niece sounded interesting. So, Mandy and I followed Shlomo to the Dupont Circle area, parked and walked along Connecticut Avenue. With Rovner in the lead, the four of us entered a small, uncrowded Indian restaurant, and were seated at a round table. The ambassador ordered *papadum*, some skewered meat and iced tea for starters. I opted for a hot, delicious curried lamb.

Rovner's niece, Ariana Kahan, was a doctoral student at Catholic University and worked as a dancer for extra money. I'd met her in McLean with Shlomo.

"She's got quite a following," Rovner remarked, chuckling. "Old men like to tuck bills in her waist band, heh heh."

We were sipping coffee when the lights dimmed and spotlights centered on a woman gliding out to soft flute music, whistles and drums. She was a tall, lissome figure clad in a filmy sari, with ankle bells and finger tambourines, flashing gold and sparkles as she whirled and stamped her feet in synchrony with the music. Her expressionless oval face peered out under a gauzy head cover and the whole effect was spectacular. She treated us to swaying hip and body movements, all done in good taste, but not hiding the erotic nature of the dance. It was quite a show.

When it was over, she joined us, demurely wrapped in a long robe with her strawberry blonde hair uncovered. Rovner was clearly proud of his niece. After a fond hug and greeting, she smiled shyly as he introduced her. He went on to describe her thesis on the origins of the Dead Sea Scrolls from Qumran and told us that dancing paid her expenses.

THE CHINESE PHOTO

"Your mother would be shocked if she knew," he chuckled, rolling his eyes.

"You know your sister is terribly proper, Uncle Av. But dancing is my form of self-expression and my escape from research! Plus, I make darn good money. Some big tippers on the weekend." She giggled. "Don't tell mother. After all, I am working on those scrolls every day." Rovner smiled.

Ariana had the hazel eyes of a Sabra, born in the State of Israel. I learned that she was fluent in French, Russian, German, Dutch, Hebrew, and Arabic. She was descended from scholars and ancient court dancers. Not a bad combination. I had a feeling Shlomo and she were much more than close friends. *Look, but don't touch, John.*

Ariana had one more performance, then she and a classmate were attending a late party near the university. "Remember the Sabbath," she murmured with a wink to us on her way out.

—— • ——

DURING A LULL IN THE conversation, I'd mentioned Mandy's project on the Nile to Shlomo and the puzzling photos. This was a tactical ploy. I was aware that Israelis were on the alert to anything which might threaten their security. Their existence depended on it. If any Chinese were in the territory, Israeli watchers would know.

When I described the body, Shlomo's eyebrows rose a millimeter. *He was interested.* He listened intently and asked, "Are you available tomorrow morning, Doctor, to meet with the Ambassador and me? Could you bring along those pictures?"

Bingo.

"Yes, sure, I can arrange that. I have no surgery scheduled. What about Miss Conant?"

"Yes, of course." The tiny hairs on the back of my neck stood up. Things were getting interesting.

Mandy was agreeable. We arranged to meet at two the next afternoon at the Embassy of Israel. She and I drove to the Embassy grounds, parked in Visitors and identified ourselves to security. We were expected.

Upon entering, I heard Hebrew, French, and English and nearly choked on the strong tobacco smoke. Thankfully, the Ambassador's office bore only the faint aroma of leather, furniture polish, and cigars.

Rovner was speaking quietly in Hebrew on the phone. Shlomo brought coffee while we waited for Rovner to finish.

I glanced around the room. There were glass shelves containing clay lamps, pottery, and a large empty wine bottle, Methusalem size. Was this Rovner's dry sense of humor? On other walls, there were photos of Masada, Yigal Yadin, Golda Meier, and one of Rovner kneeling beside a huge jar, the sandy cliffs of Qumran behind him. He was lifting a wrapped bundle from the jar. A Dead Sea scroll? Another photo showed Rovner with a group of camouflaged men on a battle tank in the sand, next to assorted diplomas and certificates. An interesting glimpse into this ambassador's life.

Rovner was wearing a tan turtleneck, gray slacks, and polished Italian loafers. His eyes had a permanent crinkle that verged on a smile. He hung up and rose to greet us.

"Please sit down. Thank you for coming." He smiled and showed us to seats at their conference table. He had a kind face for such a reputedly tough man.

Mandy seemed slightly awed. I had the feeling she had never been in an embassy before. We sipped Shlomo's coffee, the strongest espresso I've ever tasted.

"So, Doctor, you have some photos to show us?"

"Yes, Miss Conant took these photos." I explained and continued, "We are scratching our heads. Why would a Chinese chap would be near the Nile, much less *in it*? Since you've had experience in archaeology and the military, you might have some thoughts." I didn't add *possibly Mossad*, too, although I was sure both Shlomo and Rovner might have been connected to it.

"Mandy thought photos would confirm her findings if it became necessary." Rovner's eyes smoothly reassessed Mandy. "But," I continued, "frankly, we had no idea what to do next."

"And how did you learn about the Chinese character?"

THE CHINESE PHOTO

I explained again my visit to the House of Fortune. He nodded, chewed on his pipe and spoke to Shlomo in Hebrew, who rose, went to the bookcase and brought over a collection of maps, a Michelin tour map of Egypt, a *National Geographic* atlas, and cartographic maps of the Nile. Charts from our NOAA. Rovner quickly opened the last batch, spread them out.

"Now if you don't mind," said Rovner, "I'd like to ask two of my geography specialists to join us and help me get oriented on these maps. You have no objection?"

"Not a problem." I stifled a remark about his "geography experts." Intelligence was more likely.

Shlomo left the room and returned with a uniformed man and a middle-aged civilian woman. Both bespectacled and serious. They were introduced as Major Ruth Avatar and Colonel Ron Maser. They shook hands and looked at the chart Rovner had spread out.

"Your houseboat is here, Miss Conant?" He put his finger on a spot on the chart and she leaned over to look.

"Yes, I think so."

"Is that Qasr Ibrim up there?" He pointed to a speck in the middle of the Nile, close to its opposite shore.

"Yes, that's Qasr Ibrim." The two "geographers" nodded.

"The body was found here," Mandy pointed to a spot on the map.

"You said, Miss Conant, that there was another houseboat with some Polish archaeologists nearby, right? They are working on a separate project?" She nodded.

"Did you meet any of those people? Any idea what they're doing?"

"One of the men is a Professor Michaelowski. I met him at the Cataract Hotel in Aswan. His team is working a Coptic Church site over on the Nubian shore, reclaiming frescoes of Christ from its walls before the Nile rises. They've never accepted our invitations to visit, and houseboats were the only things we had in common."

Rovner nodded, chewed his pipe, and spoke to Shlomo again in Hebrew.

"Let's look at the photos, shall we?"

I spread out the photos.

Rovner scanned them quickly, and turned his attention to the blurred tattoo. Polishing his glasses, he moved the magnifying glass directly over the tattoo, grunted, and surveyed the other photos, one by one.

Sliding the tattoo print under the magnifying glass again, Rovner mumbled some Hebrew at Shlomo.

"Miss Conant, please tell us again exactly how you came to take these pictures." Patiently, she went through it all, step by step. Rovner seemed satisfied and dropped a bombshell. "You should know, those Polish archaeologists in the other houseboat are *our* archaeologists. Israeli."

Huh?

"It looks as though you've stumbled onto a little secret of ours."

Rovner was completely serious now. "We've been aware of a Chinese presence for some time. Yahr and my colleagues," a head tilt at the Major and Colonel, "assure me that nothing I tell you will endanger our people or change anything. You are in possession of information that we consider top secret, and it must be kept so. If we were in the field, it would be a different matter. We would ask you to stay put until our exercise was over, but you are here and they are there." He waved a hand dismissively. "We have plans for these Chinese. We think they are a commando team. I suspect by the time you return to your Nile houseboat, it will have returned to normal.

"But now we are faced with a slight problem," he sighed. "In the next few days, a mixed team of Israeli, Egyptian, and American frogmen plan to remove the Chinese presence from the Nile, keeping it all very quiet. This team has quietly assembled on the Polish houseboat awaiting the "go" signal. All of the men are skilled in underwater work, floating mines and the like. They'll go underwater to Qasr Ibrim, surface, take out the Chinese, detonate their torpedoes, return to the houseboat, and one by one, go back to their bases. You two will be the only outsiders who know. Can you give us your word to remain silent?"

We both nodded vigorously. *What torpedoes?*

CHAPTER 41

Return to the Abnormal

M Y LIFE QUIETLY RETURNED TO NORMAL. MY "REHABILITATION" BY THE Agency took place, without fuss, little by little. Left me feeling a little empty, though. So when Mel asked me to his office, I told him I'd get there after rounds later and scurried over during rush hour.

"Now John, what's all this jabber about going back to Egypt, to a project site on the Nile?"

I explained that I'd been invited by Mandy to join their group on the houseboat to visit the site where she'd unearthed chambers containing the votive pots. I told him about Dr. Wetmore's bird identification and the suspicion that Imhotep's tomb might be there. It was partly a Geographic research project. I hoped to accept her invitation, with Geographic's blessing, of course. I let my voice trail out, waiting for Mel's response. *How did he know so much?*

"John, I asked them to send me all the information on this project. These findings should have been in their latest updates to the Research Committee. Are you sure what you're telling me is correct?

"Mel, I'm telling you what Miss Conant told me. She found those stuffed Ibis birds in that myriad of underground chambers and thinks that the Saqqara site was just a diversion to fool tomb robbers. They think they know where the real tomb is on the Nile shore. You know how these people are, paranoid and afraid of being scooped. They'll stay mum until it's show and tell time."

Mel scratched his cheek. "Look John, I'm an editor and I have to think of my magazine first. I'm not going to send *you* out to take photos of a tomb or anything else that important. That would require a full professional; don't take offense.

"The grant people are obligated to notify us well in advance of any suspected findings, and if they do, we immediately whisk a cameraman out to do the pictures. Someone experienced in archaeology, who's done it before. This isn't the time to learn."

He shook his head like a lion. "But based on what you did in Laos and Cairo, I'll make an exception. You go out there and take background pictures of sand, hills, and the river. If and when they get ready to open a tomb, let me know and I'll send Luis Zarden or someone like him, okay?"

I nodded. "Go on down to the travel office and pick up your tickets, get a large cash advance and your camera gear and get on out of here. Let me hear from you soon." I knew he had to be tough, but he was also being kind. I'd said nothing to him about the dead Chinese man. I'd have to know a lot more before telling Mel.

Time to get things lined up. I put in a call to Mandy and left a message for her to meet me at the Cosmos Club for drinks at five. Then I called Shlomo and told him my plans. He wanted a meet right then.

Half an hour later, we met at my office and I filled him in.

He replied, "I'm going with you."

"How you figure that?"

"You're in possession of important information, and I want to make sure nothing happens on this trip, especially to you. Follow?"

I did.

"Furthermore," he said, "the major would be along to keep an eye on Mandy. You can both be of help to us. Do you suppose we can be lodged in Miss Conant's houseboat?"

I mulled that over for a minute. A simple solution popped up.

"I have a suggestion. Would you be in a position to make a contribution to her research?"

"Depends how much."

"Say about ten thousand."

"Easy. We have contingency funds for these things."

"Okay, I'm going to meet with Mandy at five at the Cosmos. Join us there with an American check made out to her for that amount, and in the lower left indicate Nile Research project."

"Done."

"Can you get identification cards and passports to say that you two are a research team from the *National Geographic*?"

"Of course."

"Well, get them started immediately, because you'll need new names and papers in Egypt."

Shlomo chuckled. "See you at five at the Club," and left.

Mandy called, saying she was finishing up her work at the Geographic and they'd be leaving on the Friday flight. It was Tuesday. Things just might play out.

"Mandy, I have some good news for you. Can you use a little extra research money?"

"Are you kidding? How much?" She was obviously delighted.

"Meet me at the Cosmos Club at five fifteen and I'll have answers for you."

I was getting organized. I had a germ of an idea that would have to percolate until I worked out the variables.

CHAPTER 42

The Cosmos Club, Washington

At five, Shlomo found me seated at a table in the Club bar. We ordered Tanqueray and tonic and a large plate of cashews. I blurted, "Got the check?"

"Yes, you want to see it?"

"No, just hang onto it. Don't show it until I give you the signal, okay?"

"Yes, but what the hell are you up to, Doctor? May I call you John?"

"Of course."

"Why the mystery, John?"

"Be patient, Shlomo. This should work out for all parties. Trust me."

A very smartly groomed but harried-looking Mandy strode in. She was slightly late and sweetly apologetic. We rose and made a place for her. She'd placed her bulky shoulder bag down on the floor beside her. I'd brought the precious photos from my car trunk to return later.

"Mandy, Shlomo is an amateur archaeologist and he's never seen any Egyptian sites. He'd like to visit your site for a few days and is prepared to make a substantial contribution to your research project for the opportunity. How's that sound?"

Mandy was momentarily taken aback. "Wow, gosh, I don't know. I'd have to talk to Dr. Oberhoffer and get his approval, but yeah, it's definitely a possibility. You're into Dead Sea scrolls, right?"

I knew she was serious and Shlomo was full of baloney, but he knew how to handle himself.

He grinned engagingly. "Frankly, all I want to do is spend a few days nosing around. Let's say I'm just plain curious."

I jumped in quickly.

"What if he came over as a researcher for *National Geographic* to write a story? How does that sound?"

"A researcher?" I had the feeling that Mandy was a bit naïve. Too much isolation from the real world.

"Well, in that case, if he was coming over for the *magazine*, then I'm *sure* that would be okay."

I nodded to Shlomo, who handed Mandy the check for ten grand. Mandy's eyes widened.

"Wow, so much."

"That's only the first payment. Mr. Yahr's colleague is coming with him, and she'll bring another check for the same amount. They'll both be staying on the houseboat, in separate rooms.

Shlomo mouthed, *you bastard*, and I gave him a warning glance in return.

Mandy acted stunned. She answered cautiously, "Yes, I think that might be possible. I'll talk to Dr. Oberhoffer tonight."

"Do you have any photos or drawings of the site?" he asked her. "I'd like to get a feel for the place."

She pulled out a packet of photos, prints, and some sketches on architect's paper. There was a series of three-dimensional drawings, cutaways, projections and phantom sketches of what might lie within the sketched outlines of the project. It showed a massive cliff side with dotted lines of what might be inside it. It looked intriguing.

I peered at the sketches of the two complexes. One pictured an underground chamber where the potted birds were found, but the other drawing was strange.

Mandy pointed at that one. "See where the cliff rises from the river at this point? It's the biggest hunk of granite interspersed with large veins of basalt outside of the Aswan quarries. That's the hardest stone combination in existence. It was formed at the same time as our planet. Part of the Big Bang. We think the tomb is in that mass of granite and its entrance has been carefully and successfully hidden for centuries. We suspect the main entrance is now under water, in this slab of stone here." She pointed to a massive projection of the cliff out into the river. "The tomb builders may have carved a tunnel from the underwater part of this cliff projection into the living rock in order to hollow out burial chambers."

"The river has risen since, and at this spot," she pointed, "it's muddy, swirls wickedly, and is full of crocodiles. We don't hold much hope of finding an underwater entrance, so we're combing all the crevasses, looking for vents or some sign of a chamber."

"These sketches are my projections of where that tunnel might be. And we're running out of time. If we don't find strong indications this season, we may not get the grant renewed."

"What about finding the stuffed birds? Doesn't that count for something?"

"Yes, but they found birds in Saqqara and then they dug for twenty years and still found nothing."

A germ of an idea flickered. I put a finger on the drawing.

"This entry tunnel," I said. "How deep is it inside the rocky projection?"

She pulled out some photos of a massive stone formation with diagonal striations jutting straight down into the Nile. Formidable!

Mandy answered, "From a side approach, I'd say about halfway into that stony mass."

It was thick, heavy rock, but it was worth a shot. I had another idea, but I'd have to talk to Shlomo. It couldn't be done without him.

Mandy loaned me a copy of her sketches, I returned her photos, and we broke up for the evening. Shlomo asked me to stay behind to chat. At first he gave me grief for the twenty thousand dollars.

I countered that his government held millions in the bank. This amount was chicken-feed that she could really use. He should be ashamed.

"Touché," he said and smiled. "And of course, we will cooperate with you and Mandy."

I began to pitch my idea. I showed him the photos and the sketches. As he studied them intently, I told him what I had in mind.

He stared at me in horror. He shook his head at the insanity of it. But, after a while, ruminating over a third drink, he wondered aloud why the archaeologists hadn't thought of it earlier themselves? We parted deep in thought.

-- • --

I WENT HOME AND PACKED my gear, hoping Shlomo would come through. Mandy called me after her meeting with Oberhoffer with good news. The professor didn't care about extra guests. He had no desire to get involved in this adventure and put her in charge. He was working another promising tomb site and wanted to be left alone. Personally, he considered Mandy's tomb theory unlikely, but if she'd found additional funding, all well and good. Bank it and go ahead.

This was a perfect set-up for what I had in mind. By the end of the week, I had things in order and was ready to leave, but an article in the *Times Herald* caused us all alarm.

> *Aswan, Egypt. (Reuters) Reports reaching Cairo from this ancient site indicate severe rain and windstorms struck the area, demolishing dwellings, boats, and power lines, with serious water damage to the famed Cataract Hotel. The storm abated after three days of strong wind and rain disrupted communications and travel.*
>
> *In rising waters, rescue workers struggled to save stranded fishermen from overturned dhows and the daily paddleboat steamer from Aswan ran aground on a Nile sandbank. Egyptian Coast Guard has been called to the scene. Two anchored archaeological houseboats also dragged anchor and moorings and ran aground. No loss of life has been reported.*

The article had my complete attention. I hoped that her houseboat would be back in position by our arrival.

We got our travel plans in order. Mandy and I would fly Swissair to Geneva, then on to Cairo, and from there to Aswan, to check into the Cataract Hotel. There, she'd make arrangements with Hochtief to take us on the twice-weekly barge to Abu Simbel. It meant traveling overnight in a huge motorized barge with a cabin section to accommodate passengers. We would be dropped off en route to Abu Simbel.

Hochtief, a German engineering firm, was part of the consortium that was taking apart the temples of Rameses II and his sister, Nefertiti, and then gluing them back together on higher ground in advance of the rising Nile. It was their policy to cooperate with visiting archaeologists for future business consideration. To that end, Hochtief often used their company plane to fly archaeologists from Aswan to the Abu Simbel worksite, and dropped others off at their own worksites, but the plane was currently undergoing maintenance. It would be another trip on a barge.

CHAPTER 43

Abu Simbel on the Nile

WE BOARDED THE JET AT DC AND WERE ON OUR WAY. AFTER LONG, grueling flights, transfers, and bad airplane food, we arrived in Cairo, and transferred to a small twin prop, landing finally in Aswan. We planned to stay at the posh Cataract Hotel until Mandy firmed up our onward passage to the houseboat. We went to our rooms and literally crashed onto our beds. Ruth Avatar and Mandy had separate rooms; Shlomo and I shared a suite.

Hours later, I joined Shlomo in the bar. I kept forgetting his phony name and he laughed. I ordered a Tanqueray and tonic; the quinine prevented malaria, I hinted to a bemused Shlomo.

"Schweppes tonic, sar?"

I did a double take. The fancy dressed Nubian waiter was serious. "Yes, of course, do you have it here?"

"Sartinly, sar."

"Thank you."

He served my drink with a thin slice of lime and placed it before me like an offering to a potentate. In addition, he plunked down two crystal bowls of huge, delicious, marinated capers and giant cashews.

Shlomo and I fell into a stupor, sipping and chewing, rendered speechless with fatigue.

A tan, fit looking man wearing the epaulettes of an aircraft captain sauntered into the bar. He ordered a beer, which meant he wouldn't be flying for a while. He looked around, saw us and smiled, and on impulse, I waved him over. I introduced myself, and Shlomo used his fake name. The pilot was Captain Hossein Najafi, chief pilot for Hochtief. We shook hands and handed out our business cards. Clearly, he was happy to be in the presence of westerners who seemed educated, friendly, and relaxed, unlike the crazed tourists who infested the Cataract Hotel. Clinking glasses, we discussed the recent storm damage to the Nile shoreline. The cataract at Aswan remained undamaged, which was good news. He mentioned, idly, that he was flying out in the morning to survey the river, check the dig site at Abu Simbel, and locate the Hochtief barge, which was due at noon, but had not made radio contact.

Najafi had a 206 long-range Cessna that he flew from the Hochtief office home base in Aswan. He lived in Cairo, but he kept a flat in Aswan for layovers. He came across as a very nice, professional chap, in his regulation shined shoes and crisply ironed shirt. I decided to ask for a ride.

"Not a problem," said Najafi. "I'll pick you up in the morning, early." After handshakes all around and my insistence on paying the tab, he left.

The others were still asleep in their rooms, so Shlomo and I ordered a delicious lamb and lentil dish, fresh vegetables and fruit, and Italian mineral water. The waiter had suggested a good French Red, the *crème brulee*, and strong coffee. We ate and felt mightily restored.

I took the plunge and tackled Shlomo once again. "Shlomo, you given any thought to that matter we discussed?"

Shlomo looked irritated.

"Relax, Doctor, it will arrive in Aswan in a day or two, and be delivered to me. Stop fretting."

Fretting, hell, I was excited! And I was a little worried. If my plan worked, I'd be a hero; if not, well; I'd cross that bridge later.

Shlomo and I sat sipping our very strong coffee when in walked Ambassador Rovner in safari attire. He ordered a Czech Pilsner and joined us. *Of course.* I should have expected Rovner!

He grinned, drank his beer, and began talking as though he'd just paused for a minute from where he'd left off in Washington. "Let me start with the geography of this area," he said, and opened a map and a chart. "You see on this shore some topography of this area," pointing to the Red Sea with his pipe stem. "But let's look at it more closely.

"Look at the Red Sea area. Notice the cliffs along the sea, and the little recesses and bays. The area is maybe two hundred kilometers east of the Nile at this point. Six weeks ago, a Japanese registered freighter, the *Tachibana Maru*, left an East African port and chugged its way to the Red Sea. On its decks were three Jeeps, each pulling a trailer, two small trucks loaded with equipment, pulling two fuel trailers carrying about five hundred liters of fuel, each, and some camels. One moonless night, the *Maru* slowed nearly to a halt, and a huge crane hefted two small World War II landing craft loaded with all this equipment, over the side. The moment they hit the water, engines running, they sped to shore, here at Wadi Abu Kassab. There's a small desert road from the coast to the Nile, just here." He pointed to a thin red line a few kilometers north of the landing point.

"The landing craft went ashore here, dropped their ramps and off-loaded everything, including the camels. The animals were quickly loaded, and their drivers set off across this *wadi*, heading west, followed by the vehicles. A half hour later, the landing craft were hauled back aboard the *Tachibana Maru* as it made a huge sweeping turn, moved down the Red Sea, around through the Gulf of Aden to put in at Djibouti. The *Maru* then took on a huge cargo of dried fish.

"We knew that the *Tachibana Maru* was, in fact, a Chinese freighter, whose identity was changed long ago for use in Chinese operational missions around the world. We believe it carried the Chinese officials in charge of this particular operation. It looks like a rusty-hulled, decrepit old freighter, but the *Maru* has powerful radios, radar, GPS, satellite connections and other such equipment. It also carries camouflaged deck guns. It has the latest Isuzu diesels and can move at 15 or 20 knots, if necessary."

Rovner stopped for a minute, and we all switched to Evian.

"This landing party is a Chinese special action group, like the Russian *Spetsnaz* guys. Not much is known about them, but they are a military bunch. They're well trained, well disciplined, and often used when their own people act up. They restore order in a hurry. They're also used for international missions. Still, we aren't sure what they're up to this time.

He glanced at Shlomo. "What they don't know is that the entire unloading was observed by members of the *Beja*, an African tribe of coast watchers on the Egyptian side of the Red Sea. The *Beja* natives sit quietly along the tops of the huge Red Sea cliffs watching the coming and going of vessels below."

He took a drink. "They're a strange people. Some of their tribal customs are frightening, but they have this unique cliff-watching pastime. They have excellent distant vision like hawks. They see everything; smugglers, crocodiles, submarines. When they're hungry, they trap little ground hogs to eat, or take the eggs and nestlings from cliffside nests, and spit them on little fires. They know where fresh water drips in the cliff crevices."

We were fascinated.

"Every few weeks, Manny Levine, the WHO representative, and his Nubian driver, both on our payroll, drive up to the village in a World Health Organization Toyota station wagon and dispense medicines. They have tea with the *Beja* watchers and ask routine questions, just to stay alert for any news. Manny has some arrangement with them, and we remunerate him. Anything of interest he learns from these tribesmen is passed to us by radio or coded telephone message.

"It was the sharp-eyed natives who spotted *Tachibana Maru* at midnight." Rovner continued. "Two of the *Beja* watchers trailed the camels across the desert and quickly realized the caravan was headed for the Nile by an indirect route. It was obvious that the Chinese were avoiding detection on their way to Qasr Ibrim.

"This Chinese incursion seemed well planned. But why would they send an action group into the Nubian Desert? Manny got on his radio. You see, we're just here at the top of the Red Sea," he pointed to Eilat and nearby Aqaba. "We take any possible threat to us very seriously.

"We learned that a Chinese survey group had obtained several World War II two-man torpedoes, one from Algeria, and the other from the Cortez shipyards in Sicily. Both were sold for a sizeable sum of American dollars in cash. Why would the Chinese want torpedoes? To use against whom? If any convoy is heading across the Nubian Desert toward the Nile carrying torpedoes, shouldn't we consider their possible target, the Aswan High Dam?"

He shook his head. "So we asked ourselves, *cui bono*? Who benefits? In the most diabolical way, we concluded, perhaps the Chinese want to blow up the new Aswan Dam to make it appear that the Russians did it.

"Russia and China have been on an expansionist collision course for years. Each wanted Africa. If they could triangulate that continent, they could control it. Russia had the same plan for surrounding America when they started with Cuba, went to Nicaragua, and then Grenada in the Caribbean. They even tried Canada, but it blew up in their faces when the Americans quietly messed up their plans.

"The Russians planned to take over Africa starting with Egypt, and despite their initial success, they ran into a brick wall once Nasser got what he wanted from them. In fact, Nasser was slowly, but steadily, reducing their presence in Egypt. The Chinese," he went on, "had a solid stronghold in Albania, and eventually got a toehold in Egypt, by paying bribes. But the Russkies struck back hard. They agreed to help Egypt and other Arabs in their *jihad* against Israel. Egypt gained control over the distribution of Soviet arms, ammo, planes, and pilots. Egypt was overjoyed; we weren't, but at least we were forewarned.

"Then Nasser got a little greedy and decided to play the Americans against the Russians. Dulles said 'no thanks' to their childish demands and backed out, and this gave Russia an immense role in Egyptian commerce. The Russo-Egyptian triumph was to be the new Aswan High Dam. But once they were dealing from a position of strength, the Russians began looking down their noses at uneducated Egyptians, who got fed up and began wooing the West and tossing Russia out. This kind of bizarre behavior can only happen under dysfunctional rulers." Rovner paused. "To blow up *Saad el Ali,* the precious Aswan High Dam, and make it look like a Russian operation? That could only come from a Machiavellian Chinese mind."

Major Avatar and Mandy joined the group and ordered some dinner. The Major interjected, "It sounds childish and destructive doesn't it? Ironically, our Kremlin insiders tell us that Russia knows about the Chinese plan and hopes it succeeds. They plan to reveal the Chinese perfidy. We contacted the CIA and met with their top Egyptian man, along with Manny Levine, in Tel Aviv."

Rovner broke in. "The friendly tribesmen who followed on camels got some very good campsite photos with a long lens. We suspected the Chinese were headed toward an old Coptic redoubt, Qasr Ibrim, because it's a great place to hide a large group. According to Manny's driver, there were twelve men, speaking Arabic, Russian, and Chinese, with a Nubian guide. They set up camp in the old Coptic fort, a huge fortress-like massif rearing out of the Nile that is riddled with passageways and points of defense. The graves of fallen Christian Copts fleeing Muslims lie at the very top of it.

"The pictures showed net-covered, camouflaged vehicles and equipment and supplies. They strung up an antenna, cranked up portable generators, and made immediate radio 'commo' with the *Maru.* Of course, we were listening. We knew the *Maru's* frequencies and we have Chinese in our shop. By the way, did you know there are Chinese Jews?"

He went on. "We deduced that they had the dismantled torpedoes to re-assemble and test there. Their heavy-duty batteries needed charging and the propulsion motors tested. Our observers watched a two-man unit ease a readied torpedo from its storage space and take several test runs under water. In fact, they made several practice runs a day. These floating navigable two-man submarine bombs would be launched at a signal."

Rovner stopped and looked around. His guests were dumbfounded. He picked up the thread. "We concluded that the first torpedo released would be carried upriver to the dam and blow the protective grates which prevent logs and debris from getting sucked into the flues. Fifteen minutes later, the other unit would slide inside and drop a charge into the huge intake tunnels to explode inside. It would take out most of the hydroelectric generators." Rovner unrolled some drawings of the dam onto the table.

"The Chinese team would be headed back to the waiting *Tachibana Maru*. They would leave the area with 'planted' Arabic trash, but not a single Chinese character in evidence. *But the team made one mistake and Miss Mandy photographed it. The dead Chinese fellow.*"

"We assume they must have searched for their team member and concluded that he was not retrievable. The man was probably testing the unarmed torpedo, and hit a log or something, flipped overboard, hit his head, and drowned. The torpedo propellers slashed his torso and arms. He later washed up on that sandbar. And thanks to Miss Mandy here, we have photos to substantiate our assumptions."

Mandy smiled at him.

"Actually, we've got to keep this absolutely quiet for our own safety. We will eradicate the Chinese team shortly and then it will be over, vanished, like so much smoke." Rovner chuckled.

"In the next few days, a mixed team of Israeli, Egyptian, and American frogmen will remove this Chinese presence from the Nile, keeping it all very quiet. It will not be in the news. It's a silent operation; one that never happened. They are quietly assembling on the Polish houseboat awaiting the 'go' signal. These men are skilled underwater operators and have worked on floating mines and oilrigs. They'll go in by rubber boat, slip over the side, swim to Qasr Ibrim, surface, take out the Chinese, detonate the torpedoes, clean up the debris, return to the houseboat, and you will be the only outsiders to know. I'm omitting some details. We might retain a Chinese operative to question. We all remain silent, agreed?"

Mandy and I nodded vigorously; Shlomo and Ruth nodded, too.

Rovner sat back, looked around and smiled. "Any questions?"

I had a million, but I just shrugged. What he said made sense. Maybe that's why he had been one of Israel's top generals.

CHAPTER 44

Aswan Port

THE CESSNA LOOKED TO BE IN EXCELLENT SHAPE. IT WAS BRIGHTLY PAINTED, white with red and black trim, looked clean and well maintained. Huge block letters on the side read: *Hochtief A.G.* and in smaller letters, a list of organizations involved in the Abu Simbel project.

Familiar with small planes by now, I jumped in the right seat and strapped myself in. Najafi handed me a set of earphones and I listened as he cleared with Tower in Arabic.

Najafi got cleared, did his checklist, and commenced taxiing to the active runway. We passed a row of huge transport airplanes that I recognized as Russian Antonov transports, all lined up behind a row of hangars, well out of general view. Beneath their wings, dun-colored ambulances were parked, doors open. Some transports bore the red hammer and sickle emblem on their tails; others had Egypt's colors. What was I seeing? Ambulances could only mean one thing. Wounded or dead soldiers. Where the hell was the action? Yemen was the only place that came to mind.

I lifted my camera, thinking, *Soviet Antonovs parked here in Aswan! Worth taking confirmation photos of tail numbers. Why not, as long as I was here?*

Najafi reached out and grabbed my hand just as I was raising my camera. *No, no,* he mouthed, shaking his head, then drew his hand across his throat. I got the message and slid the camera into my lap, just after I mashed the soundless shutter button. I might have a picture worth a thousand words.

These planes must be flying Egyptian troops out of the Yemen confict, bringing home injured, crippled or dead troops. In war, certain facts are withheld from the people, and in this case, the news media in general. Woe to anyone in Egypt who published any of this information.

Najafi toggled the mike switch. "Put that damn camera down under your seat, Doctor! The men in the tower have field glasses; a glint from your lens and I'll be ordered down." I stowed it.

Najafi cleared Aswan, then leveled low over the river, flying slowly. After the storm, the Nile was muddy and full of floating debris. We saw logs, crocodiles, bloated dead cattle, and overturned boats broached on sand bars.

Soon, Najafi came upon the yellow Hochtief barge chugging serenely up the Nile toward Aswan. The people on deck waved at us. Most were Nubians in white robes and turbans, smiling widely, pearly teeth glistening, as Najafi banked and circled. He waggled his wings. Satisfied they were okay, he advanced the throttle and we moved on toward Abu Simbel.

I could see the project long before we reached it. It looked like someone had clobbered the massive temple with a giant cleaver. Odd pieces were missing from its picture book appearance. Najafi overflew the site; I could clearly see workers suspended by cables, power saws in hand, attacking and dismantling it. There was no visible storm damage. Sweat-stained workers stopped to look up and wave. They knew his plane.

This was my chance for some great frames. I flipped up the side window and began clicking away. It was bright and sunny and I'd slipped a 50mm lens on, shooting F5.6 at a thousandth of a second for aerial photos. I bracketed and shot several rolls, just to be comfortable. One or two might be usable for a story someday. Najafi grinned and circled several times for me. He looked at me inquiringly. Had I gotten enough? I gave him the thumbs-up and pointed ahead. He nodded.

Najafi reduced power and slid us lower. There was a hydrofoil tied up at Abu Simbel's pier with the name *Hatshepsut*, the female ruler, standing out in bold letters on its stern and both sides. Banking once more, Najafi roared off toward the two archaeologists' houseboats, and circled several times, looking down. Nothing seemed amiss. Najafi gave me a thumbs-up, which I guessed meant it looked okay. If they'd dragged anchors it wasn't apparent. More smiles and waves from those on the boats below. Najafi tapped me and pointed to the controls. I'd hinted to him that I could fly. "Doctor, let's come right to a heading of ten degrees. That should put us right on course to Aswan. Stay at this altitude until I take over, okay?" He smiled reassuringly.

I was in hog heaven. I took the yoke and banked to the heading. We roared home for the barn, and I was happier than I'd been in months. The Aswan landing was a piece of cake, but the damn Cessna was a floater, I almost had to crash land it. Najafi chuckled, "Cessnas are like that. They just love to fly; landing is painful for them."

--•--

BACK AT THE CATARACT HOTEL, news awaited us. The barge had radioed the Hochtief office, which in turn, had contacted Mandy. They'd seen Najafi and advised we should be ready to leave the following afternoon, waiting with our stuff dockside. The barge had tonnage to load for the construction site back at Abu Simbel, and would take on fuel, water and us, and then move out. Everything was fine on the river, they reported. Gosh, why hadn't I landed and gotten off at Abu Simbel while we were there? But what the hell, a ride on the river might be interesting.

--•--

SHLOMO ASKED IF I'D BE interested in visiting the Polish barge after we got situated on Mandy's barge. A courtesy visit, so to speak. He explained that after we arrived, a small boat would take us over. I jumped at the chance.

"Sure."

ASWAN PORT

The barge trip was interesting, but quickly became tedious. The scenery was monotonous. After a while, one got used to muddy water, floating things, and the occasional croc. The sun beat down fiercely and the only respite was an occasional breeze off the water.

The houseboat's huge, diesel engines rumbled below, as the captain made his winding way up the river. He knew the tricky, shallow spots and where whirly water made navigation difficult. Exhaust stacks from the hull's sides issued plumes of smelly, blue smoke, as we chugged slowly towards Abu Simbel and our drop-off point.

Feluccas loaded with sand, rocks, and timber passed by. Everyone waved and cheered lustily, and the captain blasted his diesel horn. Crocodiles were everywhere; some even lazed on the surface. Occasionally, a giant Nile perch would surface, a primary food source for both Nubians and crocs. On the far shore, there were flocks of shore birds I couldn't identify, but I knew the iconic, glossy Nile Ibis, with its down-turned beak. They often twittered by in pairs, heading for swamp feeding grounds. This was a descendant of the *Imhotep* ibis, whose bones we'd shown Dr. Wetmore.

The barge crew was made up of smiling Nubians. Many VIP guests and Hochtief personnel who used the barge to get back and forth were not thrilled by the Nubian's noisy banter or body odors. Mixing body odor with diesel fumes made for a hellish, smelly journey. For old Africa hands, it was no problem.

From my perspective, it was an adventure with all its attendant surprises, despite the occasional boredom. Diesel odors were familiar to me; in the Navy, my LST had had Detroit Allisons, which put these newer ones to shame in both power and stink.

-- • --

SHLOMO AND I SHARED A cabin with twin bunks. Mandy and Ruth were given a stateroom reserved for women and high officials. As night approached, the captain announced we would overnight at a large sandbar at Kalabsha. The river narrowed there, and at dusk, unseen floating debris was too risky to the propellers. We had plenty of fresh water on board, and even hot water for showers, plus ample food. It was like an overnight stay on a floating hotel. Dinner featured grilled lamb, lentil stew, pita bread, cucumber salad, with sliced fruit and freshly brewed iced tea. I'd brought a bottle of Tanqueray and some tonic aboard and availed myself of the ice machine and some fresh, Aswan limes, for a pre-dinner drink. Shlomo was preoccupied and declined to join me.

But first, the river stop.

We beached on a large, wide bar of sand which rose several feet out of the river. Its gentle, curving bank kept out the strong river current; its kidney-shaped contour kept the current away from our projecting stern, so it was relatively calm once we'd nudged the prow onto the sandy shore. The crew quickly secured us by driving port and starboard bow anchors far up on the sandy beach.

In minutes, the men had a huge fire going under cook pots filled with river water and slung from metal tripods. They'd first run the water through cloth filters and brought it to boiling. They efficiently tossed out lines and pulled in several huge Nile perch. I watched the men clean, split, and affix the fish on huge wooden planks stuck into the soft sand in front of the fire. This was a twice weekly feast that they looked forward to. A chunk of grilled fish, boiled lentils, boiled rice, and a handful of strange-looking greens, washed down with beer. Shlomo was totally unmoved by any of this activity. He'd camped and cooked out many times during his military service. Once you've camped out in the cold desert night, he mumbled, it's not something you want to do again. He had changed into a safari jacket, khakis, ankle boots and a broad brimmed hat, like a white hunter straight out of Central Casting. I'd changed into a safari jacket, too, but somehow, he looked more authentic. There were times when I wondered what Shlomo was really up to.

I was itchy to get to Mandy's dig site. She'd remained holed up in her cabin, refusing to eat barge food, even the freshly baked bread. I found most of the food passable, uniquely seasoned and quite tasty, especially a lentil concoction that they served in a gaudily decorated bowl. It was the end of Ramadan, the feast of *Eid al-Fitr,* and I was invited to join

ASWAN PORT

in breaking the fast. Afterward, I drank a snifter of brandy and crawled into my clean bunk sheets, both courtesy of Hochtief.

Shlomo still remained uncommunicative and preoccupied. What was worrying him? He tuned his small radio to a station broadcasting news in Hebrew. *Coded messages?* It was followed by Glenn Miller music and I faded out.

— - • - —

My bunk jiggled just before dawn. I rose quickly and looked out the porthole. There was mist on the mighty Nile, and from somewhere close by, frightened shore birds squawked. I heard a deep rumble below decks as the mighty diesel engines roared to life. We were moving out.

Skillfully, the captain backed out into the current, while slowly turning his boat on course, all the while advancing power, accompanied by huge plumes of black, diesel smoke. We were on our way to the houseboats!

I dressed in a flash, tiptoed past the sleeping Shlomo, slipped into the wardroom and grabbed a huge mug of hot tea, chunks of fresh bread with real marmalade, and hurried to the bridge to watch.

Around noon, I heard a crewman yell what must have been the Nubian version of "thar she blows." He was at the bow pointing to a smudge on the river as far as the eye could see. Desert people have hawk-like vision. Peering in that direction, I made out the outlines of a long hull. Within the hour, the captain pulled us alongside the houseboat, *Anoush*.

The Nubian Hochtief barge captain usually pocketed a handsome tip after maneuvering his bulky craft tenderly alongside houseboats to discharge passengers. It was expected. Today, however, he bumped into the houseboats, despite trying to slide smoothly alongside, and thus didn't get as large a tip. There was always next time, *Ma-alish*. We quickly off-loaded baggage, supplies, plus a few workers who'd climbed on at Aswan.

— - • - —

DR. JOHN...ON ASSIGNMENT

My first impression of the *Anoush* was that we'd boarded an old, wooden-hulled steamer, like a Mississippi paddleboat. There was a section of gingerbread iron railing surrounding the bridge level. It was quaint-looking, but was not just some Cajun bateau, rather a floating residence. It was a large, floating workstation and dormitory combined, at least one hundred feet long, with a wide beam for stability in bad weather, and a squat, sturdy hull that could weather a sudden storm. It was anchored in the Nile bottom. There were two bow anchors at the ten and two o'clock positions, and a long anchor chain to another from the stern, to keep the barge from drifting.

Entering the main living quarters was like entering an old-fashioned hotel lobby. Worn oriental carpets were spread over plank floors. The decor was early turn-of-the-century, with overstuffed couches, divans, and huge lamps with weak light bulbs. *They did have a generator!*

On the table rested several upturned glasses and a clear glass water pitcher covered with netting to dissuade flies. *Fresh water and a galley too!* This place would do just fine for my short stay on the river.

Dr. Oberhoffer apparently wanted little to do with us and disappeared down the passageway to his private area. He'd turned most of the day-to-day operations over to Mandy, who turned us over to the Nubian houseman, Nabil. She excused herself, claiming some immediate business, and went off down the passageway.

Nabil, a tall, slim man in a white skullcap and long flowing white robes, majestically showed us to our cabins. He had a huge smile, dazzling white teeth, graying temples and spoke good English. He was a character right out of the British Raj.

My small corner stateroom reminded me of the Dutch canal houseboat from my earlier caper. Screened windows opened on two sides, which allowed cool river breezes. Not at all unpleasant. There was a sink, flush toilet and running water. All the comforts of home and quite plush, this far out in the Nile and miles from civilization. The river glinted outside my window and reminded me how far from shore we were. It was a floating hotel and a prison, in a sense.

I tossed my gear on the bunk, washed up and stepped out. I wanted a good look around. Passing by Shlomo's closed cabin door, I heard him speaking Hebrew. Ruth was out on deck talking to Mandy. Who else spoke Hebrew on this barge? I was actually relieved to hear him; it confirmed my suspicions that he was talking to someone on the adjacent houseboat by radio.

I headed for the outside deck. There was pleasant breeze off the river, which kept our quarters cool. We rarely needed the window air conditioners. It was good to be away from the dusty, mind-numbing heat of the desert. Mandy was lounging on deck, and looked up as I stepped out. "Doctor, I'm going to visit the dig site tomorrow morning. If you'd like to join me, we'll leave after breakfast, before it heats up." I nodded okay.

As she chattered on, I noticed a pleasant change in her appearance. She was wearing a thin blouse stretched tightly across her bosom, shorts, and flip-flops, and a large floppy hat. She sprawled in a lounge chair with suntan lotion smeared all over, wearing red-framed, dark glasses. And maybe it was my imagination, but when I'd stepped out, had she looked me over?

"Ruth is anxious to join us tomorrow, so I've ordered extra water, iced tea, and sandwiches for us. I suspect Shlomo will want to come along, too."

We all wanted to visit the dig site. After all, didn't Rovner say he'd make sure we didn't blab about the dead Chinese fellow? Shlomo would tag along to make sure.

"In the meantime, you might want to take a look at these sketches and photos of the site." Exactly what I had hoped to do. And I'd look for photo opportunities, too.

Mandy led us into a cabin with a large conference table and chairs and excused herself to change into work gear. She returned in Levis and T-shirt, and still looked quite fetching. I decided to ignore her T-shirt and stick to business. In the Navy, there was a rule: *No friggin' in the riggin'*.

The sketches were laid out on a long parsons table. Daylight filtered from skylights and the room was comfortably cross ventilated.

Suddenly, a sketch had my complete attention. I saw something that gave me a brilliant idea!

Overlying the photos of that huge stony massif were phantom dotted line projections, which she'd sketched on thin opalescent paper. Inside those dotted lines, when overlaid on the photos, I visualized tunnels that could lead to inner tomb chambers, or where they should be. If they were there, then they were deep in heavy rock. But if a trained archaeologist like Mandy couldn't find any sign of an entrance, assuming there was one, it must be well hidden.

There had to be a hidden entrance, perhaps an underwater one. Finding it was a huge challenge, so the first priority for me would be to look for a surface entrance. The next option would be plan B, and I'd have to play it carefully.

Earlier, I'd hung my few clothes and located the galley, where Nabil, the silent Nubian houseman in flowing white robes, was marinating meat. He reassured me, "Yes, we have limes, sweet melons, and wonderful Aswan oranges, sar." This was not a desert camp, but a very proper houseboat for scientists, with plenty of fresh food. Laundry service was available, too. I put his age at about fifty. He obviously ran the inside of the houseboat and the other Nubians ran the machinery and the outside areas. It was a very posh setup.

I showered, shaved, and donned fresh clothes for dinner. As I sipped my pre-dinner drink and gobbled huge cashews swiped from the Cataract Hotel, I felt a certain excitement.

I had a strong hunch that Mandy was right. *There was a tomb there, as her drawings depicted, so logically, there had to be an entrance to a tunnel. Find the tunnel and see where it led. Find the entrance...or make one. That's where Shlomo and plan B would come in.*

During dinner we all listened to the BBC world news broadcast, then a German station playing *Der Rosenkavalier*, and some Glenn Miller tunes. I was still bushed from the long trip from the States, so I had my coffee and turned in. I may have dreamt of how to get into that tunnel, even though I'd already decided on a plan.

CHAPTER 45

The Plan

IN THE MORNING MANDY TOOK US OVER TO THE ARCHAEOLOGICAL SITE. About a hundred yards from the path leading to the underground bird chambers, we nudged our small boat ashore and beached it. The massive cliffs stood farther down, along the river's edge. Another faint path, not far from where we landed, led to level desert floor. There was nothing other than stark desert, rocks, shrubs and scattered vegetation. Shore birds were wheeling and clacking in anger at being disturbed. I have never seen as large a bunch of sooty sea gulls anywhere, and curiously far from the ocean. They flew everywhere, making a raucous noise, but there was no other sign of life. It was silent, save for the occasional soughing of wind across the sand.

A breeze came off the water, but it was still beastly hot. We trudged up to the site, about a hundred yards from the shore, where a tarp hung across four poles. It shaded a large square hole in the ground, from which the top rungs of a wooden ladder protruded. A small, portable gasoline engine purred, and wires from it fed down beside the ladder. A few sweaty workmen stood smiling and holding the ladder steady. Mandy greeted them and started down, beckoning us to follow.

"Remember to put your sunglasses in a safe pocket, because you'll be blind down there otherwise." Good advice from an experienced desert traveler.

I peered over the side into the hole. Cripes! It went way down, I estimated about fifty feet. I started climbing the ladder, and at the bottom, stepped onto a fairly level, sandy floor. It was surprisingly cool, with a curious musty odor. That of a burial site?

—-•—-

DANGLING FROM THE CEILING WERE small light bulbs, feebly illuminating the tunnel walls and passageways. On each side of the ladder was a long passageway carved out of the desert and lined with stone blocks. From it, some chambers took off at right angles, along with a few blind passageways. Shlomo grunted quietly to me that this place looked like a French whorehouse. "I've seen better ones," I mumbled back. We chuckled.

Each chamber had niches and shelves crowded with the same brown clay pots she'd shown Wetmore in Washington. It could very well be the place where Imhotep was buried, or just another sneaky deception. The ancient Egyptians liked to hide things, using truth in deception. Some say they are just as deceptive today.

So what were they hiding and how?

The votive pots containing the sacred Nile Ibis were brought here, one by one, by worshippers as offerings. Did a thousand people hike this far from anywhere to pay homage to Imhotep?

What if a thousand pots were *brought* here from Saqqara by Imhotep's architects to round out the authenticity of this new site as a deception, or a reverse deception? Something to consider.

This passageway arrangement using blind tunnels that lead to blank walls was a favorite ruse employed by tomb architects to fool looters. At other sites, there was always evidence of break-ins in the form of crude, surface chisel marks, abandoned tools, traces of fire, bones and food. But nothing like that had been found here.

Mandy was satisfied that these tunnels might be a red herring, and if there was a tomb in the area, it should be somewhere in that huge stone massif down the shore. That site was next on the agenda.

—-•—-

THE PLAN

I WAS READY TO GET the hell out of this underground birdcage anyway, and gladly started up the ladder toward the patch of daylight. I followed right behind Mandy and appreciated the way her faded jeans swayed from side to side as she climbed each rung.

Once topside, we hiked along the shore with two Nubian workers in the lead. For protection, Mandy explained, because they knew the desert and could spot snakes and things from far away. Sometimes a beached log was really a crocodile. An occasional dun-colored snake lay quietly, blending with the sand. They'd killed two asps on their last trip, and there were plenty more. The Nubians killed a snake by pinning it down with a forked stick, reaching down and grabbing the snake by the tail with one hand, and behind its head with the other. Like a great bull whip, they snapped the snake by the tail, killing it instantly. They quickly skinned the large ones to sell in Aswan for attractive belts and wallets. Grilled crocodile tail, spitted and turned slowly over a fire, is quite tasty, they insisted.

I had eaten gator tail at Kalabsha, and it had tasted like seasoned chicken. Croc hides made great boots, shoes and fancy handbags. Leather buyers from Florence come to Aswan to purchase salted baby croc hides.

Finally we reached the imposing stone cliff, the massif that soared up at least a hundred feet above the river. It was a very, very hot hike, trudging in the soft sand.

I looked up at the huge mass of stone, the only such mass in Egypt, and maybe in the world, according to Mandy. More impressive than the stone quarries at Aswan. Although ancient Egyptians would not have known, it came up from deep underground as magma, red-hot liquid stone, and slowly congealed when the the earth's crust was cooling.

One could clearly see seams and cleavage lines running mostly vertical, and some at angles. Seams can enlarge to become cleavage lines that allow the stone to be split under powerful pressure.

Right in the middle, was a huge black slab, an inclusion, like meat between two slices of bread. It was dense, black basalt, surrounded by granite, and was a grand site. I'd never seen such a thing before. Was it possible the tomb architects had chosen this impressive massif to be a fitting final resting place for the great Imhotep? It seemed logical. Of course, Imhotep had to approve, but this site did have everything. It was remote and far from the pyramid sites of Giza, yet also impressive and close to the river of life, the Nile.

Mandy had mentioned Walter Emery, the noted British archaeologist who had worked Saqqara. Was this what he had been looking for, and Saqqara was the red herring? What if a young archeologist like Mandy and a rank amateur like me found the real burial site of Imhotep, Chancellor of the King of Lower Egypt and Greatest of Seers? We'd upstage the people who'd toiled here in the unforgiving desert all their lives. Sometimes, one gets lucky. *If we found him, it would be a find ranking as importantly as King Tut's tomb. Think of the photo opportunities!*

I nodded at Shlomo, pointing to the top of the cliff, and raised an eyebrow inquisitively. I'd been thinking about "blowing" the top off that rocky projection at a spot just above where a tunnel might exist, down in the solid rock.

He smiled; he'd been thinking the same thing ever since we'd seen the sketches. He nodded affirmatively. We were both looking for a short-cut into the tunnel, like bank robbers looking for a spot to insert some dynamite. But in our case, dynamite would be too tame for this job. There was far better stuff available.

"What do you think, Shlomo?"

He was nodding and pursing his lips. "It's just possible, Doctor. You may have stumbled on the best way to get in."

"You get the supplies?"

"We have to visit my friends first. Tomorrow okay?"

"Fine." *I just love it when things start to fall into place.*

— • —

MANDY SHOWED US WHERE HER workers had dug exploratory trenches on both sides of the massif looking for vent holes or signs of entry. They'd probed every cranny and indentation and found nothing to spur further activity. No holes, no vents, no signs of chiseling, or stone chips.

THE PLAN

But I was convinced Mandy's sketches were accurate and her logic correct, so it was worth a shot. We'd blow a deep hole at the top, if I could convince her it was the right thing to do. I'd use logic, charm, and a bit of blarney.

A few parts of human skeletons had been found near the deep shaft we'd descended. Skeletons were most likely of workers, whose bodies were dumped near the dig site. Mandy observed that workmen who died were usually left to rot where they fell, and since the desert climate preserved bones perfectly, they were still here. They may have been workers who died in the underground passageways and were dragged out, tossed on the massif and left to dry for vultures. Life was cheap in those times. These bones were likely very, very old. Some showed old bone damage, even healed fractures, which fit with her theory that they had been tomb workers. This material had been carefully hidden. Bones sent for carbon dating would take months for a readout. All the same, they'd eventually give her a better notion of how long they'd been there. For now, time to make an end run.

--•--

AT DINNER ON THE BARGE, Shlomo casually mentioned that he'd heard from the other houseboat. Would tomorrow be okay for a visit?

I was game, but Mandy demurred; she had work to do in her shop. We were free to have a small boat take us over. Ruth planned to join us. It seemed like a routine, friendly visit.

I went to my room tired after a delicious dinner of roasted fowl and pilaf, fresh steamed vegetables, huge slices of tomato covered with balsamic vinegar, lemon juice and olive oil. A light pastry dessert and coffee. But dammit, I couldn't sleep. Nabil poured me a snifter of Napoleon brandy and I relaxed, but still couldn't sleep.

I turned on the table lamp and began studying Mandy's sketches. I was deeply engrossed when I felt a draft. Shlomo had entered my cabin ever so quietly.

"Doctor," he said. "Bring an overnight kit along tomorrow. You never know when plans will change."

"Yeah, sure," I said, "thanks." *Why?* I decided to take more film, too. Strange guy, Shlomo, but I'd gradually become comfortable with him and he no longer seemed as wary of me. He'd become more relaxed in my presence, and usually wore a bemused, Mona Lisa smile. I suspected he was a Mossad operative and rarely saw the smile when he was in deep thought.

Tonight, he seemed confident about our situation. In my experience, confident people deal from inner strength, so I planned to go along with his suggestions, but reserved the right to ask questions.

"I can use a brandy, too," he looked serious. "I don't drink alone."

"What's the problem?" I asked.

"We have a tricky operation coming up, and it's partly my responsibility, the planning and operational part. It should go well, but I'm anxious. I brought a very fine Rémy Martin along. You have any clean glasses?"

I produced two and we toasted the fates and solemnly bid each other good night. I slept soundly.

—- • —-

Mandy's young boatman, Kharpet, took us out the next morning. It was a half hour run to the other houseboat, which looked remarkably like Mandy's. Provided by the Egyptian government, the boats had been used earlier as tourist boats until the advent of more modern ones. They were sturdy craft built in Holland in the late twenties, and still had functioning machinery and amenities that spoke well for their staff.

To the casual onlooker, they appeared similar. As we drew alongside, I heard a low greeting. It wasn't in Polish. It was Hebrew and both Ruth and Shlomo answered in Hebrew. I recognized *Shalom.* So where the hell were the Poles?

We climbed aboard and were greeted by a smiling, muscular man about Shlomo's age. He wore a safari jacket and jeans, heavy sandals, and a floppy hat.

"Allow me to present Major Baruch Minah," said Shlomo, "Excuse me just a minute. He turned and said something to Kharpet in Arabic

THE PLAN

and turned back to us. "I told him that we will spend the night and return tomorrow in a boat from here. He's going back."

A few other men sauntered out onto the deck and Shlomo introduced them. They were all very fit, tanned and rugged-looking men and they all knew Shlomo. Then to my surprise, out came a man in a bright red United States Marines T-shirt!

"You must meet Warrant Boatswain Luke Scarborough," said Minah, "He's one of yours." I smiled at this sandy haired giant of a man, with bulging, muscles and an open face.

"Hi, Boats," I said.

"*Gawd Daaam*," he said. "Yore an Ammurican, Gyrene or Navy?"

"Damn straight, Boats. Right the first time. I was a swabbie once, long time ago, did some boots with you guys. Then went Amphibs."

"Yew don't say? Well all right, happy to meet up with you, sir," he added as an afterthought. He had no idea who I was and was taking no chances.

"You're a long way from Norfolk."

"Little Creek, sir. They got thangs a-cooking over here, but it should be over soon. I'll let the major do the talking. We're under orders, sir."

"I get the picture. Nice to meet you. Any other guys from Little Creek?"

"Yeah, a Master Chief Quartermaster and a Master Chief Electrician. We all cross-trained at Little Creek. We all worked with the Gyppos and the Izzies clearing mines in the Red Sea, so we're part of a special reserve SEAL outfit ready to go at a moment's notice. We wuz settin' around playing gin rummy when this little Ops came along."

What the hell was he talking about? This group didn't look like tomb diggers. They were a highly trained commando outfit, SEALS, no less.

Minah took us inside. It was almost an identical set-up as our houseboat and smelled of beer and cigarette smoke.

"Doctor, please let me explain. We are a combined task force composed of Israeli, Egyptian, and American personnel. We are on a small mission that was delayed because of the freak storm. If we had been on schedule, you wouldn't have seen us. Things are quiet again and tonight we proceed according to plan."

"Shortly after midnight," he continued, "we will depart in our rubber boats and destroy a Chinese encampment over on Qasr Ibrim. For security, you will be our guest here until our return. Afterwards, you will be free, of course, to go back to digging and photographing. Any questions?"

I wasn't completely taken aback; I'd suspected something was afoot. But the directness of the Major made it quite clear.

"In the meantime, make yourself comfortable, Doctor. Colonel Yahr will be happy to show you around. By the way, it would be best if you kept all this to yourself. There will be no reports in the press. The Chinese, of course, will deny everything, if anything leaks out. He smiled and made to leave.

I caught up with him. "Excuse me, sir, may I have a minute?"

"Yes, Doctor?" Eyebrows raised.

"I'd like to go in with the rubber boats."

He stared at me.

"Surely, you're not serious?"

"Yes, I am. In fact, sir, I am an accredited photographer for *National Geographic*, I've had a great deal of experience..." I babbled on until he cut me off.

"You are not a commando and you would be a hindrance. We have our own photographer, if needed." The major turned and walked away.

I looked back at Shlomo. He just shook his head, expressionless.

Colonel Yahr, huh? Shlomo was a Colonel. Be damned. But why should I be surprised? Nothing is what it seems on the surface around here.

"Come, John," said Shlomo in a placating voice. "Don't ask any more questions. Just listen. Yes, I am a Colonel in the Israeli Defense Forces and I am also the Embassy military attaché. When you told me you were coming here, we had no choice but to make sure you and Mandy arrived safely, and didn't compromise this mission. We came along with you under this thin ruse as researchers for Geographic.

THE PLAN

"At midnight, the underwater commandos go to Qasr Ibrim in the rubber boats, swim ashore and take out the encampment. They may question one Chinese prisoner if the situation permits. They'll destroy everything, disarm and dismantle the two-man torpedoes and sink them. When they're finished there will be no trace of anything. If anyone looks in Qasr Ibrim, they will find nothing. Our men are very good. They may bring back technical stuff for our scientists and a series of mission photos to be reviewed by our intelligence mavens."

"I see," I said. I was still searching for a way to go on this mission.

"Come with me. I have a surprise for you." He led me to a small storeroom and pointed to three five-gallon plastic paint buckets, labeled *Caulking Compound* in English with Hebrew characters. He hefted one, and signaled for me to take the other. We went out on deck to an unoccupied area. The lounging troops ignored us.

Shlomo pried open the first pail, which was full of thin, whitish liquid. He unfolded a knife, dug the blade into the whitish stuff and carved out a chunk of what looked like putty. But it wasn't putty.

"Here's your explosive, Doc. This is Semtex, from the Holston Army site in Tennessee. Wonderful, military-grade stuff. You can do all sorts of things to it, but it won't go off without a detonator. I've used it in the desert to warm my soup. Just light a small chunk and it burns hotter and better than a campfire, but it has to be used outdoors, because it gives off poisonous fumes. Of course, I also have detonators and some lengths of det cord. I've figured out how it can be done. I think we can blast off the whole damn cliff if we use enough. With any luck, you'll find the tomb tunnel and not destroy the chambers, if there are any. John, hear me. *You don't go in the rubber boats. If you try, there are orders to shoot you. Understand?*" He was serious.

I nodded. "Loud and clear." This boom stuff was just what I needed, but it also scared the hell out of me. Dangerous, specialist stuff. And what if it actually worked? What then?

--•--

DR. JOHN...ON ASSIGNMENT

Everything was going to happen *after tomorrow*. Nothing but the mission mattered now. Shlomo was going to help place the charges, wasn't he?

"Will we see anything when the commandos hit?"

"We may hear some small weapons fire and see a few grenade rocket flashes in the sky, but it should be fairly quiet. Sound carries over the water, especially at night, when the wind has died down. We don't want the Chinese on that ship to have any idea of what happened to their team. Their damn Aswan Dam team will just disappear into thin air. John, this is not our first operation. Keep that to yourself too."

I nodded. There was nothing to do but wait. "By the way, Shlomo, how do you want to set up the explosives to blast into that cliff?"

Shlomo glanced at his watch. It was still early and the team was resting, checking their equipment, or going over their assignments. Some were writing in notebooks, I noticed one man praying. Two others had a small machine gun disassembled on a towel, checking the parts. They all smoked foul-smelling cigarettes, but as a whole, they seemed light-hearted, as though it was just another job.

Shlomo and I went inside to an office.

"Here, look at these" He had a copy of Mandy's sketches and a black and white photo of the cliff. He'd made X marks at certain locations on the massif.

"We take about a pound of this stuff for each spot, we mold it into a ball, then jam each chunk down into these cracks and crevices all along this line. You see here." he pointed to the cracks in the photo of the huge extension into the river. "Have you ever noticed when you drive along mountain roads, you sometimes see drill holes in the stone? They drill holes in solid rock to drop dynamite charges, then fire them all at once. The whole bloody mountainside drops off and *voilà*, you have your road. Well, we 'll use cracks and crevices and do the same here. We'll place the charges, connect them, put a detonator in each charge, actually I'll use two, no chance for failure that way. Something I learned from my instructor at Quantico, he was a real demo man, a little crazy, but smart as hell. I'll tuck in some det

THE PLAN

cord in the cracks, too, just for kicks. It goes off with the charges, and we should have a pretty good result. Done right, the whole chain goes off as one. If we're lucky, we find a hole into a tunnel. If not, we'll do it again. I have more paint cans in the barge and if nothing else, we'll have nice big chunks of rock to study.

"But tell me this, John, what will the other archaeologists say? Can you clear using explosives with them?"

I had a plan.

— - • - —

IT WAS APPROACHING BINGO TIME. Shlomo and I were now isolated from the men. They were operational now, and we were to keep our distance. We ate alone quietly. Dinner was lamb, rice, cucumber and yoghurt salad, sliced tomatoes, and goblets of good, Israeli white wine.

I asked about Professor Michaelowski, "He's encamped ashore at the Nubian church. Trying to lift a huge fresco of Jesus out of a collapsed temple."

I was too excited to turn in. Shlomo gave me the lower bunk in a spare cabin. He jumped up into his bunk, tossed his clothes in a pile and, unbelievably, started snoring in minutes. I finally fell asleep and imagined hearing explosions far away and seeing flashes of light on the horizon, but as I say, I must have been dreaming.

I hadn't heard them leave, but I did hear their noisy return. My photos of them crawling back aboard just after dawn would be souvenirs of a sort. It would show men returning from an exercise; nothing more and nothing with a hint of Chinese.

This bunch of happy warriors were standing around the foredeck getting hosed down, washing their hair and wiping grease paint camouflage off their faces. All had returned safely; mission accomplished without injuries. Torpedoes had been defused and sunk, trucks rolled into the Nile, or what was left of them after thermite charges had done their work. Some equipment and documents were retrieved and brought over for later study. Lastly, the operation's rubber boats had been deflated and stowed aboard.

They had picked up some "souvenirs" for the visiting doctor. "For you," said the major, with a grin. He handed me a small, waterproof package, which to my surprise, contained several large shards of ancient pottery, and a badly dented and blackened silver chalice with faint repoussed inscriptions. It looked like *Timotheos* in old Greek. And a lovely, silver filigree, Coptic cross, heavily discolored. The men had also snatched up a pair of ivory chopsticks and a complete acupuncture set. "You might have some use for it." These guys had a wry sense of humor.

They *had* taken mission photos for confirmation. Mandy's photo tattoo matched those they'd seen on several other forearms. They were all photographed. Lastly, they'd fingerprinted all the fallen combatants. Their mission was over and they'd be extracted shortly.

CHAPTER 46

The Tunnels

Back on our houseboat, I looked for Mandy, but she was ashore and wouldn't be back until dinnertime. It was only midafternoon, and the Israeli mission was over.

We'd come back with "Shalom" and my small package of artifacts. No one would ever believe this adventure, *but I would have these little mementos*. I hadn't been allowed to take any photos, other than the return of a bunch of laughing SEALs, but it was understandable.

Eventually, Mandy arrived back aboard, hair blown askew, her shirt covered with dust and looking bedraggled. She still had a freshness about her despite the streaks of dust on her face. She went to wash up and headed for her cabin.

At cocktail time, Mandy emerged refreshed, dressed in a long white dress of thin cotton. With her silhouetted against the doorway, I could see clear through it. Her hair was freshly washed and fragrant, and her face was glowing with desert sun. A good-looking lady.

There had been no sign of Oberhoffer since we'd arrived. He was working on a project on the opposite shore.

Mandy joined me for a glass of white wine. Nabil had laid out the Schweppes, limes, and a tub of ice cubes, and I was enjoying my signature gin tonic out here in the middle of the effing Nile! I plied her with a second glass right away, hoping to get her guard down.

Women are so perceptive, dammit, that I thought she might have had an inkling of what I wanted.

She began telling of her experiences ashore. It had been a tantalizing foot-by-foot search for some sign of an entryway into the massif, but it was discouraging. She was beginning to show signs of defeat. Time to make my move, carefully. I chomped on cashews and huge capers that Nabil served. *This guy was great. I wish I could take him home.*

"Mandy," I said, sipping gently at my second gin. "I wonder if you have any objections to Shlomo and me going over there and looking around? Maybe we could move a stone or two, turn over a boulder. We might find something, who knows? You don't have any objections, do you?"

She frowned fleetingly.

"Sure, you guys go right ahead. You might be a big help. See if you can bust your way in for me," she giggled. "And if you do, I've got a reward for you!" Now that was a challenge worth going after.

She said, "I'm going with Oberhoffer early tomorrow. There's a promising riverside dig site about five miles away. We'll be gone most of the day, so you guys can go ashore in the other boat. I'll send a couple of workmen who know the area with you. Make sure you take lots of water and some food. I'll give you Kharpet; he knows the place."

She'd given us the perfect opportunity.

I finished my drink. At the current rate of consumption, there'd be barely enough gin or tonic to last the week. Now my excitement began building. Shlomo had drifted in and joined us, drinking Black Label Scotch, courtesy of his buddies. He'd listened and looked satisfied that it was a go. We'd blast tomorrow.

I couldn't wait for tomorrow. The thought of blowing a hole in the rock had my adrenaline flowing at full tilt. I was really wired. First the commandos and now this. I made notes in my journal and labeled my film. Mel couldn't use any of it. I'd have these processed on my own.

— - • - —

WHEN I AWOKE EARLY THE next morning, the horizon was brightening with was morning's first light. The first rays of sunlight now slanted through my window as they must have done for centuries into the entryway of Rameses II tomb at Abu Simbel.

Mandy and her group had eaten a hurried breakfast and set off in their boat. So far, so good.

I looked over to the near shore through field glasses and stared at that huge promontory. I wondered. *Imhotep, are you there? Could you have been clever enough to hide yourself this far away from the beaten path? One good blast from the Semtex and we might just find out.*

Along the shoreline I saw brown ibis, white ibis, curlews, herons, and other birds I couldn't identify, but not a single animal anywhere, not even a crocodile showing its snout.

Shlomo stepped out on deck, puffing a lighted cigarillo.

"Where'ja get that smelly thing?" I asked. I'd gotten a whiff earlier on the Polish boat and should have known. He just chuckled and pointed to the Polish barge.

"Same place I got the Scotch, and it's a Cuban. An excellent tobacco," he pretended to be offended. "My friends leave tomorrow and can't take the booze or cigars back with them. I'm just practicing anyway. These are good for lighting firecrackers."

We loaded our stuff and headed ashore on the dory with small forty-horse outboard. Shlomo had worked out all the details for this project earlier. We'd plant one or two pound charges every six feet, a total of fifteen on the back side. There would be a loud slapping sound when we blasted, a helluva blast, but with the wind blowing our way, it should be muted. And maybe the Nubians would be blasting on the opposite shore, too.

It would be prudent to keep the complete details from Mandy as long as possible. There would be ample time for damage control later, if needed.

Shlomo first laid out a tarp and opened a paint can, stabbed a long serrated knife into it, and cut out chunks of Semtex, each roughly about a pound. He set them on the tarp. From inside the large Halliburton case, he gingerly extracted a coil of det cord. Another case held the detonators and wires and a firing box. It was clear that Shlomo knew exactly what he was doing and had done all this before.

I recalled Hank Peters at work. These bang-bang guys all belonged to the same club.

Following his directions, we carefully tucked charges in a fairly straight line into each nook and cranny, starting from the shoreline outward, using long heavy pieces of driftwood to pound them tightly into the crevices. Then he carefully stuck the detonators, wires already attached, into the charges.

"Just in case," said Shlomo, as he ran backup det cords from one charge to another up and down the line. Finally the wires were hooked from the primary detonators for the string of charges. Those not hooked up would blow immediately anyway in response to the blast. Actually, the det cord was a redundancy. But no sense taking chances, we'd only have one shot at it. It had taken the better part of an hour to get it all done right. The Nubians were openmouthed when it dawned on them what we were doing. Just like the quarry men across the river, they said. Good observation.

We reeled out a long length of wire to the beach, quickly hooked it to the detonator box terminals, then ducked behind the farthest large boulder.

A heavenly breeze blew our way, happily, away from Mandy's location. Shlomo declared it perfect. They might feel a rumble, but doubted they'd hear the blast. If anyone asked, we'd say it was the quarry men.

The two workers huddled beside us. Shlomo took a good look around with his field glasses and counted loudly in English: three, two, one and he shoved the detonator handle. At first nothing happened, then we watched as a huge cloud of dust and rocks flew up, out and in our direction. We were safe behind the huge boulder. First the ground rumbled and then a "boom" shattered the silence. Then more dust and rocks flew, as the airborne rubble finally came splattering down and settled. It was all over in seconds.

The birds scattered. I watched a large wave rush out from river's edge toward the Nile center and our boats, but it swiftly flattened.

Shlomo raised his hand. "Now we wait," he said. "No rush. These blasted stones must get comfortable in their new positions. If you get in there too quickly and start crawling over them, shifting rubble can kill you. So let's take some time to rest and think."

He called to the Nubians in Arabic, for the sandwiches and water.

How can he be so nonchalant at a time like this? I thought. It was maddening. I was anxious to see what we'd done to that mass of stone. Maybe we'd blasted our way into a tunnel!

We ate the sandwiches, replaced our fluids, and rested a spell. The river breeze kept us cool, and while I fretted, Shlomo was perfectly relaxed. He appeared to be in deep thought.

"You go first, Doctor. If we made a dent in that pile and there's a hole, you should find it."

We clambered up the rocks. There was no question, huge pieces of the massif had been blasted away. In fact, the whole side of that cliff had been sheared off, forever changed. But there was no sign of a hole and no tunnel. Just a huge pile of rubble. Damn!

We started a foot by foot search of the blasted site, top and sides, and moments later, one of the workers let out a yell, pointing down at something on the very top of the pile where he stood.

We rushed over. Grinning hugely, he pointed to a gaping hole we hadn't noticed at first glance. It went straight down into the rock, but there was no indication of how far.

A worker brought a long boat hook and I probed the hole with it. The hook was about seven feet long, and went straight down to its end before it hit resistance. Shlomo frowned and cut out another chunk of the explosive, twice the size of the first ones, and shaped it into a ball. He tied it securely with thin rope, then inserted a detonator before lowering it down the center of the hole to roughly the halfway level. He secured the string to a large slab of rock, then fed the wire back to our box behind the shielding boulder and blew the charge. If he'd guessed right, this would even off the hole in the tunnel, making it rounder and deeper.

This blast shot more dust, dirt, rocks, smoke, and a fiery yellow flame, too, straight up. Shlomo said the yellow flame was gas, which sometimes remains in the rubble and can flame up after a blast. Not a problem. So once more, we waited fifteen minutes.

The Nubian charged back to the top and yelled again excitedly, pointing down. We climbed over to him, stumbling on sharp chunks of basalt and granite.

When we got there, God's truth, we felt a steady flow of cold air streaming up out of that hole. It had a musty, slate smell, like a wet blackboard. *Wet stone!* We must have popped into something, but what? A watery tunnel? We had to find out. The hole still wasn't wide enough to lower anyone through, and something told me we shouldn't try.

But I had an idea. I rigged up my camera and set it for a timed delay flash, secured it to two lines, one at each end to keep it from spinning, and lowered it to the limit of the line, about forty feet. It negotiated the narrow spot and continued all the way down. *Holy Shit, the camera had to be in a tunnel, a passageway, or something!*

I was excited and even Shlomo looked interested, for a change. I laboriously lowered and raised the camera, each time carefully firing off an exposure: black and white film first, then fast Ektachrome. They were two very precious rolls of film. I reeled it back up. For the moment, there was nothing more to do, so we called it a day. Before leaving, I slid a large flat capstone over our new entry, and we left.

—- • —-

I NEEDED TO CONCOCT A story for Mandy about what we'd done, and more importantly, I needed to get that black and white film processed in her darkroom.

I had a few nagging concerns, too. Mel's instructions about what to do in case of a discovery now became a reality. If we found something big, like Imhotep, who should go down the hole first? Mandy, me, or maybe Shlomo? Or would it be wiser to send down Kharpet or a Nubian worker? Mel had intended that we contact him in such an event, so he could send an experienced photographer to do the magazine's photos. But there was no way we could wait for that.

Shlomo decided to ditch the explosives, detonators, and everything. We didn't need them now. Remove all evidence of our mischief. It all went overboard from the Polish boat, except the Halliburton cases. The Nubians watched but said nothing. I suspected they'd keep silent.

The small dory returned us to our houseboat, where Ruth was sunning in a lounge chair, wearing a bikini, dark glasses, and a floppy hat. She was puffing a brown cigarillo and sipping tea like a bored tourist. The bikini looked as good on her as it had on the French gals. She waved and began applying cream to her legs.

Shlomo and I had our stories for Mandy ready. I would do the honors and he would listen and play it by ear. We went to clean up.

I heard Mandy's boat pull alongside. She bounded up the gangway. The rest of her gang looked beat; they dragged themselves up and disappeared inside.

"Hi! Did you have a good day?"

"Yeah. And we may have some interesting news for you."

"Like what?" she smirked. "Find the tomb?"

"Maybe."

"What?"

"Go clean up, Mandy, and come have a drink. We'll tell you all about it."

"Okay, I won't be a minute."

Fifteen minutes later, out dashed Mandy, smelling like flowers and wearing shorts and a clean safari jacket. She'd even applied lipstick.

"Okay, guys, stop teasing. What are you talking about?"

She looked first at Shlomo, then me. Nabil picked that moment to bring our gin tonics and a glass of white wine for Mandy.

I cleared my throat, "Cheers," and took a long swallow.

"I can tell you this, Mandy. We went ashore and searched over that whole rock pile, but we couldn't find any sign of anything leading to a tomb. Then we had a brilliant idea. We'd use natural forces to move some of those top stones, and so we did." *I said it with a straight face, my niggling conscience calling me a liar.* "Maybe, just maybe, we've found an entrance. It's certainly a deep hole in the rock pile, anyway..."

She interrupted me, eyes wide. "In which part of the rock formation?"

"The part that looks like a Sphinx's left front leg. The top of the promontory part that juts out into the river. We think there's an entry hole midway between the sides of that rocky extension, between the basalt and granite layers.

"You moved stones and boulders off the top? I can't believe it. How did you do it?

"Yes, well, it was some very heavy work up there, moving those boulders, and we're beat. But it was fun."

"And you didn't use any dynamite?"

"Dynamite? Where would we have gotten dynamite out here? We used natural forces." *I wasn't telling the whole truth. She had not used the word explosive, thank heaven. We didn't use dynamite. Never mind the stuff we used was a hundred times more powerful.*

While Mandy was thinking that over, I switched topics and told her about lowering the camera. That got her attention. I pulled the black and white film canister out of my pocket and gave it to her.

Without a word, she put down her drink, grabbed the film, and headed for the darkroom. To be honest, I felt that Mandy didn't care that much about *how* we'd moved the stones. She wanted to see the negatives, and, of course, so did we.

It would be at least an hour before we could look at the dry film-strips, so we sipped our drinks, ate cashews, and waited. I assured Mandy that there had been no real damage to the rock pile. It was a stupid remark, because we had shattered the bejeezus out of the place. But I meant *inside* the rock pile, just in case there was anything there.

Thirty minutes later, just before dinner was served, we heard a yell from the darkroom, "Guys, get in here!" Mandy was holding the 35-mm negatives over a yellow bulb. One frame in particular had her attention.

"I'm gonna make an eight-by-ten print of this as soon as it's dry. Let's eat dinner first. This is very exciting! I can't imagine how you guys made a hole in such dense, heavy stone." I think she may have suspected, but didn't want to pursue that line. Plausible deniability.

It was just us three Musketeers at dinner. Beef bourguignon, with salad and fresh dinner rolls. Nabil was a great chef. We wolfed it all down with hot coffee before storming back to the darkroom.

Using large wooden tongs, Mandy gingerly extracted an enlargement that was in the hypo and held it up. We stared. "Sweet Jesus," she exclaimed. "Look at that!"

Dimly visible at the far end of a dark passageway, we could see what appeared to be a very wide door or a panel. Definitely man-made. I had a giddy feeling. No question, we'd stumbled onto something, but what?

Frantically, Mandy scanned the other negs, but they were all dark blobs with a white splash where the flash had bounced off a wall. This was the only image that showed anything other than weakly lit darkness.

We'd have to get down inside that tunnel and have a look around. But Shlomo had tossed away the magic keys. If we needed to move more rocks, it would be difficult. We had no more Semtex at hand. Shlomo still had some military grade C4, and maybe a small amount of less powerful commercial Semtex, back on his Polish barge. If we needed to do more blasting, all was not lost, but I didn't think we could get away with it again.

Mandy was smart enough to weigh the outcome. As it turned out, busting in had been the right thing to do. She was no dummy.

We stood there staring at the print. It was tantalizing. "We absolutely have to go ashore and see for ourselves," she mumbled. "I don't dare say anything to Oberhoffer until I'm sure of what we've got. Professional jealousy might erupt. After all, he's the senior investigator on this barge."

Mandy organized a party to ashore at first light.

It was hard to figure what was racing through Mandy's mind. The discovery was right where she had *thought* a tomb or passageway should be. Why wasn't she overjoyed? Maybe because *she* hadn't found it?

CHAPTER 47

The Panel

Four men strained and toiled with picks and crowbars to move aside the large amount of granite and basalt. Gradually the entry hole was widened, almost wide enough to admit the tall ladder from the other desert hole.

Mandy must have suspected we'd done some blasting, but refrained from asking. I wondered whether blasting was kosher with archaeologists, but I didn't dare ask. I had said no dynamite, and she didn't know from Semtex. Best to leave it alone.

The crude wooden ladder, made locally with three short sections haphazardly fitted together, was lowered into the tunnel and securely jammed against jutting rocks. Mandy shined a torch down the hole and confirmed it was solidly positioned and secured; there was another twenty-foot drop from ladder's end to the passage floor. We attached a rope ladder to close the gap.

Kharpet, the smallest and lightest of us, went down first, carrying a hurricane lamp, which he hung on the lowest rung of the wood ladder. Then he lowered the rope ladder, which easily reached the bottom. He hopped off and steadied the rope portion. We all clambered down, leaving one man at the top, in case we needed topside help.

We stepped onto a damp, cold floor of sand over solid stone. It was level but for some spots of wet, slippery sand. I looked around.

THE PANEL

We were standing in a long, wide tunnel about twelve feet high and fifteen feet wide. *High enough headroom enough for a procession.*

The walls were blackened centuries ago by worker's torches. That was definite evidence. Someone had been down here, right where we were standing, thousands of years ago. Amazing!

In the excitement of our discovery, it hadn't occurred to me to search from within our tunnel for its original entrance. If it existed, we'd obviously missed it. It was either ahead of us or behind us in this dank, gloomy passageway. We felt no air currents.

We advanced slowly toward the desert side of the tunnel, looking from side to side and hoping to see something. But the pale stone walls were bare, mute. Nothing more than smudges.

Suddenly *we saw it!* In the far recess of the tunnel, some fifty feet ahead, a large, white stone panel crossed the tunnel from one side to the other, completely blocking any further advance. We could see better as we advanced. It proved to be three panels placed side by side. The center panel faced us directly; the other two flanked the center panel at oblique angles toward us. It reminded me of the entryway to a deluxe hotel suite.

I didn't know if the smooth stone was alabaster or polished sandstone, but it was amazing. The light from our hurricane lamp showed the figure of a full-sized man carved into the center panel. It was a classic Egyptian relief. He stood over five feet tall, magnificently carved in haute relief and its coloring just as the artist had left it long ago. The hypnotic eyes, almost real, stared straight ahead. Even after all these years, the figure seemed alive. Who was he? He wore no fancy headgear or clothes. His hair was cut short, Dutch-boy style. He wore only a short, pleated skirt and sandals. No jewelry, no markings. Wow.

He was holding a tall staff and looking to the side, as Egyptian figures do, and beside him were stalks of some tall vegetation, papyrus or reeds. On the other side was a bird, which looked like an Ibis, with the recurved beak. It stared directly at us. There was no water depicted. Looking up at the ceiling, I saw several carved rows of exquisitely decorated hieroglyphs painted in red, black, and gold, and just below them was a small winged insignia of outspread wings. It resembled pilot's wings.

There was a set of carved hieroglyphs beside the man, also outlined in black and gold, but no red. Amazingly, the colors were just as vivid now as they must have been centuries ago.

Could it be Imhotep? The carved figure was too young. There *was* a clue, though. The carved Ibis on the panel was associated with Imhotep. The hieroglyphs would explain a lot. Mandy could read them and hadn't said anything yet. It would be too easy to call him Imhotep just because of the birds.

She was making fast notes and snapping away with her camera. I took some shots, too. I suspected Mel Grosvenor would definitely want to see them.

We all studied the panels closely. There was no sign of handles or hidden things to press. No carefully hidden cracks or a way to get behind those panels. But there had to be reasons for the panels. After all, it was there for a reason. It had to be moveable. There was something important behind it, no question. But where the hell was the clue to that riddle? How did we get beyond that panel?

These were not just plain panels stretching from ceiling to floor. Unquestionably, this all was a magnificent piece of work by sculptors who had labored with no light save for their smudgy torches, and of course no power tools. Chipping and grinding at these panels, which had been laboriously cut, shaped and fitted neatly into place without any visible seams. Amazing!

Something was nagging me. I looked again at the edges of this massive panel. And *yes,* around the panel's edges there was a thin molding, giving the panels a more finished appearance, like a photo frame. I stared, and looked around again.

Something didn't connect. The sidewalls were so bare compared to the lovely panels. Why? Then I spotted a series of holes at eye level, cleanly drilled into the solid rock wall to my left. Dark smudges surrounded them, suggesting they held torches at one time, but the smudges were heavier in one area than the others.

THE PANEL

How interesting! Some electrifying thoughts raced through my mind.

Mandy seemed perplexed. "This is like a riddle. All I can make out of these glyphs is *"The labor of tomorrow starts here."* I haven't a clue what that means. There may be a hidden message or maybe I'm not reading correctly. I was hoping for a name. They were so afraid that a tomb might be defiled. But it could mean just what it says, *if you want to go further, look further, start here.* Doncha think?

"Doctor, please take some photos. Meanwhile I'm going to look at the back part of this passageway."

That suited me fine. I set up my mini tripod, measured distances, slipped on a wide-angle lens, framed the panels, using flash and torchlight. It would give a spooky feeling to the place when the slides were viewed. I shot several rolls, including close-ups of the glyphs and the smudges on the wall. I even posed the smiling Nubians beside the panels for a few.

Shlomo stayed out of lens range. He always stayed out of photos, he told me later. It was professional.

Interestingly, no stone chips had been left except for one small thumbnail-sized piece of panel material, which I tucked into my pocket, for later analysis. I knew it was taboo, but I wanted to know if it was alabaster brought by barge from a distant quarry.

--•--

WHEN THERE HAS BEEN A major discovery, the saying at *National Geographic* is, "We've found the Curlew's nest." I thought we had. Just what had we found? For now, it was enough to have truly stumbled onto a new find.

Was this the tomb for which Mandy had been searching? Something about the place, especially the panel, nagged my subconscious. What was not quite right?

Mandy returned to announce that the entrance was probably at the back, and may have been underwater. There was a large, angled hole carved into the floor, over which a huge flat capstone sat. It fitted into the hole, like a pan cover. Around its basin, pulsating water seeped up and back, keeping the floor damp and slippery. Without that capstone, this place would have flooded. Is this how the last worker got out? He'd have had to pull the capstone down. Clever tomb builders. Imhotep was an engineer, after all, the architect of Zoser's step pyramid.

From what I had seen so far, a mighty slick hand had been at work here. But I had a sixth sense that this panel was all an elaborate door to throw off looters. And weren't we just another bunch of looters who'd been suckered?

I wracked my brain. It was nearly time to climb out, because we'd been down for over an hour. Claustrophia was setting in and after the initial excitement ebbed, we were slightly disappointed to find nothing more than the panels for the present. It was time to leave. We gathered our stuff and headed for the ladders.

But those smudges were bothering me. It meant something more.

— - • - —

WE WENT BACK TO THE houseboat to wash up, slurp down a cocktail, eat dinner, and listen to Armed Forces Radio or the BBC. Basically, I was stranded on the Nile with a mystery. Was this place a tomb site or just a centuries-old joke?

I wanted to study the photo prints of the panel wall pictures. Maybe the answer was staring me right in the face. They were spectacular panels. But if one wanted to see if anything lay *behind* them, they'd have to remove them or tunnel around them. I *sensed* that they *were* moveable panels. Something was there, I just couldn't see it.

I was also convinced that the present crew wouldn't be able to decipher, decode or otherwise find a way in behind those panels. I wondered who might have the instincts to fathom out a situation like this when Mandy, a trained archaeologist, had no clue. She was smart enough to discern an anomaly with the drowned Chinese guy. I was gonna solve this goddam riddle come hell or high water. Please, Lord, hold the water.

A consultation with others in the field would take months. I wanted to do it on my own. Why give someone else a shot at the brass ring? After all, this could be a helluva prize: Imhotep's tomb. There had to be a solution and I was running out of time. Shlomo had suggested it was time for us to leave. His mission had ended and his people were returning to their bases. I returned to reality. How was I getting back to Washington?

Not a problem, said Shlomo. A boat was coming for us tomorrow and we'd all be on our way. Reluctantly, I made ready to leave and got my gear packed. The rolls of exposed film were labeled and stored in my kit bag. Cameras cleaned and put away, but I kept one loaded and available to be ready for the unexpected. I was fidgety that I hadn't solved the panel riddle. There had to be a tunnel beyond it. Why core out a tunnel from solid rock just to end at a decorative panel? No way, I thought. The bothersome item in that panel was the Ibis. It was the sacred Nile Ibis, no question. But why was it so beautifully carved on that panel?

At dinner, I told Mandy that I'd be leaving the next morning whenever Shlomo's transportation arrived. I asked her to send a message to Dr. Grosvenor and the Research Committee. I recommended that she let them know what she'd found and what her plans were. With her permission, I wanted to show them the photos and arrange to forward to her copies of their comments to the houseboat. She said she'd get something ready.

"When are you leaving?"

"Tomorrow noon."

Shlomo contacted his friends by transceiver from his cabin. He learned that the others had already left. We'd be picked up tomorrow around noon, maybe spend the night and catch the return hydrofoil from Abu Simbel to Aswan, to fly on to Cairo the same night. Arrangements were made to have the hydrofoil make a very expensive, unscheduled stop at the Polish houseboat.

The smudges and drilled holes in the tunnel walls still nagged at me. It had taken a lot of workmen a long time to drill those holes. I imagined them hand spinning round mandrils of stone into those walls; rubbing one stone against another to wear it down is both time consuming and takes some doing. Why were some of the smudges bigger and darker than others? *Why more smudges on one wall than the other?* My mind visualized the torch holes, and suddenly I thought I had it. Of course! *More smudges meant more light was needed because more work was being done on one side than the other!* I had to go back down that hole and look again.

I found Mandy. "Listen, Mandy. I have this horrible feeling that the film I shot in the tunnel may have been accidentally exposed to light during the rewind, and I'm concerned that the entire color roll is ruined," I lied. "Would you please let me go ashore first thing in the morning and reshoot those panels? It shouldn't take long. I can be back in time to leave as planned. This is important. I need to have good color pictures for Mel Grosvenor and the Research Committee."

"Yeah, sure, John. I'll have one of the workmen, Walid, and Kharpet take you ashore at first light. You need good photos. Will two men be enough?"

"Sure."

I planned my actions so there was no time to waste, because I had to get back to the houseboat in time to leave with Shlomo. Delay was not in the cards.

-- • --

WORKING QUICKLY WITH TWO LARGE branches and the stout boat hook, we levered the capstone off like a large sewer drain top, and slid it off to one side. We went down the wooden ladder, then onto the rope ladder, and jumped lightly to the bottom.

Walid carried a hurricane lamp and my tripod slung across his back. I carried my Nikon, film, changing bag, flash gear, and Evian in my safari jacket pockets. After helping us, Kharpet sat on the rock pile above our head. He would be my upstairs man. I set up the tripod, mounted the camera, used my hand torch to shine on the panels to better focus the split image finder on those panels. I fired off two rolls of high speed and daylight film, using flash on alternate exposures. I was bracketing, in professional terms, then "accidentally" kicked the tripod knocking it and the camera to the side, but grabbed the tripod and camera before they fell, being careful not to let it land it lens down. Then, playing the silly actor, clapped my hands to my head and yelled: "Oh shit!" pointing to the camera, to myself and waving my arms to the heavens, all to impress Walid. I pulled the tripod back up, looked at the camera, clapped my hands to my head and muttered, "Oh, no."

Walid understood. *This man is struggling.* He shrugged his shoulders, mumbled a quiet *maalish* to himself and waited. I pulled out my pen, wrote *camera bag* on a sheet of note paper, then handed it to Walid, and pointed up. I'd deliberately left my bag with Kharpet, who spoke English and hopefully, read it too. It made no difference, the bag held only a few odds and ends. Walid scurried up the ladder carrying his lamp. I would be alone and I had a powerful flashlight with fresh batteries and a working camera. Now to get to work.

The carbon deposits smudges around the left side torch holes were blacker and thicker than on the other side. My flashlight slid into those holes easily. I picked one at random, jammed my torch in, lens side up. I wiggled it, pushed, lifted the torch up and down. Nothing. I repeated this in several other holes on the same side, all heavily smudged. My mind kept spinning over that fact: more smudge meant torches had been burning here longer.

Because they needed light to see...what? To see what they were doing. What were they doing? Working, building, a tunnel perhaps. I moved to another smudge hole, this was my last shot, any minute now, I'd hear Walid returning.

This time, for no good reason, I selected a clean hole. I pushed the torch handle in, waggled it up and down, and Bingo! *The stone was loose!* I pulled out the torch, eased out the stone, flipped on the light and searched. Sure enough, a stone rectangle had been cut out and replaced in the wall. The seam between the stones was almost invisible. I wiggled the stone out again and set it down by my feet. Inside a cavity, about eight inches wide and a foot deep, was a horizontal rod. I reached in, wrapped my fingers around, and moved it left. It moved silently, and as it did, I saw the left panel open and pivot outward. Then the center panel swung slowly on a silent pivot, to the other side. There was the tunnel, wide open! My mind raced, *I may have found the Curlew's nest."*

The panel doors stood open invitingly. Carefully, I edged forward and shined the light beyond the entrance. I could just make out the extension of the wide passageway, as I'd expected. I moved forward. There were more torch holes with smudges, and ahead, a chamber and entrances to other chambers off to each side. I dismantled the camera from the tripod, dashed inside and started snapping photos systematically. I had to do this quickly. I moved directly into a large center chamber. It was dazzling. In the center lay a huge sarcophagus in the same pale, white stone. A somber group of beautifully carved Ibis statues was standing in a circle, facing it. My mind screamed, *Imhotep*!

Walid had been gone about twenty minutes; I had maybe ten more. I looked around. The huge space was filled with art and furniture, and everything looked perfectly preserved. There were beautiful chairs, gracefully carved, inlaid with gold and mother of pearl, and intricately painted in blue, red, gold and black ibis designs. Oil lamps and gold trinkets were everywhere. A huge white stone statue and hundreds of scattered ceramic and stone pots and vases. There was another drawing of the man on the panel, painted and covered with gold necklaces and bracelets. I had no time to waste. I fired off the rest of the roll, fed in a new one, and dashed to the other chambers. They contained a chariot, two animal skeletons, more lamps, more gold, more pottery. I was surrounded by glyphs and paintings on all walls, even the ceilings. Red, blue and gold splashes of paint on all figures. I needed one souvenir, for *proof!* I saw a small flat saucer filled with scarab beetles. Quickly, I set the camera on self-timer release, aimed and focused, lifted the plate, faced the camera and smiled. The shutter and flash fired and I had one exposure of the scarabs and me. The date would show on the negative. I repeated this several times moving around the chamber. Then on a whim, I stuffed the small plate *and* scarabs into my jacket pocket. I had one last thing to do. I walked over to an ornate table holding blue ceramic cats, sitting artfully. I took my index finger and wrote in the dust: John Sundukian, the date and underneath it, Amanda Conant. On self timer, fired off some shots to confirm, then quickly scooted out. I had to push the panel doors shut, but because of the weight, they wouldn't stay shut. I exerted all my strength, but they still wouldn't stay shut. They needed to stay in position long enough for me to slide the wooden rod back into the hole. The tripod! I jammed the legs against the floor, the upper portion against the panel and it held. Quickly, I slid the rod back into position inside the recessed rock. Bingo! It worked.

I will always remember that shiny, black wooden rod, showing no evidence of decay. It had to be ironwood.

Where the hell was Walid? From the entry hole, I heard Walid calling *"Effendi,"* and I looked up. He and Kharpet were grinning, waving my bag. I motioned them down.

I had to go through the motions of redoing the photography. Acting as normal as possible, I smiled and thanked them. Took a few pictures, finally signaling that I was ready to return. Inside my heart raced and I was churning with emotion.

Time to get back up and out. This time, Kharpet had come down with me and Walid sat up top, enjoying the cool river breeze. Kharpet reached up with the boat hook to steady the rope section, and I moved to climb on his shoulders, hoist myself up and grab the bottom rope rung. Walid would lower a rope to tie around my waist, and would hoist me up to the wooden rungs. Then we'd do the same for Kharpet.

Disaster! Kharpet reached with the boat hook and grabbed the bottom rung of the rope ladder, and pulled. The rope must have been rotten; it snapped and cascaded down to ground. A moment later, the wooden ladder pieces loosened, and they, too, fell down into a huge a pile at our feet in front of us.

Kharpet shook his head. "We cannot not get back up this hole today, sir. Can you swim, sir?"

"Yes," I said cautiously.

"Then follow me and we'll get out. First, I tell Walid to go for help." He shouted something in their local patois and we heard Walid go running off.

"Please. Take off your clothes. Put everything you wish to save in your jacket."

I took the film and my torch and buttoned them into the pockets. The camera and gear and my LL Bean britches could stay behind. They were replaceable, the film was not. Kharpet took the jacket, rolled it up tightly, and used its belt to strap it to his body. I had no idea what he had in mind, but I was getting chilly in my jockey shorts. He seemed perfectly composed in a cotton loin cloth.

"Follow me." He cut off a long section of the rope ladder and dragged it with us. We went to the far end of the tunnel where Mandy had spotted the exit hole, she thought. Kharpet looped the rope around one side of the capstone covering the exit hole, and together we lifted it out. To my surprise it was easy.

"Now listen to me sir, and please listen carefully. We are going to swim out."

Huh?

"I have your jacket and films. They are safe with me. I will tie this rope around my waist and lower myself in the hole. You take the other end of this rope and wrap it around your wrist, then you follow me. I will swim out and up to the surface, just like my ancestors did. If they could, so can we."

I was numb with fear. "When we come up to the surface, we go to the closest shore. You understand? Sir?"

What could I say? "Yes," I croaked.

Not a moment to relish. Kharpet dropped straight down, feet first, and sank. I had to jump or get pulled. The water was dark, and so were the sides, but I felt Kharpet tugging. I may have shut my eyes. I don't remember, it all happened so fast. But I somehow negotiated myself downward into the watery tunnel, and suddenly felt a huge surge of water pulling me out. The water and mud zipped by at a frightening rate, and I was half blinded, but I clung to the tugging rope. Kharpet was pulling me out, but where the hell was the surface?

I didn't know up from down, until finally, after a few minutes, I saw faint light overhead, but we were still way underwater.

THE PANEL

The current seemed to lose its intensity and I felt myself being pulled up, and suddenly, broke through the surface. I was grateful to gulp air again, but I was being pushed downstream. Spluttering, coughing and gasping, I looked for Kharpet. He was ahead of me, fighting the current, and slowly heading for the shore to our right. I gave crocodiles a fleeting thought. Kharpet reached shallow water and stood up, pulling me with him. We were both covered with mud and slime and goose-bumps;, safe, for the moment. Despite the heat, we were both shivering, partly from fear and adrenaline. Kharpet led me to some large flat stones baking in the sun.

"Lean up against these stones, sir, and you will get warmer. Make sure no snakes are there first; sometimes they get cold, too." He grinned.

The hot stones did the job. I gradually warmed up.

Kharpet said, "The currents are difficult at the point of the massif. It keeps the crocs away. They don't like to struggle with anything but their food. Now we are safe." He shuddered.

He spied Walid and some men in a boat far upstream from us. He shouted, but the rushing waters drowned out his voice. We used my torch to signal them and they found us quickly. I watched lots of discussion and amazement, shoulders shrugged and Allah praised. We were safe, but I'd missed the last boat out. *Maalish*.

-- • --

ON THE WAY BACK TO the houseboat, I decided *I would tell no one of this little caper in the tunnel.* Not Mandy, not Shlomo. For starters, I trampled all over the ethics of the arcane science of Archaeology, including breaking and entering a burial chamber, which might have even violated agreements between Mandy and the Egyptians. Shlomo and I had entered a tomb site by blasting with Semtex. I didn't want to put him in career jeopardy for supplying me or helping to set up the blast. Well, no one would know where it came from. I could lie, but I'd be trapped no matter what I said. Keeping my mouth shut would solve many problems. A number of lies and future explanations whirled through my mind, but in the end, the only person I could talk to was Mel. I'd tell him everything, and show him the photos and trinkets, too.

The burning question was: *is the mummy in the sarcophagus Imhotep?* I'd bet my bottom dollar it was. I wished there had been more time for me to poke around. Once I had prints of the photographed glyphs on the sarcophagus, someone could read it, but that would tip my hand. It would take some first class maneuvering.

There was one disconcerting thought. I'd heard stories that tomb robbers and Egyptologists came down with horrid diseases after making a grand discovery. Should I be worried? Nah, I assured myself, it only happened in the days of poor hygiene. They were just old wives tales. I was elated. After all, I did find the Curlew's nest, and wasn't that enough? *Hell, yes.* Time to move on.

CHAPTER 48

Dr. Grosvenor and a Future Path

I WAS HEADED BACK TO WASHINGTON. WE LEFT MANDY AND DR. OBERhoffer with our profuse thanks and goodbyes. As we left, Mandy handed me a thick envelope containing her preliminary report for the Research Committee. This would solidify her possible discovery of an unknown tomb, despite the omission of information about what we'd found in that tunnel. She had included sketches and photos to dazzle the committee, and hopefully extend her grant.

Ruth, Shlomo and I stopped by the Polish houseboat before boarding the hydrofoil to Aswan. My two Israeli companions resumed their fake identities so as not to create a problem at airports. Ruth announced she was leaving us at Geneva to take a leave. Shlomo shrugged his shoulders, unconcerned. Truly laid-back professionals.

—- • --

AFTER I UNPACKED AT THE Mews, I took the film. I was burning with curiosity to see the processed material. I dropped the rolls at the Geographic photo desk and asked for one-day processing and got unpleasant looks. I remarked that Dr. Grosvenor was waiting to see these slides tomorrow. They backed down, and I pushed it. Could they go out by courier now? More black looks. I'd be back at closing time to retrieve the yellow boxes and they'd be returned for labeling later. The surly developer grunted an assent. I smiled, thanked her and left.

At five p.m., the exposures looked perfect. The new Kodachrome transparencies were not greenish at all. They told me the film required maturing before being put to use, not a problem for me. The bracketed flash shots were clear, well exposed and very usable. So I selected out dupes of the alabaster panel views, the rocky massif, the sarcophagus shots, those of the table with my name on it, and lastly me holding the scarabs. I'd keep them as "insurance." I requested immediate color identification prints and called Mel's office for an appointment.

As soon as I launched into my tale, Mel blustered at me, "*You did what? What the hell are you talking about, John? I can't believe my ears. You found Imhotep's tomb? Are you serious? Holy Cow, man! They've been looking for it for decades and you may have found it? Tell me the whole story and don't leave out a word.*" Mel stuck his head out the door.

"Karen," he yelled to his secretary. "Please call the Smithsonian and tell Professor Smedlap to get over here as soon as he can. I want him to read some glyphs for me. Send a car. No calls, no visitors. Tell Gil I'll meet him later. Tell Garrett I'll see him in the morning. Something has come up and I'm gonna be a very busy man." He locked his door.

I told Mel about Mandy, Shlomo, and our antics at the rock pile. It was surreal to see the head of the *National Geographic*, *numero uno* editor of the most famous global magazine, looking slack-jawed and incredulous. I explained that we'd studied an unsual stone massif, and found no sign of an entrance or traces of looters, in spite of Mandy's conviction that there *was* a tomb somewhere in there. Her theory was deduced from intuitions, sketches, and hard work. I explained about the votive offering pots and the human remains. In short, I told Mel everything, well almost everything. I told him the Polish archaeologists had stored explosives that we used for our tunnel entry.

"You mean to tell me that you blew a hole in the cliff? Are you nuts, John? You might have been killed! You might have destroyed the whole goddam tomb!"

DR. GROSVENOR AND A FUTURE PATH

I didn't explain I had expert help. No need to jeapordize Shlomo. I just let Mel blow up and then calm down. But it was an unsettling outburst. I didn't want him to toss me out. But I was thinking that when he came around, he'd be as excited as we had been.

So, as he stamped red-faced around the room bellowing at me and waving his arms ceilingward, I quietly pulled out the enlargements I'd ordered. They were eight by twelve prints in magnificent color.

I placed them on Mel's desk and waited. He spun spun around, spotted the prints, and stopped. He charged over to have a better look and stopped dead in his tracks. He stood open-mouthed, and grabbed the prints. Then he held them at arm's length and gawked some more. He was grinning and shaking his head. "You did find the Curlew's nest, didn't you? Amazing! Gawsh, John, I've got to think about this."

He couldn't believe his eyes. He shuffled the prints, staring at the carved panels. I was holding back the photos of the inner chambers for the boffo line at the end of my presentation. Mel was waving the prints around like a symphony conductor. He was nearly speechless, so I jumped in.

"You don't see any signs of destruction, do you, Mel? My small charge of explosive barely cracked the shell of that tunnel, just enough to let us in. It's true I agreed not to enter any new find; that I'd let you know so you could send another photographer. Well, it just couldn't be helped, Mel. It didn't work out that way. I was there, *it* was there, one thing led to another, and then suddenly, it all happened. I had no way of contacting you from the middle of the Nile. Here, this is what was found."

I pulled out the rest of the photos and continued. "We didn't know what was behind that panel. When I figured out the way to open the panel, here's what I found *behind* that paneling. Only you and I, Mel, know any of this. The rest of them never saw behind the panels."

Mel looked stunned. This was like finding Tut's tomb.

I described how I'd discovered the loose stone in the wall and the ironwood rod in the depths of a hole. Then from my attaché case, I set the exquisite ceramic tomb dish with the scarabs on his desk.

He shifted his attention back and forth from the prints to the little beetles. He sat there grinning, and I believe he was impressed. The dish and beetles were plainly in the photos, with my name scrawled on the dusty tabletop. We stared silently at the shots of the imposing sarcophagus, with its carved glyphs and golden, kingly image in vivid reds, blues, and yellows.

Transfixed by the prints and the purloined scarab beetles, Mel's eyebrows had skidded up his aristocratic forehead. The carved relief of the man with the hypnotic eyes was the most arresting print and clearly had his attention.

He must have been thinking ahead to a huge public presentation of this, the latest finding by his Society explorers. Suddenly, I felt safe. *I'd done it.* I'd convinced him I'd done the right thing and reported it all to him. He hastily skimmed my three-page report.

"Okay, John. These are some great photos. You didn't open that sarcophagus, did you?"

"Hardly, Mel. Too damned heavy," I joked.

Mel believed me. I might have tried if it had been possible. But it would have been a heinous criminal act, besides, we both knew it weighed tons. "Jesus, fella, what might have happened! You know, John, you're a bit impulsive at times."

I spent the next forty minutes describing the whole trip. Mel sat there, relishing every word, his eyes glistening. I think he secretly admired my antics and wished he could have been with me.

Karen informed us that Professor Smedlap was away, but his assistant was rushing over. Mel grunted.

"John, I want you to present this to our Research Committee and the Board as a preliminary report on this spectacular panel and tunnel find. Work supported by our Research Grant. There's no question they're going to want to know what lies behind those panels. *But we are not going to mention that you went behind that panel or hint what's behind those panels.* That information's gonna remain between you and me. More funds will be allocated to continue the research, and of course, this time we'll coordinate with the Egyptian authorities. Keep in mind, from here on out, no mention of explosions or moving the doors. Are we clear?"

"Absolutely, Mel. I may have to deal with Miss Mandy about the blasting business later, but leave that to me. I think she'll understand."

I guess Mel wasn't surprised when I turned down his offer to go back to the Nile for the anticipated "discovery" of how to open the panel. We did agree that if Mandy and her team made no discovery of the panel-opening trick, then I'd go back and "stumble" on the hollowed rock niche and open the panel.

I had copies of the color prints showing me with the sarcophagus, me holding the scarabs, and, of course, the table top with my name and date on its dusty surface. On the back of each print, the photo lab had imprinted the date and a warning against publishing it anywhere. The date would be months or even a year prior to public "discovery," just in case it was of later interest to anyone. For the present, Mel and I were the only ones who would know about my breaking and entering behind that panel.

— - • - —

INSTEAD OF WAITING TO GO to Egypt, I asked Mel to let me go right away to Guatemala. Professors Sharer and Sedat, from the University of Pennsylvania, whom I met at his Cosmos Club dinner, had invited me. They'd found a probable Mayan tomb site at a United Fruit plantation in Quirigua, deep in the Petén. I was more than willing to *recon* this and bring back photos and information to him. Did he have any interest? I allowed my voice to trail off, sounding hopeful. I had a video of the prospective find, too, if he was interested. That got him.

"More tombs, huh? Show me the video," he said, all the while giving me a look of *déjà vu*. He asked for a two-page summary with complete details of what I wanted to do and the reasons, how much film was needed, and what my expenses might be. He was in the midst of budget tightening. He said Garrett had been producing blockbuster issues lately, but production costs were rising. Available funds for research were becoming scarcer, he moaned.

I'd baited the hook again, and Mel trusted me, so I set to work outlining my request, keeping the costs in mind. Dr. Ralph Stewart had also approached me from the United States Information Agency in Guatemala to give lectures to the local physicians on the newest treatments for tuberculosis. Stewart told me the U.S. government would pick up all expenses, part of our new policy to project a caring image to the Central American community, which would spread by word of mouth, starting with local physicians.

I decided to accept Stewart's offer, and added a special request. Would they arrange to let me make rubbings at the *stela* carvings at Tikal? I'd watched rubbings being made in Cambodia, and photographed the technique as part of a *Geographic* article. I fancied that I could make rubbings myself. It would be a neat opportunity and he agreed that it could be arranged.

I wanted to parlay the lecturing with a small assignment from Mel, in order to have the *Geographic*'s imprimatur and the Guatemalan government's permission. There might be some great photo opportunities in the newly exciting Mayan finds. Mel gave me the green light to go and I vowed that I would make him happy with the information and pictures I shot in Central America. That's how I became a Mayan explorer, tromping the jungles of Guatemala's Petén District with a camera and rubbing materials.

--•--

I PREPARED FOR THE NEXT trip with serious contemplation, knowing that I was now at a crossroads of my future and it was decision time. Which road to take? Carry on with my doctoring? Or follow the adventures that beckoned so strongly? Was I making a deliberate choice or merely an escape? Was I giving up Medicine? Mel had given me a reluctant green light to go to Guatemala, so I packed my bags and considered all the implications of another jaunt.

I decided exploring, flying, and photography were temporary sidetracks, passions that engaged my mind and made my heart soar. I would always be a doctor, a damn good one, and I would carry on my noble profession by lecturing on lung disease in the tropics. Sharing my medical expertise around the world was what had first taken me to Saigon, after all, and that had been the start of an exciting series of adventures which had enriched my life and changed my perspective on the world. There would always be more surgery back in Washington, *after* Guatemala.

I was still determined to enlarge my life beyond medicine, and now, I was more confident than ever that the world needed everything I had to contribute, using all my talents. And I wanted to seize every opportunity to taste all that life had to offer.

CHAPTER 49

The Past and the Future

As great as it had been to stun the preeminent Mel Grosvenor with my tomb photos, I wished for someone else to share my secret discovery with, and felt a void in my personal life again. My professional successes were stacking up, but I found myself too much alone.

I thought about the women I'd known in the past year or so, each one fascinating in her own way, but none of them right for me. The Gigi of my memories was a *femme fatale* of the first order, a slick female operator and a seductress par excellence. But she had vanished in the jungle, and Maeve, the injured woman whom I'd seen in Virginia, was not the same. The last I'd heard, she had moved to France to start over. Lt. Witherspoon had been sweet, but needy. Katarina had been a sensuous delight, but capricious and fickle. Mandy was a dedicated and talented archaeologist, and plenty attractive, but her heart was in her work; she and I were meant to be friends. I was looking for a smart, gutsy, beautiful woman who could understand me and admire my ambitions, who'd come with me on adventures, and every triumph would be sweeter, sharing it with her.

-- • --

THE PAST AND THE FUTURE

A YEAR PASSED AND THE tomb remained "undiscovered." Mandy and the others never figured out how to open the panels, so as agreed, Mel sent me back to "stumble" onto the maneuver and pop them open. I stood back and watched as the assembled archaeologists scrambled madly inside to gawk. I must report that I sneaked in quickly and wiped off the incriminating dusty signatures on the tabletop, but I still had those dated photos, just in case.

Of course, after the tomb site had been "seen" and evaluated by members of Egypt's Antiquities program, museum officials, a representative of President Nasser's office, reporters, science writers, and representatives of the U.S. National Science Foundation, it was announced that the tomb and sarcophagus were indeed Imhotep's. It rocked the science world and made international headlines. Mel sent Luis Zarden, an old Egypt hand skilled with a Leica, to silently click away, smilingly wending his way from chamber to chamber. I later learned that he'd "retrieved" a fallen scarab beetle from a chamber and somehow brought it to Washington for close-up photographs; after all, there was to be a story.

The outside of the tunnel entrance and the top of the massif showed no remaining evidence of a blast. I'd sent Kharpet, the boat boy, and his helper, Walid, to slide the capstone back over the blast hole after we'd returned to the boat, so nothing remained for suspicious eyes. The windstorms and gusts of river water had rinsed away all signs of the explosions, so I was safe on that score. I hung around for some of the Egyptian festivities and watched as experts, money, plans and congratulations poured into that formerly sleepy spot on the Nile. Then I caught the hydrofoil back to Aswan and made my way home.

--•--

MORE PAGEANTRY TOOK PLACE IN Washington. A grand showing of artifacts was kindly loaned by Egypt for display in Explorers Hall. There was an international forum, with receptions, speakers, lecturers, a slide show, and full color brochures. Museums were lining up for the chance to hold a future exhibit.

I found myself at a huge, beautifully catered formal affair, another *National Geographic* extravaganza, and watched a proud Mel Grosvenor in his glory. Amanda and her fellow archaeologists were seated on stage with him, and thrust onto the world stage, as well, as the press breathlessly covered the event. Mandy was honored for having discovered Imhotep's hidden burial place, a discovery likened to that of King Tut's tomb. It was her shining hour, and there was enough glory to spread around. She gave me credit for my help and support, and told me she would be forever grateful that I had come to her houseboat to "nose around."

Me? I was glad to celebrate in grand *Geographic* style. I sat in the front row in my monkey suit, swilling champagne, listening, and inwardly chuckling. I had delighted in a once-in-lifetime thrill, and enjoyed exposing to the world the whereabouts of the great Imhotep, brilliant physician and architect of the past. I knew Mel and I would share my secret triumph forever.

— — • — —

AS TIME PASSED, SHLOMO AND Ariana, the red-haired belly dancer, became good friends of mine. We went out together and had marvelous times. And I saw Mandy in Washington occasionally. She'd accepted a position in the Byzantine Section of the Dumbarton Oaks Museum, where she had met a fellow scholar, and I was happy for her.

And then I met her, my fabulous Nancy Lee. She was more than everything I'd hoped for and she captured my heart. Nancy Lee even joined me on my next adventure to the jungles of Guatemala. In Quirigua, I was moved to demonstrate my strong feelings for her. I offered her a rare, gorgeous orchid, when suddenly, a howler monkey jumped from a tree and snatched it out of my hand! We laughed and are laughing still; my strong feelings have never diminished, and in fact, we married, and remain happily so.

FINIS

Author's Note

This story was ten years in the making. Originally named *Not by a Dam Site*, it was written and rewritten countless time until it finally appeared as *Dr. John*. For this we thank Nancy Lee Keshishian and, of course, the fine folks at Inkwater Press.

To lend accuracy and credibility to the material researched for this novel, the author visited almost all the sites mentioned in the book, except of course, those sites created with his inflamed imagination. He did get flight instructions in Vietnam. He did visit the late Dr. Tom Dooley at his hospital in Laos at the request of CARE/Medico. There he gave advice, took many photographs and gathered material for this story. He did not fly into China, at least didn't know if it was China.

His visit to Russia and meetings with medical colleagues were indeed real. His contacts with Russians were always harmonious, leading him to consider that medical colleagues were better representatives of the citizenry than politicians. His visit with the then Ambassador Thompson was indeed real. His Intourist mentors were a constant source of amusement. He had no trouble departing Moscow as a passenger aboard a KLM flight. And his trip aboard a barge on Dutch waterways was nothing more than a short pleasure trip.

With his Egypt visit, he went to Qasr Ibrim, the remote fortress to which early Copts fled when under duress. He went to Aswan, to Abu Simbel, and traversed the Nile by boat, barge and at times by air. He received permission to explore Saqqara to visit the possible site of the Imhotep's tomb...he of religious, medical and architectural legendry. He trod the underground excavated tunnels there which contain thousands of clay pots bearing Ibises within: votive offerings to Imhotep; this was all real, but it was not his tomb site; that still remains hidden...more, the author's "finding" of his real tomb on the Nile shores was pure imagination.

About the attack on Aswan High Dam by Chinese commandos, that was all the result of a barroom conversation with tourists from Europe.

My friend, Charles McCarry, one of the most brilliant, erudite and smoothest novelists of this generation, crafted a story, the scenario of which was in a foreign country, Siberia, I think. The bizarre goings-on made perfectly good sense to me and to his loyal readers, who were told at the end he'd made it all up.

So let me tell you that much of *Dr. John* is true. I'd been there, done that. You see, this is all called a "fictionalized autobiography."

Gigi came to an inglorious end in an auto accident in Hong Kong (very much like Grace Kelly). Antoine did die of lung cancer, François was tossed out of a helicopter—he had been a Nieman fellow at Harvard University—Dooley as many know died of melanoma. I didn't discover Imhotep's tomb...I thought we had. I faked that finding, but not the doing. Shlomo was and still is a person...name changed of course. Mandy is still around.

Photos

DR. JOHN...ON ASSIGNMENT

Margaret Keshishian with sons John, James, and Harold at their London suburb home in Willesden Green.

Mark and Margaret Keshishian with sons John and James on boardwalk in Ostend, Belgium.

PHOTOS

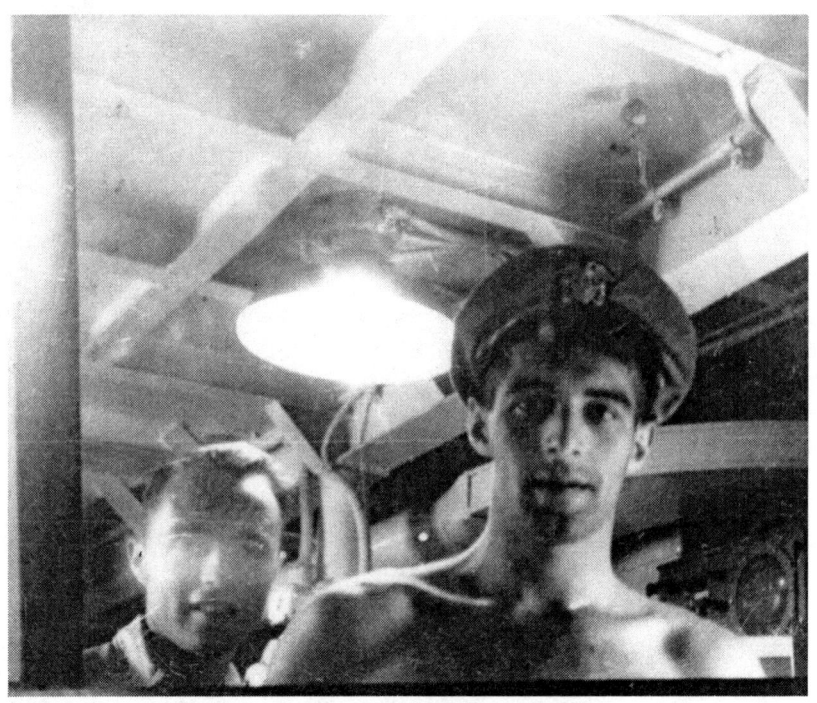

Allen M. Johnson and J. M. Keshishian aboard
LST *466* anchored in Manila Harbor.

LST *466* beached on Tarakan Island, Borneo, after the successful repossession
of that important island's fuel refinery, Royal Dutch Shell Petroleum.

DR. JOHN...ON ASSIGNMENT

Let's start with the guy on the far right. The big guy with glasses. He is Dr. Walter Bloedorn, Dean of the School of Medicine Next to him, Dr. Evarts Graham, Professor of Surgery, Barnes Hospital, St. Louis, Missouri, Next to him Dr. Brian Brewer Blades, Professor of Surgery, George Washington University School of Medicine and next to him, Professor G.M. Rees, Department of Medicine, George Washington University School of Medicine.

Celebrating New Year's greeting from King of Morocco at Cosmos Club in Washington. From left: JMK; Catherine Wrather; Royal Physician Dr. Ahmed Benabud; Mrs. Helen Kitchen; and Dr. Creighton Wright.

PHOTOS

JMK strolling along Saigon's Quai Belgique at rush hour.

Mark Keshishian toasting famed composer Aram Khachaturian during latter's visit to Washington, DC.

Dr. Tom Dooley at his piano as natives wander in and out of his hospital in Muong Sing, Laos

Lao soldier and Akha Kho woman with family in Muong Sing, Laos.

PHOTOS

Supplies being loaded on small plane to be dropped with soldiers behind enemy lines in the North of Laos.

Akha Kho family stopping for lunch in Muong Sing roadway. Wicker baskets carry all belongings, including freshly netted fish from mountain streams. These contained no iodine, leading to large goiters among native population.

DR. JOHN...ON ASSIGNMENT

JMK at Abu Simbel examining portions of Ramses II temple which have been cut apart for later assemblage at the new temple location 200 feet above the Nile River.

Photo of JMK's passport with permission to travel on Nile River appended at page top.

PHOTOS

Dr. Ali el-Kholy descending ladder into suspected tomb site of Imhotep, followed by JMK.

Tunnel containing piles of clay pots containing Nile Ibis, which were known votive offerings to Imhotep. His tomb remained to be found.

Dr. Keshishian reporting to the President of National Geographic on the occasion of his return from a quick trip to Panama. From left: Dr. Grosvenor; Gilbert Grosvenor; JMK; and Dr. Thomas McKnew.

About John M. Keshishian, MD

JOHN KESHISHIAN IS A SEMI-RETIRED ACADEMIC SURGEON. HE IS EMERITUS professor of surgery, Emeritus chief of his division, and Emeritus chief of the Medical Staff at the Washington Hospital Center in Washington, DC.

Over a span of fifty years, he has been involved in research, teaching, photography, writing, and archaeology. He has served as consultant to many organizations including the National Geographic Society, NASA, FAA, Department of State, US Air Force, Veterans Affairs, and the FDA. He served as a board member of CARE, MEDICO and the Medstar Health Care Group. He also served as Medical Director of Pan African Airways.

Later, Dr. Keshishian initiated action which prohibited smoking aboard U.S. commercial passenger aircraft.

He has appeared on VOA broadcasting abroad in his native tongue, Armenian, as well as numerous radio and television appearances, both as guest and moderator. He was sometimes known, on those occasions, as Jack Cartwright.

Taught to fly by French pilots in Vietnam, he completed his flight training under the FAA's aegis and holds a Commercial Pilot rating.

The photos of the author at Abu Simbel are real. But that episode was omitted from the story. There really were US military guys there—sweeping mines away. The author later visited Dr. Yigal Yadin at his museum to learn about Dead Sea scrolls courtesy of Shlomo.

Some of Dr. Keshishian's photos were published in *National Geographic*. He also wrote a number of small articles for World Book Science Service on Abu Simbel, wrote several articles for the *Explorer's Journal* and did a story or two for the *Smithsonian* magazine. A hundred or so scientific articles, chapters, and studies bear his name.

Many will remember the story Dr. Keshishian wrote of Burma's Long-Necked Women, which appeared in *National Geographic*.

The author and his wife live in Virginia.